Mage of Clouds

The Cloudmages #2

S. L. Farrell

D0018153

DAW BOOKS, INC.

DONALD A. WOLLHEIM, FOUNDER

375 Hudson Street, New York, NY 10014

ELIZABETH R. WOLLHEIM
SHEILA E. GILBERT
PUBLISHERS

http://www.dawbooks.com

First Paperback Printing, January 2005
3 4 5 6 7 8 9 10

DAW TRADEMARK REGISTERED
U.S. PAT. OFF. AND FOREIGN COUNTRIES
—MARCA REGISTRADA
HECHO EN U.S.A.

PRINTED IN THE U.S.A.

*For Megen, whose own march
to independence is a mirror for my characters.*

And for Denise, who is part of all that I do.

ACKNOWLEDGMENTS

Let me give a heartfelt acknowledgment to **Sheila Bading**—not for anything specifically in this book, but for the inspiration she gave me over the time I knew her. She was an excellent role model for me as well as some of my characters. May the Mother keep you safe in her arms, Sheila.

My appreciation to **Sheila Gilbert** for her vigilant editorship, for the "Wow!" moment in her editorial notes, and for making me part of the family at DAW.

This book's sonic inspirations: Once again, **Osna** often found its way onto my CD player (and my iPod), as did **Capercaillie, Cherish The Ladies,** the **Afro–Celt Connection, Loreena McKennitt, the Chieftains, Gaelic Storm,** the **Celtic Heartbeat** collections, and even **Flogging Molly.**

My apologies in advance to speakers of Irish Gaelic. Throughout the book, I have borrowed several terms from Irish and though I've made my best attempt, any mistakes in usage (and I'm certain there are many) are my own and are due to my limited understanding of the language. My intent was simply to give a bit of the flavor and cadence of the Irish language to English-speaking readers.

If you're connected to the internet, my web page can be accessed at **www.farrellworlds.com**—you're always welcome to browse through.

CONTENTS

Part One: Acolyte

Part Two: Taisteal

Part Three: Bunús Muintir

Part Four: Traitor

Part Five: Banrion Ard

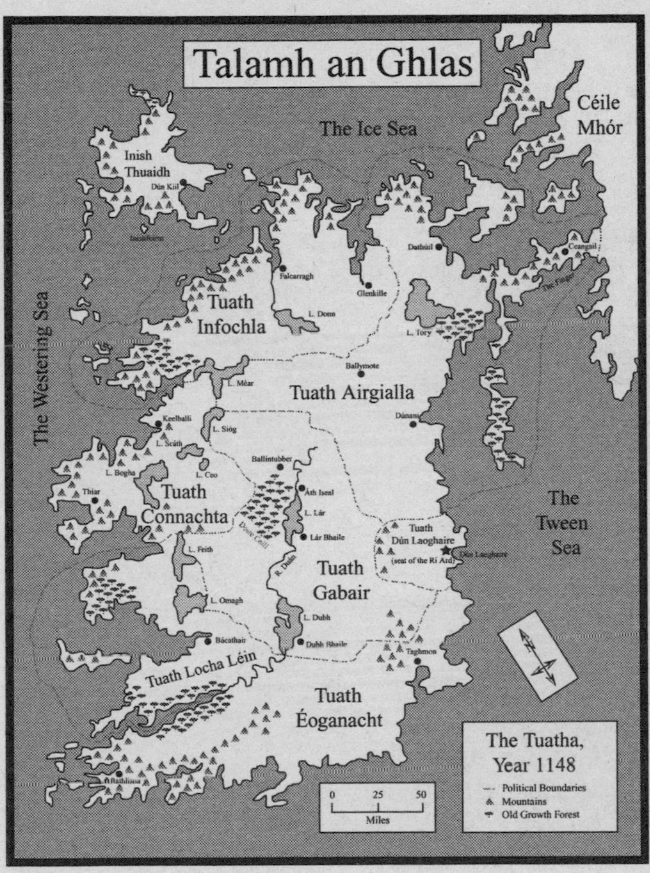

Talamh an Ghlas
The Ice Sea
Céile Mhór
Inish Thuaidh
Dún Kiil
The Westering Sea
Falcarragh
Glenkille
Dathúil
Ceangail
The Finger
Tuath Infochla
L. Donn
L. Tory
Ballymote
L. Méar
Tuath Airgialla
Keelballi
Dúnani
L. Sióg
L. Scáth
Ballintubber
L. Bogha
L. Ceo
Áth Iseal
Thiar
Tuath Connachta
L. Lár
Doire Coill
Lár Bhaile
Tuath Dún Laoghaire
Dún Laoghaire
(seat of the Rí Ard)
The Tween Sea
L. Feith
R. Duán
Tuath Gabair
L. Omagh
L. Dubh
Bácathair
Dubh Bhaile
Taghmon
Tuath Locha Léin
Tuath Éoganacht
Rathliana
0 25 50
Miles
The Tuatha, Year 1148
Political Boundaries
Mountains
Old Growth Forest

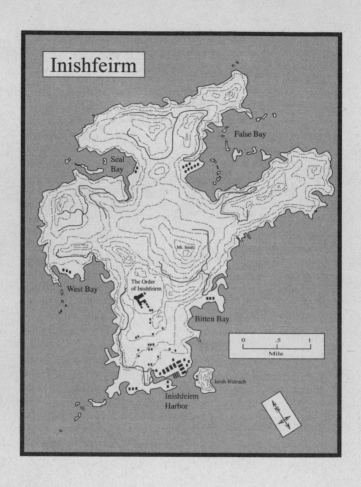

Inishfeirm

False Bay

Seal
Bay

West Bay

Mt. Inish

The Order
of Inishfeirm

Bitten Bay

| 0 | .5 | 1 |
Mile

Inish Bideach

Inishfeirm
Harbor

PART ONE

ACOLYTE

1

Fire from the Stones

RAW power smeared red and purple across the night sky, held captive in the glow of the mage-lights. . . .

Jenna raised her right hand, with the stone called Lámh Shábhála clasped in her fist, to the dazzling fury banishing the stars. The radiance snarled about her arm, the painful scars that mottled her skin glowing as she cried out in mingled relief and suffering.

She felt the man's presence before she actually saw him, sensed the attack even as the danger arced toward her: a dragon scaled in fiery red and yellow, great wings of leather beating the night sky, its taloned and muscular legs striking for Jenna as it reared back in midair, a long barbed tail lashing like a whip.

Almost contemptuously, Jenna took a part of the energy in which she was ensnared and sent it toward the dragon. The power smashed into the creature, nearly blinding Jenna with a showering explosion of white and blue. The mage-dragon howled in agony and vanished, but mocking laughter followed its disappearance: baritone, a bit too loud. She lowered her hand and the mage-lights curled reluctantly away into sky, fading. She could see him now, standing not ten strides from her—at the edge of the small courtyard enclosed within the private inner bailey of Dún Kiil Keep. He was a young man, no older than twenty, dressed in a silken, well-made clóca and léine, red-haired and thin of face, with a jewel grasped in his right hand—like Jenna's own hand, it too was scarred, though lightly, a barely visible marking that stopped at the wrist. She knew him immediately, even though she'd last seen him several years before, when he'd been a pimpled, gawky adolescent: Doyle Mac Ard.

She wondered how he'd gotten here—to her island, inside her keep, but she refused to let him see that his presence worried her. *"Strike him down while you have the chance . . ."* the voices of the old Holders within Lámh Shábhála whispered to her, but she ignored them, confronting the intruder with a scowl. "Only a fool would attack the Holder of Lámh Shábhála alone, especially when the mage-lights are out, Doyle."

"I'm not a fool," the man answered. "I was simply announcing my arrival. And you're as strong as they told me you would be, Sister."

"*Half* sister," she answered. A sudden, shivering fright came over her—she could think of only one reason why Doyle would appear here to speak with her. "How is Mam?"

Again, his noisy amusement echoed. "So nice of you to still care. I rather expected an immediate 'You're not welcome in Inish Thuaidh, Doyle' or 'I'll kill you the way I killed your da.' Of course, if you *really* cared for her, you would have actually come to see her once over the years. I hardly think your occasional letters to her count, though she stopped me when I tried to burn them."

Jenna didn't answer. She longed to justify her absence: *I asked her if she would see me in the letters, but she never answered. . . .* She waited, and after a moment, Doyle sniffed. She saw the answer to her question in the lines of his face before he even spoke the words. "Mam's dead. She passed two days ago. I thought I might tell you before you heard from your spies in the Tuatha."

"Dead . . ." Jenna didn't know what to say. "No . . ." Tears started in her eyes, brimming to run down her cheeks. She tried to speak and couldn't, the sudden grief closing her throat. An image flashed before her: Maeve, as she'd been the day Jenna had found Lámh Shábhála: the age Jenna was now, her hair a satin blackness sparked with wisps of pure white at the temples, and a smile creasing her face. Jenna blinked, and the vision faded. "How?" she asked finally, unable to get out more than the single word.

"Does it really matter to you? You're a few decades too late for genuine concern, aren't you?" Doyle responded. When Jenna just stared at him, he finally shrugged. "She hasn't been in good health for the last few years, as I'm sure your spies reported back to you, and the last winter was especially hard on her. I assure you that she was always well-cared for by Da's family. When she was lost in her final madness, they made certain she didn't hurt herself. I saw her as often as I possibly could, because I loved her and wanted her to know how much I will always be in her debt for having raised me. But *I* was never the child she most wanted to hear that from. Is that what you wanted to know?" A deliberate hesitation; a half smile. "My dear sister."

Jenna stared past him, not allowing any of the pain inside to show on her face. The residue of the mage-lights pounded in her temples, throbbing, and she longed to put a warm cloth over her eyes and take some kala bark to ease the headache. She wanted to be alone to grieve for the mam she remembered. "You sound surprisingly like your da," she said. "You're too young to be this cynical."

"I've had to grow up fast," he responded.

"Why are you here, Doyle?"

"Not *how?* I'd think you'd worry about me just showing up in Dún Kiil."

"I can guess how. The library at Inishfeirm tells of a Cloch Mór— 'Quickship,' isn't it?—with the ability to move people to places its holder has been, so one of the Rí Ard's tiarna must have found that stone and learned how it works."

"Indeed." Doyle gestured mockingly at the high, crenellated walls about them. "Aren't you glad that it was me who came and not some assassin?"

The voices grumbled inside her—". . . *kill him* . . ."—but she took a calming breath, pushing them back. "Don't threaten me, Doyle. You have no idea what I'm capable of."

Doyle gave her a wide-mouthed look of false astonishment, his empty hands palms out in front of him, then laughed again. "Actually, I think I have a *very* good idea of what you're capable of doing. I wouldn't presume that I have any ability to frighten the Banrion and First Holder. In fact, I'm here to do you a service. I'm here to give fair warning to my kin." His face went serious then, and he released the jewel he was holding, letting it fall to his breast on its chain. "I'm a man now, sister; a mage of the Order of Gabair and a tiarna in the service of the Rí Ard O Liathain and fully in his confidence."

"And also betrothed to Nevan O Liathain's daughter and to be married to her at the Festival of Fómhar," Jenna interrupted. "Given a Cloch Mór by the Rí Ard himself. I *do* hear these things, brother."

"*Half* brother." Doyle grinned. "I hear things as well. I hear what the Riocha say: about Inishlanders in general and their Banrion in particular. They think you're arrogant and above yourself; they think you've done little or nothing with the power you control; they think you're mad and dangerous and you hide here like a hermit; and they believe someone more . . . well, *deserving* should hold Lámh Shábhála."

Jenna tightened her fingers around the finger-sized stone in its silver cage. "I know at least some of those you talk about. Then let Nevan O Liathain or any of them try to take Lámh Shábhála from me." Her voice took on heat now—if she could not let herself grieve, then she'd let anger cover the turmoil inside her. "Perhaps you'd like to bring back your mage-dragon again and make the attempt yourself? I remember Snapdragon—the cloch you now hold—from Dún Kiil. I'll tell you that it will fare no better now than it did then."

Doyle simply shook his head. "We're not stupid, Jenna. Especially not the Rí Ard. But Dún Kiil was a long time ago, and memories dim and time grows shorter for the ones who were there. We young tiarna don't remember it at all. Why, I was just a babe suckling at our mam's breast when you murdered Da."

"It wasn't murder, Doyle," Jenna snapped. The headache and grief pounded at her skull; her right arm ached as if it were made of glacial ice. "*. . . smash him for his arrogance and be done with it . . .*"

"Of course, you wouldn't call it that. How do you think of it, Jenna? 'Self-defense?'—no, it couldn't be *that,* when you've already bragged to me that you don't consider one piddling Cloch Mór a challenge for Lámh Shábhála. Or was it just a happy accident of some sort, just a twist of unkind fate? What was it you told Mam when you gave her Da's body? 'He gave me no choice . . .' No, there's no blame on you, sister. There's no guilt to stain *your* soul when the Black Haunts come for you."

Jenna blinked away the memories. She set her jaw against the pain, both mental and physical. "We can dance with words all night, Doyle. If you wanted to chastise me for my past, you could have done it more easily in a letter. What is it you want?"

A sniff. "I'm telling you all this, Sister, so that I can go to Mam's barrow with a clear conscience and tell her that I warned you, that I made the attempt to avoid bloodshed between us. It's she who has protected you all these years, Jenna. You probably don't realize that. She told me that she couldn't bear to see her children fighting each other, so I obeyed her. But she's gone now. *You* may be too strong to attack directly, Jenna, but those around you, those you love, aren't so well protected and to hurt *you,* someone might decide to go after them. Your enemies might feel they have no other choice. Do you understand what I'm telling you?"

The image came to her of her lover Ennis, his throat slit open in front of Jenna as she watched helplessly . . . Jenna closed her eyes against the horrible vision etched forever in her memory, forcing back the hot tears that threatened her again. She took a slow breath and opened her eyes again. "I understand that better than you'll ever realize," she told Doyle.

"Good," he answered. "Then I've done what I came to do. As to what *I* want . . ." Doyle stared at her, then let his gaze move slowly to her hand, where she clutched Lámh Shábhála. "I want what should have been Da's in the beginning," he said quietly. "I want what should have been mine. And I *will* have it." His gaze came back to her eyes. His stare was unblinking and steady. "One day, I will have it. And aye, I know what that means."

He touched the stone at his chest and Jenna started in alarm. The voices inside Lámh Shábhála screamed at her—"*Fool! Kill him now!*"—but Doyle didn't release the power of his cloch nor did the dragon appear. Instead, he was simply gone, soundlessly, as if he had never been there at all.

Jenna let out her breath in a long, shuddering sigh.

A garda's step scrunched on gravel, and Jenna saw a face peering through the garden gate as he called out to her. "Banrion, is everything all right? I thought I heard another voice. . . ."

"Just a ghost," she told him. "The air tonight is alive with ghosts."

2

Leaving

MERIEL'S mam was at the window, staring out toward the cliffs of Croc a Scroilm, the "Hill of Screaming" atop which Dún Kiil Keep sat. "Your daughter's arrived, Banrion," the hallway garda announced, allowing Meriel to enter the room and then swiftly closing the door behind her. With the click of the door lock, her mam sighed as if in resignation and turned.

"Meriel," she said, glancing at the clock-candle on the fireplace mantel, the white wax marked with regular lines of red. "I sent for you over a stripe ago."

"Sorry, Mam," Meriel answered. "I'd had Iníon Nainsi take me down to the harbor, and we came back as soon as the page found us."

That was a lie. In truth, Meriel had been with Lucan O Dálaigh behind the rocks at the edge of the harbor, with Nainsi acting as lookout in case someone came near. Lucan was two years older than Meriel and the youngest son of Barra O Dálaigh, a tiarna under Meriel's da.

She and Lucan had started a secret flirtation—at least Meriel hoped it was secret—while she'd been visiting her da in Dún Madadh last summer. The first night there, she'd danced with him at the Festival of Méitha; the quiet romance had blossomed during long, warm days, fueled by too-rare meetings. When Lucan had been sent to Dún Kiil to serve at the keep only a few days after

9

Meriel herself had returned, she'd thought that the Mother-Creator Herself had blessed them. The relationship had already lasted longer than any of her past infatuations; she had dared, once or twice, to imagine that it might even go further. For now, though, there were only stolen moments in the corridors of the keep and precious minutes when they could both find excuses to be away and alone together. She could still feel the touch of Lucan's mouth on hers; she wondered that her mam could not see the kisses, engraved in burning heat on her lips.

Jenna MacEagan seemed to possess that sorcery: she had a strange knack of knowing when Meriel was lying and for seeing things that Meriel thought hidden. Her mam was still frowning, and Meriel rubbed unconsciously at her lips with the back of her hand. "Besides, Mam," Meriel added, "there's that Taisteal clan that has set up down by the harbor, and they hardly ever come here and I wanted to see what they had to buy. . . ."

Her mam only nodded abstractedly and without anger, as if her mind were elsewhere. Jenna tucked strands of coal-black hair (with a few, first strands of silver at the temples) behind her ear and adjusted the golden torc around her neck: the torc of the Banrion. On the brocaded clóca she wore, a chain glittered, a cage of silver wire on it holding a stone of pale green, shot with lines of white: Lámh Shábhála, the first and most powerful of the clochs na thintrí—the mage-stones. Despite its reputed power, the stone had always seemed rather plain and ordinary to Meriel.

In the shadows of the dimly lit room, motion snagged Meriel's gaze as a man moved behind the serving table to her right. He was dressed in a plain white clóca and léine. He was older, perhaps the same age as her mam, with long blond hair fading now to gray, his skull shiny-bald from eyebrows to nearly the crown of his head. His beard, though, was strangely dark and liberally spattered with white hairs; under it, a jewel the green-blue of a shallow sea glittered in a cage of silver and gold, suspended from a chain around his neck. The gem was far more impressive to look at than the one around her mam's neck. Jenna knew what that stone was, too, or at least she could guess at it: a Cloch Mór, one of the thirty major mage-stones. White raiment, the cloch na thintrí around his neck: the man was a cloudmage of the Order of Inishfeirm.

Seeing him in this room, she had a sudden gnawing suspicion as to why he was here and why she'd been summoned. Her stomach burned with the thought, roiling. *You wouldn't do this to me, Mam,* she wanted to cry out, all at once. Her mam saw Meriel's attention on the stranger. "Meriel, this is Máister Mundy Kirwan," she said, "head of the Order of Inishfeirm."

The man's eyes were the blue of glacial ice, though there was a gentleness in the folds that crinkled around them as he smiled at her. "You probably don't remember me, Bantiarna MacEagan," he said, "but we've met before, three or four times. The first time, you'd been born no more than a week before; the last time I was in Dún Kiil, you were seven or perhaps eight summers old. You've . . . grown up much since then." He glanced over to Meriel's mam, whose lips were set in the neutral near-frown she wore whenever she was talking with the Riocha—those of royal blood—who swarmed around Dún Kiil like flies around a dead storm deer. "She's ready to go?"

The burning in Meriel's stomach went to flame. "Ready to go?" Meriel asked, looking from one to the other. "To *go?* Mam, please, you can't mean that . . ."

Meriel saw confusion and embarrassment cross the Máister's face, and his hands lifted in apology. "Jenna, I'm sorry. I thought you'd already told her—"

Jenna . . . With the casual use of her mam's name, Meriel realized how well the Máister must know her. There were very few people on Inish Thuaidh who could address her so familiarly. Jenna MacEagan was "Banrion MaEagan" or at the least "First Holder." The only one she had heard call her mam "Jenna" had been Da or old Aithne MacBrádaigh, whose late husband had been the Rí before Meriel's mam had become Banrion.

"Told me *what?*" Meriel asked.

Her mam's lips tightened, the lines on her forehead grew deeper. Jenna's right hand, covered with the patterned white lines of old scars that echoed the lines of the mage-lights, brushed the silver cage of Lámh Sháb-hála and dropped again.

"I meant to tell her," Jenna said, speaking more to the Máister than to Meriel. "But she was away with Kyle all the summer and I've been otherwise occupied since then, as you know. . . ." She stopped. Took a long breath. Gold-brown eyes caught Meriel's gaze. Meriel knew what she was going to say before she spoke, confirming the apprehension she'd felt ever since she saw the Máister in the room. "You're going with Mundy—Máister Kirwan—to Inishfeirm, Meriel. I studied there, too, after I became First Holder—"

"No." Meriel spat out the word, interrupting her mam. Her head shook, her long and rather unruly strands of curly red hair swaying with the motion. She said it more loudly. "*No!* I'm *not* going, Mam. I'm not interested in being a cloudmage."

"You need this schooling, Meriel," Jenna answered. "It's vital, for your own well-being."

"Do you hate me that much, Mam?" Meriel railed back. "Have you run out of cages to put me in or places to send me so you don't have to deal with me? Am I in your way that much?"

Bright spots of color flared high on her mam's cheeks and Meriel thought she was going to spiral into one of her rages, but Máister Kirwan cleared his throat and they both looked at him. "Meriel, I remember your mam telling old Máister Cléurach fourteen years ago, in nearly the same tone, that she had absolutely no interest in anything he could teach her," Máister Kirwan said, a chuckle of subdued amusement in his voice. "The poor man damned near died of apoplexy right there and then." He did laugh then, a low rumble like soft thunder. "But your mam *did* study despite her protest, if somewhat grudgingly, and she learned. You should be an even better student: you have the gift from your mam's side, and . . ." He paused, glancing at Jenna strangely. ". . . as strong a one from your da's."

Her mam's cheeks colored again, and Meriel wondered why the man would say that, in such an odd tone. Aye, her da also held a Cloch Mór, but he always said that it was only because his wife was the First Holder and he never seemed to enjoy talking about the times he'd used it. Jenna, on the other hand, was certainly snared in magic. Meriel had heard the tales of the Filleadh, the "Coming Back" of the mage-stones for which her mam had supposedly been responsible.

Meriel had never been able to escape the history of her mam. In fact, her mam's past seemed to surround Meriel everywhere she went, and people delighted in telling her again all the tales she'd heard too many times before. She heard them in long ballads sung by the Songmasters in the Weeping Hall: the Lay of Jenna Aoire and its endless verses. Or she heard them in the whispered tales from the succession of maidservants who had watched her through her childhood, or even from her current attendant Nainsi. "Oh, your mam the Banrion," they'd say with trembling voices, "why, you wouldn't believe what she did when all she was but a young woman herself. She was chased all the way to Inish Thuaidh by the gardai of the Rí Ard and barely escaped with her life. . . ." Or it would be the flattering tongues of the Riocha she met, pressing around her in sycophantic delight. "Aye, I was there at Dún Kiil with the Banrion when she defeated the armies of the Tuatha. . . ."

The stories and songs, some of them, were so farfetched that they seemed more myth and legend than truth, impossible to attribute to the flesh-and-blood woman she called Mam: the powerful Banrion who united the contentious clans of Inish Thuaidh; the fierce Hero of Dún Kiil; the great First Holder. Meriel knew the last was true, at least: the mage-lights called Jenna nearly every night and Jenna went out to commune with them and let them wrap their silver-and-green tendrils around her.

Meriel also remembered the feel of her mam's right arm like ice against her skin, and how the fingers curled into a stiff claw. She heard her mam cry out in pain some nights, cradling that arm to herself and moaning.

Meriel had cried at nights as well over the years, wishing that her mam could simply be her mam and not some distant story.

"The Máister's right," Jenna said. "Meriel, you're seventeen. You need to start learning your way in life." She touched the stone around her neck; as she did, the sleeve of her léine fell to her elbow, displaying the scars that marred the flesh from hand to shoulder. "Someday, this may be yours to hold."

"I don't *want* it, Mam," Meriel said. "I've told you that a dozen times before. But I don't expect you to suddenly start listening to what I want now."

Jenna drew in her breath with an audible hiss, and Meriel saw small muscles twitch along her mam's jaw. She knew that the argument was lost before it was begun. *Mam,* she wanted to cry, *every time I try to make my own life, you destroy it. You can't take me away from here, away from Lucan, away from the only friends I have, away from my da, away from everything familiar and everything I have right now. You can't send me to a miserable flea speck of an island stinking of fish and seals. That isn't the life I want. Why do you hate me so much?*

She knew what her mam would say—Jenna had said it to her daughter many times over the years, so often that the actual words had lost any meaning they'd once had. It was ritual. "We rarely get what we want from life, Meriel. We have to take what the Mother-Creator gives us. I'm doing this to make you stronger."

I don't need to be strong, I need you to act like you love me, Meriel ached to retort. *It's not the Mother-Creator doing this. It's you. No one else.*

But she bit her lip, trying not to cry in front of them. "You're going, Meriel," Jenna said, her voice as implacable as the stone walls around them. "You don't have a choice."

"Da, you can't let Mam *do* this!" Meriel said desperately.

A slow, somewhat sad smile drifted over her da's features. His attendant Alby, who somehow always seemed to be in the same room as her da, sniffed as if in reply to Meriel's plea as hc poured water for tea. Kyle MacEagan's chambers in Dún Kiil Keep were unconnected to his wife's, and they seemed more comfortable and warm to Meriel. "Come here, my lamb," her da said, opening his arms. She leaned into his embrace, as soft as his features. Kyle was a short man—Meriel's head was at a level with his—and plump. Meriel sometimes wondered how the man could be her da—she seemed to have inherited everything from her mam, not him. She could also love him as she couldn't seem to love her mam. He was also affectionate with her, always willing to be interested in anything she was interested in, always able to let her be part of his life.

Her mam would never do that. Jenna was the First Holder before anything else, and Lámh Shábhála was the more demanding child.

Everything about Kyle MacEagan was relaxed and gentle: his movements, his breath, his voice. The only hardness to him was the Cloch Mór, Firerock, that he wore around his neck. He kissed Meriel's forehead as if she were still a child. "Your mam has only your welfare at heart," he whispered to her as if he'd guessed her thoughts. "I know you don't feel that way sometimes, but it's true. It's always been true."

She pulled back from him; his arms dropped back quietly and unresistingly. "You can't be taking her sidc in this, Da. She wants to send me to *Inishfeirm*—that miserable, sheep-infested island, where I'll be surrounded by old cloudmages and all the useless third sons and second daughters of the Riocha that have been sent to them."

"Ah," Kyle said. His eyes twinkled. "So you're too good for them?"

"Da, that's not what I mean," she said in exasperation. His eyebrows raised, but he didn't answer. "It's not. Why should I have to go to Inishfeirm with the Máister? I should be *here*, where I can learn to be a bantiarna and serve on the Comhairle and maybe even one day be the Banrion."

"Ah, so you've decided to be Banrion now," Kyle said, and Meriel heard Alby chuckle quietly across the room. Meriel felt her cheeks go hot, but before she could say anything, her da shook his head. "Meriel, maybe one day that burden—and it's a burden, my lamb; if you believe nothing else, you should believe that—will come to you. If it does, aye, you'll need to know much more than you do now. You'll need to know things that only Máister Kirwan can teach you."

Meriel resisted the temptation to stamp her foot on the stone flags of the room. "You're going to let her send me away? Why does she hate me so much?"

"Meriel . . ." Kyle sighed and took the mug of tea that Alby offered him. Meriel shook her head at the mug the man proffered to her. Alby nodded, though she thought she saw a disapproving half scowl on his face, and moved back to the recesses of the chamber. Her da sipped at the tea. "Your mam loves you, as I do, even if you don't want to believe that. If you're going to truly be Bantiarna MacEagan and be on the Comhairle, much less be Banrion, then you're also going to need to learn that sometimes—often, in fact—you can't do what you want, but rather what you *have* to do. Things have changed recently, and so this you have to do."

"Why?"

He lifted the mug again. His eyes closed as he sipped.

They stayed closed as he spoke. "It's for your own safety."

Meriel glared at him. "That's what Mam said. I didn't believe her either."

Kyle glanced across the room to where Alby stood. She thought she saw him shake his head at the man. He went to the window of the chamber and set the mug down on the sill. When he turned back, his face was more solemn than Meriel ever remembered seeing it. "Jenna—your mam—asked me not to tell you this. But I will. You've been directly threatened, Meriel. Your uncle Doyle Mac Ard . . . he sent a message to your mam. That's why we want you to go to Inishfeirm: so you'll not only have cloudmages around you for protection, but so you can also begin to learn to protect yourself."

Meriel was shaking her head before he'd finished. "That doesn't make sense, Da. Mam has Lámh Shábhála, and you have Firerock. How could I be safer away from you?"

"At Inishfeirm, you'll have several Cloch Mórs and clochmions around you, all the time, as well as those who know slow magics. We both agree—"

"But I don't," Meriel interrupted. "I don't."

Her da's face closed off. He wouldn't look at her and she knew that she'd lost the argument, that nothing she said would be enough. "You don't have a choice, my lamb," he said. "If Jenna's telling you as your mam isn't enough, then she'll tell you as the Banrion and First Holder. You don't have a choice."

"We could run away," Lucan said desperately. "Why, we could take one of the fisherfolk's boats and go across to Talamh an Ghlas. We could travel to one of the southern Tuatha, or maybe even cross over the Finger to Céile Mhór. They wouldn't find us. We could make our own lives."

They were on the rocks at the western end of the harbor near the noisy and busy Taisteal encampment, with Nainsi again acting as their lookout, though a trio of gardai from the keep had also been ordered by Jenna to go with them and were standing with Nainsi just out of sight. A mist was falling, beading on their clóca; the waves splashing against the black rocks were gray and thick as porridge, and seals grunted and groaned out toward Little Head. Meriel and Lucan stood together, embracing each other, their faces close. Meriel could see the thrill of adventure blazing in Lucan's green eyes. He'd already constructed a fantasy around the notion and she wanted desperately to share it, but she couldn't. "My mam and da would come after us, and your da as well," she told him.

"They won't find us. Not in Talamh an Ghlas. There are lost valleys there, and the old forests. We could hide there and an army couldn't find us." His voice was desperate and deep and the urgent certainty in it made her shake her head.

"They wouldn't need an army. They have the clochs na thintrí, Lucan, and my mam holds Lámh Shábhála. You don't know how powerful that stone is—"

"Those are folktales and myths, Meriel. Your mam doesn't know about us, does she?"

Meriel shook her head once, back and forth. "I don't think so."

Lucan grinned. "There, you see? She can't know everything. This is *right,* Meriel. Can't you feel it? Let's do it. Now, before we have a chance to talk each other out of it." He leaned down to kiss her, and she reached up with one hand to touch his black beard, short and soft and still patchy on his cheeks. The kiss was long, deep, and sweet, yet when Lucan moved back, Meriel couldn't stop the words that tumbled out.

"If they find us, Lucan . . ."

"If they find us, what can they do, Meriel? We'll have

been together. Alone. Intimate. We're both Riocha and my family name is good enough even for the MacEagan clan: they'd insist that we marry, that's all. And isn't that what we want?"

"Aye," Meriel answered, but she couldn't summon the enthusiasm she thought she should feel. She started to speak, swallowed the words, and then tried again. "We'd be two people alone in the wild, Lucan. Only the Mother-Creator knows what walks there since the land has awakened again. There are still Bunús Muintir in the old woods, and the dire wolves are bad enough here—" She didn't mention the threat of her uncle.

"Shhh . . ." He leaned down again, kissing her softly. "I'm good with sword and bow and I can teach you. And we'd be together: there's nothing in this world that could stand against that." He laughed, and after a moment she laughed with him, wanting to believe.

Believing enough that she agreed to go with him that night, before the ship to Inishfeirm sailed tomorrow afternoon. They walked out from behind the screen of the rocks, hand in hand.

"Good afternoon." Máister Kirwan waited with arms folded across his chest at the end of the harbor, with Nainsi standing sheepishly alongside him. The trio of keep's gardai stood a pace behind. "A foul day to be out, don't you think, Meriel? When I first talked to your mam, I thought perhaps she was wrong to be sending you to Inishfeirm. Now I suspect that it's exactly the right thing to do." Máister Kirwan glanced at Lucan, giving him a grim smile. "And young Tiarna O Dálaigh. It seems your da has sent a request to the Banrion, asking that you return home to Dún Madadh. You'll be leaving tomorrow morning." He nodded to the gardai. "If you'll be good enough to accompany Tiarna O Dálaigh back to the Keep so he can begin his packing, I'd appreciate it. Meriel, let's take a walk, you and I. Nainsi, you'll wait here for us."

Máister Kirwan's tone was that of a person used to obedience. Meriel saw Lucan hesitate, but the gardai were grim-faced and moved quickly alongside him, taking him by the elbows and escorting him away. "Meriel . . ." he called, looking back as they pulled him away. She would have gone to him, but Máister Kirwan took her arm and moved her back along the path through the rocks. His grip on her elbow was gentle yet firm.

"Máister . . ."

"You'll have a chance to say good-bye to him, Meriel. I promise you that," he said. "And if it is love between you and not a simple infatuation, it will be strong enough to survive the separation. Come with me for now. Please."

Meriel cast another glance back, but Lucan and the gardai were already near the street entrance, the bright tents of the Taisteal camp ahead of them. She let Máister Kirwan guide her away from the harbor, walking slowly past the hollow where she and Lucan had kissed and planned, following the rough path down to the water again, closer to the curving horn of Little Head. He didn't say anything while they walked, nor when they reached a small, rock-strewn beach where strands of green kelp lay in the tidal foam and pebbles. He stood there, looking back toward the town and the Keep high above it, and the mountains that framed Dún Kiil Bay.

"It's a rough beauty we have here on Inish Thuaidh," he said at last. "Our islands aren't soft and green like those of Talamh an Ghlas. Here, the hard bones of the land are laid bare. And we Inishlanders are like the islands themselves: we make our own way, and we prefer to be left alone—but that's not possible. We've managed it about as long as we can."

"I don't know what you're talking about," Meriel said, impatience coloring her voice. She found the voice she used on the servants when they hadn't performed as she wished. "By what right are you interfering with my life this way?"

Máister Kirwan's face twisted, as if he were trying to conceal a smile. "By the right of your mam's orders," he answered. "And my own advice to her, to which she occasionally listens. You've been kept away from most of what your mam has had to deal with; that was Jenna's choice—*against* my advice. Because of that . . ." He stopped. Just before Meriel started to speak, he began again. "Meriel, your mam wasn't much older than you when she was given Lámh Shábhála to hold, all unprepared, and was thrust into larger events than she ever imagined when she was a simple shepherd girl. I can understand why she'd want to protect her daughter from the same fate. I think that was a mistake, but it was Jenna's to make. Yet now . . . it's time you started to open your eyes."

Impatience flared into anger. "You talk to me like I'm a child. I'm not. Speak plainly if you have something to say, Máister, not in riddles and innuendos."

"Plainly?" Máister Kirwan reached into a pocket on his clóca and brought out a small rock. He held it in the palm of his hand as if admiring it: Meriel thought it might be quartz: a pretty thing, with transparent facets that were a faint blue in color. "Here's the unadorned truth, then. You are privileged, Meriel. You're even spoiled . . ." He raised a finger against her protest. ". . . even though I know you feel confined and over-protected. Because of who you are—who your *parents* are—you will almost certainly hold a Cloch Mór one day, one of the thirty great stones of magic. You may even hold Lámh Shábhála, if that's the fate the Mother-Creator has in store for you. That's a great burden, a heavier one than you can imagine. It's my job to make certain that you can bear it."

"What if I don't *want* that?" Meriel told him. "Because I don't."

"Then what is it you *do* want?"

Meriel blinked. "Right now, I want Lucan. But you and Mam took him away. She takes away *everything* I want."

A grin creased his cheeks. He put the piece of quartz

back in his pocket. "Think beyond your wants of this instant, Meriel," Máister Kirwan said. "Think beyond today."

"Then . . ." She stopped. "I don't know. I . . . I haven't . . ." Her voice trailed off into silence.

His face changed, all the lines carving deeper in his flesh, his eyes flashing as he leaned near to her. His countenance frightened her: he glared at her as if he were holding back a terrible anger, and his voice was like the low rumble of an approaching storm. His left hand caught her forearm, the fingers digging deep into her flesh. "Listen to me, child," he growled. "Listen because your life may depend on this knowledge, sooner than you think." He let go of her arm, and Meriel rubbed at her skin where his fingers had been, blinking back unbidden tears. Máister Kirwan reached for the chain around his neck, lifting the gem at the end of it.

"Let me tell you something you may know, something you damned well should know, if you don't. And if you think you've already heard it, then listen again, because it's obvious to me that you haven't understood the importance. There are one hundred and fifty clochmion—the minor stones of magic. Of the *major* stones, the Clochs Mór, there are thirty, Meriel. No more. Eight of them reside here in Inish Thuaidh—which means there are but twenty-two Clochs Mór in *all* of Talamh an Ghlas; between the seven Tuatha; between all the Ríthe who rule them and the Rí Ard himself; between all the Riocha there, the hundreds of tiarna and bantiarna and céili giallnai with royal blood in their veins, and the thousands who would like to be among the Riocha. The balance of power among all of us, now that your mam has opened the mage-lights to the stones once again, is largely determined by the Clochs Mór. To the Riocha of the Tuatha, if Inish Thuaidh has eight Clochs Mór, then we have *too* many Clochs Mór. We're smaller than any of the Tuatha, yet none of them have more than four of the Clochs Mór.

"They want our Clochs Mór, want them the way a

drowning man wants the sweet air, and it's only the Rí Ard Nevan O Liathain who holds them back from coming to take them. He hesitates because of what happened the last time, here at Dún Kiil. But the Rí Ard's health is failing—if he dies, then the new Rí Ard may not be so cautious about warring against us. Many of the Riocha have forgotten Dún Kiil or are too young to have fought in that battle, and the southern Tuatha never took part in it at all. The Tuatha look at Inish Thuaidh, and they see that we have more Clochs Mór than they like, and they think that their twenty and two are more than a match for our eight even with Lámh Shábhála also against them."

He let the stone drop back to his chest, and he gazed at Dún Kiil, his eyes narrowing and his face pained. "I remember the battle. I remember the hundreds who died here. I remember smoke and chaos and the smell of death, the crackling of magic being used in its most destructive way." He turned back to her, stricken.

"That war isn't ended. It will soon break open again," he said. "I don't think we can stop it. And you *will* be part of it, whether you want that or not. Sometimes people don't have the luxury of deciding what they want to be. *You* won't have that luxury, Meriel. That's why you're going to Inishfeirm."

"Did she hear you?" Jenna asked. "I mean *really* hear you?"

Mundy shrugged. "I don't know," he answered. "I hope so. I think I scared her, at least, and she needs to be scared. We should *all* be scared."

Jenna *hmmed* at that. Mundy could see the worry on her face, and he saw the way she cradled her right arm with her left hand, as if the scarred arm pained her. "The O Dálaigh boy?" she asked.

"I talked with him also, after I spoke to Meriel. He's just . . . a boy. We'll see how long the infatuation lasts when they're apart. I'll wager it won't be long. Some pretty lass will smile at him, and suddenly what's in front of him will be more important than what's gone."

Jenna blinked. Mundy saw her start to protest—as any mam might protest such an offhand dismissal of her daughter's charms—then close her mouth again. "And the clochmion? Treoraí's Heart?"

Mundy reached into his pocket and brought out the fragment of crystal he'd had on the beach. "I didn't give it to her," he told Jenna. "I know you asked me to, but she isn't ready, not even for a clochmion." He paused, his fingers still closed around the stone. "She may never be ready, Jenna," he said. "Not for what you carry. I think that's something you have to consider when you're ready to pass it on."

"She doesn't *need* to be ready," Jenna answered sharply. "I wasn't prepared for what was given me, but I struggled through." Jenna held out her left hand. "Give me Treoraí's Heart. I'll give it to her myself before we go."

Mundy looked at Jenna's outstretched hand but didn't respond. "Meriel's not you, Jenna," Mundy said. "She's not her da either—and I mean her *real* da, not Kyle MacEagan. She's just . . . herself." His hand was still closed around the stone. He looked again at Jenna's hand, then at her bitter frown. "If you want me to be Meriel's teacher, then you also have to trust my judgment in this, Jenna. Otherwise, you can teach her yourself. Can you really handle that responsibility, along with all the others you've taken on?"

A grimace twisted her lips. In that moment, she looked older, and Mundy realized how much the years had touched her. "It would be nice to have a daughter or a friend who simply obeyed me when I asked them to do something."

"A Banrion can demand unquestioning obedience from her subjects, but a *friend* will give the Banrion honesty instead, even when I tell her something she doesn't want to hear. Which do you want me to be, Jenna: friend or subject?"

Grimace slid into scowl. The fingers of Jenna's right hand twitched, as if she wanted to form it into a fist but couldn't. "You sound more like old Máister Cléurach every time we meet, Mundy Kirwan. You have the same arrogance and the same stubborn belief that you're the only one who's ever right."

He scowled back at her. "It's the air at Inishfeirm," Mundy answered. "It turns us all into grumpy old curmudgeons before our time. Evidently you stayed there long enough to be infected yourself." He held the scowl for a moment longer until he saw her lips relax and her head shake, and he laughed into her reluctant smile. He put the clochmion back in his pocket.

"I'll take care of your daughter as if she were my own, Jenna," he said. "I promise you that. With the help of the Order, Meriel will find the strength that's inside herself and bring it out."

3

Inside the Keep

THE ONE, the *only,* good thing about the trip to Inishfeirm was the three days at sea it would take to get there.

Meriel had loved the sea instinctively from the time she first remembered seeing it: the smell of the brine; the delicate changing colors of water under the sky, from slate gray to foaming green to cobalt blue; the aching vastness and sheer weight of the ocean, extending unbroken out to the limits of her sight and hiding unguessed treasures underneath; the raw, seething power of the storms that often swept over Inish Thuaidh from across the Westering Sea. Whether at Dún Kiil or at her da's estates at Dún Madadh, Meriel spent as much time as she could at the shore or in one of the currachs, watching the cavorting seals and the wheeling gulls.

A year ago, she'd spotted a family of blue seals just off Little Head at Dún Kiil: the Saimhóir who had their own language and who her mam claimed could also harness the energy of the mage-lights. She'd watched them lolling on rocks a few hundred strides out in the water, the sunlight striking sparkling emerald highlights from their black fur. Their craning heads noticed her watching them from the shore and they seemed to call to her, honking and moaning in their odd tongue before finally slipping back into the water and moving down the coastline. Meriel had watched for them for several weeks afterward, but never saw them again.

As much as was possible on the *Uaigneas,* the royal ship with its double masts, Meriel stayed away from Máister Kirwan and her mam, who had also accompanied them on the trip. Instead, she dutifully wrote a long letter every morning to Lucan, placing it in an envelope and sealing it. That's what she and Lucan had vowed they would do during that last unhappy (and too well-chaperoned) meeting before the ship left: they would write to each other each day. She would send the first packet of envelopes back to him via the captain of the *Uaigneas* once they reached Inishfeirm, and she hoped the first of Lucan's letters was already on its way to her.

She also prowled the decks with Nainsi, who seemed singularly unhappy to be at sea—or perhaps her gloomy face was more due to the fact that this was the last time she'd accompany Meriel. Unlike the children of most other Riocha, Meriel had never been sent away to fosterage. No, Jenna had wanted her near—"For your safety," she said curtly when Meriel had asked why—but while they lived in the same keep, Jenna rarely spent much time with her daughter, leaving her in the care of a succession of nurses and teachers and caregivers. Nainsi had been Meriel's attendant/guardian since she was ten summers old: a dour, plain girl five years older than Meriel, the daughter of a minor tiarna from the townland of Rubha na Scarbh. Meriel knew that Nainsi enjoyed the reflected glory of being in the Banrion's household, and after the severe tongue-lashing she'd received from the Banrion in the aftermath of yesterday, Nainsi was afraid that she'd be dismissed entirely.

"Your mam says that she'll try to find something for me within the keep, but after what's happened she could order me away. Then what happens to me? My da and mam would be furious, and they'll marry me to some flatulent, pig-farming céili giallnai from Tuath Éoganacht. Promise me you'll talk to her, Meriel. After all our time together . . ."

Meriel tried to ignore Nainsi's whining, finding some
small pleasure in talking with the sailors, listening to
their rowing songs and their rough jests, though Nainsi
pretended to be horrified and tried to lead her away.
Meriel also spent a lot of time simply standing at the ship's
prow, watching the waves break white against the carved
image of a sea serpent. She pretended that the voyage
would never end, that she would see Lucan coming after
her in a ship of his own, and she would leap over the
side of *Uaigneas* to him and they would sail off on an
adventure to some far, unknown shore, perhaps as far
as Thall Mór-roinn. Or if not Lucan, then a storm that
would hurl *Uaigneas* before its fury and drive them into
the rocks somewhere else, anywhere else but Inishfeirm.
But Lucan's ship never came, nor the storm, and by
evening they were rounding the long arm of An Ceann
Caol and beginning to slip westward.

Meriel took her supper in the cabin she and Nainsi
shared. When she came back on deck, she saw her mam
standing at the rail of the ship. She started to turn back,
but her mam caught sight of her. "Meriel, come
here . . ." she said. With a sigh, Meriel went over to
her. Jenna pointed down at the water. "Look," she said.
"The seals have come to say hello."

Around the ship, several large seals were skimming
through the wake of the ship, occasionally jumping from
the water. "Those are blues," Jenna said. "Saimhóir."

"I know," Meriel told her. "I've seen them before,
out near Little Head. I go out there sometimes just to
see them. I think they're fascinating and . . . beautiful."

Meriel could feel Jenna's gaze on her, and when she
turned her head, she found her mam staring at her appraisingly. "You just . . . watch them?" she asked, and
Meriel frowned.

"Of course, Mam. I tried to go up to them a few
times, but they'd just go in the water and honk and wail
at me, like they were trying to talk to me."

Jenna nodded, slowly, and her attention went back to

the seals in the water. "I love them myself. Especially the blues. But I never knew you liked them also."

"There's lots you don't know about me," Meriel answered, too sharply.

Meriel thought her mam would react angrily. She saw Jenna's fingers grip the railing tightly in the last of the sunlight, but Jenna only took a long breath. "I know," she said. "That's my fault, Meriel, and I admit it. But there's nothing I can do about it now. I can't change the past. All I can do is try to be more of a mam to you from now on."

Then don't banish me to Inishfeirm, Meriel wanted to retort, but she bit her lips, watching the seals. They were falling behind the ship now, turning back to the shore. They watched them depart as the sky darkened and turned red on the horizon ahead of them. "My own mam . . ." Jenna started, then paused. "Your great-mam Maeve . . . I've learned that she died. I'm sorry you never had the chance to meet her, Meriel. She was a good person and she would have loved you."

"Then why didn't you ever bring me to see her or have her come to us?"

Meriel saw her mam's lips tighten. Her eyes shimmered in the sunset. "It's a long and complicated story, and—" She sighed. "I'll tell you someday. I *want* to tell you. Maybe when we get to Inishfeirm and can sit down for a long chat. But the short version is that we both, Mam and I, made the choice to stay apart because . . ." Her voice became softer than the hush of the water against the hull.

"Because you killed Padraic Mac Ard."

Meriel saw her mam's eyes close with remembered pain. "Aye. Because of Padraic Mac Ard. I wrote to her, oh, once a year or so. I told her about you. I told her lots of things, but she never responded. After a while I stopped writing. We're both—well, we're both too proud for our own good. I know that was a mistake, now—and I hope the Mother-Creator will forgive me for it." Jenna turned her head to look at Meriel. "It's a mistake I don't want to make with my own daughter."

She couldn't hold back the retort this time. "Then tell the captain to turn the ship around. Don't send me to Inishfeirm."

Jenna was already shaking her head before she finished. "I can't, Meriel."

"Why not? This isn't what I want, Mam. How does it help us to get closer if I'm *there* while you're in Dún Kiil? Tell me why you're doing this to me."

Jenna had turned away from the ocean. The seals had vanished, and only the edge of the sun was still visible. In the dusk, Meriel could see her mam's eyes glistening. "There are things you shouldn't know, Meriel. Not yet. This is one of them."

"Fine," Meriel said, snapping her mouth shut with the word. She slapped the railing with her hand, the sound loud. "You treat me like I'm still a child, Mam, but I'm not. I suppose that's something else you didn't notice."

With that, Meriel pushed away from the railing and left. She heard her mam call her name behind her but she paid no attention. She went to her cabin and shut the door, causing Nainsi, still in her bunk, to glance up startled.

Meriel expected any moment to hear a knock and her mam's angry shout.

She heard nothing at all.

The next day, a small island lifted from the sea ahead of them.

Inishfeirm was a fog-wrapped, steep-walled mountain thrusting out from the waves five miles from Inish Thuaidh. As they approached, Meriel could see houses and buildings scattered up the slopes from the small harbor sheltered by a tall rock ("Inish Bideach, that rock's called," one of the sailors told her. "Tiny Island.") Smaller white dots moved along the green-cloaked, steep hillsides: grazing sheep. High up on the mountainside, a large, towered structure gleamed as if it had been molded from snow: the White Keep, home of the Order of Inishfeirm and Meriel's intended residence for the next several years.

It looked a gloomy prospect, indeed.

The sailors furled the twin sails and took to the oars, rowing *Uaigneas* into the harbor as Jenna and Máister Kirwan came up from their tiny cabins. They flanked Meriel and Nainsi. Jenna greeted Meriel with a "Maidin maith," but said nothing else to her. Those on the shore had noticed the Banrion's insignia fluttering on the forward mast, and a crowd gathered quickly around the wharf where they tied up.

"Most of the island's turned out," Máister Kirwan commented, smiling and waving to the people. "Everyone wants to see the Banrion and First Holder again."

Meriel refrained from comment: if this was "most of the island," then there weren't many people here at all. She'd seen larger crowds on nearly any day at the market at Dún Kiil, and during the Festivals the streets there were so full that this pitiful group waving back at them would have been utterly lost. They seemed to be fisherfolk or farmers mostly, with plain clothing and plainer faces, hands stained dark with work and toil. Here and there among them were a few men and women in white clócas like Máister Kirwan, some with a white léine underneath, others—mostly younger than Meriel—with red. A man all in white came forward as the lines were secured to the pilings and the planking laid from deck to wharf: slightly built, with hair so dark brown it verged on black, and eyes the color of freshly-turned earth. His beard was still downy and short, patchy on the cheeks, and to Meriel's mind he looked to be no more than four or five years older than she was. He also seemed to be rather nearsighted, for he leaned slightly forward and squinted heavily in their direction, his nose wrinkling. He wore a glittering stone around his neck "Máister! And Banrion MacEagan! Welcome!"

"Owaine Geraghty." Jenna's mam was smiling. "And in a Bráthair's colors finally. It's good to see you once again—you're taking good care of the clochmion I sent you, I see."

Owaine smiled, touching the stone. "Thank you again for the gift, Banrion. It was unexpected and very much appreciated."

"You and your family helped me once; that's just a small return of the favor."

"It was far more generous than that," Owaine answered. "I never expected to actually hold a cloch na thintrí." He gestured toward the buildings near the docks. His squinting eyes found Meriel. "So this is our new acolyte. Welcome, Bantiarna MacEagan. I have a carriage for you—we saw the ship from the keep. There's a supper waiting above . . ."

Meriel found the White Keep depressing despite its bright outward appearance. The stonework was ancient, with a central tower that appeared far older than the Keep at Dún Kiil. The stones were a pale granite coated with layer upon layer of whitewash. Inside, the structure was huge, drafty, and cold—a maze of corridors and passages, all of them seemingly added to the existing structure at various times over the centuries. The architecture varied wildly, from plain work around the oldest portions that might have been crafted by the ancient Bunús Muintir race; to ornate, fancifully ornamented archways that belonged to the Before, back when the mage-lights had last gleamed in the sky; to the stark, utilitarian lines that Meriel associated with the Great Hall of Dún Kiil; to a colorful geometric style of decoration that she didn't recognize at all. A flagged corridor might end suddenly, going down two abrupt steps to a marble-tiled hall built a century later that jutted off at an angle. Corridors never seemed to intersect at right angles, or several corridors would meet all at once in a strangely-shaped room, and a few of the halls they walked were so ancient that the feet of countless people had worn double hollows in the very stones. The entire population of the island could have lived here easily, with room left over for every last goat, sheep, and chicken.

Meriel began to doubt that she would ever come to know this place. She also doubted that she would ever enjoy it.

"This will be your room, Meriel," Máister Kirwan said, "and—ah, good, you're here—this is Faoil Caomhánach, who will be your roommate for now . . ." They had entered the dormitory wing, a dreary expanse of wide halls and spacious rooms. This particular room was undistinguished—a parlor with a peat fire burning in the grate, some dark utilitarian furniture, and two doors leading off to bedrooms. A young woman's head lifted in the warm glow of a sconce of candles, glancing up from a roll of parchment spread out on a pine desk: Faoil. Hair the color of candlelight sparked from under a white wimple; large green eyes flecked with brown regarded Meriel first, then went to Máister Kirwan and Jenna. Faoil's eyes widened even more, and a blush touched her cheeks. She rose, scattering papers in her rush, and curtsied.

"Banrion MacEagan, Máister," she said. Her voice was honeyed milk; the momentary fluster gone. She gestured to the chairs near the fire and spoke as if meeting the Banrion were something she did every day. "Please, come in. I was just studying; Siúr Meagher hinted that she might give us a small test tomorrow."

"Faoil has a great potential in the slow magics," Máister Kirwan said, "if she continues to apply herself."

"And Máister Kirwan has made certain that all of the Bráthairs and Siúrs keep me working," Faoil added with a smile. Meriel decided that Faoil was too smooth, too polished, too flattering. She'd seen the type before: the polite sycophants who prowled the halls of Dún Kiil, the width of their smiles a gauge of the relative rank of those they met. She wondered what the real Faoil was like.

She had the distressing realization that she would undoubtedly find out.

Her mam seemed to have the same curiosity. She was staring at Faoil as she might a meal set in front of her. "Caomhánach," she said, pronouncing the name as if tasting the sound of it. "There are Caomhánachs in Tuath Infochla and Tuath Airgialla. And Tiarna Iosep O'hEagjra, who is on the Comhairle, has a sister who is married to Odhrán Caomhánach of Infochla . . ."

"That would be Aisling," Faoil answered. "She's my mam, and Odhrán Caomhánach my da," Faoil answered. "We have land near Glenkille, though he's often in Falcarragh."

"In the Rí Infochla's court," Jenna said. It was a statement rather than a question. Faoil nodded. "And your da holds a Cloch Mór."

"Aye," Faoil said. "He does." She paused a moment, glancing at Máister Kirwan again. "I . . . was introduced to your mam once about a year ago, Banrion, by your half brother Doyle Mac Ard, at the Festival of Gheimhri in Dún Laoghaire. She was . . ." Meriel couldn't see her mam's face, but she could see Faoil's smile falter. The girl visibly blanched, as if realizing the gaffe she'd just made. Faoil blinked, obviously not wanting to finish the thought but thinking that it would be even more awkward to leave the sentence unfinished. ". . . a bit ill at the time, but she was very pleasant to me."

Meriel saw her mam's hand drift toward where Lámh Shábhála rested on its chain. She could only imagine her face under the cowl of her clóca. "It's good to have met you, Faoil," Jenna said. "Mundy, I remember a courtyard at the end of this hall. Does it still have the statue of Peria? I'd like to take a look at it again—shall we go there?"

With a nod toward Faoil, Jenna abruptly left the room. Máister Kirwan hesitated a moment, an expression on his face as if he'd just swallowed sour milk, then he turned to follow. "We'll be back in a bit," he said to

Faoil. "You ought to continue studying; Siúr Meagher's examinations are generally quite thorough. Meriel, if you'll come this way, please . . ."

They found Jenna already in the small courtyard, staring at a young woman caught in a moment of agony, her tortured face lifted toward the sky as if in supplication, her right hand clasped to her chest. On the woman's arm, Meriel could see the same pattern of scars that marred her mam's skin. For a moment, Meriel didn't realize that it *was* a statue—the coloring of the flesh and the clothing she wore were entirely realistic, and the figure itself was so lifelike. She almost expected it to breathe, or sound to come from that mouth.

It was instead her mam who spoke. "What in the Mother's name do you think you're doing, Mundy?" Jenna said without turning around. "Do you think I'm going to let my daughter sleep in the same chambers as a Tuathian spy?"

"She's not a spy, Jenna," Máister Kirwan answered. "Faoil's a girl, the same as Meriel. No more."

Jenna whirled around, and Meriel saw the anger on her mam's face. (Behind her, the statue remained unmoving, caught in its moment of sheer terror. Meriel moved around the outside of the small garden, wanting to get closer to it.) "You can't know that. How fortuitous that a tiarna in the court of Infochla would send his daughter here to study. And that remark about my mam and Doyle Mac Ard . . ."

"She was trying to make polite conversation and meant nothing by it. You saw her face; she realized that she'd said something she shouldn't have, but she tried to make the best of it. Faoil's an only child, and her da could have sent her to the Order of Gabair instead, but he didn't. He has family ties to Inish Thuaidh and knows that it's *here* that cloudmages are best taught. I've met the man and I trust him. Are we already back to war with the Tuatha, Jenna, or do the agreements we've made still hold? Have I missed something?"

"You know what I mean, Mundy. We might not yet be at war with the Tuatha, but you know as well as I do that we will be, and perhaps soon."

"But not *yet*," Máister Kirwan said, unrelenting. "We have several students here from Talamh an Ghlas; you knew that from the beginning. We teach anyone who comes here, regardless of their home or background or heritage—that's the way it's always been."

"Perhaps that should change, since you teach the enemies of Inish Thuaidh, who will use that knowledge against us."

"Perhaps the Banrion is seeing enemies where there are none." He lifted his hands in exasperation. "Jenna, I chose Faoil personally, myself, because she has work habits and abilities that Meriel—"

Meriel, an arm's length from the statue, heard her name and glanced over to the two. She saw her mam's face go dark as her arm slashed air, cutting off Máister Kirwan's words. "Listen to me, Mundy. I don't want Meriel in that room. Put her with someone from Inish Thuaidh or place her in a room of her own—the Mother knows you have enough to spare here. I don't care which you do, but do it. You can pretend she's just another acolyte all you want, but she's still the Banrion's daughter— *my* daughter—and I need to know that she's safe."

"Aye, she is the Banrion's daughter, but while she's here she *will* be just another acolyte. I told you this in Dún Kiil, Jenna: if Meriel is to be here, I will treat her as I think best. If that isn't to your satisfaction, then find somewhere else to put her. I'll keep her as safe as—"

Meriel reached out a hand to stroke the statue's arm and gave a startled, half-strangled cry. Her mam and Máister Kirwan both spun around to look at her. "The statue," she said, embarrassed at the attention. "The skin is soft, and warm . . ."

"Severii O'Coulghan, who was the son of Peria, the woman it depicts, made the statue," Máister Kirwan said. "He created it with the dying energy of Lámh Shábhála in the last days of the Before. There's a huge statue of his da, Tadhg, the Founder of the Order, elsewhere in the keep—it's the same: when you touch it, it seems like you're touching flesh."

"So real . . ." Meriel breathed, gazing up at the woman's face.

"Severii had a gift, and used Lámh Shábhála to help him create it. The clochs can be used for more than war, though they rarely are." Máister Kirwan sighed, turning back to Jenna as Meriel touched the statue's arm again. "I'm not your enemy, Jenna. I never will be. Trust me to do what's best."

Meriel thought that her mam would fly into a rage. She'd seen it before when her da or some tiarna or bantiarna persisted in giving Jenna advice that went against her own instincts. *"Your mam's strong-willed and independent,"* Da told her once. *"And don't misunderstand me, Meriel—I think that's good. Jenna wouldn't have survived all she's gone through without those qualities. But sometimes it does makes her blind."* Meriel watched her mam struggle internally, the cords standing out in her neck. Jenna's gaze caught on Meriel, still standing next to the anguished depiction of Peria. Her mam's hand slid over the jeweled cage of Lámh Shábhála, and the touch seemed to calm her. Her breathing slowed, her posture relaxed slightly.

"You'll watch her, Mundy," she said. "Personally. She'll be your charge."

"I'll watch her," Máister Kirwan answered. "As you would watch her yourself."

Her mam stayed the night on Inishfeirm, and for that night Meriel stayed with her rather than with Faoil. The supper was interminable, with Meriel sitting alongside as her mam spoke with seemingly every one of the Bráithars and Siúrs of the Order, all of whom also appeared to have a long history with her, as did several of the Inishfeirm residents who also attended. Meriel was introduced all around and smiled as well as she could into the barrage of greetings and well-wishing, and endless variations on "I remember when you came here as a little girl . . ." The supper was served by the acolytes, and Meriel found that the gazes of the young men and women rested curiously on her most of the evening, at least a few of them, it seemed to her, with open hostility. Afterward, there was singing—Meriel nearly fell asleep during the *Song of Máel Armagh,* done badly by one of the male acolytes whose prepubescent voice kept breaking on the high notes.

She was relieved when the night sky suddenly bloomed into shimmering brilliance. "Mage-lights!" someone called. The latest song stopped in mid-verse; the people in the hall shifted in their seats. Máister Kirwan leaned over toward Jenna. "Banrion, would you like to step outside here with the rest of us, or meet the mage-lights in your own room?"

"In my room, I think," Jenna answered, and Meriel sighed inwardly with relief. One of the acolytes guided them back; Nainsi came to the door, fluttering around solicitously until Jenna, annoyed, shooed her away. Meriel started for her own bedchamber, but her mam called to her. "No, Meriel. Come out on the balcony with me."

Never a request, only a command . . . It was the way her mam always phrased things. Meriel grimaced, then set a faint smile on her lips as she turned. "Aye, Mam." Jenna was already pulling aside the heavy, tapestried curtains in front of the balcony doors. Meriel felt the cold air sweep into the room as Jenna pushed them open, and the colors of the mage-lights danced on the walls.

Green veils of light glistened overhead, shifting to a chill blue as Meriel stepped out alongside her mam. A blood-red fold sparked directly overhead, shot through with white spirals. Mage-lights: Meriel had seen them her whole life, though she knew that it was her mam who had opened the way for them. Mage-lights: the energy that fed the clochs na thintrí, that had brought them back to life after their centuries-long slumber.

Meriel had also seen the lights fill Lámh Shábhála, and she knew what to expect as her mam lifted the chain from around her neck, closed her right hand around the stone, and held it toward the sky. The mage-lights responded, seeming to dip and sway and curl above them as tendrils of light snaked down from the zenith in long streamers. To the left, where the cloudmages of the Order had gathered below them on the grounds outside the dining hall, other light-streams were swirling, wrapping around the gathered clochs. But the largest and brightest concentration was around Jenna, sparkling coruscations that made Meriel squint against their brilliance. The lights danced around Jenna's upraised hand, and the scars etched in her arm seemed to glow themselves as the mage-lights filled Lámh Shábhála with their energy.

Sometimes, the mage-lights would dance for a full stripe of the candle; tonight, the brilliant display slowly faded not long after they began. Jenna let her hand fall, cradling the arm to herself as if it were injured. She moaned, and Meriel went to her. "No, I'm all right," Jenna said, though the words were uttered through clenched teeth. "Tell Nainsi to bring the kala bark tea. Go on."

Nainsi had already made the tea. She handed the steaming mug to Jenna as the Banrion walked slowly back into the room, then scurried away again as Jenna waved a hand at her. Meriel watched as her mam collapsed wearily into a chair near the fire. "Sit here with me," Jenna said, and Meriel took the chair on the opposite side of the fireplace. For a time, they sat silently, Meriel watching the small blue flames curling around the peat, a pale imitation of the mage-lights. Jenna sipped at the healing tea; Meriel leaned back with her eyes closed.

"It hurts, every time, and yet it feels so wonderful. So powerful."

Meriel glanced over at her mam to find her eyes fixed on her. "Someday, it might be you out there, Meriel," Jenna continued. "If not with Lámh Shábhála, then with another cloch."

"I don't enjoy pain, Mam," Meriel told her. "I prefer to avoid it."

Jenna's mouth twitched, as if she wanted to smile. "Sometimes it comes and finds you, whether you want it or not. Sometimes enduring a certain amount of pain is necessary to avoid a greater hurt later."

"I'm not you, Mam. I'm not as strong as you. Fiodóir didn't weave the same destiny into the tapestry of Fate for me." She bit at her upper lip. "I don't think He wove *anything* for me."

"Nonsense," Jenna spat out. "You have no idea yet what you're capable of. That's why you're here—to begin to learn."

"Mam . . ." Meriel started to protest, but then everything seemed to overwhelm her, all at once: her weariness; the new surroundings; the feeling of being torn away from all and everything she'd ever known; the fear of not knowing what she faced, of being surrounded by strangers; her exile from Lucan . . . everything. Tears formed unbidden in her eyes, and she wiped at them angrily with the sleeve of her léine, blinking and sniffing. Suddenly, her mam was crouched in front of her, her arms around Meriel, and she sank into that embrace in surrender, letting the tears flow.

"Hush, darling . . ." Jenna whispered into Meriel's ear. Her left hand stroked Meriel's hair; her right sat on Meriel's shoulder like a dead block of ice, cold and unmoving. "I know you're scared, Meriel. I was scared, too—many, many times. It's all right to feel that way." Meriel felt Jenna's lips brush her forehead with a soft, fleeting kiss. Her mam's face was in front of her, very close. "I'm *still* scared, Meriel," Jenna said. "Only now I'm scared for both of us. And that's worse. If something happens to me, that's one thing, but if it's you that would be hurt . . ."

"Then keep me with you, Mam. Let me go back to Dún Kiil."

"I can't," Jenna answered, "as much as I might want to, I can't let myself do that. You *need* to be here. You must start learning how to become what you'll need to become, because of who you are. And as much as I might like to, I can't stay here while you get that knowledge. My place is in Dún Kiil."

"Don't *I* have a choice in any of this?"

Jenna did smile at that. She leaned forward, kissing Meriel's brow once more. "I used to pretend that I had choices, but I didn't. Not really. The Mother-Creator wanted me to have Lámh Shábhála, or Lámh Shábhála wanted me itself, and I couldn't avoid what happened afterward, only deal with it as best I could. And you can't avoid it either. Not with me as your mam, and with your da . . ." She stopped, pressing her lips together.

"Is this what Da wants, too?" Meriel asked. "I wish he'd been there to see us leave, or to come here with us. He's never . . ." She stopped, sniffing again. "I always felt like he was never as involved in this," she gestured to include the keep—"as you are. He doesn't even come to Dún Kiil much unless he has to for the Comhairle's gatherings, and you hardly ever go to Dún Madadh to see him. I remember he told me that even if you gave Lámh Shábhála to him, he wouldn't take it because he doesn't have the skill or the desire . . ."

Meriel stopped. Jenna had risen as Meriel spoke, walking over to the curtains that screened the balcony. She stood looking out at the night; faintly, Meriel could hear the voices of the cloudmages as they spoke among themselves in the courtyard below. "Mam?"

"Believe me, Meriel," she said, though her face was to the curtains, "having you come here would . . . was . . . your da's desire, too." Jenna took a breath, and Meriel thought she heard a catch almost like a sob. Finally, she turned and gave Meriel a wan smile. "My arm hurts," she said. "I think I need to rest and let the kala bark work. And you need to sleep, also. Tomorrow, you'll be starting your new life."

She came over to Meriel, crouching down again and hugging her. "Do you know how much I love you and care for you, Meriel?" she asked. "Do you have any idea at all."

"Aye, Mam," Meriel answered. "I do."

She said it because she knew it was the answer Jenna wanted.

Jenna's arms wrapped tightly around Meriel and she returned the embrace. Then, as quickly, her mam stood again, calling to Nainsi as she left the parlor for her own bedchamber. For a while, Meriel sat in front of the fire, staring at the flames. After a time, she went to the small desk, pulled out a sheet of parchment, sharpened the point of the quill in the drawer, and unstoppered the ink bottle. She began to write, wondering how she could tell Lucan what she felt when she didn't quite know herself.

Outside, the Bráthairs and Siúrs had left and gone to their own rooms. In the quiet of the night, she could hear the chirping of insects, and—faintly—seals calling to each other on a beach far below.

4

A Delegation Refused

KYLE was waiting for Jenna when the *Uaigneas* docked at Dún Kiil, standing next to Mahon MacBreen, the captain of Jenna's personal gardai. Jenna noticed several gardai scattered around the harbor. "What's going on?" she asked as Mahon helped her across to the wooden quay.

"Just a few extra precautions, Banrion," Mahon answered. In his mid-twenties, his face and body had acquired the scars of a violent life, as had his da before him. Mahon was quick with his sword, his intelligence was as sharp as his weapon's edge, and he was fiercely loyal to Jenna. "There's a delegation here from Tuath Infochla." Jenna's eyebrows raised and Mahon nodded. "I'm sure Tiarna MacEagan will explain," Mahon said.

Mahon fell in alongside her as Kyle MacEagan came over. They embraced once, as friends would, then Kyle took a step back. His round features folded into a moue of apology as they started walking toward the carriage that waited to take them up the mountain to Dún Kiil Keep. "I'm sorry I couldn't go with you and Meriel to Inishfeirm. Did you give Meriel my apologies?"

"I did," Jenna told him. "She understood. I gave her the letter you sent."

"Thanks. I really wanted to be there, but settling the land dispute in the Comhairle took longer than I thought. How is she?"

"She blames me. She thinks I'm trying to get rid of her."

"You could have told her the truth."

Jenna sighed—it was an old argument between them. *"She's old enough to know, Jenna. About the age you were when you were given your burden."* Jenna could only shake her head. *"You can't keep her sheltered forever, Jenna,"* Kyle had persisted. *"Do that, and she'll* never *be ready to handle things herself. And that includes telling her the truth about me. She should know who her real da was."*

"I don't want to scare her, Kyle," she said. "Doyle made definite threats against her. Against all of those I love."

He didn't argue; he never did—it was one of the traits she admired about Kyle. He would make his point and speak his mind, but once she made a decision, he backed her without question. He had been a steadfast ally for her over the years, a true friend even if they'd never shared their marriage bed. He had also been a wonderful da to Meriel; Jenna had to admit that she was sometimes jealous of the easy, loving relationship the two of them had, so much different from the way Meriel was with her.

Kyle nodded in Mahon's direction. "I take it Mahon's told you about the delegation that arrived here yesterday."

"Aye. From Infochla. Is it a problem or just routine?"

"A problem," Kyle said.

"Let me guess. The north islands of the Stepping Stones."

Kyle nodded. "Aye. They're claiming that the Ards of the Northern Clans had no right to secede from Tuath Infochla, that they still owe their tribute to Rí Infochla, and that allowing them a vote in the Comhairle breaks the terms of our current treaty with the Tuatha and the Rí Ard."

"And does it?"

Kyle's lips tugged upward in a slight smile as he

shrugged. "Probably. Though that hasn't stopped us from picking off other islands in recent years. The delegation's carrying a formal protest to you and the Comhairle; they insist on meeting you today to read it."

"Today." Jenna sighed.

"Aye."

"Send them home," Jenna said, grimacing. "I don't need to listen to their whining. If Rí Mas Sithig wants to come here and complain to me in person, then I'll listen to him. But I'm not going to be lectured by his lackeys." Mahon snorted quiet, discreet laughter at that. Kyle looked less amused.

"Jenna, I'm not so certain that's the right tactic at the moment. Considering the threats Doyle gave you and the Rí Ard's health, this may be the provocation that the Tuatha are looking for—an excuse to pull their armies together again."

"They'll come at us one day no matter what we do," Jenna answered. "We all know that. Today, tomorrow, what's it matter?"

"I'd rather avoid it entirely if we can. So would you, if you still remember Dún Kiil."

"I remember," Jenna said. "All too well." She rubbed at her right arm, stiff and icy after the voyage. The scars mottling her flesh were in her mind as well, etched just as deeply. She looked at Mahon, whose da had died in the battle of Dún Kiil; his gray eyes had gone steely, and she knew that he, at least, wouldn't mind if it came to war. She suspected that there were others like him. The Inishlanders had long memories indeed, the list of grievances against the Tuatha was a lengthy one, and vengeance was a motivation that all the Inish clans knew well. Some of them would welcome the chance to go against the armies of the Tuatha with Lámh Shábhála and their cloudmages at their head and let the blood of their foes redden the soil.

Part of Jenna might agree with Kyle, but another, more visceral part of her sympathized with Mahon. *"The dead enemy cannot strike."* It was an old Inish saying.

"The Northern Clans came to us freely," she said. "We didn't go to them or ask them to join us. If the islands feel that they'd rather be aligned with Inish Thuaidh than Tuath Infochla, then perhaps Infochla should have done a better job of attending to them."

" 'Tis true they came to us freely, aye, but then you also offered to halve the tribute that they would pay to the Comhairle each year and increase the shipments of grain they were getting from Infochla," Kyle said. There was no heat in his voice, only a touch of resignation. "But still, that's a pretty speech. Should I bring the delegates into the Weeping Hall to hear it?

"No," Jenna answered. "Tell them yourself, Kyle, and send them away."

"As the Banrion wishes," Kyle said. She could see the disappointment in his face, though she knew none of it would be there when he spoke to the delegates. She held out her left hand and Kyle took it, pressing his fingers against hers. "Is it also as Jenna wishes?" he asked.

She nodded faintly. "Aye. I think so." They reached the carriage, a servant opening the door as they approached and putting down a footstool under it. Mahon snapped fingers to a garda, who brought his horse over to him. Kyle stepped into the carriage, then helped Jenna up. "Thank you, Kyle," she said. "For everything. All along."

He smiled. "I'm your husband," he said.

Edana emerged from the Rí Ard's chambers as Doyle approached.

The woman was dark-haired, fair of complexion, with eyes that were startlingly blue. Edana was the daughter of Nevan O Liathain, the Rí Ard, and his second wife—Nevan had little luck with wives. His first wife had died not long after delivering the Rí Ard's firstborn son, Enean. Three years later Nevan had married Edana's mam, who would have a series of miscarriages yet finally bring one child to term, only to die like her predecessor a few days after Edana's difficult labor and birth.

Nevan's third wife had died before giving the Rí Ard any children at all. After that, perhaps understandably, the Rí Ard had never married again (though Doyle, sensitive on the point, had heard the usual rumors of bastard children scattered throughout the Tuatha).

The hall garda and Edana's maidservant glanced politely away as Edana came up to Doyle and embraced him. Old MacCamore, Enean's guardian, was in the hall also, and Doyle nodded to him over Edana's shoulder. MacCamore did not look away; he watched.

"Maidin maith, darling," Edana said brightly. Doyle kissed her once, enjoying the soft warmth of her lips and the feel of her lithe body under the heavily brocaded royal clóca.

"How is your da today?" he asked.

Edana sighed. "No better, I'm afraid. Enean's in there with him. Is there news from Rí Mas Sithig and Infochla?"

"Aye," he told her. "Jenna did exactly what you said she would do—she sent the delegates away without even deigning to receive them. She had that fat servant of a husband talk to them instead."

"Good," Edana said with a grim satisfaction. "Then we'll use that against her with the Riocha. She'll tighten the noose around her own neck." She hugged him again. "I know how hard it is for you, Doyle. You'll take back what's yours. It's what my da wants, too. I'll help you."

"And I'll need that help. You know the politics better than anyone." Doyle kissed her again, deeply, his fingers caught in the glossy strands of her hair. "I love you," he said. The words came easily because they were true. Doyle often thanked the god Fiodóir for having his fate wound with that of Edana. Arranged marriages were not always blessed with actual warmth and affection.

"And I, you," she answered with a smile. "I'm off, though—Da's asked that I interview a new healer from Airgialla. Till tonight." She kissed him again, quickly this time, and went rushing off with her maidservant. Doyle watched her until she turned left with a smiling wave, and then he turned back to the Rí Ard's chamber as the garda opened the door for him. He entered.

The chamber high in the Keep of Dún Laoghaire smelled of corruption and stale urine that the perfumed candles seemed to enhance rather than mask. As Doyle Mac Ard leaned forward, he caught a whiff of the Rí Ard's foul breath and had to force himself not to show his distaste as he kissed the man's grizzled cheek and brushed back the stiff, gray hair from his brow. The golden torc around the man's neck looked as if it would slip off the wasting flesh of its own weight.

"You look well, my Rí," Doyle said as he straightened, then sat on a stool next to the bed. One did not stand above the Rí Ard.

Nevan O Liathain, ostensible ruler of the Seven Tuatha, grimaced and coughed wetly, spitting out a blob of green phlegm into a small silver urn alongside his bed. A chamber servant hurried forward to empty it. "Don't flatter me needlessly, Doyle," O Liathain said, his voice rough and broken. "I know exactly how I look and I'm sure Edana's already given you her opinion. I can feel the crows gathering outside my window, and I hear the human ones cawing in the hallways. Damn this disease, and damn all the healers who have tried to cure me with their wretched potions." O Liathain coughed again, a series of rattling, lung-scouring hacks. When the spasms passed, he lifted a blue-veined, thin hand on the finely-brocaded bedclothes, gesturing, and a man only a few years older than Doyle hurried forward from a seat near the window. A long and deep scar furrowed the left side of his face, running high into his skull. Where the jagged scar ran, the brown, wavy hair was interrupted by white skin.

"What is it, Da?" the man said in a childlike voice, slurred by the scar that twisted his lips. "Look! One of the ships is coming in the harbor. It's flying red and white, so it must be from Airgialla, and there's another flag below that I don't recognize at all. Can I go watch it dock?"

"Aye," O Liathain told the man, who was kneeling alongside the bed. He tousled the hair as he might a boy's. "Go ahead, Enean."

"I'll go with him, Rí," Doyle said, starting to rise, but O Liathain waved him back down.

"No, let his keeper watch after him," O Liathain told him. "Enean, make sure that MacCamore is with you. Do you understand?"

"I will, Da," Enean said, and bounded toward the door already calling for MacCamore, waiting patiently in the corridor outside. O Liathain sighed, watching him.

"Sometimes," he said after the door had closed, "I wish that the boy had died with his stepmam. That would have been more merciful."

Doyle remembered that day as well as the Rí Ard, even though Doyle had been only twelve summers old at the time. The Rí Ard had been in Tuath Gabair, staying at the capital of Lár Bhaile along the banks of Lough Lár. The Banrion (the Rí Ard's third and last wife), seventeen-year-old Enean (just named as Tanaise Ríg the year beforc) and Enean's newly named fiancée Sorcha were following a few days after the Rí Ard. The Rí Gabair's Keep had been flung into a sudden uproar when the bloodied and lame remnants of the Banrion's escort rode up the long hill of Lár Bhaile a few mornings later, bearing the corpses of the Banrion and Enean's fiancée as well as a badly-injured and unconscious Enean. The gardai hurriedly gave the Rí Ard the tale of bandits along the High Road from Dún Laoghaire. Enean had taken a severe blow to the head from a highwayman's sword while defending his mam and his bride-to-be, and he would never be the same again: feeble-minded, childish, prone to seizures and fits.

Vaughn Mac Ard, Doyle's uncle and commander of the Rí Gabair's army, had immediately sent troops from Lár Bhaile in pursuit of the attackers, largely suspected to be raiding Inishlanders—no one believed they were mere bandits, then or now. The highwaymen fled west along the High Road pursued by a squad of gardai, retreating into the haunted and feared depths of the ancient oak forest of Doire Coill, dark and trackless. None of them, attackers or gardai, ever came back out. Three days later, where the northern edge of Doire Coill touched the High Road, the heads of both the bandits and the squad of gardai were found in a field amid a black flock of feasting crows. Doyle, as squire to his uncle, had ridden with the Rí Gabair and the Rí Ard to see the sight. He still could recall how the crows took flight, reluctantly, as Nevan O Liathain rode toward the gory sight, shouting. The heads had been stripped of much of their flesh by then, the eye sockets just raw bleeding holes and the gaping mouths tongueless . . . Some would say later that they'd noticed Bunús Muintir watching from under the shadow of the oaks, but Doyle hadn't seen them, the Old People who supposedly lived there.

No one ever knew for certain who had sent the murderers. Many, including the Rí Ard, would continue to believe it was the Inish, but Doyle never believed that— it wasn't Jenna's style to be covert. But there were factions enough among the Tuathian Riocha, families who wanted to advance their own fortunes and who wouldn't be troubled over stooping to hired murder.

Doyle would say afterward that this was the day he gave up his childhood and took up his da's legacy, at once and early, driven by the awful vision in front of him. Doyle knew who the Rí Ard blamed and they were the same people who had taken Doyle's da away from him. He would take allies where he found them, justified or not.

"What Enean did was incredibly noble and brave," Doyle said to the Rí Ard. "The Mother-Creator saved him for a reason. He still has a destiny to fulfill."

"Then I wish She would whisper Her secret to me, for I don't see it," O Liathain answered. He groaned as he shifted in the bed. "And I fear that I never will."

"Don't say that, my Rí."

"Why not? For the last many months, I've been thinking this is the last summer I will see, the last Festival of Gheimhri I'll ever celebrate, the last harvest. One thing I'll *never* see is the face of the person who will take this torc from my cold body and put it on their own, but I know that will be soon." For a moment, O Liathain closed his eyes and Doyle wondered whether he'd fallen asleep. Then the gray, rheumy eyes opened again and he licked dry lips. "What of Inish Thuaidh and your sister?"

"News came from Tuath Infochla this morning—that's why I asked to see you. The rumors we've heard are true: the northern Stepping Stones have gone over to Inish Thuaidh, and the Ards of those clans are now sitting in the Comhairle in Dún Kiil. We bleed in the north, Rí Ard. The Banrion refused to see the delegation Rí Infochla sent in protest. She wouldn't even accept Rí Mas Sithig's letter. She defies us all."

"Damn that woman!" The effort cost O Liathain another spasm of coughing, his face going red then gray; he spat again, and again the servant hurried forward. When he'd recovered his breath, he shook his head. His voice was much fainter. "We should have moved against her before now. We shouldn't have let her recover after Dún Kiil—I should have renounced the oath I made to her, should have gathered together *all* the Tuatha and clochs na shábhála and come against her with an army even Lámh Shábhála and the Inishfeirm cloudmages couldn't resist. But my father and the Riocha were all afraid after our first defeat and I couldn't get them to agree, and I *had* given the Mad Holder my word. My word . . ."

O Liathain went into another fit of coughing and Doyle waited patiently, leaning over to press the cloth against the Rí Ard's lips when he'd finished. "So we waited and waited and now we pay for our cowardice," the man continued, "and it will be that much harder to pry her out and remove her." He stopped, his eyes closing again. Doyle waited, and he stirred a few breaths later. "I need you, Doyle," O Liathain whispered. "As

I needed your da long ago: a strong and loyal hand, a strong and loyal mind, someone fit to hold a Cloch Mór. That's why I've given you my daughter, that's why I gifted you with the stone you hold."

These were words he'd heard many times before. O Liathain's mind sometimes wandered along old paths now, and it was best just to nod and pretend you'd never heard the words before. "You have my hand and my mind and my loyalty, Rí Ard," Doyle said. "You know that. You treated me as a favored son when the others . . ." He stopped, remembering the mingled shame and anger he'd felt since his childhood every time he heard the taunts: *"There's that bastard child of Padraic's . . ." "Useless offspring of a tiarna's whore . . ."* He bloodied himself frequently in those first years, and as he'd grown, the taunts had come less frequently. But he still saw them in people's eyes sometimes, unspoken.

"Jenna could have been my Banrion, long ago," the Rí continued, his mind still drifting back. "I offered her that, when I first met her, but she refused me. It was not long after Enean's mam had died, when I was still Tanaise Ríg. She could have been my second wife. All this trouble would have been avoided had she accepted. But she went mad with Lámh Shábhála."

"I know. My mam told me that tale. Jenna is a murderous fool, Rí, and too proud for her own good."

A faint nod. "Your sister is an abomination and must be destroyed before she destroys us. I'm sorry, Doyle, but that's true. Still, I hate to ask you to plot against your own sister."

"Oh, I have no problem with that, Rí," Doyle answered easily. He fingered the Cloch Mór around his neck. "Someone else needs to hold Lámh Shábhála. Someone whose loyalty to the Tuatha is unquestioned. Perhaps the Rí Ard himself. It would look good around your neck." Doyle's hand went to his own neck, and in his imagination it was not Nevan O Liathain wearing the cloch.

There was no answer. The Rí's chest rose slowly; his

breath labored and loud. Doyle rose from his stool. "Rest, my Rí. Don't worry, Jenna will be weakened, and very soon. Edana and I will see to that." He touched the man's cheek and went to the window where Enean had been sitting. Far below, he could see the Rí's son and his entourage just emerging from the keep's main gates and riding toward the harbor. He glanced at the ship coming toward the docks. Enean was right; on the mast flew the banner of Tuath Airgialla, and below was another: a stylized dire wolf on a field of blue—the banner of the Concordance of Céile Mhór.

Doyle's eyes narrowed at that, wondering why Céile Mhór would be sending unannounced someone whose rank demanded the banner. He thought that perhaps Enean had the right idea, after all.

"Make certain the Rí sleeps comfortably," he said to the chamber attendant. "If he wakes and wants me, I'll be with Enean at the docks."

5

Excerpts from Letters

rd SILVERBARK 1148
   My Dearest Lucan:
  I'm alone now.

Well, in truth I'm *never* "alone" here—that's impossible. My mam left three days ago with Nainsi and I'm now in my rooms with Faoil, who I told you about in the last letter. Doors are not locked here in the White Keep—no, that's not quite true. *Many* doors are locked here, some with metal and some with magical wards. But not the doors for the acolytes' rooms; anyone can walk in on us at any time and the Siúrs seem to often do so. Faoil's usually here when we're not together in classes or doing the duties assigned to us. She's here right now as I write this, and has already asked me who I'm writing to. I told her "a friend." She didn't like the answer but she's too uncertain of me to ask any more questions. Maybe she's afraid of what I'll say to my mam, and how that might affect her family.

There are always other people around; the Bráthairs and Siúrs; visitors and supplicants from Inish Thuaidh; people from Inishfeirm; even Riocha from Talamh an Ghlas come to inquire about putting their sons and daughters here—though not too many of those. I've heard from the other acolytes that the Rí Ard has created his own "Order of Gabair" based in Lár Bhaile and he wants none of the Riocha taught the arts of the

cloudmage by "vile Inishlanders." I've been told that
several acolytes from the Tuatha left here in the last two
years to go to Lár Bhaile and the new Order, and there
are empty rooms in the keep's dormitories. Still, I can
feel people watching me, all the time, even though they
think I don't notice. Máister Kirwan seems to be around
every other corner I turn, especially. There's one Bráthair—
Owaine Geraghty—who also seems to go out of his way
to be around wherever I am. My mam knows him somehow; knows him well enough that she gave him a clochmion even though he is of totally common blood, if you
can believe that.

And my mam seems to think that some of them may
be watching me for other reasons. She warned me before
she left: "Be careful. Not everyone is your friend, and
because of who you are, you are always going to be in
some danger." I wanted to ask her why in the Mother-
Creator's name she is leaving me here if she felt that
way, but that would have just made her angry.

I'm treated like a servant. I'm expected to wash dishes,
to wait on the cloudmages and visitors at meals, to tend
to the gardens. The acolytes are little better than slaves.
You should see my hands, my love—they look worse
than Nainsi's, all red and splotched and scratched, the
nails hopelessly broken. Not the soft hands you used to
hold at all. Tomorrow morning, before my first class in
slow magic, I have to go out and help bring in the breadroot crop from their easy beds in the High Field, a good
half-mile trek, and we'll be getting up before dawn to
start.

And the classes themselves: dry, boring material droned
at us by dry, boring teachers, mostly. Histories, lists of
names and dates and events; catalogs of clochs na thintrí,
both Clochs Mór and clochmions and their names and
reputed powers and current mage-holders; all the past
Holders of the Clochs Mór and Lámh Shábhála; the skill
of letters—which many of us already know but that
doesn't matter, we still have to attend the class; the clan
names of the Ríocha and their genealogies. Máister Kir-

wan's class, once a week, is the worst waste of time, since we do nothing but sit silently with our eyes closed and "think of nothing." An impossible task, of course, since the moment you try to think of nothing your mind is filled with everything. We can't even sleep while we're sitting there—anyone caught actually sleeping gets extra chores. And I can't neglect telling you about the slow magics of water and earth, the most boring and insufferable classes of all—nothing but memorizing long chants and lists of ingredients to make little or nothing happen.

I miss you so much, Lucan. Sometimes I try to imagine your face and your touch and the sound of your voice, try to fix it all in my mind so I can't forget it. Usually I can, but the last time I saw you seems so impossibly long ago, and I want so much for my inner vision to be real and for the words I hear in my head to really be your voice, calling to me. . . .

5th Silverbark 1148

My Love:

I had such a strange, strange dream last night. At least I think it was a dream. I awoke because I heard the sound of seals—not the normal browns that one hears all the time around Inishfeirm, which by the way is positively infested with the creatures—but the mournful moans of the blues. I got out of my bed in the darkness, trying not to wake Faoil, and went to the window, pushing it a little farther open so I could hear better. The Saimhóir were making an enormous, sad racket. The sky was bright with the nearly full moon, though the ground was misty from the rain earlier in the day. I saw movement below, close by the wall of the White Keep. When I looked, I thought I saw a young man, perhaps twenty and one—staring up at me as I gazed down at him. He was entirely naked even though the night was cold. I gasped in surprise and blinked hard to rid myself of the last bit of sleep, and he was gone when I looked again.

Yet . . . the bushes near the base of the keep were swaying, as if someone had just moved through them.

I thought of mentioning this to Siúr O'hAllmhurain, who is in charge of our floor, but decided not to do so since it was probably only a dream. Perhaps my thoughts of you were too much on my mind. . . .

I *have* made something of a friend, though I'm half afraid to tell you about it for fear you'll misunderstand. His name (aye, *his*) is Thady MacCoughlin. He's a third-year. His da and mam are MacCoughlins from An Cnocan; you may have seen his parents in Dún Kiil last year for the Festival of Méitha. Thady says they were there and were introduced to me at one of the dances, though I don't remember them specifically—I end up meeting too many people to possibly remember them all. Thady's already told me several things about Inishfeirm and the White Keep I didn't know. He's promised to show me a particular outside door that's warded. He says half the acolytes know the ward-word to the door and use it to sneak out when they want to do so. I wonder if that doesn't explain the person I saw outside last night (though not his nakedness—though perhaps one of the first-years was tossed out that way as a prank by some of the fifth-years, who are insufferably superior). Anyway, he's very kind and helpful and I've told him about you, just to make sure that he understands. He's just a friend, Lucan, and from such a minor name at that. That's probably why he's been so helpful to me, hoping I'll say something complimentary about him to Mam or Da and gain favor for his family. . . .

8th Silverbark 1148

Dear One:

Thady told me the ward-word yesterday and tonight I used it. I heard the seals again, the blues, so loud they woke me. You know how I love the Saimhóir, and there was, well, something . . . I don't know . . . *compelling* about the sound. Maybe some of what's been said about my mam is true. I do know that listening to them made me want to get near them, the same way I felt every time I heard them in Dún Kiil.

I slipped on my clóca and overcoat and put on my sandals, leaving Faoil sleeping in her bed. I tiptoed down the corridor, half expecting Máister Kirwan or that squinting Bráthair Geraghty to be waiting for me around the corner, or Siúr O'hAllmhurain to be standing in the door to her room at the end of the Women's Corridor. But I could hear Siúr O'hAllmhurain snoring almost as loudly as the seals were calling, and so I went out of the wing and down the central hall to the Low Stairs in the back that we're not supposed to use. At the bottom of Low Tower was the door: a tiny opening half-hidden in an alcove. I spoke the word and it clicked open, just as Thady said it would. I went out.

The seals were still grunting and moaning. I hurried away from the keep (expecting that someone would call out an alarm as I did so) toward the trail head that leads down to the beach at the foot of the mountain. I started down.

It was stupid, I know—the moon hidden behind clouds, the ground slick from the rain, a mist all around. But I managed to get down, maybe half a stripe later, without killing myself in the process. I could hear the water slapping against rocks and the sound of the blues was almost deafening.

They were there, the gorgeous creatures, out on the rocks near the shore: a dozen of the Saimhóir, as big and beautiful as I remembered from Little Head. There was a bull and four cows, the rest juveniles and pups. They saw me, too; they lifted their snouts in my direction and called out to me, wailing and crying like keening sochraideach at a funeral. I took a step toward them. And another. It was like they had cast an enchantment on me, and I think I might have walked right out to them . . . but the water was so cold that when it touched my foot I cried out.

I was shivering, and a wave came and soaked me to the knees. I looked back up the mountain, realizing that it was going to take me a stripe or more to walk all the way back up there, and that I was going to be exhausted from lack of sleep for my morning chores. The seals called me, but I turned my back on them and started climbing back up the trail. . . .

11th Silverbark 1148
Sweetest:
I had hoped to receive a letter or letters from you by now. Whenever I hear that a ship has come into Inish-feirm Harbor, I wait for the Order's carriage to bring back the mail and supplies that have come, but so far there's been nothing from you. I hope my letters have been reaching you, and that the next ship will bring me your words.

I saw the naked young man again last night. Again it was the racket of seals that woke me, and I went to the window and saw him. I was awake this time: person or wight or ghost, he was real and not my imagination. He seemed to be coming from the Low Tower and the door there—the ward-locked one. He moved quickly across the grass toward the head of the trail, glancing back over his shoulder once or twice at the keep, though I don't think he saw me watching as I leaned back into the shadows. I could see his face clearly—black-haired, black-bearded, and thin—and it was none of the acolytes or Bráthairs here. That much I know. He ran strangely, as if he were drunk or slightly dizzy, but quickly disappeared into the heather near the beach trail.

I thought that I might follow him (I know; I can hear you saying it now: that was foolish and dangerous, but somehow he didn't seem frightening at all) and went to the door of my room. When I opened it, I stopped. In the moonlight that came through the corridor windows, I could see wet footprints on the stone flags: not boot

prints, but the prints of a bare foot. They were drying
quickly, even as I stared at them.

Whoever he was, *whatever* he was (and I'm beginning
to suspect I know) he had come down this hall. He'd
been there, just on the other side of my door. Somehow,
that changed everything.

I shut the door. For a long time, I lay awake in my
bed.

There are a dozen or more ghosts reputedly haunting
the White Keep, if you believe the tales I've heard from
the acolytes and mages. I asked Thady if any of them
involved a young man wandering about at night (I didn't
mention his lack of clothing). The only ghost on the
grounds is supposedly an old Bunús Muintir who stays
near the stand of old oak trees on the eastern flanks of
the mountain.

And I wonder . . .

Would a ghost would leave footprints? Especially
wet ones?

I probably should tell Máister Kirwan about this, but
somehow I don't want to. Whoever it is, he doesn't seem
dangerous to me . . .

15th Silverbark 1148

Dearest Lucan:

I hate this place. I hate the endless lectures, the interminable classes. Hate the other acolytes, half of whom
(like Faoil) are so infatuated with the process of becoming cloudmages that they can't think of anything else,
and the other half of which are bored Riocha here because their families either can't marry them off or put
them in the service of their Rí. (And half of those ask
me constantly if I can somehow intercede with my mam
to get them a position in the court of Dún Kiil or an
introduction to one of the Comhairle or a commission
within the gardai.)

I hate the boredom: first-years aren't permitted to

leave the White Keep at all until the Festival of Láfuacht, and even then we must stay on the island. The
Mother knows that a Festival on this miserable island
will be nothing at all like the grand fun we had back in
Dún Kiil during Láfuacht. Even the sheep here look
bored.

I hate the petty intrigues: all the talk about who is
important and who isn't, the unspoken hierarchy based
on who your family is, and who might betray whom or
who is allied with someone else. Oh, I know you enjoy
listening to that kind of talk, but I don't. Everyone's
speculating on who might be the next Rí Ard since Rí
Ard O Liathain's health is failing and he still hasn't
named a Tanaise Ríg. There's constant talk of the fric-
tion between the Tuatha and Inish Thuaidh, and they
seem to think that I should know all about it since Mam
is the Banrion.

I, for one, don't much care.

I heard the Saimhóir again last night, and started to
sneak out of the room to go see them. But I nearly
tripped over one of the stone flags and stubbed my big
toe, and that woke Faoil and she came running out of
her bedroom. She asked me what I was doing and I
made an excuse about needing to use the midden, but
I'm sure she didn't believe me. I went back to bed, and
a while later the blues stopped making their racket. I
once asked my mam about the Saimhóir because I've
always heard about how they came and helped during
the battle of Dún Kiil, and everyone always says that
Mam is one of the changelings, that we have Saimhóir
blood. "Not everything people say is always true," she
told me. That's all she'd say. I asked my da, too. He said
that he didn't know for certain. "If you believed what people say, then the entire population of Inishfeirm and half
of those here on Inish Thuaidh can swim with the blues,"
he said. "But your mam . . ." He smiled at me. "Your
mam has done more than I ever believed she could do.
And your twice great-mam *was* an Inishlander."

Thady has asked me if I want to come with him and

few other acolytes one night—they intend to slip out of the Low Tower door and visit the tavern down in Bitten Bay. Supposedly the proprietor doesn't inform the Bráthairs and Siúrs when acolytes visit them for a drink. About what you'd expect of a MacCoughlin. He said Faoil could come if I wanted, but I wouldn't even want to ask her. I told him no, of course.

When will I hear from you? It seems ages ago that we were last together, and I hate that most of all.

6

Lucan's Letter

"STUDYING the slow magics, eh? Most of the acolytes find studying the forms tedious, but I enjoyed them, myself."

Meriel glanced up from the thick sheaf of parchment on her lap. She'd sought out the little garden with the statue of the tormented woman—no one else seemed to use it much, or perhaps they simply avoided doing so when Meriel was there. In the few weeks that she'd been here, it had become her small quiet place where she could go and be away from everyone.

Owaine Geraghty was standing near the statue. "Mind you, I'll absolutely deny it if you ever say I told you this, but it doesn't help that they have Siúr Bolan teaching the first-years," he said. "Her voice is more effective than any sleeping potion ever made." He had a slightly quizzical expression on his face and his eyes were half-closed as he squinted—since he was assigned to be under Bráthair Maitias in the Order's library, his myopia was likely to only get worse peering at faded ink on yellowed parchment in dim rooms. Meriel had already decided she didn't like Bráthair Owaine, who seemed somehow thick and clumsy compared to most of the others here at the White Keep and who was too often around her. It was a rare trip through the corridors when she didn't seem to encounter him, a rare day when he didn't find some reason to seek her out and try to talk with her.

She treated him politely because her mam seemed to like him, but cold politeness didn't seem to have discouraged him at all.

His accent was solidly that of Inishfeirm, slow and drawn out, not at all like the speech of the Riocha in Dún Kiil or the thin, clipped tones of her roommate Faoil from the Tuatha. Despite her mam's evident patronage of the young man, Meriel had already noticed that the other Bráthairs and Siúrs also seemed to regard Owaine with a certain disdain. He didn't have the pedigree that the rest of the mages possessed; he didn't have the name or the lineage.

Meriel shrugged and looked back down at the parchment without answering. She thought he might leave after his initial attempt at conversation, but he remained there staring at her and she finally looked up again. "I can help you, if you'd like," he said. "Bráthair O'Therreagh said that I was well-suited for the slow magics and Bráthair Maitias has put me in charge of cataloging them. Bráthair O'Therreagh figured I'd never hold a cloch," Owaine touched the clochmion Jenna had given him and smiled, "but he was right; I have a knack for keeping the spells in my head. I might be able to tutor you."

"No," Meriel said sharply, then tried to soften the disappointment that showed visibly in his face. "Thank you for the offer, Bráthair Geraghty, but I need to do this on my own."

His head lifted. "Ah," he said. "That's like your mam—Máister Kirwan hints occasionally that she was a, umm, difficult student who always wanted to do things her own way."

Meriel looked down at the parchment again, pretending to read the letters there. "I'm sure she was," she said. She waited, hiding her face behind the red screen of her hair, listening for his footsteps. Instead, she heard his voice.

"I don't care for Peria's statue," he said. "It's so realistic that it bothers me to see someone trapped in such pain. And yet . . . I still come here often to look."

Meriel sighed audibly. She looked up again, glancing once at the figure of the woman with her mouth open in a tormented, eternal scream. "I always feel like I want to help her," Owaine continued. "Even though I know she died."

"Who *was* Peria?" Meriel asked despite herself. "My mam seemed to be fascinated by it."

"You don't know?"

Would I have asked *if I knew?* she wanted to retort as she might to one of Nainsi's remarks, but she held back the words. "No, I don't."

"Peria Ó Riain," Owaine answered. He seemed to be waiting for her to acknowledge the name, but Meriel shook her head. "If you don't know the name yet, you will—the names of *all* the Holders will get drilled into you when you take Bráthair Maitias' class later this year. Peria was a Holder of Lámh Shábhála and the lover of Tadhg O'Coulghan, the Founder of our Order. She died in 671 attempting the Scrúdú, the mythical test of Lámh Shábhála, and that's what this represents. Tadhg became the Holder after her death, but he never tried the test that killed Peria." Owaine touched the statue reverently. "They say your mam did, though, and that the Scrúdú very nearly killed her, too. Some say she passed the test and that's why she was able to call the stone creatures, the Créneach, at Dún Kiil. Máister Kirwan says not, but . . ." He stopped, squinting in her direction like a mole snared in sunlight. "I'm sorry, you already know all this."

No, I don't. My mam doesn't talk much about that time. . . . The truth was that most of what Meriel knew of her mam's past she'd learned from others. But she wouldn't admit that to Owaine. She simply nodded acceptance of his statement and looked back down at the parchment on her lap. She heard his feet shuffle on the flagstones as if he were turning to go, then he stopped once more. Meriel muttered a curse under her breath.

"Oh," he said. "I nearly forgot. This came for you; I was going to put it under the door of your room on my way to the library . . ."

Meriel look up to see Owaine holding out an envelope to her. The wax seal was unbroken and pressed into the red globule was the sigil of the O Dálaigh clan. *A letter from Lucan . . .* "Thank you," she said, brightening despite herself. Owaine smiled back at her.

"You're welcome," he said. He gestured at the parchments on her lap. "Remember, if I can help . . ."

"I'll remember," she said hurriedly, wanting to do nothing else but rip open the envelope and read Lucan's words. All those long letters she'd sent to him, telling him everything that had happened to her; she wanted to hear how *he'd* been, all he'd gone through since, how he was feeling . . . "Thank you, Bráthair Geraghty," she said again, this time with impatience in her voice. Owaine's cheeks colored, lines creased his forehead and smoothed again. He nodded his head.

"Well, if you need me, you can find me in the library, or . . ." His voice trailed off and he smiled, quickly, before scurrying off. Meriel had looked away before he reached the garden's entrance, ripping open the seal and pulling out the thick paper inside. Lucan's writing was large, the handwriting clumsy and hasty, with splotches of ink from where the quill pressed too hard and had to be blotted. It was dated the 11th of Silverbark, four days previously.

Dearest Meriel—I'm sorry I haven't written to you before now, but my da's kept me busy. I've received your letters, though. Inishfeirm sounds awful. I miss you. I'll write again when I can.. With affection, Lucan.

That was all. The writing ended halfway down the page. Meriel turned it over, her smile fading to puzzled frown. She looked inside the envelope: it was empty. *He's not gifted with words the way you are,* she told herself. *It's harder for him. This doesn't mean what you're afraid it means.*

The inner words did nothing. They were as empty as the page in front of her.

The letter swam in her vision and a drop of water hit the page, the ink blurring where it fell. She folded the letter carefully and placed it in the pocket of her clóca.

That night, for the first time, she wrote no letter at all.

7

The Changeling

THE moans and warbles echoed like the sounds of wraiths. Meriel blinked away sleep, reluctantly throwing back the covers on her bed and padding toward the window. Outside, the horns of a crescent moon tore holes in scudding clouds. Earlier that evening, the magelights had come, shimmering curtains of brilliant, multicolored light, but now the sky was dark, the clouds silver-white with stars salting the blackness between them. A low fog blanketed the knees of the mountain a few hundred yards down from the White Keep, masking the sea and lending a plaintive, desperate tone to the cries of the blue seals.

She wanted to see them. Their calls pulled at her.

Quickly, she threw on her léine and a heavy clóca, then slipped sandals over her feet. She shuffled out of her bedroom and into the common parlor she and Faoil shared, careful to make as little noise as possible. She could hear Faoil's heavy, slow breathing, and moved quickly across to the door, grimacing a bit as the hinges creaked. She peered out into the hall: no one there. Sliding out of her room, she closed the door behind her.

Footsteps . . .

Meriel hurried back inside, leaving the door open a crack. She saw Bráthair Owaine Geraghty turn the corner of the hallway, an odd look twisting his face as he came toward her room. Meriel closed the door fully; she heard him approach and stop just outside the door. At the bottom of the door, she could see his flickering torchlit shadow as he stood there; she could hear his breathing. It seemed that he waited there for long minutes, though it might have only been a few seconds. She was afraid he would knock, or try to open the door and find her there. She wondered why he was there, where none of the male cloudmages should have been this time of night; she wondered what would happen if she called out in alarm and Siúr O'hAllmhurain saw Owaine there in the dormitory. Then the shadow moved and his footsteps receded. She waited for several breaths after she could no longer hear him, then glanced out again.

He was gone.

Siúr O'hAllmhurain's room was placed at the end of the corridor, where it met the stairs leading to the Common Hall between the two wings of the dormitories. Siúr O'hAllmhurain was snoring again: she had been with the other cloudmages earlier, filling her clochmion with the power of the mage-lights, and was no doubt exhausted. Meriel moved quickly past the door and down the stairs.

The Low Tower butted against the western end of the Common Hall, and she moved through the archway into the musty, narrow staircase, taking it down to the small door at ground level.

Meriel placed her hand flat on the door above the handle. "Oscail," Meriel whispered: *open.* The simple ward-word worked; the door seemed to shudder once in its frame and the inner bolt sprang back. She pushed it forward, and stepped out into the ivy-clad alcove in which it was set. The cold night air made her blink; the grass was wet under her feet. She ran quickly toward the trail leading down to the water, toward the sound of the seals.

The fog made it difficult to see and she stumbled and nearly fell more than once, but finally broke through the bottom of the cloud before she reached the beach. The blues were there, waiting for her, their black eyes watching her, the moon striking sapphire highlights from ebon fur. The bull, hauled out on a rock fifty yards from the shore, roared immediately at her; a cow alongside him warbled a long string of musical notes.

A lightness moved to her left, and Meriel turned her head. A naked human form took a step toward her. She recognized him immediately: the long, damp hair the color of night, eyes so penetrating and black that they seemed almost pupil-less, the beard flowing into a mat of ebony curls on his chest, the tautness of his belly, the . . .

Meriel took a step away. "Stay back," she told him. "Who are you?"

He tilted his head, as if puzzled by the sounds she made. He smiled at her. He spoke, and the words were like the sounds she might make trying to imitate the language of the Saimhóir—decidedly a changeling then, a Saimhóir who could briefly take on human form. For a moment, she held her breath, just staring at him. He held out his hand, as if he wanted her to come toward him, and with the gesture, she saw that his right arm— and indeed, much of his body under the masking hair— was mottled with swirling curliques of scars.

Exactly as her mam's arm was marked . . .

Is he a cloudmage, then? "What's your name?" she asked again. She tapped herself on the chest. "I'm Meriel. Meriel."

"Meriel," he echoed, the name sounding strangely liquid with his voice. He touched his own chest. His hands were large and long-fingered, and bits of sand clung sparkling to the flesh. The cold air didn't seem to bother him at all, nor the icy water that lapped around his ankles. "Dhegli," he said. He reached forward, laughing, and his hand caught her forearm. He pulled at her, dragging her toward the water.

"No!" Meriel cried out in alarm, but he was stronger than she was and the sand and rocks were slippery under her feet. "No!" A wave crashed in, soaking her to the waist, her clothing was at once sodden and impossibly heavy. The coldness of the water took her breath away and she tasted salt. Dhegli's hand was still on her, pulling her farther into the deepening water and the next wave crashed over her head, the swift undertow taking her from her feet. He pulled at her, taking her down, and she flailed in panic, eyes wide despite the sting of the salt water. Her lungs cried for air, and she fought not to take the next breath. She felt something snap within her, an audible crackling that seemed to radiate throughout her body and within her mind as well.

She was no longer being held. She kicked instinctively for the surface, thrashing in the clothing that dragged her down, but the clóca and léine slipped easily away from her. She still needed to take a breath of air, but the feeling was no longer quite so urgent and the water seemed warm as bathwater. The water was as bright in the waning moon as if it were sunlight, and the dappled surface of the ocean rushed toward her at impossible speed. She broke out of the waves with a gasp that was a moan, sliding high above the water. And as she glanced down . . .

. . . the body she saw was not hers, but that of a blue seal. Her body sense shifted; she floated easily on the surface of the rolling water, flippered arms and fluked tail moving easily, naturally. Another seal's head broached the foam near her, utter black eyes glittering. The muzzle twitched; blue highlights sparked in wet fur. He snorted, the nostrils flaring. "Dhegli," he said, unmistakably. "Meriel."

"No!" Mcriel tried say again, but her voice was strange and different and the word came out more as a mewl of protest. Dhegli vanished underwater with a ducking motion and a quick flip of his tail. He emerged a few breaths later: watching her, his head bobbing questioningly. "Meriel," he said, and went under again.

Meriel took a breath. It all felt so . . . normal. She could sense the shifting water; she could feel the vibrations along her body as Dhegli swam around her, along with the smaller movements of fish nearby. She took another breath, deeper this time. She went under once more, this time of her own volition.

She found herself in another world, one she hadn't suspected existed. The water supported her, cradled her, and she flew through it as a bird might fly through air. Waves of moonlight swayed as bright as shafts of dusty sun, through which fish fluttered in shifting schools. There were sounds, too: the thunder of the waves on the rocks of Inishfeirm, the grumble of sand being shifted by the tides, the song of a whale far out in the Westering Sea, the chittering of shellfish and lobsters. She could sense the subtle changes in salinity and temperature and pressure.

In the wonder, the fear and panic left her for the moment and the tenseness in this new body relaxed. She felt the presence of Dhegli before she saw him, rolling lazily back to front to back as he fluttered past her, nipping her fin as he passed. She barked in surprise and chased after him; he increased his speed, angling down to slide and twist among waving strands of kelp and the outthrust arms of rocks. Suddenly they were flying upward along a length of mussel-encrusted granite and flopping out of the water onto the angled slope of a rock. As Meriel hauled herself out of the water, pulling herself awkwardly up with her stubby flippers, Dhegli waddled toward her, touching Meriel muzzle to muzzle. His black-blue fur was marked with the same pattern of scars as his arm had been. A voice spoke in her head, though her ears heard nothing, and he spoke in her own language.

"You are Jenna's pup."

Meriel gasped (the sound more a snort) and pulled away, and the voice in her head vanished. The feeling of panic returned. Meriel tried to speak but her words were garbled and nearly unintelligible, and Dhegli lowered his muzzle to Meriel again. Meriel felt that the touch was somehow less and yet more intimate than it might have been had they been in human form. *"Hush, young land-cousin,"* the voice said. *"You are safe here, for the moment. Think of what you wish to say; don't speak it."*

"How is it that you're talking to me? How do I understand you?"

A sound that might have been laughter rang in Meriel's head. *"Because I swallowed the Great Salmon that was birthed in the mage-light. You don't recognize my name, but Garrentha, who held Bradán an Chumhacht before me, was the milk-mother of my milk-mother. Do you know the name Garrentha?"*

Meriel started to speak. Dhegli snorted wetly, and Meriel thought the words instead. *"My mam told me a little of her. Garrentha was at Dún Kiil, wasn't she?"*

"Aye. At the shallow waters between the arms of rock, when the stone-walkers came from the Winter Home with their stones of lightning. Your mam swam with us, too."

"She did . . . ?" The words *felt* true, and with them Meriel realized how little she did know of her mam, how much like strangers they seemed. *"But she never told me."*

"Perhaps because she didn't know if the blood would run true within you. It's rare that it does. Garrentha could not change, nor my milk-mother, yet I can." Deghli paused, his muzzle leaving Meriel's as he glanced about him. The bull grunted on a nearby rock, his heavy, jowled neck lifting, and Meriel sensed a change within the blue seal, a darkening shift in mood. The muzzle came back down, shot with blue highlights. *"I came here for a reason, land-cousin. Bradán an Chumhacht, the Salmon of Light which lives within me, sent me here as it sent Thraisha-the-First and then Garrentha to your mam. You're in danger—those who would hurt Jenna will try to hurt her through you."*

Meriel nearly slipped back into the water, breaking contact with Dhegli before wriggling her body closer again. *"What kind of danger?"* she asked. *"And from whom?"*

"For that, I don't have an answer," he responded. *"I have only glimpses of a stone-walker far away. I see strings from his hand leading to others, and they do his bidding. I see one of those strings leading here, very close*

to you, and I see the stone-walker who holds the string ready to pull it."

"That doesn't help me," Meriel answered. This was the way her mam talked, all innuendo and suspicion; this was the fear and paranoia that had kept her hidden away and protected all her life and she was tired of it. She wondered whether her mam had sent Dhegli to her, another little trick to keep her confined. *"And what if I am in danger? Why should you care at all?"*

"I don't know that either. But yet I do care." Dhegli pulled back from her. He raised his muzzle and moaned toward the bull, who called back. Two of the cows slid from the waves onto the rock alongside the bull, and Dhegli's head brushed her flank once more. *"It's time to go back,"* Dhegli told her and he was gone in a moment, sliding into the water with a wriggle. She followed him more slowly, her new body rejoicing instinctively at the gliding embrace of the sea. It was with reluctance that she followed him out of the waves that crashed on the tiny beach, that she dragged herself out of the foam and brine onto the pebbles. Dhegli was already there and his head lay on top of her back. *"Just think of your true form,"* his voice whispered. *"Imagine yourself as you were. . . ."*

She felt more than saw the change. One moment, she was a Saimhóir; the next the world was cold around her and she was sprawled naked on the wet shingle, her red hair dark with the water and clinging in curled strings to her face and back. Dhegli lay there also alongside her: in human form. Meriel rolled away from him, pushing herself up into a sitting position, one arm across her breasts, her legs pressed tightly together. He lifted himself slowly from the sandy rocks. He stretched his scarred hand out toward Meriel. She shrank away but her back struck the slick, hard curve of a boulder and she was unable to retreat farther. His hand touched her shoulder, strong fingers curling around her upper arm, his face very close to her. His lips opened slightly, the breeze off the water snatching away the mist of his breath.

This touch was different. This touch frightened her more than anything she'd yet experienced this night, intimate and dangerous.

"Come to me again," his dark voice whispered in her head, even though his mouth didn't move. *"Tomorrow night. We'll swim together again."*

Meriel shivered. She gave him no answer. *"The dead things you stone-walkers wear are there, on that rock. The others of my family brought them here . . ."* He pointed to one of the rocks, where her léine and clóca were piled up, water dripping from the ends of the cloth. His hand left her arm, and she half crawled, half ran toward the clothing, pulling the clóca around her without feeling the cold, soaked cloth. When she turned around, Dhegli was gone.

Out in the surf, she saw a seal's head, moving outward to where the rest of the blue seals waited.

She shivered with the cold.

8

Lure of Water

THE Waking Bells tolled ominously: the high-pitched small bells chattering while the low droner tolled once for every five strokes of the others, so low and powerful that it was more a presence transmitted through the stone and wood rather than heard. Meriel cracked an eye open, unwilling to believe that it was already morning, but the room was grudgingly visible in the wan light of a rain-drenched dawn. Meriel groaned while the bells continued their clamor, and she heard Faoil awake and puttering about in the adjoining common room.

Faoil stared at Meriel strangely as she blinkingly stumbled into their shared parlor. "You look a mess," she said. "Your hair's all tangled and it looks a bit damp, too. Do you have a fever?" Faoil started to reach out to touch Meriel's forehead, but Muriel drew away from the girl's ministrations.

"I'm fine," she said. "I . . . didn't sleep well last night, that's all. I was tossing and turning. Nightmares."

"My mam always said you get nightmares whenever a ghost touches you while you sleep." Faoil went to the fire and pulled away the crane. She took an iron pot from the hook, folding her clóca around her hand to protect it from the heat. "Considering how old and haunted this place is, it's a wonder we have any good dreams at all. I've made tea—would you like some?"

Meriel nodded. Faoil continued to talk while she pre-

pared the tea; Meriel sank down into one of the chairs.
Last night: the memory of it seemed so impossibly far
away, so improbable. But she touched her hair, and it
was damp around her forehead and at the base of her
skull, and the curled strands were stiff with salt. When
she brought her hand to her face to rub at her eyes, the
scent of brine clung to the flesh.

It was real. You swam with the Saimhóir. . . .

The realization made her draw breath in sharply,
caused the light in the room to seem to shift. In that
moment, she realized that her life had been altered, irrevocably and unutterably, in some new direction. This
was nothing she could tell Lucan—in fact, she wasn't
sure that she would ever tell Lucan anything again. This
was nothing she could mention to Faoil or Thady or
Máister Kirwan or anyone else here. The only person
who might understand, who might be able to give her
guidance, was her mam . . . and that wasn't possible
either. She'd learned long ago that her mam was not the
kind of person to whom a child could run when she
needed comforting.

Whatever fate had touched her, it was one she would
have to face alone.

"Here . . ." Faoil handed her a steaming mug, fragrant
with mint and honey. Meriel started, then reached out to
take the mug, cupping her hands around the warm glaze.
"Thanks."

Faoil sat down on the chair across from Meriel.
"So . . . are you going to tell me?"

Meriel sipped the tea to cover her discomfiture; the
brew scalded the roof of her mouth. "Tell you what?"

"Something's happened. I can tell. Is it Thady, maybe,
or did this Lucan of yours finally write you another letter? Oh, I know," she said too brightly. "You've finally
fallen for Bráither Geraghty!" Faoil grinned at her own
jest, and Meriel tried to smile in return.

"I don't know what you're talking about," she said,
as casually as she could, and Faoil arched an eyebrow.

"All right, then, keep your secrets, Meriel MacEagan,

but I can tell that something's changed with you. Look at the way the color's rising in your neck, and you look as if you didn't sleep at all last night."

"Nothing's changed, Faoil." *And if it had, I certainly wouldn't be telling you.* Perhaps it was the residue of her mam's suspicion, but Meriel had rebuffed Faoil's occasional attempts to be a friend. She was just the person with whom Meriel shared a room. In fact, Faoil's insistence on continuing to make the attempt at friendship hardened Meriel's skepticism. *"I see one of those strings leading here, very close to you . . ."* That's what Dhegli had said, and no one here was physically closer to her than Faoil. Meriel shook her head firmly. "I have no idea what you're talking about."

"Fine," Faoil answered, a touch of irritation coloring her tone. "Then keep your secrets to yourself."

"I don't have secrets."

"Everyone has secrets, Meriel. Everyone." Faoil took a long drink of her tea, looking away from Meriel to the hearth. "Everyone," she said again, the word nearly a whisper.

The rest of the morning went no better. Meriel's morning duty was to peel breadroot tubers for breakfast. By the time the sun was fully up and the kitchen's fires blazing, the Bráthairs and Siúrs seated at their tables along with the fifth- and sixth-year acolytes and the servers taking the plates out, Meriel was already exhausted. She picked at her own breakfast, helped the other first-years clear the tables, and stumbled along the hallways with the others as the First Bell rang. She slumped into her chair at her desk with a sigh, propping her head on her hand.

It was difficult to concentrate on Siúr Meagher's lecture on the Lay of Caenneth Mac Noll and the North Dragon, and the deeper meaning within the text. Meriel's thoughts were more of the sea and the caress of water on dark fur. Somehow, the White Keep and the Order and Inishfeirm, her mam and Dún Kiil and Lucan, all the politics and intrigues and power struggles—they all seemed to have dissolved in one night, washed away in her exhilarating alteration. For the first time, she wondered whether her mam might not be right, that there was a power within her that she hadn't suspected, a power that would shape her life into some new and uncertain form.

She wanted to go back to the beach now. She wanted to strip off this life and plunge into this new ocean. She wanted to hear Dhegli's strange, low voice in her head . . . and that made her think of the Saimhóir in his human form, and that . . . well, that made her feel strangely uncomfortable and conjured up unsettling, disturbing images. The sea welled up inside her, pulsing and pounding, the tide rising and swelling, the taste of it in her throat . . .

". . . and what is *your* opinion, Meriel?" Meriel came back to the present with a start and the muffled laughter of her classmates. Siúr Meagher was standing beside her desk, frowning down at her. Her spidery fingers, thick-knuckled with arthritis, stroked the clochmion hung around her neck.

"I'm sorry, Siúr. I . . . I wasn't paying attention."

"That's vastly apparent. Is there a reason?"

"I'm . . . not feeling well, Siúr."

Brown eyes regarded her down the length of a long, thin nose. Those eyes did not seem convinced, but Siúr Meagher nodded. She let go of the clochmion around her neck and rubbed at her fingers as if they pained her. "Then perhaps you should see Siúr Khennhi in the apothecary. Perhaps one of her tonics might enhance your ability to concentrate."

Meriel grimaced; she hadn't yet experienced any of Siúr Khennhi's tonics, but she'd heard of them. Siúr Khennhi looked to be half Bunús Muintir, with a wide flat face, grizzled thick eyebrows, and an encyclopedic knowledge of herb craft. The apothecary always smelled of strange herbs and odd potions. Meriel started to protest, but Siúr Meagher was already pointing toward the door. "We'll leave it to Siúr Khennhi to decide what's best for you," she said, "since it seems not even a dragon can hold your attention today. I'll let Máister Kirwan know of your condition."

Wonderful, Meriel thought. *And Máister Kirwan will tell my mam . . .*

She heard Siúr Meagher's voice resuming the lecture as she padded down the cold hallway toward the apothecary. Turning a corner, she nearly ran into Bráthair Geraghty, carrying an armful of scrolls. "I'm sorry, Bráthair," she said. Owaine smiled at her. All she could think of was the memory of him standing in front of her door last night.

"Don't worry about it, Bantiarna. Happens all the time—I'm not the best at seeing what's in front of me." Then he frowned. "Why aren't you in class? You look tired . . ."

"I'm not feeling well. Siúr Meagher told me to see Siúr Khennhi."

Scrolls rustled dryly in his arms. He squinted. "Do you know where the apothecary is? I could walk with you—"

"I know where it is, Bráthair," she answered hurriedly.

He stared at her, eyes narrowed. "Of course you do," he said. His arms tightened around the scrolls. "I hope you feel better, then." He blinked. "You didn't sleep well last night? I didn't either; the seals were making such a racket at the bottom of the cliffs." He paused expectantly and seemed to be waiting for her to comment.

"Really? I didn't hear them."

He shrugged, looking at the wall of the corridor rather than her. "I hear them. I listen for them. I've always loved them, especially the blues. I thought you might, too, especially since your mam . . ." He stopped; he looked at her and his face went red, and he quickly glanced away again. "I was just a child when I saw her, coming out of the ocean with them."

"You *saw* her?" Meriel asked, interested despite herself.

"Aye," he answered. "I was four or five. I was on the beach and the first to find her after her swim from Thall Coill after the Scrúdú. My mam took her to Máister Cléurach, who was still alive then and afterward we heard about Dún Kiil and the great battle there. When I was thirteen, one of the Bráthairs came to our house from the keep and told my parents that the Banrion had requested I be sent to the Order. When I passed the mage-test, your mam sent me this . . ." Juggling the scrolls, he showed her the clochmion on its chain.

"What does it do?" Meriel asked.

Bráthair Geraghty shrugged. "Very little, like most clochmions. I can find things with it. Lost things." He shrugged. "Bráthair Maitias thinks that's a great skill for a librarian, to be able to find even the most hidden of the scrolls in the library." His eyes widened suddenly, as if startled. "Oh, please don't think that I'm not grateful to your mam for the gift. Why, so many of the cloudmages don't have any cloch at all, only the slow magics. I'm very pleased and humbled that she would give me this."

"I'm sure you are, Bráthair." He seemed so harmless, almost laughably so, and yet last night . . . She remembered him, standing just outside her door, where he shouldn't have been. And he was *always* around her. . . . *those strings leading here, very close to you* . . . "I need to get to Siúr Khennhi," Meriel said.

He nodded, squinting toward her again. "Aye, you do. I didn't mean to keep you . . ." He stepped out of the way, and she hurried past him. She could feel his gaze on her as she walked quickly away, and she knew if she looked back, he'd still be standing there, watching.

Thady MacCoughlin came up to Meriel as she sat down next to Faoil at supper. Faoil openly snickered as he approached, and she heard whispers from the others, especially those who were Riocha. Thady must have heard them as well, but he pretended not to notice. "I heard you were sick, Meriel," he said.

"I wasn't feeling well," she answered. "I'm better now. Siúr Khennhi gave me some herbs."

"Did they taste like ash and dirt?" Thady asked, and Meriel grimaced at the memory of the cloying, thick paste that Siúr Khennhi had made her eat. Thady laughed at her expression. "I know; I've had a taste or two myself over the last few years. They say that once Máister Kirwan was walking by the apothecary with a pot of new flowers for the garden, and the flowers wilted just from the smell in the hallway."

Faoil sniffed disdainfully. Thady didn't look at any of the acolytes with Meriel; he watched only her. His eyes were hazel, and strands of long, light brown hair slid over the side of his face as he leaned down across the table from her. "Well . . . get yourself better," he said. "Remember that little jaunt I suggested a while ago? I'd still like to try it, if you're willing."

Meriel felt conspicuous, as if the attention of everyone in the room was on her. She glanced over at the mages' tables: Máister Kirwan was looking her way, as was Siúr Meagher and, aye, Bráthair Geraghty. The other mages though were talking among themselves, and Máister Kirwan turned to one of them, as if he were answering a question. "Meriel?" Thady asked. "Did you hear me?"

"Leave her alone, Thady," Faoil told him. "You think the Banrion's daughter is interested in a 'jaunt' with you and your lowborn friends?"

He ignored Faoil, and Meriel felt a flash of irritation at Faoil's interference. "I have to think about it," she told him.

"Good," he said. "That's not a 'no.'" He smiled again, tapped the table with his fingers, and walked over to his friends, already enmeshed in another conversation. Meriel stared down at her plate.

Under the table, Faoil nudged her with a knee. "What?" Meriel asked.

"Nice of Thady to care so much about your health," Faoil said. "And nice of you to even notice him. His father has a bit of Riocha in him, but the man makes his money from keeping sheep. He's really no better than a shepherd. I'll bet you can smell the dirty wool on him. Just like you can smell the fish on Bráthair Geraghty."

"I don't care. Thady's helped me a few times. He's a friend."

A nod. A grin. "Or is he something else? I'll admit he's handsome enough. He could almost make you forget the sheep. Or someone else."

Meriel closed her mouth on the reply she wanted to make. *Actually, I find Thady very attractive and nice. I like him well enough and my own great-mam herded sheep and so did my mam when she was our age. For that matter, I'd hardly worry about sheep since last night I swam with a seal who could turn into a man, and I found him handsome, too. . . .*

None of that was anything she could say to Faoil.

"How many letters have you received from your Lucan?" Faoil asked.

"You know the answer as well as I do," Meriel answered. There'd been only the one letter, long days ago now. "But a dozen things can delay a letter."

"Oh, absolutely," Faoil agreed, though her eyes were laughing. "Answer one thing for me. Are you going to write to your Lucan tonight?"

Meriel glanced over to where Thady was sitting, talking with the other third-years. And she heard, in her mind, the sound of seals. "No," she told Faoil. "I don't think I am."

In the moonlight, she pulled the clothes from her body and draped them over a rock a few steps from the high tide line. Naked, she stepped toward the first onrushing wave, ducked her head, and dove into black water, feeling the delicious changes ripple through her body . . .

"May the currents bring you fish, Meriel." The words came with the touch of warm fur as Dhegli's body wriggled over and around hers in the water. The touch was delicious and more sensual than Meriel remembered, and it awakened a strange desire and yearning within her. The intimacy was too much for her and she swam away from him. He pursued, faster and more agile than she, but he let her stay ahead, occasionally nipping at her flukes as the sound of his laughter rippled through the water. She laughed with him, enjoying the luxuriant false chase, the sense of freedom that came with swimming this way, the heightened senses that flooded her. *"This way . . ."* Dhegli circled around her, then dashed off. She followed, and the sea bottom rose to meet them, until they hauled out on the sandy half-moon of beach near the foot of the keep trail. Dhegli was beside her, his black, pupil-less eyes staring at her . . .

. . . and though the pupils remained that strange utter black, they were no longer the bulbous eyes of a seal but human orbs set below the ridge of brow, his sable hair matted over his forehead. And she was no longer a seal either, but herself again and lying on her back in the sand, and Dhegli's face was very close to hers.

The kiss, when it came, was very soft and very tender, and his lips tasted of salt. He drew back, finally, looking down at her solemnly. His hand cupped the side of her face. *"I shouldn't have . . ."* she heard his voice say in her head, though his lips remained still and slightly parted.

"It's all right," she told him. "It was what I wanted, too." She knew, as she thought the words, that they were true: despite all reason, despite logic, despite the fact that she knew him not at all, despite the unalterable fact that he was Saimhóir and she Daoine. It didn't matter in that moment. She reached up to draw him back down to her, but he resisted, instead kissing the palm of her hand.

"Later," he said. *"There will be time later."* He looked down the length of her body and she could feel the touch of his arousal. "If that's what we both want."

"Why wouldn't it be?" she asked him, confused by the twin pulls of his desire and restraint as he smiled sadly.

"What life can we have, Meriel?" he asked. "We meet here between our two elements, you the stones and me the sea, but neither one of us can truly live as the other. Even if we could, Saimhóir lives are shorter than stone-walker lives. What would we have together—a dozen journeys to Winter Home? You wouldn't give up the stones for me, even if you could, and I wouldn't give up the water. We have our fates, Meriel, and they aren't—they can't be—together."

Meriel blinked away salt. "Then why . . ." she began, and he pressed her hand against his face and shook his head.

"Who can know the WaterMother's whims?" he said. He kissed her hand again, and started to pull away, but she caught him and pulled him toward her, and this time he didn't resist. They kissed again, longer this time, as she pressed him to her, as his hands moved along her body. This was not like the times she'd been with Lucan. Her blood roared in her ears, her breath burned.

"We can be together here, in between our worlds," she whispered to him. "For this little time."

"Aye, we can," he told her, as softly. "But not this night." He lifted himself from her and for the first time she was cold, the wind raising goose bumps on her skin. His hand touched her foot as she rose up on her elbows. "Come swim with me some more," he said. "We'll catch the sweetfish . . ."

They swam. They caught the sweetfish, and Meriel swallowed them, tasting their delicious flesh, and when she was exhausted and the night well on its way to morning, she returned to the beach, dressed, and walked back up the steep path to the White Keep, while below the seals sang of the sea.

9

A Dead Creature

IT SIMPLY wouldn't do for the Rí Ard of Talamh an Ghlas to receive a delegate from the Concordance of Céile Mhór from his bed. Instead, the initial meeting took place in the Great Hall, with Rí Ard O Liathain sitting on the throne that had been occupied by Daoine Ríthe since the time of Crenél Dahgnon, a thousand years before. In truth, it wasn't the same seat on which Dahgnon had reclined; it was far newer than that, having been rebuilt several times over the long years, though pieces of that most ancient seat of power had always been incorporated into its structure. And in truth, the Rí Ard was able to remain sitting mostly because he was tied firmly to the back of the throne under his clóca.

In both cases, appearances were maintained and that was the most important thing.

The curious among the Riocha of Dún Laoghaire had crowded into the Great Hall as word spread of the delegate's arrival. Though none of the Ríthe of the Seven Tuatha were in Dún Laoghaire, their representatives were and those privileged Riocha were arrayed to the Rí Ard's right alongside Enean, who fidgeted restlessly in his chair with MacCamore standing behind him and whispering gentle encouragement. Noticeably, Tiarna Labhrás Ó Riain sat near to Enean also. Doyle wondered at that: Labhrás Ó Riain was no friend of Doyle's or to any of the young Riocha who were part of the Order of

Gabair. Ó Riain was the protégé of the established Riocha of ancient lineage, arrogant and middle-aged, though he was held in high esteem by the Ríthe of Connachta, Airgialla, and Éoganacht. Doyle had wondered, once or twice over the years, if his half sister had not been responsible for the attack that had killed the Banrion O Liathain and addled poor Enean, whether Ó Riain might not have been among those responsible.

Ó Riain was also the Holder of Wolfen, one of the Clochs Mór. His lineage was impeccable: Peria Ó Riain, Holder of Lámh Shábhála, had been a distant ancestor; another of his ancestors had been Rí of Tuath Airgialla; his cousin was Rí there still. Labhrás had made it clear that he considered Doyle little more than a tuathánach: a commoner, a bastard and half-breed who had no right to be holding a Cloch Mór, an upstart whose betrothal to Edana was a ludicrous mockery.

Doyle knew that if his own ambitions were ever to be realized, it would be Ó Riain who would be standing in his way.

Doyle himself sat at the Rí Ard's left, next to Edana. Because their engagement was public knowledge, Doyle and Edana held hands and smiled at one another as the Hall Máister approached to announce the delegate. They both knew their roles, but the affection between them was no lie: Doyle would have asked the Rí Ard for permission to court his daughter even if Nevan hadn't pushed them together. The Hall Máister approached the throne, struck the shaft of his spear twice upon the flags, and bowed. "The Toscaire Concordai, Ulán Rhusvak, most excellent emissary from his august majesty, Aeric the Third, Thane of the Concordance of Céile Mhór, requests an audience of the Rí Ard."

"I wonder if this Toscaire is as tall as his title is long?" Edana whispered to Doyle as the Rí Ard waved a tired hand in acceptance and the Hall Máister strode back down to the tall doors of the Great Hall to usher the man into the room. Ulán Rhusvak was nearly as impressive as his introduction. He *was* tall, half a head taller than Doyle and dressed in the fashion of Céile Mhór: high leather boots; loose pants of brown cloth decorated with bits of shell and bone; an elaborately embroidered linen undertunic. Over his head and cascading down his shoulders and back was the hide of a bear, the skull and upper jaw still intact and placed atop the man's head, so he looked out at the assembled Riocha through a screen of yellow-white incisors. A necklace of claws adorned his throat; at his waist a wide leather belt held twin, long daggers with pommels of carved whalebone. His arms were bare and muscular, and on the sun-browned skin, Doyle could see the marks of battle scars.

Behind the Toscaire came four attendants, dressed similarly though without the skins; between them, they bore a long box which, from the look of strain on their faces, was heavier than it appeared.

Rhusvak strode up to the dais of the Rí Ard and bent one knee, his head down so that the black stone eyes of the bear seemed to regard them all. "Rí Ard O Liathain, your cousin Thane Aerie MagWolfagdh bids you good health and prosperity. I bring you his words."

"I would like to hear them," O Liathain answered, his voice weak but audible. "You may rise, Toscaire Rhusvak. Please accept the hospitality of the Tuatha."

"Thank you, Rí Ard." Rhusvak bowed his head again, then stood. Under the bear's jaw, Doyle could see the shadowed face, as tracked with white scars as the arms. "The Thane will be pleased to know that you're well."

O Liathain almost seemed to smile at that; at Doyle's side, Edana smothered a chuckle, though the faces of the other tiarna remained stolidly expressionless. Edana answered for her da. "I'm sure he'll also be pleased to know his Toscaire has the gift of flattery," Edana said. "I'm also certain that Thane Aeric didn't send you here to see if the Rí Ard was still among the living. Why *have* you come to Dún Laoghaire, Toscaire Rhusvak?"

There was silence in the hall at the temerity of someone speaking before the Rí Ard could reply. Then the

Rí Ard chuckled, and after a moment, the rest of the Riocha followed suit, seeing that the Rí Ard took no offense at Edana's interruption. Doyle, throughout his youth, had experienced the interminable, gratingly polite back-and-forth of diplomacy. Edana had known that the conversation should have dragged on for a candle stripe or more yet before the real subject of the meeting was finally broached, and she could also see the drawn weariness in the Rí Ard's face and the way he sagged against the hidden bonds holding him upright.

He squeezed her hand; she returned the pressure.

Rhusvak regarded the Rí Ard silently for a moment, then gestured to his attendants. They brought the box forward and set it down alongside the Toscaire. "I apologize for this, Rí Ard, but it is easier to show you than to tell you," he said.

He nodded to the others, who opened the seals and immediately turned the box on its side. As Doyle, Edana, and the rest of the onlookers rose to their feet in horror and shock, as Enean's voice rose in an audible childish shriek, a body tumbled out onto the flagstones, a massive scythelike weapon clattering loudly to the ground alongside it. A foul stench filled the hall. Only the Rí Ard, bound to his throne, remained seated.

Whatever it was, it was not a Daoine or any creature that Doyle had even seen. The thing was clothed only in a filthy cloth around its hips, bloodstained and torn, with what seemed to be a crest or insignia at the right hip. The creature's thighs were huge and muscular, the massive, platelike joints articulating backward, powerful lower limbs ending in long, clawed feet. The upper body was rippled with corded muscle; the arms too long, the four-fingered hands as large as dinner plates, looking easily capable of handling the oversized pole arm beside it. The skin was a mottled pattern of yellow and brown, finely scaled like that of a snake. The face was snouted, with large eyes set close together at the juncture of a nasal ridge, a small mouth set underneath. A thick bony crest extended from the crown down to where the spine met the neck; to either side of the neck were large, tympanic ears, the soft flesh there an oval of bright orange.

Doyle tried to imagine the thing standing; it would have towered over any of them, looming like a creature from a nightmare. The Tiarna around him were all shouting and gesturing, some with hands reaching for weapons that—following the etiquette of the Great Hall and the Rí Ard's presence—were missing. Doyle's hand, though, like a few others, had gone not for iron but for stone; he closed his right hand around the Cloch Mór he held, ready to open it and release the mage-dragon at need.

But the body wasn't moving, and slowly the uproar dimmed. Doyle sat, gently pulling Edana down with him. The others took their seats again more slowly, Labhrás Ó Riain among the last to sit. "Again, I apologize, Rí Ard," Rhusvak said when his voice could be heard. Next to Doyle, Edana pressed her perfumed sleeve over her mouth and nose, trying to ease the stench. Rhusvak caught the motion. "That isn't simple corruption you smell, Bantiarna," he said to her. "That is mostly the reek of the Arruk."

Enean alone remained standing now, and O Liathain gestured to his son to sit down; MacCamore came forward and pushed down gently at the confused young man's shoulders while Labhrás Ó Riain stood again at Enean's other side and whispered in his ear. Enean reluctantly took his seat. Doyle wondered at that interchange, wondered why Ó Riain was suddenly so solicitous toward Enean.

"What *are* these Arruk?" O Liathain asked. "What have they to do with the Tuatha?"

Rhusvak glanced down at the body with obvious distaste. His lips puckered as if he were about to spit on the creature. "I'll make the story as short as I can, Rí Ard," he said. "It began fifteen summers ago when word first came to the Thane of attacks on the Daoine villages in Lower Céile nearest Thall Mór-roinn. Bands of these Arruks had come over the Thumb into our land."

"Your land?" the Rí Ard interrupted. "Does Thane
Aeric now claim Lower Céile for the Concordance?"

Rhusvak took a long, sighing breath. "Perhaps that
overstates things, Rí Ard," he continued. "We have but
a few settlements in Lower Céile, well separated and
rarely visited by anyone except the Taisteal and other
traders. Certainly Thane Aeric has never been to Lower
Céile himself. There is empty land enough there—which
was part of the conflict. Rather than spread out into
unclaimed land where they might have had only sporadic
contact with us, the Arruk established their own settlements near ours. They planted no crops, tended no herds.
Instead, they took food from our fields and killed our
sheep, goats, and cows, as well as thinning the storm
deer herds that have lately become common. There were
encounters and brutality on both sides. More of the
Arruk came; they began to raid and burn our villages
and kill our people. Five years ago, Thane Aeric sent
an army past the Uhmaci Wall into Lower Céile to deal
with the growing threat. Only its tattered remnants came
back, the commanders telling the Thane of hillsides bristling with the Arruk weapons, of the frightening strength
of their warriors protected by a natural armor and the
cunning of their generals. They also spoke of a magic
the Arruk mages wielded, a magic not from clochs na
thintrí but from staves of wood, a slow magic but more
powerful than any of the little spells we know, more like
that of the clochs na thintrí of the Tuatha.

"Last summer, a new army was raised and sent out
beyond the Uhmaci; it, too, came back in decisive defeat.
And in the month of Longroot . . ." He paused. "The
Arruk brought their own army against the Uhmaci Wall.
The Wall was broken."

"Uhmaci Wall? Broken?" O Liathain leaned forward
as far as his bonds would allow him, staring at the Arruk
as if the body could give him answers. *Uhmaci Wall . . .*
The name of the legendary demarcation of the Daoine
lands brought to Doyle a vision of imagined white towers
and stone buttresses undulating over green hills. The

Wall was impossibly far away, so distant as to be only a legend, but in those legends and tales, the Wall was impregnable. It had stood for over a thousand years.

"The Arruk now hold all of Lower Céile," Rhusvak continued, "and we no longer control all of the gates of the Uhmaci. The Arruk have made raids well past the wall into the midland where many of our Riocha have their estates. Our people flee in front of them—already, thousands in Mid Céile nearest the Uhmaci have left their homelands. More come to our main cities in Mid Céile every day: hungry, homeless, lost. And the Arruk continue to come northward."

They were all staring at the body now, Doyle as much as any of them, imagining hordes of the Arruk moving over the green and fertile hills from which their ancestors had once traveled. "We ask for help from our sundered cousins," Rhusvak said, more softly now. "We know the power of the clochs na thintrí, and Thane Aeric would see the army of the Rí Ard ride with the army of the Thane: one great Daoine army against a common enemy, the power of the Clochs Mór against the power of the Arruk."

"Let me go there, Da!" Enean half-shouted, his voice too loud. "I want to fight the beasts."

O Liathain nodded indulgently to his son, but Doyle saw the subtle hand motion the Rí Ard gave to MacCamore. The old warrior crouched alongside Enean, whispered something, and quietly escorted him away, Enean still chattering about fighting, his hands flailing the air as if he were holding a sword already. The Rí Ard watched his son's departure, then his eyes closed for a moment, the eyelids fluttering.

Doyle noticed that Labhrás Ó Riain watched also and that the man slipped out of the room quietly a few moments later.

"These Arruk have done nothing to us," the Rí Ard answered finally. "And while the Concordance and the Seven Tuatha have never been enemies, neither have we always been friends. Céile Mhór is far from Dún Laoghaire in more ways than simple distance." There was a murmur of assent from the Riocha around the Great Hall, but Rhusvak shook his head.

"Look at this creature, Rí Ard. Look at it with the wisdom of your years. Imagine tens of thousands of them, hundreds of thousands, an endless horde descending on this keep. In another five years or ten or fifteen, if this continues, the Arruk will come through the Neck into Upper Céile, and from there, one day, across the Finger into Talamh an Ghlas. Perhaps we can hold them back longer, but if in the end the Concordance fails, then the Arruk *will* come to the Seven Tuatha. We have a chance now—together—to end that threat. If you fail to act . . ." He shrugged, and the fur on the bearskin rippled with glossy highlights. "Then the swords of the Concordance will be rusting in the ground and will be of no help to you, and our ghosts will be laughing at your fate."

The rumble of whispered conversation rolled about the hall as the Rí Ard stared at the body alongside the man. Edana leaned over toward Doyle. "Are you thinking as I am, my love?" Her sapphire eyes glistened in torchlight; the hint of a smile touched her lips.

Doyle almost smiled. "I might be," he answered, "if you're thinking that the Toscaire Concordia may have put another weapon in our hands."

She did smile then and turned in her chair, leaning over toward her da with a rustle of cloth. Doyle could not hear what she said, but the Rí Ard stirred. "We thank the Toscaire Concordia for this warning," he said formally. "And we will consider our response. In the meantime, have the gardai remove this carcass from the Great Hall. Toscaire Rhusvak, if you will follow the Hall Máister, he will guide you to your chambers and have the servants bring you and your people refreshment." The Hall Máister came forward and escorted the Toscaire away. The Rí Ard leaned back against the throne, nodding in turn as each tiarna and bantiarna bowed and took their leave.

When the last echoes of footsteps had died in the vaulted ceiling, Doyle and Edana untied the Rí Ard. He sagged wearily against Doyle's shoulder with a long, audible exhalation. "I'm so tired," he said simply.

"I know, my Rí," Doyle said. "Let us help you back to your chambers." He started to lift O Liathain, Edana under the man's other arm.

"It's time," O Liathain said to them as they helped him to his feet. "Edana's right. It's time for us to act."

"There are some who will disagree," Doyle said cautiously. "Tiarna Ó Riain will be one and he speaks for Ríthe Connachta and Éoganacht, at least."

"Let them disagree," O Liathain snapped with sudden energy. "I don't have time to waste on politics. Not anymore. Edana knows. Listen to her, Doyle."

Doyle caught Edana's gaze as they walked the Rí Ard slowly away from the dais. She was watching him, staring at his face as if she could see the thoughts chasing each other inside his skull.

She smiled.

"Then we'll proceed, my Rí," Doyle answered. "It's all in place. I just need to send the messages and get my people together. . . ."

10

The Truth-Stone

GRAY waves rolled in from the west, and dark forms
flew through the cold water.

Meriel shivered in the brisk wind, her body stiff and
reddened from the icy sea, her tightly-curled hair darkened to rust-red with salt water and plastered down her
back in twin clinging strands. The sun hadn't risen yet,
but false dawn shimmered golden on the horizon. She
felt again the weary happiness that followed the exhila-
ration of being in the water.

Of being with *him*. . . . " 'Bye, Dhegli," she called to
the water; there was an answering wailing call. She hurried to the blanket and clothing she'd left neatly folded
behind a large rock just out of the reach of the foaming
tide. She dried herself with the thick blanket, and quickly
put on her underclothing, then the red léine, white clóca,
woolen stockings, and boots.

The seals warbled and honked at her, out on the flat
rocks beyond the surf. She waved once more toward
them and started toward the trail leading up from the
tiny, rocky beach, holding tight to the memories of the
last few hours.

"Awfully cold for a swim," a familiar male voice said,
and a young man dressed in the same colors as Meriel
stepped out from behind the screen of a large boulder.
"Not to mention that Máister Kirwan doesn't like acolytes out by themselves at night."

Meriel stopped, feeling a sudden heat on her face. "How long have you been standing there, Thady Mac-Coughlin?" she asked.

"Probably not long enough," he answered, with a slight, almost shy grin, "judging by appearances."

Her blush deepened and she scowled at the fact that he could affect her that way. She wanted simultaneously to run from him, to shout at him for spying on her, or to simply disappear in sheer embarrassment. If he'd taken a step toward her, she would have fled back to the sea, uncaring of what he might witness then, but he stayed where he was without moving toward her or away. Meriel wondered if Dhegli had noticed Thady, and she hoped he wouldn't come out of the sea, naked and dripping water, to confront him.

"Why are you here at all? Were you following me?" Her voice snapped, anger covering her embarrassment as Thady spread his hands apologetically, ducking his head as if Máister Kirwan had lashed him with one of his legendary furies. Meriel wished it was her own personality that had that effect; she knew the subservience was because of who her mam was.

"I woke up early and couldn't get back to sleep," Thady explained. "I was wandering around the grounds when I heard the seals down here, so I came down to see them." He glanced out to the rocks. "Those are blues, aren't they—the Saimhóir? Half the island claims to have Saimhóir blood in them." He cocked his head toward Meriel. His gaze was appraising, and she saw the sudden certainty in them. "Some even claim to be changelings who can swim with them."

"Most people swim simply for exercise and enjoyment," Meriel answered. "And if you don't stop talking, neither one of us is going to get up to the White Keep quickly enough to keep from getting caught at First Bell." With as much dignity as she could muster, Meriel pushed past Thady. After a moment, he followed.

It was a long and steep climb along the winding path and Meriel hurried so that they had no chance to talk.

They crossed a foaming, quick stream of cold water and scrambled upward through bracken and heath before reaching the crown of the mountain where the keep brooded, higher than anything except Mt. Inish looming just east across a narrow, deep valley. Meriel and Thady could look southward down to Inishfeirm Harbor, where the houses of the island's main town clustered near the docks; behind them, the keep rose ever upward with its towers of whitewashed, pale stone, the forbidding walls pierced with the dark eyes of windows.

The two half ran to the side wall of the Low Tower and the tiny, ivy-covered door. "Oscail," Meriel whispered— the opening word that Thady had taught her—and waited for the faint *click* as the latch slid back. But there was no answering click: there was no sound at all except for the wind in the trees and the faint hammering of the surf far below. Meriel looked worriedly at Thady; he went to the door and put his hands on it.

"Oscail!" he said, more loudly, and pushed. The door shivered in its frame but didn't open. Thady shook his head. "What's the matter? It's never done this before. You don't think—"

"No, you *don't* think, Thady MacCoughlin. 'Tis exactly the problem, I would say. I expect better of a third-year." The voice was deep and stern, and both Meriel and Thady drew in their breaths. A man's form stepped out from the shadows of a nearby oak tree, his white clóca and léine swirling around him.

"Shite!" Meriel heard Thady curse under his breath, then: "Máister Kirwan . . ."

"Aye," the man answered. "It never fails to amaze me just how *surprised* acolytes are when they're caught." Máister Kirwan's eyes glittered, icy blue, and his mouth was pressed tight into a frown. He stared at Meriel especially hard, his gaze holding a long time on her face framed by water-matted hair. "I was once an acolyte here, too, as were all the Bráthairs and Siúrs. I know that's hard to believe, but it's true, and I learned the same things you did. I've also learned since how to make a door tell me when it's been used and to change the ward-word."

He went to the iron-banded oaken planks of the door and laid his hand on it, whispering a phrase to the wood that neither of them could hear. The lock clicked in response and he pushed the door open with a creak of ancient hinges. "Bantiarna MacEagan, An-tUasal Mac-Coughlin, if you'll follow me . . ."

Máister Kirwan's office was a small chamber high in one of the southern towers. The dawn caressed the rough-hewn beams of the ceiling with yellow-gold fingers. When Máister Kirwan moved the scrolls on his desk aside as he sat, motes of dust rose to spark in the shafts of new sunlight. "Sit," he said sharply, the first word he'd spoken to them since they'd entered the White Keep, and pointed to two high-backed and uncomfortable-looking chairs against the walls. Thady sat as if his legs had just been chopped out from underneath him, the wood creaking under the sudden weight. Meriel forced herself to sit more slowly, as if she were attending one of her mam's interminable state dinners back at Dún Kiil, but she very carefully kept her gaze away from Máister Kirwan's eyes and she couldn't seem to stop her chin from trembling. She told herself it was the chill from the water.

The Máister fingered the Cloch Mór around his neck, grunting to himself. A soft knock came from the door to the chamber, and another of the teachers entered: Siúr Alexia Meagher. Her clochmion stone glittered like a small diamond against her white clóca she nodded to Máister Kirwan. "Ah, Siúr, thank you for coming. You know these two."

"I do, indeed." Siúr Meagher sniffed, looking down the length of her thin nose at them. The long length of her braided brown hair swayed as she turned back to Máister Kirwan. She rubbed her arthritic hands together as if trying to warm them, grimacing as she did so; after clenching her fingers a few times, her left hand closed over the stone at her breast. She closed her eyes and sighed, then her eyes opened again. "I'm ready, Máister."

"Good." Máister Kirwan took a long breath, steepling his hands before his face and resting his chin on his thumbs. "Now, I suppose you knowledgeable acolytes also know what Siúr Meagher holds?" He looked hard at Meriel.

"A clochmion," Meriel answered. "One of the minor stones. I don't know what it does, though."

Meriel saw Siúr Meagher give a slight nod to Máister Kirwan as she answered. A faint smile touched the man's lips. "Aye, you don't. An-tUasal MacCoughlin, do *you* know what power this clochmion has?"

Thady shook his head. "No, Máister," he began, but Siúr Meagher cleared her throat. Thady glanced at her, startled; Siúr Meagher lifted her right hand, a forefinger raised warningly. Meriel heard Thady sigh. "I really don't *know*," he said, staring at the Siúr. "But the rumor among the acolytes is that Siúr Meagher has a truthstone, that it can tell her when someone's lying. Evidently," he added, his gaze going back to Máister Kirwan, "that's more than a rumor."

"Indeed it is," Máister Kirwan answered. "Frankly, Siúr Meagher might possess a clochmion, but she holds a power that some holders of a Cloch Mór might wish they had. The two of you will bear that in mind as you answer me. Now . . ." Máister Kirwan leaned back in his chair. "Thady MacCoughlin, exactly how did you come to be outside the keep before First Bell?"

Thady glanced again at Siúr Meagher before answering. "I woke up to use the chamber pot," he answered. "Kharidi, my roommate, well, he was snoring, and once I woke up I couldn't get back to sleep . . ." He stopped; Meriel saw tiny muscles tug at the corners of Siúr Meagher's lips and wondered what the woman heard in Thady's comments. "Our room is close to the Hall of the Low Tower. I heard the door to the Women's Wing open. I thought I might see who else was up, so I went to see."

"And?"

Thady's eyes flicked toward Meriel. "It was her."

"And what did you do then?"

Meriel could see a blush rising up Thady's neck as a corresponding irritation welled inside her. Thady's tale certainly didn't match what he'd told her down on the beach. "I thought I might follow Meriel and see where she was going, so I went back to my room, dressed quietly, and followed."

Meriel turned to Thady, feeling the heat rising to her cheeks again. "You sneak! You told me you were just 'wandering around' and heard the seals," she retorted, not caring that she was interrupting Máister Kirwan. *Acting like your mam's daughter . . .* that's what her da would have said.

"That's enough," Máister Kirwan snapped at her, though Meriel thought she saw him smother a laugh. "Your turn will come, Bantiarna MacEagan, and we'll see how well you fare." Meriel shut her mouth, cutting off her protest though she could feel her forehead bristling in a scowl. Máister Kirwan nodded to Thady. "Please continue."

Thady kept his face firmly pointed at the Máister. "She was gone by the time I came out, but I heard footsteps at the bottom of the tower, so I figured she was heading for the Acolyte's Exit—that's what we call it, Máister—so I just headed down that way. When I came out, I caught sight of her just starting to head down the beach trail. She was well ahead of me, already. That trail's difficult enough in the daytime, so I thought she was just going to look at the water from the top of the path. I decided to wait there for a while for her to come back up. I waited a long time, maybe half a stripe of the candle or more before I realized that she must have gone down farther than I thought. I wondered whether she was in some trouble, so I started down myself. I went slowly, looking for her all the time and expecting to see her at one of the grazing fields for the sheep, but I never saw her. I went all the way down to the water, but I still couldn't see her anywhere. I didn't know where she was."

Siúr Meagher raised her eyebrows, and Thady hurried to amend the statement. "But I found her clothes, fairly quickly, and I figured she'd gone into the water."

"And what were you intending to do if you *had* found her?" Máister Kirwan asked. His eyes glittered under the shadow of his thick-hedged brow, his chin lifted slightly.

"Nothing," Thady answered, but again Siúr Meagher cleared her throat. Thady's head swiveled toward her and back again. "I wasn't intending to *hurt* her or anything," he said hurriedly. "I just thought . . . I thought we could talk, that's all." His eyes flicked over to Siúr Meagher and back; Siúr Meagher said nothing.

"And did you call out for her then and announce that you were there, or did you go down toward the water, knowing she was unclothed and hoping to see her in that state?" Máister Kirwan asked.

The blush rose over Thady's face like a swift tide and his gaze dropped to his hands folded on his lap. "I went down to the water, Máister, 'tis true, but when I looked I couldn't see her at all, only a family of blue seals, and I started to get worried, especially knowing who she is. I started back up the trail to get someone, but then the seals started making a commotion and I came back. That's when I saw her . . ." He stopped, but Meriel could hear in the way his voice trailed off that there was more. She knew Máister Kirwan and Siúr Meagher heard it as well, and her stomach twisted and burned. *Please, Mother-Creator—don't let Thady have seen Dhegli and me together. Please . . .*

Máister Kirwan cocked his head and leaned forward. "And?" he prompted.

Thady looked at Siúr Meagher. "It's nothing," he said. "Really. I was mistaken."

"I'll make that decision," Máister Kirwan answered. "What were you mistaken about?"

Thady's face was blotched with red. "I thought . . . I thought for a moment when I first saw her that there was someone there with her, a young man. But when I looked again, he was gone." Thady's hands lifted, palms up. "I was mistaken in that, Máister. I had a good view of the beach; if there had really been someone else there, I would have noticed him. There was only Meriel. No one else."

Meriel felt the knot in her stomach loosen a bit. Máister Kirwan seemed satisfied with that, leaning back in his chair and nodding. He didn't ask the additional question that she might have asked: *"Did you see Meriel clothed or naked?"* Instead, he grunted and turned his attention to her. "Did An-tUasal MacCoughlin harm you in any way, or make you feel threatened?"

Meriel shook her head. "No, Máister. I was . . . startled when I saw him, that's all. But he . . . he behaved as he should."

Thady gave a relieved exhalation. From the corner of her vision, Meriel saw Siúr Meagher nod to Máister Kirwan, who grunted. "An-tUasal MacCoughlin, you may leave us, then. It's well past First Bell and the others have already eaten, so you've missed breakfast. In fact, you will miss *all* your meals today, I think. Perhaps a little hunger in your belly will help you sleep better tonight. You'll report to Bráthair O'Therreagh today—you'll assist him in cleaning out the midden. You may go now."

Thady grimaced, biting his lower lip, but said nothing. He rose, bowed to Máister Kirwan, and left the room without looking at Meriel again.

"The young man seems to be rather infatuated with you, Bantiarna MacEagan." Meriel's eyes widened with Máister Kirwan's statement. "You're surprised?" he continued. "You shouldn't be. These things happen, especially at your age. Especially with someone of your lineage."

"I'm not infatuated with *him*." She denied it emphatically, then glanced at Siúr Meagher, who was smiling.

"All right, aye, I find him interesting and attractive, but that's still not 'infatuated.' Does that satisfy you, Siúr? Thady's been helpful to me when others haven't and I'm grateful. I don't care that the others call him just a tuathánach—that's what my mam's family was, once. But that's all. I haven't done anything else."

"Good." A half smile lifted one side of Máister Kirwan's mouth. "Jenna would have my—" He paused. Started again. "Banrion MacEagan would be upset if she found out you were involved in a serious romance here."

"You needn't worry about that with Thady, Máister," Meriel answered, but she glanced over at Siúr Meagher as she said it. The woman still wore that amused expression, but said nothing. Her hand, with their arthritis-swollen joints, remained clasped around the clochmion on its chain.

"When I last corresponded with the Banrion, she told me to be especially watchful with you regarding the Saimhóir; understandably, I think, given your family history. This isn't the first time you've gone . . . *swimming* at night, is it?"

The burning in her stomach returned. Meriel saw Siúr Meagher's fingers tighten around her clochmion. " 'Tis the very first time, Máister," Meriel answered with as much conviction as she could muster. Siúr Meagher snorted as if stifling a laugh. Máister Kirwan *did* chuckle, shaking his head.

"Well, I must admit that I would have made that test, too," he said to her. "But I'm afraid that Siúr Meagher's cloch works quite well. In fact, your mam can do the same—it's one of the many abilities of Lámh Shábhála, as well." Meriel's eyebrows lifted; that bit of information explained several events in her childhood. *She'd climbed up on the chair to reach her mam's favorite vase, the one with the glittering golden threads in the glaze, but the vase had slipped out of her hands and shattered loudly on the floor. Her nurse at the time, who was sleeping near the fire, awoke with a snort. Worse, her mam happened to be in the next room, taking her tea and talking with one of the tiarna on the Comhairle. The Banrion came hurrying into the room at the bright explosion of noise.* "I didn't do it, Mam." *Meriel blubbered, unable to stop the tears.* "The cat must have knocked it over." *Her mam's right hand was touching Lámh Shábhála, and she simply glared until Meriel dropped her head in shame.*

"Are you hurt?" her mam asked. Meriel shook her head. She didn't dare look up. "What happened here?" her mam had asked the nurse, her voice icy.

"I . . . I didn't see it, Banrion," the woman stammered. "I turned my back for just a moment, and—"

"That's enough," Jenna snapped, and Meriel glanced up to see anger on her mam's face, but thankfully directed at the nurse rather than her. Jenna's disfigured right hand dropped away from the cloch, and she rubbed at the marked skin. "Just . . . clean up this mess." Without another word to either of them, she'd turned to return to her meeting. That night, Meriel was given no supper, a new nurse attendant came in to put her to bed, and she didn't see her mam for another day or more. . . .

"Meriel, I asked you a question," Máister Kirwan said, interrupting her reverie. Meriel blinked. "This wasn't the first time, was it?"

Meriel grimaced, lowering her head as she had that day long ago. A drop of cold water dripped from the end of a strand of hair onto her lap. "No, Máister. Not the first time. I heard the Saimhóir down on the beach nearly a month ago, and I went down to see them. My da, he told me some about Mam and the seals and I love looking at the Saimhóir, so I thought . . ."

"You went in the water with them?"

A nod.

"As *one* of them? As your mam is reputed to have done?"

Meriel nodded again.

"The young man Thady saw—he was Saimhóir, wasn't he? What's his name?" Máister Kirwan asked.

Meriel's head came up. Her lower lip trembled. She remembered the exciting brush of fur against fur, the disorienting moment of transformation and his smile, the touch of his fingers against her skin and the way she shuddered deliciously in response . . . "Dhegli," she said. "He can keep the human form for only a few hours, as I can keep the Saimhóir."

She thought he would ask the obvious next question, the one she didn't want to answer. He didn't. His gaze drifted away from her toward the window and the sun that was beginning to lift above the sloping shoulders of Mt. Inish and the fog from the valley. Máister Kirwan seemed lost in reverie, his long fingers stroking the facets of the Cloch Mór around his neck. Meriel squirmed in her chair, the fist that held her stomach tightening and twisting. Finally he turned back to her. "Meriel, I don't expect any more excursions like this from you while you're here with the Order. If we find you outside the keep again without permission, you will be immediately dismissed from the Order and sent back to Dún Kiil. I don't think I need to tell you how your parents would react to that."

"No, Máister." That was easy for Meriel to imagine. Her da would be disappointed and quietly sad, but her mam's reaction . . . well, that wasn't anything Meriel would care to endure. Meriel felt the fist slowly release its grip on her intestines: at least it seemed that Máister Kirwan was going to say nothing about this. But never to see Dhegli again, never to swim with him again, wasn't something she would accept.

You're going to have to be very careful now. Very careful.

"I'm sorry, Máister," Meriel said. It was easy enough to sound contrite—the tremble in her voice and the shimmering in her eyes were both genuine, even if the sentiment was not.

"You should be," Máister Kirwan answered sternly. He rose from the chair, going to the door. "You'll go immediately and join An-tUasal MacCoughlin and Bráthair O'Therreagh at the midden. Perhaps you'll remember the stench the next time you're tempted to take a

late night stroll." Meriel opened her mouth to protest,
then shut it again at the look Máister Kirwan gave her.
He opened the door. "That's all, Bantiarna MacEagan."

Meriel grimaced. She rose from the chair with a sigh,
bowing her head to Siúr Meagher and the Máister, then
walked out into the cold corridor. A trio of acolytes
approached, heading for class and looking curiously at
her before they noticed the Máister and scurried quickly
past. The door shut firmly behind her.

Meriel did something she hadn't done in years: she
stuck out her tongue at the wooden planks. The gesture
did little to make her feel better.

Máister Kirwan sighed, his hand still on the door handle.
"Obviously I need to replace Siúr O'hAllmhurain as
ward of the Women's Wing, since she's failed in that
capacity. Actually, it's *my* failing in choosing her and I'll
tell her so. And I need to find a quick replacement."

"I'll do it," Siúr Meagher said, then raised her eyebrows as she slowly clenched and unclenched her left
hand on her lap, grimacing at the stubborn ache in her
knuckles. "That is what you were going to ask me,
isn't it?"

"Aye, it is. Thank you, Alexia." He nodded toward
her hand. "And thank you for this morning. I know your
hands have been bothering you."

"It's fine," she told him. "The joints are stiff in the
morning, that's all." She put her right hand over her left.
"Siúr O'hAllmhurain's going to blame Meriel for this;
she's not one to keep a grudge secret, or not to act on
it in some way."

"Actions have consequences. If Meriel hasn't learned
that already, it's time she started. I just hope the consequences aren't . . . well . . ." He ran a hand over his
skull from forehead to crown, as if brushing back the
hair that once had been there. "I'm going to have to

send the Banrion a report on this," he said. "Jenna's *not* going to be happy."

"You can't lock the girl in a closet for her whole life, Mundy," Siúr Meagher told him. "This is an issue we have with *all* the acolytes. How many their ages are already married, already well into their adult lives? They come here at the most difficult time in their lives and we ask them to give up everything their peers have. They *will* find ways to listen to their emotions."

"I know that, Alexia. But that won't matter if someone needs to be blamed, and I'm the one who's ultimately responsible for looking after her. I wish it were something as simple as a youthful infatuation, but it's not—not when it's the daughter of the Banrion and First Holder we're talking about. It was bad enough that she was flirting with the MacCoughlin boy, but that was relatively harmless and easy enough to watch. The Saimhóir . . ."

"Even Lámh Shábhála can't stop her from growing up. She's going to fall in—and out—of love, Mundy; she's going to fight against the restraints we 'old folks' put on her. That's what happens at her age. It's part of the reason the Banrion sent her here. Banrion MacEagan knows you and trusts you, Mundy. She'll understand."

"I hope so," Máister Kirwan answered. He managed a wan grin. "But even if she does, it doesn't make things any easier. After talking with Jenna, I was most worried about attacks from the outside, and that's what we've been watching for. Now I wonder if we weren't looking the wrong way for the danger."

11

In the Midden

THE MIDDEN was a malodorous, room-sized hole in the keep into which all the kitchen scraps were dropped. In addition, two latrines also deposited their visitors' aromatic leavings into the space. The midden was cleaned out twice a year, spring and fall, and the black, rich compost from it mixed into the soil of the fields behind the keep.

It was the dirtiest, nastiest work Meriel had ever done.

Bráthair O'Therreagh, who also taught the slow magics to the fourth- and fifth-year acolytes, didn't seem to be bothered by the horrendous stench that wafted out from the refuse heap. He fingered a small leather bag corded around his neck, and handed two similar pouches to Meriel and Thady. "Weed of sticklebur, sage, and mint," he said, "with a spell of enhancement on it. I don't smell a thing, myself. A good thing I made a few extra, eh?" To Meriel, the charms only seemed to make the air around her sickly sweet—the overpowering mint made her nearly as nauseous as the odor of corruption wafting from the midden. Wooden-bladed shovels were placed in their hands. "Máister Kirwan suggested that the two of you start inside; shovel the muck out the door, and the others will load it into the carts. When we have the carts filled, we'll take it out to the fields and spread it. The faster everyone works, the sooner we're done. Go on, now . . ."

There were six other acolytes working with them—four boys, two girls, all second- and third-years and none of them anyone Meriel knew well—each with one of Bráthair O'Therreagh's bags around his or her neck. They didn't look any happier to be there than Meriel; she wondered what they'd done to get this nasty duty. "I'll need to burn these clothes and bury the boots afterward," Meriel muttered as they stepped through the door into the darkness of the midden.

"And scrub off the top layer of your skin with that gritty brown soap of Siúr O'Flagherty's," Thady responded, "the one that leaves your skin looking like it's been boiled." He plunged his shovel into the mountain of black filth in front of them, the blade entering with a wet *kchunk*. He flung the heap of refuse back through the door. ("Eewwww," someone groaned outside. "That's *nasty . . .*") "I'm sorry, Meriel," he said. "I really am. I didn't intend this. I hope you know that."

Meriel plunged her own shovel in and sent another sopping bladeful through the door. At least very little light filtered into the midden—she couldn't see much of what was squelching under her feet. "I doubt it would have made much difference. It wasn't you at all. Even if you hadn't followed me, Máister Kirwan would still have been waiting for me. You just happened to get caught in the same trap." She tried to rekindle the irritation she'd felt toward Thady in Máister Kirwan's chambers, but it was gone, buried under the filthy reality in front of her. "Why *did* you follow me, really?" she asked.

A scrape of shovel blade on stones: another load of foul matter went through the door. "It was stupid."

"I *know* that," Meriel answered. "But why?"

She heard him take a long breath. "Because . . ." he began, then stopped again. "I'll bet Faoil told you the only reason I'm interested in you is because of your name."

"She's suggested it," Meriel answered. "Is it true?"

They continued to shovel silently for several breaths.

"You weren't what I expected when I heard the Banrion's daughter was coming here," Thady said finally.

"What did you expect?"

"I don't know. Someone haughty and cold, I guess, all full of her own importance. Someone who acted above *all* the rest of us—after all, your mam holds Lámh Shábhála, and she may pass it on to you sometime. I can't imagine holding that much power. I never *will* hold that much power, or possibly any at all. I'll be lucky to have a clochmion."

He lapsed again into silence except for a grunt as he heaved another mound of black filth from the midden. Meriel waited. "My da's just a minor céili giallnai," he continued after a time. "About the only person here with less nobility in his ancestry is that strange Bráthair Geraghty, who's a total tuathánach. My da fought at Dún Kiil, though, when your mam stood in the storm of mage-lights and called the stone creatures to defeat the Rí Ard's army. He says it's different in Dún Kiil now than it was before, better then when old Rí MacBrádaigh was alive. Better for the céili giallnai and the tuathánach. He says that it's because of your mam since until she married Tiarna MacEagan she was barely Riocha herself, and she remembers how those of royal blood treated her then. I think you're the same, that way. I watched you, like everyone has, from the first day you came. You don't act like you're any different than any other first-year; in fact, you're quieter than most even though everyone's always so damned polite and interested around you because of your name, even the Bráthairs and Siúrs, sometimes. You even talked to me those times I came up and spoke first. But even though you don't seem all high and mighty, you also don't let them push you about. It's like you know who you are and you're satisfied with that, and it doesn't matter what the others think or say."

"Most of the others don't follow me around at night, though." She couldn't see his embarrassment in the midden's twilight, but she could feel it.

"That was stupid. I already said so."

"And you still haven't said why you did it."

"I'm not sure I really know. It just seemed the right thing to do at the time. I thought . . . I thought if I seemed to accidentally come across you outside, I might get to talk to you and know you a little. I'm not—" He stopped.

"You're not what?"

She saw him shrug, leaning on his shovel. "I'm attractive enough. I know that. But I also know that's not anything special. I've seen the girls who are willing enough to look at me but who won't talk to me because my family's not important enough. I'm hardly the best student here, but even if I were, I'd never hold a Cloch Mór—and I've heard that the mage-test is . . . well, *harder* for some students than others, that the final examination isn't as hard for Riocha as for people like me."

For a moment, she felt something tug at her, deep inside—a different feeling than what she experienced when she was with Dhegli, but yet . . . Meriel plunged her shovel into the pile in front of her. She felt confused: in her heart, she'd already given up Lucan—where he'd once been, thoughts of Dhegli filled her. But still . . .

"You're attractive enough," she repeated, as if musing. "Tell me, Thady MacCoughlin, since you were down at the beach when I finished . . . swimming . . . do you happen to know what *I* look like?"

Meriel saw the flash of his teeth even as he looked down at the blade of his shovel. "It was dark there."

"But could you see well enough?"

Again, the quick, hesitant smile. Thady nodded. "Oh, aye," he said, in a voice that was almost reverential in tone. "I could indeed. And 'twas worth the trouble it's gotten me, too."

Meriel tossed the load of sludge. Somehow, it managed to miss the open doorway and splatter mostly over Thady. "Oops," Meriel said.

She tried not to grin too widely.

Only the stony tip of Mt. Inish was still sunlit when
they finished. The rest of the mountainside was already
shrouded in the purple shadows of evening and the folds
of the valleys below were hidden in full darkness. Meriel
was covered in filth, her palms and fingers were blis-
tered and sore, and she was exhausted. With the rest of
Bráthair O'Therreagh's group, she staggered back to the
White Keep from the fields, pushing the stained planks
of the cart they'd used to haul the stinking mounds of
compost. The charm around her neck seemed to have
lost its potency; the stench surrounded them. "All right,
then," Bráthair O'Therreagh said after they'd pushed
the cart back into its shed. "The boys may come with
me. Siúr O'hAllmhurain will take the girls. Go on
now . . ."

Siúr O'hAllmhurain was a grim-faced woman in her
mid-twenties, unmarried, who like Bráthair O'Therreagh
taught slow magics. Given the Siúr's usual demeanor,
Meriel was fairly certain why she was still unmarried.
She glared hard at Meriel as she shepherded the girls
into the bathroom on the lower floor of the Women's
Wing. She stopped Meriel, letting the other girls go past
and shutting the door behind them. "I want you to know
something," she said to Meriel.

"Siúr?"

The woman's lips pressed together; her eyes narrowed.
"Your little expedition has made me a laughingstock,"
she said. "I don't care who your mam is or whether
Máister Kirwan is your protector. I won't let you do that
to me."

"Siúr O'hAllmhurain, I didn't—"

The lines on her face tightened. "Inside," she said.
"I've said all I'm going to say and the stench of you is
too much to bear." She opened the door.

With the others, Meriel pulled off her soiled clothing
and—shivering—climbed into the large tub at the center
of the room, filled with water that was quickly murky

and lukewarm. Siúr O'hAllmhurain tossed in cakes of hard soap. "Use that," she told the girls. "Then empty the tub; I'll have clean water brought in."

Half a stripe later, Meriel and the others were done, dressed in clean léine and clóca as Siúr O'hAllmhurain herded them back upstairs to their rooms. She handed them each a small loaf of fragrant, warm bread, with a pat of butter melting golden in the middle. There was none for Meriel. "What a shame," Siúr O'hAllmhurain said. "The kitchens must have made a mistake." With a small smile, she turned and left.

When Siúr O'hAllmhurain came to the door of her old room, she passed it, turning instead down the corridor toward the common hall between the dormitory wings. Meriel saw Siúr Meagher standing in the open door at the end of the hall. She nodded to Meriel.

Meriel went into her room.

"You'd better not still be stinking."

Meriel ignored Faoil, leaning back against the door, exhausted, famished, and wanting nothing more than to fall into bed. "And you'd better not be thinking of sneaking out of the room again at night," Faoil continued. "Ever. I got an interrogation and a lecture from Siúr Meagher today about whether I knew you'd been leaving the keep, and she as much as told me that Máister Kirwan will hold me responsible if I don't stop you next time. And you'll notice that we now have Siúr Meagher watching us, so we'll all suffer." She sniffed in Meriel's direction, as if she could still catch a whiff of manure and rot over the strong lye scent of the soap. "I certainly don't intend to spend *my* time wallowing in the midden."

"I'm sure you won't, Faoil," Meriel answered, her voice tired and hoarse. She went to her bed and lay down, unable to stop the long sigh that welled up from inside her. Her eyes closed almost of their own volition— *no excursions tonight, that's for certain.* But thinking of it made her recall Dhegli, and the wonderful white smoothness of his skin when he walked toward her.

"Was it awful?" Faoil asked, her voice banishing the image of Dhegli. Having delivered her ultimatum, Faoil now sounded almost conciliatory—*or perhaps she'd decided that it wasn't to her own best advantage to remain angry with the Banrion's daughter,* Meriel thought. She forced her eyes open again to see the young woman staring at her in the wavering glimmer of the candles.

"What? The work? It was nasty, aye—foul and hard." Meriel lifted her hands, palms out toward Faoil. "Look at these blisters. My arms feel like they're about to fall off."

Faoil glanced from Meriel's hands to her own, smooth, soft, and unblemished: the hands of a Riocha. "Why in the Mother's name would you go outside, when you knew what would happen if you were caught?" she asked. "Why would you take the chance?"

Meriel had no answer to that, or—more accurately— there were too many answers. "I don't know," Meriel answered. "Because I wanted to." *Because I had to. . . .* That was more accurate, but she couldn't say it.

"Where did you go? There are all sorts of rumors. They say your mam—"

"My mam," Meriel interrupted, "has nothing to do with this. Leave her out of it."

Faoil drew back as if Meriel had slapped her, and the girl's gaze went distant and cold, as if she'd slipped transparent armor over her face. Meriel remembered other exchanges with Faoil and the other young women among the acolytes, and seeing that same guarded look go suddenly over their features also. A sudden realization came to her. *The problem's with you, not them. Faoil and the others aren't really being aloof or unfriendly. They're making the effort; it's* you *who won't let them get close.* "I'm sorry, Faoil," she said. "I'm just . . . tired. I didn't mean to snap at you."

"I understand," Faoil answered in a tone that indicated she didn't understand at all. "Why don't you get some sleep?"

Sleep was easy; Meriel only had to lay her head down. Her dreams that night were of the sea, but Dhegli's hair and eyes were sometimes dark and sometimes, sometimes strangely fair.

12

Sheep and Bridges

"WHEN they told me that the Banrion was out watching sheep, I didn't believe them."

Jenna turned to see Kyle standing near her on the slope, breathing heavily as he leaned on a walking stick. She gestured at the flock of black-headed sheep grazing on the steep pastureland beyond Dún Kiil Keep. A black-and-white herding dog was circling the flock, nipping at the heels of any sheep who strayed too far from the group. Well down the slope, a trio of gardai pointedly looked the other way.

"It's meditative," she said, smiling at him. "I come out here every once in a while. The keep shepherd lets me take them out for a little bit, but first I had to convince him that I could manage to bring them back without losing any. Being out here with them reminds me of home; I can pretend that I'm just a little girl again."

"And how is it that I never knew this?"

"I'm sorry," Jenna answered. "I wasn't deliberately keeping it a secret. It just never seemed to be anything you'd want to know, and you're usually in Dún Madadh looking after your own townland. It's not that important."

"The captain of *Uaigneas* tells me that you've decided not to go visit Meriel tomorrow."

Jenna looked back to the sheep, not liking what she saw in Kyle's eyes. "The Comhairle's still all in an uproar because of the seat I gave to the Northern Clans of the Stepping Stones. They're all afraid that will be enough provocation to bring the Tuatha down on us again. I thought I should remain here while they're meeting to make certain that everything stays calm. Aithne thinks that there will be a motion to fix the number of voting seats to what it is currently—"

"And if there is a motion, Aithne and I can squash it without your being there," Kyle finished for her. "We both read the last letter from Mundy. You should go talk to her, Jenna. You understand what she's going through. I don't."

Jena turned around to face him. "Did *you* listen to your parents when they gave you advice at that age, Kyle? I know I didn't. I knew better than my mam. I thought she was stupid and couldn't possibly understand what I was feeling or what I was going through. She would—and did—give me advice that I wasn't prepared to accept and didn't believe." Jenna gave a self-mocking laugh. "So now she has her revenge on me with my own daughter."

"Because you didn't listen doesn't mean that Meriel won't."

"Maybe. But you know what, when I look back at it, I still think my mam was wrong and that if I'd taken her advice I'd have ended up in a far worse place. So maybe it's the same for me and Meriel. Maybe all I have to give her are empty and useless opinions that would in the end make her miserable and unhappy."

Kyle sniffed and he shook his head, pressing his lips together before speaking. "Give up the self-pity, Jenna. You don't believe any of what you just said, and we both know it."

"How *dare* you!" Jenna shouted back at him, flashing into sudden temper. The dog barked once at them before returning its attention to the sheep.

"You and your mam ended up apart for half of your life," Kyle continued, ignoring her protest. "I'm sorry that happened, but you can't change it now. Maybe you haven't been the mam to Meriel that you wanted to be, but all you have the power to change is what happens from this moment forward."

"I couldn't *be* just her mam," Jenna spat back heatedly. "I'm the Banrion. I'm the Holder of Lámh Shábhála."

She remembered once saying the same thing to Meriel. She must have been five or six then, sitting in the middle of the room with a trio of dolls arrayed before her like supplicants. . . . *"Mam, why can't you play with me. I want you to play with me."*

"I can't, Meriel. I'm already late for a meeting. Saraigh will play with you." She started to gesture to Saraigh, Meriel's nursemaid at the time, but Meriel was already crying.

"Mam, stay. I want you to stay . . ."

She hadn't. Couldn't. But by the time she closed the door to the chamber to shut out Meriel's howls, she was crying herself. . . .

"Aye, you are the Banrion and the First Holder," Kyle was saying. "No one can deny that. But right now you also have a child who needs you."

"You go to her then. She calls you her da."

"And I *will* go to her, if you won't. I love Meriel, as much as if she really were my own child. But I can't talk to her about what she's feeling right now. Only you can do that. I know you love her, too, Jenna. I can see it. And I know she loves you also."

"The Comhairle . . ." Jenna stopped herself. The ram started away from the flock and the dog ran after it, barking angrily until the sheep turned grumpily and went back to the others. Jenna sighed. "You're right," she said. "I'll go. In a few days, once I know that the Comhairle's settled." She pressed her lips together, studying his face. "It's what I have to do, my husband," she told him. "It's the task you and Aithne gave me. A few days. That's all."

Kyle grinned at her. "Then a few days is what it will be. But you'll go. You'll promise me that?"

"I'll go," she told him. "And if I'm going to take

another jaunt to Inishfeirm, I can't be daydreaming out here. Kesh!" she called to the dog, and it cocked its head toward her. "Bring them!" The dog barked once and then began running about in earnest, yapping at the sheep and nipping at their legs as they bleated in protest. The flock began to straggle back down the hill toward the keep, moving more steadily as the sheep realized that they were heading home. Jenna linked her arm in Kyle's and followed alongside them. The gardai started moving out ahead of them.

"Thank you, my husband," she said. "You're a better friend than I deserve."

He laughed, the sound causing Kesh to stop barking at the sheep for a moment. "And you're a better friend than you believe," he told her. "And a better mam as well."

The Order of Gabair in Lár Bhaile was still a pale imitation of the Order of Inishfeirm. Even those in charge of the institution would have admitted that had it been politically safe to utter those words. But the Toscaire Concordai Rhusvak knew none of the Order of Gabair's short history, and Doyle wasn't about to enlighten him. The delegate from Céile Mhór had overheard Doyle's plans to go to the Lár Bhaile and had asked about the Order. Edana had suggested that Rhusvak accompany Doyle. *"It gives you the chance to see if he can help us, and it masks your true reason for going,"* she'd said. *"You've seen how Ó Riain is hanging around the man."*

Three days later, they'd entered Lár Bhaile.

Doyle, the Toscaire Concordai, and their entourage rode up from the lower town around the lough to the stony flanks of Goat Fell, the mountain on which both the Ri's Keep and the Order's blue-painted tower sat. Finally, their horses sat snorting at the jagged edge of a deep ravine. Far below, the stream called Deer Creek thrashed its way to the lough, as the riders stared upward to the heights where the keep stood. The road ended here, abruptly, at a broken stone bridge, and if Rhusvak looked at the fallen edifice and wondered, he said nothing.

"The Order of Gabair was established by Nevan O Liathain on taking the title of Rí Ard from his da in 1132," Doyle told Rhusvak. "The Rí Ard had experienced firsthand the defeat at Dún Kiil, and he realized that at least part of the blame for that defeat was the lack of training for our Tuathian mages." Doyle gestured up at the Order's tower looming far above them. "The Order of Gabair now teaches our own cloudmages. Many of the Holders of Clochs Mór—at least those who live in the various Tuatha—have taken their study here."

"As you did?" Rhusvak asked.

"Aye," Doyle told him. "I spent five years here, thanks to the patronage of the Rí Ard and my uncle Vaughn Mac Ard, may the Mother-Creator keep him in Her embrace."

Rhusvak scratched at his beard under the bearskin. The man smelled strongly of pungent oils and musk. Doyle wondered whether all the people of Céile Mhór exuded the same odor. If so, he was glad that the wind rarely blew east to west across the Tween Sea. The ride from Dún Laoghaire had been a trial for Doyle's sinuses. "I must say that Tiarna Ó Riain seems less impressed with the Order of Gabair," Rhusvak said carefully, the smile on his leathery face taking away the edge the words might have had. "He didn't seem to think that Céile Mhór would find the help we want from your Order."

"Tiarna Ó Riain is . . ." Doyle paused, allowing himself a small smile. ". . . *older*. Most of the cloudmages who have come out of the Order of Gabair are within a few years of my age. Also, his allegiance is to those Ríthe who have historically been Tuath Gabair's enemies: Tuath Connachta and Tuath Éoganacht. Tiarna Ó Riain was also *at* Dún Kiil, and his Cloch Mór Wolfen was one of those that were defeated by the Inish

cloudmages. So perhaps his opinion . . ." Doyle paused
again, deliberately, and this time said nothing.

"So you believe your dragon is stronger than his
wolves?" Rhusvak suggested. "Because of your Order's training?"

Doyle lifted a shoulder. "Perhaps if the Order had
been in existence twenty years ago, your Thane wouldn't
have to be asking for help against the Arruk. Perhaps
the Holder of Lámh Shábhála would also be one of the
Order of Gabair's cloudmages and there would be no
question about sending a force into Céile Mhór to help
our cousins."

"Perhaps," Rhusvak mused. "Still, Tiarna Ó Riain
seems inclined to offer us aid in our plight where the Rí
Ard continues to avoid giving me a direct answer. How
did Tiarna Ó Riain say it the other day . . . ? 'The young
mages look west and north with the Rí Ard, while I see
that the true threat is coming from the east.' "

"When an enemy is holding a knife to you, it's not
wise to ignore them no matter what you suspect might
be at your back," Doyle told him.

"And you'd deal first with the enemy before you,"
Rhusvak nodded. "You believe that Lámh Shábhála is
that knife."

Doyle shrugged. "You'll forgive me if I must think of
Talamh an Ghlas before Céile Mhór. But come," he
said, "let me show you the Order's Tower and let you
talk to my good friend Tiarna Shay O Blaca, who
teaches there now."

"Tiarna? Not Máister?"

"No Bráthairs or Siúrs, either," Doyle answered.
"We've all traveled the same road; we're all peers."

Behind the screen of bear's teeth, Rhusvak smiled. He
glanced down at the wreckage of the bridge in the ravine
far below. "It seems our road ends here."

Doyle grinned. "It does—for those who aren't friends
of the Order or Rí Gabair. Which are you, Toscaire
Concordai?" With that, he grasped the reins of Rhusvak's horse and kicked his own mount. Rhusvak shouted

in alarm as the horses galloped onto the broken span of bridge and rushed toward empty air and the long fall.

But as the hooves struck the last stones, the air shimmered before them and the furious crash of stone against stone boomed in their ears. The missing span was suddenly *there* under their feet, gleaming white and solid. Rhusvak still shouted, but his shout was now one of glee and surprise. More slowly and cautiously, the rest of the entourage followed. When the last horse had ridden across, the bridge vanished once more; before any of them could draw breath, the sound of thunder rolled down the ravine.

"They say the Mad Holder destroyed this bridge after she killed the Banrion Cianna and set the keep on fire," Doyle told Rhusvak. "Tiarna Ó Riain and those who think like him would have simply rebuilt the bridge as it had been. The Rí Ard, though, saw a better way. I'd ask you to consider, Toscaire Concordai, that the right solution isn't always the obvious or the easy one."

Rhusvak's lips twisted upward momentarily. He stared at the empty air where the bridge had been. "Ah, spoken like the Rí Ard himself."

"I'll never be Rí Ard, Toscaire Concordai. That's not one of my ambitions."

Another brief smile. Rhusvak leaned over toward Doyle, whispering so that none of the others could hear. "But perhaps your future wife is interested in putting the Ard's torc around her neck, eh? As to your ambition, I think I can guess at it."

He looked pointedly at the Cloch Mór on Doyle's chest. When Doyle only shrugged, silent, Rhusvak chuckled and scratched at his oiled hair again, leaning back once more. "Tell me, Tiarna, is your Order strong enough to stand against the Order you intend to replace?"

"That," Doyle told him, "we'll find out sooner than some might think. But for now, it's enough that the keep has a fire, warm food, and cold stout after a long ride. If you'll come with me, Toscaire Concordai . . ."

13

Friendship

IF MERIEL harbored any hope that she would still be able to slip away from the keep, it was dashed quickly. One of the Bráthairs or Siúrs was always within sight of Meriel whenever she ventured from her rooms, and none of them bothered to conceal the fact that their task was to watch her. Generally her shadow was one of the senior mages, sometimes Máister Kirwan himself. Even the other acolytes' attitude toward her had shifted from a cloying deference to a more distant attentiveness, especially among the fourth- and fifth-years, and she suspected that Máister Kirwan had passed a warning to them. Only Thady seemed unaffected, and—unfortunately—Bráthair Geraghty, whose strange and awkward attention to her remained unflagging.

Worse, Siúr Meagher was a far more vigilant presence than Siúr O'hAllmhurain and a much lighter sleeper. After an exhausting day that the mages of the keep seemed determined to fill with tasks for her to complete, Meriel heard the seals and tried to leave and go to Dhegli. She managed to slip out of her bed, dress, and move into the parlor without actually waking Faoil, but Siúr Meagher's door opened the instant Meriel's did. No words were exchanged; under Siúr Meagher's eyebrow-raised stare, Meriel closed the door again.

As the latch clicked, there was the scrape of a footstep behind her; Meriel turned and saw Faoil standing in the doorway to her room. "I don't care who you are or that your mam's the Banrion," Faoil said, her voice still groggy with sleep. "I won't let you ruin my chances of being a cloudmage. If you leave, or if I find you gone again one night, I won't cover for you or pretend not to notice. I *will* go to Siúr Meagher."

With that, she turned and went back to her room, leaving Meriel standing in the parlor, cold despite the glowing embers of the night's fire.

"It wouldn't have done you any good, anyway," Thady told her the next morning, catching Meriel as she hurried down one of the long corridors of the keep with a pouch of aromatic herbs for Siúr Khennhi. "Máister Kirwan had put additional spell-wards on the door. He evidently gave a demonstration to the acolytes while we were in the midden—had one of the fifth-years try to open the door. The warding held his hand fast to the handle while the door shrieked like a mad thing until Máister Kirwan released him with the ward-key." Thady shook his head. "No, no one will be going out that way again. Not soon."

"That's not all the Máister's done." The voice was Bráthair Geraghty's, who seemed to have materialized an arm's length away, his arms again full of scrolls that exuded the scent of must. He nodded to Meriel and gave Thady a long, lingering glance, his eyes narrowing as if he were trying to focus on the young man's features before he turned back to Meriel.

Despite wishing that Bráthair Geraghty wouldn't look at her so fixedly, Meriel couldn't help asking the question. "What do you mean?"

"I mean that there are other eyes watching, not all of them like ours, if you take my meaning," Bráthair Geraghty answered. "Be careful, Meriel. You don't want to alienate those who only want to help you." The scrolls shifted in his arms; he adjusted them, causing a pouf of dust to rise around him. He sneezed. Nodding again to Meriel, he moved past them, the leather soles of his sandals slapping against the stone flags.

"What a strange man," Meriel said as he left. She shivered. "I hate the way he stares at me."

"Don't worry about him," Thady said. "Don't worry about the others, either. They don't understand you, Meriel."

Meriel, watching Bráthair Geraghty's receding back, turned to Thady with a smile. "And you do?"

She thought he'd grin, and perhaps return her question with a jest. He didn't. His face was solemn as he looked at her. "I understand how the name a person has or what their family's history is can force someone to take paths they don't want to take. And I can understand how desperately someone can try to find another way." Then the solemnity vanished, and he did grin. "You'd better get those herbs to Siúr Khennhi," he said. "Unless you're interested in going back to the midden."

He touched her arm, as if shepherding her past him. His fingers lingered there; she could feel them through the cloth of her clóca. Then his hand dropped away. "Thanks, Thady," Meriel said.

"For what?"

"For being a friend. For understanding."

He blinked. His lips moved as if he were about to say something. Then he nodded and walked away.

Night, and the sound of seals . . .

Meriel awoke, sitting up abruptly in her bed. The room was silent, and yet her head echoed with the calls of the Saimhóir and the swirling currents of the sea. She wrapped her blanket around her and slipped from the bed quietly, not wanting to wake Faoil. Going to the window of her room, she pushed open the shutters.

The night was clouded, the stars and moon hidden, the landscape wrapped in fog and shadow. Yet . . .

She saw him, in the high grass near the base of the keep: Dhegli. As if he felt the pressure of her gaze, he looked up to her and she could see his smile, though his eyes were closed and his hands raised. Sparkling light shimmered around him, as if he were standing in a cloud of wind sprites. The air smelled as it did during a lightning storm, full of power.

And the fog . . .

It was rising, as if it were the breath of the ground itself, swelling and thickening. Dhegli, naked, was awash in it, standing in a pool of swirling white cloud, and still it rose until it swallowed him entirely, engulfing the base of the Low Tower and rising toward Meriel's window far too quickly for any natural mist. Meriel closed the shutters as the first tendrils snaked over the sill, writhing like ghostly fingers. The keep was encased in spell-fog now, the sounds of the outside world lost.

The mist filled the keep and held it in its white hands.

She heard the door in the parlor open, then footsteps. He stood at the door to her room as she turned, still clutching the blanket to herself. She went to him in a rush, kissing lips that tasted faintly of brine, her fingers tangled in his wet curls. His body pressed against hers. "I couldn't go to you," she said to him in her mind-voice. "I wanted to, but they've made it impossible." Then she stopped, holding him at arm's length. "You have to leave, Dhegli. You can't be here. Máister Kirwan—"

She heard the laughter in her head. "Do you think I worry about some stone-walker's cloch? There are other magics in the world, just as powerful as those you're studying—did you forget that I hold Bradán an Chumhacht? If your mam were here with Lámh Shábhála, then perhaps I'd still be standing outside, but only then. Don't worry about the Máister or the others. They all sleep and dream of the sea." He kissed her again, more softly this time, and when he drew back, she tried to move with him but he shook his head. "I came because I have to tell you something: I have to go away for a time. I have to leave tonight."

A tightness gripped Meriel's chest. "Away? Why? For how long?"

"For a time," he answered. "We Saimhóir don't try

to bind time as you stone-walkers do. I'll be gone for as long as I must be—I don't know more than that. As to why . . ." His shoulder lifted. "That's simple enough: because I hold Bradán an Chumhacht and because the gift of power also gives me obligations and duties I can't refuse, even when I'd much rather ignore them. Even when part of me says that I should stay here." He touched her face, stroking her cheek softly with the back of his hand. "Your mam knows that. It's the same with her."

"You're going into danger," she said, knowing suddenly that it was true.

"Aye, that may be," he agreed, but she could hear a soft amusement in his mind-voice. "Just living is a danger. And there's danger here, as well. I've seen it in the dreams Bradán an Chumhacht gives me."

"But if there's danger for you, what if . . . if . . . ?" She couldn't finish the sentence.

He touched her forehead and she felt a tingling, a burning that remained even when his hand left her. It faded, slowly, but the warmth remained, like a banked fire in her mind. "There. Now you hold a tiny scale of Bradán an Chumhacht's power yourself and you are linked to me. If Bradán an Chumhacht ever passes from me, you'll know it because the connection will fade from you. And if you begin to worry too much, then come to the sea and call for me with the power in the scale. I'll hear you, even at great distance, and I'll come as quickly as I can."

"Dhegli . . ."

A laugh. "Hush. I'll be back as soon as I can and we'll talk again. There are decisions we must make, you and I, together." He pulled her to him. The umber sound of his voice whispered within her. "Come with me. Swim with me again, tonight, for a bit. Before I have to go."

His hand tugged at hers. She resisted for only a moment, then let him guide her away through the fog.

14

Clochmion

MERIEL knocked on the door to the chamber deep in the bowels of the keep, clutching the note written in Máister Kirwan's ornate scrawl and hoping she'd correctly followed the directions written there. The note had been placed in an envelope tacked to the door of her rooms; she'd discovered it when she groggily pulled herself out of a deep and too short sleep. The tapping of her knuckles on wood seemed too loud, reverberating against the coarse granite walls of this deep corridor, so unlike the finished marble of the upper halls. The only light came from witchfire pots set along the walls: Meriel had been taught the slow magic involved in making witchfire in Siúr Bolan's class, but she had yet to produce much more than a soft momentary glow. These were brighter than torches, the nest of herbs in the pots burning brilliantly and cold.

"Speak your name," a voice whispered, seeming to emanate from the oaken planks in front of her. "Meriel MacEagan," she answered, and the door swung open.

The chamber inside was dim, but as she stepped inside and the door—untouched—closed behind her, she saw a hand pass over a witchfire pot on a table in the center of the room. The light swelled rapidly, making Meriel blink and shade her eyes for a moment. There were two chairs at the table, but both were empty. Máister Kirwan stood alongside the table; while standing near the side wall to the right was Siúr Meagher. The room itself was small, low, and plain, the floor, walls, and ceiling all cut from the living stone of the mountain on which the keep sat. Meriel could still see the marks of the chisels in the walls. Even though the room wasn't cold, she found herself shivering. The room felt like a dungeon; it was easy to imagine clinking chains and rotting skeletons here.

She wondered whether Dhegli had been wrong and Máister Kirwan knew where she'd gone the night before. "Máister," she said. "Your note . . . you wanted to see me . . ."

"Aye," Máister Kirwan said. "Do you know where you are?" Meriel shook her head mutely, and Máister Kirwan continued. "Bear with me for a few minutes then, even if you know what I'm telling you." He drew a long breath. "The White Keep was finished in the time of Severii O'Coulghan, the Last Holder of Lámh Sháb-hála in the Before. By the time the last stone was in place, the mage-lights were failing and only Lámh Sháb-hála was still awake of all the clochs na thintrí. One of the tasks Severii placed on the Order of Inishfeirm was for us to obtain the clochs na thintrí that were sleeping, so that when the time came for them to awaken again, it would be the cloudmages of Inishfeirm who held them."

"Máister, I know—" Meriel began to interrupt, but Máister Kirwan raised his finger to his lips.

"Indulge me," he said. "I'm sometimes surprised at what acolytes *don't* know or what they have wrong, and I want to be certain you understand this. Over the centuries, we did exactly what Severii had ordered us to do. Through various means, we were able to acquire many stones reputed to have been clochs na thintrí, though we would never be certain that they were true stones of power until the mage-lights came again. And over the centuries, we also became careless—because for all we knew the jewels we gathered were just pretty stones. After several centuries, my predecessors began to doubt whether the mage-lights really would ever come again and it was easy to disregard how precious the clochs would be if they were awakened once more. The clochs were originally kept down here, but one Máister brought them out and moved them to the library, in a separate case that was under the protection of a Keeper. The stones were often shown to visitors or to the few acolytes we had during those times." Máister Kirwan took a breath, glancing at Siúr Meagher, and she took up the tale.

"Three quarters of a century ago, one of the stones was stolen: a small, plain stone with what was believed to be a severely-inflated history. The claim was that the stone was Lámh Shábhála itself, which had been lost after Severii's death." Meriel shuffled restlessly, wanting to interrupt—she knew this all too well: it was the tale of her own family. But Siúr Meagher glared at her and she closed her mouth on the words. "No one believed that claim," Siúr Meagher continued. "The Clochs Mór were beautiful gems and the clochmions were fine stones as well; how could Lámh Shábhála be something so utterly ordinary? The fact that *any* of the stones could be stolen should have been a warning for us, but because we believed the stone to be worthless and the theft trivial, nothing was done beyond disciplining the Keeper and changing the ward-words—after all, the acolyte who stole the stone was found drowned a few days later. The young woman of Inishfeirm with whom he fled and the stone he stole were never seen again. We assumed both were lost forever." Siúr Meagher paused, tilting her head toward Meriel, and Meriel hurried into the opening.

"Aye, I know that story," Meriel told the two mages. "I've heard it a hundred times from my mam. The young woman was Kerys Aoire, my great-great-mam, and the acolyte was Niall Mac Ard, my great-great-da. Niall gave the stone to Kerys, she gave it to my great-da, and my mam found it when the mage-lights came again. The stone *was* Lámh Shábhála. Why tell me this now?"

Máister Kirwan answered. "Because the Order hadn't learned its lesson. Just before the Filleadh, when your mam awakened all the clochs na thintrí, raiders came to

Inishfeirm from the Seven Tuatha. I was just a new Bráthair myself then, but I remember that day, how the two ships came into Inishfeirm Harbor and soldiers spilled out, rushing up the long road to the White Keep and overwhelming what little resistance the Order could muster—most of us couldn't handle a sword and the slow magics we had were too few. The raiders knew where they were going, knew the ward-words to open the library doors, slew the Keeper who tried to keep them out, and wounded the Librarian. They took the clochs and went back to their ships. When the Filleadh came, not long after, the cloudmages of the Order had none of the clochs that should have been ours, none of the stones we'd spent so many long centuries gathering."

Máister Kirwan gave a self-deprecating laugh, short and bitter. "Think of what the Order could have been, Meriel—with the Máister wielding Lámh Shábhála and our cloudmages holding perhaps twenty of the Clochs Mór and most of the clochmions. Instead . . . Well, we've learned to shut the pasture gate even though the sheep have escaped the field. This room is where the clochs na thintrí will go when the mage-lights fail again, long centuries from now, and hopefully this time the Order will remember its task. But . . ." he paused. "This is also where new clochs we gain will stay until they're given a Holder. We already have a few stones here, one a Cloch Mór that belonged to your—" He stopped, and Meriel saw Siúr Meagher glance at Máister Kirwan curiously. ". . . that your mam brought to us to hold," he finished.

Meriel looked around the dreary room. It seemed a sad place to lock away the stones. "If this is supposed to impress upon me the importance of the Order and what you have to teach, well, that's something I already know. I can't change what I am. I doubt that I'm the first acolyte to disappoint you, or do you bring all of us down here for this lecture?"

Siúr Meagher drew her breath in through her teeth, hissing, but Máister Kirwan only shrugged. "I *am* disappointed, I'll admit—"

"Because I'm not *her?* Because I'm not my mam?" Meriel spat out before he could finish. She could hear the stridency in her voice but couldn't stop the words, not knowing if it was because she was exhausted or because they were feelings she'd wanted to shout for too long now. "I kept telling her and telling her that I didn't *want* to be her, didn't want to be like her, and she never listened. And you're not listening, either. I didn't *ask* to come here, Máister. All this was forced on me, but I've done what I can with it. I've tried. I really have, and I don't care if you believe that or not, or whether Mam believes it. I broke your rules, aye, but I had my reasons and I'd do the same thing again if I were given the choice. Tell Mam whatever you want. If I don't have the ability or the attitude to be a cloudmage, that's not my fault. Send me back, then—that's where I wanted to be in the first place."

Siúr Meagher stared at her, her left hand over her clochmion but not closed about it. Máister Kirwan stood, patient, waiting until the tirade failed her, until she stood there shaking her head and breathing hard, her hands gesturing as if they could say what she couldn't find the words to express.

"If I actually believed you could never be a cloudmage, you'd already be gone, Meriel," he said, his voice quiet against the storm of her anger, the set of his eyes in the flicker of witchfire more amused than angry. "And I think you're more like your mam than you want to believe. Now, if you'd let me finish . . ." He paused, and Meriel waited. "I *am* disappointed, as I was saying, but mostly in myself. I've made some of the same mistakes of arrogance that Máisters have made before me, and *that* was largely the point of the lecture. Because there's no one to tell us that we're wrong, we think we're always right, and we're not. *I'm* not. I've been treating you as if you were any other acolyte, and as much as I wanted to believe that was true, it's not. It's time I stopped pretending and time we actually *know* whether you should be here instead of simply guessing at it."

With that, Máister Kirwan went to the back wall of the room. He put his hand close to unbroken stone and spoke a few soft words that Meriel couldn't hear. The wall glowed softly for a moment, then a small rectangular piece fell out into the Máister's hand. He reached into the darkness beyond it, pulling out a fine necklace from which dangled a small gem caged in silver wire. He placed the rectangle of stone back into place; there was a flash of white light, and when Meriel could see again, the wall once more was unbroken stone. Máister Kirwan held the gem and chain out to Meriel in the palm of his hand. "Your mam had wanted me to give this to you before you came here. I thought she was wrong then and maybe she was."

"Then why isn't she here to give it to me now?"

She thought he hesitated at that, but it might have been a trick of the light. "Because this is *my* decision, not hers. I thought you weren't ready. But it's time now, regardless. Take it. Go on . . ."

Hesitantly, Meriel held out her own hand and with a turn of his hand Máister Kirwan let the chain and stone slide into her palm. Witchfire sparkled on the polished facets, shimmered on the silver links. "You had this in Dún Kiil," she said, looking at the pale blue captured in the stone. "On the beach, when we talked."

"Aye. And do you know what it is?"

"I can guess. A cloch?"

"A clochmion. One of the minor stones. A gift from your mam, until you're ready to take a Cloch Mór." Máister Kirwan gave her a wry smile. "Or more."

Meriel stared at the gem. It felt heavy in her hand. "What does it do?"

His white clóca rustled as he shrugged. "I can tell you where it came from—it was given to your mam during the Battle of Dún Kiil, a gift of self-sacrifice from one of the Créneach, the clay-creatures. Because of that, your mam has always called the stone Treoraí's Heart. As to what the Heart is capable of doing . . . We'll know when you tell us, because you're the first person to hold it. Meriel, I've talked enough for one morning and I have other duties. I'll leave the rest for Siúr Meagher."

He nodded to Meriel and Siúr Meagher, and left the room. The older woman came forward and sat at the table as his footsteps receded down the corridor toward the stairs. "Why did he leave?" Meriel asked Siúr Meagher.

"Because he didn't want to make you nervous, watching." She gestured toward the other chair. "Sit."

Meriel sat. Witchlight played over Siúr Meagher's thin, serious features. Her right hand cupped her left, kneading the swollen knuckles of the fingers unconsciously. She saw Meriel glance down at her hands. "The cold and damp down here makes my hands ache," she said. Then she regarded Meriel for a long time, saying nothing as Meriel waited. "*Are* you nervous?" Siúr Meagher asked finally.

"Aye, Siúr."

The woman's chin lifted. "Good," she said. "That's the wisest thing I've heard you say. Take the clochmion and put the chain around your neck . . . aye, like that. You remember Máister Kirwan's sitting lessons, the ones all of you first-years find so boring and useless? You're about to be tested on how well you paid attention. Close your eyes and try to be as still as possible inside. A clochmion's not like a Cloch Mór, which comes to your mind with a great roar and with its own ability burned into it by the mage-lights, the same for every Holder. A clochmion is quiet and sometimes difficult to hear, and each Holder will find that it has a different skill, one unique to you and the stone."

"How will I know what that is?"

"Hush. You won't *ever* know if you can't open your mind better than this. The clochmion will tell you, or rather the two of you will discover it together. Close your left hand around the stone; gently, girl, you don't have to try to crush it. Imagine it becoming part of you, opening like a crystalline flower as you touch it with your mind. See it growing within you, larger and larger, and you're drifting with it, the energy of the mage-lights sparkling around you and captured there . . ."

Siúr Meagher's voice faded, lost in the inner sight that suddenly opened to Meriel. She was snared in a lattice-work maze of crystal, flooded with the sapphire hues of the stone, only the shades were deeper and more saturated and nearly the color of a summer sky. They pulsed and throbbed in time to the beat of her own heart. She opened herself to the energy and felt it fill her, as achingly cold as if she'd plunged into an icy sea, and yet . . . it was welcoming, and comfortable. She could hold it, gaze at the power, and turn it within herself. The brilliance flooded her.

"Oh," she said, her eyes suddenly widening. Still holding the clochmion, she covered Siúr Meagher's hands with her free one.

The pain of contact was intense and sharp and Meriel gasped in response, an involuntary cry. Opalescent power ran in a kaleidoscopic whirl around her, and the pain piercing her right hand turned it into a frozen claw and dug deep furrows in her brow. At the same time, her awareness shifted, and she found herself listening to thoughts that weren't hers . . .

. . . he doesn't realize that I love him also. He never sees me the way I want him to see me. All he feels is the affection he carries for the Banrion, and I can never tell him, never show him . . . this poor girl is trapped and doesn't realize the danger she's in or that there's no escape and only the Mother knows if she really has the talent or will grow up in time . . .

With the thoughts came the emotions that swaddled them, emotions she didn't understand but she felt, stabbing as deeply into her as if they were her own. Then the pain in her hands and the thoughts and feelings were gone, swirling past her with the bright hues and Meriel opened her eyes, sitting back in the chair, her breath too fast and the clochmion clutched in her left hand, now simply a stone and emptied of any power.

"What happened?" she asked. In answer, Siúr Meagher

lifted her own hands. For a moment, Meriel saw nothing. Then the woman flexed her hands, closing and opening the fingers, and Meriel realized that the swollen knuckles were smaller and no longer reddened. Siúr Meagher almost laughed. "By the Mother, I've not been able to do this for five winters or more.

"I felt it," Meriel said. "The pain that you felt. Like the joints of my hands were burning and aching, and if I moved them, it was like a knife cutting through the bone. I felt it, so harsh that I wanted to cry, and then everything went away with the light . . ." For a second, she experienced the pain again, a memory, and she winced. *And I knew your thoughts. I was you, for the few moments we touched . . .*

She didn't tell her that.

"There's always a price for power," Siúr Meagher said. "Even with a clochmion. You held my pain, if only for a few seconds—I suspect that will always be the case when you use the cloch; you must bear the burden before you can remove it." She was shaking her head, still looking at her hands. She gave a long sigh that shook as if with a stilled sob. "You've been given a tremendous gift, Meriel: the stones that heal are the rarest type. None of the Clochs Mór has that ability and I've heard of only a few of the clochmion who have ever displayed it. That Treoraí's Heart found such a skill within you, well . . ."

She stopped. Her walnut eyes held Meriel's. "That answers a lot of questions."

Her newly-healed hand stretched out and found Meriel's. Meriel looked down at their intertwined fingers, at the fine wrinkles that netted the back of her hand. Meriel's hand was trembling under Siúr Meagher's and she was more frightened now than she had been before.

"Now listen, Meriel—this is nothing you should tell any of the other acolytes. Some of the Bráthairs and Siúrs will know, and that's bad enough even though Máister Kirwan will talk with them. But keep the fact that you have this cloch from the others."

"Why?" The word was a breath, visible in the cold air and the witch-light.

"Because it's already hard enough for you being the child of the First Holder and Banrion. What will they say if they see that you hold a clochmion despite what happened the other night? For that matter, you don't want them to know the truth about *that*, either—and Máister Kirwan has told Thady that if he hears even a whisper of a rumor that you swam with the Saimhóir, then Thady will be gone the next day. I doubt that you're so naive that you don't realize that if some here thought they could raise their own status by pulling you down, they'd do it happily. There also may be people on Inishfeirm who wish you and your family harm. People have died for far less treasure than a clochmion, Meriel."

She pushed herself back from the table and stood. "Put the stone under your léine for now. If someone happens to see it, laugh and tell them that it's just a pretty gem and not a cloch. You'll need to fill it with the mage-lights the next time they come, but Máister Kirwan and I will teach you that skill away from the other acolytes and any prying eyes, and we'll arrange for you to take the mage-lights in privacy. Now, do you have any questions?"

Meriel lifted the stone on its chain, holding the cloch in the palm of her hand so she could see the cerulean facets nestled in the silver cage. She had heard, many times, how the clochs bound their holders to them, how ripping a Cloch Mór from its owner would send that person into screaming grief and insanity as if a part of themselves had been torn away. She'd always thought such reports exaggerations and myths, amusing tales to scare the populace (and to make them less likely to want to hold a cloch themselves). But now . . .

Siúr Meagher said that Treoraí's Heart was but a clochmion, yet already in these few minutes she couldn't think of being without the cloch, of taking it off or giving it away. Holding the cloch felt right, feeling it against her skin was comforting; it belonged to her. The cloch-mion filled an emptiness within her that she hadn't even known existed until now. She could feel its crystalline bonds thrusting deep within her mind and she knew that to tear them out again would be agonizing.

She could also think of another reason why Máister Kirwan might have made this decision. "You did this to keep me here, didn't you?" she said. Siúr Meagher didn't deny the accusation. One shoulder lifted under the white clóca.

"If it was a mistake, then give the cloch back—there are too few stones already for the cloudmages and many others who would love to hold what you have."

"You know I can't do that. Not now."

A nod. The woman's features softened then, a sympathetic half smile touching her thin lips. "Every gift also bears a debt, Meriel," she said. "Those of us with a cloch na thintrí know that best of all."

As Meriel slipped Treoraí's Heart under her léine, she noticed that the skin of her left hand was touched with pale swirls, so faint that Siúr Meagher couldn't see them from across the table. The marks were familiar; she'd seen them all up and down her mam's arm, and marking one hand of those with Clochs Mór: the scars of the mage-lights. But those with clochmions never took those marks—the stones were too weak. Yet . . .

She smiled at Siúr Meagher and kept her hand in the pocket of her clóca as they walked back up the long corridors to the dormitories.

15

Attack on the Keep

GLOWING draperies of bright color flared overhead the next night; as promised, Máister Kirwan and Siúr Meagher taught her how to open the clochmion to the mage-lights and fill it with the energy from the sky. The marks she'd seen on her skin had faded. For that she was grateful; she had no desire to be so conspicuously scarred as her mam or the cloudmages. Afterward, in her room, Meriel lay in her bed holding the cloch in her hand, feeling the gem seeming to throb under her touch with the power to dance along her very bones. As she lay there, she also listened, wanting to hear the call of the Saimhóir, wanting Dhegli to come to her again, to hold her and be with her.

She would tell him. No matter what Máister Kirwan asked, she would keep no secrets from him. *He will know, anyway,* she told herself. *He'll know because of the gift he holds.*

But the night was filled only with the sound of the wind in the trees, the buzz of wind sprites, and the distant baying of wolves in the valley. Meriel touched her forehead where he'd placed the gift of Bradán an Chumhacht. She could feel, inside, the connection to him still burning, and she knew he was still somewhere distant.

That night was long, and sleep came late.

"What's your secret?"

Meriel laughed guiltily, her hand going involuntarily to her breast where the clochmion lay hidden under her léine. "What do you mean?" she asked, and Thady laughed.

"Everyone knows that Máister Kirwan sent for you the other day. You were gone for hours and you've been very careful to say nothing about it to anyone. I know—I asked Faoil. So what's your secret?"

He leaned on the rake he was holding. Most of the acolytes were working the breadroot lazybeds under the direction of Bráthair O'Therreagh and Siúr Bolan, clearing them of weeds. It was a rare warm day, with a bright sun beating down and a blue sky uninterrupted by clouds. Thady had managed to slowly move away from the other third-years until he was near Meriel. She let her hand go back to her own rake. She smiled back at him, feeling a twinge of guilt at the way she was drawn to his grin, his dancing eyes, the easy way he moved, the sheen of sweat on his forehead and the muscular forearms revealed by the rolled-up sleeves of his léine. She shoved a vague sense of guilt away. *Dhegli has no claim on you, nor you on him . . .* "I'm sure I don't know what you mean. I certainly have no secrets from you, An-tUasal MacCoughlin."

"Ah, so you've gone formal on me, Bantiarna MacEagan, and after all we've been through. Is that how it's to be?" He frowned, but his eyes laughed.

"Aye, 'tis," she told him, trying not to break into laughter herself. "And there's no secret about what Máister Kirwan wanted of me. He warned me about you."

"Oh, did he now?" The laughter in his eyes faded. "And what did he warn you of?"

Meriel did grin then. "You," she told him, "are too easy to tease, Thady. All Máister Kirwan wanted was to tell me that my mam was extraordinarily displeased with my behavior and that if I persisted, I'd find myself back in Dún Kiil."

He sighed, as if relieved, glancing away over the field and the other acolytes bent to their work. When he looked back, the flirtation was back in his voice and face. "There you go, then—your mam's given you a way to get just what you want."

"And what is it *you* want, An-tUasal MacCoughlin?" a breathy male voice intruded. "It certainly isn't the joy of a good day's work in the sun." Bráthair Geraghty panted from the exertion of climbing the steep hill from the keep. He leaned heavily on his wooden-toothed rake, glancing squint-eyed back down the slope. From here, they were above the highest towers of the White Keep and could see, far below, the houses of the town and the bay. Bráthair Geraghty squinted at the panorama, his mouth half-open as if struck by the beauty, though Meriel doubted that his poor eyes could see much of it. Then he turned back to them. "Maidin maith, Meriel. And to you, Thady."

"Maidin maith, Bráthair," Meriel answered, though now that Bráthair Geraghty was here the morning seemed less good than it had.

" 'Tis," the young cloudmage answered, "especially since the mage-lights came last night." He gave Meriel a lingering glance as he touched the clochmion around his neck. "A particularly beautiful display, I thought."

Meriel flushed, remembering the touch of the mage-lights, curling around her uplifted hand, the wondrous sensation as they filled her clochmion, the sense of communion with the web of clochs na thintrí scattered over the land—even to her mam's, a lurking, huge presence. She'd gasped in wonder and Máister Kirwan had chuckled even as he replenished his own Cloch Mór. " *'Tis worth it all, these moments . . .*"

Bráthair Geraghty had already started digging at the lazybed with his rake, dislodging a tangle of foulweed and tossing it toward the compost pile. Thady grimaced and shrugged simultaneously with Meriel—it was obvious that the Bráthair intended to work near them. "Let's get to work, then," Bráthair Geraghty said. "These weeds aren't going to go away by themselves."

Thady sniffed. Meriel shook her head at Thady behind the Bráthair's back and lifted her rake. She pulled out a clump of foulweed, threw it in the direction of the compost. She started to bend down again.

Stopped.

A thunderclap rolled over the mountainside, impossible in that cloudless sky. The sound echoed from the surrounding peaks as everyone looked up in astonishment, peering around. It came again, and now they could see an impossible dark cloud massing just above the front of the keep. As they watched, lightning arced from cloud to ground, thunder following. They couldn't see where it struck, the towers and walls of the keep obscuring their view. The sound of a gale-force wind shrieked close by, yet the air hung still around them. Distantly, a man's voice screamed in pain. Beyond the walls, more light flashed: a red brighter than the sunlight. Black smoke rose above the roofs, streaking across the sky as if torn by a storm.

Bráthair O'Therreagh and Siúr Bolan went running past, their faces pale. Bráthair Geraghty dropped his rake and started to run down the steep hill with them, but Bráthair O'Therreagh waved him back. "Stay here!" Bráthair O'Therreagh shouted over his shoulder to Bráthair Geraghty. "Those are Clochs Mór—Tuathian raiders! Keep the acolytes with you!" He glanced significantly at Meriel. "Especially the Bantiarna."

Alarm bells were ringing throughout the keep now, and they could see the cloudmages—Bráthairs and Siúrs—in the open courtyard at the center of the oldest section, rushing toward the gates. As they watched, helpless, blue streamers like twisting ropes of fire snapped about some of them, hurling them backward. More lightning flashed from the thunderhead around the gate and a fireball splashed red flame.

Meriel heard Faoil scream in fright, heard the other

acolytes shouting or crying out in confusion. Several of them, mostly the fourth- and fifth-years, ignored Bráthair O'Therreagh's admonition and began to run toward the keep themselves. Bráthair Geraghty shouted at them; a few stopped, the others continued to hurry toward the keep.

"Come on!" Meriel felt a hand tug at her sleeve: Thady. He gestured toward the rear of the keep and the tangle of pines fringing the mountainside to the west beyond the Low Tower. "There's nothing we can do about this, Meriel, and we can hide there." Thady said urgently. "You heard Bráither O'Therreagh. You're the Banrion's daughter and may be the target—you don't want them to find you. Come on!"

"No!" Bráthair Geraghty pushed Thady away from Meriel. "Bráthair O'Therreagh said we're to stay *here*. Besides, Máister Kriwan told me—"

Thady gestured violently toward the keep, where the smoke had thickened. A small group of men dressed in undyed leathers were sweeping around the side of the keep, shouting as they spied the acolytes rushing down the hill. Metal glinted in sunlight. "See!" Thady shouted. "Those are gardai! The Máister will thank us for making sure that Meriel's safe. She's *not* safe out here in the open where anyone can see her." He looked at Meriel, his gaze steady. "Trust me," he said. "You have to trust me."

Mcricl nodded.

"Meriel, no," Bráthair Geraghty persisted. He reached for her arm; she pulled it away. "It's vital that you stay here. Máister Kirwan was quite specific . . ."

"Why?" Thady interjected. "*You're* the one who's always around her, always watching her. Is that why it's vital, Bráthair? Because you *knew* about this? Is that why you came up here this morning? Your timing was just about perfect."

With the accusation, Bráthair Geraghty's mouth dropped open, and Meriel wondered. She remembered all the times she'd looked up to see the man watching her . . .

The smoke was thickening, the flash and thunder continuing to roil. The soldiers were coming closer. A fireball came streaking from somewhere in the confusion, striking the hillside between the soldiers and Meriel.

"Let's *go!*" Thady said to Meriel.

"Meriel, you can't listen to him!" Bráthair Geraghty wailed, reaching for Meriel again. Meriel pushed his hand away. "I think that he's . . ."

"Let's go," she said to Thady. As they started to run, Bráthair Geraghty moved as if to stop them and Thady pushed the man down. He picked up one of rakes, raising it. "No!" Meriel stepped between them. "You don't need to do that, Thady." Thady shook his head, but he tossed the rake aside.

They ran.

The smell of smoke was stronger as they approached the oat field near the back wall, and they could hear the clash of arms not far away. Someone shouted orders— it sounded like Máister Kirwan, Meriel thought—and thunder rolled loudly enough that she felt the sound hammering at her chest. Crouching, they ran down the rows of the field and clambered over the stone wall bordering it, pressing close behind the flat rocks. Between them and the shelter of the trees there was only the green swath of grass where Meriel had first seen Dhegli. "You'll be safest near the sea, where you can escape," Thady told her. Meriel nodded. That felt right—if she could reach the sea and change . . . or perhaps Dhegli might, impossibly, be there.

"I'll go first," Thady whispered to her. "That way, if they have archers, or if someone with a cloch is watching this side . . ."

"No!"

"Don't worry," Thady said. "Just follow me once I'm across."

Meriel could barely hear him over the sound of her panting breath and the pounding of blood in her temples. She nodded. Thady took a deep, shuddering breath. He pushed away from the wall. Meriel watched him run, head down, and push into the brush across the green sward. She saw him wave to her, and she gathered her own breath and ran.

She expected at any moment to hear an outcry, to feel the piercing stab of arrows into her back or the screaming fire of a Cloch Mór. None of it came. She could hear only the sound of her breath and her boots pounding the grass, then she was across and Thady's arms were around her. For several seconds, they simply huddled there, then Thady's arms loosened. "Come on," he said. "This way. Let's move down to the beach . . ."

She followed him, half sliding down the narrow, twisting path in their hurry. "This way," he said at the first turnoff, where a smaller trail led out to an overlook. "Go on. I'll be right behind you—I want to cover up our tracks."

"Why?"

"Only a few moments," he told her. "You should get off the trail while I make sure they won't follow us." Meriel pushed through brush and came out onto the jutting ledge, where the ocean crashed far below.

Meriel halted, her breath frozen in her mouth.

"A spectacular sight, don't you think?" The man stood only a few feet away. He looked to be no older than herself, but he carried himself with a confidence that Meriel had seen only in those with much experience. His hair was a brighter red than hers though his eyes were the same shade of green. Around his neck he wore a yellow stone with veins of scarlet, and a sword was sheathed under his clóca. Meriel took a step back, ready to turn and run, but Thady was standing at the edge of the path and the look on his face made her stop.

"Thady?" The word came out almost as a sob.

"I'm sorry, Meriel. I really am."

The man behind her laughed. "I suppose I should apologize as well," he said. "This is a terrible way for an uncle to have to meet his niece for the first time."

Meriel drew in her breath through her teeth. She looked back over her shoulder. "Doyle Mac Ard?"

He gave an exaggerated bow, the Cloch Mór swinging

forward with the motion. "Aye, you have the name. I
see my sister hasn't neglected giving you the family ge-
nealogy, then."

A sour burning filled her stomach and the back of her
throat. Meriel felt disoriented and yet strangely calm, as
if she were watching this happening outside herself. "All
that up there . . . ?"

"A diversion designed to allow Thady to bring you
down here. I should think you'd feel flattered by the
attention. I know I would. We all underestimated how
much resistance there would be and how well-prepared
the Order was for an attack. This has cost more than a
few people their lives."

"Are you here to kill me?" The words sounded
strange and impossible.

Doyle seemed to shiver. "Commit an act of fingal and
be cursed by the Mother-Creator for the rest of eternity?
I would never slay my own kin, Meriel—that's an ugly
crime. No, you're far more useful alive." He glanced
upward to where the trees fringed the lip of the steep
cliffs. Meriel could hear nothing of the battle above; it
had stopped, or the mountainside blocked her hearing.
A falcon fluttered down through the trees. It landed on
Doyle's shoulder and seemed to lean forward as if
speaking into his ear before fluttering off again. Doyle's
face went solemn. "Things have not gone well above
and we really must go now. This can be easy or hard,
Meriel—we're going to go down to the beach where we
have a currach waiting to take us out to our ship. You
can walk between Thady and myself, or—if you insist—
you can be bound and carried." His lips twisted. "The
path is steep and treacherous, though. I really can't guarantee you won't be dropped a few times."

"I'll walk," Meriel told him. She glared at Thady.
"Bastard," she said. "You'll get all you deserve for this."

For a moment, she thought she saw remorse and guilt
cross his face, then his mouth tightened and his gaze
steadied. "I'm certain I will," he said. "That's why I did
it." With that, he turned and started back down the path.

After a moment, with a glance back at Doyle, she followed.

Her thoughts raced as they made their way slowly down toward the beach. Through the bracken clinging to the rocky soil, she could see the currachs—a quartet of the small boats were pulled up on the pebbled shore; out in West Bay, a larger ship rode the waves, its mast significantly empty of any banner or colors; she stopped to stare at it curiously. She wondered how it could have reached the island without being noticed— surely someone should have seen the ship and warned the keep. Behind her, Doyle gave her a small push; she glanced back angrily, then continued on, clambering down.

If you could get to the beach first, and into the water . . . make the change to Saimhóir and dive . . . they could never catch you . . .

The decision crystallized and she acted before any doubts could arise. Thady was just ahead of her—she took a running step and pushed at him hard, her hands striking him between the shoulder blades. He overbalanced, falling forward with his arms out and a wail. Meriel didn't wait; she rushed past him, slipping and sliding over the rocks, not even noticing the pain as they tore at her clothing and skin. Behind her, she could hear Doyle's shout of alarm. She didn't dare look back; she half fell, half ran the rest of the way down, tumbling out onto the spray-wet shingle. Panting, she got to her feet. The water was but a few strides away—

The air in front of her shimmered. A beast appeared, snarling on the rocks: a dragon with scales of yellow tipped with fiery red, rearing twice as tall as Meriel with jaws of daggered teeth and talons of razor-edged ivory. It hissed; it fumed; it roared. Meriel gathered her breath—she ran, hoping to get past the apparition, to dodge the blow that would come. *All I need to do is reach the water . . .*

The dragon reared. *One more step . . .* The tail, barbed and long, curled like a whip. Meriel tried to duck, but it was too fast. She tried to throw her hands up: as the coils hurtled toward her, as they crashed into her and flung her back onto the boulders at the foot of the cliffs.

Then, for a long time, she remembered nothing at all.

PART TWO

TAISTEAL

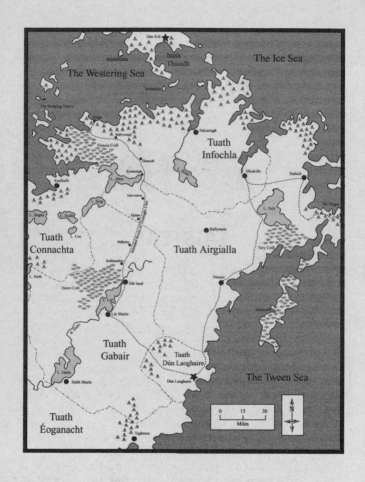

16

Awakening

BRIGHT light flickered beyond her eyelids and she could hear faint querulous voices. Meriel blinked, trying to focus eyes that didn't want to work and realizing that the blankness in front of her was the white roof of a tent with the sun gleaming through, the fabric. She was lying on her back on a carpet spread directly on grassy earth, with an uncomfortably hard rock digging into her hip. Her head throbbed, and the hair on the left side of her head was stiff and matted; when that side of her head touched the ground, it was tender and sore. Wooden boxes were stacked near her, the symbol of a dragon burned into them. That brought back to her all too vividly the dragon on the beach: she remembered the snarling mouth, the lash of its tail snaking toward her too fast . . .

She tried to shift her weight and realized that her legs and arms were bound, far too well for her to work free of them. For a moment, she had the terrible thought that the clochmion Máister Kirwan had given her was gone, but she could feel its reassuring heaviness around her neck. *Where am I? What's happened?*

Frightened, she lay still and listened to the voices.

". . . and keep her. You will keep her *safe* as well—in all ways—or I will personally come find you. Do we have an understanding, Nico?" That was Doyle's voice, Meriel knew, sharp-edged and quick.

Someone laughed, low and quiet and mocking, the words lilting with an accent Meriel had never heard before. "If you can't trust my word, then take the girl with you, Tiarna, along with your little threats. They don't frighten me."

For a moment, there was silence. She could imagine Doyle's thin face, and she wondered whether there was anger in his eyes now and if she would hear the ring of a sword being drawn or the roar of the dragon unleashed. Then Doyle spoke again. "I trust your word as Clannhri, Nico. Aye."

Another laugh. "Trust is fine, but it needs to be displayed in gold."

Meriel heard the jingle of mórceints being dumped from a purse. "That's the amount we agreed upon," Doyle said. "And a bit more, which no one in your clan but yourself need know about."

"Aye, you may be young, but someone has taught you well, Tiarna," said the man who must have been Nico. "It's good doing business with you." The mórceints rang again, as if Nico were hefting them in his hand.

"Then it's done. She should be nearly—" A flap was flung aside on the tent, and more light flooded in, causing Meriel to blink and take in a breath in surprise. Three men were silhouetted against the glare. "Ah, she is awake." The flap dropped back down and the trio stared down at her. Two of them Meriel recognized: Doyle and Thady. The third was a large, older man with long, braided gray hair and an impossible shock of dark beard that went halfway down his barrel chest. He was dressed in leather breeches and skins that, from the smell of them, had been imperfectly cured; a bone-handled knife hung prominently from a belt around his waist. He also wore colorfully painted wooden beads in the braids of his hair, and Meriel had seen similar beads in the hair of the Taisteal clan that had recently been in Dún Kiil.

So this was a Taisteal encampment and Nico was the Clannhri, the head of the clan. The realization made

Meriel shiver: the Taisteal rarely came to Inish Thuaidh, since they weren't a sailing people, but she had heard tales of them: wanderers, selling pots and pans and anything else that might have a value, even orphaned children if the rumors could be trusted. Thady crouched down beside her. "Meriel, I hope you—" he started to say.

She spat at him. The globule landed on his cheek as he belatedly scrambled away. He brushed at his cheek, his face flushed. Nico gave a roaring laugh; Doyle might have smiled, Meriel's head pounded madly with the effort and motion. Thady lifted his hand, but Doyle caught it before he could strike. "Touch her, MacCoughlin," Doyle said, his deep-set eyes flaring, "and any arrangement you and I have is over."

The rage in Thady's face slowly subsided. He pulled his hand away from Doyle and wiped his cheek again, standing up. "You'll wait outside," Doyle told him. Thady hesitated and Doyle lifted his chin. "Outside," he said again, his voice deceptively quiet. Thady grimaced and obeyed, with a final scowl in Meriel's direction.

"I never liked you," he said to her before he left. "You're a spoiled, coddled bitch."

Doyle sighed as the tent flap closed behind Thady. He crouched down near Meriel—but, she noted, not so near that she could easily spit on him. "I can understand your defiance, Meriel," he said. "But in your place, I'd be considering what's best for me right now. You saw how poor Thady reacted, and I won't be here the next time if you try it with Nico or one of his clan. I wouldn't blame Thady too much. He wanted something very badly and the price of getting it was to befriend and betray a person who stood in the way. Most of us would make the same bargain. Your mam did; in fact, there are several people dead, including my da, because of that. And her own mam and mine—your great-mam—was half-mad for the rest of her life as a result." Meriel could see an inner pain cross the young man's face. "You would have loved Maeve, and she you, if you'd ever had the chance to meet her. I would have enjoyed taking you to her. But that's no longer possible—your mam saw to that. Maeve should never have had to bear the suffering your mam caused her. Can you imagine the grief of having to light the pyre of the man you love while his child is still suckling at your breast?"

"My mam only did what she was forced to do. She said Padraic Mac Ard would have killed her otherwise."

Doyle rocked on his heels. "That's what she'd tell you, aye. That's the same excuse she gave the Comhairle for her fingal, too, and they all nodded their heads and forgave her and even made her Banrion. It's hard to argue with the person who wields the power of Lámh Sháb-hála. But talk to the ones here in the Tuatha, the ones who knew her at the start of the Filleadh—the ones whose relatives and friends she killed. Their opinion of your mam is quite different."

Doyle sighed and stood up. He stared down at her, almost sympathetically. "Nico and his clan will watch after you. If you don't give them cause, they won't harm you."

"Why are you doing this?"

Doyle smiled. "I think you can figure that out. Good luck to you, Meriel. I wish we could have met under better circumstances. I want you to know that I don't hold any of your mam's actions against you. I have no animosity toward you at all."

She spat at him because it was all she could think to do or say in defiance, but the moisture darkened the carpet a fingertip away from the toe of his boot. Doyle raised an eyebrow as Nico chuckled. "Take excellent care of her," Doyle said to the man. "With what I've paid you, she's worth more than anything else in your wagons. You will remember that or you'll pay me back more dearly than you'd like. I think you understand me, Clannhri."

Nico snorted. "You can trust the word of Clan Dranaghi."

"I'm sure I can," Doyle replied. He looked down again

at Meriel. She held his gaze, glaring back at him and
after a moment, he lifted the flap of the tent and went
through into the sunlight.

Nico said nothing for a long time, rummaging about in
the tent. Meriel heard Doyle and Thady talking, then
the sound of horses riding off. Other sounds came to
her: the noise and clatter of a busy encampment. Nico
came back over and sat on a stool near her, his fingers
prowling his beard as he stared at her as if appraising a
piece of merchandise. He seemed pleased enough.

"Where am I?" Meriel asked the man.

"A well-schooled woman-child like you, she would
know about maps and where things are and eventually
would figure it out anyway," he answered, as if talking
to himself. Then he nodded. "What does that matter? I
will tell you, then. You are near the west coast of Tuath
Infochla. Do you know the village Kirina?" Meriel tried
to remember all the maps she'd seen in Dún Kiil and at
the White Keep. She couldn't see that name in those
memories, and slowly shook her head. "No? So you
don't know the maps that well. Too bad. Well, we came
from Kirina a few days ago."

"What day is it?"

"By Daoine reckoning, it's the twenty-first day of
Wideleaf."

*Two days . . . You have no memories of the last two
days, not since the dragon struck you on the beach . . .*
Nico must have guessed her thoughts, for he stirred.
"The tiarna, he said that they used a slow magic to keep
you sleeping because it was easier that way. He said that
the other tiarna, the one you spat on, claimed you were
a changeling and that you would throw yourself into the
ocean, become a seal, and escape. Your uncle—he seems
young to be your mam's brother, does he not? He's
more like your twin than your uncle—told me that we
should watch you carefully around the loughs and rivers

for the same reason. And we will." He smiled at her. "As the young tiarna said, you're valuable to us."

Two days . . . At the thought, her body asserted itself. "I need . . ." Meriel wriggled in her bonds.

"What do you need?" Meriel could feel the blush on her face, and Nico lifted his chin. "Oh," he said, standing up. He went to the tent flap. "Sevei!" he called. "Come here."

A woman stepped into the tent a few moments later. She was small and slight, her head coming only to the middle of Nico's beard-obscured chest, but the face that stared at Meriel showed a woman in her twenties. Her eyes and long unbound hair seemed preternaturally black in the dimness of the tent. "Our guest needs to relieve herself," Nico said, and the woman's hands went to her hips.

"You're not making me her nursemaid, Nico." Her voice was a rich contralto. "I don't want to be responsible for her. You took her in; you watch her."

"I'm making you her guardian for the time being, Cousin," he answered. "As Clannhri here. Unless you've decided to challenge that."

Sevei glared at the man. Then, hands still on hips, she sighed. "Get your carcass out of here, then," she told him. Nico sniffed, rubbed his beard, and left the tent. Sevei stood over Meriel, scowling. "Here are the facts," she told her. "I'm faster and stronger than you and even if Nico doesn't want you permanently hurt, that still leaves me a number of options you'll find sufficiently painful. Give me trouble and I'll give it back to you doubled. Do you understand that?"

Meriel nodded.

"Good," Sevei said. "Then we'll be fine. Stay still; I'm going to cut these ropes." A knife flashed in Sevei's left hand—bone-handled, long and curved, and well-honed and oiled—though Meriel wasn't sure where it had come from: the unsheathing had been sudden and fast. One quick slash cut the ropes binding her ankles; another, the leather wound about her wrists. "Don't try to stand yet," Sevei said. "Rub your limbs and get the blood flowing again."

Meriel did as she said, grimacing as ankles and wrists first tingled, then burned. When the sensation finally passed, she pushed herself up, standing shakily. "It's not your moon time, is it?" Sevei asked. "If it is, I'll get some blood cloths . . ." Meriel shook her head; Sevei nodded toward the tent flap. "Outside, then," she said tersely. "And move slowly."

Slow was all Meriel could manage on legs that were still tingling and numb. The sunlight forced her to shade her eyes, half-closing them against the glare as she glanced around. The Taisteal encampment was like the one she'd seen a few months ago in Dún Kiil, possibly even the same one: a collection of wagons and tents huddled together alongside the rutted, wandering path of a road. The air carried the faint scent of the sea, but they were far enough away that the ocean wasn't visible. Across the road, Meriel could see the green-and-brown spines of mountains lumbering into the distance; behind her, very close, was a forest dominated by old oak trees growing thick and close. There were a dozen or more people moving about, all of them dressed similarly. Meriel assumed they were all part of the clan. Some of them stared at her openly before turning back to their tasks.

There was no town or village within sight and no one on the road. Wherever they were, it was desolate.

"This way," Sevei prodded, pointing toward the forest. "And don't think of running into *that* forest. It's bad enough here at the edges." When Meriel glanced back at her quizzically, the woman laughed. "You *are* naive, aren't you? That's Foraois Coill, one of the Old Forests. Nothing in there but Bunús Muintir, beasts out of myth and legend, and death. I won't even follow you if you run that way—all I'd find is your bones."

There was no glimpse of amusement on Sevei's face; if she was teasing Meriel, it was impossible to tell. But the name . . . Foraois Coill . . . Meriel knew *that* name— she'd seen it on the maps, knew its boundaries. And

Nico had mentioned Kirina: she was willing to bet that village was on the coast of the Westering Sea. And if she could get there: the scale of Bradán an Chumhacht throbbed in her mind, and Dhegli's face swam in her mind, far away . . .

They'd walked just past the first trees. "This one'll do," Sevei said. "It looks like it needs watering. And if you need to do more . . ." She tossed a trowel at Meriel's feet. "Bury it so we don't have dire wolves or worse prowling around tonight. I'll wait here."

Meriel went behind the tree. As she relieved the pressure on her bladder, she stared into the forest. Farther in, it was as shadowed as twilight with the occasional beam of sunlight only making the surrounding air look darker, and the ground under the oaks was brambled and green with ferns and brush. If someone was lying on the ground, you'd have to step on them to find them. *I won't even follow you if you run that way* . . . All Meriel needed to do was lose Sevei and she could move along the fringe of the forest to the west and the sea— she doubted that they were more than five miles from the shore, not with the briny odor so strong in the air. There might not be another better opportunity—with Doyle's warning about Meriel's changeling ability, the Taisteal would undoubtedly move inland from here.

Meriel ran.

She'd gone perhaps five strides when she heard the crash of running footfalls behind her and felt Sevei's hands grip her shoulders. The woman pulled backward, and at the same time Sevei's leg swept around Meriel's ankles and took her down hard onto the carpet of fallen leaves. Sevei landed on top of her, Meriel's breath going out with an audible *uumph!* as Sevei's elbow dug into her stomach. She couldn't breathe, couldn't move, and Sevei's hand grabbed her wrists and pinned them high above her head. The woman's face was very close to hers, her body fully on top of Meriel's and her legs wrapped around Meriel's. She smiled strangely. "I rather like this position," she said. "Don't you?"

Meriel struggled, trying to get the woman off her but Sevei only tightened her hold. Meriel cursed, and Sevei put a finger to Meriel's lips with her free hand. "Spit on me or try to bite, and I just might have to do something you wouldn't like at all. Now, I'm going to let you go, and you're going to sit up slowly and not try that again, or I'll have to tell Nico what happened, and he won't be happy at all. And you won't be, either. He can't hurt you, but that doesn't mean he can't treat you like an animal he's afraid will run off. We've had children given to us before and we know how to keep them until they're sold. How would you like to be collared and hobbled for the rest of your time here?"

Sevei released Meriel's wrists abruptly, rolling away from her in a lithe movement and standing, her hand on the hilt of her knife. Meriel sat up slowly, brushing bits of leaf and dirt from her clóca and hair. She glared at Sevei, rubbing her stomach and trying to get her breath back.

"I admire that," Sevei said easily. "I do. I'd have done the same, in your place. I want you to know that this incident is just between us."

"Is that supposed to make me feel better?"

A shrug. "No. I'm just telling you that I understand. I'm also telling you that if you try it again, you'll spend the rest of your days and nights here with chains. Nico won't be at all happy, and as a result, neither will you. It's your choice."

"If I had a *choice*, I wouldn't be here."

"But you are, and now you have to decide how it's going to be for you. No matter what you've heard of the Taisteal, we're not cruel people and when we give our word, we keep it."

"Aye. You're just fine folks. Like that bastard Doyle Mac Ard."

Sevei pressed her lips together. Her hand drifted away from the knife and her stance relaxed. "Say what you will about your uncle. I don't know the man, but he could have just as easily killed you or done worse. He could have made you a prisoner of the Rí Ard and you would have become a pawn in that struggle with all the Riocha trying to use you for their own best advantage. He didn't. He kept you safe and brought you to where you'll be treated as well as possible and where those who might wish you harm can't get to you. You didn't want to be a hostage, I know, but if that had to happen, I'd say you should be grateful to him for bringing you here, to people who know the value of their word."

"To thieves and liars and orphan-sellers."

Sevei grimaced, her breath sharp between her teeth, black eyes narrowing under the fall of hair. "You're just showing your ignorance, girl. Now, make up your mind. I'm going to turn my back now and start back. You can either follow me, or you can try to escape again. But when I catch you, I'm not going to be as understanding. After all, I'm only a thief and a liar."

With that, Sevei spun gracefully on the balls of her feet and started walking away, her boots crunching against the dry leaves. Meriel sat on the ground, watching her go. It would be easy to get up and run; the woman was already a dozen strides or more away, not even visible through the tree trunks. The sound of her footsteps was receding, growing fainter.

Meriel pushed herself to her feet, bits of leaves falling from her clothes. A breeze stirred the tops of the oaks and the scent of must and rot wafted from the shadows farther in. The limbs of the trees around her groaned and swayed. There was a feeling of eyes watching, all the hairs on the back of her neck rising.

Meriel hugged herself. Dhegli's presence throbbed once in her head—faint and far, far away.

She followed the sound of Sevei's boots back to the tent.

17

A Name

THE FRAGRANT aroma of the cook fire filled the meadow as the sun eased itself down behind the trees of Foraois Coill and the light shifted to the gold-green of evening. Meriel found a log near Sevei's tent and sat, watching as the clan busied itself preparing for departure. There seemed to be several family units within the clan. The heavyset, large woman by the black iron cook pot was Keara, Nico's wife, and their children and respective spouses, their grandchildren and a few assorted relatives like Sevei made up the rest of the clan, ranging in age from infants still nursing on up to gray-beards. Meriel had been introduced to each of them, though most of the names had already escaped her. She hoped she wouldn't be here long enough to need to know them.

"Here . . ."

Sevei handed Meriel a bowl of meat stew and a wooden spoon. Meriel glanced curiously at the bowl. She'd never seen pottery like this: a translucent blue glaze on top of fired brown clay, the glaze forming intricate curlicues of vines and leaf forms. "It's from Céile Mhór," Sevei said in answer to her unasked question. "We brought them over with us when we came. We sold most of the stock in Falcarragh to a newly-married bantiarna for her estate, but I kept a few for my own use because I liked the way they looked."

"You've been to Céile Mhór?" It seemed so far away, a place of dreams.

"I was born on the *other* side of Céile Mhór from here, in Thall Mór-roinn," Sevei answered and Meriel's eyes widened at the thought of being so impossibly distant from the place of your birth. "One day, perhaps a year from now, we'll be back there."

"How can you stand it, traveling all the time?"

Sevei tossed her hair back. "How can *you* stand it, staying in the same place all the time?"

Nico came up to them before Meriel could answer, sitting down with a grunt on the log next to Meriel. He belched once. "Sevei says that you can be trusted and that I don't need to shackle you for the night. This is true?"

Meriel glanced at Sevei, then nodded slightly. "Good," Nico said. "Now, I must talk and you will listen. We leave with the sun tomorrow, and we hope to find a village before dark where we can offer our services and sell our wares. Unless I silence you while we are there— which I *can* do—I can't prevent you from blurting out to them who you are, even if Sevei stays near you."

Meriel imagined being bound and gagged for all of the day in the stifling atmosphere of a tent. "Clannhri—" she began, but Nico lifted his hand.

"I talk, you listen. This is how it will be and you need to understand. You need to remember where you are— in the Tuatha, not in Inish Thuaidh. Those we meet won't be your allies, and will go to the Tuathian Riocha and not the Inishlanders—*if* they bother at all. Most won't; they don't want to be caught up in the affairs of the Riocha; they learned long ago that they are happier and safer when the noble folk are far away in their cities. That's assuming they even believe your tale at all. They'll look at you—dressed like one of us, as road-dusted as us, and think that you're just some useless fourth or fifth daughter who was sold to us . . . and one we've been unable to sell away to anyone else because she's obviously addled and too much trouble. And *if* that happens, we'll laugh with the villagers and take you back, and then I'll let Sevei deal out the punishment. Maybe we'll even do the lashing in front of the villagers, just for the pleasure they'll have watching it. They'll laugh while you scream."

Meriel's eyes widened. "You wouldn't."

Nico's eyebrows climbed, deepening the furrows of his brow. "My promise to Tiarna Mac Ard was that I would keep you safe and alive, and we Taisteal have learned long ago how to tame those we sell without leaving permanent marks. You'll have no scars that anyone can see, but I guarantee you'll remember the pain. I keep my word. Always. Look at my face, girl—you can see the truth there. None of this is anything I want to do. But if I must, I will. You will make the choice, not me."

Meriel could see no anger in the lines about his eyes, only an earnest seriousness. If he didn't smile, neither did he scowl. "My mam will find me," she insisted. "You don't know how powerful she is."

"If she does find you, she can have you: alive, and with Clan Dranaghi to thank for it. The Riocha's squabbles aren't ours."

"Unless you can make a profit via them."

Nico shrugged at that. "There's no sin in profit. In the meantime, you will need a new name. You will be . . ." He hesitated, eyes rolling upward as if the answer were written in the smoke curling up from the fires. ". . . Cailin. Aye, that's a good name; we would have named our next daughter that." He patted her leg as a da might, and she moved away from him. He laughed, getting up. "Do you hear that?" he called out loudly to the others. "The new filly's name is Cailin." There were calls of acknowledgment from around the wagons and tents as Nico walked away toward the cook pot, still chuckling. Meriel stared at her untouched stew.

"Cailin."

Mam will find you, or your da or Máister Kirwan, or you'll find a way to the sea and Dhegli will come at your call . . .

"Cailin?"

Meriel started at the unfamiliar syllables. Sevei was standing there, watching her in the deepening dark. "Eat your stew before it gets cold," the woman said. "Then come to the tent with me."

With the stew heavy in her belly, Meriel entered the tent as the Seed-Daughter's Star appeared just over the eastern horizon. "Take off your clothes," Sevei said as she let the tent flap close behind her. Sevei was sitting on the nest of pillows to one side, watching Meriel in the light of several candles set on a box.

"What?"

"Take off your clothes. Give them to me."

"No." Meriel clutched the filthy white clóca to herself.

"You don't have a choice. You can't wear the Order's colors anymore. Here—" She tossed a pile of clothing toward Meriel. "Put those on."

"Then leave the tent."

"I'm comfortable. If you don't want me to watch, then go outside and do it. I'm sure my male cousins would appreciate the view."

Meriel hesitated, her hand on the clóca. She could feel the clochmion underneath her palm. "Turn away, then," she said. Sevei shook her head, but she turned. As quickly as she could, Meriel stripped off her clothing. As she reached for the clothes Sevei had given her, she heard the rustle of cloth and saw Sevei staring at her.

"So *that's* what you're hiding. What is that?"

Meriel put her hand over the cloch and herself. "It's nothing. A stone my mam gave me, that's all."

Sevei's eyes moved from Meriel's hands to her face. Her head tilted to one side, the black hair falling in a satin waterfall over her shoulders. "One might be suspicious of a stone around the neck of someone from the Order of Inishfeirm. I know Nico would be."

"It's a pretty crystal, that's all, and not even an expensive one. I was just an acolyte and they don't give clochs na thintrí to us. This is all I have from my mam now." Meriel could feel her breath coming fast and hard, and it was difficult to look back into those eyes. She hoped Sevei wouldn't notice, that the curling of her lip and the lifting of an eyebrow was only coincidence.

"You were no common acolyte. You're the daughter of the Banrion."

Meriel gave what she hoped was a scoffing laugh. "The Máister hardly worried about that. Besides, my uncle—Tiarna Mac Ard—he would have taken it if it had been a cloch."

"Aye, I'm sure he would have, if he'd thought it to be a Cloch Mór and if he even thought to look for it, hidden as it was. But it *wouldn't* be a Cloch Mór, would it? You would have used such a stone trying to escape from him or from me. But a clochmion with one small gift . . . I've heard that if you take a cloch away from the Holder, that the loss can drive them mad—even a clochmion. Your uncle—the uncle you think is such a heartless bastard—would know that. He'd understand how it would hurt, but if he saw a clochmion, he might not be so concerned. And perhaps he isn't quite so heartless as you think and didn't mention it to the others and let you keep it to spare you the pain. Or, as you said, it might just be a pretty crystal gift for a daughter."

Meriel could feel her hands and legs trembling as if she were chilled. Sevei stretched, yawning. She swung her feet around and stood, walking over to Meriel. She seemed to tower over her even though they were the same height, her gaze too insistent and intimate. Still staring at Meriel, Sevei bent down and picked up her old clothes. She was standing close to Meriel, so close that she could feel the heat of the woman's body against her skin. "I'll get rid of these," Sevei said, her voice quiet and low. "You can get dressed."

Her eyes released Meriel. She went to the tent flap and out into the night.

Her breath still fast, her hands shaking, Meriel dressed as quickly as she could.

In the darkness, Meriel could hear the deep, slow breathing from Sevei across the tent and a rattling snore from someone—probably Nico—in one of the wagons nearby. The night was quiet enough that she could hear the call of night insects from the forest and the rustling of moths' wings against the fabric of the tent. A horse nickered softly.

Mage-lights swayed in their rippled patterns through the tent roof, but though Treoraí's Heart called to her, it was still full and the urge to go to the lights was weak enough to ignore—she was grateful for that. The faint light, though, was a help. She could see Sevei's form, a mound under woolen blankets.

Watching Sevei and trying to move noiselessly, Meriel slowly pushed her blankets aside. She pulled leggings and boots over her feet and stood. Stepping quickly to the tent's flap and untying the strings there, she slid out.

The dew was wet on the grass, and the small area between the tents and wagons was deserted. As Meriel passed near the glowing embers of the cook fire, a flight of wind sprites swept by her in a gust of cold air and a flurry of green, sparking light. Meriel felt the touch of a thousand ghostly hands on her face and arms and heard their breathy, indistinct voices speaking in a language far older than that of the Daoine. They curled around her as if curious and then were gone, flitting toward the shadows of the forest and vanishing among the trunks of the oaks.

Meriel glanced up at the mage-lights, curling bright and low below the cover of massed thunderheads, their brilliance illuminating both ground and cloud. The smell of rain was in the air, still distant but approaching quickly.

Meriel took a breath and held it. She was alone. The night seemed to be waiting.

She took a step toward the wagon where Nico snored, closest to the trees. She slid past the rear of the wagon, the night under the trees beckoning. She didn't run, afraid that the pounding of feet would awaken someone, but she walked as quickly as she could toward the trees without daring to look back, the skin at her spine crawling as if waiting for a call, a shout, the stab of a blade. . . .

A shape moved from behind the nearest trunk, just to Meriel's left. In the darkness, the apparition seemed huge and forbidding, and eyes glittered menacingly in the shadows of its face. Meriel stopped with a gasp, recalling tales of Black Haunts, of Blood Wolves that walked upright. "It's not safe to be out here," a voice said. The specter moved out from the trees into the mage-lights: Sevei.

"I just . . . just needed . . ." Meriel began and stopped.

"There's a chamber pot by your bed for that." Mage-light curled over her face. In the depths of the woods, a long shuddering howl echoed and the sound of the trees moving in the stiffening breeze sounded like low voices. "I should just let you go," Sevei continued. "It would be a lesson for you—a final one, I'm afraid. But then Nico would be angry with me and I'd lose my tent-mate. So . . ." She crossed her arms under her breasts. "I suppose I have to be understanding again." She looked up at the sky as the first heavy drops of rain began to fall. "I sleep light, and you already know I'm faster and stronger than you," she said. "Like the last time, I probably would have tried this myself, the first night. But after two unsuccessful attempts I would have learned my lesson. Have you? Someone who accepts the name Cailin would understand her situation very well, and turn around now and walk back to the tent all by herself, and I wouldn't have any trouble with her again. Meriel would *make* me bring her back and I'd have to become the most awful teacher she's ever experienced until I broke her of all her bad habits. So who are you: Cailin or Meriel?"

It was starting to rain in earnest now and the mage-lights were fading. Rain hissed on the leaves and Meriel blinked away droplets from her face. Sevei stood unmoving, waiting.

Meriel shivered. Dropping her head, she turned and started walking back toward the camp. "Cailin," Sevei called. Meriel stopped and glanced back at the woman. "This was the final chance. You can't try anything like this again or you'll force me to take actions I really don't want to take. Do you understand that? Do you *really* understand that?"

A sheet of cold rain washed over them and Meriel blinked into the droplets. Faintly, thunder grumbled in the west.

"I understand," she said.

"Good." Sevei stirred, striding quickly toward her. "Come on, then. Let's get out of the weather."

She walked on past Meriel without looking back. For a few breaths, Meriel stood there, looking at the forest. Then she followed.

18

Responses

THE MESSENGER peregrine that Mundy Kirwan sent to her found her already on her way to Inishfeirm aboard the *Uaigneas,* and the spellbinding on the bird spoke the horrible news of the attack on the Order: one Bráthair dead, three other cloudmages seriously injured, and two acolytes missing—one of them Meriel. Jenna shouted her impotent fury to the sky as the peregrine, startled, took to the air. She ordered the captain of the ship to put on all sail they could and to have the crew unship the oars as well. They reached Inishfeirm the day after the attack.

"Where *is* she, Mundy? That's the only thing I care about."

Jenna found it difficult to control her rage. The fury burned inside of her, throbbed in her heart and her blood and whetted the edges of her sharp words. She paced the floor in the Máister's chamber while Mundy watched her from behind his desk. Bráthair Geraghty and Siúr Meagher pressed against the wall nearest the door as if they would flee at a run as soon as they were released. Jenna couldn't stand still; she needed to be in motion. She yearned to use the cloch around her neck, to have one of those raiders who had stolen her daughter standing in front of her—half a dozen of the invaders had remained behind, but all were killed during the attack. She rubbed at her scarred and disfigured arm; it ached today, ached worse than it had in years, making her long for the treacherous relief andúilleaf had once given her.

Guilt gnawed at her, as well as anger. *If you'd listened to Kyle, if you'd come even a day earlier, you'd have been here when the attack came, and it all would have gone much differently with Lámh Shábhála against them . . . .*

"We don't know where she is, Banrion. Not yet," Mundy answered.

"You told me Meriel would be safe. You told me you would protect her."

"I know." Mundy himself had a burn scar mottling one cheek and a long gash across his forehead now scabbed with brown. His left arm had been broken and was bandaged and bound across his body. "I thought we could."

"You've done a wonderful job of guarding her."

She saw Mundy swallow the words he might have said. He composed his face in careful stoicism. "I'd taken all the precautions I'd told you I would take when we first discussed this in Dún Kiil. Then, you also thought it would be adequate. No one believed they would dare to use this much force. Not even you, Jenna. If you look at your heart instead of your anger, you'd realize that."

She felt the heat rise in her face as if he'd slapped her, and she very nearly closed her hand around Lámh Shábhála and tore at him with the cloch's power. The voices yammered at her: ". . . *kill him for his insolence. That's what I would have done* . . ." A familiar voice arose out of the babble: Riata, whose ghost had befriended her. *"The man is your friend and your ally. You can't hurt him more than his failure already does* . . ." Mundy waited, patient and solemn as he looked at her. She could see the pain in his eyes, the self-flagellation, the guilt.

Jenna felt her pulse slow. She bit at her lower lip, forcing herself into the same calmness. "You're right, Mundy. I'm sorry."

"There's no need to apologize—I understand how you feel, and believe me, I'm furious with myself for not having anticipated this. Jenna, they came at us with at least four Clochs Mór and a full squadron of gardai. We had the islanders watching the sea; we'd slow-spelled the gulls around the island to warn us of approaching ships, but none of them came to us to tell us about the ship in West Bay until after the attack began; the raiders must have another cloch that can hide such things. We had wards set around the White Keep's grounds; that's why we were actually able to strike at them first with at least a few breaths' warning. But none of us, not even you, thought they'd attack with this many clochs. One or two, perhaps, and after Doyle Mac Ard's warning to you, we were watching for someone being sent in by Quickship. I only have three Clochs Mór here, Jenna. Even so, we were winning—with the clochs, with the clochmions, with the slow magic we'd prepared. We'd stopped them at the keep's gate when they fled as quickly as they'd come, abandoning the attack. The whole encounter was no more than a quarter of a stripe, and it took a while to find that Meriel was missing. Bráthair Geraghty saw Meriel and Thady MacCoughlin last."

Jenna swung around to the Bráthair. "Owaine?"

He blinked owlishly at Jenna, his mouth open. He sputtered, then licked his lips and began again. "They were together," he said. "I told them to stay there, in the field, but Thady MacCoughlin insisted that Meriel should follow him. I tried to stop them, but MacCoughlin . . . he's stronger than me and I couldn't stop them, and Meriel wanted to go with him . . . ." Owaine stopped. "I'm sorry, Banrion. It's my fault."

Jenna forced herself to stop, to smile. "No, Owaine," she told him. "It's not your fault. You did what you could."

Owaine shook his head in miserable disagreement, and Jenna felt the last of her fury dissolve, leave behind a cold lust for revenge against those who had done this.

Doyle. He warned me this would happen. . . .

"Bráthair Geraghty believes that Thady's responsible," Siúr Meagher said. "For everything."

Owaine shrugged. "I don't know that, Banrion. But I know that he was around Meriel all the time and that he'd gained her trust. I also know that he was unhappy here, feeling that he was looked down upon by the Riocha acolytes—which was true." Owaine sniffed, glancing once at Mundy as if for confirmation. "I know how that can be myself."

Jenna could hear the hurt in his voice and she nodded, remembering how she and her mam had themselves once been treated by the Riocha. She could imagine how difficult it had been for Owaine here, with nearly all the acolytes the sons and daughter of tiarnas and bantiarnas or at least the minor nobility. Being the offspring of common fishing folk as well as having such poor sight, Owaine's treatment would have been harsh even with Jenna's patronage and Mundy's support. The Order of Inishfeirm might declare that its gates were open to any who had the talent and desire to be a cloudmage, but the reality was that it was rarely anyone but the rich who walked these halls.

"You may be right, Owaine," Jenna said. "Thady would have been a good inside contact for the Tuathians." She looked back at Mundy. "Was my brother here?"

"Doyle Mac Ard? I don't know," he answered. "If he was, then he didn't use Snapdragon in the attack—no one saw any sign of his Cloch Mór. One of the clochs was Bluefire, the one Árón Ó Dochartaigh held years ago, which we know was given to one of the Tuathian tiarna after he died. Another was the one called Weaver that fought against us at Dún Kiil, and Tornado and GodFist. So these were definitely Tuathians, and judging from the way they handled the clochs, probably mages from the Order of Gabair. We broke Bluefire and emptied Weaver, though we didn't recover either stone. Whether Doyle was actually involved . . ." He sighed. "There's no way to know. Jenna, I think the attack was a feint, something to cover the real danger. Owaine may be right—MacCoughlin may have been the one to take Meriel away.''

"And you've searched everywhere? Meriel's not on Inishfeirm?''

"If she is, she's well hidden,'' Mundy said.

"She's not here at all, Banrion,'' Owaine interjected. He lifted the stone around his neck. "I . . . I would know, with this. It finds lost things; people as well as anything else. I would have to be close to feel her, but I've walked all over the island yesterday and earlier today. I would *know* if Meriel were here, and she's not. She was taken.''

Again, Jenna smiled at the young Bráthair. "Thank you for your efforts, Owaine.'' She heaved a long sigh. "Then there's nothing we can do now but wait. If she was taken, she's now over in Talamh an Ghlas. The ransom demands will follow soon enough, and we'll know who's responsible and what we might be able to do about it.''

Her hand closed around Lámh Shábhála, tightly enough that she could feel the pulse of the cloch's power. "And I swear that if they've hurt her, they'll pay a hundredfold.''

Tiarna Shay O Blaca, using the Cloch Mór Quickship, brought the news to Edana. Even expecting his appearance, it was startling to hear a *phoomp* of air and see him standing near her. The knot that had been in her stomach for the past few days tightened viciously at the somber look on his face. "Doyle?'' she asked him immediately. She couldn't trust her voice to say more than his name, afraid of what Shay might say.

"He's fine,'' Shay answered, and Edana breathed a long sigh of relief as the knot loosened and vanished. "He said to send you his love.'' But Shay went on to tell her the rest, and her relief at hearing that Doyle was safe was tempered by the losses they'd suffered. "We knew that we couldn't hide the Order of Gabair's involvement in this," Shay said as he paced the common room where, for propriety's sake, they'd agreed to meet. It was well past the evening supper, and the balcony near where they stood showed a sky that was nearly fully dark, already gleaming with stars. A few other Riocha were there, gathered near the massive fireplace at one end of the long room, but all stayed politely out of earshot. "But we didn't expect the losses we took or that level of resistance. We almost failed; we *would* have failed if we hadn't had the inside help. Even so, we nearly lost more Clochs Mór to the Inish."

"But we didn't," Edana reminded him. "And now we have the Banrion's daughter and we can play out the rest. Shay . . ." Edana placed a hand on the burly man's arm. "The Order of Gabair will have what we want. Soon. And once we have that . . ."

Shay still looked worried, though that was a normal expression for the man. "You're ready for the protests from those Riocha who think this was an unnecessary and dangerous provocation of the Mad Holder? By tomorrow, Rí Connachta and Rí Éoganacht will know, and you can expect the delegates to be presenting their formal protests to the Rí Ard."

"I said that I would take care of my da," Edana reminded him. "He'll say the right things when the time comes." She glanced outside to the balcony, where the first strands of the mage-lights were beginning to appear. "You'll want to go to the lights," she said to Shay. "Will you be staying? I can have the Hall Máister prepare a chamber for you."

Shay was already shaking his head. "I need to get back to Lár Bhaile; Bluefire will need a new Holder, I'm afraid. I'll send word to Doyle that you're handling things here."

"Tell him also that I'll meet him in Lár Bhaile. I'll leave in a few days, once I know that my da understands what he needs to say."

Shay nodded to her. "Then I'll go replenish Quickship.

With your leave, Bantiarna . . ." He bowed and left for
the balcony. Edana watched him lift the cloch to the sky
and then left the common room, moving past the gardai
at the entrance to the residential wing of the keep and
up the stairs to the Common Hall. She'd intended to go
to her da's chambers, but she saw Enean and Tiarna Ó
Riain in the hall, huddled together speaking while old
MacCamore hovered nearby, obviously excluded from
their conversation. MacCamore saw Edana first and his
eyes widened hopefully.

Ó Riain saw her also; he rose languidly to his feet,
giving her a bow that was so slight as to be on the verge
of an insult. His Cloch Mór just barely swayed on its
chain. "Bantiarna O Liathain," he said. "I was hoping I
would see you . . ."

Enean had leaped up from his chair, his eyes bright
in his horribly scarred face. "Edana!" he half-shouted.
He strode over to her and gave her a fierce hug that
she returned with affection. She kissed her half brother's
forehead, brushing back his hair gently, but her gaze
over his shoulder was on Ó Riain, who watched the exchange carefully. "Edana," Enean said to her after giving her a kiss on the cheek, "Tiarna Ó Riain says that
I would be a good cloudmage because I can focus so
hard on things when I want to."

She kissed him again, her attention still on Ó Riain
and the amused smile playing on his thin lips. "I'm sure
you would be, Enean. Tiarna Ó Riain, I'm surprised
you're not outside with the mage-lights."

"I was just leaving to do exactly that," he told her.
"In fact, that's why Tiarna O Liathain and I were discussing his being a Holder. I was giving him my opinion
regarding the Order of Gabair."

"Labhrás says that he thinks that I would be better if
he taught me himself," Enean interjected.

Edana smiled at Enean. "I'm sure that's exactly the
way Tiarna Ó Riain feels," she told him. "Enean, why
don't you go with MacCamore? I'll come up and we'll
both go see Da."

MacCamore came forward at the mention of his name, the old man touching Enean's shoulder. "All right," Enean said to Edana. "You won't be long?"

"Promise," Edana told him. She kissed his forehead again and watched him follow MacCamore from the room.

"I'm sorry if my opinion offends you, Bantiarna," Ó Riain said as Enean left the room. "But the Order of Gabair doesn't impress me. I would hate to believe that they'd threaten the peace of the Tuatha by, let us say, doing something to provoke the Mad Holder." The way he looked at her then, with that toad's face draped with stringy, balding dark hair, made her realize that some whispers must have reached his ears. "Many of us remember Dún Kiil and the terrible power of Lámh Shábhála," he said. "We'd hate to see the Mad Holder bring that kind of destruction here in revenge for some foolish act. The thought of that would be upsetting to some of the Ríthe. Terribly upsetting."

"The Rí Ard supports the Order of Gabair," she told him.

"Aye, he has thus far. But the Rí Ard's voice is weak these days, and getting weaker. It's such a shame that your da is so ill," he said in a voice that indicated he believed no such thing.

Edana flushed at that. "He's not so ill that he can't be Rí Ard," she told the man. "And I would prefer that you stay away from my brother, Tiarna Ó Riain."

"Your brother is an adult with the capability of making up his own mind, and he likes my company," Ó Riain answered. "Perhaps he's tired of having others tell him that he can't do things, or treating him like a child rather than a man."

"You feed him useless flatteries."

The cold, polite smile was cemented on his lips. He shook his head. "I see the possibilities in front of him, and I suggest to him how he might achieve them. Each of us needs allies, Bantiarna, even the most powerful among the Riocha. I'm sure you realize that. I believe in Enean." One eyebrow raised as he stared at Edana, though the smile remain fixed and unchanging. "A pity some of those closest to Enean do not."

"I know what Enean was before and what he is now, Tiarna. And I consider anyone who would hurt him or use him to be an enemy."

The smile widened slightly but the eyes were hard and almost scornful. "Surely you don't think of *me* as your enemy, Bantiarna? That would be . . . unfortunate. I only have the welfare of your brother at heart, just as you do."

"I'm certain," Edana told him. "But I still intend to speak to my da about my concerns."

Ó Riain shrugged. "That's certainly your prerogative, Bantiarna. But until the Rí Ard expressly orders me to do otherwise . . . well, I consider Enean a friend, and I'm pleased to be able to act as a mentor to him." He glanced to the window, where the mage-lights were in their full glory. "If you'll excuse me now, Bantiarna, my cloch calls to me . . ."

He brushed past her as the smile—finally and completely—dissolved.

The seals moaned and wailed on the rocks, craning their thick, muscular heads. The wind off the bay flapped the loose folds of his clóca and made his eyes water, but even through his blurred vision, Owaine could see that they were Saimhóir, midnight bodies gleaming with sapphire highlights in the intermittent sun. He'd heard them that morning. He'd gone scrambling down the path to the shore, knowing that it was what Meriel would have done.

"She's gone!" he called to them, knowing they couldn't understand him but hoping that somehow they would understand. "She can't come swim with you!"

A young man stepped from around a screen of boulders wet with spray. He was naked, his dark hair plastered wetly to his skull, and Owaine remembered a similar morning, many summers ago, when he'd seen Jenna, as bare as this man, walk from the sea. . . .

A changeling.

The man smiled, walking slowly toward Owaine, who took a step back. He started to speak and the man shook his head. He lifted his hand, showing his empty palm to Owaine before touching his shoulder. He spoke, and Owaine's ears heard a sound like that of the Saimhóir out on the rocks. But inside . . .

"Be calm, land-cousin. My name is Dhegli, and I know why you came here."

"You know?" Owaine sputtered. "How . . . ?"

"She and I are . . ." Dhegli hesitated, as if searching for the words. ". . . bound together," he continued. "That's how I know." He gazed solemnly at Owaine with whiteless ebony eyes. "We feel the same about her, you and I."

Owaine shook his head. "No," he began, but Dhegli laughed, short and gentle.

"You stone-walkers are strange about these things. How can you deny that you can be attracted to more than one person? The hearts of Saimhóir are not different than yours and can hold more than one love. Meriel is no different than me or you. You find yourself pulled to her even though you don't know why, even though you know you shouldn't listen to that feeling, don't you?"

Owaine nodded.

"I do, too," Dhegli laughed. "We're brothers in that." Then his face went solemn, and his hand tightened on Owaine's shoulder. "I felt the power of the sky-stones loosed here, felt it all around here. I came as quickly as I could, even though I knew I would be too late to help in that. When I came here, I reached for her and couldn't touch her."

"She's gone," Owaine told him. "They took her."

"I know. She's gone to Winter Home, the larger land

to the south. She's far away and once they take her from the water, I can't go to her."

Salt spray whipped through the wind, stinging Owaine's eyes. "She's gone to Talamh an Ghlas, then," he said. "That's what Jenna—the Holder—thought. But no one knows where . . ."

Dhegli tilted his head to one side, as if listening to something only he could hear. Out on the rocks, the other Saimhóir wailed and grunted. "You can find her," Dhegli said. "The sky-stone you wear, it has that gift."

"No," Owaine said. "It's not strong enough. I would have to be close to her."

"I could take you there," Dhegli said. "I can follow their path and bring you to where they will take her ashore on Winter Home. From there, you would have to find her on your own, but I can bring you that far." A pause. A heartbeat. The wind tore gray rags of cloud across the sky. "I can do that only if you go now. If it's something you dare to do."

"Now?" Owaine nearly pulled away. He glanced back up the mountainside to where the White Keep was hidden.

"Now, or too late," Dhegli answered. "I'm leaving to follow even though my heart tells me it's hopeless. It may be too late already."

Owaine knew what he had to say. There was no choice. He had no permission for this. Máister Kirwan would *never* give permission for this, not to Owaine. Perhaps to one of the other cloudmages: someone of Riocha blood, someone with a Cloch Mór who could stand against another tiarna. Not Owaine the Poor-Sighted. Owaine the Fisher. Owaine the Banrion's Charity. To leave now and tell no one where he was going . . . There was only one answer he should have given, but he gave another.

"Aye," he said. "Take me with you."

Dhegli nodded. He released Owaine's shoulder and motioned for him to follow. Around at the end of the crescent of beach, a currach was pulled up, its mooring rope wrapped around a boulder. Dhegli unknotted the rope. He gestured for Owaine to push the boat into the water.

Owaine hesitated. Twice before, he had felt the moment where life branched irrevocably for him: the first time as a child when he'd seen Jenna climb from the sea; the second time when Máister Kirwan, then just a Bráthair of the Order, came on behalf of the Banrion to offer Owaine the chance to become a cloudmage himself. The first time, the moment had simply come to him; the second time, the choice before him had been crystalline and clear-cut. This time . . . This time there was no certainty to his choice.

Only a vague hope.

Owaine put his hands to the boat and shoved it into the waves. As he clambered into the tiny boat, he wondered whether he would ever see Inishfeirm again.

19

The Healer

"**C**AILIN!" The call was hushed, barely more than a whisper and yet urgent enough that it woke Meriel from sleep. A low, unidentifiable rumbling accompanied the voice, like an erratic and enormous drumbeat. "Cailin, come see this!" Sleep-groggy, it took Meriel a moment to realize that she was the one being called; when she opened her eyes, she was disoriented, seeing the interior of the tent rather than the familiar ceiling of her room at the White Keep.

A head poked through the tent flap from the outside: Sevei. "Come on! Hurry!" she whispered huskily. Her eyes were alight, dancing. Meriel threw the blankets aside. The undertunic she wore was stiff; the clothes she threw on felt strange and unfamiliar and she fumbled with the ties. Sleepily, she stumbled out.

The sun had yet to rise. The meadow where they were camped was a misty dreamscape white with fog, with the forest a hidden darker gray lurking in the background. The world was hushed, quiet and ethereal, except for the persistent bass thudding. She could feel it through the soles of her boots, as if the heart of the earth itself was throbbing. "What?" Meriel started to ask as she came out of the tent to stand alongside Sevei, then she saw them.

They plodded slowly and majestically through the tall grass, striding out from the forest just past Nico's wagon.

There were perhaps a half dozen of them, all close by. At first she thought it was simply a herd of deer, but then the scale of the scene struck her, how the mantled crown of the nearest stag loomed over the top of the wagon: nearly ten feet from the ground to the head, and yet another arm's length to the tips of the rack of antlers. The animal's fur was as ruddy as the eastern sky on a cloudy morning, the chest gleaming snow, the legs thick and rough-furred. And the sound . . . Black hooves as large as Meriel's hands cupped together pounded the earth with each step, and each step was the strike of a beater on the bodhran of the world. They walked with solemn grace, unhurried and confident, the thunder of their passage growing louder as more of them came from the wood: a dozen; two; more—stags and does; adults, yearlings, and fawns that were the size of full-grown red deer. Occasionally, one of them would glance over in Meriel's direction with eyes that seemed to hold a wise, ancient intelligence. All the Taisteal were awake now, tumbling from wagons and tents and staring at the herd moving past them on all sides: the children gaping open-mouthed, the adults standing awed.

"Fia stoirm." Meriel heard Nico say. "Storm deer . . ." They filled the meadow now, and the lead stag lifted his head and called, an urgent ululation that several of them answered.

And they ran . . .

The herd lurched into motion: sudden, exhilarating, and frightening. The sound . . . So deafening it was nearly solid, hammering at Meriel's chest, dinning in her ears so that she could not even hear her own startled scream as one of the stags hurtled over a wagon and through the middle of the camp not two strides from her, its hooves shattering pottery placed on a shelf of one of the wagons. For a few moments, the Taisteal and Meriel stood in the midst of a red thundercloud while the world itself seemed to roar. Then, just when Meriel thought she could bear it no more, the sound began to fade as the herd moved past the camp, across the road, and up the long slope to the north. In a few minutes, they passed the lip of the rise and were hidden from sight, though the faint sound of their passage remained, like the grumbling of distant lightning.

The children were laughing and pointing. Meriel felt an elbow nudge her ribs; she blinked. Sevei was grinning at her. "You should see your face," she said. Her voice seemed thin and weak after the barrage of sound.

"I've never seen anything like that," Meriel said. "I mean, I've seen one or two storm deer in the distance, but never . . ." She stopped, shaking her head.

"No one has seen this," Nico answered, coming over to them. "Not in seven hundred years or more. The storm deer returned with the mage-lights, like the dire wolves or the wind sprites. New things and ancient things both now walk the world since the Filleadh. We know best, we Taisteal. We see what others don't: those who are born, live, and die in sight of the same hills. And now we see what twenty generations of Taisteal haven't seen." He stared off at the hills where the storm deer had gone, a tight smile of satisfaction on his face. " 'Tis glorious to live in a new-awakened land. More opportunities for profit."

He sniffed and rubbed his jowls. "But there's no profit to be made here. Let's break our fast and move on. There's a village we can reach by this afternoon if we hurry. Cailin, it's time you started to earn your keep; Sevei, keep her busy."

Sevei did that, and more. Meriel was quickly introduced to the routines of the Taisteal—preparing the stirabout for the clan, taking care of the children, striking the camp and packing everything in the wagons, feeding and caring for the horses that drew them, and in between it all taking care of her own needs. Sevei was never more than a stride or two from her, and every time that Meriel stole a glance to see if the woman was watching, she met dark eyes and an amused smirk. A stripe later, the caravan was lurching slowly down the road, heading farther inland with pots and pans jingling as the wagons bumped and swayed.

For most of the day, Foraois Coill stayed close at their right hand, then as the afternoon shadows started to lengthen, the ranks of twisted, old oaks curved away from the road until the wood was a dark line to the south. The road stayed near the higher hills to the north, moving along at the feet of long, steep slopes blanketed by heather and stands of maple and fir. Bogs sat steaming in the hollows.

After several stripes of travel, they moved into land that was recognizably inhabited. Occasional flocks of sheep watched them pass, their woolen flanks splotched with patches of pale blue or red that marked them for their owners. Low drystone fences defined fields where farmers labored, and here and there were dirt lanes leading from the road back to one-room, thatched cottages. Sometimes, someone would lean against the fence and watch them pass. Meriel could see their faces; streaked with dirt, browned and leathery with the sun: plain faces well-marked by their labor. "That's the look of the true people," Sevei said to Meriel as they passed a woman, clutching one child to her breast with another hanging snotty-nosed at her ragged, torn cloak. "The Riocha in their stone cities never think of the thousands out here who spin their fine cloth and grow their food, who bring in the lumber and cut the stone, who do all the work that makes it possible for the Riocha to live as they do. It doesn't matter to *them* who sits on the throne—their lives won't change. Their lives *never* change."

Meriel glanced back over the side of the wagon at the woman. She'd turned away as the child coughed, a phlegm-rattled rack, her thin chest heaving. The woman stroked the child's matted curls of red much the color of Meriel's, crooning gently to her.

Meriel touched the cloch hidden under her clothing as the woman and her children slowly receded behind them. She could feel the warmth of its power, tingling in her fingers.

When she turned back to look at the road ahead, she felt Sevei watching her.

By the time the sun had dropped two fingers in the sky, they came across a village at a small crossing where another road wandered in from the northern hills and drifted out toward the now-unseen Foraois Coill. There were no signs, no posting—Meriel knew she would have been one of the few who could have read them, even if there had been. At Nico's call, a man herding a small flock of sheep with his dog told them that this was Ballicraigh, that the Ald for the village was Toma Macsnei, and that they'd best put the wagons on the Eastlawn, a small field just past the inn.

Ballicraigh seemed to consist of less than a dozen buildings: a ramshackle inn, a mill alongside a quick-running stream, a smithy, a Draíodóir's hut with the Mother's circle painted above the door. There was a tanner somewhere near; Meriel could smell the ripe odor of dead animals. They were immediately noticed: small clots of children ran around their wagons and adult faces peered at them from windows or watched from open doorways. By the time they pulled into the Eastlawn, a gray-haired woman was striding purposefully toward them on the arm of a someone who might have been her daughter, an oaken stick held in one gnarled hand stabbing the earth.

"Here we go," Sevei whispered to Meriel. "There's always a bribe or two to pay."

"Aldwoman Macsnei!" Nico called out as if he'd known her all his life, hopping down from his seat on the wagon. "Clan Dranaghi is pleased to be welcomed here. I am Clannhri Nico."

The woman sniffed. She grinned, showing the few teeth remaining in her mouth. "Well, Clannhri Nico," she said, "I hope you're better than the last group of Taisteal who came through here. I gave them five crocks of my best honey for a cook pot, and the handle fell off not two hands of days after they left."

Nice's face stretched in almost comic horror, as he placed a hand at his breast. "Aldwoman, I am *appalled*. A few, a very few, of the clans . . . well, they are just not to be trusted. Perhaps the pot you purchased came from Inish Thuaidh; the workmanship there is so poor, as you know. I assure you that what we have is only the finest, the best . . ."

Aldwoman Macsnei waved a hand. "I'm sure, I'm sure," she said in a tone that indicated the opposite. "Your wares have had slow magics of metal chanted over them as they're made. They've been certified by the twelve Great Mages of Thall-Mór-roinn and will never rust or leak. I've heard all the fanciful Taisteal guarantees that mean nothing. Spare your breath."

Nico gestured to Sevei, who rummaged about in the back of their wagon for a moment, then brought out a small hammered copper cook pot. She gave it to Nico, who presented it to Aldwoman Macsnei. "Ald-woman, let me give you this as a token of goodwill, and a small repayment for your troubles."

The Aldwoman took the pot, turning it over in her hands and tapping it with the head of her walking stick as her daughter steadied her and the metal rang like a gong. She tugged at the handle, then shrugged, handing the pot to her daughter. "You'll stay on the Eastlawn while you're here," she said. "I don't want any of you Taisteal wandering about stealing things. I'll call out the village gardai the first I hear of any trouble. If we find any of your men with our young women, I won't be responsible for the reaction. Do we understand each other?"

"We understand each other perfectly, Aldwoman. Thank you for welcoming us to Ballicraigh."

Aldwoman Macsnei grimaced sourly, sniffed, and spat, and waved her hand again. She started walking away,

and Sevei nudged Meriel. "Time to work," she said.
"Stay with me, and don't talk to the villagers unless they
talk directly to you, and even then watch what you say.
Nico wasn't joking about what he'd do to you if you try
to make contact with one of them or escape. You don't
want to be treated like a wild animal. Stay near me, and
keep your mouth shut."

The clan quickly unloaded tents and set up the camp
as a few of the villagers started drifting out toward the
meadow. The wares the Taisteal sold were as varied as
their travels, as Meriel knew from the clan who had
visited Dún Kiil. They were traders and barterers, crafts-
folk and entertainers. There were the usual pots and
pans showing a variety of origins and styles; blankets,
clothing, and bolts of woolen cloth, some with geometric
designs that spoke to Meriel of foreign hands and minds;
exotic spices and flavorings; powders and elixirs interred
in clay jars stoppered with wax and marked with unfamiliar symbols; jewelry that glittered and sparked on
scraps of dark cloth, with stones of dubious origin hanging from silver and brass links or plain thread. The Taisteal would accept coins as payment if they had to, but
they preferred barter: new-baked bread; the local honey;
suckling pigs, chickens, or even the occasional sheep;
grains and cereals; the work of a local potter that they
could sell elsewhere—all the niceties that an itinerant
lifestyle couldn't provide.

Meriel realized quickly that the Taisteal also provided
another commodity: news. In a land where most people
lived their entire lives within walking distance of the
place they were born, the Taisteal and other travelers
along the roads provided the link with the greater world,
and news now months old would be listened to with
eager ears. If the Taisteal embellished it or twisted it to
the advantage of the listener, so much the better.

Each of the clan members had their role to play in
the economic dance. Meriel found that Sevei was, among
other things, the Teller of Fortunes, and Cailin/Meriel
was now to be her silent assistant. In their tent, they set

up a small table draped with bright gauze with two rickety chairs, and lit racks of thick scented candles so that
the tent's interior glowed with warm, shifting light. Sevei
produced a small wooden box and set it on the table.
Lifting the lid, she let Meriel glance inside at the rectangles of thick, oiled paper. The cards were brightly colored and much-handled, the paper soft around the edges
and covered with strangely-dressed figures and fanciful
creatures. There were numbers in the corner of each
card. "The cards came from Thall Mór-roinn, and were
my mam's and great-mam's before me," Sevei said in
answer to Meriel's unasked question. "There's a true
power in them, whether you believe that or not, and
they tell me what to say. That, and what I see in the
person before me."

Despite herself, Meriel found her interest drawn to
Sevei's routine and soon developed a grudging admiration for the woman's skill. The first person to come into
the tent was a young woman of the village, who wanted
to know about her future love life. Meriel listened, marveling as Sevei teased hints from the woman about her
expectations and experiences and wove them all into a
tale suggested by the fall of the dog-eared cards, their
placement and arrangement. Sevei watched the woman
closely, and Meriel realized that Sevei fine-tuned her
words by the body language and facial expressions she
saw. The performance was impeccable, and the woman
left marveling at the cards' ability to see her life and
predict its future course.

"The power's in you, not the cards," Meriel said after
the woman had left. Sevei lifted one shoulder as she
shuffled the cards.

"Just now it was," she answered. "I simply told her
what she already knew and what she wanted to hear.
It's easy once you've mastered the knack of reading the
person across from you. Watch me, and in a moon's time
or less you can take a turn at it. Now—go let the next
one in."

For the next few stripes, Meriel witnessed a slow procession of people coming through the tent. There was the grieving mam who was distraught over the fate of her son, who had been conscripted by the Rí Infochla's gardai six summers before and had never returned; the farmer who wanted to know if the blight would hurt his barley crop again this year and how he might prevent it (the latter answer involved sending him to Nico for a potion to sprinkle in his fields); the couple who asked if Sevei could tell them whether they would remain childless (yet another potion, this time provided by Nico's wife); the coincidental series of three men in a row, each of whom asked whether his wife was being faithful—which made Meriel curious to know if they'd managed to cuckold each other. "Is there anyone else out there?" Sevei asked after the last of the husbands had departed, smug with the knowledge that his wife had kept her vow.

Meriel started to the tent flap, but before she could reach it a hand slid the cloth aside. The face of the woman who entered gave Meriel a start of recognition: she was the mam they'd passed on the way into Ballicraigh. Her children were still with her: the babe in arms, now sleeping in a folded shawl sling wrapped over one shoulder, the redheaded one clinging shyly to her mam's clothing. In the candlelight, Meriel could see the hollowness of the child's eye sockets, the dark pouch of flesh hanging under them, the distended, swollen belly and crusted sores covering her lips and nostrils. The child wheezed as she breathed, her breath rattling in her lungs. The woman hesitated, as if unsure if she should be here, and started to turn away.

"What do you want to know, good lady?" Sevei called to her softly. She tapped the cards on the table. "I have the answers to your life here. You could know what the future holds for you for just a few coppers, or perhaps something you have to trade . . . ?"

The woman smiled, shaking her head.

"Nothing?" Sevei urged. "Some bauble that isn't important to you, a trinket, perhaps a single coin. It needn't be much." Her eyes were on the woman's wrist, where a half-dozen or so small coins hung from a bracelet of twisted string.

"I shouldn't," the woman answered. A thin hand twisted the coin bracelet around her wrist. "Though I wish—"

The red-haired girl coughed, a chest-racking paroxysm that left her gasping for breath. They all watched, the mam holding her concern in her face. "You want to know how it will be with your daughter," Sevei said. "That's the question you've brought to me. That's what you most want to know."

A nod.

"One coin," Sevei told her. "The smallest one you have. That's all I ask for the answer to that question." A moment's hesitation: then the woman untied the string and slid one of the coins from it. She placed it on the table and retied the string as Sevei took up the cards and gestured to the chair in front of her. She began laying out the array.

"This is very odd," Sevei said, staring at the cards. She seemed genuinely shocked as she touched the cards with her fingertips, so different from the way she'd been all night that Meriel's gaze went away from the little girl to Sevei. "Very odd, indeed . . ." but another cough took Meriel's attention away again.

Meriel crouched down next to the girl. The child was wheezing badly, her chest moving rapidly. Meriel could smell the sickness on her breath and hear the rot in her lungs. The girl stared at her, venturing the smallest of shy smiles between the labored breaths. Meriel crouched down in front of her as Sevei laid down the last card and started giving the tale of the cards. The girl coughed again, a sound full of liquid and exhaustion. Blood flecked her lips when she looked at Meriel again. "Here," Meriel whispered, and she reached out with the end of her sleeve to brush at the girl's lips.

The cloch throbbed at Meriel's breast. She touched it under her tunic, unthinkingly, and the power within it slipped out: burning, rushing through Meriel's body to the point of contact with the girl and inside. Meriel gasped as a crushing weight slammed down hard upon her chest and her lungs seemed to fill with water. She was suffocating, feeling as if she were drowning from the inside. She tried to take a breath, and the effort made her cough, and the cough sent splinters of bone stabbing through her chest, skewering her. Meriel moaned, eyes wide in fright as she stared into the equally wide eyes of the little girl.

. . . so tired, but Mam made me walk here and my chest hurts so much but I like the colors of the Taisteal's clothes . . . the lady has pretty hair Mam says that I'll have pretty hair one day if the Mother-Creator doesn't take me back the coughing hurts so much . . .

Then Meriel's vision shifted, as if she were falling rapidly toward and through the girl. A red-imbued, nightmare landscape was all around her and the sound of a breath bellowed in her ears. Around her, there were clots of white, writhing fibers wrapped around scarlet nodules, and the power of the cloch went to each of them, searing the white to nothingness. Meriel felt each flare of power within her own chest. She screamed.

She pulled her hand away from the girl as if she'd touched a stewpot hung over a fire; she fell to the ground, and the girl tumbled in the other direction. "Cailin, what's wrong?" she heard Sevei shouting, dimly, and heard the cry of the girl's mam.

Her breath coming hard and fast, Meriel let go of the stone. The pain receded; the weight on her chest lightened and vanished, but the memory stayed. Of being inside the child. Of *being* the child. *Áine—that was my name. I was Áine.*

"Cailin?"

Meriel shook her head and pushed herself up, standing shakily. "I'm fine," she said. "Just . . . leave me alone a moment."

The woman had picked up her child. "Mam, I can *breathe,*" the girl said wonderingly. She pointed at Meriel. "That lady took the hurt away." She laughed and took a comically deep breath with her mouth wide. "See, Mam?"

The mam sobbed once, a great heaving cry as she hugged the girl tightly. They were all staring at Meriel.

It was Sevei who broke the silence. "You see the answer here," she said, her forefinger stabbing one the cards, where a red-haired woman walked along the edge of a cliff, holding an oaken branch toward the sun. "That card's called the Healer. And there, next to it, that's the card of the Mother-Creator, and beside it, the Gifting Hand. That tells all: Cailin's mam was gifted with the Healing Touch by the Mother-Creator, as was her great-mam before her. We have always wondered whether the Mother-Creator would give Cailin the Touch also." Sevei's gaze flicked over to Meriel; a glare that dared her to contradict. "It seems She finally has."

"Is it true?" The hope and need to believe in the woman's eyes was frightening to Meriel. The infant in the sling was crying. "Áine's not going to die?"

Meriel's hands were still shaking, and flashes of the awful sickness in the girl's lungs kept returning. "No," Meriel answered, realizing that they were all waiting for her to speak. "No, Áine's not going to die. I see a long life for her."

The woman gave a choking, abrupt sob, tightening her arms around her daughter. "Mam, you're crushing me!" Áine said, and the woman laughed and cried at the same time as she released her, twin tears tracking down her cheeks. She pulled the coin bracelet from her wrist and placed it on the table atop the cards.

"Thank you," she said. "Thank you both."

"You don't—" Meriel started to say, but Sevei's hands had already clapped down on top of the coins.

"It's the favor of the Mother-Creator," Sevei said. "She has blessed Cailin, and Cailin has, in turn, given the blessing to Áine. Go on your way now," she continued. "Look at poor Cailin; the effort has tired her and she must rest now."

With profuse thanks, the trio left, Áine laughing and

scampering ahead of her mam. When the tent flap fell back behind them, Sevei hurried over to it and tied it shut, dismissing the man who was waiting outside for his fortune to be told. Arms crossed, head tilted, she regarded Meriel. "You realize that the story's going to be all over this village in the next stripe or less," she said finally. "The girl's cured? Truly?"

"Aye," Meriel answered quietly, eyes downcast. "I think so, anyway. I don't really know."

"The clochmion?"

Meriel nodded.

"You might have told me what it could do." When Meriel remained silent, Sevei finally sighed. Her arms unfolded. "Well, there's nothing I can do about it now. How often can you do this?"

"I've only used it twice," Meriel admitted to her. "Both times the cloch was empty afterward. I can't do anything until the mage-lights fill it again."

"Fine," Sevei said. "Then we save it for the really big miracles—make sure it's somebody prominent or obviously sick and we're getting well paid for it; half of the rest will end up thinking that they're cured anyway even if you do nothing; the inevitable failures we'll blame on a lack of favor from the Mother-Creator. And we'd best dye your hair black and straighten those curls so you look more like a Taisteal—we don't want word getting to the wrong ears that someone matching the description of the Banrion's daughter is performing healings. That will work."

Meriel was shaking her head. "What are you talking about? I'm not going to do anything like that or let you dye my hair."

Sevei snorted. "Oh, aye, you will. After the tale gets out tonight that we have a genuine healer in the clan who has the Mother's Touch, they'll come swarming in. If you think Nico's going to miss the chance to relieve them of what they're willing to pay for a chance to have their ills cured, well . . ."

Sevei walked over to the table and gathered up her

cards. "He won't entirely like it because it will bring attention to you and you're supposed to be our little secret, but he also won't be able to resist the profit. We'll want to keep the clochmion hidden—the last thing we need is for the Riocha to figure out you have a cloch na thintrí; that would be too dangerous. We'd have ti-arna coming here saying the Taisteal must have stolen it, and using that as an excuse to take the cloch . . ."

"Sevei—"

". . . Maybe we'll say that the Touch weakens you—that way we can control the number of people who see you, and help explain away the failures . . ."

"Sevei!" This time she heard Meriel and she stopped, the lid to the card box open, the cards in her hand.

"Was that card really the Healer?" Meriel asked. "And the rest of them? You said the pattern was very odd."

Sevei gazed at her, the golden light of the candles reflecting on the glossy, satin strands of her hair. "There has to be a touch of truth in every deception," she told Meriel, "or it will never work."

"That doesn't answer my question."

"No," she said. "It doesn't."

Sevei came back to the table. She pointed to the chair across the table from her. "Sit," she ordered Meriel, and placed the deck of cards in front of Meriel as she obeyed. "Shuffle the cards and then cut the deck once," she said. With Sevei's dark gaze on her, Meriel picked up the cards and did as she was told, finally lifting half the stack and setting it to one side. Sevei picked up the deck again, placing the cut portion on the bottom and dealing out the cards: three cards in the center of the table, then a spiraled array around it, then a line of five cards over and under the spiral. Meriel could see the one called the Healer again. Sevei sighed as she stared at the cards.

The woman said nothing for several breaths, gazing intently at the cards. "Sevei?" Meriel asked finally, and

Sevei shook herself from reverie. She swept the cards together with a sweep of her hand.

"I'm too tired to do this right now," she said as she gathered the colorful rectangles back into a deck. She pushed away from the table, went to the box and placed the cards inside as Meriel watched. "If you're really interested in having your fortune told like some fool tuathánach, I'll do it later."

"But—" Meriel began, but Sevei slammed the lid down with a hard *crack*.

"Right now we need to talk to Nico," Sevei told her. "Before he hears about this from someone else. Come with me."

20

The Searcher

"SHE was here, two mornings ago. I can feel that much. But this is as far as I can go, Owaine. It's up to you now."

The gulls wheeled and cried overhead. Dhegli, even in his human form, was obviously drawn and exhausted. He knelt on the wet shingle, his hair plastered across his forehead, a strand of kelp draped over one shoulder. Dhegli's hand clutched Owaine's, allowing Owaine to understand him. The currach in which Owaine had ridden lay on its side nearby. Owaine had been on the Westering Sea many times in his life, fishing and sailing, and he knew that it would have taken a normal vessel two or three days to get from Inishfeirm to where they now stood on the shore of Talamh an Ghlas. Dhegli had managed it in a day and night, pulling the currach tirelessly through the waves, calling on the power of Bradán an Chumhacht within him.

Owaine touched the cloch na thintrí around his neck and thought of Meriel, recalling her face. He let the power of the clochmion radiate out as far as he could send it, but there was no answering flare in his mind showing him where she was: Meriel wasn't close. Dhegli shook his head, seeing Owaine's attempt. "You waste your efforts, land-cousin," he said. "They've already taken Meriel well inland. They wouldn't have kept her near the water, knowing she could slip away from them easily if she escaped here."

"I'll try to find her," Owaine said. He squinted at the landscape in front of him, to his eyes mostly a blur of green and brown. "But I'm not a woodsman, and my eyes . . ."

Dhegli gave him a weary smile. "I believe that you'll try or I wouldn't have brought you here. You'll have help, Owaine—I see that with Bradán an Chumhacht; you'll have help from sources that will surprise you. And if you succeed in finding Meriel, bring her back to the sea and have her call me and I'll come for you. Both of you. Now go. Go . . ."

He released Owaine's hand, and his voice faded in Owaine's head. His mouth still worked, but the sound that came from it were like the sounds of the seals. As Owaine watched, Dhegli's form began to change: the skin darkening and becoming covered with fine black hair, his body pulling into itself, the legs fusing together, the arms shrinking. In a few moments, it was a young bull Saimhóir with a scarred body who gazed back at Owaine.

"I'll find her if I possibly can, Dhegli," Owaine said. "And I'll bring her back."

Dhegli roared once, lifting his snout. Owaine waved to him and turned his back to the sea, trudging up the steep slope to where the green roof of a forest blanketed the hills beyond. In a few minutes, he was at the top of the nearest rise and he stopped to look down at the beach, peering myopically at the tiny crescent of sand. The dark blob that would have been Dhegli was gone—he'd returned to the sea.

Owaine was alone in this world. He'd never in his life been off the few square miles of Inishfeirm, had never even been as far as Inish Thuaidh, and now he stood on Talamh an Ghlas, unfathomably far from anything familiar.

A bit to his left, away from the edge of the oak forest, Owaine glimpsed a barely-discernible footpath, a pale tan in the wash of emerald and yellow. Near where the path cut through the dunes of the shore rise, there was a dark circle in the heather. Curious, he went toward it, discovering a ring of field stones and the white-tipped ends of burned logs: the remains of a campfire. He could imagine the scene: a beacon fire burning on the shore, guiding in the ship. In his imagination, Meriel was seated in the vessel between grim tiarna with her hands bound. He reached down to touch the ashes—they were cold and dead, but the heather around the end of the path was torn and marked by the ruts of wagon wheels and the horses' hooves, as well as the boots of several people, including— if the size of the footprints were any indication—children. Whoever they were, there had been several people here to meet the ship when normally there were rarely any people here at all. They had to have come here to meet with those who had taken Meriel. And there was only one way they could have gone, unless they were all changelings. Owaine could almost see it all.

"Maybe I can do this after all. How hard can it be?" He tried to say it confidently, but his voice sounded thin and uncertain in the wind off the sea, and only gulls answered him, mockingly.

Owaine turned his back to the water once more and followed the trail eastward, his head down—at least if he looked at his feet things were almost in focus and he might not miss too much. The footpath itself curved off toward the forest and vanished, but the wagons had stayed on an eastward course. The marks of the wheels took no skill to follow—the wagons had been heavy enough to crush the grass into the wet earth. But . . . from the edge of the deep forest to his right—a blur of green so dark it seemed brown, with hollows of purple verging on black—Owaine thought he could feel eyes watching. As he turned to look, pressing his eyelids together in a futile attempt to focus, a flock of black crows took flight, mocking him with their calls. The crows circled around him once, their shadows running cold over him, then they vanished into the green smear of the forest. The sense of being observed remained even in their absence. Owaine shivered, forcing himself to ignore

the feeling and concentrate on the tracks at his feet,
crouching down to look at them again. Aye, there was
a boot print caught in mud, and the toes pointed eastward, away from the water.

He wondered how much of a head start they had on
him, how many miles from here they might be.

" 'Tis only one way to find out," he said aloud, more
just to break the oppressive quiet of wind and rustling
leaves than for anything else. But again his voice sounded
dead and dull in this place and he shut his mouth firmly
as he lengthened his stride, following the trail and hoping that if the wagons turned away from the path it
would be obvious enough he'd see it.

Hoping that he wasn't simply following the trail of
some family who'd had a picnic on the beach and knew
nothing of Meriel at all. No . . . he couldn't let himself
think that. He wouldn't.

A few more half-used trails, all from the hills to the
north, came down and merged with the one Owaine followed, and the route gradually shifted from being nothing more than crushed heather and grass to an erratic
path of bare dirt to—as the sun climbed in the sky—a
twin-rutted lane, traveled often enough that the grass
grew only fitfully where the wagon wheels passed along
it. By that time, Owaine was no longer following any
markings he could recognize. There were the rutted
signs of wagons, but they could have been any wagons,
from any time. Owaine began to wonder—even more
than he had before—about his wisdom in coming here.

The road, at least, was easy to follow, even for a nearsighted fool. He continued to follow along the indistinct
edge of the forest to the south. Occasionally an arm of
trees would sweep across the road and Owaine would
be traveling through lightly-forested hills; at other times,
the wood was only a dim dark line well off in the distance as he strode through what might once have been
plowed fields now long gone fallow. Once he passed a
line of old barrows and he turned his face away as he
hurried past the dark gaping mouths of the graves.

The road was well-used enough that Owaine expected to meet others. Dressed in the colors of the Order, he knew he should hide, but he also knew that it was far more likely that anyone he encountered on the road would see Owaine before his poor eyes glimpsed them unless he was lucky enough to hear them first. He wondered what tale he could give them, and whether he might find out from them whether the wagons he hoped he was following had passed this way—if they didn't kill him outright. But as the stripes went by and the sun began to fall, no one came walking the other way or passed him riding from behind. Once, well ahead of him, he saw a rider turn onto the road from out of the northern hills and canter away, the sound of the horse's hooves coming belatedly back to him. Owaine could make out no details from that distance—the rider was a vaguely man-shaped blur on top of a horse-shaped blur in the midst of a landscape blur. The rider could have been man or woman, tiarna or tuathánach, in plain clothing or rich. If whoever it was saw Owaine, he or she made no sign and vanished in a few minutes around the next turn.

By evening, despite the signs of more frequent travel along the road, he'd yet to come across any other human habitation. Though he'd slaked his thirst in a few streams, Owaine was desperately hungry and beginning to realize just how horribly unprepared he was for this trek. He'd left Inishfeirm with nothing but the clochmion around his neck, and the clothes on his back, his purse holding a few coppers without even a lone mórceint. He had nothing else. "You are a stupid jackass," he muttered, cursing himself. "You're going to do Meriel a hell of a lot of good when you die out here. Won't the Banrion be impressed with that? Won't Máister Kirwan love the fact that some Tuathian will get my clochmion?"

He trudged on, his belly growling and his legs aching, any optimism he might have felt at the start of the day long ago replaced by a dull realization that he was going to fail. The sun eased itself below the horizon behind him, throwing a long shadow angling ahead. As the sky turned purple-black and the Seed-Daughter's Star shimmered into existence on the western horizon, Owaine noticed a rocky outcropping extending from the margins of the forest. There were no signs of fire anywhere that Owaine's eyes could see, not even a cultivated field that might have promised some nearby farmhouse where he might have begged shelter. The folds of stone at least promised a shallow cave or some outcropping that might give him shelter during the night, and he moved off the road toward it. Walking along the flank of stone, he found a low shelf of limestone arching over darkness and he crept into the recesses of the overhang, dragging with him a few branches to serve as blanket and bed.

He was exhausted enough by his long hours of walking that sleep found him almost immediately despite the protests of his stomach.

He didn't know how long he slept, or what it was that woke him: some crack of branch or leafy rustling or the sound of distant singing. He opened his eyes to darkness alleviated only slightly by starlight. There *was* singing, a compelling susurration like the chant of a thousand deep voices, far off in the darkness under the trees. The sound seemed to call to him and he lifted his head in response. Something small skittered away from him, chattering as it scampered out toward the forest; startled, Owaine rolled back farther into the recess. He squinted out to the lighter patch of world past the overhang. He thought . . . he thought he saw something darker there, like a round boulder set atop another larger one. He rose up on an elbow, peering out with a frown.

The mysterious singing swelled as a wind shook the trees.

"Now here's a curiosity, Léimard: a Bráthair of the Order of Inishfeirm out here all alone." The voice—deep and male—came from the dark shape, startling Owaine. As he gasped, the shadow moved, and he saw that it was a person, crouched at the lip of the overhang and looking in at him, two arm's lengths away. A smaller shadow leaped from the ground to his shoulder: a squirrel. "At least he had the good sense not to light a fire here so close to the Old Ones."

The words were strangely accented, and as the figure pulled back slightly from the overhang Owaine could faintly discern the face in the wan starlight: a man of middle age, the features flat, with eyes sunken deep below the ridges of eyebrows, and the hair starting low on the brow, the lips thick under a dark beard. He was wearing furs and leather, his feet wrapped in skins. *By the Mother, that's a Bunús Muintir . . .* Owaine realized with a start. Owaine was staring at one of the Old People, the ones who Owaine's own tribe, the Daoine, had defeated and had driven into the depths of the ancient forests.

Owaine shivered, as much from the cold of the night as seeing the apparition in front of him. "Go away!" Owaine grated out. "I warn you; I have a sword and I'll use it."

The Bunús seemed to hiss; it might have been quiet laughter. "Since when does a Bráthair prefer iron to a cloch? You've nothing with you to frighten me, but if you're at all intelligent, you should be scared . . . Do you hear the singing of the trees, Bráthair Lost? Maybe you'd like to go closer to it so you can listen to the Old Ones and sleep forever at their feet." The Bunús took a step back from the overhang, gesturing toward the trees. The chant, with strange long syllables woven into it, pulled at Owaine.

Aye, I should go listen . . . They call me . . . They know me and want me . . .

A hand touched his chest, and Owaine realized that unknowingly he'd crawled out from the shelter, that he was standing and walking toward the sound, that if the Bunús Muintir hadn't stopped him, he would have found himself deep among the trees. He blinked, startled, as the song wrapped around him and tugged at his will.

"Should I let you go, or not?" the Bunús said, almost

musingly, as if talking to himself. "A difficult decision . . ."
He spoke another few words, his hand still on Owaine's
chest, then let his hand drop.

Suddenly, there was no song at all, only the formless
sound of harmless wind in the treetops. Wide-eyed,
Owaine scrambled back away from the man, crouching
under the lip of rock.

"Here . . ." The Bunús reached into a large leather
pouch strung over one shoulder. He held out something
in Owaine's direction. "I suspect you need this." He
placed a leaf-wrapped packet on the ground between
them, then sat back. The squirrel chattered on his shoulder and the man stroked the animal with one hand.

Owaine hesitated, then leaned forward and took the
packet. The smell hit him first: the fragrant, smoky perfume of cured meat sprinkled with aromatic spices. The
odor filled his mouth with saliva and made his stomach
growl. "Eat," the Bunús said. "It's not poisoned. If I
wanted you dead, I'd have let you go with the Old One's
song." Watching the Bunús suspiciously, Owaine took a
bite and sighed helplessly with pleasure. He chewed the
leathery meat, swallowing quickly and tearing off another chunk.

He realized that the man was watching him. "Thank
you," Owaine said.

The Bunús' face split with a smile. The squirrel
hopped from shoulder to ground again, taking a few hesitant steps toward Owaine. "My name is Cataigh," the
man said. "And that is Léimard, my friend and companion. And this . . ." He gestured with one hand toward
the tangle of oaks behind him. "Foraois Coill is my
charge to protect and nurture."

"I'm Owaine Geraghty," Owaine answered, "Bráthair
of the Order of Inishfeirm, as you realize. So this is
Foraois Coill . . ." He remembered the forest from the
maps in the library of the White Keep, one of the remnants of the ancient oak-dominated forests that had once
covered Talamh an Ghlas in the times of legend. He

remembered some of the other tales he'd heard about the ancient woods, and he shuddered. *The singing of the trees* . . .

Cataigh seemed amused. "You don't know where you're walking and you wear the léine and clóca that identify you as one of the Order—clothing that marks you as an enemy in this land." His eyes closed momentarily, and Owaine felt a tingle at his breast, as if a feathery hand had brushed the stone there. "*Without* a sword, too, despite your bluster, and that's but a clochmion around your neck, not a Cloch Mór. No horse, no pack, no food, no companions, though the smell of the sea lingers around you. There must be an interesting tale here. Are you shipwrecked, Bráthair Geraghty, or are you simply a madman?"

"How did you know—" Owaine began, then shut his mouth.

"Ah, so you remember your history," Cataigh chuckled. "Aye, we Bunús Muintir are better with the slow magics than you Daoine, and we have our own ways of knowing things. Come, Léimard, there's no danger to the forest with our Bráthair Geraghty." Cataigh clucked his tongue and the squirrel hopped onto his arm, climbing rapidly to the man's shoulders as he rose. "Stay here tonight if you wish. Perhaps we'll talk again," the Bunús said, and began walking away into the darkness.

"Wait!" Owaine called, but by the time he scrambled out from his shelter he could no longer see the man at all. The forest was an impenetrable wall with inky darkness pooled under the canopy of the trees, and there were sounds and calls from within it that made the hair on his arms rise. He was afraid the trees would begin singing again, and that he might go to them . . . .

This was not a place in which to go wandering at night. "Cataigh!" Owaine called, but the sound of his voice sent the forest silent for a moment as if it were annoyed at his interruption, and Owaine shivered again. Wrapping his clóca around him, he crawled back beneath the overhang. For a long time, he lay there with his eyes open.

He thought he wouldn't be able to sleep, but he drifted somehow into dreams of oak trees whose limbs were like thin, grasping hands and he was running through bramble that tugged at his clóca, pursued by wolves with bright, glowing eyes that laughed at him. Overhead, a dragon flapped leathery wings as it circled, searching for him. The dragon belched fire and stooped with an awful cry, and its talons reached for Owaine. . . .

"Ow!" He jolted himself out of sleep abruptly, striking his head on the rocky overhang. He rubbed his bruised head, blinking his eyes in the daylight, wondering if the Bunús Muintir had also been a dream brought on by the nearness of the oaks. He pushed aside the screen of branches and clambered out, shading his eyes at the dawn. The forest was wrapped in mist and fog.

At the edge of his shelter, closest to the trees, he saw a pile of objects. Crouching down alongside, he found leather breeches and shirt, and a clóca of rough wool such as a farmer might wear. Underneath the clothing were sandals of soft fur and a small pouch out of which tumbled a knob of flint, a striking steel, and a wooden tinder holder. Another packet of the jerky was there as well, and a skin filled with cool water.

Owaine picked up the gifts. He looked at the trees. "Thank you!" he called. "I'm in your debt, Cataigh!"

There was no answer.

The road stayed near the forest all that day, never far from the ranks of gnarled oaks, but even looking for signs as he was, Owaine would have missed it.

As the sun neared its height on the second day of his search, Owaine suddenly walked into an invisible wall with an audible *thump*. At the same moment, a pair of invisible hands grasped his temples and turned his head gently but firmly to the right. *"Look!"* a half-familiar voice said, seeming to come from the air in front of him.

"Cataigh?" Owaine called to the air, but no answer came. The hands held his head and Owaine squinted. In a field on the forest side of the road, there were marks in the grass. The invisible hands released him, and Owaine stumbled off the road, trying to see the field clearly. This was evidently a campsite: wagons had been pulled off the road here and the remnants of black, stone-encircled campfires marred the lush grass. The deepest layer of ashes were still slightly warm—given the weather, they could have been a day, or perhaps two, old. None of that, though, was a guarantee that these were the same people who had Meriel. Owaine let the power of the clochmion drift out around the area. Nothing came back to him. If she'd been here, she was still too far away for him to find. Some huge herd had crossed here as well— the earth was pockmarked with the imprints of hooves twice the size of Owaine's hands, coming from the direction of the forest and moving over the road toward the northern hills.

He wandered about the old campsite. A few shards of broken pottery had been abandoned in the heather; the pieces were like nothing Owaine had ever seen. He turned them over in his hand, squinting at the lines of blue-green glaze that marked the fired clay.

"They're the ones you call 'Taisteal,' Bráthair Lost." Owaine glanced up hurriedly to find the Bunús Muintir from the night before watching, leaning against the nearest oak while the squirrel Léimard clucked and fussed in the branch above him. "My people call them Corrthónach, the Restless People. They wandered here even before you Daoine came."

"Cataigh? Did you . . . ?" Owaine put his hands to his own head and turned it as the unseen hands had done on the road.

The Bunús grinned and pushed himself erect. Owaine realized that the Bunús was short, the crown of his head no higher than Owaine's shoulders—somehow he'd seemed huge last night. The man came forward, a large staff of yew in his hand. "Aye, I did that. And I'm pleased to see you remember my name."

"Aye," Owaine told him and plucked at the clothing he wore. "I wanted to thank you for this."

The staff prodded the ashes of the campfire, sending a pout of ash swirling into the breeze. "Then reward me for my efforts. Tell me why the Taisteal would come all the way down to the sea to this lonely road when the nearest village is a full two days' walk north on the coast. Tell me why they met a ship that flew the flag of the Rí Ard, and why several tiarna with their clochs na thintrí rode with the Taisteal as far as this place before leaving them and riding on that way alone." Cataigh jabbed the sooty end of his staff eastward. When Owaine hesitated, Cataigh frowned at him. "This is my place to protect, Owaine Geraghty. If you have an answer, I would hear it. I could have as easily let the forest take you last night as helped you."

Owaine had listened to the tale with increasing certainty. Dhegli had brought him to the right place, and it seemed he had managed to find the correct path. "The ship and the tiarna you saw brought a young woman here—a bantiarna—against her will. At least that's what I suspect happened," Owaine told him. "Tell me, when the tiarna left, did they have a woman with them?"

Cataigh shook his head. "It was late afternoon when they rode off. There wasn't a woman with them; I would have known. The Corrthónach—the Taisteal—stayed the rest of the night, then went eastward in the morning. There were women enough in the clan."

Owaine let out a sigh. "Then she's with the Taisteal for some reason."

"Perhaps." Cataigh shrugged. He brushed back his long, bedraggled hair. His heavy-boned face looked back toward the forest. "Why is the young bantiarna so important? Is she your lover?"

Owaine could feel heat on his cheeks. "No," he answered quickly. "I mean, I could wish so, but . . ." He stopped awkwardly. "She's the Banrion MacEagan's daughter."

Cataigh blinked. "The daughter of the First Holder, of Jenna Aoire?" he asked, his face turned up to Owaine's, his eyes narrowing and his head cocked to one side. Owaine remembered the tales of the First Holder, recalling that she had stayed with the Bunús Muintir for a time after she found Lámh Shábhála, and Cataigh was one of the Protectors.

"Aye," Owaine answered. "Though the Banrion's name is now MacEagan. Meriel is her only child."

The man hissed between yellowed teeth like a boiling teakettle. "I should have realized . . . This Meriel has hair as red as a cloudy sunset, is perhaps as tall as me and as thin as a sapling. And she holds a cloch." He paused, as if thinking of something. "A strange stone, that one."

"The person you describe sounds like her," Owaine said, puzzled, "except for the cloch . . . As far as I know she doesn't have a cloch na thintrí."

Cataigh didn't seem to be listening to him. "I must tell Keira; she will want to know this." He nodded as if to some inner voice. "I did well to listen to my heart when I saw you," he said. "You bring interesting news with you, Bráthair Lost."

"Who's Keira?" Owaine asked, but Cataigh was staring upward, sniffing as if scenting the wind.

"There will be mage-lights late tonight," the Bunús Muintir said. "And tomorrow will bring rain." He looked at Owaine with eyes the color of soil. "I'd take you with me, but your way lies along this road, I think, and not yet to the south. May the Greatness walk with you, and give you Her blessing." He shook his head. "Tell me, Bráthair Lost—how many crows are there on that tree over there?" He pointed to a tree fifty or so strides away; Owaine could see the tree and—barely— the limb, but though he tried, he couldn't distinguish any birds in the blur. "I thought so," Cataigh said. He gave a sigh. "Come, Léimard . . ." The squirrel, which had been foraging in the mistletoe curling around an oak's trunk, scampered over to him and clambered up his leg to his shoulder. He spoke to the squirrel, a soft whisper in words Owaine couldn't understand. The squirrel chattered, almost angrily it seemed to Owaine, then when Cataigh spoke again, skittered down Cataigh's body and up Owaine's to perch on Owaine's left shoulder. He looked at the squirrel, which was staring back at him.

"The squirrel has far sharper eyes than Bráthair Lost," Cataigh said. "And Léimard knows what you're searching for. He'll stay with you for a time." Cataigh seemed amused. "Unless you think a squirrel is a poor companion," he finished.

"No," Owaine said. He glanced at Léimard's furry face, in focus because it was so close to him. "I don't think that . . . I just don't understand . . ." He looked back at Cataigh, but the man was gone. He caught a glimpse of the Bunús Muintir walking toward the forest, already almost among the trees.

"Wait!" Owaine called after him. "Where are you going?"

"To where you couldn't walk alone," Cataigh answered without looking back, his words coming back to Owaine on the breeze. "The roads are the way of the Daoine, not the Bunús Muintir. Perhaps we'll find each other again where the oaks and the roads meet, or perhaps not. Take good care of Léimard." His voice drifted away as he walked between two oak trunks. In Owaine's fuzzy vision, the man seemed to merge with green-brown shadows under the leaves.

"Cataigh!" he called again, but he couldn't see him anymore. "Wait! I still have questions to ask you!" There may have been a shifting of light where he'd gone, but then even that was lost.

21

Cailin of the
Healing Touch

As the last of the villagers were wandering away from the encampment, Sevei escorted Meriel to Nico's wagon.

Though she watched his face closely as Sevei told him about the incident with the girl, Meriel wasn't sure what Nico was thinking. The Clannhri sighed and grumbled through the story, rubbing his stubbled jowls and fidgeting on the other side of the little table in the wagon that also served as his home. Keara, Nico's wife, chatted with one of her daughters, sitting on the bed at the front of the wagon as several grandchildren ran about underfoot. "So our little Cailin has a clochmion," Nico said finally, grabbing one of the granddaughters and putting the child on his lap. "And not just any clochmion, but a healing stone. Damn Tiarna Mac Ard for handing me such trouble without telling me," he finished, though he said it without the heat that Meriel might have expected, and if he didn't quite smile neither did he frown.

"We won't be able to keep this quiet, Clannhri," Sevei said. "It's already too late for that. The woman has no doubt already been telling all her friends about the healer in our camp. They're probably all in the tavern now discussing it."

"Which means that tomorrow morning, anyone with anything from a hangover to the Bloody Cough is going to be coming around looking for Cailin of the Healing

Touch," Nico sniffed. He ruffled the head of the grand-daughter and set her down with a kiss. "Well, it's done and can't be undone, so we might as well gain what we can from it." He gazed at Meriel the way he might examine a bag of coins. She could see him toting up her value in his head. "Let me think on this. The girl will do what I say?"

Meriel started to protest, but Sevei kicked her ankle sharply under the table, causing Meriel to gasp and close her mouth. "She will, Clannhri," Sevei answered, "or she'll answer to me."

"You can't do this," Meriel said, glaring once at Sevei. "I'm not one of your clan performers, doing tricks for the peasants or bartering worthless merchandise."

"No," Nico nodded. "You're a hostage we're holding for Tiarna Mac Ard, and the merchandise *you* have around your neck is potentially worth more than you are as a hostage. I'd remember that if I were you." He shrugged. "If you'd rather be treated as an unruly hostage, well, that can be arranged. It doesn't matter to me. In fact, just keeping you hidden and quiet when we're in one of the villages would be simpler and more profitable. I could take the clochmion from you and sell it— the selling would have to be done carefully, but when we reach one of the cities there will be a surplus of Riocha who would be *extremely* happy to buy a clochmion from us. None of them would care or ask questions about where or how we obtained it or what might have happened to its previous Holder. Of course, you'd have to bear the pain of losing the stone. But if that's your preference . . ."

He cocked his head toward her, his eyebrows lifting in question. Meriel felt a cold finger brush her spine and her hand went involuntarily to Treoraí's Heart under her léine. "I won't deceive anyone, Clannhri." She tried to keep her voice steady. If he had made a motion toward her, she would have bolted. "I'm not a thief and liar like you."

"Oh, I know," Nico answered. "You're completely

honest with everyone. That's why you wear your cloch-mion so openly. That's why you ran away when you gave your word to Sevei that you wouldn't—you think I didn't know about that? That's why you answer to the name we've given you." The mockery was so gently and sympathetically spoken that it took a moment for the sting to color Meriel's cheeks. Keara and the daughter chuckled at the front of the wagon.

"The trick," Nico said to Meriel, "is to let those who come to you deceive themselves, and that's easier to learn than you might think—your mam is likely as good at it as we Taisteal: most successful Riocha are. You'll find that it's a rare person who actually wants the raw truth. Most of us would much rather believe a comforting half-truth or outright lie, if it matches what we want to believe." He paused. "Just like you want to believe that someone will find and rescue you tomorrow or perhaps the next day."

Máister Kirwan and my mam know that I have the clochmion. If they heard of a True Healer traveling in Talamh an Ghlas, perhaps they'd wonder if it was me. . . . The thought came to her suddenly, giving her a brief moment of hope. The realization must have shown on her face, for Nico smiled. "Aye, now you see, I would be wanting to believe the same thing in your place," he said. "But I'd also be making certain that until such a rescue actually occurred I was as comfortable as I could be, even if that meant cooperating with those who held me. You should make the same decision." He raised an eyebrow in question.

Meriel bit her lower lip, looking away from him. *Do this and be free, or refuse and be a prisoner.* "I'll do it," she said. "I don't like it, but I'll do it."

"Good," Nico said, as if he'd expected no other answer. "Now, it's time to rest and think about what we'll do tomorrow. Dye her hair, Sevei, so that those who come tomorrow won't see the red. Then you two should get some supper and sleep. Tomorrow will be . . . interesting."

As they left the wagon and went over to the cook fire, Sevei nudged Meriel. "I think Nico likes you," she said.

Meriel found that she wanted to believe that, also, because her well-being depended on it.

The mage-lights swarmed in the sky late that night and Meriel's clochmion called to her, yearning to be filled again with the power. Sevei woke at the same time Meriel did. "Come on," she said, nodding to the tent flap.

They went outside. The lights played over the roofs of the village and across the field, waves of color that washed over the land and vanished again while the curtains and streamers swayed in the night sky just below the gathering clouds. Nico was sitting outside his wagon with Keara and a few others of the clan, watching the mage-lights. He nodded to Sevei as they came out from the tent, and she guided Meriel behind another of the wagons where they were hidden from the village, though not from Nico, who stared curiously from his perch. "Go on," Sevei said. "Do what you need to do."

Meriel loosened the neck of her tunic and brought out the clochmion, holding it in her right hand as she lifted it like an offering to the sky, opening her mind as Máister Kirwan and Siúr Meagher had taught her. The mage-lights circled above, snaking down to wrap about her wrist; with their touch, Meriel could feel the web of clochs na thintrí throughout the land, many of them replenishing themselves in the same energy. Out there in the distance, Lámh Shábhála was feeding on the mage-lights, a huge presence like a mountain glimpsed on the horizon. Meriel wondered if her mam could feel Treoraí's Heart, and if she knew it was Meriel.

Meriel sighed as the power of the mage-lights filled the cloch, relief and pleasure flooding through her, a strange warmth surrounding her so that she seemed to breathe charged air.

A hand touched her shoulder; she glanced around at

Sevei, who was staring at Meriel's light-wrapped hand. "It's wondrous," she whispered. "Does it . . . does it feel as beautiful as it looks?"

The cloch's reservoir of power was full, and Meriel reluctantly let her hand loosen around it. Tendrils of glowing color lingered for a moment, then drifted away. "Aye," she said. "I don't know that I can describe the feeling. It's like . . . when I've been with . . ."

Meriel stopped. She remembered Dhegli and the feel of his body against hers.

Sevei gave her a twisted half smile. "Ah. I think I understand," she said. Her hand drifted slowly down Meriel's back and then away. Meriel turned toward Sevei and, in the shimmer of the mage-lights, saw a sadness in the woman's eyes that surprised her. Meriel started to slip Treoraí's Heart back under her tunic, but Sevei caught her hand. "Look," the Taisteal woman said. Meriel glanced down. The faint scars that snaked around her hand to the wrist were more defined now, and faint traces of them could be seen on the skin halfway to her elbow. "The cloudmages get those marks, I know," Sevei said. "I've seen them on a few of the most powerful Riocha, those with the Clochs Mór. But they don't go so far up the arm, and are usually fainter than these. I've never noticed that you can see any markings on anyone with a clochmion." Sevei's gaze went from Meriel's hand to her face. She leaned in, very close to her. "I hear that the First Holder's arm is marked all the way to the shoulder because of the power of her stone. Is that true, Cailin?"

Sevei's eyes held her. Meriel nodded. "But this is a clochmion," she said. "That's what Máister Kirwan told me. I'm certain that's what Máister Kirwan *believes,* also. They wouldn't have given me anything else. No matter who I was." But she started to wonder. It's also *Treoraí's Heart, a life gift from the Créneach to the First Holder.* She tried to keep that thought from showing on her face.

Sevei's stare held her for a moment longer. Then she released Meriel's hand. The night air was cold on her

skin and Meriel rubbed at the hand. The scars had faded
somewhat. She could still see the marks on her hand,
but the scarring on her arm was faint enough to be
unnoticed.

Sevei seemed to be debating within herself. She was
looking at Nico, who was now staring at the smoke curling up from the Taisteal's campfire. Sevei blinked heavily and rubbed at her eyes with her sleeve. "Come on,
Cailin," Sevei said. "We still have work to do tonight,
and we're both already tired. We'll have a busy morning."

It started raining before dawn. The rain pattered on the
tent like a thousand fingers and droplets fell from the
patches and tears in the fabric. Outside the tent, Meriel
could hear the sounds of the Taisteal breaking down the
encampment in the steady rainfall and preparing to
leave. Several villagers were huddled outside as well; she
could hear them complaining softly to one another about
the foul weather. "Remember what Nico said," Sevei
told her, "and let me do most of the talking this time—
later on you'll be able to do it yourself. Right now, follow my lead as best you can."

She went to the tent flap, untied it, and motioned for
the group to enter. They did, three men and four
women: ducking their heads, shaking the raindrops from
cloaks and hats and gazing around them, all of them
bowing their heads politely to Meriel as she sat with
hands clasped on the stool Sevei had covered in red
cloth. The hood of Meriel's clóca was down, and her
newly-dyed hair gleamed as black as a moonless sky.

"You need to know that Cailin is very tired," Sevei
said over the drumming of rain. "The Mother-Creator's
touch isn't gentle, as you can imagine, and she used up
most of her healing strength yesterday with the little girl,
who was near death. We mortal folk find it difficult to
hold a god's power in our fragile bodies. You also must

understand that the choice to heal or not to heal isn't Cailin's, but the Mother-Creator's—Cailin is but Her vessel. Because this is the gift of the Mother-Creator, we ask you for nothing but what you wish to give freely." A few of the people grinned at that, and Sevei held up a forefinger. "Only remember that the Mother-Creator watches what you choose to do for Cailin, and it's Her favor—coming through Cailin—that you ask for."

The grins faded as quickly as they'd come. They stared at Meriel while Sevei talked, making her squirm uncomfortably on the stool and look down at her own hands. Sevei had covered both her hands with fingerless gloves so that the scars of the mage-lights on the right hand couldn't be seen. When Sevei had finished, Meriel motioned to one of the men to approach, as Sevei had instructed her beforehand. He hobbled forward leaning on a crutch, his right foot swaddled in thick bandages. Meriel's left hand rested over the hidden clochmion while her right took the hand he offered to her: blue-veined, callused, and thick-skinned, crosshatched with fine wrinkles, the tip of his middle finger missing from the first joint—the hands of a field worker. She glanced at Sevei, who nodded.

"How can I help you?" she asked.

"It's my foot," the man said, the words punctuated by a grimace of pain. "The gout is in the joints and sometimes I can barely stand to walk on it. I can't work much anymore, and the pain's been getting worse lately."

Meriel slid from the stool and crouched down in front of the man, running her hand softly along the bandaged foot. She could feel the injury, throbbing as her fingers brushed her cloch, and with the touch came faint traces of the man's thoughts: curiosity about whether she'd be able to help him, a rather minor ache as he flexed his toes under the bandages, and—shockingly—a disturbing surge of lust as his gaze traveled her body. She stood quickly, her face reddening as she nodded to the man and she sat again on the stool. "Let me see the others," she said to Sevei.

"We'll keep the group small, and Sevei will choose them—she knows how to do that," Nico had said. "Since you can truly heal only one, see them all first. At least a few of them will have phantom complaints or illnesses that will go away on their own. Just your touch and their belief will heal them, at least for a day or so. Beyond that . . ." He'd shrugged. "Hopefully you know the cloch's limitations and yours. You can choose to perform whatever healing you want, or even none at all."

One by one, they paraded forward: the woman with complaints of chronic back pain (though the cloch seemed to find nothing at all wrong within the woman, and her thoughts were strange and wild); a young wife whose three pregnancies had ended in miscarriages, and who grieved so deeply inside that Meriel found herself wanting to weep; a man whose broken arm had been badly set and was now unusable; the elderly widow whose skin and face were covered with warts and growths; and finally the man troubled by frequent kidney stones—she could feel the memory of the stones as he spoke of them, and the horrible pain of them until they passed.

She touched them all. The woman with back pain straightened as soon as Meriel stroked her back, letting out a shout. The man with gout was standing without putting any weight on his cane and leering at her. The young wife and the man with kidney stones were smiling at her expectantly. The man with the badly-set arm and the well-warted woman alone seemed disappointed, and Meriel avoided looking at them, not wanting to find their gazes on her. She heard Sevei usher them all outside. ". . . I know the weather is terrible, but wait a moment; I'll see if Cailin wishes to see any of you separately. Nico, our Clannhri, is just outside; you may give him any offering you wish. . . ."

Sevei ushered them out, then closed the tent's flap and came over to Meriel. "This is too hard, Sevei," Meriel said. Her hand was on her breast where Treoraí's Heart burned. She could sense that it wanted to be used, yet the responsibility weighed on her. *You can't fix everything or everyone. Only one or two, here and there* . . . "I don't know if I can do this. What if . . . what if the cloch only helps for a little bit? What if that little girl from last night gets her cough back in a few days, or if it's even worse afterward . . ." She stopped, imagining Siúr Meagher's hands turning arthritic and clawed, or perhaps worse.

"If that's what happens, well, we'll be that many days down the road. Nico will keep us moving faster now, with Cailin of the Healing Touch traveling with us." She pursed her lips in a wry smile. "The Taisteal are used to that kind of reputation following behind us—people sometimes regret the bargains they made. We don't mind as long as their remorse can't catch us. Why do you worry about the healing failing?—do you *know* that's what happens?"

Meriel shook her head. "No. I don't . . . I don't know enough at all."

Sevei took a step to her and put her hands on her shoulders. "This is hard for you," she said, "and it'll only get harder. The word will spread, as fast as we can travel. Faster. There will be more people coming to see you in each village, and when we reach Áth Iseal and Lár Bhaile, well, we'll need to be very careful. But by then, you'll be used to the routine, and it will all be easier. So . . . do you want to call one of them back?"

"I don't know . . . They're all hurting in one way or another."

"Cailin, it doesn't matter. Half of them already think they've been cured or that at least there's a chance of it. The woman with warts—if the cloch won't help her, I can tell her that you've asked Keara to fix her a potion."

"And will *that* help her?"

Sevei lifted a shoulder. "It won't hurt her. She might even enjoy the effects, since Keara uses the poteen she brews. What about the man with the bad arm?—that would have an immediate, visual impact. Can the cloch help him?"

"I think so, but . . ."

"But what? You want one of the others? None of them? Tell me."

"I don't *know* . . ." The last word was nearly a wail. Who should she heal? For the first time, she realized that holding a gift like Treoraí's Heart could cut both ways, and that made her think of her mam with Lámh Shábhála. *She must wrestle with this dilemma every day, having to make choices about how to wield her power, knowing those choices will inevitably affect other people's lives and might even lead to their deaths. How can she do that? How does she find the strength and certainty?*

Sevei had crouched down in front of her. She felt the woman's thumbs brush away the tears that had started from her eyes. "You have a good heart, Cailin. The heart of a True Healer—I'd say that the cloch chose a good Holder for itself. Look at this as a chance to use it for people who ordinarily don't have access to this kind of resource. Not for the Riocha, not for the privileged ones who hold the clochs and power but the ones who get their hands dirty and who live short lives full of toil and poverty."

"And in return you take what little they have."

Sevei shook her head. "Even we Taisteal have to make a living, and we take no more than they can afford. When we get to a real town, when the Riocha and the céili giallnai and the rich landowners come around, *then* see what Nico charges." She brushed away Meriel's tears again, softly, and stood. "Who do you want to see? I need to know now."

There was no good choice, yet she remembered the look on the young woman's face, the sorrow and grief that aged her as she spoke about the unborn children she'd lost. If the cloch could help her, then it would also bring new life to the world. "The one who miscarries. I think I—the cloch, that is—can help her."

"I'll send her to you." The woman's gaze was full of empathy. "There was a reason you were given the clochmion, Cailin. There was a reason you were placed here. Maybe this is the reason—so you'd start to use the stone."

"Is that what you saw in the cards last night?"

Sevei's face went guarded. "Aye," she said. "I saw that."

"And what else?"

"You don't believe in the cards. You saw what I do with them; there's no magic there."

"Tell me what they said. Afterward. Will you do that? After I use the cloch. Please."

After a moment of silence, Sevei sighed. "All right," she said. "I'll send the young woman in."

Sevei fiddled with the cards, sitting across the table from Meriel. She gazed at the colorful pasteboard. "I'm a fraud," Sevei told Meriel. "Now my mam . . . she was a true reader, when she wanted to be. Oh, she rarely did that with our customers; for them, she did exactly what I do—she gave them the reading they wanted to hear and no more. But when she took the cards in truth and placed the array . . ." Sevei sighed. "The cards would tell her things, things she couldn't otherwise know."

"The future?" Meriel asked. "Truly?"

Sevei shook her head. "Only Fiodóir the Fate-Weaver truly knows your future. The cards—if you believe in them—can show the shape of what's possible and what's likely. They can indicate where the path you're treading is likely to lead and act as a guide or a warning, but you can still choose to change your direction and your fate. Mam could see clearly through the cards, though. Nico says she was better with them than anyone he'd ever known. Sometimes she scared people with what she told them; I know she did me, more than once." She set the card down and placed her hands on top of them, looking at Meriel. "I don't have her gift."

Meriel waited. Sevei licked dry lips and her forefinger prowled the ragged edge of the cards. "I know what it's like not to share your mam's gift," Meriel told her. "I understand that very well."

Sevei smiled sadly at that. "I suspect you do. Yet sometimes, every once in while . . ."

"Like last night?"

A nod. "Like last night. I touched them and . . . and the cards seemed . . ." She lifted her hands, let them drop again. ". . . right," she finished. "I can't explain it any better than that. I could feel the truth of them *here*." She shook black hair away from her eyes and touched her hand to her forehead. She gave Meriel a fleeting smile. "Or maybe I was just tired and influenced by what I'd seen you do. You told me that you don't believe in the ability of the cards, so why should you care what I think I saw?"

"I *shouldn't* care," Meriel answered. "But . . . I'm curious, that's all. No, I don't believe it, but I still want to know. And you promised."

A laugh. "Aye, I did." Sevei took up the cards. "Here," she said, and spread them out as they had been last night. She touched the card in the top of the array: a red-haired young woman surrounded by several unsheathed swords held by skeletons. "That's you: in the midst of strife, surrounded by forces you can't control. There, next to you—that's the Tiarna Mac Ard, your uncle; you see, he's also sword-caught and the coin cards flank him also, the needs of the rich. Toward the center of the spiral is the Clannhra—what you would call a Banrion. One of the most powerful of the cards and, I think, your mam. She sits by the Traveler, which means she is closer to you than you believe." She pointed to the line of cards above the spiral. "These are the forces who would help you: the Blind Man, along with three cards which are all staves—those represent natural forces. That influence is unusually strong, and I don't quite know how to interpret it. And these"— Sevei touched the lower line of cards, "—are the forces that you see as opposing you: the Mage and the Single Sword wielded by the king."

Meriel was already shaking her head. "How is this any different than what you did for those who came here last night? You could say the cards mean anything you want them to mean and I can't say differently."

"That's true," Sevei agreed, nodding. Her gaze came up from the cards and found Meriel, challenging. "Do you want me to stop?"

Meriel looked away. "No."

A nod. Sevei's finger touched the cards at the center of the spiral. "This is the heart of it," she said. There were three cards in the center of the array, two placed side by side, the last placed horizontally across the others. The bottom cards were obscured; on one, Meriel could see the face of a dark-haired woman holding a card with a strange symbol aloft over her head. A skeletal figure in a cowl dominated on the other, the skull grinning obscenely. And the top card . . . On the painted surface was a seal—a Saimhóir, with azure highlights in the ink-blackened body, but as Meriel looked more closely at the card she realized that the face of the seal was that of a human woman and she was pulling herself onto the rocks with arms and hands rather than flippers.

"The Changeling," Sevei said. Meriel felt her face go hot. The scale of Bradán an Chumhacht in her head seemed to burn on her forehead. "The Changeling sits atop the place of sacrifice, and that alters the meaning of everything else in the reading. You believe that the ones set against you are your uncle and the Rí Ard, but the Changeling says that you look the wrong way. The reading indicates that it's those you love you should fear the most, for they hold the greatest danger for you."

"That makes no sense."

Sevei's face seemed to close up, her lips tightening and eyes narrowing. "It's what the cards say. I didn't choose them; you cut and shuffled the deck."

"And that's all? What of these?" Meriel pointed to the two cards underneath the Changeling. The dark-haired woman holding the card, the grinning skeleton leering at her . . .

Sevei shook her head. "I won't talk of them. They don't concern you."

Meriel stared at the woman, who gazed steadily back at her, almost defiantly. Yet, somewhere underneath, there was something else in those eyes . . . "How can they not concern me if this is my reading?" Meriel asked. A sudden realization struck her then. "The woman with black hair . . . That's *you*, isn't it?"

In answer, Sevei swept up the cards and shuffled them quickly so that the array was lost. "I shouldn't have done this," she said. "I told you I don't have my mam's skill. I'm just what you suspect: a charlatan."

"Sevei." The Taisteal stopped shuffling the cards and looked at Meriel. "What happened to your mam?"

Sevei took in a breath that whistled slightly between her teeth. "She died," she answered curtly. "A long time ago."

"How?"

"That's none of your business."

A glimmering suspicion came to Meriel as she watched Sevei handling the cards . . . an inkling born in the obvious reverence she had for them. "I can guess," Meriel said. "Your mam saw something in the cards . . . a foretelling . . . an event that concerned you." Meriel watched Sevei as she spoke, watched the way the muscles along her jaw slid under the skin, the way she breathed, the slight widening of the eyes. "Or something that concerned *both* of you. That's why you say you don't have your mam's skill with the cards—not because you don't, but because you're afraid that you do."

Sevei's face had gone stiff, her eyes almost angry. "You've learned my tricks far better than I expected, Cailin. You're good at this. A natural. Maybe I'll just let you read the fortunes for the fools in the next town." The woman put the cards back in their box and shut the lid. "We need to get ready to leave here," she said abruptly, getting up from the table. "We have a long ride yet today."

22

Other Places Revisited

THE FALLS of the Duán roared with white rage, the water foaming and spraying on its way down to Lough Lár far below. Rainbows shimmered in the mist. The lough stretched out blue in the distance; as Doyle turned to watch Edana's entourage approach, he could see the checkerboard pattern of fields near the High Road and beyond them, the somber presence of Doire Coill, one of the ancient woods.

Tuath Gabair: this was the home of his ancestors, the land where his da had been born and lived, the land where he'd been conceived. Every time he was here, he thought he could feel the very soil calling to him. He felt content but for one minor annoyance . . .

"I hear them talking about me behind my back. I hear what they call me," Thady MacCoughlin said loudly.

Doyle arched an eyebrow as he watched Edana's entourage disappear behind the trees at the last bend approaching the falls. He could hear Thady shuffling his feet alongside him. He forced himself not to look at the boy—that's all he was, Doyle had decided; a stupid boy, even if he was actually a year older than Doyle. Thady had become increasingly tiresome on the long, hard ride across half of Talamh an Ghlas and what little patience and gratitude Doyle had for the young man had long since evaporated. He would be glad to get rid of him. "And what is it that they call you?" he asked Thady, although he knew perfectly well. He just wanted to watch Thady's face as he said the word.

Thady's lips pursed and his eyes narrowed. He looked as if he'd just swallowed a fish bone. "Oathbreaker," he spat out. " 'Oathbreaker MacCoughlin.' They'd stop saying that if you told them."

"Would they?" Doyle asked gently. "These are my peers. My friends. Not my servants. Why would they listen to me?"

"Of course they would," Thady answered. "You're the fiancé of the Rí Ard's daughter. They *have* to listen to you."

"And now *you're* a tiarna, just as you wanted," Doyle responded. "You're one of them. Why don't you tell them yourself? Inform them that you take offense at the name and demand satisfaction for your honor if they don't immediately apologize. If you'd like, I'll lend you my own sword."

The expression on Thady's face was impressive: horror mixed with a slowly-dawning comprehension. His lower lip trembled. "This isn't what I wanted. You said I'd be a tiarna, that I'd have an estate. . . ."

"And you have the scroll from the Rí Ard that names you as Tiarna MacCoughlin, and you will have your own land: on the Outer Island of Tuath Locha Lein. In fact, you'll be leaving for there today." Doyle nodded to the approaching riders. "This is where we part ways, Tiarna— you to your new home and me to Dún Laoghaire."

"Locha Lein? The Outer Island?" The protest was a squeal. "But that's so far away, and the Outer Island's nothing but stones."

Doyle glared at Thady, his hand brushing his cloch, and the boy shrank away. "Aye, 'tis far away, and you'll have to work hard to pull a living from the stones and pay your bóruma to Rí Locha Lein, and the people you rule will call you 'Oathbreaker' behind your back and maybe even to your face until the day you die and for-ever afterward." Doyle snorted mocking laughter. "Did you think being Riocha solves everything? Didn't you see that a tiarna might wear better clothes and eat better than the common rabble, but there are still struggles and responsibilities in our lives? If you manage to prosper, MacCoughlin, maybe your children or their children will lose the 'Oathbreaker' part of your name. But you . . . you will always be MacCoughlin the Oathbreaker and no Riocha will ever trust you completely because of what you've done."

"You didn't tell me!" Thady half-shouted. His face contorted, he reached out toward Doyle, twisting a hand in the cloth of Doyle's clóca. "I didn't know it would be this way!"

"No, I didn't tell you," Doyle agreed quietly, glancing down at the fisted hand, then to Thady's flushed, angry features. "But you *would* have known it if your greed had let you think at all. So listen to me now. You will let go of me and apologize, or you'll be forever known as MacCoughlin the One-Hand, as well."

Thady blinked into Doyle's flat, unblinking stare. Slowly, his fist loosened, dropping back to his side, and his face changed. Doyle saw a bland and careful subservience slip over his features, the familiar mask the boy must have worn all his years. "I'm . . . I'm sorry, Tiarna Mac Ard," he said. "I lost control of myself."

"Good. It's forgotten." Doyle looked past Thady to the road. Edana and four other riders had come into view again, dust rising from under their horses' hooves. They were riding hard and fast, and that caused Doyle to wonder. "Go see Tiarna Salia; he also has holdings in Locha Lein and will be accompanying you along with his gardai. You'll leave within a stripe's time, as soon as we break camp."

With that, Doyle strode away from Thady, ignoring the mutter of veiled protest. He lifted a hand in greeting to Edana as she rode into the encampment. He watched her jump lithely down from her sorrel gelding, unconsciously acrobatic, and he smiled, feeling the affectionate, eager glow that seeing her always created in him.

Doyle had no illusion that love was necessary in a marriage, but when it was there, such a union was at its most powerful, and he had long ago found that he enjoyed power.

"Maidin maith, my sweet," he called out in greeting, holding out his hand for her to take. "What a surprise. I didn't expect to see you until we returned to Dún Laoghaire. But I'm glad you came; it will make the rest of the trip much more pleasant." She took his hand, but though she smiled at him there was something in her gaze that made him stop. "What's wrong, Edana?"

"Come look at the falls with me," she said. "Away from the others."

He led her away from the encampment and up the path to the overlook, passing Thady on the way without a glance. With the spray moistening their faces and beading in their hair, he heard Edana sigh. "I came to bring you back to Dún Laoghaire as quickly as possible, Doyle," she said. "It's Da. The news isn't good, I'm afraid. He's taken a sudden turn and his health is failing quickly. The healers are thinking that he is now lying on his death bed. It's possible he may already be gone even as we're speaking here. I would have sent a messenger to tell you, but I wanted . . . I needed . . ." Doyle heard the break in her voice. She was crying now, openly, the spray from the falls mixing with her tears.

"Edana . . ." He took her in his arms, holding her close. Of the two children of Nevan O Liathain, she had been the closest to her da, especially after Enean's accident. He could feel her tremble, then take a long, shuddering breath and lift her face again. When he looked, tears still glistened in her eyes but her mouth was set firmly.

"I know what he'd say," Edana told him. "He'd tell me to grieve later and do what I need to do to take his place," she said. "And I will. We need to hurry back to Dún Laoghaire. This changes everything—all the plans we made. Your niece . . . ?"

"She's safe for the moment—where I can find her when I need her. And by now, my sister should have received my note. As to what she'll do then . . ."

Edana shuddered. "That's exactly what scares me, Doyle. Everything's different now. We thought we had months yet to play this game and we don't. We thought we would have the Rí Ard's authority behind us and now we may not. Only the Mother knows how the Ríthe will react if Da does pass, and we're not ready. All the old alliances and agreements die with my da . . ." She didn't need to finish the thought; they both knew. When the Rí Ard died, the bloody clawing and fighting among the claimants to the throne would begin, and it could easily spill into physical bloodshed—that had happened far too often in Daoine history.

"This will work out. It's our time. It's *your* time," Doyle whispered to her. His lips brushed the nape of her neck, gently kissing there. "Just remember that. It's your time. No matter what Jenna does or what the Ríthe think or who else wants to be Ard. We can handle all of that and my sister too. Together, we can handle it all. . . ."

Máister Kirwan started to hand the roll of parchment to Jenna, but she shook her head. "Read it aloud for me, Mundy." A small, wry smile touched her lips. "One thing the Order never could quite drum into me was my letters."

"It certainly wasn't for lack of trying," Mundy answered. He pulled at the ribbon and the wax seal broke. He unrolled the parchment on his desk and smoothed it down, placing an inkwell and blotter at the top to hold it down. "It's from Doyle Mac Ard," he said.

Jenna grimaced. "I guessed that much. This whole situation has the Mac Ard smell about it. Go on. I'm ready."

Mundy took a breath. He began to read:
My Dearest Sister:

*As you've undoubtedly guessed by now, I have Meriel.
Actually, I don't physically have her with me, since cloch
lore and the Rí Ard's experience both tell me that Lámh
Shábhála might be able to find me too easily—so coming
after me directly won't work, Jenna. Meriel's in good
hands where I can reach her. Don't, by the way, be
tempted to come after me just in anger; since the people
holding Meriel have instructions that if they don't hear
from me at certain prescribed times, they are to kill her.
I assure you that those instructions will be carried out if
you interfere. But then you're already familiar with the
truth of that type of threat, aren't you?*

*You know what I want: Lámh Shábhála. I expect that's
already occurred to you, since you're hardly stupid. I
want what should have been mine in the first place, and
I'll have it or you'll lose the only other thing that's precious to you.*

*Here's how this must happen: we'll meet on Inishduán
on the 7th day of Straightwood, the day of the Festival
of Láfuacht. You used that island to give my da's body
back to my mam; it seems appropriate that I use it now
to get the cloch. You'll come alone except for the crew of
the ship that will bring you home—I know you could get
to the island through the power of the cloch, but you
won't have it afterward for the return, will you? I assure
you that I won't be alone, that there will be enough
Clochs Mór there to overcome Lámh Shábhála should
you decide to resist. If I find that there are cloudmages
with Clochs Mor with you—and the Order of Gabair has
slow magics that can tell me—I'll immediately send word
to have Meriel killed and no matter what the outcome of
our battle, you'll have lost her. But assuming you follow
my instructions, once I have the cloch I'll have Meriel
sent safely back to Inish Thuaidh. I give you my word
on that.*

*I'm sure this all sounds familiar to you. Mam told me
how Árón Ó Dochartaigh tried a similar ploy with you
once. I assure you that I won't make Ó Dochartaigh's
mistake. You have a simple, clear choice, Jenna: you may*

*have Lámh Shábhála or you may have your daughter.
Not both. If you choose Lámh Shábhála, then I'll know
when you fail to arrive at Inishduán . . . and I hope you
can live with yourself afterward. As to the pain you'll
suffer after you give me Lámh Shábhála . . . I have no
sympathy for you whatsoever. All I have to do is imagine
the pain my da felt when you killed him, or our mam's
grief and madness afterward; your suffering will be simple
justice for that.*

*Of course, should you make any aggressive moves on
the Rí Ard or the Tuatha of Talamh an Ghlas before we
meet in Inishduán, I'll take that as a signal that you prefer
the cloch to your daughter and will take appropriate action. I'll make sure, however, to show you the same great
kindness you showed our mam and return Meriel's dead
body to you. . . .*

Mundy looked up from the parchment. Jenna was
standing near the window, her face nearly as pale as the
thin white clouds masking the sun. Her scarred right
hand was clutched around Lámh Shábhála, the knuckles
white with tension. She stared outward, unblinking, hardly
seeming to even breathe. When she did draw in a breath,
it was half sob. "Doyle's right," she said quietly. "I
knew. I knew what he would say."

"Today's the twenty-third of Wideleaf," he reminded
her. "That means he intends to meet you at Inishdúan
in twelve days."

She stared.

"What are you going to do, Jenna?"

She turned to Mundy. He saw her face, ashen and
almost skeletal, and the agony and interior struggle written there frightened him. She shook her head. "I don't
know," she told him. "May the Mother-Creator help and
forgive me, I truly don't know."

*". . . you can't give it up. It would be more merciful to
kill you . . ."*

*". . . I lost Lámh Shábhála to another. I went mad with
the agony and threw myself over a cliff into the sea . . ."*

*". . . she's your daughter. The guilt of causing her death
will be worse . . ."*

Jenna walked along the shore, her thoughts as jumbled
and chaotic as the stones and boulders scattered there, not
caring that the steady hard rain seemed to find every crease
in the oilcloth she wore over her clóca. The voices of the
long-dead Holders of Lámh Shábhála assailed her like the
rain and salt spray that licked her face, a thousand contradictory wails of advice. She tried to block out the chorus, but
her own doubts made it impossible to hold them back.
The dead voices pounded at her head, yammering and
shouting, and she pulled the cowl of the oilcloth close
around her ears as if she could blot them out that way.

The tears came then: hot, racking sobs that she had
held back while she was with Mundy, not wanting him
to see her weakness and uncertainties, and they mingled
with the cold rain. She sat on a boulder in the brine-
laden wind off the Westering Sea and let the sorrow and
terror and guilt wash over her.

I hope you can live with yourself afterward . . . Doyle
had written. And yet she knew that to tear Lámh Shábhála away from herself would be like ripping out her
heart. She didn't know if she could survive that with her
sanity intact.

Once, she had tried to keep Lámh Shábhála and yet
save Ennis—her lover and Meriel's da—at the same
time. She'd failed and lost Ennis. His death had nearly
shattered her, and the cracks in her soul were still there,
unhealed. She didn't know if she could stand the guilt
of knowing she'd also killed the living result of the love
between Ennis and her, all that was left of him left in
the world.

"First Holder . . ."

The greeting sounded in her head, louder than the
voices of the ancient Holders, and at the same time she
heard a grunting cough and, through Lámh Shábhála,
felt the nearness of a familiar power. She lifted her head

and blinked away the tears to see a naked man standing knee-deep in the surf, his body scarred in a familiar pattern, his eyes the unrelieved brown-black of the Saimhóir, his hair plastered tight to his skull with the rain. He held his hand out to her in greeting. "I felt you here with Bradán an Chumhacht," he said. "It's been a long time since Bradán an Churnhacht and Lámh Shábhála have met. I am Dhegli, milk-son of Garrentha."

Jenna closed her hand around Lámh Shábhála and let a trickle of energy flow outward, changing her words as she spoke so that he could understand her. In the clochvision, she felt Dhegli open himself to her and allow Lámh Shábhála's energy to surround him; at the same time, she let Bradán an Chumhacht's power sweep around her, though she kept all the inner barriers up. "I knew your milk-mother well, and Thraisha before her, who was the First of the Saimhóir. I owe them both my life, more than once."

Dhegli nodded at that, taking a step forward. "And I," he said, "know your daughter well."

"Ahh . . ." There were undercurrents in his words that made Jenna clench her jaw. "So it was you . . ."

"That she swam with, and more?" Dhegli finished for her. He opened himself fully to her, and she found herself looking through his mind and his memories, and Meriel was there. "Aye," Dhegli said. "This is how it was with us."

Jenna gasped at what she saw and she pulled herself away from him. Dhegli stood complacent and confident in front of her in his nudity. "How dare you . . ." she began, then snapped her mouth shut.

"It was Meriel's choice to make," Dhegli told her, his voice calm. "Not yours, First Holder." For a moment, he smiled, then his face went somber "Not even mine. You and I share the same pain and concern right now, First Holder. We both want Meriel back. That *is* what you want, isn't it?"

"Aye," Jenna answered sharply, glaring at the changeling. " 'Tis."

"Then look at me again with Lámh Shábhála."

In her cloch-vision, she saw a new mind-place open up within him. Tentatively, she pushed the energy toward Dhegli once more and this time she saw Owaine, standing on a beach in Talamh an Ghlas. She heard their conversation, saw Owaine as Dhegli had seen him.

"So that's where the boy went." Jenna sighed. "Poor gentle Owaine . . . May the Mother keep him safe."

"Aye," Dhegli answered. "Yet I think the Water-Mother has a role for him to play in this. And you, First Holder? Will you open yourself to me as I have to you?" When Jenna didn't respond, Dhegli spread his arms wide as if offering himself. "Who does it help if we don't trust each other, First Holder? It certainly doesn't help Meriel."

Jenna still didn't respond and Dhegli started to turn away from her toward the sea, and she knew that he couldn't stay much longer in human form. "Wait," she said at last. "Do you love her?"

A nod. "Aye. I do."

Jenna closed her eyes, seeing only with the cloch-vision. She lowered the mind-barriers and the blue fire that was Dhegli slid toward her and into her, mingling with the green-gold fire of Lámh Shábhála. She pushed memories to him: Mundy's reading of Doyle's ultimatum; her last meeting with him back at Dún Kiil, and—much farther back—the difficult choice she made once before, back on the terrible day when Ennis had died.

When the blue fire receded and she opened her eyes again, Dhegli was no longer in human form. Instead, it was a bull seal who looked at her. He lifted his whiskered snout and grunted, and Dhegli's voice sounded again in her head.

"So that's the way it was and that's what you face," he said. The chocolate eyes of the seal held her, full of sympathy. The wind threw curtains of rain over them, but Jenna didn't feel them. "You needn't face it alone, First Holder. Not this time."

23

Trust

A SULLEN rain followed the Taisteal caravan all that day and the next, well into the morning of the following day. The weather matched Meriel's mood quite well.

The wagons of the Dranaghi Clan traveled slowly down the muddy road, the iron-shod wheels and the hooves of their horses tearing new ruts in the grass. If someone emerged as they passed a house they might stop and trade, perhaps bartering a pot for a chicken or mending a pot or bucket in exchange for bread. They camped where they were when it became too dark to travel, unless they came across one of the far-flung villages in the afternoon or late evening. Then Nico would meet with the Ald and arrange to stay for the night.

It was in the villages that the sad ones—the halt, the lame, the sick, the ones with broken bones, the ones with addled minds, the one with lesions and sores and wounds oozing pus—would come around because they'd heard the whispers spreading slowly through the Tuatha abut the Taisteal healer with the true touch. Some of these Nico and Sevei diverted to the potions and herbs that their wagons carried; most of the others were told that Cailin was simply "too exhausted" to see them, or that the Mother-Creator's presence was weak that evening. A few of them—a select few—they passed on to Meriel.

Luckily, the mage-lights appeared regularly each night

and she could renew the clochmion. There was, in each of the villages, a healing made possible by the cloch; there were others healed simply because they believed. A few of the false healings amazed even Meriel—such as the man in a village called Glenmill who (his daughter swore) had been unable to walk more than a few steps without pausing from exhaustion. The moment Meriel touched him, before she could even feel what he was feeling and hear his thoughts, he sprang up and capered about like a boy as Meriel blinked, wondering if perhaps she'd unknowingly used the cloch.

"There is the magic of the sky," Sevei said to Meriel afterward, "and then there is magic that exists only in here." She touched her forehead, grinning.

The country through which the Taisteal moved was ancient. They passed the occasional bog where peat was being cut in black rows, but many other bogs lay wet and forever untouched; they passed plowed and planted fields undulating with obvious barrow-graves, where unguessed kings of the Bunús Muintir or the earliest Daoines lay buried. They saw the stone rings, the ruined foundations of stone forts that had once guarded these lands and were now gentled and conquered by weather, by grass and heather. Standing stones with incised lines and patterns leaned atop hilltops or ringed a meadow, half of them now fallen and broken. Once, the road wound alongside the squared foundations of some ancient temple with the weather-blurred and tumbled images of old gods set in the grass, whose names must once have been feared or adored and were now forgotten unless the few Bunús Muintir who remained still remembered and worshiped them.

Near the villages, the land was tamed, the trees cut down for fields and the rocks pulled from the soil to make fences that lined the road for a time. But large areas of the land lay unpopulated by Daoine, looking as it must have looked for centuries: covered with thin forests of beech and elm, yew and sycamore, maple and pine that were airier and less grimly and defiantly dark

than the oldest woods. Yet there were swaths of land
where the trees were gone that might once have been
cultivated land or perhaps were the sites of ancient battles that had soaked the fields in blood and torn bodies.
There were roofless stone houses and abandoned settlements. There were places where people had once been
born, raised their children, and died, and then those children or their children's children had gone elsewhere,
leaving the land to return to itself.

Ancient things were awake in the land. Twice, herds
of the storm deer crossed their path, thundering madly
as they flowed like a russet tidal wave over the earth.
Dire wolves howled and muttered in their own language
in the evening shadows; wind sprites glittered and chattered in the dusk. Once, they passed a quartet of tumbled rocks that slumped in a field like human forms and
Meriel wondered if they might not be sleeping Créneach,
the clay-beings her mam had found in Inish Thuaidh and
who had come to her aid in the battle of Dún Kiil—and
one of whom, Treoraí, was the source of the cloch around
her neck. There were glimpses of strange forms in the
trees, calls and cries that Meriel had never heard before;
when the Taisteal heard them, they muttered and made
arcane warding motions in the direction of the apparitions.

The third morning, as they departed just before dawn
from another village, a heavy mist came rolling out from
the marsh across the road, seemingly moving against the
wind. The fog was heavy and strangely cold and so thick
around them that for a moment, Meriel was tempted to
jump from the wagon into it and run, certain that no
one could find her in the fallen cloud. But Sevei stirred
next to her and Meriel felt the woman's hand on her
arm.

"You don't want to do that, Cailin," she said. "That's
a sióg mist. Can't you feel the chill, and didn't you notice
that it's not damp like a normal fog? See the way it
moves and how it muffles some sounds and yet you hear
other things clearly? Wander into *that* and when it

clears, you'll be in *their* world, never to find your way back here."

Meriel believed none of it, thinking that Sevei was simply trying to stop her from running. She could pull away from the woman, still. *A simple jump from the wagon's seat and start running as soon as you touch the ground* . . . She leaned away, and Sevei's fingers tightened around her arm. "Let me go!"

"I can't. Not when it puts you in danger."

Meriel scoffed at that. "You don't care about *me,* just what Nico might do if I got away."

"You can believe that if you want." There was an undertone to Sevei's words, and a hurt in her eyes as she held Meriel's gaze. Then the sióg mist swept over them. For a moment Meriel could see nothing, not even Sevei's face alongside her. The only connection to Sevei was the clenching of her fingers on Meriel's arm, the hand seeming to appear disembodied from the fog. The horses nickered; the wagon lurched once as Sevei used her other hand to pull up the reins so they wouldn't run into Nico's wagon ahead. Meriel thought she could hear laughter in the mist and the plucking of spectral fingers in her hair and clothes. Voices seemed to call her, tantalizingly. *"Come with us . . . Come. . . ."* and then that sensation, too, faded as the fog slid off to the north.

There was only the normal morning haze in front of them, a gray, thin curtain. Sevei still gazed at her with that strange concern. The wagon lurched forward as the horses started moving down the road again. Sevei's hand loosened on Meriel's arm. The sióg mist, if that's what it was, had passed, and with it any opportunity to escape. If she leaped down from the wagon now, Sevei would only jump after her, probably followed by some of the clan from the third wagon behind. A dull anger pressed her mouth into a scowl.

"How would you know about a sióg mist or anything?" Meriel sniffed. "You don't even come from Talamh an Ghlas. This isn't your land."

Sevei shrugged again and clucked at the horses, flicking the reins as Nico's wagon, just ahead of them, started forward again.

"I know these things because my people have come to this land since before the Daoine," Sevei answered. "We have tales as old as those of the Bunús Muintir. As for me—I was here once before. Before you were born, I spent several years in this land as a child when my mam wandered here and I have been here again with Nico for three years in the Tuatha. I've seen the changes with my own eyes and heard your people talking with my own ears. We Taisteal *know* this land and know its tales and those creatures that walk and swim and fly in it, far better than most of you Daoine who cower frightened on the same piece of land for all your lives and never see what's beyond the horizon."

The scolding tone of her voice dampened Meriel's anger. "Sevei, I'm sorry," Meriel said. "I didn't mean—"

"I know you didn't," Sevei said quickly, her voice gentler. "You don't know how it is with the Taisteal. We wander—it's in our blood and our souls. We stay nowhere for too long. Our home is our family and the wagons in which we ride, not the soil and rock under our feet. It's been seven years now since I last saw Thall Mór-roinn and it will be another two before we return there for the Klaastanak, the meeting of the clans. Many of our children were born here or in Céile Mhór as we came north; they'll be seeing Thall Mór-roinn for the first time." She stared straight ahead at the rear of Nico's wagon, but her gaze seemed to be focused somewhere beyond it. "I wonder if they'll see the same place I remember."

"The world's changed that much?"

Sevei laughed. "The world's *still* changing. The change has just begun, really. One of our lives is just a moment to the world; it is still just waking to the Filleadh. We're seeing the quickening of the earth, when it returns to the time of legends—when you've slept for seven centuries and more, it takes time to wake up. It'll be several generations yet before everything is the way it once

was." Sevei glanced over at Meriel. "You're part of it,"
she said. "Whether you like that or not. You're part of
the change."

"Are you playing fortune-teller again? Should I go get
your cards?" Meriel tried to gentle the sarcasm with a
smile, but Sevei's face was solemn.

"Are you mad at me, or at yourself for listening to
me a few minutes ago?" she said finally. "You could
have jumped; you didn't and I'm glad. I won't let you
hurt yourself, Cailin, and—"

"That's not my name," Meriel interrupted harshly.
"You don't *know* me."

A shrug. "—and I won't let anyone hurt you, not even
Nico. You can believe that or not. While I'm with you
I'll keep you safe. If I think it's *not* safe for you to be
here, then I'll help you leave myself."

Meriel snorted her derision for that and moved as far
away as she could on the wagon's seat. She stayed there
for the rest of the day, silent, wishing she could believe
Sevei and knowing she couldn't.

Toward the end of the fourth day, Meriel began to catch
glimpses of a large lake through the trees and between
the hills. The lough stretched out long and dark under
the slate sky, covered with a froth of choppy waves
pushed by a steady wind: Lough Méar, Sevei told her, a
name Meriel remembered seeing on the maps at Inishfeirm. Meriel gazed at the water longingly. If she could
reach the water's shore, even for just a few moments . . .
Lough Méar grew closer as their road descended out of
the hills toward a village set at the end of the lake. This
place was somewhat larger than the villages they'd
passed through: a few dozen buildings and a small stone
temple of its own, with fishing boats pulled up on a
stony shingle.

As they came toward the village gate, Nico pulled his
cart over and let Sevei come alongside. He leaned over

toward Meriel. "You wouldn't be thinking of running for the lough, would you, Cailin? Mind you, I remember what the tiarna said about you and the water. We'll be watching you, all of us."

"And especially me," Sevei added, with a lifting of eyebrows. "They say the waters of the western loughs are haunted by Uisce Taibhse, the water ghosts, ever since the Filleadh."

"I don't believe in ghosts," Meriel answered. "Any more than I believe in sióg mists."

Sevei shrugged. "I'd love to hear you say that in the middle of night when the mage-lights play over the barrows and the dead kings come out to walk, with glowing eyes and anger in their hearts and bright swords in their hands. But the Uisce Taibhse aren't true ghosts at all; they're creatures all too alive who live under the water and who prefer flesh to fish for their dinners. Still, I'm sure your lack of belief will be a comfort as they drag you under the waves to their lair. Wait until we get to the village, then talk to the fisherfolk. Ask *them* if they believe."

Nico, as usual, negotiated with the Ald of the village, a wizened dwarf of a man with a bald head so shiny it might have been polished. At his direction, they moved the wagons to a sheep pasture on a hill just outside town and well away from the shore, and the clan began unpacking and setting up for the night. The clouds had opened in the west and the lough was touched with golden fire as the sun fell toward the hills at the far end of the water. The sight reminded Meriel of similar sunsets in Dún Kiil and Inishfeirm, and the ache in her heart deepened. Somewhere not too far past those distant peaks must be the sea, and that realization made Meriel think of Dhegli. She could still feel the warmth of his gift in her mind: *call me, and I'll come to you . . .*

I will call for you, she whispered silently. *Soon . . .*

Several of the villagers were already plodding up from the town center toward the Taisteal encampment, and she felt the sick dread starting again in her stomach coupled with the throbbing of Treoraí's Heart under her tunic. "Do you want to wait?" Sevei whispered to her. Her hand stroked Meriel's shoulder. "I'll have Nico tell them that you're ill and can't see anyone until late to-night or tomorrow."

Meriel shook her head. "No," she told her. "I'll see them. I *am* tired, though."

"I'll keep the group small. Go get yourself ready and I'll work with Nico to see who we have. We'll be there in half a stripe."

Meriel started toward the end of the pasture where two of Nico's grandsons were erecting the small tent for Sevei and Meriel. Halfway there, she stopped. Sevei and Nico were well down the hill talking with the villagers; everyone else was busy readying the camp and paying little attention to her. Meriel sidled away from the tent, drifted behind one of the wagons. A small copse of haw-thorns sat a few yards away on the other side of a stone fence. She ran, hopping the fence and darting into the sparse cover of the trees.

No one shouted alarm. No one seemed to notice at all. Meriel started to dare to hope.

She pushed through the bramble to the other end of the stand, then hurried across another pasture—startling a small flock of black-faced sheep—to a wooded hillside. She stayed within the shelter of the trees and started to work her way down the slope toward the lough, follow-ing a brook that leaped and danced on its way to the larger water. The wood skirted the southern edge of the village, and the brook soon fanned out into a thousand rivulets as it hit a bog. Meriel was forced to move away along the edges of the swampy hummocks, staying to firmer ground and fighting her way through thick under-growth and thicker clouds of midges. The ground oozed black water under her boots; she told herself that soon she would strip the boots away entirely, along with her captivity.

As the sun vanished beneath the crown of hills and the eastern sky turned purple, she came out onto a rocky meadow that ran down to the shore of the lough. Meriel ran toward the water. She stripped off the furred over-cloak of the Taisteal and flung it to the ground; she pulled off her boots. She began to loosen the ties of her trousers.

"Cailin! Meriel!"

The call came from behind and she knew the voice well. She looked over her shoulder to see Sevei stepping out from the trees, still several yards away. Meriel turned her back and started to move toward the water.

"Wait! I won't come any closer. Please wait!"

Meriel paused. Glanced back again. "You can't stop me," she said. "By the time you reach me I'll be in the water. Take one step toward me and that's what I'll do."

"I won't," Sevei said. In the rising gloom, she carefully sat on the ground. "See? You've won, Meriel. You've escaped. But . . ." She closed her mouth, lowered her head.

"What?" Meriel asked.

"How safe will you be afterward, Meriel? Think about this. Even if you don't believe what I said about these waters, what happens when you reach the end of the lough? You'll be naked, alone in the wild, and still miles from the sea. You'll have no food, no provisions, no fire to keep you warm, no weapons if dire wolves or bandits or anything else that walks here attacks you. Worse than that, you'll still be in the Tuatha and any tiarna you meet will be your enemy, if not actively looking for you."

"I'll take my chances with all that."

Sevei nodded. "I might, too, in your situation. But I have another offer."

Meriel shook her head, wondering if Sevei was trying to trap her, if the woman wanted to hold her here until boats came from the village. She could see firelight reflecting from the waters of the lough from where the village quay jutted out around the curve of the shore, but there was no one out on the lake. "I'm listening."

"I have to give you a story first. I have to explain something you asked me before."

"Then do it. Quickly."

Meriel could see Sevei draw a long breath in through her nose, her eyes closed. "You asked about my mam and the cards," Sevei said at last. "I told you I was here with Mam when I was a child. I didn't tell you how my mam died."

"Scvci—"

"No, I've started this. Now listen . . ."

I told you that my mam was a true reader, and the clans knew it. My da had left not long after I was born; I never knew him. But Mam was well-known among the clans and always welcome in a caravan. I used to watch her give readings to the Clannhra with whom we were traveling, after all the locals had gone. I was no more than six or seven, then—this was a few years before the mage-lights returned. I'd sit on her knee and watch as she laid out the cards on the table, fascinated by the colors and the drawings and the way Mam's voice took on this mesmerizing tone when she was lost in the reading, speaking of things only she could see.

One day I asked my mam to read my fortune for me the way she did for our cousins—I handed her the cards, awkwardly shuffled, and cut them in front of her the way I'd seen the others do. She looked at the cards, then at me, and finally laid them out in the true spiral array. I stared at the cards, fascinated: all the pretty drawings and strange symbols. Mam stared at them also, then swept the cards up again and placed them in their cloth bag. She pulled the tie-string and knotted it. "Mam!" I complained. "You didn't *read* them."

She reached across the table and patted my cheek. "No, *moj ljubav.* You don't know it, but I've read the cards for you many times. Someday I will tell you, when you're older."

"Tell me now," I insisted.

She shook her head. "You wouldn't understand."

"I would, too," I said fervently. "Mam . . ."

She smiled, a bit sadly, I thought. "You know the suits?" she asked me, and I nodded. "Good. What cards did you see the most of?"

"The Major Arcana and Swords," I told her.

"Aye. The Major Arcana are great influences that you cannot affect, and Swords . . . they indicate strife and conflict. Do you know what I mean?" I nodded, though I didn't really understand, and she went on. "I did a reading when you were first born, touching the cards to your body and breaking the deck where you put your finger when I held them in front of you. I saw then that you have a role in life to fill, Sevei. You'll come to know someone when you're older, someone who is destined to be important, and you'll have a chance to help that person."

"Really?" I said, and I grinned, thinking of myself as the hero of some bard's tale. "Then I'll be important, too."

She was already shaking her head. "No, Sevei," she told me. "You won't. If you take that path and help that person, very few will ever really know about it. Your part in the tale ends there."

I was disappointed, though I tried not to show it. *What's the good of doing something heroic and dangerous if no one ever knows about it?* I wanted to ask her. Instead, I asked Mam if she ever read the cards for herself. She just smiled at that. "I already know my fate. I'm destined to be your Mam. My fortune is to make certain that you grow up. And I'll do that, *moj ljubav.* I'll do that."

I reached over and picked up the cards in their bag, feeling their edges through the soft, smooth cloth. "I still want you to do a real reading for me, Mam."

She patted my hands and took the cards from me. "I will," she told me. "One day I will."

She never did. She never had the chance.

Back then, I didn't really understand what happened, though I do now, having seen what I've seen over the

years. It must have been no more than two seasons or
so later. We were somewhere in the Tuatha, in the south
of Talamh an Ghlas, in some village that looked no different than any other village that we'd been to. Mam
was reading the cards and I was bored. I wandered away
from the tents and across the field where we were
camped toward a grove of fruit trees. Though I couldn't
see our wagons or the buildings, I could hear the noises
of the village and every once in a while someone's laughter. There was still daylight left, so I felt safe. So when
I heard footsteps behind me and turned to see a man
standing there close to me, I just turned around, curious.
"Enjoying your walk?" he asked. I remember his voice,
gruff and low with a sound like a rasp on hard wood.
"It's a lovely day, isn't it?"

I nodded as he came closer. In my memory, he's huge,
standing over me like a mountain, so big he blocked the
light. He smelled of sheep and earth and sweat. One of
his hands reached down to cup my face. "You're the
pretty one," he said. "Very pretty. I noticed you right
away yesterday, when you came here. Did you see me?"

I shook my head. He was crouching down in front of
me now. His face was grizzled and lined, and he was
missing several teeth. He was breathing strangely and
his breath was sour. Both of his hands were on my shoulders and the fingers of his right hand were stroking my
neck. "I saw you walk out here," he said. "So I followed.
A girl as pretty as you . . ." He stopped. His tongue
brushed his upper lip. I didn't like his fingers on my
neck or his face so close to me and started to back away.
His left hand tightened on my shoulder and his right
flashed down to his belt and came back. He held a knife
blade in front of my face. "Do you see this, pretty thing?
You know what it can do?" I nodded, so frightened now
that I couldn't speak. "Good. If you scream, if you yell,
it will be the last thing you do. Do you understand?"
His fingers dug into the skin of my shoulder and the
blade of the knife pressed against my throat. I quickly
gave him another nod.

He flung me down on the ground. I could feel his hand on my clothes and hear the cloth ripping and his weight on me . . . Then it was gone as I heard him grunt, and he went rolling off to one side in a flash of bright cloth and I saw my mam struggling with him. "Run!" she screamed at me. "Run, Sevei!"

I obeyed her, crying and screaming for help. I ran out of the grove as others came at my wailing, villagers and Taisteal both. The Clannhra took me in her arms and hurried me back to the tent. "Mam! Where's Mam?" I kept asking her.

They found Mam on the ground in the grove, deep stab wounds in her chest, her breath rattling in her lungs and blood on her lips. Four of my cousins brought her back to the encampment while the others went after my attacker. Mam . . . she died less than a stripe later. The man, they caught him, too. They would never tell me what they did to him.

For a long time afterward, I wondered why Mam hadn't seen the danger in the cards, why she didn't know what would happen to her. Finally, I realized that she almost certainly had known and that it didn't make any difference. As she'd told me, her destiny was to be my mam—and she would perform that task, no matter what the cost might be for her. . . .

"Sevei . . ." Meriel said, but Sevei shook her head.

"No, don't say anything. There's nothing to say. Nothing to change it. You wanted to know what I saw in the cards. Well, I saw that I am tied to you. Mam said that I was destined to help someone who would be important—I would think that a Banrion's daughter is important enough, eh? You've escaped. I'll grant you that. I couldn't reach you before you were in the water. But this isn't the time or the place, Meriel. I don't want you to die out there—and I think that's what will happen if you leave now. I want you to come back with me now.

Come with me and I promise you that when the right moment comes, I'll help you escape. I've made you this promise before and I'm making it again: until then, I'll make sure you're safe, no matter what."

Sevei rose to her feet and Meriel took a long backward step into the water. A wave lapped at her calf and she felt mud squelch beneath her bare foot as the bottom dropped sharply away. The water was dark and frigid, and strange ripples erupted on the surface of the lough not far from shore as if something swam out there. She could feel the change starting within her and all she had to do was let it happen—dive in as she was and emerge a few seconds later as a Saimhóir. But she held back the transformation. "Why should you care?" she shouted back to Sevei. "You're just trying to trick me."

"No." The denial came simple and sad; in the twilight, Meriel could see her lips press together in a frown. "But I can't prove it to you. You need to believe me, on your own."

"How can I believe it? Why would you be willing to betray Nico and your clan for me?"

Sevei spread her hands wide. "You just have to trust that it's true, Meriel. You have to feel your choice inside and know it's the right one. My mam knew that feeling; I know it, too. If you can't do that, I'll understand. But I'm going to walk toward you now . . ."

She took a step and Meriel retreated into the water, standing knee-deep in the lapping, cold waves. The desire to change swept over her again and she shivered in response. She turned her back to Sevei. The ripples were gone now, as if whatever was out there had gone still, waiting for her to make a decision. Meriel took a long, slow deep breath. She could smell the peaty fragrance of the lough. The water was beginning to feel nearly warm around her legs.

She could hear Sevei's slow, deliberate steps behind her.

You trusted Lucan and he forgot you as soon as you left Dún Kiil. You trusted Thady and he betrayed you.

You trusted your own mam and she sent you away and wasn't able to protect you even with Lámh Shábhála. Maybe she didn't even try. You trusted Dhegli, but he wasn't there when Mac Ard snatched you away. You've made nothing but bad choices. How can you trust Sevei? Dive in. All you have to do is dive in . . .

Gentle arms went around her from behind, hugging her. A sweet, warm breath touched her hair, whispering in her ear. "Come back with me? For a little while?"

Meriel leaned back into the embrace. She was crying now, unable to keep the tears back and yet not knowing exactly why they came. A few drops splashed from her cheek into the lough. "I escaped," she said. "I did. You have to remember that."

"Aye, I will," Sevei said. "You'll be free again as soon as the right moment comes. I promise."

24

Travelers

THE QUESTION didn't seem to be *if* he would die. Rather, it was only matter of what would kill him first.

Owaine sneezed violently and loudly.

The rain was persistent and thorough, finding every crack in the skins and clothing Cataigh had given him. Owaine was shivering and ill from the cold before he'd walked more than a few miles, and he could visualize himself being found weeks later lying stiff just off the road, dead of a fever. He blinked away the thought with the rain and kept walking. If his fate was to die of this rain-begotten sickness, there was nothing he could do about it now.

Owaine's feet were sore, his legs tired. The squirrel Léimard was still with him; at least he thought it was the same squirrel that scampered through the branches of the trees lining the road. So far, the squirrel had been no help at all; he wished that Cataigh had given him a horse instead—that would have been far more useful. Owaine thought about how nice it would be to let a horse do the walking while he snuggled himself in a blanket on its back, and how quickly he'd cover the miles. But he had little money in his purse, just about enough to buy a tankard of ale. Enough to pay for a night's stabling, but not the horse itself. No one was going to lend a stranger a mount, espccially someone as bedraggled looking as he, with the accent of Inish Thuaidh in his voice.

If he wanted a horse, he would have to take it.

A stripe or so later, the squirrel chittered and bounded down onto his shoulder, startling him. Then it ran down his arm, leaping away and bouncing off down the road before turning abruptly into the underbrush alongside. "Where . . ." he started to say, then he heard the sound of hooves from around a bend in the road. They grew louder, then abruptly stopped. A few breaths later, there was the sound of wood crashing against wood. Owaine went forward several steps until he could see around the curve. He could make out a building at a crossroads not far ahead. Squinting, he thought he could see a signboard mounted above the door: probably an inn, then, though he was too far away for his nearsighted eyes to make out either picture or words there. A horse was hitched to the rail in front of the building, with the green-and-gold colors of Infochla draped over the back of its brown flanks: a Riocha's horse, well-cared for and strong. Léimard leaped out from the underbrush onto the road in front of him, scampering to the building and springing up on the railing where the horse's reins were looped. The horse snorted and pulled back. Owaine blinked.

If you want a horse, you'll have to take it.

A knot was beginning to form in his stomach, but with it was a new resolve. He waited to see if a servant would come from the inn to take care of the horse or if the tiarna would come back out himself. Neither happened. The inn's door remained firmly closed. If he could reach the inn without being noticed . . . He remembered the slow magic incantation that muffled sounds, but it would take a quarter-stripe to prepare—there wasn't time for that.

The longer you wait, the more likely it is the tiarna comes back out. Owaine took a breath and hurried forward as quietly as he could.

Léimard had jumped down from the railing and vanished. Owaine didn't care—he'd happily trade the squirrel for a horse. The horse nickered, turning its head toward Owaine as he approached and moving nervously away to the limit of its reins. Owaine patted its flanks; muscles flexed underneath and shook raindrops from its hide, but the animal made no other sign of nervousness. The horse was a gelding and looked gentle enough, though Owaine's knowledge of the animals was limited to the few lethargic and spoiled horses in the Order's stables.

Owaine watched his own hands unknot the reins from the post near the door as if he were seeing someone else performing the task—it didn't seem possible that he could be stealing a horse. The worst theft he'd ever committed in his life was snatching a few extra slices of bread from the Order's kitchens and now here he was taking a tiarna's mount, a tiarna who would certainly kill him without asking any questions if he happened to come out the door now or glance through the slats of the inn's shutters. From within the darkness of the inn, he heard a woman's voice and then a man's, then an unmistakable groaning sigh of arousal.

Owaine blushed. His hands shook as he took the reins. He forced back the sneeze that threatened to reveal his presence.

"Shh, softly now," he whispered to the horse as if the animal could understand him. He pulled himself up on the straps of the soaked livery and dug his heels into the horse's side as he'd seen others do, then nearly fell off as the beast wheeled and started to canter away. The sound of its hooves on the sloppy ground seemed impossibly loud. Owaine hung on, waiting for the shout from behind and perhaps an arrowhead slicing into his unprotected back to tear the life from him. The rain drummed at his face and body as the horse began to trot away. He didn't begin to relax until the inn had vanished behind a screen of trees. As soon as he dared, he stopped and tore away the banner of Infochla from the horse, burying it under rocks well away from the road—people might wonder how a bedraggled traveler managed to afford a fine horse, but at least they wouldn't see immediate evidence of the theft.

The tiarna had also left his pack on the horse. In it, Owaine found a boot knife, a roll of hard bread wrapped in cloth with a brick of yellow cheese, a small purse with two gold mórceints and several smaller coins, and a pouch of papers. He riffled through the papers; they were all addressed to the Rí Infochla in Falcarragh and appeared to be from the court of the Rí Connachta in Keelballi. The tiarna, then, must be a courier, perhaps one who came this way frequently enough to stop at the inn regularly for a liaison. By now, the man must be regretting his decision to soothe his baser instincts.

Léimard scolded him from a nearby branch, then jumped down to land on the horse's back just in front of Owaine. The horse half-reared nervously, nearly sending Owaine off it again. Léimard was unperturbed, sitting up on its haunches, and Owaine broke off a piece of the loaf and held it out to the squirrel, who took it in its paws and began chewing contentedly.

"They'll hang me for a common thief," Owaine muttered to Léimard as he tossed the pouch of papers into the deep brush alongside the trail and gnawed at the bread himself. "Taking the man's horse and his money, and destroying the correspondence of the Rí . . ."

Léimard didn't answer, absorbed in his meal.

By midafternoon, Owaine decided that simply riding a horse might kill him before the rain and cold. His back ached, his buttocks had long ago gone numb, and his legs screamed with the effort of holding to the gelding's sides. The only advantage was that he was covering the miles more quickly now, and it was the horse's hooves and not his boots that were thick with mud. Even Léimard seemed content to let the horse do the work.

As the day began to fade, they came upon a village. Owaine sent a tendril of energy out from his clochmion, searching for Meriel, but there was no answering resonance—she wasn't here. He decided he would ride straight through, not wanting to face the questions that would come if he stopped. But Léimard hopped off the horse and away. "Léimard!" he called, but the squirrel ran toward the ramshackle stone cottages at the edge of the settlement and vanished into the blur that was the village. As Owaine squinted into the dusk, the thought of a night alone and unprotected on the road seemed suddenly far more dangerous than a night here. The tiarna hadn't come from this direction; the horse wouldn't be recognized and with the tiarna's purse, he had money enough. Two villagers nodded to him as he passed the open gate of the town, and their gazes were merely curious, not suspicious. The inn beckoned, with yellow light already flickering beyond its shutters. He pulled up the horse and dismounted with a groan and a cough. He looked around for Léimard, didn't see the animal, and shrugged. He went in.

Owaine nodded to the proprietor—a skinny man behind a table placed over two barrels—as well as the local couples huddled near the peat fire drinking and smoking pipe weed, and placed a copper on the planks. "Stout," he said. "And can you tell me what village this might be?"

The man grunted, snatched a wooden mug from a grimy shelf behind him, and opened the tap in the bunghole of one of the barrels. Dark foam dribbled out. "You're in Ballycraigh, may the Mother help you," he said finally. "And where would you be from? There was an Inishlander who came through here once. He had an accent like yours." He glanced up and down Owaine's length as he placed the mug on the table. "You're not dressed like fisherfolk, though." Owaine could plainly hear the unspoken: *you're not dressed like* anyone *from around here . . .*

"I'm from—" Owaine paused momentarily. "—the Stepping Stones, one of the south islands, not those traitorous northers. Still, we sound a little like the Inish sometimes, being so close to the island. I'm on my way to Falcarragh." The last half of the sentence was a rush of words followed by a sneeze. Owaine wiped his nose on his sleeve and sniffed loudly.

"Strange that someone from the Stones would be riding to Falcarragh rather than sailing."

"Believe me," Owaine answered heartily, "the way my backside feels, I *wish* I'd sailed." The proprietor chuckled at that, though he still stared at Owaine curiously. Owaine blinked and sneezed again. "You wouldn't have anyone here who's good with potions, would you? I've caught a chill from the damp."

"You might call on Ald Macsnei; she's a good eye for the herbs," the man told him. "Too bad you weren't here a few days back; there was a young woman with the Healing Touch traveling with the Taisteal. Had an accent more like yours than the Taisteal, though, so perhaps she was from the Stones, too. She healed Widow Martain's daughter Áine of the Bloody Cough, she did. Did it in an instant, just laying hands on her. Better than a bloody cloudmage."

Owaine remembered the wheel marks he'd seen at the campsite near the ocean: *the Taisteal would have their wagons, and the Bunús Muintir had said something about Meriel having a cloch . . .* He had the feeling that he knew now why Léimard had made him stop here. If he'd followed his own instincts . . . "The woman had an accent like mine, you say?"

"Aye. And hair red enough that it flamed like a sunset, Widow Martain said, though others who went to her the next day said the woman's hair was raven black. A young one to have the Healing Touch, if you ask me, though the Taisteal said it was in her family."

Owaine frowned. He had no idea why Meriel would be traveling with a Taisteal clan, or why she'd be pretending to possess a "healing touch," or why she might dye her hair black. None of it made any sense. Meriel should be with Thady and the tiarna who had taken her, yet . . .

Owaine's clochmion might not know that it was Meriel, but his gut screamed that it was.

"Will you be staying the night?" the proprietor was asking. "I've a room for you, and the wife has a good side of lamb roasting in the kitchens tonight. 'Tis a foul evening, as you already know . . ."

Owaine sniffed and sipped at the brown head of the stout. The bitterness played along his tongue and throat. He wanted nothing more than to fall into a real bed and sleep, and the thought of lamb roast started him salivating. "I'll have some of the roast and another stout," he told the proprietor. "And if you have someone who can feed and take care of my horse while I'm eating, I'd appreciate that. But I can't stay."

The man's chin lifted. "That must be important business you're about if you intend to ride through the night in this weather and in these parts," he mused. He tilted his head, leaning on the table and obviously waiting for Owaine to elaborate—as a good traveler was expected to do. Owaine noticed the other people in the room had stopped their own talking and were listening as well. After all, tales from strangers were likely to be more interesting than the well-gnawed gossip they all knew anyway.

"Aye, it's important enough to me," Owaine said. It was clear that they weren't going to leave him to sit in silence. It seemed easiest to mix a bit of the truth with the outright lies he would have to tell. "I'm looking for someone I've lost."

"Ahh," one of the women breathed and beamed a gap-toothed smile. " 'Tis love, then."

Owaine nodded. "Aye, 'tis that indeed," he said. The bartender nodded; the woman who'd spoken grinned.

"That's good, that's good. Love makes for the best stories. Come, sit over here and tell us about it while you eat. . . ."

The bedroom of the Rí Ard appeared to Doyle as a battleground, or perhaps a game board for ficheall, with the combatants arrayed on either side of the dying man and glaring across at each other. Doyle sat alongside

Edana at her da's left side, and Doyle kept his arm around her shoulder as she grasped the Rí Ard's hands, clasped over his chest as if he were already dead.

Across the bed was her brother Enean, his scarred face made even more distorted with a mute and sour fury, as if he waited there to slay the Black Haunts when they came to take the Rí Ard's soul to the land of the dead. MacCamore, Enean's guardian, stood behind the young man, which was natural enough, but Tiarna Labhrás Ó Riain also sat alongside Enean, his Cloch Mór glittering prominently on a brocaded, silken léine. Ó Riain's hand was on Enean's shoulder, but his gaze kept drifting to Edana and Doyle with open malice.

At the foot of the bed sat the Toscaire Concordai, Ulán Rhusvak, dressed again in his bearskin garb. The emissary watched the stuttering breath, the erratic lifting of the Rí Ard's chest, and Doyle could not tell what the man might be thinking past the curve of yellowed bear teeth that masked his face.

Outside the chamber more Riocha waited: each with his own agenda, each with his own thoughts. Doyle wondered how the alliances would eventually play out, and realized that he would find out all too soon. *Those who were with me at Inishfeirm must hold together. That's what matters most. None of them can talk about our capture of Meriel until I meet with Jenna at Inishduán, or we're lost.*

The current healer hovered around the Rí Ard's bed, occasionally leaning over to help Nevan sip a bit of water or drink a potion of andúilleaf to ease his pain. A pair of Draíodóiri—a priest and priestess of the Mother-Creator from the Dún Laoghaire temple—stood in the far corner of the chamber near the open window, quietly chanting while incense curled around them. The room smelled of herbs and illness.

The Rí Ard was no longer conscious, though his eyes were open and staring. His Cloch Mór—named Demon-Caller for the apparition it could summon—lay heavy on its chain, sparkling in the candlelight. "He may be able to hear you, even if he can no longer see," the healer whispered to Edana. Doyle leaned over to her and added his own whisper into her ear:

"And be careful what you say, my love. Too many ears listening . . ." He felt more than saw her nod.

"Da," she said. "It's Edana. I made it back, as I promised. Doyle's here with me."

"I'm here, too, Edana," Enean said, too loudly. "I've been here the whole time, even though it's boring and it stinks in here." He started to rise from his chair and old MacCamore took a step forward to press him back down, whispering softly into the addled young man's ear. Tiarna Ó Riain nodded at Enean's protest.

"Indeed you have, Enean," he said. "You're a good, beloved son, and your da is proud of you, as he should be."

Edana smiled at her brother, though Doyle could see her cold glance to Ó Riain. "Enean's here, too, Da," she added, patting her father's hands, and Enean subsided, sitting down again. "We both love you very much. We'll take care of everything you've started. Don't worry; just rest. You'll be in the Mother's arms, Da. She'll keep you safe forever."

There was no answer, no flicker of eyelids or anything that indicated he might have heard. There was only the slow gasping inhalations and the long pauses between. No one said anything.

A stripe passed. Another. The healer kept up his ministrations; the Draíodóiri continued to chant in their corner. Doyle sat, patient and watching. Watching them all.

He suddenly realized that he hadn't heard the Rí Ard take a breath in a long time. The silence stretched on too long. The healer shuffled forward, touching his fingers to the Rí Ard's neck. "He's gone," the healer said simply.

Edana sobbed once, a choking gasp, and Doyle put his arms around her. Enean screamed, flailing his arms as if he were wrestling with ghosts that only he could see. "No!" he screamed. "Bring him back! Bring him back!" He lurched forward as if he were going to fling himself on his da's body, and it took both MacCamore and Ó Riain to hold him back. When the grief subsided as suddenly as it had come, MacCamore led Enean away out of the side entrance, calmly talking to the distraught, quietly weeping man. As they left, the Toscaire Concordai pulled himself from his chair with a groan and started toward the main chamber doors. "I'll let the other Riocha in to pay their respects to the Rí Ard," he said.

"Thank you, Toscaire Concordai," Ó Riain said, and at the same time, Ó Riain reached over toward the chain of the Cloch Mór on the Rí Ard's still chest. Before the tiarna could touch the cloch, Doyle stretched his arm and caught Ó Riain's hand by the wrist.

"That's Edana's legacy," he said, "and not yours to take."

Ó Riain stared at Doyle. "Remove your hand, Mac Ard. Now."

"I meant what I said, Tiarna. Demon-Caller belongs to Edana."

"That cloch goes to the new Rí Ard."

Doyle smiled grimly. "Certainly you mean the *Banrion* Ard."

Ó Riain opened his fingers and pulled away; Doyle let him go. The Toscaire Concordai watched from near the door, masked by the bear's teeth; Edana stood at the side of the bed. The healer retreated from the confrontation as the chant of the Draíodóiri faded. "The Rí Ard wanted Enean to be his successor," Ó Riain snarled. "That's what he whispered to me two days ago while his daughter was riding away from his deathbed, and I've told the other Riocha here in Dún Laoghaire. Many of them agree. So will the Rithe, when they come."

"*I* don't believe that happened," Edana spat before Doyle could answer. "Nor does Doyle or the Riocha who are with us. Nor will all the Rithe agree and certainly not the cloudmages of the Order of Gabair. When I left, Tiarna Ó Riain, my da was unconscious and the healer tells me that he never—*never*—woke again or spoke to anyone. As to Enean . . ." She paused. "It's not my brother's fault, but he's not capable of being the Rí Ard and we all know that. My da said so many times, when he could still speak. The Riocha have all heard *that,* and from his own lips. Not from yours."

Ó Riain scoffed. "They've also never heard the Rí Ard say that he wanted his daughter on his throne, while he has in the past said that of Enean, his firstborn and son."

"My da did say that," Edana agreed, "before Enean was injured. Enean was the firstborn and had been named Tanaise Ríg, as he should have been—but that was *before* he was hurt."

"Your brother was wounded while defending his mam and his betrothed, and the Rí Ard admired that," Ó Riain retorted.

Edana nodded. "Indeed, and we've all wondered who might have been behind that attack. Perhaps it wasn't the Inish. Perhaps it was someone closer."

Ó Riain's smile touched nothing but his lips. "Whoever it was, they didn't succeed in assassinating Enean or in killing his spirit. Enean hasn't lost his courage, nor his strength or his desire. All he needs is guidance."

"And you'll be happy to provide that," Doyle said.

Ó Riain smiled. "Indeed. Enean . . . *trusts* me."

"I don't," Edana said. She reached for the Cloch Mór on her da's chest; at the same time, Ó Riain closed his hand around his own cloch. A wolf's howl shimmered in the air and a black form leaped between Edana and Doyle, close enough that Doyle felt the wind of its passage. Edana gasped, snatching her hand back as hungry jaws snapped at her. Doyle opened his own cloch even as several spectral wolves shimmered into existence around Ó Riain. Doyle felt the golden dragon rise behind him, snarling and familiar.

A wolf sprang toward him; Doyle sent the dragon's tail whipping out, snatching the wolf in mid-leap and hurling it backward against the wall where it dissolved in black and yellow sparks. Ó Riain staggered with the impact. From the corridor, they heard muffled shouts of alarm as those with clochs sensed that something was happening inside the Rí Ard's chambers.

"Is this the way it has to be, Ó Riain?" Doyle asked. "Do we tear at each other with our clochs over the body of the Ard?"

"There are more outside who would follow me than you, and they have clochs as well," Ó Riain answered. "You can't win this battle." He turned as if to call to his allies, but the Toscaire Concordai was watching in seeming fascination, and he held the doors firmly shut even as the waiting Riocha knocked and called.

"I *will* kill you before I fall," Doyle said. "You know that, Ó Riain. Whether or not you like or agree with the Order of Gabair, you know our training is good. You know how well I handle the power; you know I could hold even Lámh Shábhála. How are you going to advise Enean when you're laying cold in your tomb with the Rí Ard? Go on—send your wolves now if you believe that's an empty threat."

The dragon snapped its tail and hissed; the wolves howled but remained huddled around Ó Riain. "Take Demon-Caller, Edana," Doyle said. "Go on. It's yours."

Edana reached over the bed. She kissed her da's cheek as she lifted the chain from him. O Riain released his cloch and the wolves vanished.

"This isn't over," Ó Riain said. "None of this is finished." He lifted his chin and glared at Edana as she slipped the chain of the Cloch Mór over her own head. "You can hold Demon-Caller for the moment, Bantiarna, but you're not the Banrion Ard yet," he told her. "Not until all the Ríthe of the Tuatha declare it during the Óenach, and that's not going to happen. I'll make certain of it."

With that, Ó Riain stormed from the room, rushing past the Toscaire Concordai and pushing open the doors. He gestured angrily, and several of the tiarna outside left with him. One of them, Doyle noticed, was the court representative of Rí Connachta. Edana noticed as well;

he heard the hissing intake of her breath. The others
stared curiously into the chamber as the Toscaire Concordai shut the doors once again. Doyle glanced inquiringly
at the man. "Are *you* taking sides, Toscaire Rhusvak?
I'd think that's a dangerous thing for the Concordance
at the moment."

Rhusvak's face was solemn behind the gaping jaws of
the bear. "No, Tiarna. I'm simply a neutral observer who
will work with whomever becomes the new Rí Ard." He
nodded to Edana. "Or Banrion Ard. The Concordance
has its own worries with the Arruk and the Thane's attention is there, not on the Tuatha. Though . . ." Rhusvak paused for a breath, and Doyle waited. The Toscaire
lifted a shoulder under the bearksin. "If the two of you
can offer the Concordance the help of Lámh Shábhála,
as the late Rí Ard promised me privately, perhaps the
Concordance can be persuaded to be . . . less than neutral in this. Certainly a few of our troops could be spared
to come west, if they are joined later on their return
with an army from the Tuatha."

"The Rí Ard made that promise with our knowledge,
as you know, Toscaire," Edana said to him. She moved
alongside Doyle; he took her hand in his. "We will have
Lámh Shábhála soon. We will also have the throne of
the Tuatha. And we'll keep the promise my da made
to you."

"The Thane will be pleased to hear that," Rhusvak
answered. He glanced back at the door through which
Ó Riain had gone. "Though it seems that not all Riocha
agree with you, and who knows what *they* may promise
the Concordance." He bowed to both of them. "I should
retire to my own chamber and give my scribe a message
for my Thane. My condolences to both of you on your
terrible loss." He glanced at the door. "The other tiarna
and bantiarna should have a chance to pay their respects."

"Aye," Edana said. "Please let them in, Toscaire
Rhusvak."

The Toscaire left the room, opening the doors wide

as he did so. As the Riocha started to file into the chamber, Edana pressed Doyle's hand and leaned toward him. "You *will* have Lámh Shábhála, won't you, love? If we have that behind us, the Ríthe—and all the Riocha—will have no choice when they come together for the Óenach."

"I'll have it," he told her. "On Festival Day. Jenna will come to Inishduán. She will."

He hoped he was right. He closed his right hand in the air as if he were already grasping Lámh Shábhála.

The *Uaigneas* rolled in the heavy waves coming in from the west as it left Inishfeirm Harbor for Dún Kiil. Jenna stood at the railing of the deck shifting her weight easily with the movements of the ship, her hand closed around Lámh Shábhála as the head and shoulders of a young woman rotated slowly in front of her, suspended in the air and glowing with the energy of the cloch.

"That's Meriel," Mundy said behind her. "A good likeness, too. So you've discovered how Severii O'Coulghan used Lámh Shábhála to make the statues in the White Keep."

"It was Severii who told me," she answered. "I just rarely listened to his voice before. I used to think Severii wasted the mage-light's energy with his sculptures and architecture, but now I wonder if he didn't use Lámh Shábhála better than the rest of us."

Jenna brought the bust down until it came to rest in Mundy's hands. She released Lámh Shábhála and the glow around the figure faded, leaving Mundy holding an image of Meriel that seemed achingly lifelike, even to the color of her flesh and hair and the open and gleaming eyes. Jenna reached forward to touch the image. The stone felt warm and yielding under her hands, almost as if she were actually touching her daughter. Her breath caught in her throat; she blinked heavily. Her arm and head ached with the pain of using Lámh Shábhála. "I . . .

I was afraid I'd forgotten what Meriel looked like. I needed to see her again."

Mundy's voice growled, gentle. "You don't need to be afraid of that, Jenna."

"I am, Mundy. I'm afraid I'll never see her again. I'm afraid that I'm doing the wrong thing." She laughed scornfully. "You know, I was angry with my own mam for years and years because of the way she acted toward me after she fell in love with Padraic Mac Ard. I never forgave her for that betrayal—which is how I thought of it, then—and I never had the chance to reconcile . . . no, I'll be fair; I never made a real effort to reconcile with her before she died. Now I wonder if I haven't treated Meriel far worse than I ever treated my mam."

"You can't mean that."

"I do. Mundy, I can remember a thousand times when I was too busy to listen to her or play with her because some clan leader needed something or there was a conflict or the Comhairle was in session or I was in pain from Lámh Shábhála or . . ." She stopped. "Now she's gone and I may never see her again. She's gone, and I'm not willing to give up Lámh Shábhála to get her back. I'm about to do the one thing that Doyle warned me would result in her death."

Mundy handed Jenna the sculpture; she hugged it to herself. She was afraid to look into the eyes, afraid that they might stare back accusingly.

"You're doing the one thing that will allow you to have both of them," she heard Mundy say. She looked out at the waves, turning her back to him. Well out from the ship, she could see a seal break the water and dive again.

"I hope so, Mundy." She kissed the top of the statue's head as she might Meriel's. "By the Mother-Creator, I hope so."

25

Hunters in the Wilds

NOT LONG after leaving Ballycraigh, Owaine was regretting his decision to continue his journey. He seemed to have lost Léimard; the squirrel hadn't returned to him as he rode away. The rain was persistent and steady, never a raging downpour but hard enough that it dripped constantly from every surface and discovered every halfway dry patch of clothing on his body. He'd bought a small clay pot in the village and filled it with some herbs, and spent most of the first stripe of his ride recalling the witchfire spell, finally managing to get the pot alight. He wasn't sure it helped. Aye, it illuminated the road a bit, but it turned the rain into silver streaks all around him, it glared in his eyes when he held it up so that the darkness was even more profound, and it sent shadows to swaying so that it seemed the night was alive around him.

Which it was.

The witchfire pot might not have helped his already poor sight much (though he hoped it aided the horse), but there was nothing wrong with his ears. Even through the persistent drumming of the rain and the patient *clop* of hooves, he could hear the sounds of movement around him. The road had curved back toward the edges of Foraois Coill once more, which made him wonder if Léimard hadn't returned to Cataigh. The trees around him didn't seem to be oaks, however, and the road turned and twisted through the valleys between high, wooded hills. Wolves—normal ones—howled in the distance, and he heard the barking of what might have been feral dogs. Once, not long after he'd lit the witchfire pot, there came from startlingly close by the muttering growl of a dire wolf speaking its own language, though Owaine saw nothing and—thankfully—the creature didn't attack. He heard the warbling cry of red deer and the hooting of an owl, the low grunting of some animal scrabbling in the brush and a high warble as branches above him shook heavy drops down on him. A thousand insects trilled and rasped in the thickets. Up on the hill to his right, as the rain subsided for a few minutes, he saw a snaking line of blurred but bright lights like a flowing river of cold blue-and-green fire: wind sprites, he guessed.

People might sleep in the night. The world did not. It seemed more awake than asleep.

Owaine shifted his sore rear in the leather cup of the saddle; he swung the witchfire pot, hung on the end of a stick, from the right to the left. As he did so, he heard a coughing roar and what sounded like great wings beating. A stand of young maple saplings at the edge of the road just ahead suddenly collapsed as something huge and dark moved out onto the road. Owaine's horse reared backward and he barely managed to stay on, dropping the witchfire pot in the road and spilling the glowing herbs. In their wan illumination, baleful red eyes glared at him from the wrinkled folds of a leathery, snouted face. The mouth of the thing opened, showing white, daggered teeth, and it stood on its hind legs, spreading batlike wings with jutting, clawed fingerlike-spines.

Owaine had seen something like this only once before, a hideous creature drawn in one of the books in the Order's library, a book depicting the near-mythical beasts of the Before. Under the illustration had been a single word.

Dragon.

The horse reared again, but less urgently this time as

it backed up. The apparition did the same, hissing like
a boiling teakettle as it dropped down again and scuttled
away a step. Grounded, it moved like a bat, the wings
its hands; as the witchfire sputtered and threw fitful light
over glinting, reddish scales, Owaine realized that it
wasn't as big as his fright had made it—no larger than
one of the brown bears he'd glimpsed in the forests on
Inishfeirm. The book in the Order's library had spoken
of dragons as big as houses, creatures that could perch
on a keep's tower as if it were a tree stump.

If this *was* a dragon anything like the dragons of the
Before, it was also a very young or a very scrawny one.
But young or scrawny, it looked big and powerful
enough to make a snack of Owaine and a meal of the
horse.

"Shoo!" Owaine shouted, as if he were scolding one
of the Order's cats. He waved his hands in the creature's
direction. "Go away!"

The dragon snarled, a low gurgling deep in its throat.
Its head reared back on its long neck and the scales at
its neck rose like a collar of hard petals. Its wings
flapped, the wind showering drops from the branches
above them. Gray smoke jetted from its nostrils.

"Shite!" Owaine cursed.

It spat fire.

The attack wasn't the great gout of searing, awful
flame that the ancient books had depicted. Rather, the
dragon disgorged a ball of phlegm the size of Owaine's
head that hissed and fumed and dripped burning gelati-
nous globs. The largest mass of it hit the road a few feet
shy of Owaine, sizzling as it struck the mud of the road
and spread out as if it were made of soft pitch. The mess
burned there like a soggy bonfire.

His horse reared up again at the same time, wide-eyed
and frightened, and this time Owaine went down. He hit
the road in a splash of mud and water. The dragon
lurched forward, crawling awkwardly on its winged front
legs. It hissed again, the massive jaws opening and snapping shut again. As Owaine frantically tried to regain

his feet and his horse went galloping back the way they'd come, the dragon took a half-hop, half-flight with a beat of its wings and landed a few feet from him. Its head snapped back; Owaine grabbed the witchfire pot from the road, flinging it as hard as he could at the dragon with a shout. The pot hit the beast directly on the snout, the fired clay shattering as if it had hit a stone. The dragon roared and lifted up on its hind legs again.

Owaine waited to die.

Sounding vastly annoyed, the dragon's great wings battered the air and its muscular hind legs pushed at the ground. The dragon crashed through tree limbs and into the night sky, showering Owaine with bits of leaves and small branches. Well above him, the creature roared again and wheeled away to the west.

Owaine sat on the road for several long breaths, gazing up through the broken limbs where the dragon had gone and feeling the rain on his face. He squinted back down the road: his horse was standing there a dozen paces away, already grazing contentedly at the grass on the side of the roadway as if nothing had happened. Léimard had returned as well, sitting on the horse's rump with a nut between its paws and chewing contentedly as if nothing at all had happened. In the middle of the road, dragonfire fumed and hissed in the drizzle.

"I think," he said to Léimard and the horse, "that the Mother is trying to tell us to camp here and get a fresh start in thc morning."

Meriel healed a man with a mangled leg in Kenleelagh, a woman with a deformed spine in Garventon, a child with lackbreath in Elphin. There were some who seemingly healed themselves at her touch, and unfortunate others who were turned away or found that the magic of Cailin of the Healing Touch failed to work. The villages were more numerous now and closer together, and the Taisteal spent one night in each with an early departure the next day. Always moving, always just ahead of someone who might be disappointed in the Taisteal wares and promises, though the rumor of the True Healer who traveled with them seemed to keep pace with their movements.

They moved on from Elphin, following the road southward. The wagon Sevei drove rocked and bounced along the rough lane.

"Do you ever get tired of the traveling?" Meriel asked Sevei, who shook her head.

"Not really. Sometimes, aye, of course it all seems too much the same, but then we'll pass mountains or some deep hidden lough, or see something that none of us have ever glimpsed before. Those with the Taisteal blood would be bored being in one place and seeing the same faces every day. We want new landscapes, new people."

"And new pockets to empty."

Sevei grinned. "Aye, and that. There's more than one reason we—" She stopped, a frown furrowing her brow as she rose up in the wagon's seat, peering forward along the curve of the road. "Hey, Nico!" she called to the wagon in front. "Look to the east."

Meriel followed Sevei's gaze, leaning over toward the woman. Approaching from a hill just off the road were several riders. The sunlight glinted on ring mail and helmets, and the horses they rode were armored as well. A green-and-brown banner fluttered from a pole held by one of the riders. They came down the slope and stopped in the middle of the road ahead of them. They heard Nico call to the horses and bring his wagon to a halt several paces from them. Behind, Meriel and the others did the same.

The riders came forward.

"Sevei," Nico called out as they approached. "Come here and bring our Cailin with you."

Sevei nodded to Meriel and hopped down from the wagon. Meriel followed, standing next to Sevei as the riders came abreast of the wagons. At a nod from the lead rider, the others moved carefully to either side and effectively surrounded the clan. None of them had weapons drawn, but neither did they smile at the faces of the clan staring out at them from the wagons. "Maidin maith, Tiarna," Nico called up to the rider. "A pleasant day, 'tis."

"And who are you?" the rider grunted without returning the pleasantry.

"Nico, Clannhri of Clan Dranaghi." He paused, as if waiting for the man to give his name. When the tiarna simply stared, Nico continued. "We're on our way to Lár Bhaile, then to Dún Laoghaire and up the coast and across the Finger to our own long-unseen homes. I note by your colors that we've entered Tuath Gabair. The most pleasant of all the Tuatha, as I would know, having seen them all. The lush green hills, the—"

"I want to see everyone out of the wagons," the man snapped, interrupting Nico. "Now."

"As the tiarna wishes . . ." Nico called to the rest of the clan, and a few moments later the entire group was standing alongside the wagons, the small children hugging to their mam's legs. "This is all of you?" the tiarna asked Nico. The horse nickered restlessly and the man pulled at the reins to calm him.

"Aye," Nico answered. "My family, which I love as the tiarna no doubt loves his own family."

A grunt. "None of them are orphans you've picked up to sell, or slaves?"

Nico shook his head. "No, Tiarna. Everyone here is of Clan Dranaghi. Everyone."

"Check the wagons," the rider ordered his men. "Make sure they're not hiding anyone else." He rode slowly up and down in front of them as the other riders dismounted, staring at each of them. Meriel could feel Sevei's hand firmly gripping her arm.

"If the tiarna would tell us who or what he's looking for, perhaps we could help," Nico suggested.

The rider laughed. "I'm sure you'd be happy to tell me whatever I'd like to hear, especially if I crossed your palm with coins. I know how well the Taisteal can lie."

His gaze swept over them and stopped on Meriel. He stared hard at her. "Odd skin color for a Taisteal," he said. "All the rest of you so dark, and she so pale. And I'd swear the sun finds red highlights in her hair . . ."

"The tiarna is very observant," Nico said. "You are to be complimented. Cailin was an, ah, unfortunate mistake by her mam, I'm afraid, who dallied with one of the local young men on our last trip here to Talamh an Ghlas. Cailin wanted to see her da's homeland, so she came with us this time."

"Is that true?" the rider asked. He looked directly at Meriel. "Answer me. You've nothing to fear from me if you tell the truth. Step out here to me, away from the others."

Meriel felt Sevei's hand loosen on her arm. "Careful," Sevei whispered as Meriel moved out from the crowd, going up to the tiarna's horse.

"What's your name?" he asked her.

The man stared down at her: green eyes, a face furrowed with a scar along the chin, the skin tanned by sun and wind: a warrior's face. He would do as he was ordered to do no matter what that order might be. Meriel remembered what Nico had told her when she'd first tried to escape: *"Those we meet won't be your allies . . ."* This tiarna, if she told him the truth, would more than likely take her to the Rí Gabair. Meriel knew that in Lár Bhaile the name of Jenna MacEagan, Holder of Lámh Shábhála, was a curse to be spat upon once uttered. Jenna had slain the Banrion Cianna, the mam of the current Rí Gabair, when she was last here and that deed was still well remembered and reviled. The Mad Holder's daughter would be a prize indeed here. She would be a prisoner here, or perhaps worse.

"I'm Cailin," she said, imitating the Taisteal accent as well as she could, shortening the vowels and making the consonants harsh and guttural. "Of Clan Dranaghi." She thought she could almost hear Nico's sigh of relief. "It's just as Clannhri Nico told you. My mam was seduced by

a man from Falcarragh long ago, and I have some of
his coloring."

The man nodded, though his eyes glittered as they
continued to hold her. Then he looked away, calling to
his men. "Well?"

"Nothing, Tiarna," one of them answered. "Just the
usual Taisteal junk."

"All right, then." The rider flicked the reins, moving
up to Nico. "Then tell me, Clannhri, if you've seen other
travelers on the road. In particular, I would be interested
if you've seen a young woman, perhaps of about seventeen cycles, with red hair and an Inishlander's accent.
She may have Riocha around her or gardai, and they
might try to prevent her from talking to others."

Nico stroked his chin. "Oh, we Taisteal must see a
thousand travelers on the road, Tiarna, and remembering is hard work. . . ."

The tiarna reached into his belt pouch and flipped a
coin. Silver glinted at Nico's feet. "Fortunately, I have
the memory of an Ald," Nico continued, glancing down
once. "But, alas . . ." He shook his head gravely. "I
recall no one like the girl you describe or any such travelers. I would certainly have remembered them." He
turned to the others. "Do any of you remember such
a woman?"

The clan shook their heads as one. The rider released
an irritated sigh. "A shame," he said, "for the Rí Gabair's reward would be in gold, not silver, and there
would be a substantial pile of it. If you see this woman
or if your overtaxed memory recalls her, then leave word
with the Ald of the nearest village to send the message
to Lár Bhaile. And should I hear of any Taisteal thievery
in this part of the Tuath, I'll know where to come, won't
I? Perhaps I'll see you again in Lár Bhaile, if that's indeed where you're going."

"I pray to the Mother-Creator that we meet again,
Tiarna," Nico told him. "It would be a pleasure. Perhaps
we may even do some further business then."

The man's smile was devoid of mirth. "Perhaps," he said. He nodded to his companion and kicked at his horse's flanks. They rode off to the west. Nico spat in the dirt where the tiarna had been. *"Svinja sin od pas!"* he uttered, and spat again. Nico leaned down to pick up the coin and placed it in his pocket. He stalked back to his wagon.

"What did Nico say just then?" Meriel asked Sevei as they pulled themselves back into the seat of their cart. The pots and pans hung inside jangled and clattered as they started off again.

"It's Taisteal," Sevei answered. "He called the tiarna a 'bastard son of a dog.' "

Meriel laughed. "I'll have to remember that," she said.

Meriel had thought that she'd see nothing that day more intriguing than the riders. She was wrong.

By late afternoon, the clan had seen little of other humans. The northern stretch of Tuath Gabair was dominated by drumlins, low but very steep hills one after another with marshland at their feet. There were occasional small woods of elm, maple, and pine around the bottoms of the drumlins, but the tops of the hills were bare as if generations of unknown people had logged the forests that had once been there, leaving the hills green with high grass dotted with purple heather and flecks of pure, startling color from wildflowers. Birds—sparrows and larks—called to each other and flitted through the bracken. They passed an occasional farm or spied a thatched roof well off on a tiny lane that meandered away from the main road, but for the most part the country was still wild. Nico had said that they were making for a village called Ballyrea some fifteen or twenty miles below the border of Gabair. "It's the first glimpse of civilization in this Mother-forgotten part of the world, but it's as beggarly a place as we've seen," he said. "We won't find much profit in Gabair until we cross the River Duán at Áth Iseal. Then we'll finally be in a true city again."

The sun was already dipping low in the sky before they caught sight of Ballyrea. They moved in alternating dusk and sun as the road climbed the drumlins and then fell again into the marshland. At the top of one of the hills, they could see smoke wafting skyward from several chimneys and the gleam of whitewashed walls under thatch, just at the foot of the next drumlin.

And there was something else.

A black cloud swirled over the land. It was low, skimming the treetops at one side of the village, moving too fast and against the wind. The cloud broke apart and re-formed, the edges breaking into distinct particles that wheeled and swayed. Faintly, Meriel could hear a noise from the cloud's direction, a strident din as if a thousand voices were calling. The cloud was moving southwest to northeast across the road, but it seemed to sense them and sent a questing tendril in their direction. Then the entire cloud followed, the dark bulk of it sweeping in an impossibly wide turn.

The noise intensified and Meriel suddenly realized what she was seeing and hearing.

"Crows!" Meriel shouted.

"Aye," Sevei said. "A larger flock than I've ever seen before . . ."

The cloud of birds, as it approached, grew more distinct and more ominous. The birds were enormous, with wingspans as wide as Meriel's outstretched arms. The thunder of their wings boomed, a low accompaniment to their screeching, strident voices. Meriel could almost imagine them talking to each other, their calls more varied than the barren screeches she'd heard from normal birds. The flock flew overhead once, so low that the Taisteal could almost reach up and touch them as they hurtled past, blocking out the sun. The horde passed and then wheeled around once more.

This time they circled above the caravan, and some of the birds landed on the roofs and wheels, on the horses' backs, on the ground around them. Two of the birds flapped down just above Meriel; as she turned around to bat at them, they hopped back, cawing with beaks open and black eyes glittering. One of the crows, she noticed, had a patch of white feathers above its left eye. The two creatures seemed to nod to each other, then flew heavily away again.

Sevei struck at another bird that landed momentarily on her shoulder. The horses reared in the harnesses, nickering in fright at the noise and commotion; around them, Meriel could hear the rest of the clan shouting and cursing as the crows landed around them. Their world was suddenly confined to the whirl of black bodies and their shrill calls, the landscape around them blotted out in the ebony storm.

In the chaos, a crow landed again next to Meriel. A flash of white told her that it was the same bird as before. But as Meriel lifted her hand to strike away the creature, she stopped. The crow held something in its beak: a twig with an oak leaf attached to one end. As Meriel stared, it placed the twig carefully at her side and cawed once. When Meriel didn't respond, it bent its head down and—with its beak—nudged the twig closer to Meriel before taking flight again.

The flock swept over the wagons and disappeared northward.

Meriel picked up the twig. As she did so, she heard a voice in her head: a woman's voice, the words touched with a strange guttural accent. *I will meet you in Doire Coill. The branch will show you the way.*

Then it was gone. The twig, a straight branch no longer than her hand, was trembling between her fingers as if it were alive, pulling her hand. When she relaxed slightly, the leafed end of the branch quivered as the notched leaf pointed south-southwest. When Meriel tried to move her hand away from that direction, the twig resisted, as if it were comfortable only when it lay in that direction.

"Cailin?" Meriel was suddenly aware that Sevei was

talking to her, and she started. "I said, what's that in your hand?"

"I don't know," Meriel answered honestly. "One of the birds dropped it."

Sevei's brow knotted. "Let me see . . ."

She held out her hand. Reluctantly, Meriel placed the twig in the woman's palm. Sevei twirled it around, looking at it from all sides. If the branch spoke to her or moved in her hand, Sevei gave no indication. She handed it back to Meriel. "It's oak," she said. "There's another old forest not far from here. Probably got it from there. Damned huge noisy things they were. I'll bet the farmers hereabouts are in an uproar. A bloody big flock like that could strip a field in less than a stripe."

Meriel nodded. The twig was trembling again, and she loosened her fingers slightly to let it move. It turned on its own in her upturned palm, the tip of the leaf pointing unerringly in the same direction.

Meriel said nothing to Sevei.

They saw the flock once more less than half a stripe later as the sun was going down, moving past them just off to the west, this time streaming by as if trying to beat the last rays of the sun and paying no attention to the caravan at all as they approached Ballyrea.

They flew, Meriel noticed, along the path of the twig.

26

Unexpected Movements

AFTER the night encounter with the dragon, Owaine thought that nothing worse could happen. For the next several days, that appeared to be the case. He continued to chase the Taisteal. Whenever the road reached a turning or intersected another road, Léimard would leap unbidden from its perch on the horse and flit quickly around the ground, finally scampering several strides up one path or the other until Owaine nudged the horse forward toward the squirrel, who would leap back up again. In each village they passed, or when they came across other travelers on the road, Owaine would inquire about the Taisteal; he kept the story he'd told those in the inn of Ballycraigh—that he was chasing the Taisteal because his love was ill and needed the True Healer who rode with them. From the reports he garnered, they seemed to gain somewhat on the Taisteal with each day; Owaine grew increasingly convinced, despite the lack of any hard evidence, that Meriel was the healer with them. In the village of Elphin, with the sun—finally emerging from the clouds—at the zenith, he was informed that the Taisteal had left just that morning, still moving south into Tuath Gabair. With a hard ride, the villagers said, he might even catch them by evening.

Owaine rode on with an optimism that was quickly dampened. First, not long after he crossed into Tuath Gabair, Léimard suddenly chattered and leaped away from the horse. Not ten breaths later, several gardai riders in the colors of Gabair accosted him on the road and interrogated him endlessly, stretching Owaine's ability to lie and seemingly jabbing at every inconsistency in his story. From their questions, it was obvious that it was Meriel that they were searching for, and they had ridden up from the direction Owaine was headed; that worried Owaine. If the riders hadn't found her with the Taisteal on the road ahead, was he also chasing a chimera?

There was little choice but to continue, though. There was nowhere else to go in this place—his choice had been made. Owaine plodded on— Léimard returning as soon as the gardai had departed—as his mood soured.

Then the crows came, more of the nasty, loud things than Owaine believed anyone could count. They swarmed around him like monstrous black gnats, cawing and screeching, and then hurrying off back the way they'd come.

Worse, the sun was falling far too quickly in the sky and the cursed drumlins lay mockingly across his path as if the gods had set them there deliberately to slow him down, and he'd neither caught up with the Taisteal nor found the village the riders had told him was just ahead: Bally-something-or-other, though half the villages and towns in Talamh an Ghlas seemed to start with that. There was nothing around him but marsh, a copse of trees just ahead, and the bare heads of the drumlins front, back, and sides. He'd have to spend another night out in the weather. After the encounter with the dragon, Owaine had no intention of riding in the dark.

He flicked the reins and the horse moved into the shelter of the trees. Léimard chattered at him scoldingly. Owaine ignored the creature.

"All right then, Máister Cléurach," he said to the horse, "we'll stay here for the night. It looks like good enough grazing here for you." Owaine doubted that the old Máister would appreciate Owaine's naming of the horse (especially since the beast was a gelding), and it really wasn't fair to the horse, either, who wasn't nearly as ancient, cantankerous, or decrepit as the Máister had been during Owaine's first two years at the Order. Owaine was certain he wasn't the only one who failed to mourn when Máister Cléurach suddenly died one morning and Bráthair Kirwan became Máister.

He hobbled Máister Cléurach, then gathered wood for a fire and set about making a camp. Léimard ran up the nearest tree trunk and vanished. When Owaine had a small fire going and a bit of stirabout sizzling in the pan, he leaned back against his bedroll and ate, staring at the veiled landscape around him, which could have hidden untold thousands of crows or several dragons. "I hope we're going the right way," he said to the horse, who lifted its tail and deposited a steaming pile on the ground. Owaine decided not to take that as a sign, but he wondered. "We'll catch up with the Taisteal tomorrow, maybe even before they leave the village," he told the horse. The horse was a worse conversationalist than Léimard, who at least looked at Owaine when he was talking. "We'll find out whether it's really Meriel we've been chasing." He touched his clochmion for reassurance; there was no sense of Meriel's presence, but he told himself that he still was confident in his choice. Yet . . . a few times, especially during the rainy, dreary and empty days, he'd doubted.

In all the villages, those who described the healer invariably said she was dark-haired and a few had given her name as Cailin, not Meriel. But there also were those who said her accent wasn't quite that of a Taisteal and some who said without Owaine's prompting that she might sound a bit Inish.

Hair could be dyed. Names could be changed. And Meriel may have been given a clochmion, and perhaps the stone could heal. . . .

He'd know for certain soon. His clochmion would tell him, as soon as he was close to the Taisteal he'd been chasing.

There was nothing he could do about it now. With a sigh, Owaine scraped the last few scraps of stirabout on the ground in front of Máister Cléurach and unrolled his blankets. He looked around again for Léimard, who remained hidden. He stared up at the blurry stars and the fuzzy rags of light clouds until he fell asleep.

He woke, suddenly, with the remembrance of a sound. It was still full night, and the fire had gone to glowing coals. Eyes open, Owaine lay still, listening—aye, there it was again; the crack of a dry limb, somewhere nearby. Máister Cléurach was snuffling with flaring nostrils, the horse's hooves shuffling nervously, its ears standing straight up and eyes wide.

Owaine let his hand ease down to the hilt of his belt knife and slipped it from the scabbard. Carefully, he moved the blankets aside as he gazed around. He could see nothing and no one. The road lay empty under the stars a few paces away, but there were shadows enough around him, and the tree trunks were black as obsidian and numerous enough to conceal a dozen men. Robbers were common enough and single travelers were easy pickings—that was why Owaine had kept to the villages at night when he could. But he'd thought that with the gardai out riding, robbers would have decided to stay off the roads tonight.

A crow cawed once, overhead. Owaine glanced up. It was difficult to make out the bird in the darkness, but a patch of lighter color shone in the glow of the coals. The crow cawed again.

A low growl answered, just off in the trees . . .

Owaine scrambled to his feet as Máister Cléurach whinnied in fright and fought its hobbles. Owaine saw it then, a form sliding fluidly out into a patch of starlight and close enough that he had no difficulty seeing it: a wolf, but one as tall as Owaine at the shoulders. The beast was massive and huge, with muscular limbs as thick as Owaine's leg and curved talons sprouting from the paws; yellow, angry eyes; twin rows of ivory spearheads set in its open jaws; a blood-red tongue lolling out hungrily as the creature stared back at Owaine.

A dire wolf, a beast of legend . . .

The knife in Owaine's hand looked ridiculous, suddenly: no more threatening than a knitting needle set against a sword. The dire wolf gave two barking exhalations, fog coming from its mouth with each explosion of breath—it sounded suspiciously like laughter. Owaine shivered. He imagined those jaws closing around him, tearing and ripping . . . a shiver crawled his spine. He backed away toward Máister Cléurach, the wolf staring at him without moving, and stooped down. He envisioned cutting the hobbles and leaping onto the horse's back in one swift motion, holding on for his life to Máister Cléurach's neck and bare back and praying to the Mother-Creator that the gelding could outrun a dire wolf.

The wolf laughed again, as if it could hear his thoughts.

Owaine reached down and, sawing desperately, severed the rope around the horse's front legs. Máister Cléurach reared away as Owaine straightened and tried to vault onto the horse's back. He managed to get his leg up and his arms around the gelding's neck as Máister Cléurach turned and started to gallop away in utter fear.

Owaine's leg slipped off; Máister Cléurach's flight tore his grip from the horse's neck. He fell to the ground as the gelding pounded away through the trees. He pushed himself up. The knife was gone, lost somewhere, and the dire wolf glared at him. He knew, for a certainty, that he couldn't outrun the creature.

He knew he was going to die here.

As he stood there, waiting, he heard another sound behind him. Before he could turn, something struck him in the back, like the stabbing of an arrow. He reached for it, spinning, but as he did so the world dimmed around him. A darker night closed in from the edges of his sight, growing until it seemed he was staring through a pinprick at the stars, realizing that he'd fallen and was staring up helpless. He tried to rise, but his body wouldn't obey and the nothingness closed over him like a storm wave and he was lost.

"You're certain you can do this, my friend?" Doyle asked Shay O Blaca. "We've talked about this so long, and I agree with you: I'll need three other cloudmages with Clochs Mór with me for us to be certain we can overcome Lámh Shábhála; if we can't be four against the One, then none of this will work."

Shay nodded grimly, touching the irregularly-shaped, clear crystal around his neck. In many ways, O Blaca had been the da Doyle had never had, taking the much-younger Doyle under his tutelage at the request of Doyle's uncle. Shay had become adviser, mentor, guide, and friend; as Doyle had come into prominence in the Rí Ard's court, he had also become co-conspirator.

O Blaca glanced over to Edana, who was listening to the two of them while staring out the window at the inner courtyard of the Rí Ard's keep, then his gaze returned to Doyle. "I've never been to Inishduán, so I had one of the Infochla fisherfolk take me over to the island so I could see well enough to use Quickship. I think I can send all four of you *there* with the cloch, Doyle, but I won't be able to bring anyone back and I won't be able to go myself. It will take everything Quickship has to do just that one task."

Doyle waved a hand in dismissal. "I've already sent word to Falcarragh to have a ship waiting for us off Inishduán." He gave O Blaca a quick grin. "Getting back won't be the issue, Shay—we'll either have Lámh Shábhála or we'll be dead."

Shay chuckled darkly at that. "You'll have Lámh Shábhála. I know you."

Doyle grinned back at him. "Aye, I will. But just in case . . . You remember that bantiarna in Falcarragh with a clochmion called Messenger?—a useful little stone. I know she's not of the Order or even Riocha, but she wants to study with us, and I told her that if she'd help in this I'd make sure she had a personal invitation from you to come to Lár Bhaile. She's agreed to be aboard the ship and will send word back immediately as to the outcome."

"I'm worried about the number of people involved in this, Doyle. Too many people know too much."

"I know," he told the man, clapping him on the shoulder. "I am, too. But the cloudmages of the Order will work together. Think of how prominent we'll be when the Order of Gabair holds Lámh Shábhála."

Edana stirred. She lifted the Cloch Mór around her own neck. "I'll be one of the four, Shay," she said. "Demon-Caller has already met Lámh Shábhála and nearly won." She stood up and went to Doyle before he could protest. She hugged him, placing her index finger on his lips. "No, love," she told him. "I know what you'll say, and no. I *will* be with you. Consider that an order from your Banrion Ard."

Doyle kissed her finger. "You're not the Banrion yet. And you've not used Demon-Caller yourself."

"I was trained at the Order, too." She inclined her head to Shay. "I had the same excellent teacher."

"I know, but . . ."

She lifted her finger again. "I have a few days still to learn the cloch. And I *will* be Banrion. When we return with Lámh Shábhála."

He wanted to simultaneously smile and sigh. He realized, more and more, the cost of love. Even his love for his mam had been tempered by pity for her broken soul and mind; in truth, there had been a sense of relief in him when she'd finally died. But he looked at the vital, comely woman before him, and he knew he was where he wanted to be. Aye, he was ambitious. Aye, he wanted to share the power she would have and that was why he had first courted her, but they had both been snared— unlooked-for—by the fickle bonds of tenderness. He knew now that love imposed its own burdens, for when he thought of Edana in danger or hurt, he ached inside. He was more frightened for her than for himself. "Edana, the training and your desire don't matter. You've had no experience fighting with another Cloch Mór. This would be an empty, useless victory if we win Lámh Shábhála but lose each other."

She leaned forward. She kissed him deeply and long, uncaring that O Blaca watched. When she pulled back, she put her forehead on his, her hand curled around the back of his neck. "And what kind of leader would I be if I stayed and let the other Riocha whisper that I was too afraid to risk myself?" she asked him softly. "What kind of lover would I be if I didn't do all I could do to protect the person I care most about? I have to do this, Doyle. I *will* do this."

He sighed. He nodded. He hugged her fiercely.

O Blaca cleared his throat noisily. "Ó Riain has already sent people to Rí Connachta, Éoganacht, and Airgialla," he said. "There are too many Riocha who would like to see Enean on the throne for my comfort. No offense to your da, Bantiarna Edana, but he was strongwilled and forced the Tuatha to cooperate, sometimes against their will. Some have made no secret of the fact that they resented the power given to your da—Rí Connachta and Rí Éoganacht definitely made their feelings known privately as well as in their dealings with him. They'd prefer to see a weaker person on the throne in Dún Laoghaire so that their own power is elevated."

"Which makes it all the more vital that we take Lámh Shábhála from the Mad Holder," Edana answered. "Once Doyle holds the cloch, the Ríthe can make their feelings known all they like, but they can't stand against us. They'll *have* to—" She stopped as the door to the chamber was flung open and Enean stalked in, followed by two protesting gardai. "I'm sorry, Bantiarna," one of the gardai said, "but he—"

"You took Da's cloch, Edana," Enean shouted over the garda's explanation, going up to Edana. Doyle started to interpose himself between the two, but Edana raised her hand to hold him back. "Tiarna Ó Riain says it's mine and so I want it back." Enean stamped his foot on the floor.

"Enean," Edana said soothingly, as one might talk to an angry child even though the man towered over her by a head, his muscular arms corded where they emerged from his clóca. "Have I ever taken anything of yours? Have I ever hurt you before?"

Enean's anger dissolved, his face melting into an uncertain frown. "No," he admitted. "You haven't." Then he scowled again, his hands fisting at his sides. Doyle watched, ready to intervene. "But Tiarna Ó Riain said you took it from Da after he died and that Da said it was supposed to be mine."

"If it had been yours, I would have given it to you," Edana said quietly, brushing back the man's long hair from his scarred and disfigured face. "I'm afraid Tiarna Ó Riain's mistaken. Do you remember how Da sent me away for a few years to Lár Bhaile so I could study magic with Tiarna O Blaca?"

Enean glanced quickly over at Shay, then nodded grudgingly, his face still angry. "Aye. I didn't like it because you weren't here."

"I know. I didn't like being away from you either, Enean. But you see, Da knew that you were already strong and could protect yourself with your sword; he sent me to the Order because he wanted me to have his Cloch Mór—that would be *my* strength."

Enean's face went stern, but he no longer looked angry. "I'll protect you, Edana."

"I know you will, Enean." She touched the cloch at her breast. "But this is in case you're not there, or in case I might need to protect you."

"Ah . . ." Enean blinked heavily and tears glittered in his eyes. "Da was smart. I miss him."

"Aye, he knew what was best and I miss him, too. We all do, very much. Enean, where's MacCamore? Why isn't he with you?"

"Tiarna Ó Riain sent MacCamore away. He said . . ." Enean grimaced, his eyes searching the ceiling as he concentrated. "He said that I should be doing things on my own now if I'm going to be Rí Ard." The emotions flitted over his face like racing clouds. "Edana, do you think I'd be a good Rí Ard?"

Edana smiled up at him. Doyle glanced at Shay, shaking his head to make sure that the tiarna said nothing. "I think you would try your very best to do exactly that, Enean," Edana said.

"I would," he agreed proudly. "I really would."

"I know." Edana hugged him; when she released him, he was smiling distractedly, as if he'd already forgotten the confrontation a moment ago. "What are you thinking about, Enean?" she asked.

"Tiarna Ó Riain introduced me to a pretty woman, almost as pretty as my Sorcha was." For a moment, Doyle saw the man's face cloud with the memory of his murdered fiancée. Then the expression slid away. "She likes me, and I like her, too."

Doyle caught Edana's wary glance. "That's wonderful, Enean," he said. "And who is this beauty you've met?"

Enean's forehead creased in concentration. "Bantiarna Toiréasa De Danaan. She's a niece of the Rí Connachta's, and she's Tiarna Ó Riain's cousin, too."

Doyle didn't need to look at Edana to know what she was thinking. They both knew the young woman—she'd been in Dún Laoghaire for the last few months; her father was one of the Rí Connachta's representatives in the court. Once widowed, though childless, she was a few years older than Enean. "You've been introduced to Bantiarna De Danaan before, Enean," Doyle said, "back when she first came to court. She didn't seem to take any particular special interest in you then, as I remember. It's strange how love can bloom all of a sudden, isn't it?"

Edana raised an eyebrow warningly at Doyle, but Enean missed the irony and merely grinned. "Aye," he said. " 'Tis." Then he frowned again. "But what about the cloch, Edana? Tiarna Ó Riain . . ."

Edana raised her finger to his lips. "You can tell Tiarna Ó Riain that you've talked to me about it, and that you want me to keep it because you know it will help

me stay safe. You want me to be safe, don't you?"
Edana hugged him once more. "And you should also
take these two gardai, find old MacCamore and tell him
that Tiarna Ó Riain was mistaken and that I wish him
to stay with you at all times. I'll tell Tiarna Ó Riain that
myself as soon as I'm finished here. Can you do that,
Enean?" The man nodded solemnly as Edana nodded
to the gardai. "Good. Now, go on. I'll come find you in
a bit—I'd love to hear more about this bantiarna of
yours . . ."

After Enean had left, Doyle let out a sigh. Shay stirred
from his place by the window. "You—we—have a huge
problem there," O Blaca said.

"Ó Riain oversteps his bounds," Edana hissed, the
fury she'd been holding back seething undisguised. "I'll
see him strung up by his entrails before this is over.
Using my brother this way . . ."

"We'll be in worse trouble if Bantiarna De Danaan
shows up big-bellied with child a few months from now,"
Doyle said to her. "Enean's mind is addled, but the
body . . . I hate to say this, but we should play the same
card, Edana."

She grimaced. "That's not right. To trick poor Enean
that way . . ."

"No, it's not right, but Ó Riain's already done it and
we need to be careful. The right bantiarna, someone we
know who will work with us . . ."

"Nuala Chathaigh," O Blaca interjected. "She's young,
comely enough, and Riocha if not as well-connected as
De Danaan, and her family has no love for the Connach-
tans. I know the family—they're from the same area of
Tuath Infochla as mine. Her parents would be pleased
to be so closely bound to the O Liathain family. Nuala
understands how the game is played and she has no better prospects. Her family sent her to the Order—I've
been teaching her. She's smart and fast to learn."

"I don't like it," Edana repeated, sighing. "They're
using my brother as a pawn and it's not right. We'd just
be doing the same."

Doyle took her hands in his own. He kissed her brow. "I know, love," he told her. "But we should have expected this, now that your da's gone. The Rí Ard would never declare Enean incompetent and so now he has to be considered as potentially much more than a pawn. Even if—when—I have Lámh Shábhála, Enean will still have a legitimate claim to be Rí Ard, and there will be those who would use that against us if they can. It would be best if *we're* the ones who have the most control over Enean, whether we like doing that or not. Who's going to keep Enean's interests most in mind: you, or the Rí Connachta through his puppet Ó Riain?"

He saw the decision form behind her eyes. Her lips tightened as she nodded. "How soon can this Nuala Chathaigh be here?" she asked Shay.

Shay smiled grimly. "At this time of day, she'll be in Tiarna O'Murchadha's class . . ." He closed his hand around the Cloch Mór around his neck. Doyle's hair stood out on his arms as energy crackled around them. Tiny lightnings crawled over Shay's figure; a moment later he vanished entirely with a faint thunderclap. They waited. After a few breaths, Doyle shrugged. "Perhaps she wasn't in the class today . . ." he began, but then the air near the fireplace shimmered and a puff of a breeze washed over them, laden with the scent of pine trees: an odor Doyle knew well from Lár Bhaile.

Gasping in surprise, a young woman with brown-gold hair and a blue embroidered clóca stood where Shay O Blaca had been a moment ago, her eyes and mouth wide with surprise. She saw Edana and sank to one knee with a deep curtsy.

"Welcome to Dún Laoghaire, Bantiarna Chathaigh," Edana said. "Tiarna Mac Ard and I have a proposal for you . . ."

27

Ballintubber and Inishduán

"WE'RE MAKING for Ballintubber today," Sevei said.

Ballintubber . . . That name woke echoes in Meriel. Her mam had told her the tales—on those far-too-rare nights when the mage-lights stayed hidden and no one else demanded her mam's time, when Meriel would snuggle up against Jenna in the huge bed her mam slept in every night alone. Then Jenna would talk about her own childhood.

Ballintubber . . . In Jenna's stories, it was a place of laughter and friendship, a simpler place made for simpler times where life might have been poor but was yet full, where her days had been uncomplicated and far happier.

There, too, would sit the looming presence of Knobtop, the mountainside on which Lámh Shábhála had been found, and the dark, gloomy recesses of Doire Coill, which Meriel imagined now as a larger and even more tangled version of Foraois Coill where she'd first met the Taisteal. In Ballintubber, Meriel might find the charred remnants of the two-room stone cottage Jenna had lived in until the cloch had found her, and perhaps the burial mounds where the bones of the people Jenna had known back then rested as their children and grandchildren led the same lives that generation upon generation before them had experienced.

Ballintubber . . .

For the first time, Meriel found herself looking forward to their arrival in a village. And yet, when they did arrive . . .

Ballintubber looked no different than any of the other places she'd seen. In truth, it might have been the smallest of the villages through which they'd passed, a collection of poorly kept buildings strung out along a half mile of road, the village center defined by a grimy tavern at a dusty crossroads—*Tara's,* the sign declared, and Meriel remembered that name also. Jenna had described Tara's as a joyous inn where the stone walls gleamed with whitewash (the stones looked as if they'd last seen paint when Meriel was born and the thatch roof sagged badly at the crown), where golden light shone dancing in the windows (the shutters, which were hung all askew and didn't match, were closed and there was nothing but darkness behind them), where the glad voices of the inhabitants could be heard talking and laughing and singing (Meriel heard nothing but the bleating of sheep in the fields, the lowing of a few cows in the stables behind the tavern, and the buzzing of flies on the excrement in the road).

The townspeople who came out to watch the Taisteal caravan arrive stared suspiciously at them with scowls on their dirty faces. And Knobtop . . . The glorious and magnificent peak inhabiting Meriel's imagination was in reality nothing more than a bare-topped hill, far less imposing than any of the mountains at Dún Kiil and positively diminutive against the lofty spine of crags that ran along the center of Inish Thuaidh or clustered on the island's western coastline.

Reality was a disappointment. Meriel knew it was unfair, but she wondered what else her mam's memory might have altered.

Nico guided the clan to a field across the street from Tara's Tavern, behind the tumble-down shell of a ruined house. The Ald of the village, an ancient, hunched-over graybeard with only one hand, caned his way over to the wagons as the clan started to climb down from the wagons. "You the Clannhri?" he barked at Nico.

"Aye, and you must be the Aldman of this fine town,"
Nico answered. The Aldman snorted and wiped at his
nose with the sleeve of his tunic. Meriel could smell the
alcohol on the man's breath.

"Bailey's the name," he said. "An' don' you be for-
gettin' it. We don't like Taisteal 'round here. Thieves
and worse." Bailey's besotted gaze drifted over to Meriel. "She be the healer?"

"Ah, so you've heard of her," Nico said, still smiling.
"Aye, that's Cailin, and she has the true gift."

Baily snorted. "Can she be fixin' this?" he asked, his
scornful laugh showing pink, toothless gums. He lifted
his handless arm; he waved the puckered stump nearly
in Meriel's face. "If she can, I'll be first there." Meriel
took a step back as Sevei jumped down from the wagon
alongside her, scowling at the Ald. Nico hurried in between them, smiling and clapping the Ald on the
shoulder.

"Now then," he said with a warning glance back at
Sevei, "Cailin's indeed a healer and a true wonder the
likes of which Ballintubber will never see again, I promise, but even she can't be bringing back what's not there,
I'm afraid. But I do know something that will help take
away the pain for a time—a little liquid fire in the belly,
eh? Keara, where's that poteen of ours, woman? Wait
'till you taste this, Ald; made by an ancient, secret recipe
known only to my clan." He led the Ald away, still
talking.

"What's the matter?" Sevei asked Meriel.

"What do you mean?"

"Something's wrong with you," the woman answered.
"I can see it. You're looking around at this place like
you're searching for something, or more like you're
afraid to see what you're expecting to see."

Meriel hesitated, not knowing how much she should
confide in the woman but remembering how she'd come
after Meriel at the lough and the promises she'd made
then. *Perhaps this is where I need to leave the clan, and
if it is then I'll need her help.*

Sevei's hand touched Meriel's shoulder, jolting her from her reverie. "I won't do anything to hurt you," the woman said. "Remember that."

Hesitantly, then, Meriel told Sevei about her mam and Ballintubber, and slowly Sevei's eyebrows rose. "Here? The Banrion MacEagan was born *here?*" she said, whispering so that no one else could hear as the clan began setting up the camp around them.

"Aye," Meriel answered. "But her surname was Aoire, then."

Now it was Sevei who glanced around. "Stay," she told Meriel. "Help the others set up our tent. I'll be back soon." With that, Sevei strode away. Meriel saw her go to Tara's Tavern, open the door, and go in. Meriel stared after her for a few breaths, then when the door didn't open again, turned to the wagon and started helping unload the tents and bedding. It might have been half a stripe later that she felt a tug on her sleeve; turning, she saw Sevei nod her head. "Come with me," the woman said. "Don't worry; the family will take care of the rest of the work. We have something to see."

Sevei said little. She had unhitched one of the horses and placed riding livery on it. She pulled herself astride the animal and then reached down to help Meriel up. Meriel put her arms around Sevei's waist as the woman twitched the reins and kicked once at the horse's side. They rode south down the road for a bit in the lengthening shadows, then Sevei turned the horse into the opening of a lane that was nearly obscured by overgrown foliage. They ducked under overhanging tree limbs, the horse pushing through high, choking weeds. The lane was defined only by the top of what had once been a stone fence; there was nothing left of the ruts that must have once been there and the grass was as high here as elsewhere, with a few young trees growing up between. The fence curved, and then stopped. Sevei urged the horse forward, then pulled up on the reins. "There," she said, pointing.

Meriel could see nothing at first. Then she saw what

must have once been the corner of a house, the stones now tumbled down but for this one section with weeds and trees filling the interior. "I asked at the inn," Sevei said, answering Meriel's unvoiced question. "I talked to a man there who said he was the son of the Tara on the sign, and he told me where the Aoires had lived." She pointed at the stones. "Here."

"Here," Meriel repeated wonderingly. She slipped down from the horse. "So it started here." She gazed around, stunned, trying to visualize what it might have looked like a few decades ago and failing—she couldn't see it, couldn't even imagine her mam at Meriel's own age, walking down this lane with a flock of sheep, with Meriel's great-mam Maeve standing in the doorway of the tiny house. She couldn't think of her mam and great-mam coming out to stare at a Taisteal clan like the rest of the Ballintubber residents. The Jenna Meriel knew was too distant from here, too changed.

Meriel walked over a low jumble of stones into the small rectangle of the house. A piece of an old cooking pot lay in the remnants of the hearth, brittle and thin with encrusted rust. Jenna might have once touched this same piece of metal. Meriel stooped to scoop it up; the metal nearly disintegrated in her hand, pieces of it flaking away.

The horse nickered and a chill breeze came in from the west, swaying the tops of the high grass. Meriel shivered. She went over to Sevei, who stood watching from horseback. The older woman smiled down at her. "The old places are never as you remember them," she said. "That's why we Taisteal are always traveling, because the places you leave won't stay still."

Meriel wanted to cry, not knowing why. There was a melancholy here, a deep sadness that grasped at her like a hand from a barrow grave. "Thank you for bringing me here," she said to Sevei. "I needed to see this. But I want to leave now."

Sevei nodded to Meriel, reached down with a hand, and pulled her up.

Jenna stood at the window of the High Chamber of Dún Kiil Keep, staring out at the Croc a Scroilm, the Hill of Screaming where soldiers from Tuath Infochla had long ago massacred women, children, and old men. It was a foul day, with sheets of gray rain pounding the earth and hiding the dawning sun.

She wondered if the weather would be the same on Inishduán.

"Jenna?"

She turned at the call. Kyle had entered the chamber, accompanied by Mundy Kirwan. Kyle came up to her as she turned, giving her a brotherly hug while Mundy went over to stand near the hearth, holding his hands out to the fire and shivering. Kyle MacEagan might have softened over the years, his hair gone gray and sparse, his body full and round. But his smile had remained the same. She wondered, strangely, how Ennis might have aged. . . .

Ennis. She blinked away the tears that still threatened whenever she thought of her long-dead love. She'd never told Meriel about Ennis, never told her who her true father was. She wondered now if it was too late. She might never have the opportunity if she failed today.

If Kyle guessed at her thoughts, he gave no indication. "You're certain this is what you want to do?" Kyle asked.

Jenna nodded, taking a long slow breath. "Aye."

"The Comhairle wouldn't agree with you," Kyle told her. "Even Aithne would be furious at the risk for Inish Thuaidh. If Lámh Shábhála were to go over to Doyle Mac Ard and the Order of Gabair . . ." He didn't need to finish that thought. They all knew what it would mean: Inish Thuaidh would fall. The Rí Ard in Dún Laoghaire, whoever that person might be, would rule all.

"That's why I haven't told any of them, especially Aithne," Jenna answered. "And I appreciate your silence, Kyle."

"I'm your husband and you are the Banrion. You have my affection and my loyalty."

"I know," she told him with a faint smile. She hugged him once more. "Mundy? You're quiet this morning."

Mundy turned from the fire. She saw him try to smile at her and fail. "Nothing needs to be said. Words don't matter now."

Jenna did smile at that. "No, they don't." She closed her right hand around Lámh Shábhála, feeling the cloch's strength throbbing within her with the surging power of the mage-lights. "If you don't see me here again in a few hours, know that you both have always had my love and appreciation, no matter how rarely I ever told you."

She opened the cloch without waiting for a response. The fury of the mage-lights rose around her and took her away.

Inishduán was a flyspeck in the ocean, a piece of rock barely poking above the waves. A few wind-bent trees and grasses clung to the thin veneer of soil. No one lived on the island, which had been claimed by first Inish Thuaidh, then Tuath Infochla, and now Inish Thuaidh once more.

In truth, no one really cared much on which side of the island the imaginary boundary lines were drawn.

Jenna imagined Inishduán as she'd last seen it. Mage-lights whirled around her, a searing rainbow, and swept away again. She was standing on the rocky shore not three strides from where waves pounded against black rock. Rain and wind pelted her, making her blink, and she was almost immediately soaked through, though whether it was the fault of the rain or the salt spray was difficult to tell.

A currach was pulled up on the shingle, its anchor tossed farther up on the beach. Out in the gray waves, half-hidden in the squall, a ship waited. Just upslope, a tent sagged under the assault of wind and sky, the flag of the Rí Ard hanging tattered from the central pole. Jenna recognized the spot; once, nearly two decades ago, she'd been the one sheltering in a similar tent as she waited to give her mam the body of Padraic Mac Ard, Doyle's da. Jenna touched the cloch and let a wisp of the power spread out, feeling within the shell of energy for the presence of other people.

There were four, and all four had Clochs Mór. At the touch of Lámh Shábhála, she felt them all wake. A moment later, the tent flap opened. Doyle stood there, backlit by the glow of a lantern.

"Sister," he said. "Won't you come in out of the rain? You're looking all bedraggled."

Jenna shook her head. "We're not here for talk," she told him.

A quick, half-amused smile flitted over his lips. Again, she was struck by how young he was: a bare year older than Meriel. Yet she could see the man he had become in the faint lines of his face. "No, we're not," he answered. He glanced out over the water. "You didn't come by ship as I suggested," he said.

"No."

His face told her that he understood the implications of that. He held out his left hand; his right hand was conspicuously closed over the Cloch Mór called Snapdragon. Jenna knew the other three as well, had felt their unique energy-shapes before: Sharpcut, Weaver, and Demon-Caller. The last was the Rí Ard's cloch. She wondered at that: why would Nevan O Liathain himself come here, as old and frail as he was? After Dún Kiil, he'd taken an oath to never come against her again and had kept his word over the intervening years. Had he decided to go against it now?

"You shouldn't be foolish here, Sister," Doyle said. "Give me Lámh Shábhála and I'll send word that Meriel is to be released and sent back safely to Inish Thuaidh. I'll make certain that you're returned to Dún Kiil as well."

"I can't do that, Doyle."

A genuine sadness pulled at his features and sagged his shoulders, but there was also concern in his eyes, and she knew that he'd hoped not to fight, that he wasn't entirely as confident as he appeared. "I thought you might say that. Jenna, you must have felt the Clochs Mór that are here with me; you can't defeat us all alone and I warn you that you condemn your daughter by trying."

"This isn't about Meriel. It's about you and me. And about Mam's ghost."

His posture stiffened. He shook his head. "I'll ask you one more time, Jenna. This is your last chance to save your daughter. Give me Lámh Shábhála."

"If the Order of Gabair has the knowledge you claim to have, then you'll understand that I can't do that, Doyle. Not willingly."

"Then I'm sorry," he answered. He half-turned, glancing back into the tent. *"Now!"* he called, and his fingers tightened around his cloch.

Jenna barely opened Lámh Shábhála in time. The first assault was tremendous, battering at the shield she hastily erected in front of her. Her vision was suddenly doubled: in the cloch-vision, she saw the yellow-and-red dragon form around Doyle and rush at her. The tent ripped apart, fabric flying into the gale: a thicket of bright yellow spears hurled toward her; a snarl of curling force lines gleamed as they flowed toward Jenna. And behind them, a creature rose from the wreckage: brick-red and immense, with leathery bat wings sprouting from a muscular back and talons scything at its fingertips, fire spewing from its mouth—the mage-demon.

They came at her at once.

Jenna snarled defiance at them and lightnings crackled from her hand, slicing through the energy spears and scattering them. She sent her own twisting strands of power to entwine the constricting mass around her; she threw raw mage-power at the dragon and saw the radiance smash against golden scales, hurling the creature

backward even though her counterblow was weak, her
attention and power diluted.

Nor could she be everywhere at once: the mage-
demon roared and its wings beat as its hands raked
across and through Lámh Shábhála's power, and Jenna
felt the blow as if the talons had gouged her own skin.
She screamed in pain, staggering back and nearly falling
in the uncertain footing of the stony beach.

The others saw her weakness. "Again, together!" she
heard Doyle call, and the clochs gathered themselves,
surrounding her in her cloch-vision like columns of patterned, aching light. She knew that she couldn't resist
this next attack, that this time one or more of them
would get entirely through.

As they charged toward her, she opened Lámh Shábhála fully in desperation, the coruscating energy of the
cloch flooding away from her. The spears tore at her
wall; the curling flails of Weaver ripped it open. The
mage-demon snarled and its fisted hand sent her gasping
backward; the dragon roared and sent flames that
seemed to boil Jenna's skin. She screamed with the pain;
blood-mist filled her eyes. The dragon's mouth arced forward and closed around her upraised hand, shaking its
head savagely so that she was lifted from the ground.
Her right arm felt as if it were tearing from its shoulder socket.

She could not stand, not against them all.

"I'm here, as I promised . . ." The words whispered
in her head and in the same moment, another force—in
Jenna's cloch-vision it was the blue of the sea—sent a
tidal wave of power at her assailants. None of the mages
were prepared for the unexpected attack: both Weaver
and Sharpcut vanished under the foaming crest; the
mage-demon roared as it was tossed away; the dragon
was hurled backward yet again, its teeth scoring Jenna's
arm as it left her.

The wave washed past. "Edana and I will take the
Holder," Jenna heard Doyle shout, and she realized that

it was the Rí Ard's daughter who now held Demon-
Caller, not Nevan O Liathain himself. She had less than
a breath to wonder at that. Through Lámh Shábhála,
she felt the attention of the Tuathian mages shift: Sharpcut and Weaver turned to face Dhegli as the Saimhóir
hauled out from the sea onto a rock just offshore. Jenna
could pay little attention to her ally, though, for the
mage-demon and the dragon stalked her, both of them
hovering about her in the cloch-vision, wings drumming
against the air. Her arm ached from the dragon's attack,
true hot blood pouring out to soak her clothing; her
mind ached with the mental wounds of the first two attacks and she knew that she'd done little to hurt them
as yet.

But *two* Clochs Mór she might be able to handle, even
wounded as she was. She gathered Lámh Shábhála's remaining energy, watching the world mostly through her
cloch-vision. Edana, she could tell, was by far the weaker
of the two—new to her Cloch Mór and unused to handling
the full energy of the mage-lights. She might one day be
a formidable opponent if she lived to become as practiced
as Doyle, but not yet. Not yet. Both of them had thrown
up walls against Lámh Shábhála, but Edana's shimmered
uneasily, thin and uneven.

Jenna hurled more lightning at the demon as the furious, ululating battle cry of the Inishlanders, the *caointeoireacht na cogadh,* tore from her throat. The crackling,
wild energy battered at Edana's wall, colliding with her
cloch's energy in a brilliant burst of white and blue sparks,
and then—as Edana's defenses crumbled—smashing into
the chest of the mage-demon itself. The beast roared,
not in defiance but in sheer agony, and through her own
ears Jenna heard Edana's answering wail. The mage-
demon staggered and nearly went down, and even
though the dragon hurled fire at her, Jenna ignored
Doyle to send another barrage toward the crippled
demon. Edana's shield was entirely down; the lightnings
enveloped it and Jenna felt Demon-Caller empty itself
as Edana collapsed to the ground: unconscious or dead,

Jenna didn't know which, but she had no time or inclination for guilt.

One . . .

Jenna hurriedly glanced around her with her cloch-vision. The other two clochs had vanished, but so had all signs of Dhegli—she could feel none of them with Lámh Shábhála's probe. She had no time to search for the changeling: wings beat and claws struck her, knocking her to the ground once more. The dragon hovered above as the rain sheeted down on her.

"Neither one of us can win here now, Doyle," Jenna shouted up at the awful, red-and-gold face of the creature. She held up Lámh Shábhála, showing him the glittering emerald-and-azure energy cupped in her hand. The dragon hissed; with her true eyes, she saw Doyle standing alongside the crumpled form of Edana. "Release your cloch, Brother, and I'll do the same. It's over; it's just the two of us and I'm stronger. I've no wish to kill you unless you've harmed my daughter. . . ."

She wondered if he would know her words for the bluff they were. There was little energy left inside Lámh Shábhála: enough to return Jenna to Dún Kiil. Not enough to defend herself against Doyle. She could feel the remaining strength of Snapdragon, and it frightened her. But she scowled at him and pretended.

The dragon roared once more, but it didn't attack. Instead, it faded in her sight until the ghostly outlines were driven away by the wind. Jenna let go of Lámh Shábhála, nearly losing consciousness herself with the shock of returning to the world.

Jenna managed to stand, though her body screamed in protest. Doyle crouched over Edana. Her face was bloodied and she didn't move, but Jenna thought she saw the woman's chest rise with a breath. When Doyle glanced back at Jenna, his eyes were full of hate and fury. Near them, the bodies of the other two mages were sprawled—they had the surreal stillness of death about them.

Dhegli was nowhere to be seen.

Out on the waves, sailors were shouting and a small boat had been launched. She could see four people rowing toward the shore. She could not stand against even gardai; they might be able take Lámh Shábhála from her with plain swords, weak as she was. She saw the same appraisal in Doyle's face and watched his hand stray near the Cloch Mór.

"Don't, Brother," she said, her voice raw. "Please . . ."

Doyle spat on the ground, a red stream of spittle. His fingers closed around the cloch.

Her hand leaped to Lámh Shábhála. She saw the dragon begin to appear around him once more, rearing up on hind legs, wings spread and mouth wide. Muscles bulged in its neck and it struck like a snake.

At the same moment, Jenna used the dregs of power within Lámh Shábhála, imaging her chambers in Dún Kiil. The colors of the mage-lights gathered around her and snatched her away.

As Inishduán vanished, she heard Doyle's scream.

"Damn you, Jenna! You lose your daughter for what you've done here! Do you hear me? You lose her!"

PART THREE

Bunús Muintir

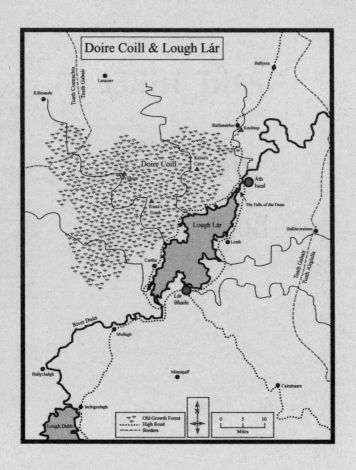

Doire Coill & Lough Lár

Ballyrea

Tuath Connachta
Tuath Gabair

Laracor

Killenaule

Ballintubber
Knobtop

Doire Coill

Keira's
Cave

Áth
Iseal

Village

The Falls of the Duan

Riata's
Tomb

Lough Lár

Balliteorainnn

Leath

Cartha

Tuath Gabair
Tuath Aingealla

Lár
Bhaile

River Duán

Mullagh

Ballycladgh

Minnigaff

Cairnbaarn

Inchigeelagh

Lough Dubh

—❦—❦ Old Growth Forest
.... High Road
– – – Borders

N

0   5   10
Miles

28

Battle at Doire Coill

LEAVING Ballintubber was no different than leaving any other tiny village. The clan was up just before dawn, taking down their tents and storing away the goods. A few villagers were there as well, picking up pots that the clan tinsmith had repaired overnight and bringing payment in grain or poultry or eggs. Meriel had performed once more as Cailin the Healer the night before, using the clochmion to cure a child of poxboils. Meriel had found it difficult to pull herself away from *being* the child, caught up in the horrible fear of death that their linkage revealed. The nightmares the girl had experienced for the last few weeks as the pox spread became Meriel's as well, all the horrors gibbering and clawing in the darkness of her mind. She found herself clinging, as the child had, to the light of affection and love that welled from her parents, allowing her to find her way back as she released Treoraí's Heart.

The mage-lights hadn't come last night and Treoraí's Heart hung around her neck empty of power, so Sevei had diverted or sent away the quartet of villagers who came to see her as the Taisteal broke their camp.

The wagons jangled and clattered as Nico slapped the reins of his horses and the wagons started lumbering out of the village. Meriel sat with Sevei at the front of their own wagon, following immediately behind Nico. They rode through the dawn mist, passing the lane where Jenna's farm had once been, crossing a rickety bridge over a small, boggy creek and finally passing Knobtop, rising on the other side.

These all would have been familiar sights to her mam, but they meant nothing to Meriel.

It was nearing midday when Meriel noticed that a forest was creeping closer to the road: dark oaks wrapped with vines, the woods dense and old. That would be Doire Coill, she knew, through which her mam had fled after she found Lámh Shábhála. Doire Coill was another remnant of the ancient old growth forests where the Bunús Muintir had lived. Where, if legend was true, they *still* lived, what few of them were left. *"We all feared Doire Coill. . ."* Meriel could hear her mam's voice as she recalled those precious times when Jenna had pulled Meriel onto her lap and talked to her about her own childhood. *"And there was good reason for that, too. Doire Coill is alive, in its own way, and the Eldest Trees aren't friendly. But there's also great beauty in the Old Forests, and I found a friend there who would save my life more than once. Maybe one day we'll go there, you and I. Would you like that?"*

Back then, Meriel had nodded her head eagerly. Looking at the woods now, she was no longer so certain. There was nothing welcoming about these trees. Even the sunlight seemed unwilling to penetrate the canopy of green. As with Foraois Coill in the north, there was also the sense of being watched, of eyes peering from the darkness. Meriel could swear that she saw shadows flitting through the bramble under the trees and crows lifted high to land in bare branches sticking above the main mass of green, their heads turning to watch them pass. Cold air drifted from under the trees across the road at times, almost as if the forest were breathing slowly. It seemed to be waiting.

In the pocket of Meriel's clóca, the oak twig the crow had given her quivered. She reached in and touched it: the small branch was vibrating. She brought it out quietly so that Sevei didn't notice, and the twig bent imme-

diately in her hand, pointing at the woods. The single
leaf, still green, fluttered as if in a wind even though the
air was still. *Here,* it seemed to be saying. *You should
go here . . ."* Meriel put it back in her pocket.

Sevei hadn't seen the twig. She was laughing and smiling as they moved along the road. "You'll be surprised
when you see Áth Iseal, Cailin," she was saying. "Or
maybe not—I keep forgetting that you've seen actual
cities. Anyway, Áth Iseal isn't like these tiny places
we've been moving through. It's more a real town, even
if it's not as big as Lár Bhaile where the Rí of Tuath
Gabair lives, and as for Dún Laoghaire where the Rí
Ard stays, well, there's no place larger in all of the Tuatha. Even so, we'll be in Áth Iseal for a few days, I'm
fairly sure. At least that's what Nico did the last time—"

She stopped. The road curved here slightly eastward;
ahead, they could see several mailed gardai on horseback standing in the middle of the road. Two riders
waited in front of them: Riocha, judging by the way they
were dressed. Nico called the clan to a halt and the
tiarna rode forward, their green-and-brown clóca flowing
in the wind. Rings of mail jingling, the gardai followed
them. Meriel didn't recognize either of thc tiarna, but
she felt a shiver, seeing them. Outside the stiff boiled
leather jackets they wore under their clócas, each had a
heavy chain that held a jewel . . . and those could only
be clochs na thintrí. "You're Clannhri Dranaghi?" one
of the tiarna called out to Nico. His right hand stroked
his chest near his cloch.

"Aye, Tiarna," Nico called out. "We're traveling to
Áth Iseal. Has our fame reached so far that the Riocha
come out to meet us? Surely we've done nothing to of-
fend, especially to a tiarna who I don't know . . . ?"
Nico laughed as if no one could seriously believe that
the Taisteal would be under any sort of suspicion, but
the tiarna's face remained grim.

("Sevei?" Meriel whispered as Nico was speaking. "I
don't like this." She touched the twig again, feeling it
wriggling like a live thing against the cloth. "You said

you'd help me when the time came for me to leave. I think that time's now."

A frown. "Hush," Sevei answered. "Wait a moment. Nico will handle this.")

The first tiarna glanced at the second wagon with Sevei and Meriel. His gaze stayed with them as he spoke. "I'm Nyle O'Murchadha, cousin and friend to Doyle Mac Ard, and this is Tiarna Shay O Blaca of the Order of Gabair, sent here by Tiarna Mac Ard. We've come to take the young woman he left with you, Clannhri."

"Tiarna Mac Ard spoke of Tiarna O Blaca," Nico answered. "Though sadly he didn't give me a description. Why didn't Tiarna Mac Ard come himself?"

"He's away to the north on pressing business," O Blaca answered. "And I assure you that I'm who Tiarna O'Murchadha said I was—though I would think that our clochs might be identification enough for a Clannhri who wanted to avoid trouble."

Nico raised his hands. "Now there's no need to take offense, Tiarna. After all, Tiarna Mac Ard made it clear that I was to—"

O Blaca shifted in his saddle, grimacing. "The girl, Clannhri. Now."

"Ah, aye, the girl," Nico nodded, stroking his chin. "There was a question of additional payment, you see—" Nico's words trailed off as O Blaca nodded to O'Murchadha, who tossed a leather pouch toward Nico. It jingled heavily as he caught it.

"Payment in full and more," O'Murchadha said. "Tiarna Mac Ard thanks you for your service and looks forward to seeing you again when you reach Dún Laoghaire. Now, the girl. Quickly."

The tiarna looked again at Meriel, then away, and Meriel realized that he was searching for red hair. ("Sevei?" she whispered again. "Please . . .") Nico was laughing.

"Ah," he said. "Nico Dranaghi is more clever than that. Do you think I would let my charge be seen so easily? No. A bit of hair coloring . . ."

("Trust me," Sevei said. "I said I would help you, and I will.") Nico hopped down from the wagon's seat. He pointed at Meriel. "There," he told O'Murchadha. "She's the one."

Sevei's hand gripped Meriel's arm. "And I have her for you, Tiarna," Sevei said. "Come alongside and I'll put her on your horse for you."

"Sevei!" Meriel gasped at the betrayal.

"Be quiet, child," Sevei laughed. "Tiarna, here's what you paid for. Come take it."

Grim-faced, O'Murchadha nudged his horse back to the second wagon; O Blaca waited, his hand on his sword as he watched Nico. Meriel struggled to get away but Sevei's hand held her, fingers digging into flesh. As the tiarna came alongside, he reached out for Meriel. But rather than pushing Meriel toward the man, Sevei pulled her backward, whipping her across the board and off the wagon entirely. Meriel tumbled to the ground. "Run! Now!" Sevei shouted to Meriel. As Meriel scrambled to her feet, she saw Sevei fling herself at O'Murchadha, her knife flashing. She pulled the tiarna from his horse as Nico hollered in dismay, shouting to his sons.

She had no time to wonder who Nico would help, Sevei or the tiarna.

The forest lay a hundred strides ahead of her; to her back there was nothing but the road and the gardai. Meriel ran for the trees through tall grass, the weeds seeming to grab at her ankles. She heard the gardai cry out in alarm and start after her; she half heard, half felt a sound like a gigantic boulder striking the earth followed by a woman's piercing wail; she heard Nico and the others shouting in new alarm and panic. Hooves pounded behind her, too close, and she realized that she wasn't going to make it, that the gardai would have her long before she found the trees.

A black mass streamed from the forest above her. A wolf howled, answered by another. The dark mist rushed noisily past Meriel and she realized that it was a dense flock of crows like the one that had appeared the day

before. A quartet of wolves the size of small horses
emerged from the cover of the oaks at the same time.
Even from this distance Meriel could see their eyes
glowing red, and two of them . . . two of them had riders
astride them, and one of those riders . . . One of the
wolf-riders leaned forward, his eyes narrowed as if he
were trying hopelessly to bring the scene into focus.

"Bráthair Geraghty?"

Hooves thudded behind her and Meriel dropped to
the ground. She heard the *swish* of a blade through air
as she dropped. With the dangerous sound came the
realization that they were not here to capture her; they
intended to kill her. The garda pulled his horse up and
leaped off as Meriel rolled and pushed herself up on one
knee, readying herself to run again. She got no farther.
The man lifted his long sword. Meriel was frozen as if
caught in prayer; she could see the metal and the
brighter scratches where he'd whetted the edge and between his hands the skin-polished patina of the leather
around the hilt. There was a hint of pity in his eyes, but
also a resolve that was her death. His mouth opened as
the blade began to move . . .

. . . a wolf hit him from behind, the beast's dagger-
filled mouth closing around the garda's weapon arm. The
massive head shook like a dog with a rabbit, tearing the
arm entirely from the socket as the garda screamed.
Blood flew through the air, spattering over Meriel as the
wolf flung the arm—still clutching the sword—away with
a final jerk of its head. The garda had collapsed to his
knees: screaming, his eyes wide with panic, his remaining
hand closed around the ragged stump at his shoulder as
a red torrent flowed unchecked between his fingers. The
wolf looked at Jenna with eyes the color of the blood
and growled—not an animal sound, but a sound which
seemed to have words—before bounding away past her.

The garda collapsed facedown in front of her, his head
at her knee. The body twitched. Close behind her, she
heard other growlings and a scream. A riderless horse

went galloping past her, neighing in terror. She started
to run toward the forest again, but there was the clamor
of hooves and movement as a man jumped from his
horse, and now O Blaca was standing before her. His
hand dropped from his cloch to his sword, and he
grinned as he raised the weapon.

The cloch gleamed at his breast; she wondered why
he didn't use it.

The crows saved her. Dozens of them flew at the man,
enveloping him in a loud flurry of black wings and bodies. He flailed at them with the sword and birds flopped
dead to the ground, but more came to replace them.
Meriel couldn't see O Blaca behind the screen of ebon
feathers.

"Meriel!" Owaine, clinging to the back of another dire
wolf, was there also, his hand reaching for hers as she
stared at the crows' assault. "Come on! We have to get
out of here before those tiarna use their clochs on us."

She took his hand and he pulled her onto the wolf,
her feet nearly touching the ground. "Hold on!" he cried
and the wolf raced away, turning back toward the forest
at a run. Meriel wrapped her arms around Owaine's
waist; even so, she nearly fell off as the wolf, panting,
rushed toward the shelter of the oaks. Meriel felt . . .
something, a pressure or presence above her. She glanced
up and the sky shimmered just above them, as if a nearly
transparent giant's fist were moving there. It came down,
and the force of the blow was tremendous, all the air
going out of her lungs as the mage-force slammed into
her back. The wolf collapsed with a high-pitched yelp as
she heard its legs snap, Owaine and Meriel sprawling
onto the ground. On her back, Meriel could not breathe;
she tried to suck in air, but her lungs complained with
a loud wheeze. She tried to move her arms and every
muscle along her spine went into spasm. She wanted to
scream from the pain but couldn't gather the breath.
Her body trembled, helpless.

She saw air gathering above her again, the fist forming

and starting to hurl down directly toward her. For the second time, she saw her death approaching. She closed her eyes.

For the second time, she was saved.

She heard a crackling and saw light through closed eyelids. She opened her eyes to see the ethereal fist outlined in brilliant, snapping fireworks, quivering not three feet above her. Meriel rolled, her body protesting; as she did, the light flared and vanished and the fist slammed into the earth, the soft earth cratering where she'd just lain. At the edge of the forest, she saw the other wolf-rider: a woman holding a wooden staff in her hand, the end of the stick broken and smoldering. The twig in Meriel's pocket seemed to sing and tore away from Meriel entirely, rushing toward the woman as if blown by a storm wind and falling at her feet. As Meriel watched, the woman flung the staff aside and called out, her voice howling like a dire wolf. The wolves came thundering toward her, two of them stopping where Meriel and Owaine were trying to stand.

"Get on!" she heard Owaine say, and she clasped her arms around the nearest wolf's massive neck, throwing her leg over its back.

It ran as Meriel desperately hung on. She heard calls behind her, then abruptly they were in the woods. The branches of the nearest oak cracked and snapped, the massive trunk splintering as the mage-fist pounded earth again, but they were already moving deeper into the cover of the forest. Branches whipped and cut at Meriel as the wolf tore through bramble and cover before emerging into a small glade. The wolf stopped and Meriel half climbed, half fell from the wolf's back. "Thank you," she said. The wolf stared at her, ears up, then ran off back the way it had come.

She was not alone for long. A few minutes later, another wolf deposited Owaine in the glade. He ran to her. "Bráithair Geraghty? Owaine? I can't believe—" she began, but then the tears came, and she felt Owaine's arms go around her as he tentatively held her. The touch brought Meriel's head up and Owaine's arms dropped immediately away. He stepped back as if he realized he'd overstepped his bounds. "I'm sorry, Bantiarna," he said. "But you needn't worry now. Keira will take care of everything."

Meriel blinked. She tried to take a deep breath but pain stabbed her side; she groaned instead. "Who's Keira?" she managed to say.

As if in answer, a woman stepped into the clearing. She was dressed in furs, her body short and bulky, and a huge black crow was perched on her shoulder. Her long, dark tresses were bound and wrapped with ivy and vines, and a collection of leather pouches were tied to a belt looped over one shoulder. She looked to be older than Meriel's mam, though not much so. Her hair was pure white at the temples and abundant strands of gray ran through the rest of her hair; her eyes and the corners of her mouth were caught in webs of fine wrinkles. Her face was flat and broad, the brow prominently ridged: a Bunús Muintir's face.

"I'm Keira," she said. "Welcome to Doir Coill."

29

Into the Woods

"**Y**OU don't have to worry," Keira said. "I told Arror to lead any of the soldiers who come after us down the Fastwater Dell to where the Elder Trees are. Those who go there won't return, not even if they hold a Cloch Mór. If the tiarnas are at all familiar with Doire Coill, they already realize that and won't come in here at all. For now, you're safe."

They were still in the glade not far within the borders of the forest. Keira had first checked on Meriel before going to Owaine. The Bunús Muintir woman rapidly cleaned and bound the worst of the cuts on Owaine's arms and legs. She spoke to him in a whispered conversation that Meriel hadn't been able to overhear; he'd nodded and left the glade, moving deeper into the woods. Then she came to where Meriel was reclining in soft grass and wrapped Meriel's ribs with a poultice that first burned like fire before turning colder than a winter's morning. She moved quickly, her gaze frequently flicking outward in the direction from which they'd come, from where they could hear a canine whining in the distance. She knotted the cloth holding the poultice under Meriel's léine and brought the tunic over it. She brushed Meriel's cheeks with thick-padded fingertips. "I have to leave you here for a bit—the wolf you rode also needs attention. I'll be back as soon as I can."

"What about Bráthair Geraghty?"

"You mean Owaine?" Keira asked. "He may be back before me."

With that, she rose and hurried off, the crow flapping away in front of her. In the space of two breaths, Keira vanished under the trees. Meriel lay back, shading her eyes against the sunlight that filtered down through the overhanging boughs. She tried to sit up and succeeded, groaning with the effort and the sharp pain in her sides. She remembered the scream she'd heard after Sevei had attacked Tiarna O'Murchadha and guilt flooded through her. Sevei might have lost her life keeping her word to Meriel. At best, she would be seriously injured, and what the tiarna might do to her now that Meriel had escaped . . .

Meriel remembered the cards and the reading Sevei had performed what seemed ages ago now: *the dark-haired woman and the skeleton.* She was afraid that she knew now what Sevei had not been willing to tell her then. She wanted—needed—to see Sevei again, to find out what had happened.

She pushed herself to her feet and took a few limping steps after Keira. Every muscle protested and knife blades seemed to stab into her right hip with each impact of her foot on the ground. *There's nothing you can do, and you'll only put yourself in danger after these people have risked themselves for you,* some rational part of her mind yammered, but she ignored it. She imagined Sevei lying in the road bloody and hurt, and O'Murchadha or O Blaca screaming angrily above her, ready to strike again with cloch or hand, to make Sevei pay in pain and blood. She couldn't bear that image. Better to go back, to let them finish what they'd started if doing so meant that they'd leave Sevei alone.

The Riocha wanted Meriel dead, which meant that was what Doyle wanted, too, assuming they had told Nico the truth. She knew that. O'Murchadha hadn't come to take Meriel away somewhere; he'd come to kill her. With the realization came another: there was only one reason she could think of for Doyle to order her

death: her mam refused to pay the ransom Doyle Mac
Ard demanded. That could be the only explanation. Her
mam had decided that Meriel's life was secondary to
something else.

She leaned against a tree, closing her eyes against the
pain and trying to take a breath that was more than a
sip of air through her broken ribs.

"Meriel! There you are!" She heard Owaine behind
her, and turned her head to see him entering the glade
from the other side, leading a dappled gray horse. There
was no bridle or harness on the animal, but leather
straps were drawn around its chest and belly, to which
two long branches were attached, their ends bound together several feet in back of the horse, dragging the
ground. Between the poles a length of cloth had been
tied, creating a hammock of sorts. "Keira said you
shouldn't be walking; you don't want one of those ribs
to puncture a lung."

She tried to push away from the tree and had to hang
on once more as the movement sent pain stabbing
through her chest. "Sevei," she managed to gasp out.
"Have to . . . see . . ."

"You can't do anything for them now," he told her.
He hovered around her. "I'm sorry. I know that's not
what you want to hear right now, but it's true. Let Keira
do what she can. Here, put your arm around me and I'll
help you walk."

"I have to go to Sevei," she insisted. She took a step,
but the jolt of her foot on the ground sent the pain
lancing through her again. She drew in a breath, and
that only made the pain worsen. She felt herself starting
to fall, then Owaine was alongside her, lifting her arm
and ducking under it. He put an arm carefully around
her waist. "I'm taking you to the carrier," he said, and
she finally nodded. She was crying, and she didn't know
if it was from her fear for what had happened to Sevei,
or the pain, or relief at getting away from the Taisteal.
"Hang on," Owaine said. "One step at a time . . ."

They moved back to the glade. The horse came

toward them, and Owaine brought her over to the improvised stretcher. "Here, lie on this. I'll lift the other end when we're ready to move so it doesn't jolt you too much. We'll go slow . . ."

She realized how tired and hurt she was when she let go of him. Her legs trembled and she could barely stand. She sagged to the ground. "Not yet," she said. "Need to rest first. How . . . ?" The single word was all she could get out of the question, but he seemed to understand. He sat down in front of her.

"It started with Dhegli," he answered.

"Dhegli?" The word brought his face back to her, along with a fleeting sense of his presence in her head.

Owaine's face took on a strange expression as she spoke Dhegli's name, but he nodded. He told her about the search for her on Inishfeirm, and how he'd gone to see the Saimhóir. He gave her a short version of the tale of his long pursuit, how Dhegli brought him over, how Cataigh and Léimard had aided him, and how they'd tracked the Taisteal. "I figured that the healer had to be you, using a cloch, and I was right. Léimard led me along your path, and when I was close enough, Keira sent the wolves to find me. She tells me Cataigh and Léimard have gone back to Foraois Coill. That's a shame; I wish you could have met them, too."

Despite the pain, Meriel found herself caught up in Owaine's story, smiling at the thought of the nearsighted Bráthair leaving Inishfeirm without so much as a change of clothes and pursuing her through Talamh an Ghlas. "I can't believe you did all that." But she saw how his face changed with her smile and her attention, and she knew why: she could see the infatuation in the way he gazed at her, in the tone of his voice. She remembered that he'd looked at her the same way back on Inishfeirm, and all the times she'd come across him in the corridors. . . .

It explained everything.

No, she wanted to tell him. *You can't think about me that way. I don't want you to think about me that way. It's not fair—to either of us.*

He was smiling shyly and now she found herself frowning in response. "I can't really believe I did it either," he continued. "I thought I was going to die at least a dozen times—remind me to tell you about the dragon. But I was lucky enough to find the right people. Cataigh was the one who really made it possible; he told Keira to watch for me and for you. That's what saved us both." Owaine glanced back to where Keira had gone, back to the road. "Who were those tiarna and what did they want? Who put you with the Taisteal in the first place?"

Meriel shook her head. She didn't want to explain anything to him. "That's far too long a story for right now. Where's Keira? I'm worried—if the tiarna uses that Cloch Mór—"

"I'm here and safe," Keira's voice answered, heavy with the accent of the Bunús Muintir. Meriel turned her head to see the woman standing near them. The crow was back on her shoulder, but Meriel could see no sign of the dire wolves. "We were lucky; there were two Clochs Mór here, but one was empty and couldn't be used. The Riocha are gone. They've taken what remains of their gardai and fled. They took the Clannhri and most of the Taisteal men with them."

Meriel struggled to sit up. "And the other Taisteal? Sevei?"

"Was she the woman who attacked the tiarna?" Keira asked, and her voice and gaze softened. "You were her friend? I'm sorry."

"No!" Meriel couldn't stop the scream of protest even though it racked her lungs and set her coughing. She wept, putting her hands over her eyes. "Oh, Mother-Creator, no!" She couldn't imagine Sevei dead: her smile, her eyes, her laugh. *"I promise you that when the right moment comes, I'll help you get out,"* she'd said. *She made the promise knowing that it might come to this. She made the promise knowing it was the path the cards had shown her.* "Sevei . . ."

Meriel sobbed at the emptiness inside herself.

She felt Owaine's hand on her shoulder and she

shrank away from him; the hand left. Keira's voice continued, calm and soft. "The other Taisteal have your Sevei's body and will send her to the Greatness in their own way. I told the wolves not to hurt them, though I don't know what the Riocha will do later. That's their fate, not yours—your path goes elsewhere. For now, though, you can rest and grieve if you need to. Owaine, help her over to the carrier . . ."

He held out his hand. Meriel ignored it and tried to rise by herself but quick sharp pain racked her sides and she fell back again. She could see a reflection of her pain in Owaine's face as he held out his hand again. She nodded, and he crouched down alongside her, helping her to her feet and over to the horse, where he eased her down slowly onto the cloth between the poles. Meriel felt the carrier lift as Keira clucked at the horse. They started forward, Meriel prone in the hammock with the oaken limbs of the forest shielding her tears from the sun.

The cave entrance was a few hours' walk into Doire Coill, halfway up a bare knoll. By the time they reached it, Meriel was stiff and sore and barely able to rise from the carrier. Owaine and Keira both helped her stand, then Owaine almost carried her into the cavern, which opened out into a large room.

She noticed that he was careful where he placed his hands.

"Your mam was here once," Keira said as Owaine helped her down on a straw pallet to one side of the torchlit room, which emptied into a black void leading farther back and down. Cold air welled outward from the dark. The crow had settled on a ledge near the entrance. A peat fire smoldered in the center of the room, the smoke curling upward to some unseen opening; around the fire were several racks—herbs laid over wooden poles to dry. The smell of the herbs was nearly

overpowering to Meriel, as if she'd put her nose in one
of the spice jars in the White Keep's kitchens. "This was
one of Seancoim's homes," Keira continued. "Now it's
one of mine."

"Seancoim? I remember my mam talking about him."

Keira nodded. "His fate was bound with hers. I was
his pledge-daughter; now I serve as the Protector of Doire
Coill as he once did." She went to a shelf at one side
of the cavern and poured water from a jar into a wooden
cup. Dried herbs were scattered on the table; she broke
a leaf from one of the stalks and crushed it to powder
in her palms, then brushed the tan dust into the cup of
water. She brought it over to Meriel and crouched down
next her. "And I get to care for you as Seancoim did
for Jenna. Here, drink this."

Meriel sniffed at it suspiciously. "What is it?"

Keira's face creased in a smile. "I'm not likely to hurt
you after spending so much energy saving you, girl.
Drink it—it's to stop the swelling."

Keira slipped her hand under Meriel's neck and lifted
her head to the cup. Meriel drank, grimacing at the taste
of the potion. Keira laid her head back down, but her
hand remained there. She slipped her fingers around the
chain there and pulled Treoraí's Heart from under Meriel's léine. Meriel reached out her right hand to stop
Keira, and she saw the Bunús Muintir gaze at the mage-
scars on her skin. "I'm not going to steal it," she said. "I
only wanted to see it. Tonight, when the mage-lights come,
you can fill this and heal yourself instead of others."

"How do you know—" Meriel began, but Keira was
laughing, her wide face bright with amusement.

"It's not magic," she said. "Just Owaine. He told me.
You should be grateful to the Bráthair—his clochmion
told us where you were far better than my slow magics
could have. Without him, we might have been too late."
At the foot of Meriel's pallet, Owaine grinned. His mouth
seemed too large in his plain face, his teeth were
crooked, and his nose wrinkled as he squinted.

"Don't let her try to tell you the slow magics are

weak, though," Owaine said. "From what I've seen here and in Foraois Coill, I think I should have paid more attention in Siúr Bolan's class back at Inishfeirm. You saw what she did with the Cloch Mór out there—that must have been the one called GodFist; it was one of the Clochs Mór stolen from Inishfeirm just before the Filleadh A Cloch Mór, and she turned it aside."

Meriel remembered the hammer blow of the cloch and the force that had stopped it, but she said nothing to Owaine. Instead, she looked at the Bunús Muintir. "Thank you," she said to Keira. "They were going to kill me."

Keira nodded. "So it appears."

"That was slow magic?"

Keira shrugged. "Aye. You Daoine have forgotten most of those skills. You're likely to ignore it even more now that the clochs na thintrí are awake again and in your possession. The slow magics can be as powerful as a Cloch Mór—perhaps even more so—but the spells require time and patience to build and can be used only once. You don't have time to create them during an urgent need, nor can most people hold more than a few of them within themselves for any amount of time. That's why those who hold the clochs don't care about the slow magics—the clochs are easily used and easily renewed; the stones themselves hold the magic, not the person. But the slow magics are all we Bunús Muintir have had for many generations; we never forgot them."

"Teach me," Meriel said impulsively.

"And me," Owaine echoed, causing Meriel to tighten her lips.

Keira scoffed. "Oh, and when you each have a Cloch Mór around your neck, will either of you remember the slow magics or even care about them?"

Owaine answered first. "Right now all we have are clochmions, Keira."

"Aye, that's what you have, Owaine." Meriel heard the faint stress Keira put on the word "you," but Owaine seemed not to notice. "I'm not talking of now, though, but later."

Owaine shook his head in disagreement. "Meriel's the Banrion's daughter. She'll have a Cloch Mór one day. But not me. I'm just an unimportant Bráthair of the Order and there are too few of the great stones to go around."

Another shrug. "Perhaps not, but you have your clochmion, your head has been filled with the lore of the clochs na thintrí, and only the goddess Pauk sitting in her web of fate knows what you might possess in the future. You may not be as unimportant as you think, Owaine." The young man beamed at that, and the obvious friendship he felt toward the woman made Meriel frown. "The slow magics are also terribly slow to learn," Keria continued. "It took years and years for Seancoim to give me the skills I have, and I can't match what he could do yet. Do you have years to spend here in the shade of the oaks? Do you want to become like the Bunús yourselves and show me your dedication by binding yourself to me as pledge-daughter and pledge-son? Do you want to never see your home again or your parents or friends?"

Keira paused, her gaze going slowly to each of their faces. She smiled, shaking her head. "I didn't think so. Your fates aren't tied to Doire Coill. You can't learn everything in one life; the best any of us can do is learn what we need to survive. While you're here, I'll teach you what I can, but it won't—it can't—be much. After all, you can't stay here."

"Why not?" Meriel asked. The thought of leaving Doire Coill filled her with fear. The world outside, the world of the Riocha, seemed hostile and dangerous.

"Because even though what's outside scares you right now, you don't belong here," Keira answered softly, as if she'd seen the fright pass behind Meriel's eyes. "But there's time enough to worry about that later. For now, rest. I'll call you when the mage-lights come."

The mage-lights pulled her, and Meriel managed to rise and limp from the cave on her own despite Owaine's offer of help though he insisted on walking alongside her, too close for her to feel comfortable. She could see the mage-lights' dazzling ballet reflected on the stones of the passageway as she climbed toward the entrance. She felt the urge of Treoraí's Heart to be filled with their power.

Keira was already outside. She said nothing, only watched as both Owaine and Meriel closed their hands around their clochs and lifted them toward the sky that glowed from horizon to horizon with the shimmering curtains of light, rippling as if in some unseen spectral wind. The mage-lights curled above them, tendrils of glowing blue and green snaking down to wrap about their wrists and arms. Meriel sighed, feeling relief as the cloch sucked hungrily at the energy. In the mage-vision, she could see the lattices of crystal inside the stone, sparkling as they took in the mage-lights. She could feel the faint tendrils of connection between all the clochs and their Holders, as all of the cloudmages performed the same duty. It seemed but a few minutes but was probably half a stripe or more before it was done and she released the cloch. The mage-lights were already fading.

Meriel let herself return to the world around her. She could see the scars on her right hand in the moonlight. She saw Owaine looking at them also, curious, and she covered them with her other hand.

She was aware, suddenly, that Keira was not the only other one on the hillside with them, that a dire wolf stood near her. She could hear the growling voice of the creature, its red eyes seeming to glow in the night, though perhaps it was only the reflection of moonlight.

"Arror wants to know if you were worth his mate's broken legs and the arrow wounds his pack suffered," Keira said. Meriel's jaw dropped at that and she stammered as Keira laughed. "Aye, they do have their own language, as Owaine could have told you," she continued. "And I told Arror that, aye, I think this will be worth the pain they suffered, and that as a reward they can hunt the storm deer in Doire Coill below Misty Fen."

"Tell Arror that I thank him and his pack, too," Meriel told her. "I know I wouldn't be here now if it weren't for their help, and I'm sorry for what happened to his mate."

Keira nodded, and turned to Arror with a series of growls and grunts to which the dire wolf responded in kind. "He says that two-legs are unwise creatures if they apologize for what wasn't their fault. It wasn't you who hurt Garrhal, but the one with the magic stone whose face Arror will remember." Keira visibly shuddered under her robes. "And I wouldn't care to be the tiarna if Arror finds him. The dire wolves are difficult enough as friends; they make terrible enemies. But now . . . it's time to heal yourself, Meriel."

Meriel brushed the clochmion with her fingers, feeling the power tingle with the touch. She felt the ache of her muscles, the sharp knives that slashed along her spine when she shifted her weight, the slow purpling of the bruises everywhere. It would be wonderful to make herself whole and free of pain.

It would be a delight, but . . . Arror stared at her. She could feel his gaze. "Keira, ask Arror where Garrhal is."

Keira looked at Meriel curiously, her chin lifting. "I don't need to ask. I know their dens. Down at the bottom of the hill, and a short walk under the oaks."

"Then take me there."

"You can't walk that far," Owaine said and Meriel glared at him.

"I'll manage," she said.

"Then let me help you."

"Leave me alone, Bráthair," Meriel started angrily, then stopped at the stricken look he gave her. "Bráithair Geraghty," she began again, more gently. He smiled tentatively.

"Call me Owaine. I've never been entirely comfortable with 'Bráthair.' "

"Owaine, then," she said, "I appreciate everything you've done. Coming after me . . . that was incredibly foolish but also incredibly brave of you, and I'm glad you found Keira and came for me, but . . ."

Owaine's eyebrows raised. Behind him, Arror seemed to be listening and sniffing the air around them at the same time, his mouth half-open in canine amusement.

"It doesn't change anything," Meriel finished. "Do you know what I mean?"

She could see the disappointment in his face and the futile struggle he made not to show it. Too late, he shrugged. "Oh, I understand. Actually, it is Dhegli who's ultimately responsible. He didn't give me a chance to think about consequences; he just brought me here."

Dhegli . . . The name made her smile momentarily. *His face, the touch of his fingers on her skin, the sound of his voice.* A sense of loss and yearning threatened to overwhelm her. *I want to call him. I want to see him again, be with him . . .*

Keira had gone into the cave as Meriel and Owaine talked. When she emerged, she was holding an oaken staff burnished at the knobbed top by what must have been years of use. "Here," she said. "This is one of Seancoim's old staffs. I keep them, figuring I'll need them one day myself." Meriel took the stick in her free hand as Keira turned to Arror and growled something in his language. The huge wolf barked once, and padded off down the hill and into the cover of the trees as the three of them followed slowly, Meriel trying to find a rhythm that would allow her to walk over the broken ground with the least amount of pain, Owaine hovering unasked at her side. At the bottom of the knoll, they turned under the oaks and were plunged into darkness, the moon hidden by the dense foliage above. They could hear animals moving nearby and feel the pressure of eyes on them. Wind sprites glittered a few strides away, the bright stream of them flowing between and around the trees like a fast-moving creek, their voices a high chattering. Wings fluttered heavily above them; to their

left some animal suddenly wailed, the sound eerily and
abruptly cut off.

Keira seemed untroubled by the dark and the noises,
walking quickly ahead of them. "The forest is most alive
at night," she said, glancing back at Meriel and Owaine
as they paused, trying to adjust to the dimness. "The
trees and most of the creatures who live here rest during
the day. They prefer the darkness. Doire Coill is a dangerous place for travelers at night; the trees will hinder
you deliberately and try to lead you to the Eldest and
your death, and there are other animals out here who
would also prey on humans—Arror's people not the
least of them. If the Eldest, the Seanóir, were singing
tonight, then even I might be cautious, because ever
since your mam brought the Filleadh, Meriel, the song
of the Seanóir has been growing stronger and drawing
the unwary from greater distances. But they're quiet tonight and the trees know you're with me, and you have
Arror's protection as well for now."

It seemed to Meriel that they walked for a full stripe,
though it was probably far less. They came eventually
to a small opening in the trees where steep, thorn-
covered slopes ringed them on three sides. A bit of
moonlight trickled down through the overhanging
branches, and Meriel could see the dark, round opening
of several holes in the cliffside ahead of them. Red eyes
gleamed in the hole just ahead of them and Arror
stepped out. Other dire wolves came from the dens until
they were surrounded by well over a dozen of the beasts.
They sniffed and muttered and growled, and Meriel
found herself staying close to Owaine. "Arror says that
he can smell fear on the two of you, and says that you
should calm yourselves—no harm will come to you
here tonight."

"Tonight?" Owaine repeated, and Keira laughed.

"Tonight," she repeated. "Among the packs, they
have a saying I've heard: 'No throat goes unbared forever.' They know that the one who is strong today may

be beaten tomorrow, and their social order is always in flux. As a result, they make promises very carefully."

As Keira was speaking, Meriel saw a gray form limp out from Arror's den—a female wolf, her rear legs splinted and bandaged so that she seemed to half drag herself along. As she appeared, some of the other wolves growled, their mutters obviously aggressive and angry as Arror snarled back at them and showed his teeth. Four cubs—the size of normal wolves but tiny by comparison with the adults around them—came out with her. "Dire wolves don't generally save someone injured as badly as Garrhal was," Keira told them. "She's protected only by Arror's status in the pack—if he was less dominant, they might have killed her or driven her out of the pack already. They say she's a danger, that she can't contribute to the pack or her cubs and should be left to fend for herself to heal or die."

"Tell Arror I need to go to her," Meriel said. As Keira translated, Meriel hobbled to Garrhal, kneeling beside her with a sigh of exhaustion. The wolves watched, growling softly. "Thank you for carrying me today," she told the wolf, even though she knew Garrhal couldn't understand her. "I'm sorry you were injured; if I'd known that would happen, I wouldn't have let you do it."

Garrhal watched her warily, her tongue lolling from her open mouth as Meriel pulled Treoraí's Heart from under her léine. She closed her hand around the stone as her other hand touched Garrhal's side. Her sight doubled; in the cloch-vision, she could see the fractures like shimmering blue lines in Garrhal's bones, with orange-and-red lines of pain radiating away from them. The legs had been set well by Keira, but the Cloch Mór's blow had shattered bone and scattered fragments of bone were buried deep into the muscles. Now Meriel let the clochmion's energy out, wrapping it about the legs. The pain slid along the lines of energy, coming to her; Meriel accepted the hurt, crying out helplessly at the feeling of

the broken bones, the torn ligaments, the ripped muscles. Closing her eyes, she let herself see only in the
cloch-vision, tightening the energy around the wolf's injured leg before releasing it all in one burst. She fell into
the wolf's mind. She became the wolf.

There was the pain, aye—terrible and agonizing, like
being stabbed repeatedly with a spear. But there were
also new dimensions to the world: Meriel was awash in
odors which assaulted her from every direction—the
scent of the cool mold under the trees; the sharp tang
of Owaine and herself, both with the undertone that she
could recognize as fear, and the slightly different smell
of Keira, overlaid with strong herbs; the incredibly distinct aromas of each of the wolves; the sweet milk-scent
of her young ones. She could hear the rustle of fur, the
panting breath of the wolves. Her vision lacked a strong
color sense, but the moonlight might as well have been
daylight—she could see easily, with an acute sharpness
that made Meriel's vision seem like Owaine's.

And the thoughts . . . Meriel found herself caught in
a mind that was totally unlike any of those Treoraí's
Heart had revealed to her before. There was primal heat
in Garrhal's thoughts, a purity of attention. There was
hunger in the belly and a lust for bloody, rich meat.
Meriel saw herself in Garrhal's thoughts, felt the appraisal of how she might taste. She felt also Garrhal's
own acceptance of the pack's attitude toward her, and
there was a disgust and self-loathing for her own injuries
below the pain. Meriel realized with a start that the only
thing holding Garrhal here was Arror, that if he had not
stopped her, she would have slunk off on her own to
die—but Arror was dominant in the pack, and not to be
questioned. So she stayed when she didn't want to be
here.

She wanted to die. She wanted to end this disgrace.
Meriel wanted to die with her. Garrhal shifted her weight,
and the searing agony of the smashed limbs washed over
Meriel once more.

She fell back, howling with Garrhal as if her own legs had been crushed, her own discomfort lost in this greater misery. She sent the power of Treoraí's Heart rushing out from the stone, and it was like handling fire. Meriel howled again, a sound enough like a wolf that the other members of the pack lifted their muzzles and howled with her. With a gasp, Meriel released the stone. She fell backward to the ground as Owaine rushed over to her, as Garrhal rose and shook herself before loping over to Arror with a howl that held relief and joy. The wolf cubs danced around them, yipping. Owaine's hands were under her. "I can get up," she managed to say. It felt strange to use words; part of her wanted to growl. "Just leave me alone a moment."

"Are you sure you're all right?"

"I will be," she told him. Already the pain and the touch of Garrhal's mind was fading. She let go of the emptied cloch as Arror padded over to her with Keira at his side. The dire wolf looked at her, red eyes staring into green. He growled long and low, and Keira nodded.

"He calls you Meriel Wolf-friend," Keira translated. "He says that as long as he is master of this pack, you are safe and will be treated as part of them."

She understood that, better than she had just moments before. "Tell him that I'm grateful," Meriel told her. "Tell him that I hope he and Garrhal live long lives."

Keira spoke to Arror in his language, and the wolf barked once and went back to Garrhal and their cubs. "You didn't need to do that," Keira said to Meriel as they watched the wolves. "You could have used the cloch for yourself. But that's what your mam would have done also. She was generous with others, too."

"My mam?" Meriel nearly laughed, forcing the sarcasm back. *My mam generous? The hard, cold Banrion? The "Mad Holder"? The mam who never seemed to have time for me? The mam who never paid the ransom Doyle Mac Ard must have demanded?* She wanted to scoff and protest, but she closed her mouth.

It was Owaine who nodded in agreement.

"Aye," he said. "The Banrion's a generous woman. I know that well."

Meriel thought it best to say nothing. She took a breath, watching Arror and Garrhal. "I'd like to get back to the cave," she said. "I'm exhausted."

Meriel could feel Keira studying her for a moment. "Aye," she said, "and we need to send word to your mam that you're safe, before she does something she'll regret. . . ."

30

Recovery

"I DON'T know what's happened to Meriel, or what that bastard Doyle may have done to her, or if he's carried out his threat . . ." Jenna raged and sobbed at the same time, pacing back and forth in her chambers, high in Dún Kiil Keep. Kyle MacEagan and Máister Kirwan watched her—she could feel their gazes on her. "Mother-Creator, if I've killed her because . . . because . . ." Her intake of breath was a shuddering gasp. She couldn't say more. She gave in to the tears that had threatened ever since Inishduán, sinking to the floor in front of the fire in a silken puddle.

Lámh Shábhála throbbed at her chest in time to her huddled grief.

She heard the rustle of cloth, felt the heat of Kyle's body kneeling behind her just before his arm came around her. "Jenna . . . Jenna, you did what you had to do," he said softly, almost a whisper. "You had no choice. Mac Ard and Lámh Shábhála gave you no room to do anything else. Don't blame yourself."

Jenna lifted her head, her face stricken with anguish, the lines of tears on her cheeks but sudden fire smoldering in her eyes. "If he's hurt her, I'll hunt my bastard half brother down and kill him. I don't care what it costs me, I don't care what happens afterward or how many clochs stand between me and him." She saw the troubled glance that Kyle threw to Mundy and that only fueled the rage. "I know what you're both thinking. *I don't care.* I condemned my daughter so I could keep Lámh Shábhála. Do the two of you understand that? The flesh of my blood, the flesh of *Ennis'* blood, and I couldn't give up this damned stone around my neck to save her. Blame myself? Who else is there to blame? I *still* can't give up the stone, even now—curse the Mother-Creator for giving it to me. Meriel was all I had and *I couldn't make the sacrifice for her.* I'm her mam; I should have laid down my life for my daughter, but no, I had to keep the bloody Lámh Shábhála—"

She stopped. Kyle and Mundy were staring, their faces stricken, and she realized that she was raving.

There's so much I never told Meriel or had a chance to do with her, and now it may be too late. It's almost certainly too late . . .

"Who are you angry with, Jenna?" Mundy asked gently, as if he could read her thoughts. "Doyle Mac Ard or yourself?"

She glared at him. Sniffed. "Shut up, Mundy."

The Máister shook his head slowly and deliberately. "Jenna, I'm going to speak to you as a friend. If you take offense at that, so be it, but here it is: we don't have time for this self-flagellation. If there's a chance for us to save Meriel, we have to act and we have to act *now.*"

"And do *what* exactly?" she railed at him. She pushed herself from the floor, standing again. "Do you know where Meriel is, oh, great Máister? If so, please tell me so I can go to her. Do you know where Doyle's gone?— then I'll go there next and kill the bastard this time. Have you talked to Dhegli?—we don't know whether the Saimhóir's alive or dead or what might have happened with him afterward, and without him, I *would* be dead and Lámh Shábhála gone. . . ." She waved a derisive, mocking hand, not caring that Mundy's face had gone stiff and white. "So do *you* have a plan, Máister Kirwan?—then tell us about it. I'd much rather be doing something—*anything*—rather than sitting here."

Mundy stared at her, all the muscles of his face tight as if he were trying to control his anger before he replied. Kyle sighed loudly, and Jenna looked to her husband. "I know where Doyle will be," Kyle said. He'd risen with Jenna, standing on the other side of the hearth from her. "Dún Laoghaire. Or at least he'll be there as soon as he can reach there."

"Why?"

"You said Edana O Liathain was the one wielding Demon-Caller," Kyle answered. "Rí Ard O Liathain is no more capable of just giving up his Cloch Mór than you or any of us are. We know that the Rí Ard was ill; if his daughter has Demon-Caller, then we can assume that the Rí Ard died in the last several days; the news just hasn't reached us yet. The Tuatha will be stirred up—I didn't like Nevan O Liathain any more than you did, but none of us can deny that as Rí Ard he managed the Ríthe even better than his da. He brought the Tuatha together and made them act as one, and that was his best accomplishment. Now all the old, half-buried conflicts between the Tuatha will surface again when the Ríthe meet to name a new Rí Ard. Your brother's a political animal and ambitious, and Edana is the Rí Ard's daughter; Doyle will return to Dún Laoghaire to protect his interests, which almost certainly have been damaged at this point, since he undoubtedly expected to be holding Lámh Shábhála."

Jenna nodded. "I suspect you're right, Kyle, but I may have killed Edana during the battle. I don't know for certain."

"If you have, then I don't know where Doyle will go—I would think his ascent among the Riocha is linked to her. But you don't know that she's dead. That he'll go to Dún Laoghaire is still the best bet."

"Then Meriel's there, too?"

"I suppose that's possible, Jenna. But we don't know—Doyle may have put her somewhere else for safe-keeping against the other Riocha. You say that Doyle, Edana, and two other cloudmages of the Order of Ga-

bair were at Inishfeirm, and Doyle was involved in the
kidnapping of Meriel . . ." Kyle shrugged heavily. "I
don't think all this is something the Ríthe agreed to. I
think this was concocted by the Order of Gabair. Even
the Rí Ard might not have known what his daughter
and future son-in-law were doing. If that's the case, then
Doyle would put Meriel where only he and those he
trusted knew where she was."

"But it's *possible* she's in Dún Laoghaire?" Jenna
asked, and Kyle shrugged again. "Then that's where
we go."

Mundy's incredulous laugh brought her head around.
"How, Jenna?" he asked. "With an army? It would take
weeks to get troops and ships together. If we go through
Falcarragh, the Rí Infochla isn't going to let us march
unchallenged from Falcarragh across the Tuatha. As for
the sea route, it would take weeks to sail around Talamh
an Ghlas to Dún Laoghaire, not to mention that doing
so would leave Inish Thuaidh completely unprotected.
You know all this as well as I do, or you would if you
took a moment to think without letting anger and revenge get in your way. Even if you wanted to, you can't
go alone using Lámh Shábhála—you've never been to
Dún Laoghaire, so you can't visualize it and have Lámh
Shábhála take you there. Even if it *were* possible, the
cloch would be half-empty from the effort. You don't
know exactly where Doyle is in the city or when he'll
arrive, and there will be several Clochs Mór there with
him. The tiarnas and bantiarnas may be squabbling with
each other now, but they'll happily set aside their own
quarrels for a few minutes to unite against the Mad
Holder."

Jenna could feel her face flushing red from irritation,
even though she knew that Mundy was only speaking
the truth as he saw it. "You're good at telling me what
I can't do, Mundy," she told him, unable to keep the
edge from her voice. "Are you equally good at telling
me what I *can* do?"

Mundy pressed his lips together. He remained silent.

Jenna glanced from one to the other of the two men. "Are both of you saying that I have to accept that Meriel's dead if Doyle carries out his threat?" Neither of them answered immediately. Finally Kyle stirred. His hands lifted, palms up.

"I don't have a good answer for you, Jenna. I only know this: if the Rí Ard's dead—and I think we'll hear that news confirmed very soon—then the oath that Nevan gave you so many years ago is also dead. With what's happened between you and Doyle, I would say that there's a good chance the Tuatha will soon declare open war against us, and we need to prepare for that." He paused, biting for a moment at his lower lip as if not wanting to say the next words. "You know I love Meriel, too, as much as if she were my own daughter. I was as upset as you were with her capture; if she's been harmed, I'll grieve as her da and you have my vow that I will be at your side to avenge her blood, no matter the cost to me and no matter what you decide to do. But . . . I think Mundy's right and you need to listen to him. If we knew exactly where Meriel was or who was holding her for Doyle, maybe then—" He stopped, exhaling loudly. "But we don't. We have to trust to the Mother-Creator to help Meriel because I just don't see a way for us to protect her right now. I think we will help her best by strengthening ourselves here for the struggle that's coming, and if revenge is all we have left, then we'll make our revenge awful and strong. We need Lámh Shábhála here in Inish Thuaidh to do that. Meriel's beyond our help, wherever she is."

Jenna looked from one man to the other. Mundy was nodding at Kyle's words.

"I won't accept that as the answer," she told them. "I'm sorry. I can't."

When he first went to Edana, Doyle had been terrified that he was going to find her dead.

He still shivered every time he remembered seeing Edana lying on the beach of Inishduán, her face bloodied and bone-white, her fingers clenched tight around the emptied and defeated Demon-Caller. If Jenna *had* killed Edana, Doyle would have followed the Mad Holder even to Dún Kiil. He would have stalked into the Weeping Hall there and confronted his sister without caring what it meant to him. He would have emptied his cloch at her and when it was empty, he would have clawed at her with his bare hands until one or the other of them was dead. He would have speared her with the lance of his rage.

He still might do that. Inishduán had been an unmitigated disaster. The Saimhóir Jenna had used to deceive him had killed the other two mages—both Sharpcut and Weaver needed new Holders now. Doyle swore that he would kill every blue seal he saw from that day forward as payment for the treachery, but the thought of revenge was cold. Even now, a day and more later, Edana remained unconscious in the Rí Infochla's Keep in Falcarragh, her breathing shallow and her skin pale. Doyle remained at her side, watching the procession of healers come and go. They anointed Edana with unguents, poured potions down her unresisting throat, muttered spells, and burned aromatics. They gave opinions that were just empty words. "She's mage-snared, Tiarna Mac Ard," they said. "Perhaps if she were taken to the Order of Inishfeirm, where they have long knowledge of such things . . ." And when Doyle glared at that, they would protest that the Order of Gabair was simply too new to have experience with something like this. They would shake their heads and suggest that perhaps the prayers of the Draíodóiri in the Mother-Creator's temple couldn't hurt.

Edana remained caught in the world of the magelights, her eyes sometimes moving under closed eyelids or her lips parting with unheard words. Doyle remained at her side and he prayed to the Mother-Creator to bring her back. He stroked Edana's cheeks, made her sip

water. When he was alone with her, with no servants
about, he allowed the tears to come because it hurt too
much to hold them back anymore.

As for the rest . . . he'd sent Shay O Blaca to handle
that as soon as he'd reached the ship off Inishduán . . . .

Doyle heard the low clap of collapsing air behind him
as he sat alongside Edana's bed. He turned to see Shay
standing in the middle of the room. O Blaca stared at
Edana. "No change?" he asked.

Doyle shook his head. Looking at O Blaca, he knew
the answer to his question before he asked it. "Where's
my niece, Shay? Did you and O'Murchadha do as I
asked?"

O Blaca released the Cloch Mór around his neck,
Doyle saw the fading glimmer of the stone's energy.
There were long scratches on the man's neck and arms
as if something had clawed at him, the blood clotted and
scabbed, the skin angry and red around the wounds.

"I rode with Tiarna O'Murchadha out of Lár Bhaile
to get her," O Blaca said. His gaze drifted past Doyle
to Edana's pale face before returning. "The news isn't
good, I'm afraid. If Quickship had been full it would
have been different—I could have just snatched the girl
away with the cloch, but I'd used up everything moving
you and the others to Inishduán, and the mage-lights
didn't come that night to let me replenish it . . ." He
shook his head, grimacing. "We found the Taisteal near
Doire Coill, but we were attacked before we could get
Meriel."

Doyle's eyebrows lifted. "Attacked?"

O Blaca related the tale as Doyle listened with in-
creasing anger and a sickening sense of doom. "By the
Mother, I'm cursed. Crows, dire wolves, and Bunús
Muintir . . ." Doyle grimaced. "What of O'Murchadha?"

"Wounded also. Worse than me; he'll walk with a limp
for the rest of his life; that witch of a Taisteal woman
nearly severed his hamstring when she came at him. We
had six gardai with us; two are dead."

"The Taisteal?"

"The woman who attacked O'Murchadha and allowed your niece to escape died there. As for the Clannhri, O'Murchadha took him and the older men to the Order's keep at Lár Bhaile for . . ." O Blaca sniffed. ". . . further questioning," he finished. "The Clannhri Nico insists that he's innocent, but we'll see how long his protests last in the donjons. I think O'Murchadha will be rather persuasive after what happened to him."

"The Rí?"

"Rí Mallaghan is aware of what happened. The death of the gardai and O'Murchadha's injuries . . ." O Blaca spread his hands. "I'm sorry, Doyle. He wasn't pleased, I have to say. He asked me to tell you that the next time, you should consult with him before engaging Tuath Gabair and the Order in a diplomatic incident."

"Damn!" Doyle let his head drop, then lifted his chin again. "I'm sorry, Shay. I'm sorry you had to take some of the consequences for my failure."

"It could be far worse," O Blaca said. "I think Rí Mallaghan suspected what you were planning to do since our visit with the Toscaire Concordai, but what he didn't know he didn't have to acknowledge. He supports the Order, and by association, both of us. He didn't denounce you publicly but only in private with me. But he knows everything is public now. He may have to respond."

"He doesn't know everything. There was one thing I didn't tell you in the message I sent—worse news yet. Sharpcut and Weaver are Holderless."

O Blaca sucked in a breath. "No . . ."

"Aye," Doyle answered. He went to the hearth and took down a large wooden box banded with iron. "Both of them died on Inishduán; here are their Clochs Mór. As head of the Order, they're yours to give to their next mage-holders." As O Blaca took the box, Doyle sat heavily in the chair beside Edana's bed. "The attack on you was somehow Jenna's doing, damn her," he told O Blaca. "I'd wager my life on it. My da took Jenna and my mam through Doire Coill after that bitch found

Lámh Shábhála originally, and she lived there again for a time after she murdered Banrion O'Mallaghan. Jenna wasn't actually there or neither you or O'Murchadha would have lived, but I'm certain she was responsible. I seriously underestimated her; I won't do that again."

Doyle sighed. O Blaca looked at Edana again, and something in the man's face made Doyle cock his head. "What else, Shay? I've had my fill of bad news."

The man raised his eyebrows. "You'll have to absorb more, I'm afraid. I've news from Dún Laoghaire. Labhrás Ó Riain and his crowd have been busy in your absence. From what I hear, Rí Connachta and Rí Éoganacht have put together a proposal for the Óenach. They want Enean to be named Rí Ard, with Ó Riain acting as 'Regent Guardian' for him. I think we both know what that really means."

Doyle scoffed. "Aye. Ó Riain would be the real Rí Ard, no matter who Enean might marry or what title the Ríthe bestow on him. The Rí Infochla's already on his way to Dún Laoghaire for the Council; he was gone when we returned from Inishduán. The timing couldn't be worse, especially with poor Edana . . ." Doyle stopped, looking back at her, his gaze softening with the sight of her face. He sighed. "I can't wait here, no matter how much I want to. Can Quickship send me to Dún Laoghaire and take you back to Lár Bhaile, Shay?"

O Blaca touched the cloch, closing his eyes momentarily. He shook his head. "Not until the mage-lights come again."

"Then we'll hope they come tonight. I told Jenna what I intend to do for her treachery, and I will keep that vow."

"We can't go into Doire Coill after your niece, not even with a small army, Doyle. The Rí Gabair wouldn't allow it. Besides, the tales I've heard . . ." O Blaca shivered.

"Perhaps," Doyle answered, "but that's for later. We need to take care of Labhrás Ó Riain first; even Rí Mallaghan would agree with that." Doyle rubbed the back of

his neck, weary, but with his mind roaring with nascent
strategies. He clapped O Blaca on the shoulder, guiding
him to the door. "I don't deserve such friends as you,
Shay, and I'll make all this up to you. I promise. Rest
for now. One of the Rí's servants will get you a chamber
and I'll have them send you his best healer. We'll talk
more later . . ."

Dhegli would have drowned but for his milk-clan, who
came to him as he drifted down into the cold, black
embrace of the WaterMother. They lifted him to the
air again.

Dhegli was utterly drained, his body aching from
snout to flukes with the effort of fighting the two stone-
walkers with their sky-stones. He'd never felt the power
of the sky-stones before, but Garrentha—who had swallowed Bradán an Chumhacht before Dhegli—had told
him that her predecessor, Thraisha, had died fighting
sky-stones.

They were extraordinarily powerful. He knew that
now.

For a time, Dhegli had been afraid that he would follow Thraisha's example. It had taken every last dreg of
power within him to finally extinguish the lights of the
clochs, and afterward . . .

He didn't remember afterward. He didn't know whether
Jenna had prevailed or fallen or where she might be.
He'd come back to consciousness to find his milk-clan
gathered around him, having pulled him up on a rock
on the far side of the island. They were still there with
him, and they had brought him fish to eat and had
placed kelp over the worst of his wounds to start the
healing. Slowly, he felt the power of Bradán an Chumhacht returning within him.

With it, he also felt the portion of that power he'd

given Meriel. He half dragged his body down to the sea, and he looked southward.

"You can't be thinking of going to Winter Home, Dhegli," Challa, his milk-sister and sometimes-mate, said. "You still need time to recover. The stone-walkers aren't worth this, not even our land-cousins. All they hold for you is death and misery. Look at what happened here—what did *you* gain for helping the First Holder? Thraisha, Garrentha . . . Do you plan to add your name to that list?"

"She's there," he answered.

Challa coughed derisively. "What can you offer her, or she offer you beyond a dalliance for a few hours every so often? You're Water-snared, Dhegli; she's Earth-snared. Neither one of you can ever change that, and the *Saimhóir* are your charge, not the stone-walkers."

"Yet the water does meet the earth, always."

Challa snorted. "Aye, it does. The water pounds against the earth endlessly: beating at it, tearing it down, frothing in anger and frustration the whole time. You really should choose a better metaphor."

Dhegli bobbed his dark head in acknowledgment. "You're right, Challa. And I know that your judgment in this is probably better than my own. But . . ." He took a breath, not quite knowing how to say it.

"But my advice comes from my head and your heart is singing too loud for you to hear it," she finished for him.

He brushed his flank against her. He barked a short laugh. "Aye," he answered. "It sings very loudly."

Challa jumped from the rocks into a crashing wave. A few moments later, her whiskered head appeared in the surf well out from the shore. "When?" she called, her voice thin against the roar of the wind and the incessant pounding of the waves against the rocks.

"Now," he told her. "Before my head realizes that I should listen to you." Grunting with the effort of moving his stiff and sore body, he waddled to the edge of the rock and waited. A green wave rose, cool and inviting.

He plunged in as it crested and foamed, relishing the embrace of the water. He saw Challa's body against the bright roof of the sea and rose alongside her, breaking into the air again with a sniff and shake of his head.

"I'll come with you," she said to him. "Saimhóir should always have milk-kin with them."

"Thank you. I may need your strength."

"I've no doubt of that," she told him. "I've no doubt of that at all."

31

By the Lough's Waters

THE MAGE-LIGHTS did come the next night, and Meriel filled the clochmion once again. Keira, with a thoughtful expression on her weathered face, crouched nearby as Meriel lifted the cloch to the sky. The mage-lights began to fade and Meriel sighed and released the cloch though tendrils of color still netted the stars. Meriel leaned on the staff Keira had lent her, exhausted, not daring to take too deep a breath because of her broken ribs. She didn't want to cry out, knowing it would bring Owaine—watching her from the entrance of the cavern—over to her.

When Meriel had recovered her breath, she closed her hand around the cloch again, this time opening it to release the captured energy. In the cloch-vision, she could see herself and the pus-yellow threads of the pain through her body, the red-orange of the fractured ribs. She send the mage-light toward them, expecting to feel the pain redoubled for a moment, then ease and relief as Treoraí's Heart healed the damage within her.

The mage-light burned in her cloch vision but it didn't—it wouldn't—touch her, even though she bent her will to it. There was an unseen barrier around her; she couldn't reach into herself as she did with the others. The power of the clochmion flared all around her as a nimbus of power, but it came no closer.

She could not heal herself.

She brought the energy back into Treoraí's Heart and opened her fingers, blinking back tears and trying not to show her disappointment. Keira was still watching and Meriel lifted her eyebrows toward the Bunús as she leaned again on the staff.

"You knew?" Meriel said, as much statement as question, and Keira shrugged under her furs.

"I wondered all along," the woman answered. "Look at the mage-scars on your hand—the cloch you bear is far more than a simple clochmion. They don't scar their Holders at all. Also, it is truly Treoraí's Heart, the most personal gift the Créneach could give; it isn't meant for the selfish. The stone allows you to take away another person's pain; but your own you have to bear by yourself."

Meriel noticed Owaine squinting curiously in their direction. She flicked a quick glance at him but looked quickly away, not wanting to give him the chance to say anything. Keira noticed the movement, even in the darkness. "I'd say this to you, also. Owaine risked everything to come after you when no one else did," Keira said quietly. "He did it without orders, without thinking about his own safety, without any reason but his gratitude to your mam and his affection for you. He followed you with nothing protecting him but a belief he might be able to find you."

"I didn't ask him to do that. I didn't give him any reason to think that I might like him the way . . ." She hesitated. ". . . the way he wants me to like him. I don't. I can't. It wouldn't be fair. I'm in love with someone else."

"I know you are. He knows it, too. And yet it changes nothing for him. He came here knowing that if he managed to bring you back, you'd go to the Saimhóir instead of to him. But to Owaine, that didn't matter, not if it was what you wanted. That, I think, is a pure love."

"You seem to know a lot about him," Meriel answered, the words edged. "You also seem to think that I'm ungrateful."

Keira didn't answer. She rose from her crouch, sniffing the air and stretching, looking out into the darkness of the forest rather than at Meriel.

"I *am* grateful to him," Meriel persisted. "I am. I know I might not even be alive if it weren't for him."

More silence. Treoraí's Heart pulsed against her chest, and she realized what Keira was saying to her. "Oh." She took as deep a breath as her ribs would allow. "Owaine, would you come here?" Meriel said, though she looked at Keira before turning to him. He squinted, pushed himself away from the stone walls and walked over to them quickly, stopping a few feet in front of her.

"Didn't it work?" he asked. Concern lined his face. "The way you're holding onto the staff . . . I can help you back inside . . ."

"Just be quiet a moment," she told him. She closed the distance between them and opened the cloch again, reaching up to touch his head with her free hand. There was no pain within him, but her true vision went soft and the leaves of the trees around them, once etched sharply against the night sky, became blurred and indistinct. She couldn't imagine seeing the world so hazy and smeared, much less navigating through a totally unfamiliar landscape that way. *He can barely focus an arm's length away, yet he came after you. . . .* She sent the cloch's strength into him, and it pulled her awareness into his. She saw herself as he saw her. She saw *him*. She drew in a breath.

There was nothing hidden in Owaine. She could feel all the hurt and pain he'd accumulated over the years, all the abuse he'd taken at the hands of the other students and even some of the Bráthairs and Siúrs of the Order: the whispered jests he'd overheard, the taunts, the barely-disguised prejudice, the jealousy over Jenna's and Máister Kirwan's favor toward him. She felt the cuts she'd put in his soul as well with her curtness. And yet . . . yet there was no anger in him toward her, no resentment, no bitterness. She was him, and she looked at herself and she felt only a forgiveness for every time

she'd shunned him or turned away coldly or answered
him sharply.

For the first time, she felt regret for the way she'd
treated Owaine. For the first time, she looked at him
and saw him as he was, and he no longer seemed quite
so clumsy or ugly. She found herself comfortable inside
him. She felt protected here.

But she couldn't stay. She let the mage-light fill his
eyes and shape them gently. "This is all I can give you
for what you did for me, Owaine," Meriel whispered to
him. Owaine gasped.

Meriel released the cloch and stepped back from him.
She blinked, the remnants of his poor vision blurring the
world around her, feeling his thoughts fade from hers.
Owaine, wide-eyed, turned in a circle, giving a cough of
amazement and then a long, full laugh as he looked at
the world around him.

"I think your mam and the Máister chose the stone's
bearer wisely, Meriel," Keira said.

Two days later . . .

"Come with me. Quickly!" Keira gestured at Meriel
and Owaine from the entrance of the cavern. Then she
was gone, hurrying down the slope of the knoll. They
followed after her, but she'd vanished among the trees
by the time they emerged. One of the crows—they
seemed to take turns being with the Bunús Muintir, and
though Keira knew all their names, Meriel could never
remember them—was waiting for them in the branch of
a nearby oak. It cawed and flew off for a short distance,
then landed with a hop, cawing at them again. They
followed: fly, hop, caw—Meriel hobbling along with the
aid of Seancoim's old staff; Owaine staying at her side.
They chased the crow for what seemed to be a stripe of
the candle or more, finally half pulling themselves to the
top of a hill overlooking the High Road that followed
the western side of Lough Lár. Here, the oaks of Doire

Coill came nearly to the shore, and the High Road was crowded between trees and water.

The crow gave a cry and flew away.

Meriel gazed at the lough, its peat-stained waters glistening in the sun, the far shore blue-gray in the atmospheric haze. She saw—faintly—a smear of white smoke from a small village on the hillside across the water. Here, the lough was four or five miles wide, though its length stretched nearly thirty miles end to end. From the southernmost end, the River Duán flowed down to Lough Dubh, and from Lough Dubh on an ever-widening course to the sea.

The sea . . .

Meriel suddenly, desperately, wanted to get to the shore. The water called her, the gift that Dhegli had placed within her burning in her mind. If she could touch the water, she could call him, and he would hear her longing and respond, swimming up the river's current from the Westering Sea.

He would come to her, she would go to meet him and they would swim away together. . . .

Heedless of the aches and protests of her body, she started down the hill. "Meriel!" she heard Owaine shout behind her. "Wait!" She paid no attention to him, almost falling down the hillside through the bramble, the staff somehow managing to keep her upright. She could hear Owaine thrashing through the woods after her.

At the bottom, she slogged through a marshy fen, the cold black water filling her low boots and soaking her clóca to the knees. Midges rose in a cloud around her, biting incessantly, but she ignored them. Then she was on the firmer ground of grassy hummocks, and the oaks were thin and far apart, and the High Road was just ahead of her on the other side of a low fieldstone fence, and not more than fifteen strides beyond it, the water.

"Meriel!"

The rolling embrace of the sea pounded in her head. She could almost feel Dhegli, as if he were standing invisible alongside her. If she could reach the water, she could touch him, she could send her words flowing out to him . . .

She heard the sound, so sudden and loud that she knew that she must have been hearing it for some time without realizing it: the thudding of hooves on soft earth. She looked to her left: from the north, two riders were coming fast: gardai, she saw, bearing the colors of Tuath Gabair, and each with a spear in his right hand. They'd seen her: one garda jumped the wall of the High Road as she watched, the hooves of his mount tearing at the loam of the field. Meriel hesitated—the shelter of the trees was too far away; the water now seemed terribly distant. She reached the wall and clambered over it onto the road, every muscle screaming protest, the binding around her broken ribs not enough to stop her from crying out in pain. Her staff clattered onto the rutted ground as she half fell onto the road.

"Meriel! Use the staff!" The voice wasn't Owaine's but Keira's. Meriel bent to pick up the staff: as the first of the riders thundered down at her, as she saw the blade set on its long pole gleam in sunlight as he lowered his spear to run her through. She grasped for the staff and lifted it in a desperate, late attempt to strike the spear and knock it aside.

She expected the stunning shock of yew against oak or, worse, the terrible ripping of the spearhead through her body. She was unprepared for the scream of the rider: in the instant spear touched staff, Meriel seemed to see the staff leap outward, the wood flowing like water around and through the weapon, up the man's arms, spreading and twisting even as Meriel was thrown back by the force of the contact and went tumbling on the dirt of the roadway. But her attacker had stopped in mid-charge, and when she pulled herself up, she stared at a living sculpture: rider and horse caught and frozen, the expression of murderous intent still on the man's face, the horse captured in mid-stride, its head turned and mane flowing with the wind of its movement.

Made of oaken wood now, not flesh. Meriel's staff itself was gone, consumed.

The other garda reined in his steed. For a moment, Meriel and he stared at each other and she could see the fright in his wide eyes. When Keira and Owaine came out from the shadows of the trees, the man visibly shuddered, taking a final glance at his wood-snared companion. Keira gestured at him, as if she were about to cast a spell.

The garda yanked at the reins of his horse, turning his mount so hard that they almost went down as hooves flailed at muddy ground. He fled.

Meriel crouched in the dust of the road, panting. A crow landed on the wooden-bladed spear of the transformed garda and cawed once at her. She heard Keira and Owaine climb over the stone wall.

"Rather pretty, isn't it?" Keira said. "Very lifelike." She patted the horse's neck. The crow flapped from the spear to sit atop the rider's head. It lifted its tail and a splotch of white dropped, leaving a streak from the top of the garda's armored cap to his ear.

Meriel had no words. It was Owaine who spoke. "Slow magic?"

Keira nodded. "I said that the staff was one of Seancoim's. He had enchantments in all of them. Seancoim had an ability that only a few who use slow magic can master—that of being able to place the spell into an object, where it stays until released."

"You can do that, too," Owaine said. "Can't you?"

Keira only smiled in answer. She nodded appreciatively at the rider. "I didn't know what the staff would do, only that it would do something." She tilted her head appraisingly at the garda and horse. "That's a rather nice effect, I think."

Owaine came over to help Meriel up but stopped when she shook her head at him. She rose slowly to her feet on her own, holding her side. Keira turned to her. "There are several encampments of gardai around Doire

Coill," Keira said to her, "and they're sending patrols to ride the High Road on this side of the lough. They're also around the north and west reaches, or so the crows tell me. That's why I sent for you; to show you and warn you. I really didn't expect you to go wandering out to give yourself to them."

"I . . ." Meriel released a loud sigh. "I'm sorry. Are the Tuatha at war, then?"

Again it was Owaine who answered. "It's *you* they want, Meriel." He gestured at the wooden rider. "He wasn't looking to capture you; he wanted you dead. Which means Doyle Mac Ard still wants you dead."

Keira nodded her agreement. "I watched the patterns of the mage-lights; there are clochmions and a few Clochs Mór among those watching the forest. They know you're in Doire Coill."

"Are they going to attack?" she asked, but Keira was already shaking her head.

"They're not that stupid. A few foolish gardai went in, but the trees sang to them and took them into the hidden places—they won't return. The soldiers remember the wolves and crows, too. And now this will be a further reminder." Keira shook her head. "No, they won't attack; not yet, anyway. For now, they're willing to have Doire Coill act as your prison."

"But now I'm out of the prison." Meriel gazed at the lough. "I need to go to the water before they come back."

"Meriel," Owaine started to protest, but Keira put her hand on his shoulder.

"Let her go, Owaine," Meriel heard her say. "She will make her own decisions. All you can do is help her. Go on."

In a few running footsteps, Owaine was beside her. "Here," he said, and swept Meriel up before she could protest, lifting her over the wall on the far side of the road and climbing over after her. "You really don't need to come with me," she told him.

Owaine shrugged. "I get to make my own decisions,

too," he told her. He walked alongside her as she limped across the rocky verge to where wind-driven waves lapped at the rocks. Meriel walked into the achingly cold water until it reached her knees before glancing back. Owaine had stopped at the shore; Keira remained standing where she'd been, alongside the immobile horse and rider in the road. Meriel could feel this water's connection with the distant sea and the sense of that link made her tremble with the remembered change, caused the gift Dhegli had placed within her to awaken fully. The scale of Bradán an Chumhacht burned in her mind and she could feel Dhegli—far distant to the north and west—answer the call. *I hear you,* he seemed to say. *I'm coming to you, Meriel . . .* Then the bond vanished, as quickly as it had come, making her wonder whether she'd truly felt it at all. She called to him again, her lips moving with his name, but there was no answer.

I'm coming to you, Meriel . . .

It would be effortless to let herself change, easy to go and meet him. It would be simple, and it would be what she wanted. Dhegli would have to come up the Duán; there was no other way for him. All she need do was fall forward and the feel of the water would turn her and she could swim down to meet him as a Saimhóir with the flow of the water.

Effortless. All she need do was desert Owaine, who had followed her all the way from Inish Thuaidh. All she need do was leave Keira behind, who had rescued her a few quick breaths from death. All she need do was forget about Nico and the Taisteal, who had at least treated her kindly enough. All she need do was forget about Sevei, who had sacrificed her own life for Meriel just to keep a promise she'd made.

All Meriel need do was to think of herself first and follow the easiest path.

She glanced back at Owaine and Keira. Following the path of least resistance was what she'd done most of her life. She'd done that with her mam, with her da, with her life as the Banrion's daughter. It was what she'd done in her personal life as well: with Lucan, with Thady, and—aye—with Dhegli. If she left now, she was abandoning those who had helped her to the revenge of Doyle Mac Ard and the Tuatha when they realized that she was gone.

The water lapped at her thighs, beckoning to her and warm with promise. The change tingled inside her skin, making her forget the bruises, the torn muscles, the broken ribs. The desire to go into the water tugged at her, but this time she resisted its allure.

She turned. She walked out of the water onto the rocks and mud and chill air.

"I need to go back to the cave and dry these clothes," she said to Owaine. "Do you mind if I lean on you while we walk?"

32

Casting Bones

"WHY DID you bring us here? Who are those people?" Meriel asked Keira.

Meriel, Owaine, and Keira stood on a small rise deep within the forest, looking down at a small, hidden lough. Well out in the water were three crannogs: lake dwellings—artificial islands on which thatched wattle and daub huts stood. Small herds of sheep and cows grazed in fenced stockades on the crannogs; chickens pecked at the dirt among the huts. Smoke from peat fires drifted low over the water and through the branches of the trees huddling close around the lake, and they could hear the ring of a smithy working metal somewhere on the shore. A few people were visible on the crannogs: feeding the cattle, milling grain in stone querns, placing herbs over racks to dry.

"They're my clan," Keira answered. "This is where I was born. And I brought you here because I was asked."

"There're more people over there," Owaine said, pointing to another group of a half dozen men and women along the shore of the lough, tossing a weighted net over the black water. He grinned at Meriel. "I can *see* them."

The Bunús Muintir pulled at the net; with high-pitched shouts: water foamed suddenly, raging and white, and the ropes were nearly torn out of their hands. Something scaled, manlike, and large emerged from the water, tear-

351

ing at the strands that snared and held it. The captured
animal—if that's what it was—charged toward one of
the net holders, sending those behind sprawling and
bearing the man in front down onto the reed-choked
mud of the shore. They heard a thin scream as the creature tore savagely at the man's arm with claws and teeth.
The others pulled at the net, yanking the creature away
as a few more Bunús rushed in to stab at the thing with
spears. It grasped one of the spears and pulled the
woman wielding the weapon toward it; she released the
shaft and retreated as the water-beast slashed at her, but
another spear impaled it from behind, the barbed stone
head emerging from the scaled, blue skin of the abdomen. The creature shrieked, then the Bunús Muintir
closed around it, forcing it down onto the muddy shore.
The blood that pulsed from the beast glinted the pale
yellow of a winter sun.

"What is *that?*" Meriel and Owaine asked together.

"A water ghost, a Uisce Taibhse," Keira answered.
"Not ghosts at all, but creatures that live in fresh water.
Sometimes one will come into Doire Coill through the
river and come over to our lake—they can cross short
distances out of the water, though they can't breathe air.
You'll find them in many of the lakes in the west and
north—like other races, they were awakened in the Filleadh. They're intelligent and strong, and they like human
flesh too much. Where we find them, we kill them."

*Lough Méar . . . Sevei told me that water ghosts lived
there and I didn't believe her.* Meriel imagined one of
these Uisce Taibhse grabbing her, bearing her down
under the water: she shuddered as they hurried down to
the shore. At close range, the body of the Uisce Taibhse
was a horror. Its body was a mottled blue-black like the
deep water held in an underwater canyon. Sharp-pointed
spines lifted from the crown of its head down its back
to the waist, the spines linked by leathery webbing; the
long-fingered hands were also webbed. The face was
smooth except for the slits of gills on either side of its
neck and two tiny eyes. The eyes were dead black and

shining—emotionless, cold shark eyes—and thin fanged teeth glistened in a gaping round fish mouth smeared with the blood of the man it had attacked.

The others were talking loudly to Keira: the guttural, odd cadence of their language sounding eerie and strange to Meriel. One of the women had gone to the injured man; another of the men strode away a few steps, calling across to the nearest crannog until someone called back.

Hidden, Treoraí's Heart warmed between Meriel's breasts. She went to the injured man; he was moaning and rolling from side to side as the woman crooned to him, the tone of her voice belying her worried eyes as she tried to staunch the bleeding with cloth torn from her skirt. The wound along the man's forearm looked awful, the skin laid open in a trio of parallel tears, the white of bone showing through the gushing red flow of blood that soaked his shirt and dripped to the muddy ground. "Let me help," Meriel said to the woman, who glared at her almost angrily before her gaze flicked over to where Keira was standing. Keira said nothing, but the woman moved aside with a grunt. Meriel reached for the chain of the cloch and brought it out, closing her hand around the stone and touching the man at the same time.

. . . *the horrible rotten-fish smell of the water ghost's breath, the claws ripping at skin, tearing it . . . the mouth closing around the arm and the awful feel of tooth scraping bone, severing muscles and ligaments, sinew and nerves as the creature shook its head, the teeth ripping, tearing, gouging . . . the burning of the creature's saliva . . . the sharp, searing pain . . .*

Meriel shouted, falling away from the man as she released Treoraí's Heart, unable to bear the shared agony any longer. The contact faded more slowly than Meriel liked. She gulped air as the pain radiating from her arm slowly receded; the scars on her hand burned, and she could see that the lines were snaking past the wrist now. The man gave a shout, holding his arm aloft in wonder. Where a moment before the arm had been scored and torn, there were now only three angry red streaks like healing scabs. He flexed his hand, laughing and holding it up before him in amazement.

The Bunús woman, still holding the shreds of bloody cloth, also gave a cry. She hugged the man, speaking fast words in her own language to Meriel over his shoulder. "She asks you to forgive her for her suspicion before," Keira told Meriel. "She thanks you for healing her husband."

"Tell her that she's welcome, that I owe the Bunús Muintir far more than that for rescuing me."

As Keira translated, Meriel caught glimpses through the trees of someone rowing a skin-covered currach across toward them. An elderly man stepped from the boat and approached the group on the shore. Like Keira, he wore skins and fur and around his neck was an ornamental collar made of a beaten gold sheet decorated with raised patterns that reminded Meriel of the scars on her and her mam's arm.

"Ragan!" Keira cried, going to him and embracing him. He kissed the top of her head, laughing. His eyes, a startling ice blue, gazed at Meriel and Owaine over the top of her head, then to the Bunús gathered around the dead water ghost. Keira pulled away from him and spoke to him at length in their own language, pointing at Meriel and Owaine, then to the newly-healed man. He nodded. He spat carefully on the body of the Uisce Taibhse, then came over to them with slow, shuffling steps.

"I don't speak the language of the Daoine well," he said, his voice so heavily accented that they had to listen carefully to understand it. "Forgive me. Keira has told me about you; I was the one who asked her to bring you here, and after what you've done here today, I'm glad for that. I am Ragan, and I am Ald here. You know the title?"

"Aye," Meriel said. "In some of our towns, there is an Ald."

He nodded again. "You Daoine borrowed the term

from us, but even for us it means less than it once did. Come, I'll take you across to the island."

Ragan's hut was larger than it had looked from the shore. Inside, the single large room was partitioned off by hanging tapestries, with the center area left as a common kitchen. A table formed from a slice of a huge oak trunk dominated the area, its surface polished and smooth, the three legs that supported the table flowing from the top in seamless curves down to the rush-covered floor. A wide, shallow bowl of cut flowers floating in water sat in the middle, their sweet smell filling the air. A small leather bag slouched alongside the bowl. Ragan gestured to the half dozen stools arranged around the irregular perimeter. "Please sit," he said. "Let me get you some refreshment after your long walk."

The Ald called out and a young Bunús man scurried in with a tray holding a pitcher and several wooden mugs. Ragan poured a pale liquid from the pitcher into the mugs and handed them to Meriel, Owaine, and Keira. Meriel sniffed at hers—an aroma of mint and honey drifted up from the liquid; when she tasted it, a cool, lush sweetness filled her mouth. "That's wonderful," she said. Owaine muttered agreement

Ragan nodded. "It's an infusion of tree barks, a few herbs, honey, and water from a sweet spring." He smiled as if with a gentle, inward amusement. "There's also a fermented version, but that's for other occasions." He reached across the table for the pouch. As he picked it up in his knobby-fingered hand, Meriel heard a sound like small stones clinking together. Ragan fiddled with the knotted string holding the pouch closed, but didn't open it. "You Daoine have your cities and your steel. Your stone houses are better than any we Bunús ever made. But there are a few things we Bunús Muintir know that you have yet to discover, or perhaps have simply forgotten."

Meriel thought of Keira, of her slow magics and her woodlore, of the wolves and crows who did her bidding. "Believe me," she said, "I realize that. Sometimes . . . well, I've heard people say that the Bunús are savage people, half wild, but my mam . . ." Meriel could almost see Jenna as if she'd invoked her, and with the vision an intense, surprising longing filled her, not just for her mam, but for Inish Thuaidh and Inishfeirm and everything that had once been familiar. *One minute you hate her, and the next you miss her so terribly* . . . Meriel hesitated, swallowing hard. ". . . she never would say anything like that or let anyone talk that way in her presence," she finished. "She always talked fondly of your people, and especially of Seancoim. She's made laws in Inish Thuaidh—no one is allowed to harm a Bunús Muintir there or to go into Thall Coill without their permission."

Again, the slow smile. "That's good to hear. The First Holder is a true friend to us and if one of us can no longer hold Lámh Shábhála, we're glad that she wields the First Cloch. But we're seeing the long twilight of the Bunús Muintir, I'm afraid, and darkness is gathering even while the magic returns."

"Because of us?" Owaine asked. "I know about the old wars between Daoine and Bunús Muintir, and I've heard that the Tuatha still kill Bunús Muintir whenever they find them."

"Maybe in Talamh an Ghlas that's true," Meriel said. "But not in Inish Thuaidh. It can be stopped here, too . . ."

Ragan's graying head was moving slowly from side to side. "No, you don't understand. We're not failing because of the Daoine. Oh, that's part of it, perhaps, but it's not the illness that kills the root. No . . ." He untied the string on the pouch, his fingers trembling slightly. "We were never many, we Bunús, even when the Daoine came to Talamh an Ghlas. A Daoine mam might have four or six or even more children in her lifetime, if the Greatness wills it; a Bunús will be lucky to have two or three, and some of those will die before they reach the age of childbearing themselves. When you Daoine came and filled the land, some of our women became Daoine brides; a few of the men lay with the

Daoine women, too, though that was rarer. You, Owaine, or especially you, Meriel, may have Bunús blood yourself; I know Seancoim wondered about that with Jenna. And some of us here have a trace of Daoine ancestry. So a part of the Bunús Muintir has blended in with the Daoine—become part of you. But the rest of us . . . we fade, slowly, without any help from the Daoine at all. I wonder, when the mage-lights fail again, centuries from now, if any Bunús Muintir will be left under the old trees. I can hope so . . . but I doubt that any of us will see the awakening after the long darkness. I don't think we'll survive to awaken once more."

Ragan jiggled the pouch and upended it on the table. Bits of polished ivory bones spilled out along with a single black feather and three blood-red, polished half circles that might have been seashells. They rattled on the tabletop. "Bones of crow and scale of dragon," Ragan said.

"Dragon scales?" Owaine said. "Really? I saw a dragon . . ." He leaned forward, reaching out toward them but Keira touched his wrist, shaking her head, and he reluctantly pulled his hand back.

"These oracles give a similar pattern every time I cast them," Ragan said. "See there, farthest out?—the wing tip is under the claw, and see how far the bit of spine has gone from the rest? And look next to it: the feather is covered by a scale. I see our time passing. Here, closest to me, the bones jumble—a war, perhaps, or certainly a great struggle coming soon. And just beyond that, the dragon scale covering a rib bone: a threat from outside that is still hidden." He scooped up the pile and placed them back in the bag, then handed the bag to Meriel. "Throw them again," he said.

Meriel remembered Sevei in her tent, placing the array of cards on the table and peering down at them. She shivered, afraid suddenly. "I don't believe in this," she said, but the truth was that she was afraid that, like Sevei's cards, she believed in them all too much.

"You don't have to believe," Ragan answered. "The

bones will feel what's in your heart whether you have faith in their ability or not. Go on." He peered at her with ancient eyes. "I'm not afraid to see what they say," he told her. "Your Taisteal friend accepted what she saw in the future, also."

"How do you—?" Meriel stopped. Shivered. Ragan smiled at her gently.

"Cast them," he said. She jiggled the bag as she'd seen Ragan do and turned over the bag, letting the contents scatter on the table. Ragan bent forward, squinting so that his white, bushy eyebrows seemed to curl together around the wrinkles above his nose. "Interesting," he said. "Not what I expected."

"What do they say?" Owaine asked. Ragan didn't answer, looking instead at Meriel. She shrugged at him.

"I don't care," she said. "Whatever it is, you can say it."

A nod. "The dragon scales touch there," he said, jabbing at the table with a thick-nailed hand. "And see how the feather floats free while the claw and beak touch. I thought . . ." Ragan looked up, staring at Meriel. "You reject the path others would set for you. Instead, you follow what calls to your soul. That will bring you danger and possibly an early death."

A coldness gripped her chest. Meriel stared at the artifacts, trying to see in them what Ragan saw. "The parts within you are at war," Ragan continued. "You are pulled in many directions—toward something or someone different than you and away from what someone else wants you to be, even though I see that you would do well in that place."

Meriel felt the brush of cold fingers along her spine. "You're saying I'm making a mistake," she began, but Ragan was already shaking his head.

"No one can say that. The bones indicate that you stand at the branching of paths. There are several futures for you: some where you fulfill a great destiny, others where you turn away from that destiny because the choice is being imposed on you rather than being

your own. I also see here—" he touched the bones that
had fallen closest to Meriel, "—that the most risk for
you comes from someone close to you, not from those
you think of as your enemies."

Meriel drew in a breath. *It's what Sevei said, also.
". . . that it's those you love you should fear the most,
for they hold the greatest danger for you."* Meriel nodded, but Owaine spoke, almost angrily. "This is nonsense," he said. "You can't see the future in a few bits
of bone. You're talking in such vague terms that of
course Meriel imagines it applies to her."

Ragan looked placidly at the young man. He scooped
up the bones and placed them back in the bag. "Would
you like to cast them?" he asked Owaine, holding out
the pouch to him. "There might be enough of the spell
left within them for one more telling." Owaine blinked
and Meriel saw the anger slowly fade, replaced by a
grudging curiosity. He held out his hand and Ragan
placed the pouch in Owaine's upturned palm.

"I still don't believe in this," Owaine said. Ragan said
nothing and Owaine upturned the pouch. Bones chattered on wood, bouncing. "Well, what do you see?"

Ragan peered at the array. "The beak is down while
the rib bones have opened to enclose the scale . . .
You've given your love to someone who doesn't return
it. You're afraid to speak too much of your feelings to
her because you think you know what her answer would
be, so you stay silent. And the claw holds the feather . . .
You would protect that person even at the cost of yourself. That speaks of an unselfish and brave heart."

Owaine looked up from the table and his gaze caught
Meriel's. Owaine blushed; Meriel looked quickly away.
*We both know what Ragan is implying, and I don't want
you thinking that way about me,* she wanted to say to
him. *I don't want to hurt you after all you've done, but
I don't love you. Not that way. Dhegli has that part of
me . . . I'm sorry.*

She didn't say it; she pressed her lips closed, staring
only at the bones. "You talk of now, Ragan," Owaine

said. With his voice, Meriel stole a glance at him, but he kept his gaze fixed on Ragan. "What of my future?"

A soft smile. "I thought you didn't believe?" Owaine sputtered, and Ragan laughed. "I didn't need the bones to give you the reading just now, Owaine," Ragan said. "I could see all of what I said in your face and your eyes. The bones were empty of the slow magic; I could feel that when you put them on the table. I'm sorry. But I can tell you one other truth without needing magic: you haven't thought much of your future. Someone who would rush away to find someone without any preparation or concern for himself doesn't look that far forward. Right now you see little hope that there will *be* a future." Ragan scooped up the bones again and knotted the string around the neck of the pouch. "There will be one, of course, but whether you or I will be in it . . ." Ragan shrugged and gave a low laugh. "Only the gods know."

"That's hardly comforting," Owaine said. "And hardly magic."

Ragan sighed and straightened. "Comfort is for fools, and only fools depend on magic." He set the pouch aside on the table and folded his hand on the polished surface. His wrinkled gaze returned to Meriel. "I wanted to meet you because the bones tell me you'll be here for a time yet, and that affects us."

"I'm sorry," Meriel told him. "I didn't want to bring trouble to your people. If you want, I'll leave. All I need do is go to the lough."

"And leave Owaine behind, trapped here?" Keira asked.

She could feel his gaze on her and wouldn't look his way. "Owaine can't travel the way I'd go. The Riocha aren't after Owaine, but me. Once the Riocha realize I'm gone, it would be easy enough for him to leave."

Ragan shook his head. "The bones don't see you leaving, Meriel," he said. "And having you here isn't a great danger for us. Or rather, only a little more than we already had. I see allies coming here to find you. So rather than escape from Doire Coill to return to your mam and your home, I would propose that we bring your mam here."

33

A Game of Ficheall

THE sense of failure sat in the pit of his stomach,
indigestible and heavy and booming with every pulse
of blood in his body.

. . . my fault, my fault, my fault . . .

*"I need you to take care of Edana," he told his cousin,
the young tiarna Aghy O'Máille. "I've sent word to my
family and a dozen of our retainers should be here in a
few days to ride with you and your own gardai. I'm giving you the thing I treasure most in this world, Aghy.
Take her to the Order of Gabair. Shay will begin a search
for a healer who understands this type of mage-caused
injury. But if she wakes, bring her back to Dún Laoghaire
as quickly as you can. Trust no one you might meet on
the road. Send me regular messages on your progress. I'll
be waiting to hear from you in Dún Laoghaire."*

*He'd kissed Edana then, tenderly, wanting to cry at the
sight of her pale, thin face. "I love you," he whispered,
his lips close to her ear. "Please come back to me, Edana.
I need you, now more than ever. I hope you can hear
me. Let me tell you again: I love you." Then he'd straightened and nodded to Shay, and the tiarna had closed his
fingers around his Cloch Mór and the coldness of the
Between had gripped Doyle . . .*

*You have to wake up, Edana. You have to return to
me . . .*

. . . my fault, my fault, my fault . . .

"It's your move, Doyle."

Doyle started. Torin Mallaghan, Rí of Tuath Gabair, waved a hand at the ficheall board set up on the table between them. Torin was more like his mam Cianna—murdered almost twenty years ago by Jenna—than the da after whom he'd been named. Torin was thin almost to the point of appearing fragile, with fine-boned and soft features, though those who made the error of mistaking appearance for reality had paid heavily. Rí Mallaghan had arrived in Dún Laoghaire a day after Doyle, and had called Doyle to his chambers within a stripe. But since Doyle had been ushered into the Rí's presence, Torin had mentioned nothing about either Meriel or Jenna. Instead, they'd played ficheall, Doyle engaging in carefully circumspect small talk as he waited for the Rí to come to the real topic.

"It's your move. You should really pay attention," the Rí repeated with a hint of annoyance that came easily to him—in that, he was like his da.

Doyle glanced at the board, then slid one of his gardai forward between Torin's Rí and his remaining dragon. "Marbhsháinn," he said—*death trap*. Torin hissed and glared at the board. "I'm sure that you're just distracted with the coming Óenach, my Rí."

Torin's face clouded. "Don't patronize me, Doyle."

Doyle lowered his head at the rebuke. "My apologies, Rí. But you do generally play better."

"Aye, but you still generally win. That's why it disturbs me when you make a mistake in the true game."

"Rí?" . . . *my fault, my fault* . . .

Torin reached out with a thin finger and toppled his Rí. It clattered onto the marble board. "What's happened to her, Doyle?"

Doyle shook his head. *Does he know about Edana? By the Mother, if that's common knowledge, then I'm truly lost* . . . "Edana? She's on her way here, as I mentioned . . ."

Rí Mallaghan grimaced in annoyance. "Not Edana; the Mad Holder's daughter Meriel. Do you realize the

cost of placing my gardai around Doire Coill? Do you
think that none of the other Ríthe will wonder why I'm
doing that? Do you comprehend what it will mean if
they realize that you snatched the Banrion Thuaidh's
daughter but managed to lose her? Have you thought of
the consequences if the MacEagan girl should fall into
another Rí's hands or even—may the Mother-Creator
protect us—finds her way back to Inish Thuaidh? Can
you imagine the repercussions?" His eyes narrowed, his
lips pressed tightly together for a moment. "Do you
know how furious I was to find that you and Shay with-
held all this from me? Does my patronage of the Order
of Gabair and my advice mean so little to you?"

Doyle could feel the heat on his face. Small beads of
sweat had formed at his hairline. He wanted to wipe
them away but instead closed his hand around one of
the ficheall dragons. *Dance with words as best you
can . . .* "My Rí—" Doyle began, then closed his mouth
as Torin waved a hand.

"Don't misunderstand me, Doyle. Frankly, the raid on
Inishfeirm showed your initiative and leadership skills;
even your enemies would grudgingly admit that—though
I wish you'd seen fit to consult with me beforehand. I
have to assume that the Rí Ard knew and approved, but
your home is Tuath Gabair and I still rule there."

"Rí Mallaghan—"

Torin raised a hand and Doyle again subsided into
silence. "You're arguably the most accomplished mage of
the Order of Gabair. You're young, yet you've shown ma-
turity beyond your years and despite your . . . well, let's
call it a dubious lineage, you've managed to convince several of the other Riocha—especially those among the
Order—that it's worth their effort to follow you. Those
qualities are why I suggested to O Liathain that you'd be
a good choice for his daughter and, as I expected, you
managed to win him over before his death. In the ficheall
of life, you managed to place the pieces of your life well
in the opening. But I'm troubled now."

Torin gestured at the board and his fallen piece. "A

good opening isn't enough. A missed move anywhere in the game can be fatal. I want to know that my backing of you isn't a mistake that I'll regret."

"The game isn't over yet, Rí, and sometimes a mistake can uncover a new strategy or cause the opponent to become overconfident."

"Not if your opponent's also a skilled player. Then, one misstep is often enough, and I fear that your opponent in this game is a very good player herself." Torin leaned back in his chair, sighing. One of his servants hurried forward and poured ale into the hammered gold cups on the table, then scurried back to the wall; another poked the fire in the hearth, sending sparks whirling upward. "You didn't get the ransom you wanted from your sister, did you?" Doyle blinked at that, but Rí Torin only waved a hand again at the ficheall board. "Oh, come now. I have eyes and ears out in the world, as does every Rí if he wants to survive, and I know both your history and your style of play. I can guess as to why the Rí Ard's daughter, her fiancé, and a few other of the Order's mages with Clochs Mór would suddenly go to Falcarragh even though the question of the Rí Ard's successor is at risk . . . because if you'd gotten what you were after, there'd be no question as to who the next Rí Ard would be—or should I say Banrion Ard? But you didn't get your ransom, did you?" He looked significantly at Snapdragon hanging around Doyle's neck.

"No," Doyle said, grimacing. "I didn't." *My fault . . .* The guilt moved through him again, leaden. He'd done nothing but replay his decision ever since he'd seen Edana fall and he thought he'd found the fatal flaw in his own ego. *You wanted the battleground to be Inish-duán because you wanted to defeat Jenna where she'd sent your mam spiraling into her depression and madness, and it was too close. You chose the ground and you chose wrongly. You forgot about her affinity with the damned Saimhóir. You didn't weaken her enough . . . It's your fault . . .*

"A pity. I would have loved to have seen Rí O Seach-nasaigh and Rí Taafe pretend to be pleased when they learned that Lámh Shábhála was in Doyle Mac Ard's hands and the Mad Holder was no longer able to trouble us. Now that would have been a move to win any game. But . . ." Another sigh, then Torin leaned forward, one eyebrow raising, his face serious and grim. "What else should I know, Doyle? Tell me now, because if I find that you're not telling me everything, I'll withdraw my protection from you and simply watch when your enemies—and you have enough of those—take you down. We're approaching the endgame, Doyle, and *I* am the Rí, not you; I can't afford pieces that hide themselves from me. I'll use them for sacrifice to protect myself first. Do you understand me?"

Doyle swallowed hard. He stared into the Rí's face, weighing options and seeing no way out. Too much had happened, and Torin would eventually know—he might already know. This could simply be a trap. Doyle's gaze flicked over to the servants; Torin caught the movement. "They're my people and know when to close their ears," the Rí said. "You can speak freely here."

Doyle nodded. Haltingly, then with increasing urgency, he told Torin everything: the ransom he'd demanded, how Jenna had betrayed him, how he thought that he should never have used Inishduán, how two of the Order's cloudmages were now dead and Edana was lost in a dreamworld. Torin said little, but by the time Doyle had finished, he had sagged back in his chair, shaking his head.

"I'm sorry, Rí Mallaghan." Doyle could think of nothing else to say. "This all went so wrong."

"You realize this changes everything."

"Aye, Rí Mallaghan." . . . *my fault* . . .

Torin's lips twisted, as if his thoughts tasted sour. "I came to this Óenach believing that we might just be able to leave with Edana as Banrion. Now . . ." He shook his head and exhaled at the same time. "I think the best we can hope for is to somehow keep Enean from the throne. Does Rí Mas Sithig know any of this?"

Doyle lifted his hands and let them drop back to the table. "We took ship out of Falcarragh for Inishduán, so he would have known that, but the Rí had already left for the Óenach when we returned. He may have heard from his people, but I tried to keep Edana's condition secret from those in the keep. Still, he'll eventually know if he doesn't already."

Torin nodded at that. "Aye, he will. I'll need to tell him and Banrion O Treasigh as well, since this also affects Locha Léin." Torin took a long breath, rubbing at his eyes.

. . . my fault . . . But a new thought was forming. He could see the pieces in the game and there was still room to maneuver. "Rí—"

"Unless you have more news for me, I'd rather not hear from you, Doyle," Torin said.

"Not news, my Rí, but a request."

Torin blinked heavily, wearily. "I'm listening," he said. "But this had better be good."

"Meriel is still in Doire Coill. We know that much." Doyle hurried into the obvious impatience in Torin's posture. "My mam always told me how the Bunús Muintir in Doire Coill helped them when she, Jenna, and my da fled Ballintubber. Meriel will try to send word to her mam that she's safe and the Bunús will help her. That hasn't happened yet or Jenna would already be here— and we would *know* that." Doyle shuddered at the thought. "I would think that we should put your best archers around the north of Doire Coill and any birds, especially crows, leaving the woods for the north should be shot. There are a few mages of the Order who can help if the archers miss, and we should use them."

"To what end?"

Doyle took a breath. "I made a mistake with Jenna, my Rí. I fully acknowledge that. It's not a mistake I would make again, if I had the chance to meet her again."

Torin rubbed his bearded chin with thin fingers, looking down at the ficheall board. "I know what you're thinking. But the game is getting rapidly dangerous for those in it and I fear some important pieces are going to be removed from the board very soon. And with Edana one of them . . ."

Doyle lifted his chin. "Edana is only temporarily gone," he said. "Only that."

Rí Mallaghan looked unconvinced. "We need her *now,* Doyle, but you allowed her to be placed in danger. That was another mistake you made, along with the choice of Inishduán. Oh, I can understand why you'd choose that Mother-forsaken dirt speck, but it was a poor choice of ground. You should have made the Mad Holder come here or to Lár Bhaile. You also let your affection for Edana and your desire to avenge your mam cloud your judgment. Edana should never have been there, not when she's so important. I don't expect those I support to make such elementary mistakes. I don't expect you to make another mistake. Ever."

Doyle allowed himself to breathe. "I won't, my Rí."

"Good. Now leave me. I need to go speak with Rí Mas Sithig and Banrion O Treasigh and see what we can do to minimize the damage."

"And the archers?"

Torin smiled. "They're already in place, along with the mages. I know your family's history, too."

"Thank you, my Rí." For the first time, the knot of tension in his gut started to uncoil.

As Doyle started to leave, Torin stirred, turning in his chair. "Doyle, you should know this: in your place I would have taken the same chance. The prize was worth the risk."

"Thank you again, my Rí," Doyle said, bowing low to the man.

Torin sniffed. "That forgives nothing, though. You failed. Fail again, and you and I will no longer be friends. And I make a ferocious enemy."

Doyle knocked on the door to Enean's chambers. Mac-Camore opened the door, the old man's face brightening at seeing Doyle. "Tiarna Mac Ard," he said, opening the door wide. "I'm pleased to finally see your face again. Come in, come in."

"How's it been?" Doyle asked as he entered and Mac-Camore shut the door behind him.

"Not good," the old man answered quickly in a low voice. "Tiarna Ó Riain . . ." The old man growled in the back of his throat.

"I know," Doyle said. "We'll deal with him soon enough. How's Enean?"

"We need to speak quietly, sir," he said, lifting a forefinger to his lips. "I kept Toiréasa De Danaan away from Enean as much as I could, as Bantiarna Edana asked, and I've tried to do the same with Tiarna Ó Riain, though with less success. But . . ." He managed a quick grin. "Nuala Chathaigh, that young woman Tiarna O Blaca brought here from the Order, tells me her moon time is a week late. If she's pregnant, the arrangements for the marriage have already been made with her parents. She's good with Enean and seems to genuinely like him. I thought that might have settled things, but then after the Ríthe got here I started hearing all the talk of making Tiarna Ó Riain the Regent Guardian . . ." Again, the growl. "He uses the boy. It makes me want to—" He stopped. "Well, that's not for now, and we do need to keep our voices down. Tiarna—"

"Doyle!" Enean shouted, interrupting MacCamore and grinning widely as he came into the foyer from another room. "Where's Edana? I want to see her."

"She's on her way from Falcarragh, Enean," Doyle told the young man, clasping him in a fierce hug. "She'll be several days, I'm afraid, but she's looking forward to seeing you, I know."

Enean managed to frown and smile at the same time.

"I wanted to tell her about Nuala. I like her. She reminds me of Sorcha. I might even marry her."

"Why, that's wonderful news," Doyle said, clasping Enean around the shoulders as he glanced back at Mac-Camore. "I know Edana will be delighted to hear this."

"Tiarna Ó Riain doesn't like her, though. He says that she's too common and Toiréasa is a better match for me. He thinks I'm going to be the Rí Ard, like Da, so I should marry someone with a better name. He says that the Óenach will say the same thing."

Doyle managed a smile. "Not everything Tiarna Ó Riain says is right." His arms still around Enean's shoulders, Doyle guided Enean away toward the hearth. Behind him, he heard MacCamore clear his throat warningly, then a flash of motion from the archway of the room from which Doyle had just come caught his eye.

"Not always right? Why, Tiarna Mac Ard, I would never deliberately tell Enean an untruth."

Doyle gave Ó Riain as small a bow of acknowledgment as etiquette allowed. He didn't bother to smile. "Tiarna," he said. "Why am I not surprised to find you here?"

"We both have an interest in Enean," Ó Riain answered. "He's not only a good friend to me, but I also have his da's dying request to consider. And *I* . . ." Ó Riain went over to Enean and tapped him on the cheek as he might a small child. "I will be pleased to see him wear the torc of the Rí Ard." Standing in front of Enean and Doyle, Ó Riain raised his eyebrows as he looked at Doyle. "Is that what you and Bantiarna Edana want for Enean, Tiarna Mac Ard? Do you want to see him as Ard?"

"I would like to see him happy," Doyle replied. "And that's what Edana wants as well."

Ó Riain's lips stretched in a tight, toothless smile. "That's so good to hear. I've been entertaining Enean with tales from our history. It's interesting how often siblings have turned into enemies when an empty throne was placed between them. Why, I had just mentioned an incident from your own family history: Sinna, the second wife of Teádor Mac Ard, who wanted one of her children to be the successor despite the better claims of the children of Teádor's first wife . . ."

Doyle flushed. "That was many generations ago, in another time."

"Ah, but history can sometimes illuminate the present, don't you think?"

"I think that every family has its dirty tales, Tiarna," he said, "and I hope yours doesn't fall in this generation." He was pleased to see Ó Riain stiffen at that and his smile go cold. "I need to speak with Enean, Tiarna. Privately. If you'll excuse us . . . ?"

Ó Riain gave Doyle a quick bow rimed with frost. "Certainly. Enean, I'll speak with you again soon. Tiarna Mac Ard, MacCamore . . ." With that, Ó Riain left the chambers. MacCamore slammed the door shut after the man.

"I try to keep the tiarna away," MacCamore said to Doyle, but Enean shook his head.

"Tiarna Ó Riain's my friend," the young man insisted. "He likes me."

MacCamore rolled his eyes and lifted his hands. Doyle clapped Enean on the shoulder. "I know," he said. "But he's not my friend or Edana's."

"He told me that you and Edana don't want me to be Rí Ard. Is that true, Doyle?" In Enean's clear eyes, there was a hint of the old Enean, the man Doyle remembered from a few years before: ambitious; courageous; very much his da's son, who would have taken the torc of the Rí Ard without hesitation and worn it deservingly; who would have immediately challenged any person who stood in his way or who threatened those he loved. Suspicion and doubt colored Enean's voice now. "He says that you want Edana to be Banrion Ard because you're going to marry her."

"I will marry Edana, aye," Doyle answered, smiling at Enean and holding his gaze. Watching those eyes carefully. "I love her, Enean, the way you loved Sorcha and the way you're feeling now with Nuala. And Edana loves you also, Enean. She wants only what's best for you. Think of her, Enean. Can you imagine Edana doing anything to hurt you?" As he spoke—soothingly, slow and soft—Doyle saw the uncertainty dim in Enean's eyes as the corners of his lips turned up again. "None of us know what the Ríthe will decide. But if you're chosen as the Rí Ard, Enean, I will never be your enemy. I promise you that."

Enean brightened like a child praised by a parent. "I know, Doyle. I know." He clasped Doyle to him, laughing.

Doyle hugged the man in return, hoping that what he'd just pledged was true.

"Tiarna Mac Ard!"

Doyle heard the call from behind him and turned to see the Toscaire Concordai waving at him from down the corridor. Rhusvak came up to Doyle with the odor of grease and oils, his face shadowed under the upper jaw of the bearskin. "Toscaire," Doyle said. "I understand you enjoyed your tour of the Order of Gabair."

"Indeed I did," the man smiled. Doyle had made certain that Rhusvak was well fed and entertained while at the Order, and had also made certain that two of the female acolytes would be particularly interested in the Toscaire Concordai during his stay. From the reports, Rhusvak had found his short stay with the Order quite satisfactory in all regards. The bear's head tilted slightly on Rhusvak's shoulders, and the man's glittering eyes went from Doyle's face to his Cloch Mór and back. "I'm very impressed. Though perhaps the Order isn't quite as powerful as I thought. I'd hate to have to rethink my position. I had hoped that the Concordance would be able to unequivocally state its preference for the new Rí Ard in light of a newly-acquired power, but . . ." He stopped. Eyebrows lifted in shadow.

Long practice was all that allowed Doyle to keep his smile from faltering. "I assure you, Toscaire Rhusvak, that the power you hint at *will* be acquired. Very soon."

"Ah." Rhusvak sniffed, a loud, wet clearing of nostrils. "Before the Óenach?"

Doyle shook his head. "I'm afraid that's no longer possible. But soon after."

The eyebrows lifted again. "In your position, I might worry that 'after' would be too late. I'd prefer to tell you that I can urge my Thane to support Bantiarna O Liathain and yourself, but I can't do so with vague promises. Not at this point. I need to make a decision, since I've been asked by other parties to give them the same kind of support you and I have discussed. If I knew more, perhaps . . ."

Doyle hesitated, not wanting to confide in the man, not trusting him. But Edana was out of reach, two of those who had followed him dead, and the Rí Gabair's support wavering. He couldn't afford to lose more. He would have to hope that the man's promises were genuine or he'd lose him.

He didn't think he could afford another piece going to the other side of the board.

"Come walk with me," he told Rhusvak. "We'll talk of power and how it might be acquired."

34

The Óenach of the Ríthe

FOR the Óenach, the Ríthe of the Tuatha met in Tuatha Halla, a circular and ancient edifice outside the walls of Dún Laoghaire. There, the leaders of Talamh an Ghlas had met for long generations to name and certify the Rí Ard, their high king. Once, when the fiefdoms had been smaller and more numerous, over fifty Ríthe might have filled the expanse of cold stone thrones enclosed within the hall's stone walls.

Now only five men and one woman were there under the painted gaze of ancient kings and battles: Torin Mallaghan, the Rí Gabair—the second Torin, son of Torin the First and Cianna; Harkin O Seachnasaigh, the Rí Connachta; Brasil Mas Sithig, the Rí Infochla; Mal Mac Baoill, the Rí Airgialla; Kerwin Taafe, the Rí Éoganacht; Siobaigh O Treasigh, the Banrion Locha Léin. There should have been a seventh, the Rí Dún Laoghaire—ruler of Tuath Dún Laoghaire. Often, the Rí Dún Laoghaire was also chosen to be the Rí Ard; that had been the custom now for several generations. But Nevan O Liathain had left his successor as Rí Dún Laoghaire in doubt and so there was another empty stone throne in the ancient circle.

The six were not entirely alone, however. Several tiarnas and bantiarnas—bound to silence by custom and the presence of gardai who would escort them away if etiquette was breached—watched and listened from outside the circle of thrones as the Ríthe conversed.

Doyle was among them, as was Labhrás Ó Riain, too near to Doyle for comfort. Enean was not—he remained at the keep under the watchful eye of MacCamore. That decision had been Doyle's, but when Enean complained, Ó Riain had agreed. Both men doubted that Enean could have remained quiet and neither of them knew what he might say or how that might influence the Ríthe.

None of the onlookers wore weapons—swords and knives were forbidden at the Óenach except for those worn by the Ríthe and the trusted gardai of the hall. But there were clochs on many chests; those could not be taken away. Each of the six Ríthe displayed a Cloch Mór.

A large turf fire burned in the pit at the center of the hall, smoke curling upward to the hole in the high thatched roof, but the warmth never seemed to reach the thrones. All the six were huddled in blankets and looked unhappy to be here rather than in the more comfortable and hospitable keep.

By the time Doyle and the other Riocha had settled in the hall, Rí Taafe had already broached the subject. "I feel strongly that the best course we can follow is the plan that Rí O Seachnasaigh and I have already proposed: we name Enean O Liathain as Rí Ard and Rí Dún Laoghaire. At the same time, we appoint Tiarna Labhrás Ó Riain to act as Regent Guardian. That way, the interests of the Tuatha are best protected." Rí Taafe shifted uncomfortably on his stone seat despite the cushions, pushing himself up with flabby arms. Doyle knew that the man suffered from piles. He hoped they were particularly inflamed today. To Doyle's left, Ó Riain smiled modestly as the Riocha gathered around him— the older families, mostly—nodded. Rí Taafe shifted again, grunting. "*Damn* these seats," he muttered.

Torin Mallaghan couldn't quite keep the smile from his lips, Doyle noticed. "That would serve the interests of Connachta and Éoganacht, perhaps," Torin said. "But not necessarily Gabair. After all, Tiarna Ó Riain is Rí O Seachnasaigh's first cousin and your nephew, Rí Taafe."

"If we're going to look for someone unrelated to any of us, we'll be here for a cursed month," O Seachnasaigh answered heatedly, but Rí Taafe cleared his throat. O Seachnasaigh waved a hand, his protest falling off to a mutter.

"The relationship of Tiarna Ó Riain to any of us doesn't matter," Taafe said easily to Torin as O Seachnasaigh scowled. "Labhrás Ó Riain has proved himself many times over the years. Who else would you have as Regent Guardian for Enean, Rí Mallaghan?"

"I wouldn't have Enean at all," Torin replied. "Let's at least say aloud what we're all thinking and what all the Riocha listening already know—we all realize that Enean will never be capable of being Rí Ard or Rí Dún Laoghaire on his own, not in the way of his da or great-da. This idea of a 'Regent Guardian' is just a pretense."

"Rí Mallaghan's conveniently forgetting that Enean is the person Nevan O Liathain designated as his successor," O Seachnasaigh grumbled. "He's the firstborn and a son."

Banrion O Treasigh snorted derisively at that. Her hair, ringleted and full, flowed over her shoulders and around the golden torc she, like the others, wore around her neck. Once the hair had been flaming red; now it was mostly white, with the barest shadow of its former color, but the face underneath still appeared young. "If all that mattered was the equipment hanging between his legs, any fool could be a Rí," she said. "Or perhaps that's already the case." Torin barked a quick laugh as the Banrion hurried on before any of the others could react. "The Enean of a few years ago would have been a fine Rí Ald. I don't disagree with that at all—if that Enean were still here, I think we'd already be back at the keep enjoying our meal tables and making plans to return to our own keeps. But the Mother-Creator decided otherwise, despite Enean's undoubted courage. But if we look to Nevan O Liathain's family as his successor, there's still Edana."

Doyle felt his heart leap at the mention of his fiancée.

He knew that Torin had already informed Rí Mas Sithig and Banrion O Treasigh—yet the Banrion pretended that there was no issue with Edana. That gave him hope.

It was too early for Doyle to have heard anything from his cousin Aghy. He wondered how Edana was and if she might have awakened, where she might be now on the road from Falcarragh to Dún Laoghaire. Ó Riain had glanced over at him with the mention of Edana and his flat-lidded gaze lingered appraisingly on Doyle's face, his attention making Doyle wonder if the man suspected the truth. Edana's condition couldn't be kept secret indefinitely—undoubtedly the rumors were already starting to spread. The money Doyle had paid the healers and servants in Falcarragh would only keep their silence so long, and all the Ríthe had spies within each others' courts.

If the other Ríthe knew, this was over.

Mac Baoill of Airgialla responded. "I'm not surprised that the Banrion O Treasigh would consider Edana a viable option," he said. "But I don't. Aye, she has a mind as sharp as her da's, but there's never been a Banrion Ard over the Tuatha. There may yet be one in the future, but now's not the time. Look what a Banrion has done to Inish Thuaidh."

He doesn't know . . . Doyle started to breathe again as Mas Sithig scoffed.

"Aye," Mas Sithig answered, his tone openly mocking, "and no one is closer to that cursed island than my Tuath Infochla. What's the Mad Holder done? Well, let's see . . . She's unified the clans there as no Rí before her ever could. She's taken back far too many of the islands that have been with Tuath Infochla for generations. She's managed to bring the Order of Inishfeirm's cloudmages back to prominence. She's made Inish Thuaidh strong enough that though we might all talk about returning with an army there, that's *all* we do. Aye, having a Banrion Ard who could accomplish something like that for the Tuatha would be a *terrible* idea."

The sarcasm drew blood to Mac Baoill's cheeks. Ban-

rion O Treasigh laughed, a crystalline sound in the chill;
O Seachnasaigh cleared his throat loudly and spat. The
globule landed near the fire, hissing on the stones.

"No one would trust a Banrion in war," O Seachnasaigh said loudly. "That's the plain, unadorned truth our
Rí Mallaghan seems to find so lacking here, and not just
my opinion. And war *is* what's coming, if not from the
west, then from the east. I've talked with Toscaire Concordai Rhusvak and my emissary gave me a quite vivid
description of the monster the Toscaire brought from
Céile Mhór. I tell you that the armies of the Tuatha will
fight for Enean because his bravery is unquestioned and
because he had his da's approval." He sniffed. His gaze,
too, found Doyle, challenging. "If you want to know in
what esteem Nevan O Liathain held his daughter, look
at who he threw her to: the bastard son of a failed
tiarna."

Near Doyle, Labhrás Ó Riain chuckled audibly, the
sound loud in the quiet hall. Doyle could feel the heat
fill his head at the insult to him and his da, the muscles
at his neck tightening at the affront, rude even under
the expected honesty of the Óenach. He lifted his hand
toward Snapdragon, already imaging the serpent of the
mage-lights coiling around Rí O Seachnasaigh. Doyle
saw Ó Riain reach for his cloch as well and around the
hall there was a rustling as the Riocha prepared to defend themselves and their leaders in any way they could.

But Torin had risen from his seat with a shout.
"Enough!" For a moment, Torin's gaze and Doyle's met;
Torin shook his head slightly. Then there was the bright,
unnerving sound of metal ringing as Torin drew his
sword. As the other five Ríthe rose in alarm, hands going
to their Clochs Mór as the onlookers cried out and the
gardai of the hall belatedly put hands to their own weapons, Torin threw his sword at the stone flags between
then. The weapon clattered loudly, coming to rest near
the fire pit.

"You dare to draw a weapon in the Óenach!" Rí
Taafe roared at Torin.

"I do," Torin shouted back at the man, "when the Óenach turns to name-calling and division." He pointed at the sword, the polished metal glittering in the firelight. "That's the legacy of this Óenach if we continue this way. We're here to name a Rí Ard, not to reopen old wounds. Do we want war between the Tuatha once again while the throne in Dún Laoghaire sits vacant? Wouldn't the Mad Holder love that, or those monsters from the east that you seem so worried about? We'll kill ourselves without our true enemies having to raise a finger, and they'll laugh as they pick over our corpses."

Rí Mac Baoill, his hand still on the hilt of his own sword, spat. "And Rí Mallaghan has a suggestion? Perhaps he thinks we should elevate *him* to be Rí Ard."

Torin laughed scornfully. "The Óenach could make a worse choice, if you want the truth. At least I wouldn't be someone's boot-licking lackey, as Tiarna Ó Riain would be." Doyle was pleased to see Ó Riain color at that, his hand fisting near his cloch. Doyle watched the man, ready to loose the dragon if Ó Riain moved to open his own cloch.

"This is ridiculous," Rí O Seachnasaigh muttered, loudly enough for everyone to hear. "Now who is flinging names? We waste our time with these insults."

"Aye, we do," Torin agreed, turning to face the man. "And we waste our time as long as you insist on Ó Riain as Rí Guardian. Rí Mas Sithig and Banrion O Treasigh agree with me on this. We won't have Enean as Rí Ard."

"No. Instead you'd elevate a woman who couldn't even bother to be here. 'Unavoidably detained . . .' " O Seachnasaigh sniffed and spat again. "I think we all see that as a flimsy excuse or some subterfuge. I wonder if Bantiarna Edana could tell us the identities of the unknown persons with Clochs Mór who attacked Inishfeirm, an open act of aggression that could have consequences for all the Tuatha. Or perhaps the Rí Mas Sithig could enlighten us, since the bantiarna inexplicably traveled to his Tuath after the Rí Ard died. I've heard rumors of a ship leaving Falcarragh with Tiarna

Mac Ard and at least three other of the Order of Gabair's mages aboard and returning two days later. Where,
I wonder, would they have gone?"

Mas Sithig simply glared at O Seachnasaigh. For several long breaths, the tension held. Doyle knew that it
all balanced on a knife's edge here. A wrong word, a
gesture, and blood would be spilled in the hall, blood
that would quickly spread out to all the Tuatha, a drowning, violent tide.

*Because of you . . . At the core, this is because you
failed . . .*

Banrion O Treasigh spoke into the dangerous silence.
"This Óenach is over," she said. "We all know it.
We're three set against three and there can be no
agreement. We should return to our Tuatha, consider
our options, and return here in three months to try once
more. The throne of the Rí Ard can sit empty for now,
as it has in the past."

"And the throne of Tuath Dún Laoghaire?" asked O
Seachnasaigh. "What of it, Banrion?"

"Perhaps in three months we'll be seven Ríthe instead
of six, and the Óenach won't be deadlocked." A mutter
went around the hall. It was clear to most of the Riocha
what the Banrion was actually suggesting, Doyle no less
than any of the others: *let this mess sort itself out. Leave
the question of the Rí Ard alone for the time being and
allow the strongest person to claim the throne of Dún
Laoghaire. They can try to hold it while the rest of us
watch from a safe distance, sending whatever help we
wish. Blood will spill here in Dún Laoghaire, aye, but at
least it will be confined to this one place. Someone will
eventually triumph, the other Tuatha will hopefully remain at peace, and when the Óenach resumes, there may
be no dispute at all.*

Torin was staring angrily at the Banrion, and Doyle
knew that this was something Torin, Rí Mas Sithig, and
Banrion O Treasigh must have discussed and rejected.
It meant that O Treasigh had not been convinced by
Torin that Doyle could eventually win Lámh Shábhála.

It meant that the Banrion felt safer looking for a compromise and the fragile coalition Torin had put together was already cracking, if not altogether broken.

O Seachnasaigh laughed, slapping the arm of his chair, and the tension in the air dissolved with the sound. "Done! You have my vote, Banrion. We'll return here in three months. What say the rest of you?"

"Éoganacht says aye," Rí Taafe echoed immediately, followed by Rí Mac Baoill: "As does Airgialla."

Rí Mas Sithig shook his head, but the word he spoke was the same. "Aye. Infochla will agree."

They were all looking at Torin Mallaghan. Again, Torin's gaze found Doyle, and it was angry and tight, the face he wore when he looked at his pieces on the ficheall board and saw that he had lost the game. He strode down from the dais into the fire pit. Backlit by the flames, he picked up his sword. "I don't like it," he said. "But Gabair will also say aye since that's the will of the Ríthe." He sheathed the blade in its leather scabbard. "May the Mother-Creator have mercy on us if we're wrong."

35

Water and Blood

IN THE moonlight, the waters of Lough Lár were black and silver, alive with shifting promise. But that had been true every night for the last three. Meriel had waited almost a week in Keira's cave, then awakened from sleep that night with a certainty in her mind. "He's coming closer," she'd said to Owaine when he'd also stirred. "I have to go to the lough and wait for him." She didn't need to tell Owaine who "he" was; she'd felt the way Owaine had watched her over the last several days, like a puppy waiting for its master's hand to be raised without knowing if it would be a gentle stroke or a slap. He'd nodded at her words as if turning the thought over in his mind, examining it from every side before deciding to speak.

"You should have someone with you," he said. His mouth was set somewhere between smile and frown, the lips pressed so tightly together that they paled.

When Meriel told Keira, she'd shrugged, not even turning from the herbs she was laying on racks over the fire. The air around her was heavy with their scent. "Your mam will be coming here soon—we've already sent the messengers. I wouldn't want her to find you gone already."

"I won't leave," Meriel told her. "I promise. Not until Mam comes."

Keira nodded slowly. "I'll take the two of you to

where the trees come closest to the water, south of here," she said. "You can cross over to the lough from there if you're careful and watch for the gardai. They don't pass by that often, and when they do, they hurry by because of the trees. As long as you don't light a fire, it will be safe enough there at night; in the day, come back here."

That was what they did, finding a brush-covered jumble of stones on the shore that shielded them from anyone passing on the High Road. Dire wolves howled close by in the darkness, their shuddering wail no longer frightening to Meriel. Indeed, she found it comforting because when gardai did come along the road, they galloped quickly by with the sound of the wolves pursuing them.

Meriel and Owaine waited. Sometimes, they talked, huddled in their blankets near each other, whispering as they stared out at the water. "You don't need to stay here with me, Owaine," she said to him the second night. "I mean, I appreciate the company, but it's cold and—" She stopped, not quite knowing how to articulate what she was feeling. *I'm waiting for my lover, and I know how you feel and I don't want to hurt you . . .*

"It's all right," he answered. "You shouldn't be alone. It's not safe."

"It's not safe for you either."

"It wasn't safe for me to come here at all."

They sat silently for a time, staring out. "I've never thanked you enough for coming after me," she said at last. "If you hadn't been here, I might be—"

She didn't look at him, but she felt his smile. "And in return, you fixed my eyes," he told her. "That was a better gift than you can imagine for someone who saw the world as I did. I'll always be grateful to you for that."

"That wasn't me . . . it was just the cloch." *It was nothing I haven't done for strangers and for the coins they'd give Sevei or Nico. I did it because I couldn't heal myself. I wasn't thinking of it as a gift.*

Owaine was still talking, not hearing the accusations

in her head. "Knowing where you were wasn't anything,
Meriel. Keira, she brought the wolves, the crows, and
the slow magics. I just pointed the way and she did the
work. I'd say that I've been more than repaid."

The honesty and humility in his voice pulled at her.
"You're too modest, Owaine Geraghty. And braver than
I would have been. I think my mam was wise when she
brought you to the Order. If I were Máister Kirwan, I'd
make sure you had a Cloch Mór to hold."

"With all the Riocha cloudmages waiting for one?
That's not likely," he said, but she caught the hint of
pleasure in his voice. "I'm happy with what I have."

"Are you?" she asked.

"Aye," he answered, though Meriel thought the answer came slow and drawn out, with a finishing rise that
sounded uncertain.

"There is nothing more that you want?"

"There is." The two words were heavy in the darkness
and she knew what he was thinking. She felt him shift
in his blankets. "But none of us get all we want. At least
not people like me. Maybe for you, Meriel. Maybe the
Riocha. But not me."

Impulsively, she reached out and found his hand in
the dark. His skin was warm. She pressed her fingers in
his and he squeezed her hand back, his fingers strong
and yet gentle. "I hope you find someone who deserves
you, Owaine," she told him, the words quiet in the night.
She started to pull her hand away and for an instant he
tightened his fingers, as if reluctant to let her go. But
he did.

For a long time after that, neither of them said anything.

It was the third night of their watch.

"There," Owaine whispered softly, touching Meriel's
arm and pointing out to a ripple where something—
someone—moved. Meriel pushed herself up from the
damp grass at the verge between the High Road and the
lough, then ran down into the lapping waves, laughing,

toward the naked, dripping man who miraculously rose knee-deep from the water.

"Dhegli!" Splashing, she nearly leaped toward him, her still-knitting ribs pulling so that she winced at the same time she laughed.

Laughing with her, he swept her up in his arms, twirling her around once and kissing her. She returned the kiss fiercely, hugging him to her without caring about the cold water that soaked the front of her léine and dripped from the hem of her clóca. "By the Mother, I thought I might never see you again," she said when they finally broke apart, gasping for breath. She kissed him again, laughing and crying all at once, pulling his head to hers. "I've missed you so much. Did you know that Owaine managed to find me after you brought him over here . . . ?"

She glanced over her shoulder, gesturing to where Owaine had been sitting, but her voice trailed off as she realized that no one was there. "Owaine?" she called. She let go of Dhegli to turn. She saw Owaine then, walking quickly away from the lough, already over the second stone wall of the High Road and nearly to the trees. She started to call to him, but Dhegli touched her shoulder.

"It hurts him to see us together," he said, her ears hearing the sounds of the Saimhóir language while his words echoed in her head. "He's in love with you, too."

"I know, but . . . ." She turned back to Dhegli, touching his face with her hands, enjoying the feel of his wet skin.

"Do you like Owaine?" Dhegli asked.

"Owaine? Aye, but not . . . ." She stopped, puzzled, wondering why Dhegli was saying these things. "I love *you,* Dhegli."

"And I, you," Dhegli answered with a laugh that pulled at the corners of her mouth. "But it's possible to love two people at once in the same way, Meriel." He kissed away her protest. "Come," he said when they broke apart. "Come swim with me again."

She felt the change surge within her with the words. He helped her strip away the clóca and léine, tossing her clothing onto the shore until she stood as naked as he. Together, they dove in with human shapes and emerged as Saimhóir.

The lough was different than the ocean: murkier, the water tasting sweet, the sounds hushed and quieter. Distantly, she could hear the roar of the falls of the Duán where the river tumbled into the deep rift in the land that held the lough. Where there had been schools of brightly-colored fish in the water around Inishfeirm, the fish here were smaller and plainer, quick to scurry away to hiding places.

They swayed and fluttered through the shoals—Meriel more gingerly than she would have liked; she was still not completely healed and the change hadn't altered that, the effort of swimming sending minor twinges through her body—down the muddy, algae-slick slopes into the starlit darkness of the water, chasing each other. They surfaced in exuberant sprays of water, huffing as they inhaled the cold air and dove again. They rubbed flanks, slid glistening furred bodies over each other, tasting each other's arousal.

After a time, in human form again, they hauled out on rocks near the shore. Meriel was laughing, her hair streaming in curls down the bare curve of her shoulders and back. She hugged Dhegli, bringing him to her.

She heard the bark of a seal, and turning her head on his chest, saw another Saimhóir watching them, a cow. Dhegli called back to her in their own language as Meriel regarded him quizzically. After the exchange, the seal dove back under the water and vanished. "Her name is Challa," Dhegli's voice sounded in her head, and she heard the deep affection in it. "She saved my life at Inishduán when I went to help your mam and came with me here."

Meriel stared at the blackness that was the seal's eyes, the moon touching them with silver. "Can she . . . ?"

"Change? No. She has none of your people in her blood."

Meriel nodded. Somehow, that made her glad. There was another question she wanted to ask, but though her mouth opened she said nothing, afraid she knew the answer, afraid to hear it. She clutched Dhegli to her.

Under the leaves of Doire Coill, a dire wolf howled.

The Ríthe left Dún Laoghaire the morning after the Óenach, six trains of retainers and gardai taking six different directions on the High Roads. Doyle was at West Gate to give his leave to Rí Mallaghan, returning to Lár Bhaile, but Torin said little to him. "Do what you can," he told Doyle, "but it may be all you can do just to stay alive. I can't do anything to protect you now—none of the Ríthe can without risking open war between the Tuatha, and I'd rather see the Order of Gabair retain the Clochs Mór we have than lose them in a futile battle. Without knowing whether Edana will ever . . ." He shrugged. "Do you understand me, Tiarna Mac Ard?"

"I do, my Rí."

"I hope you do." He sat back in his seat, looking away from Doyle, and gestured to the driver. Doyle watched the Rí and his entourage leave the city, feeling more afraid than he'd ever felt in his life.

Dún Laoghaire—both the city and the keep that brooded on a low rise near the harbor—vibrated with tension. The streets were uncommonly empty that morning, half the market stalls closed, shutters latched on the shop windows in the business sector, worried faces peering out between the slats. Those who went out hurried quickly about their business, giving furtive glances around them. The gardai still walked slowly through the streets but their hands stayed near the hilts of their weapons and under their cloaks one could catch the glimpse of leather armor or hear the clinking of the iron rings.

Shay O Blaca had sent, via Quickship, two new cloudmages to Doyle. Alaina Glanchy and Shéfra Cahill had been given the Clochs Mór whose Holders had been lost at Inishduán. Alaina now held Weaver while Shéfra carried Sharpcut, but though O Blaca had chosen the two for their skill and their loyalty to the Order (and the political strength of their families), both were new to their Clochs Mór. Together with Doyle's Snapdragon, the trio made a formidable force, but Doyle wondered how the two would handle the rigors of fighting cloch against cloch, if it came to that. He was afraid that he would find out.

Dún Laoghaire moved warily through that day and slept uneasily or not at all that night. The first killings came the next day: a battle at the morning shift change between squadrons of the Dún Laoghaire gardai whose families had come from different Tuatha left four dead and several injured; then a midday riot in Findhlay Market put the casualty figures in the dozens while half the stalls in the market were destroyed and looted; in the evening, news came to Doyle that a tiarna of Tuath Locha Léin who had remained behind at the Banrion O Treasigh's request had been attacked and killed in the bailey of the keep itself—by what appeared to be either slow magic or a cloch na thintrí.

Doyle met in his chambers that evening with two of the lieutenants of the Rí Laoghaire's gardai—significantly, the keep's captain had refused to come to the meeting. ". . . you all know Enean and his difficulties," he was saying to them, trying to see some hope in their set jaws and averted eyes. "I know you have sympathy for Tiarna O Liathain and admire his courage. But you also know his limitations and you know Edana. I think it's obvious which of the two would make the better ruler for Dún Laoghaire."

"We know what you're saying, Tiarna Mac Ard," one of the men said finally. "But Bantiarna O Liathain isn't *here* and some of the rumors that are flying around the city are troubling. Tiarna O Liathain, at least—" He

stopped, eyes widening as a long wailing scream came
from beyond the door to the chamber, trailing off into
a horrible wet gurgle. The gardai drew swords and rushed
from the room, Doyle following. Across the hall, Alaina
and Shéfra came from their rooms. "Clochs?" Alaina
asked, but Doyle shook his head. "Not yet," he told her,
"but be ready." They followed the gardai, running down
the hall and turning at the stairs that led up to Enean's chambers.

Dragonfire smoldered in Doyle's stomach.

The door to Enean's private chamber was open; they
rushed in. MacCamore was sprawled faceup on the tapestried rug near the door, mouth and eyes open, his abdomen slit wide with a horrible, long diagonal wound
that his blood-soaked, still hands could not hold shut.
An irregular pool of red was still spreading from the
body; a knife lay near the edge of the stain. Enean was
there, half-dressed, the back of his hand to his mouth as
he stared at MacCamore; Nuala, a blanket wrapped
around her form, leaned against the doorway to the
inner bedroom, weeping with her face turned away. And
Labhrás Ó Riain . . .

Ó Riain was there also, his sword drawn though held
down at his side as blood drooled from its tip.

"Take him!" Doyle barked to the gardai, pointing at Ó
Riain. None of them moved. Ó Riain's mouth twitched.

"What's the matter, Tiarna Mac Ard? Having trouble
with the gardai?" More footsteps came from the corridor. Doyle knew others had arrived but he didn't dare
look behind.

"What happened here?" he demanded. "Enean?"

Enean shook his head. "I don't know, Doyle. I heard
a knock and MacCamore went to the door. Then I heard
MacCamore arguing with Labhrás and I came out. Mac-
Camore had a knife, and Labhrás unsheathed his sword,
and . . ."

"The old man came at me," Ó Riain said. "I had to
defend myself." He tossed the sword down contemptuously. "And Enean."

"MacCamore would do nothing to harm Enean," Doyle spat.

"I believe his exact words were 'I'd rather see Enean dead than under your influence.' Ask Enean. He heard."

Doyle glanced at Enean, who was nodding. "He did say that, Doyle. Then he took a step toward Labhrás."

"There it is," Ó Riain said. "Are you satisfied now, Tiarna? This was simple defense—both of myself and Enean."

Doyle glanced down at the knife on the rug. "That knife is Connachtan-made," he said. "Strange, isn't it, that MacCamore should have that?"

Ó Riain gave him a tight-lipped smile. "A weapon like that is easily obtained here in Dún Laoghaire. Perhaps MacCamore had a taste for expensive weapons. Or perhaps he was at Findhlay Market this afternoon with the other scofflaws and found a weapons shop open for the taking." Ó Riain gave a sniff and a contemptuous look at the corpse. "It doesn't matter. The old bastard won't interfere anymore."

The insult stoked the fury and frustration in Doyle, blowing the coals into sudden white heat. His hand found Snapdragon and his mind ripped open the cloch: as Ó Riain responded in the next breath; as he felt Alaina and Shéfra do the same behind him, as out in the hallway, other clochs opened as well. The dragon appeared in his cloch-vision, snarling and ready and he would have sent it rushing forward against the shadowy forms of wolves that were rising around Ó Riain, heedless of the consequences.

But it was Enean who stopped him. "No!" he heard Enean shout, and he pushed himself between Doyle and Ó Riain as Nuala screamed from the bedroom archway, as the bright clochs sparked into life around him. "I won't let you do this!"

The dragon coiled, rising until it seemed to fill the air, fire spouting from its open mouth, ready to strike. Enean glared up at it as if daring Doyle to unleash the beast—

as the wolves howled around Ó Riain. "Enean! Get out of my way!"

"No!" Enean shouted back. "You told me that if I were Rí, you'd obey me, Doyle. Edana's not here, so right now I'm the Rí."

You can win here. You're stronger than Ó Riain. The temptation made his body tremble with the effort of holding back the power. *You can win . . .* He could have ignored the boy-man. He could have sent the dragon's head snaking around him, could have tried to avoid hurting Enean as the clochs came together in rage. But the others, the allies Ó Riain had here, the gardai . . . The conflict would spread out from this center, engulfing the entire keep and the city and the countryside all around, and even if Doyle did take Ó Riain and even if he did manage to spare Enean, eventually he would have to ride against him because Enean *wanted* to be Rí. Doyle could see that in Enean's face and stance. Even damaged and scarred, he wanted the legacy that should have been his, and if Doyle won this battle, it wouldn't be the last. The Enean standing between Doyle and Ó Riain wouldn't go back to being the pliable child-man: not without Edana, not without MacCamore. Enean had tasted power; he would try to keep it and those behind Ó Riain would help him.

Doyle might win this battle, but the war would come and Enean would have to fall. Doyle couldn't do that. He would lose Edana as well as Enean if that happened, because Edana wouldn't hurt her brother.

There were times when the only way to continue to fight was to retreat. It was the hardest lesson he'd ever had to learn.

"Enean, tell Tiarna Ó Riain to release his cloch," Doyle said. "If he does that, I'll do the same. I'll kneel to you as Rí, Enean. Right here and now."

Ó Riain scoffed, the wolves snarling, but Enean smiled warmly at Doyle, his eyes full of trust. He turned to Ó Riain. "You heard Doyle," he told the man. "Let go of your cloch."

"Enean, it's a trap . . ." Ó Riain began but Enean's face flushed. He reached down and snatched Ó Riain's sword from the floor, brandishing it in front of the man.

"You will *do* it!" he snapped. "For your Rí!"

Ó Riain glared at Doyle over Enean's shoulder, then bowed his head slightly. "Everyone here heard Tiarna Mac Ard give his word. You're all my witnesses." He released the cloch; the wolves vanished. Enean spun around to Doyle, the sword whistling in the air.

Doyle opened his fingers, letting Snapdragon fall back on its chain. The dragon faded and blew away as if on an invisible wind. Around them, the other clochs went out, one by one.

"Now the rest, Mac Ard," Ó Riain said. The man dropped to one knee; Doyle heard others doing the same behind him. "Say it."

You could win. Now more than ever. Just open Snapdragon . . . Enean was watching him, the sword trembling in his muscular hands. Doyle sank down and bowed his head. "I acknowledge Enean O Liathain as Rí Dún Laoghaire," he said. He rose up again and embraced Enean. The sword clattered on the ground as Enean's arms went around him. "You're still the bravest man I know, Enean," Doyle said to him. "Despite everything. I've never met anyone braver."

"I wish Edana were here," Enean said. Doyle could hear the tears in his voice.

"I wish she were, too," he said. "Very much so. I wish you luck, Enean. I do. I hope you understand when I tell you I can't stay here. Not right now. I have to go to Edana."

"Bring her back here," Enean told him. "I want her to see the torc around my neck."

Doyle smiled at the pride in Enean's voice. "I will," he told him. "She'll be proud of you." Doyle released Enean's hands and took a step back. He glared once at Ó Riain, grinning with triumph behind Enean. Crouching down beside MacCamore's body, Doyle closed the

old man's eyes and mouth. "Rest well," he whispered
to the corpse. "I'm sorry."

Ó Riain was staring at him, waiting. The tension still
hung in the room, a fog. *You could have won . . .* "Let's
go," Doyle said to Alaina and Shéfra. "We're done
here."

They pushed through the crowd that had gathered,
most of them Riocha attached to Ó Riain, and left the
floor for his own chambers.

The Toscaire Concordai knocked on the open door.
Doyle saw him glance at the baggage waiting there for
the servants. "So you're leaving."

"Aye, Toscaire," Doyle told him. "As soon as the
servants prepare our horses. It's dangerous for my people to stay."

"I understand that the Riocha of Dún Laoghaire have
decided on a new Rí." The Toscaire moved a step into
the room and shut the door behind him. "Will Rí Enean
become the new Rí Ard when the Óenach meets again,
I wonder."

"I truly don't know, Toscaire," Doyle told him. He
pulled an overcloak from a hook near the door and
swept it over his shoulders. "Perhaps. But perhaps not."

The Toscaire nodded, the bear's head moving. "While
fighting the Arruk, our generals had to give way and fall
back, yet we remain confident that we will eventually
prevail. I, too, find it a foolish bravery to continue to
fight on a field where there's no hope of victory."

Doyle inhaled, a long breath through his nose. "I'm
glad you understand, Toscaire Rhusvak."

Eyes gleamed behind the death scowl of the bear.
"Despite the day's events, I would still advise Thane
Aerie to throw the might of the Concordia behind the
one who holds Lámh Shábhála. I wonder how the Riocha of Dún Laoghaire would react to a flotilla of troop

ships from Céile Mhór in the harbor and—let us say—
the chief cloch and several cloudmages of the Order at
their front door. I think the new Rí's guardian might
tremble. If there were a way for that to happen . . ."
The Toscaire paused.

For the first time that day, Doyle felt a renewal of
hope. "There is a way," he said to the Toscaire. "There
will be a way. I'm certain of it."

"Then send me word when it might happen, so that I
can tell my Thane." The Toscaire came close to Doyle,
grasping his arm. Doyle could see the man's bearded
face, could smell the oils and the scent of his dinner. "I
like strength," he told Doyle. "It's what Céile Mhór
needs more than anything now. And I see strength in
you, not in this new Shadow Rí and his puppetmaster.
I'll deal with them if I must, but I'd rather see Lámh
Shábhála around your neck and its glory sending the
Arruk fleeing back to Thall Mór-roinn."

Doyle put his hand over Rhusvak's. "I promise you
that will happen," he told the man. "You have my
word."

36

The Crow's Note

MERIEL returned to the lough the next night. Owaine had wanted to go with her, but she had told him to stay there. Keira listened to their discussion from the other side of the fire in her cave, sorting the pile of herbs she'd gathered that afternoon and saying nothing. Owaine was persistent, and eventually Meriel agreed to let him accompany her as far as the edge of the woods.

The trees were singing that night, the Seanóir, the Old Ones' voices so loud and compelling that Keira gave Meriel and Owaine tufts of soft moss to put in their ears. "Keep your minds on what you're doing," she told them, "or you'll find yourselves deep in the forest feeding their roots with your blood and flesh." Even through the moss, the song of the trees was insistent. Meriel was glad to leave the forest behind. She lifted a hand to tell Owaine to stay, checked the road in the moonlight, then ran quickly toward the water, vaulting the low stone walls bordering the road and crossing the dew-damp grass to the shore.

Dhegli was already there, the Saimhóir lolling on a grassy shingle half in the water. He moaned and warbled at her as she stripped off her clothing and ran into the water, feeling the change touch her as soon as the cold, then quickly warm, water touched her. He came to her, brushing up against her seal body, laughing. "Hello again, my love," he said, the voice husky and low in her mind. "Follow me—I want to show you a place I found . . ." He nipped her furred neck, making her shiver. Then he was away and she swam joyfully after him.

He took her northward along the lough's shore to where the lake narrowed and deepened, and they began to hear the low, constant roar of the falls of the Duán. Dhegli dove deep, suddenly, and she followed: through a shimmering cascade of frothing water that hammered and buffeted her, the sound of it nearly deafening. Then they were through and rising again, and Dhegli hauled out into a hollow behind the falls. The falls howled and bellowed and hissed several yards in front of them; the air was filled with wet spray. And the walls . . .

It was dark here and human eyes might have seen nothing. But she was in Saimhóir form, and enough moonlight filtered through the water of the falls for her to see the glimmer of crystals lining the cavern. It was as if she stood in the center of a jewel, surrounded by glittering facets. Dhegli lay alongside her, his head resting on her back, his body warm along her length. "It's beautiful," she said, then laughed at the sound of her voice, amplified and changed by the crystalline walls and the sheet of falling water in front of them.

Dhegli laughed with her. "Wonderful, isn't it? And even more delightful in the daylight," he told her. "You'll have to come here then, when rainbows dance in the air and the walls shimmer with color. This is a place of magic, though like everything, it's ephemeral."

"What do you mean?"

"Look up."

She lifted her head. Above them, a shelf of granite hung out into the falls, white water pouring over its jagged lip. "The falls are eating away at that, every day," Dhegli said. "One day, it will break away and whatever's up above will fall into this space while the falls of the Duán fill this place, tear it down and destroy it."

Meriel shivered at the thought and Dhegli laughed.

"Ah, not for years yet. But it will happen. Nothing and none of us last forever. But we're here now, and we've seen the beauty and we'll remember it always." His head moved on her fur; his flipper stroked her flank. "Do you want to make love in this form, or in yours?" he asked.

"In mine," she said, and she felt him change even as she allowed herself to slip back. She shivered at the touch of the damp air. "Though it's cold this way," she said.

"Not for long," he answered, and his arms went around her.

Afterward, he let himself return to Saimhóir form, though Meriel remained as she was, cuddled against his warmth. She couldn't see the crystals now, but she imagined the place in the daylight, as Dhegli had described it. She stroked his fur, luxuriating in the thick softness of it. "How did you find this place?" she asked him.

"I didn't," he told her. "It was Challa. She found it and brought me here yesterday."

"Oh." The mention of the Saimhóir's name brought her presence between them. Meriel bit her lower lip, wanting to ask him a hundred questions and yet not wanting to know the answers. If she didn't know, she told herself, then nothing had changed. If she didn't know, she wouldn't have to respond. If she didn't know, everything was fine.

If he'd stayed silent, it would have been finc. But he didn't. "Why do your voice and your face change when I say her name?" Dhegli asked.

"What do you mean?" His featureless black eyes remained on her; she could see herself twice reflected in their glistening surfaces. She looked away. "It's just . . . you said you loved me, but I hear you talk about Challa. . . ." She couldn't stop the rise in her voice on the last word.

"I do love you." A pause. She knew what he would say next. She kncw and she didn't want to hear it. "I love Challa, also."

She remembered what he had said about Owaine and

her, and a chill made her shiver. *Don't ask* . . . But she
couldn't stop herself. "Have you and Challa . . . ? Are
you . . . ?"

"Aye," he answered without hesitation. She heard no
apology in his voice. No guilt. No shame. It was simply
a word like any other. "I love her also. Why wouldn't
we enjoy each other's bodies?"

He started to say something else, but she pushed herself away from him, breaking the contact, and all she
heard were the moans and wails of a seal. She huddled
in the middle of the small space, shivering, her knees to
her chest, hugging herself. "No," she said when he waddled near her, though she knew he couldn't understand
her. "Stay away from me."

He would not. He pushed up to her even though she
backed away until her spine touched the hard points of
the crystals. The chamber was no longer beautiful; it was
a prison lined with a thousand spears. His head touched
her legs and his voice returned to her head. ". . . think
differently than you. Not wrong, not right, Meriel. Just
different. If you want me, you have to accept that, just
as I have to accept the way you are. I can be a stone-
walker only for a short time, just as you can be Saimhóir
only for a bit. We each have to live most of the time
apart, in our own worlds. We can't be with each other
always. Aye, if one us stayed in the other's form for too
long, we'd find ourselves caught in that form forever—
but we'd both be dreadfully unhappy that way. Even if
you chose to be Saimhóir, you'd eventually start to yearn
for the land and your own kind; you wouldn't know or
understand or even agree with our ways. You couldn't
use the sky-stone in that form, and you'd lose it. If I
chose to be Daoine, then Bradán an Chumhacht would
leave me and that would torment me the same way
you'd be tormented if you lost your sky-stone, and I
would always want the sea. Meriel, we meet here in the
middle for a few fleeting moments before we have to go
be among our own again. I want you to be happy there,
Meriel. If you had a lover on the stones, I'd be happy

for the joy you'd take with him. How would that change
anything between us?"

It all sounded so logical, but Meriel was shaking her
head long before he finished, her eyes closed to try to
hold back the tears. "No," she shouted, the word echo-
ing against the crash and thunder of the falls. Her stomach was knotted; she wanted to vomit, wanted to scream
with the inner pain. "Can't you see? That would change
everything. *Everything!*"

"How?" he persisted, his head nudging her lap. "I
don't understand. Do you doubt my feelings for you,
Meriel? I helped your mam because of you. I came when
you called, all this way. I came because you're part of
me."

"Maybe you should have stayed where you were." She
pushed him away. "I want you to leave me alone," she
said, not caring that with the loss of contact he could no
longer understand her. She pushed away from the rocks,
padding over to where the water lapped at the rock and
the roar of the falls drowned out even the contradictory
voices inside her, where the cold spray mingled with the
tears that she could no longer hold back. She heard
Dhegli come up behind her, in human form now. She
started to leap out into the water, but in the hesitation
his arms went around her and his mouth kissed the nape
of her neck.

"I don't want to hurt you, Meriel," she heard his voice
say in her mind. "I never wanted to do that."

"But you did," she told him. "You did. And the worst
thing is that you'll never really understand why."

Owaine was there when Meriel emerged from the lough
before dawn. When he saw the black heads of two seals
creating twin wakes in the still surface, he turned to
stand with his back to the water near the pile of her
clothing, staring stolidly away from her. He heard Meriel's voice and the coughing moans of a seal, then the

splash of water again. He heard the quiet shush of bare
feet on the grass as Meriel approached.

Hours ago, after she'd entered the water, he'd gone
back to Keira's cave and returned with a soft blanket,
which he'd laid next to her clothing. He imagined Meriel's nude form bending down to pick it up, wrapping
herself in its warm folds. . . .

"Thank you, Owaine," she said. "That was kind of
you." There was something wrong with her voice, a som-
berness that surprised him.

"I thought you might be cold when you came out,"
he answered, still staring out into the night. "That's all.
I know you didn't want me to come with you, but I
thought someone ought to be here to watch in case one
of the patrols came by. Not that I could do anything if
they did but hide. I mean, I'll bet that Keira has some
of her crows watching and she'd be here quickly if there
was trouble, or maybe the dire wolves would come. The
trees were still singing, too, or at least they were a while
ago—" He was babbling and knew it, but it was better
than silence. Meriel evidently realized it as well. Her
voice interrupted him, without responding to anything
he'd said.

"You can look now. I'm covered."

He turned. He studied her for a moment as she stood
there, shivering a bit, her lower lip trembling with cold.
He wanted to go to her, to hold her close and warm her
with his own body. He shifted his weight from foot to
foot but stayed a careful few steps away from her. The
look on her face in the false dawn's light wasn't what
he expected. He thought she'd be weary but ecstatic,
illuminated with the joy of being with Dhegli again. Instead, her mouth was drawn down and her shoulders
sagged. In the lough behind her, he saw a seal's head
staring back at the shore, then it vanished under the
water. "How's Dhegli?" he asked. "I'll wager he's happy
to see you again. Did you enjoy your swim?"

A shrug.

"Meriel, what's the matter?" he asked. "I mean, I know it's none of my affair and I shouldn't pry, but—"

Meriel blinked. Water dripped from the curled strands of her hair. "I didn't tell you the last time. There's another Saimhóir with him," Meriel said flatly.

"Aye? I'm not surprised he brought someone with him. It's such a long way from Inishfeirm up the Duán—"

"A female," Meriel interrupted and the tone of her voice told him the rest. Owaine didn't quite know how to respond. Meriel shook her head, her chin lifting slightly. "You don't have to look quite so pleased with the news," she said.

Belatedly, Owaine stirred and forced his mouth into a frown. He could feel an exultation stirring in his soul and it was difficult not to show it. "That doesn't mean anything," he said, blinking. "The seals . . . well, I don't know about the Saimhóir, but the others, they always travel in packs and probably don't have the same kind of relationships with each other that we . . ." He stopped, seeing the confusion and pain in her eyes. "I'm sorry, Meriel. I am."

"Dhegli said . . ." she began, then had to stop to wipe at her eyes with an edge of the blanket. She glanced at the lough. "He says it doesn't change anything about the way he feels about me. Maybe it doesn't. I want to believe that. I want to so much, but she's out there now with him, in the form that he prefers, and the way he talks about her and swims with her . . ." Her voice broke; she sniffed. "I don't know why I'm telling you all this. It's so *stupid*." Owaine felt the urge again to hold her and this time he did, going to her and putting his arms around her. She stiffened at the touch, then relaxed, letting him embrace her.

"Does it change the way *you* feel?" Owaine asked, and regretted the words even as he spoke them: he could hear the hope buried under the surface in his voice and wondered if she could as well. But she only shook her head against his chest.

"I don't know. I still love him—" the hope in Owaine's heart sank like a stone tossed in the lough, "—but now I don't . . . don't know . . ." Her hands clutched the blanket tighter to her, hiding her face when he looked down at her. "I don't know what to think right now."

"You don't have to think now. Let's just go back to Keira," Owaine told her. "We don't want to be out here in the daylight for the gardai to see, and you need to warm up. Keira said she sent another crow out to your mam, not long after we left; she expects the Banrion will be here soon."

"Mam?" He could feel her tense in his arms. "I'd nearly forgotten about that. Dhegli said he talked to her and told her about us, and that she wasn't pleased. He also said that the ransom Doyle Mac Ard wanted for me was Lámh Shábhála and that she wouldn't give it up for me. She nearly killed herself and Dhegli, too, rather than do that."

"She *couldn't* do it," Owaine said. "At Inishfeirm, I was taught enough about the history of Lámh Shábhála to know that. She *couldn't* give it up, Meriel, not without destroying herself. That has nothing to do with how she feels about you. She loves you. I know she does. I've heard her talk about you, I know what she's done for you. She loves you more than anything."

"Than anything?" Meriel repeated, scorn burring her voice. "What about the cloch?"

"That's not love," he told her. "That's something embedded so deep in her that Mac Ard might as well have asked for her to rip out her heart and give it to him."

Meriel nodded again. "Maybe," she said. "Maybe that's true. Or maybe if he'd just asked for her heart, she might have given it to him." She glanced back at the lough, and he knew what she was hoping to see. But Dhegli was gone. When she turned back, she was shivering under the blanket.

"Let's leave here," she said.

Rí Torin Mallaghan refused to see Doyle when he and the cloudmages returned to Lár Bhaile. Doyle announced himself to one of the heralds at the doors to the audience chamber, who nodded and went in. Doyle then stood outside in the hall for three hours, the dust and filth of the road on his clothes and face, waiting. The doors remain closed; the herald never returned. People passed by and none of them spoke to him. He seemed to be invisible, standing there.

Finally, when Doyle was considering breaching etiquette and leaving, one of the court underlings emerged, a young stripling whose name Doyle didn't even know and whose smug face showed a decided glee at Doyle's discomfiture. "The Rí requests that you give *me* your report, Tiarna Mac Ard," he said, holding out his hand.

"It's important that I speak to the Rí himself," Doyle persisted. The boy's smile was irritating, especially in someone who was at best lesser nobility—he was probably the son of some distant cousin of the Rí, sent off to court in hopes that he'd marry better than his station or gain the favor of some Riocha. Doyle decided that he'd actively work against those dreams—the boy enjoyed his current task far too much. "I'd prefer to give Rí Mallaghan the report myself."

The smile widened. "The Rí was quite clear about his wishes, I'm afraid, Tiarna Mac Ard. Unless you'd prefer that I go back to the Rí and tell him that you refused . . . ?"

It was obvious Doyle could not win this argument unless he wanted to open his Cloch Mór, have the dragon trample this upstart underfoot and push past the gardai at the door, at which point it would be doubtful that he'd reach the throne alive. Doyle set aside the delicious thought of the boy's broken body and plunged his hand into the pouch at his side, pulling out the report he'd carefully composed the night before. He'd tried to stress the untenable position in Dún Laoghaire and emphasized the fact that the Toscaire Condordai was still their ally. He put the best spin possible on the circumstances, but knew that there was no concealing the fact that he'd lost and that Ó Riain was now effectively the Rí Dún Laoghaire with Enean as his puppet.

He'd lost completely.

Doyle slapped the papers into the underling's hand, taking a small pleasure in the cloud of road dust that rose and caused the youth to sneeze and brush in annoyance at his clóca. Doyle spun on the balls of his feet and strode off to his chambers in the Order's keep to brood. He was surprised later that evening by the knock on his door. He opened it to find the same underling as before standing in the hall with two servants, each holding a cloth bag that sagged heavily. "Rí Mallaghan asked me to deliver these to you, Tiarna Mac Ard," the boy said. "He said to tell you that it's in your best interests to do something with them, and quickly." He gestured to the servants, who placed the bags just inside the door. The boy grinned, bowed at Doyle, and left.

Doyle hefted one of the bags—it was heavy, and he could feel a dead weight at the bottom, as if sand had been poured into it. He opened the tie-string.

The smell hit him first; the distinctive odor of decaying flesh. Doyle covered his mouth and nose with the sleeve of his léine and peered in. A heap of black feathers lay at the bottom of the bag: he was staring at the body of a large black crow. Doyle retied the sack and took both of them outside. In the bailey, with a few curious acolytes trying hard to appear as if they weren't watching, Doyle dumped out the contents: four crows, two in each sack, each with at least one arrow through it. Lying on the ground, as well, were hollow cylinders of wood about the size of his little finger. He plucked one of them from the dirt. Inside, a piece of parchment had been rolled and placed inside. Doyle pulled out the parchment— there was writing on it. He read the words, read them again.

"Martin!" he called to one of the acolytes. "Go find

Tiarna O Blaca and tell him that I need to see him in my rooms. Quickly, boy! It's urgent!''

Jenna listened as Kyle read to her the Comhairle's schedule for the next morning's session. ". . . the clan heads of Baile na Oiléanach want to define the limits of fishing from the Northern Stepping Stones to be the Foaming Shoals. That's been under contention even before the Northern Clans came over to us, and it's unlikely either side is going to want to budge. Then there's the issue of the annual fees due to Inishfeirm from the townlands. I'm hearing muttering from the Comhairle about the increase over last year.''

They both heard a strange *pop* from the sill of the window overlooking Croc a Scroilm, followed immediately by a flutter of heavy wings. Jenna turned her head to look: a crow was perched on the sill. It dropped something from its beak onto the wide polished marble, cawed loudly, then flew off. Jenna glanced at Kyle, eyebrows raised, then went to the window. A narrow wooden tube lay there; Jenna plucked it up.

"What is that?" Kyle asked. He set the Comhairle's schedule on a table and rose to his feet.

"I'm not sure," Jenna answered. "A piece of bog reed, I think; I used to see them around the fens in Ballintubber. I don't—" She stopped, her breath frozen. Turning the reed, she could see a slip of parchment rolled up inside it, with a bit of colored string attached to one end as a pull. "Kyle?" She showed it to him and tugged on the string. The parchment came out in her hand. She unrolled it; saw the writing there. Wonderingly, she handed the note to Kyle, who scanned it with an intake of breath. "Kyle? What's it say?"

"By the Mother-Creator, Jenna," he said, gasping with sudden laughter, a grin splitting his round face, "it's from Meriel. She's alive in Tuath Gabair, in Doire Coill!"

Jenna nearly staggered. She closed her eyes as Kyle's arms went around her, and she sobbed, the relief surging through her and releasing a tension she'd been holding for weeks. "Alive!"

"Aye," Kyle said, "and Owaine with her. The note says: 'We'll meet you at Knobtop mid-moon night.' That's two nights from now. Where's Knobtop?"

"At Ballintubber, in Tuath Gabair," Jenna answered. She stared at the reed, rolling it with her fingers. "Near Doire Coill. It's where I found Lámh Shábhála. Two nights from now . . ."

"Jenna . . ." Kyle scanned the small sheet of parchment again. He glanced at the sill, Jenna following his gaze—the crow was gone. "My heart just took the same leap yours did, and, aye, I look at this and I see Meriel's handwriting. But . . ." He handed the note back to her. She stroked the parchment with a fingertip, feeling the ridges of dried ink. "We have to at least consider that this isn't from Meriel at all, or that she might have written this under duress. What if this is just another of Doyle's traps? Using Lámh Shábhála to go to Inishduán is one thing; using it to go all the way to Ballintubber is another; you'll have drained much of the energy from the stone. In two days, there's no way to get any support for you in place, and you'll be inland where the Saimhóir can't help even if you could find them and they were willing. If Doyle is waiting for you again . . ."

He must have seen her gaze, fierce and determined, for he stopped. "What would you do in my place, Kyle?" she asked. She held up the paper in front of his face. "Tell me what you'd do."

He didn't look at the paper. Instead, he did something he'd rarely done over the years. His hand reached past the note to stroke her cheek. His fingers were soft and warm and when his hand dropped away after a moment, she found herself missing the touch.

"I'd do the same thing you're going to do," he said.

37

Reunions

" **A**NY CHANGE?" Doyle asked Aghy, but the look on the younger tiarna's face had already given him the answer. "Where is she?" he asked before Aghy could answer.

"In a room in the back off the courtyard. I have two gardai outside." Aghy glanced at the riders with Doyle, at the bright Clochs Mór around their necks, and his eyebrows raised a bit: Doyle could see what he was thinking—four Clochs Mór here, five if Demon-Caller around Edana's neck was included: Snapdragon, as always with Doyle; GodFist, held by the glowering and angry Nyle O'Murchadha; Sharpcut and Weaver, in the hands of the new cloudmages Shéra and Alaina. The tiny village was awash, all unaware, in great magic. The Riocha dismounted and gave the reins of their steeds to two wide-eyed stablehands. "I've told the innkceper that we'll be using all his rooms tonight. He seemed happy enough once a few mórceints crossed his palm."

The inn was a ramshackle affair, the village small and ugly. Doyle and his companions had ridden north from Lár Bhaile to Áth Iseal and across the Duán to meet Edana's caravan. "How was the journey down?" Doyle asked Aghy as they brushed the dust of the road from their clóca.

Aghy shrugged. "Mostly uneventful. The story you concocted worked perfectly." Doyle had told Aghy to tell those who asked that the bantiarna with the large escort was ill and disfigured and preferred to stay in her room with her trusted servants. "I did the same thing here when we arrived yesterday evening. The proprietor— name's Eliath; he's the man over there yelling at the stable boys and looking nervous—says he's the son of the 'Tara' the inn had been named after. The place looks like it hasn't been cleaned since his mam died, I'm afraid, but the ale's good."

"That's for me, then," O'Murchadha said. "I need to clear the damned dirt out of my throat." He limped heavily toward the tavern door, leaning on a cane, with Shéra and Alaina following. The proprietor, seeing them start toward the tavern, wiped his hands quickly on his apron and scurried inside.

"I'll take you to Edana, Tiarna," Aghy said. "How're are things in Dún Laoghaire?" he asked as they walked toward the side entrance of the inn.

"It's better not to ask," Doyle told him. "Enean— Tiarna O Liathain—is now the Rí Dún Laoghaire."

"Oh," Aghy said, and the falling tone of the word said it all. "And Rí Mallaghan?"

Doyle managed a small laugh as Aghy opened the door and gestured for Doyle to enter. "Suffice it to say that if I fail here, you should look for another patron because mentioning my name would no longer be beneficial for you."

"It's that serious?"

"It's worse," Doyle told him. "But it's my problem, not yours, Cousin." They climbed the stairs to the inn's second floor in silence.

"Shabby accommodations," Aghy told Doyle as they walked down a dingy and badly-lit corridor. At the end of the hall, two gardai straightened as they saw Doyle and Aghy approach. "Still, they're the best to be had in this sty of a town outside of commandeering one of the houses—which frankly aren't any better. Unfortunately, the villagers are already gossiping; you should have seen

the tavern last night—it was packed, and as close to
Doire Coill as we are, I was worried."

Doyle clapped Aghy on the back. "You've done perfectly fine," he told the young man. "I'm in your debt.
Why don't you go join the others in the tavern? I'll be
down soon."

Doyle embraced Aghy, clasping the youth to him.
He knocked on the door. One of the maids let
him in.

It was indeed a shabby room, with whitewash peeling
from the stones of the outside walls and bedraggled,
dusty tapestries covering the others. A large bed dominated the room with torn and patched linen draped over
it. Doyle pushed it aside; Edana lay there.

She looked as if she were sleeping. Doyle bent over
and kissed her, half-hoping that this time she'd open her
eyes and gift him with her soft smile. But she didn't.
Her chest rose and fell in a steady rhythm. Behind her
closed eyelids, he could see the flutter of movement, the
ghost of the dream she inhabited. "Sometimes she smiles
a bit, Tiarna, and I know she's thinking of you," the
maid said.

Doyle nodded to her—a woman who reminded him
of his mam in the last few years before she died: thick-
waisted with graying white hair, and the memory of old
beauty held in a lined and weary face. "She's never
woken?"

A solemn shake of the head. "Once, the first day we
left Falcarragh, I touched her hand and she pressed my
fingers. I thought she was going to open her eyes, but
she didn't. I've never seen anything like this. It's like
she's been enchanted, Tiarna, and you need the right
charm to bring her back."

Doyle chuckled grimly. He took one of Edana's hands,
half-hoping he'd feel the returning pressure of her fingers, but she didn't respond at all. "I think you're exactly
right," he told the maid. "And I intend to take that
charm. Tonight."

*The First Holder was high on a hillside, the rain lashing
her face, and she was looking around as if for someone.
She searched for Meriel, he knew with sudden clarity. For
Meriel, and Meriel was coming to her mam . . .*

Dhegli could feel the pattern in the air. He lifted his
snout, looking north. "No," Challa said, alongside him.

"What do you mean?" he asked.

"You saw something and no, you shouldn't go." Her
dark eyes looked at him imploringly. "I can feel it, too,
in the throbbing of Bradán an Chumhacht's fingerling
that's inside me. The great sky-stone is coming and you
want to go there. And I'm telling you to stay."

"Challa, Bradán an Chumhacht has given me a foretelling. Jenna may need my help again."

"Aye, and what did you achieve for the Saimhóir the
last time you helped her, other than nearly die yourself?"

"She's Meriel's mam."

"And Meriel hasn't come here in two days now and
may never again. In the meantime, you ignore the needs
of the Saimhóir for a stone-walker. How will you get
there, Dhegli—walk on the stones like one of them,
naked and vulnerable and lost? Dhegli . . ." Challa
nudged her head against his thick, warm neck. "I know
how you feel for her. I understand that. But I also know
that this isn't our concern. Bradán an Chumhacht's do-
main is the sea and the Saimhóir, not the hard earth and
the stone-walkers. I love you, Dhegli, and I'll follow you,
but listen to me first. I can't fill the part of you that
Meriel fills; I'm glad that she can and I share your joy
with her. But as long as you have Bradán an Chumhacht,
you have a greater duty. We should be back at the Nesting Land now, not surrounded by stones in sweet water
and all alone."

Dhegli's body shivered, blue-black fur rippling in starlight. He smelled the coming rain on the wind. "Saimhóir have followed stone-walkers before. We have a debt

to the great sky-stone for bringing Bradán an Chumhacht back to us."

"Aye, and that debt's already been paid—and more,
in my opinion—by Thraisha and Garrentha. And by you
with what you've done. If anything, the stone-walkers
now owe *us*, but do they worry about the things of the
WaterMother? No." He heard her voice go frightened,
as if a Biter was swimming close by. "You weren't in
the foretelling you just had, were you?"

"No . . . Though if I had been, at least then I'd know
what I needed to do." He sighed, lifting his snout and
letting his voice call out over the still dark water toward
the hidden trees. He could feel the pattern of the great
sky-stone approaching, but it would arrive far from the
lough, where a Saimhóir couldn't walk. The day star
would come before he could reach that place and he
couldn't hold the stone-walker form for that long. . . .

Dhegli moaned as another flash of premonition came
to him: if he went, he would be too late. This was, as
Challa had said, an affair of the stone-walkers. "I hear
you, Challa," he told her sadly. "We'll stay here. And
if Meriel doesn't come to me tomorrow, we'll go home
to where we belong."

"You're certain Mam will come here?" Meriel asked
Keira. She tried to keep her misgivings and uncertainty
out of her voice and knew she didn't quite succeed. The
older woman raised an eyebrow and lifted one shoulder
under her skins.

"We told her mid-moon night. She knows this place
and Lámh Shabhála has the power to bring her here.
We'll just have to wait."

Meriel shivered in the darkness and moved closer to
Owaine and Keira. So far there had been no mage-lights
even though the sun had gone down over two stripes ago.
The night air was chilled and wet in the valley to which
Keira had led them; the moon snatched shreds of fast high

clouds to veil itself and the stars to the west were obscured
by a wall of looming black clouds that promised rain. Keira
had stopped Owaine when he pulled flint and steel to start
a fire. "Not here," she said gruffly. "You don't want to
wake some of the ones sleeping here."

They sat alongside a dolmen erected in the center of
a ring of barrow graves. Keira had named the Bunús
Muintir kings buried around them, though Meriel had recognized only one of the names: Riata, who had figured in
some of her mam's tales about Lámh Shábhála. Riata had
once supposedly held Lámh Shábhála as well and Jenna
had met his ghost. Just thinking about that made the fine
hair rise on the back of Meriel's neck and along her arms,
and she kept looking at the dark and open entrance to his
barrow-grave as if an apparition might appear there at any
moment. Every touch of the freshening wind made Meriel
think that the ghosts of long-dead kings were walking
close by and the clouds that raced past the moon sent
spectral shadows slipping over the valley. The trees rim-
ming the small bowl of land swayed and dipped, as if
dancing to an unheard reel. Dire wolves howled in the
distance; she could hear the flutter of wings and the
hooting of great owls, and a pair of eyes seemed to
gleam in the blackness under the dolmen.

No—eyes *did* gleam there, caught in a spectral outline
of a face. Even as Meriel started to open her mouth to
scream, Keira stood and bowed her head in its direction.
"Riata," she said. "You honor us."

A thin, breathy laugh came from the darkness below
the eyes. "You wait for Lámh Shábhála and the First
Holder," he said. His regard seemed to drift over them,
one by one, at once frigid and searing. "And you," he
said to Meriel in those same breathy tones that might
have been mistaken for the soughing of the wind. "You're
her child, perhaps even the next Holder."

"Aye," Meriel answered. "I'm her child. But I don't
want Lámh Shábhála."

"Neither did your mam," Riata told her with another
eerie laugh. "But the cloch didn't care. It only worries

about itself." The form drifted out from under the dolmen, the misty outline of an old man dressed much as Keira was with a torc around his neck. Through him, as if through a cloud of pipe weed smoke, Meriel could see the landscape behind. His head lifted as he glanced up at the moon; his long hair rippled in a wind they could not feel. "There will be no mage-lights tonight," he said. "The Holder will be disappointed." He looked back at them. "You're waiting here, but this is the wrong place. She isn't coming here."

Keira cocked her head at the specter. "What do you mean? She knows this place; this is where we told her we'd be."

Riata sighed. "Lámh Shábhála is still far away, but I can feel its pattern approaching and I know its power is not focused here but to the north. Is there still a flat-topped hill close to the forest, near the fens . . . ?"

"Aye, we know that place," Owaine said. "Knobtop, near Ballintubber. Where the First Holder found . . ." Riata's gaze turned to Owaine. He gulped at the sight of the glowing eyes. ". . . Lámh Shábhála," he finished.

"Those names aren't the ones we used," Riata said. "But, aye, the Holder comes to where the stone was found."

"Why would she go there?" Meriel asked Riata, but she was drawn by Keira's face. It had gone nearly as pale and bloodless as Riata's. Meriel found that her own apprehension at seeing her mam again had shifted; she was suddenly more frightened for her mam than for herself.

"So far away," Keira said. "Something's wrong. Riata, are you sure?"

"I can feel Lámh Shábhála as if I held it still," he said. "I know where it goes."

"We have to get there," Keira said. "And quickly."

"That's twenty miles or more," Owaine told her. "It would be midday tomorrow before we arrive."

"If we walked, it would be," Keira replied. "But we won't walk. I just hope we won't be too late."

38

The New Holder

JENNA hadn't seen Knobtop in nearly two decades, not since she'd fled Tuath Gabair with Ennis. As the icy cold of the cloch-world slowly receded and the fog of her passage faded, she found herself gazing at a landscape that didn't appear to have changed in all that time. The faint lights of Ballintubber twinkled in the distance across the fens and the Mill Creek, and the high pasture of Knobtop looked as it had when she and old Kesh had brought their small flock of sheep up here to feed. The smells filled her lungs: the heather and grass, the moist richness of the fens, the western wind heavy with the promise of rain. The half-moon glittered once above before cloud hid its face and it might have been the same night the mage-lights had first appeared, when she'd found Lámh Shábhála here.

She was still clutching the stone in her hand. The effort of the long journey had taken nearly half of the stored energy from Lámh Shábhála; she glanced above, hoping to see the mage-lights, hoping that she could quickly replenish the cloch and not feel so vulnerable here, in the land where they still called her the Mad Holder.

A cold pattering of rain splashed across her cheeks and she pulled up the hood of her clóca. The voices of the ancient Holders yammered in the quiet: *"You've made a mistake, weakening Lámh Shábhála by coming to them. Soon you'll just be one of us, another dead voice in the stone . . ." ". . . You've let sentiment rule you, and that's always the downfall of a Holder . . ."*

And Riata spoke also, comforting. *"Be vigilant, Jenna. You're stronger than your enemy, even now."*

Jenna pushed the voices away until they were only the hush of the wind in the trees. "Meriel?" she called softly into the darkness. "Meriel, are you there?"

The answer that came was the one she feared. Still holding Lámh Shab-hala, she felt the hidden one with the ebbing remnants of the power that had brought her here, saw it in the landscape of her cloch-vision: a Cloch Mór, and a specific one at that—Doyle Mac Ard's cloch Snapdragon. She could feel the pinprick presence of other clochs here, still unopened by their Holders, and there were more people with them: a dozen, perhaps more, all in the small stand of trees just down the slope.

". . . You should have known it was just a trap . . ."
"You foolish woman . . ."
". . . leave now while you have the chance!"

Jenna blinked against the hissing drizzle and saw Doyle step out from the shelter of trees just down the slope; in her cloch-vision, the dragon walked with him, gold and red and snarling and looming gigantic over the high meadow. Jenna opened Lámh Shábhála, ready to pull the energy from it to take her away from here, but the attack came immediate and sudden. "Not this time," she heard Doyle say.

The dragon belched fire. Its claws raked toward her, its barbed tail swung and she had no time to form the image of Dún Kiil Keep in her mind that would whisk her away. She could only defend herself. Jenna took the energy and reshaped it, screaming with frustration and fury and fear as she brought up a wall of bright emerald. The dragon's fire splashed into it like a wave striking a rock. The shield shuddered under the impact of claws and tail, and Jenna staggered backward herself with the impact. Before the dragon could recover, she counterattacked, reshaping the wall into a lance and hurling it

full force at the dragon's exposed chest. The lance struck
the scales there, penetrating deep, and the dragon (and
Doyle, down the mountainside) shrieked in pain as the
lance exploded in a shower of bright meteors. The
dragon reeled and faded. "Where is she?" she shouted
at Doyle, on his knees in the grass. "Damn you, where's
Meriel? I'll kill you right now if you don't tell me!"

She shaped the power remaining in the cloch, ready
to send it smashing down on him . . . but she felt two
more clochs open: Sharpcut and Weaver once more, renewed and with new Holders. They were clumsy—she
could feel the awkwardness and inexperience in the minds
behind the energy, but they were fresh where she was
tired and their clochs were full. Had they attacked together as one, as weakened as Jenna was, she might have
fallen . . . but they didn't.

Sharpcut sent its bristling spears toward her first, a
hundred arrows streaking through darkness and rain as
if shot from hidden archers, and she caught them with
a wind from Lámh Shábhála and sent them rushing back
toward the Holder before he could react. He tried to
deflect them, but there were great holes in the shield he
flung up and Jenna held them open, sucking the energy
from the Cloch Mór. He went down with a cry and the
light of his cloch vanished in Jenna's cloch-sight. With a
silent snarl, she turned to the other.

The Holder was a woman, she realized, and Weaver
was already sending out its shimmering blue tendrils.
They snaked around Jenna in her cloch-sight like the
arms of some gigantic creature. Jenna sent her own
streams of energy out to meet them before they could
close around her, and she was nearly blinded as they
met in an eruption of white light and noise. She was
encased in cloch-light, and though the woman holding
the Cloch Mór was more skilled than the Holder of
Sharpcut, Jenna had held Lámh Shábhála for decades
and knew the ways of the cloudmage far better. Rather
than trying to block Weaver's energy, she deflected it
and let it pour into the shell about her, spraying outward

like hard rain splattering on stones. The Holder faltered, and in the hesitation, Jenna imagined the shell, still burning with the power of the mage-lights, closing around the woman. She held up her open hand, squeezing it closed into a fist as in her cloch-sight she watched the cage contract around Weaver's holder: tighter, tighter . . . Jenna felt the woman pushing back, loosing all the power within the Cloch Mór in one desperate burst. Jenna's fingers opened, a burning agony radiating up her arm as if she'd plunged her hands into a bed of red-hot coals. She screamed away the pain, closing her eyes and pushing her mind deep into Lámh Shábhála's crystalline core, pulling from it all the last dregs of power she could find.

Jenna's fingers closed again. The fire around the woman contracted to a white-hot core, a sun that threw blinding light over Knobtop, a dawn of fury.

The sun went out. Jenna collapsed to her knees in the rain-wet grass, exhausted. Lámh Shábhála was nearly emptied.

Jenna heard the sound of bitter, ironic applause in the sudden quiet: two hands clapping slowly.

"I *am* impressed, Sister," Doyle said. "Very much so. I swore after Inishduán that I'd never underestimate you again, but I see that I very nearly did." She saw the corners of his mouth lift as he walked up the slope toward her. His head was bare to the rain, his dark hair, so like his da's, clinging to his skull, neck and shoulders in wet ringlets. "Nearly. But not quite."

"Where's Meriel?" Jenna gasped, her throat raw. "Is she . . . ?"

"Dead? No. As to where she is: she's somewhere in Doire Coill and not in my hands, I'm afraid. You can take that solace with you. Your daughter's still alive."

His hand went to his cloch. The dragon arose again, shimmering into existence to his side, horrible and leering, smoke writhing about its horned head. The creature's wings boomed, sending a rush of hot air over her like the blast from a smithy's forge. Jenna tightened her

grip on Lámh Shábhála, reaching into its depths for what
was left of its cold stores of power.

There was very little—certainly not enough to flee as
she had at Inishduán even if she had the time to image
a place close enough to here that the dregs of Lámh
Shábhála's power could take her there. She saw her defeat. The voices within her laughed or cried or wailed.
Riata's familiar voice rose above the babble. *"I'm
sorry,"* the ghost said. *"I'm so sorry . . ."*

The dragon roared. It lifted a clawed foot. She looked
up at it, the talons flexing in the air above her. With a
roar, the dragon brought the foot down and she emptied
the cloch, trying to hold it back, but she could not . . .

It struck her, bright and hot and hard, and she heard
her own wail as she fell away into darkness and oblivion.

His hands trembling, Doyle slipped Lámh Shábhála's
chain from around Jenna's neck, lifting it over the
golden torc of the Banrion and around her long, dark
tresses of hair. He did it with surprising gentleness,
seemingly almost sad as he saw her face, lost in uncon-
sciousness, tighten in a rictus as Lámh Shábhála left her.
Rain beaded on her cheeks. "I'm sorry, Sister," he whispered, then his eyes narrowed. "This is for my da, who
you killed with this very cloch. And it's for our mam,
too, because you killed her that same day with a far
longer and crueler death. This is their revenge. I won't
savor the pain and suffering you're going to feel, but it's
no less than you deserve. It's no less than you gave
Maeve."

He rose to his feet over her.

He held Lámh Shábhála in his hand. It was *his*—
emptied of its vast power now, but he would fill it when
the mage-lights next came and take it as his own. It was
his, as it should have been his da's. He closed his fingers
around it, grinning.

"Nyle!" he called. "Have the gardai tend to Shéra and

Alaina, and I need you and two others to carry the Banrion. We'll take her back to Lár Bhaile for Rí Mallaghan—he'll be delighted to have the murderer of his mam in his donjons." No one answered him. "O'Murchadha?"

But it wasn't Nyle who strode out from tree shadow and mist. . . .

He saw the faint shape of wolves rushing from the forest, and he reached immediately for Snapdragon. As he opened the Cloch Mór, he could see them fully, glowing with mage-light: the spectral wolves from Wolfen, Ó Riain's cloch. Doyle called the dragon, and its claws raked into the wolves, tossing them away as it roared and flamed. But though the wolves howled and screamed, they kept coming, more and more of them, veiled in dragonfire and smoke but always advancing, jaws snapping and slobbering, tearing great chunks from the dragon's legs, leaping onto its scaled back, tattering the leathery wings to shreds.

He could not do this, not for much longer—he'd been terrifically weakened by the fight with Jenna, and Wolfen was fresh. Doyle shuddered; the dragon's tail, lashing out at the blackness, struck him and sent him reeling backward. He closed his eyes, trying to clear his mind, searching with the Cloch Mór for some reservoir of energy, some hidden well he could tap.

There was nothing.

In desperation, Doyle took the power that remained, squandering it all in one violent counterattack. The dragon lifted from the ground, its wings restored, shaking away the ethereal wolves and sending them howling into the night. It arced its serpent's neck and slashed down jaws wide at Ó Riain. But the wolves came rushing back, stronger than before, and they met the dragon, pushing it backward and down. They covered the golden scales, they tore open its belly and snatched up its heart, howling in triumph.

Doyle felt the dragon die as the last ounce of power drained from the cloch, and he felt himself go with it,

the wolves staring at him as Ó Riain walked from the
cover of the trees; the world narrowing as if he looked
through a tunnel that was closing in on him. There was
someone with Ó Riain, and that man wore the skin and
head of a bear over him.

The Toscaire Concordai . . . So I was betrayed . . .

Doyle fell to the ground, fighting to retain consciousness. He heard them approaching. He waited for the
wolves to come, for Ó Riain's Cloch Mór to ravage him
as he lay there helpless. It was too much effort to even
blink away the rain that fell onto his face. But it was
only Ó Riain's face that appeared above him. "I must
give you credit, Tiarna Mac Ard," the older man said.
"You were indeed a masterful cloudmage. Far better
than me. But you never learned that it's best to delegate
someone else do your work for you rather than to do it
yourself. Then, when they're weak, you can take what
you want." He bent down, and Doyle felt a tugging on
his left hand. He tried to close his fingers around the
stone, but they refused to work. Ó Riain's face returned.
"So this is Lámh Shábhála . . . A plain thing to hold
such power, don't you think?"

Doyle opened his mouth to protest, but no sound
came out. He couldn't lift his hand or stir; it was all he
could do to cling to consciousness, to watch as Ó Riain,
holding Lámh Shábhála, moved away and the half-
hidden face of the Toscaire Concordai took its place.

The bear grinned; Rhusvak grinned. "I should thank
you, Tiarna Mac Ard," the man said. "You've given the
Concordance what it wanted and more. Lámh Shábhála
will come to Céile Mhór with an army for our aid, and
we'll have a Cloch Mór of our own in the battle against
the Arruk. Tiarna Ó Riain has promised to teach me
how to use it. A dragon to fight against the Arruk . . ."
Doyle felt hands under his head and the chain holding
Snapdragon was lifted from him. At the moment it left
him, a wave of searing, awful loss—physical, agonizing—
swept over him and this time he did cry out, a wail of
distress and grief.

Doyle had been taught that to lose his cloch was the worst trial a cloudmage could ever endure. Now he *knew* the truth of that lesson, knew it to the marrow of his existence. It was as if Rhusvak had plunged his hands into Doyle's abdomen and ripped out his entrails. He moaned: a whimper and sob. Rhusvak looked down at him, almost sadly. "So it hurts that much? A pity . . ." The man's face came close to Doyle, whispering. "I'm a merciful man," Rhusvak said, "and when I hunt, I never let my prize suffer." Doyle heard the ring of steel leaving leather. He waited for the strike, for the feel of the blade slicing between his ribs or slashing across his throat.

It never came.

He heard wings in the rain. He heard thundering and felt the ground tremble underneath him. He heard the howl of wolves, somewhere down near the base of Knobtop. He heard Rhusvak call out and Ó Riain answer, then running footsteps and the sound of horses in flight.

He tried to rise, to see what was happening, but he couldn't. He lay there lost in misery.

39

Convergence

AFTERWARD, the inhabitants of Ballintubber would call it the "Night of Visitors." They were first awakened by the sound of rain on their thatched roofs, and they peered from their windows at a display of strange and colorful and silent lightnings on the bare high slopes of Knobtop. Some would swear that they saw a dragon there, limned in golden, spectral light as it belched flames. It was as if the mage-lights that curled and swayed in the sky most nights had come down to earth near them. Knobtop was lit in an awful fury for several minutes, then went dark again.

And as it did, they heard the sound of low thunder, the howling of wolves and the beat of unseen wings. They gaped at the sight of monstrous crows, so many (they would say later) that they blocked the very sky and stopped the rain as they flew past at the level of the rooftops. Then came the thunder itself: the fia stoirm, the storm deer, their antlers so high that they tore the very clouds, their hooves shaking the earth so that pots and pans clattered and fell from their hooks and sparks shuddered up from banked fires. There were three of the storm deer, they said the next day, though some later remembered six, or perhaps it was more, an entire herd of them that left the fields pockmarked and all the crops for the village trampled underneath. Some would later say that the fia stoirm had riders: cloudmages from Inish-

422

feirm, clad in robes of white and shrieking imprecations and spells as they went. Others claimed that there were Bunús Muintir with them, the wild people of Doire Coill, an army of them howling in their guttural, strange tongue and wielding staffs that glowed in the night and ensor-celled hammers and axes.

But all agreed that after the fia stoirm came the wolves, gigantic dire wolves that snarled and slavered over the fields in the wake of the deer, their red eyes like pinpricks of fire in the night and their teeth gleaming, and the villagers slammed their shutters and barred their doors as the man-high wolves rushed past. The count of them would grow from a hand to a dozen to a hundred to a thousand as the tale was told and retold over the years.

They all—crows, deer, mages, wild men, and wolves—rushed through the village in the direction of Knobtop, though no more lights were seen there. Afterward, in the morning, the curious and brave few who went up to the mountain found the stones charred and broken, with pits and craters everywhere, as if some vast and unimaginable battle had been fought in the high pasture. . . .

Meriel, Owaine, and Keira were seated astride three storm deer. Keira had called them from the valley of Riata's tomb and they'd ridden through the forest at an impossible speed, Meriel simply holding on to the creature's neck in desperation, closing her eyes as limbs and branches lashed at her as they rushed along and the low booming din of their hooves nearly deafened her. Somewhere, she realized, two dire wolves began running with them: Arror and his mate Garrhal. Their presence made the storm deer shiver and quicken their own pace, and Meriel could feel her own mount shake its head, snorting at the smell of their enemies. But Keira shouted something in her own language and flung a powder from

one of her pouches into the air, and the storm deer settled once more, seeming to ignore the wolves.

A half dozen or so crows swept by her, staying close
to Keira before swooping off ahead as the strange group
left the shelter of the old oaks and came out into thinly-
wooded rolling land just as the rain began to fall. She
could see, faintly, a few points of yellow light in the
distance that must be Ballintubber.

"Look!" Meriel shouted to Keira and Owaine, pointing to the east and south. They'd come out of Doire
Coill farther north than Meriel had expected; over the
roofs of the village they could see lights flickering on
Knobtop, as if the storm that now soaked their clothes
had decided to spend all its fury there.

"Go!" Keira shouted, and the storm deer answered
with their high, bleating voices. The wind threw rain
hard into Meriel's face as they redoubled their pace.
They came through and passed the village in what
seemed a moment, tearing across fields, road, and fen,
pounding over a bridge and rushing up the flanks of
Knobtop. Arror and Garrhal howled, leaping over rocks
as they climbed. They entered a small stand of trees,
emerging from the other side, Meriel saw men fleeing
on horseback, several of the crows diving futilely at them
as the riders headed through the high grass at an angle.
The wolves started to pursue, but Keira called to them
and they returned, red tongues lolling over white teeth
as they panted.

"Let them go! There are too many for us, and they
have Clochs Mór," Keira told them. "We're needed
here." She nodded her head upslope, where through the
darkness and rain Meriel could see two figures in the
wet grass. There was a disturbing familiarity to one of
them. . . .

"Mam!" Meriel leaped from the storm deer and ran,
Owaine following. She sank down on the grass next to
her, stroking Jenna's cold cheeks with her hands. With
relief, she saw her mam's chest rise with a wheezing
breath. Meriel lifted Jenna's head onto her lap and the

woman's eyes flew open, feral and strained. Her mouth opened in a wide "O" and she wailed, a wordless, bottomless grief that seemed to shake the rain from the clouds. Her hand, the arm scarred white to the elbow, clutched desperately for something at her breast, and Meriel saw then that the chain holding Lámh Shábhála was gone.

"Oh, Mam . . ." Meriel found her own breath caught in empathy. She looked around, hoping desperately that Lámh Shábhála had only fallen off somehow, that she would find it in the grass. "Mam, I'm here. I have you; Keira's here, and Owaine. You're safe, you're all right . . ." Jenna continued to scream, long and distressed, pausing only to take a breath, her eyes open but unseeing. Meriel was sobbing with her, a panic rising. "Mam, please . . ." Meriel pleaded, looking up bleakly at Owaine. "Lámh Shábhála's gone," she said to him, and he grimaced as he nodded.

"I know." He stared at Jenna's madness, flinching as another ragged scream tore from her ravaged throat. Keira had come over also, crouching down alongside Meriel. Arror and Garrhal padded about the meadow, growling.

"Please help her," Meriel said desperately to Keira. "Listen to her! You must know something . . ."

Keira shook her head, her soft brown eyes watching Jenna's agonized face. "She's beyond anything I can do," she said. "But perhaps not for you, if you can stand the pain, too."

"Oh." Meriel clutched at Treoraí's Heart around her neck. She could feel the energy within it aching to be released. She hugged Jenna to her. "I'm here, Mam. Let me try to help you . . ." She closed one hand around the azure facets and opened her mind to it, still holding Jenna.

She found herself lost.

Before, it had been difficult enough to keep herself separate from the person she was trying to heal until she could send the clochmion's power through them. Meriel

had learned how to use the clochmion to explore the
body she touched and find the source of the injury; she'd
learned to accept the linkage of her personality with that
of the person she was healing. But this . . . this was
more, and worse . . .

Meriel found herself caught in a maelstrom from the
first moment. Her mam was the center of the storm, a
vortex of blood-red and black that immediately engulfed
Meriel. Jenna's wail was the world-voice of the Mother-
Creator, a deafening sound beyond sound, a thousand
needles driven hard into Meriel's flesh. The emotional
matrix of her mam's torment caught her up and swept
her inward, and she found herself screaming in concert,
lost. *Lost, lost . . . I need it. I can't live without it . . .*
Meriel flailed out even as she screamed, trying to pull
away from the darkness inside Jenna that clutched at
her with fingers of misery and loss and anguish, dragging
her back to the midnight core like some great swallow-
hole of the sea.

Meriel was drowning in this misery. There were no
other thoughts in Jenna/Meriel but this awful pain, this
terrible mind-grief. *Lost, lost . . .* Fleeting images of years
past flitted by, but they were colorless and stretched, the
faces skeletal. She saw herself once, much younger, but
her face was that of a corpse, and maggots wriggled in
the sockets of her eyes. Meriel/Jenna screamed, thrashing out with her fists at the apparitions. Meriel could
barely hold onto herself and remember that she held
Treoraí's Heart. This was no broken leg, no simple injury, no ordinary illness. This was a madness of mind
and soul. Lámh Shábhála had driven its roots all the way
to the core of Jenna's being, and having that connection
torn away had left great wounds that were beyond anything Treoraí's Heart could heal. Meriel knew in the
midst of her coupled pain that if she stayed here longer,
the agony radiating from those lesions would consume
her as well. She tried to feel her own hand and could
not; she might as well be trying to lift a phantom limb.

"Mam, I'm sorry," she said. "I can't help you. I have

to go." The words were submerged in the wailing. Meriel searched for herself in the nightmare inner landscape, forcing herself to focus through the shared pain. She couldn't heal what the loss of Lámh Shábhála had done, but she could perhaps give her mam some temporary solace. She found the thread of memory, followed it deeper. She found Jenna, huddled frightened in the midst of the storm . . .

She tried to find her own thoughts, a whisper against Jenna/Meriel's linked cries. . . . *Once you use Treoraí's Heart, your own protection is gone. If you can't release quickly enough, you'll be trapped here* . . .

"Mam?" In her mind, she saw her mam's face lift toward her, recognition dawning in her tortured face. "I'm here with you, Mam." Meriel took a breath, bracing herself for the full impact of the pain she knew would come. She took the cloch's power in her mind, gathering and holding it. In one inner motion, she placed it around her mam like a clóca; in that instant of total connection, the waves of deep, endless loss swept into her. She took the grief, hearing her own voice screaming, her own throat scraped raw with the sound, the pounding surf of red and black dragging her under, sucking her back into the well of agony.

She willed her fingers to open, to break the connection . . .

Meriel gasped, the world snapping back into focus around her as the sound of a scream seemed to echo from the summit of Knobtop. "Meriel!" Owaine was shouting, his face very close to hers. Meriel gasped, the pain still throbbing inside her. If she closed her eyes, its insistent grasp would still drag her back. She could feel the connection, pulling even as it began to dissolve. "Meriel!"

"I'm—" she started to say, but her throat ached, and her hand burned cold where she had been holding the cloch. She looked down to see the faint, curled lines of white scars on her arm had reached nearly to the elbow, fading slowly back to flesh "—here," she finished with

a gasp, swallowing hard. "I never thought—" She looked
down at her mam's face, still cradled on her lap. Jenna's
eyes were closed now, and though the face reflected the
pain, she was no longer thrashing in Meriel's arms. She
seemed to be only sleeping, perhaps snared in a nightmare. "That was awful. I can't . . . couldn't . . . It was
too strong for me." *Lost, lost* . . . She shivered, the
memory of the interior horror receding slowly. Her body
ached, as if she'd been pummeled and bruised.

Owaine stroked her hair and her back; Meriel leaned
back into his touch, enjoying the silent comfort of it.
Keira grimaced, as if she'd expected to hear Meriel's
assessment. "The legends all speak of cloudmages driven
mad by the loss of their clochs, especially those who
have held Lámh Shábhála," she said. "I don't know that
anyone can help your mam now. She has to find her
own way."

"She's hurting so terribly, Keira," Meriel said. "I
could give her a little comfort, that's all. And it won't
last. It can't." She took a long breath that threatened to
break into a sob. "I don't know if I can go there again.
I don't know if I'm strong enough."

"I can do a little more, once we're back in Doire
Coill," Keira said. "And we can pray to the Greatness
to help her. But all the old Holders who had Lámh
Shábhála taken away from them died when the cloch
was stolen, or not long after. The First Holder is stronger
than most, but . . ." She looked away, nodding to where
Arror and Garrhal sat on their haunches, several strides
down the hill. "There's still something we have to do
here. Come with me."

Gently, Meriel laid her mam's head down on the grass,
kissing her cheek. Owaine helped her to her feet. She
started to shake her head and shrug away his hands, but
the movement caused the world to spin around her and
her knees crumpled. She nearly fell and had to let
Owaine support her weight for several seconds until the
ground settled once more. She let him keep her arm as
they walked toward the dire wolves. As they approached,

she saw a person on the ground between them. His face was turned up to them, the eyes open; his hands were clasped together at his chest. "Doyle Mac Ard." She spat out the name.

He said nothing in response, though his lips moved and she thought he could see recognition in his gaze. "His Cloch Mór's gone," Keira said. "There are two more tiarna farther down the hill; Arror says they're the same way. Whoever we saw fleeing here left with Lámh Shábhála and three Clochs Mór—that's a prize worth a Rí's ransom. That's enough to shift the balance of power in Talamh an Ghlas."

"Then let's go after them before they're too far away," Owaine said. "With the storm deer, maybe—" But Keira was already shaking her head.

"What would we do then? They have the Clochs Mór with them, and several gardai. By the time we reached them, they could be near Áth Iseal, where there's a garrison. No, we'd fall, and there'd be no one to care for your mam. The crows will watch them and tell us where they've gone."

Meriel listened to them, staring at Mac Ard. His eyes gazed back at her, and in them was reflected the same pain she'd felt inside her mam—perhaps not as intense and all-consuming but still a mirroring of that grief and loss, of a part of him torn bodily away and carried off. His scarred right hand clutched over and over again at his chest for something that wasn't there. His lips opened. "He took it," he said. "Ó Riain. He took it. By the Mother, it hurts, it hurts . . ."

Arror growled in his own language, long and low. "He says he'll kill the man for you," Keira said, "and to turn away if you don't want to see."

Arror rose from his haunches and started to lunge at Mac Ard, his terrible mouth open, but Meriel shouted. "No!" Arror stopped in mid-strike, as Mac Ard brought his hands up belatedly. "I don't want him killed."

Arror growled again, as did Garrhal. "He says one should never leave a wounded enemy alive," Keira translated. "And Garrhal adds that mercy is giving your opponent another chance to bite you. You may smell sorrow on him now, but that's an odor easily washed away."

"I agree with them, Meriel," Owaine said. "Mac Ard didn't give you the same consideration. Did you, Tiarna?" he asked Mac Ard. The man shook his head.

"No," he answered, closing his eyes as if trying to push the words through the pain. "I would have killed you, Meriel, to get back at your mam. I'm sorry. I was angry. I thought . . ." His eyes opened again. "I know now why she couldn't simply give up the cloch. I know very well." He seemed to almost laugh, then his face twisted again in pain. He curled up on the ground, groaning.

The rain fell harder, lashing Knobtop in sweeping sheets. The lights of Ballintubber were lost. They stood alone on a dark island lost in clouds and mist. Arror growled and Keira nodded. "We should leave here," she said, "before others come. Everyone for miles around will have seen the lights on the mountain. Meriel? What of Mac Ard and the others? I leave you with that decision."

Meriel's fingers brushed against her clochmion: Treoraí's Heart, her mam had named it. She imagined someone taking it from her and the pain that would follow—the gift itself had cost Treoraí its life. Now it was hers, the stone that could only heal, not harm.

A vital part of her.

"Leave them," she said.

"Meriel!" Owaine protested. "Arror and Garrhal are right. If we leave them here alive, the Mother alone knows what could happen."

"Exactly," Meriel answered. "None of us know."

"They wouldn't have been so kind to you," Owaine retorted. He pointed at Mac Ard. "That bastard admitted it."

Mac Ard was watching, silent. Meriel caught his gaze, and he looked away. "He'll know. He'll remember.

Won't you, Uncle?" Mac Ard nodded, misery clouding his face. "It's done, then," Meriel said. "Let's get my mam and leave."

Arror growled, looking as if he would ignore Meriel's decision, but Garrhal stepped in front of him. She sat on her haunches and lifted one of her huge front paws, displaying to him the leg that had been broken, speaking to him in a bark and low howl, nudging him when he persisted in moving closer to Mac Ard. Arror growled again, but he turned his head away. The two dire wolves padded away down the hill. In a few moments, their gray forms were hidden in the rain and darkness.

Owaine stood over Mac Ard, still holding Meriel's arm. "I hope it hurts," he said to the man. "It doesn't begin to pay for what you've done to Meriel and the Banrion." Mac Ard remained mute, blinking against the raindrops that pattered on his face. As Keira called the storm deer back to them and Owaine and Meriel went back up the hill to Jenna, Mac Ard called after them. Meriel turned to see the man push himself up to a sitting position, a hunched figure in the wet night.

"Meriel," he called. "I'm sorry. For all of it. I'm sorry."

She didn't answer. She had nothing she wanted to say to him. She was empty and exhausted and tired and she seemed to feel nothing, or perhaps everything. Her emotion were a welter, a confused jumble. It was all she could do to help Owaine and Keira lash together a carrier for Mam, then mount the storm deer for the slow journey back to Doire Coill.

The sky stormed the rest of the night, and the mage-lights did not come.

40

A Father's Cloch

THE ODOR was overpowering and bitter, and just sniffing the fragrance wafting from the small bronze kettle made Meriel feel dizzy and lethargic. "It's an infusion of andúilleaf," Keira said. "It helps a person to forget the pain for a little while."

"Mam told me about it once," Meriel said. "She also said that once she started taking it, she couldn't stop. She said that it made her crazy and that's why she killed Banrion Cianna in Lár Bhaile."

Keira nodded, stirring the brew with a wooden spoon. Thick white liquid clung to the wooden handle. "That could be true. If you use too much of it too often, the leaf makes you dependent on it. It does cloud your judgment and makes your emotions climb higher and fall lower. But right now, your mam needs help with the pain she's feeling, and andúilleaf does that better than kala bark or anything else I know from the herbcraft Seancoim taught me. But if you don't want me to give it to her . . ."

Keira raised an eyebrow; Meriel shook her head. Since they'd returned to Keira's cave, her mam had become increasingly distraught and inconsolable. The calming effect of Treoraí's Heart was wearing off and it wasn't yet night, when the mage-lights might come and Meriel could refill the cloch. But even if she did have Treoraí's Heart to use, she wasn't certain that she could attempt another journey into the wailing, chaotic interior of her mam's injured mind. The thought of being inside her mam's mind again terrified her.

"Go on," she told Keira. "Whatever you think best."

"I think for the time being all we can do is ease her pain. She'll bring herself back on her own, in her own time, if that's what the Mother wills."

"Let me help you, then . . ."

Meriel lifted her mam's head and shoulders, and Keira touched a wooden bowl filled with the andúilleaf brew to Jenna's lips. Jenna seemed to stir at the odor; her lips opened and Keira let some of the brew trickle into her mouth. Meriel could see her mam's throat convulse as she swallowed. Jenna sighed; her mouth opened. "More," she said, her voice a bare croak.

Keira glanced at Meriel, then brought the bowl up again. Jenna sipped at it eagerly, her hands coming up to cup Keira's. She drained the bowl, and Meriel could feel her mam's body relax, the tenseness leaving the muscles as she lay her back on the pallet. "Mam?" she said. "Can you hear me, Mam?"

Jenna's eyes flickered open, her tongue licked cracked and dry lips. The wisp of a smile touched her mouth. "Aye," she husked. "I hear you, my darling." She lifted her hand; Meriel took it, feeling the fingers trembling under hers. She leaned over and kissed her mam's forehead.

"I was so afraid, Mam," she began, then could go no further, her throat closing with a sob.

"I was scared, too," Jenna said. "I was frightened I'd never see you again, never hold you . . ." Her eyes closed, opened again. "I felt you, when you used the clochmion on Knobtop. I felt you inside me when I was lost, and you brought me back. You're a true cloudmage, Meriel, even more than me. If you can do that with Treoraí's Heart, then you're strong enough to hold Lámh Shábhála, perhaps even to do what I couldn't." Jenna licked her lips again, and Keira leaned over to moisten them with a dampened cloth. Jenna watched the

Bunús Muintir. "You must be Seancoim's apprentice," Jenna said to her. "I never met you, but this is his cave. I remember it . . ."

"Aye," Keira said gently. "We never met, but I saw you in these woods. Then, you looked much as Meriel does now. I see you in her. You both have the same inner strength."

Jenna nodded. Then her face clouded and she moaned. "Lámh Shábhála. Doyle took it—"

"Not Doyle, Mam," Meriel said. She told Jenna what they'd seen on Knobtop, what they'd learned from her uncle. When she'd finished, Jenna lay with her eyes closed, her breath harsh and fast. Meriel thought for a moment that she was sleeping again, then the eyes opened again, clouded with subdued pain. "I'd have killed him," she said. "For what he's done to me. And to you."

"I couldn't, Mam. I'm sorry if you feel I was wrong."

"No," Jenna said. "Not wrong. At least he's suffering for what he's done. But . . ." She scrabbled in her clóca, her hands thrusting into a hidden pocket under the folds. "Thank the Mother—I brought this for you, Meriel."

She brought out her hand, holding a thin silver chain at the end of which dangled a jewel of pure, bright red. "This is Blaze," Jenna said. "A Cloch Mór. I brought it to give to you."

"Keep it, Mam," Meriel said. "Maybe it would help you."

Jenna shook her head. "No, it would make it worse. If I'd had another Cloch Mór, perhaps Blaze could replace it. But holding it now would just remind me of everything I've lost. Besides, this was . . ." She paused, holding out the cloch to Meriel. Her eyes suddenly filled with tears. "It was your da's cloch. I took it from Padraic Mac Ard after . . ." She stopped.

"Da's cloch?" Meriel asked, frowning. She didn't move to take the stone. "But Da has one, and it's brown and tan."

"Meriel." The tone of Jenna's voice sent ice through

Meriel's chest, made her quiver as if the world had shifted around her. She didn't want to hear the rest, afraid now of what her mam was going to say. When it came, it was worse than she could have imagined.

"I should have told you a long time ago," her mam said. "Kyle said I should, but I didn't listen. Now I wish I had—it would make this easier." Gold-brown eyes held Meriel, and the deep sorrow in them frightened her. "Kyle's been a true and good da to you, a better da than I could have hoped for and a good friend and companion to me. But you share no blood with him, Meriel. Your da, the man I loved, was named Ennis O'Deoradháin, though he died before you were born." Groaning with the effort, Jenna sat up and grasped Meriel's hand. She put the Cloch Mór in Meriel's palm, letting the fine links of the chain flow around it, and closed her fingers around the stone. "Take this. Take it and when the mage-lights come, make it your own."

"You should keep it yourself, Mam," Meriel protested. A hundred questions whirled in her head. Jenna had smashed her worldview with a few words and Meriel reeled, not knowing what to say or how she should feel. She stared at the jewel in her hand, wanting it to be gone, wanting everything to be the way it had been just a few moments before. "You don't know; in a few days, with the andúilleaf . . ."

"Blaze is *yours* now, Meriel," Jenna said, and for an instant her voice had again the imperiousness of a Banrion, sharp with the expectation of obedience. "Yours." The effort exhausted Jenna, she lay back again, panting. "I need more andúilleaf," she said to Keira.

"How's your mam?" Owaine asked as Meriel emerged from the cave mouth. He was standing a little farther up the slope, gazing back over the treetops of Doire Coill to the north. It was nearing dusk and most of the forest was already in shadow. Blaze lay heavy in a pocket of her clóca; she could almost feel its yearning to be filled again after long years of emptiness.

"She's awake and resting," Meriel told Owaine. "Keira gave her a potion that seems to have helped some."

"That's good. I'm glad to hear that. After all I was taught about the old Holders, I'm worried about her. If we could get her back to Máister Kirwan, perhaps . . ." He shrugged.

Meriel had heard nothing of what he'd said; it had been just a babble of sound. "I'm going down to the lough," Meriel told him, and Owaine stirred himself, coming down the slope toward her.

"I'll go with you." Her face must have shown her emotions, for he lifted his hands. "Just as far as the High Road," he added. "In these woods, it's better for two than one, and it's getting near dark."

"I'll be fine," she told him. "I don't really want company."

"I'll follow you anyway."

His face was so serious that she had to smile at that. "You already followed me from Inishfeirm, and look at where that's got you."

Slowly, he returned the smile.

They walked through the deepening gloom, following the path and landmarks that Keira had shown them: *"There's no absolutely safe path through Doire Coill, but don't stray and you should be fine."* Where the oaks thinned and the softwoods and firs began, they paused and surveyed the road, a hundred strides away. Two riders were approaching, heading north toward Áth Iseal; they watched them pass. When the last sound of the hooves had faded, Owaine nudged Meriel. "Go on," he said. "I'll stay here and watch for a bit."

Meriel started to protest, then stopped herself. She nodded to Owaine and slipped over the fences and through the brush and willows to the shore of the lough.

She wasn't certain what she wanted or what she wanted to say to Dhegli. She only knew that she wanted to see him again, that she needed to talk with him about what had happened last night, to look into his black, sympathetic eyes and hear his deep voice singing in her head.

She kicked away her sandals and let the cold waves lap over her feet. She could feel the urge of the change dancing in her blood, but . . . There was an emptiness out in the water. She looked out over the wide expanse reddened with sunset and saw nothing. The ripples of russet and flame-orange were mesmerizing, and she found herself staring at them with the certainty that there would be nothing out there for her, that Dhegli was no longer here. The scale of Bradán an Chumhacht still burned in her head, but the pulse of it was distant now and growing more distant with each moment.

The water was icy around her toes and she no longer wanted to let the change happen. She stepped back away from the lough, sitting down hard on the grass and mud there. She clasped her knees to her chest.

She waited, hoping she was wrong and knowing she was not.

"Meriel?"

The sound of her name startled her, coming from behind without warning. She hurtled to her feet with a cry, thrown roughly out of reverie. Belatedly, she recognized the person who had materialized in the moonlight and the throbbing of her pulse in her temples started to slow. She didn't know how long she'd been sitting at the lough's shore. Somehow the landscape had gone dark without her knowing and the stars of the Badger twinkled high above, holding the half-moon.

"By the Mother, Owaine, I thought you were a Black Haunt calling for my soul."

Buttery light dappled his cheeks. "Sorry, Meriel." His gaze went past her to the lough, and she answered the question he didn't ask.

"He didn't come. I've just been sitting here, thinking."

"The mage-lights are coming," Owaine said. He pointed to the zenith, where Meriel could see the first tendrils of blue-green and pale yellow beginning to curl above. Noticing them, she felt the insistent yearning of Treoraí's Heart and was surprised that she hadn't noticed it before. She also felt the hunger of Blaze, still in her pocket.

Take it and make it your own, her mam had said. Yet now she wasn't so certain. To take Blaze would mean she would lose Treoraí's Heart and its healing abilities. Aye, Máister Kirwan had thought it just a clochmion, not one of the terrible and powerful Clochs Mór, yet . . . she could see the scarring on her arm, and she found she had little interest in the destructive powers of the clochs. She remembered Siúr Meagher and the joy and wonder that had filled her face when Meriel had taken away the pain in her hands; remembered little Áine, the girl she'd cured of the lung sickness in Ballycraigh, Owaine's wonder and surprise at being able to see clearly. She could recall the faces all of those she'd healed over the past few months.

In recalling them, it was Sevei's face that came to her the strongest. *You have to feel your choice inside and know it's the right one,* Sevei had said to her.

Meriel remembered her choice on Knobtop to leave Doyle alive. *The right choice . . .* "I'm not like my mam. I'm not like the others."

"What?"

Meriel shivered, not realizing that she'd spoken aloud. "Nothing. It's nothing." The mage-lights were brightening, beginning to spread over the rest of the night sky. Soon, they'd be in their full glory, radiant curtains and dazzling swirls as bright as a dozen moons. She wondered if her mam could see them and she imagined the redoubled pain that they must cause her, knowing that on any other night she would be standing under this sky, filling Lámh Shábhála as all the other clochs na thintrí fed on the energy with her. Knowing that somewhere

not too far away, Tiarna Ó Riain would be holding
Lámh Shábhála and claiming it as his own.

Owaine dug under the collar of his léine and brought
out his clochmion. He started to close his hand around
the stone and open it. She saw the mage-lights reflecting
on his upturned face.

His face . . . In the moonlight, it was as if she saw
him for the first time, as if it had been her eyes that had
been clouded and dim all along, not his. "Wait," she
told him, putting her hand over his. "Not yet."

He looked at her questioningly. Meriel reached into
her pocket and brought out Blaze. She put it in his palm.
"Take this one."

He stared down at the jewel in his hand. He took a
breath. "Meriel . . ." His head was shaking. "I can't . . .
Where'd you get this?"

"It was given to me. Now I'm giving it to you."

"Why? Meriel, this is something even most Riocha
don't have; you can't give this to me."

"Why not?" she told him. "From what I've seen,
you're a better person than most of them, and as skilled
a cloudmage."

"*You* should have this. A Cloch Mór instead of that
clochmion . . ."

He tried to hand the stone back to her; she pushed it
away. "I don't *want* it." She said it more forcefully than
she intended, and softened the next words. "Owaine, I
only want Treoraí's Heart. Nothing else."

"This is too much of a gift for me to take." He stared
at the blood-red stone, black in the night.

"It's not a gift," she told him. "It's a burden. Because
it's a Cloch Mór, everyone who sees it will covet it. Because you're not Riocha, those who are of the blood will
think that you don't deserve to hold a Cloch Mór and
will believe they have the right to take it from you with
impunity. If they succeed, then you'll suffer like Doyle
Mac Ard or my mam. That's the 'gift' I'm giving you."

He was still shaking his head, still staring. "I know

this one from the scrolls at Inishfeirm: Blaze. It hasn't been seen since just after the Filleadh. How did you come to have it?"

She closed Owaine's fingers around the stone; this time he didn't resist. "How doesn't matter. All that matters is that it's mine to take or to give away. And now it's yours if you want it." She nodded to the sky. "The mage-lights are full," she said. Multicolored shadows slid over and around them; they could see the colors of the stones in their light. Owaine lifted the chain of his clochmion from around his neck.

"The last thing I did with this was to find you," he said. "Since it was given to me by your mam, it seems fitting to let you find someone else to give it to." He dropped the clochmion into her hand; as he did so, he hunched over, his forehead creasing with deep lines as he sucked in his breath with a cry. "It hurts, more than I thought," he said, almost with surprise. "It's like I just cut off my own arm." He tightened his hand around the Cloch Mór and Meriel saw the lines in his forehead slowly ease as he straightened. "That's better," he said. He lifted his hand to the sky and the mage-lights began to dance and swirl above him.

Meriel slipped Owaine's clochmion into her pocket and took up Treoraí's Heart, opening the cloch as she lifted it to the lights. The gem sucked hungrily at the power, filling the glittering hollows within her clochvision and sending a deep, icy satisfaction through herself.

For the moment, that was enough.

41

A Temptation

TWIN DEMONS tore at his soul with filthy talons, gibbering with the faces of his mam and da as he half walked, half dragged himself down the hill toward the river. "You failed us!" they roared as one. "You failed us!" He sobbed like a child at their accusations.

"I'm sorry," he wept. "Please, just take me. Kill me. Don't make me suffer this way . . ." But Maeve and Padraic only laughed, tearing strips of Doyle's living flesh away from bone but leaving him miserably alive. He reached the fens and they vanished in a hot wind that scoured his raw, bleeding skin with desert sand. He looked up with bloodshot, ruined eyes at the bridge. He forced himself to move toward it even as light glinted from a massive, winged body rising alongside.

Dragonfire erupted from a yellow scaled snout and the flames played over his body as he pulled himself over the bridge leading to the village. He screamed, his flesh turning black with boils and the odor of his own charred flesh filling his nostrils as he staggered toward the tavern where Edana lay. Dark shapes came running toward him, wearing the faces of the dead, rotting flesh falling away from white skulls; he pushed at the apparitions even as they took him, wailing. The sound of his distress ripped the tapestry of the world and he fell away into the void beyond. His da was there, immense and gigantic, and he took Doyle in one huge fist, his fingers crushing Doyle's chest. His eyes were moons, his mouth a yawning crevasse, and his breath a hurricane. "So this is the son I never knew," Padraic said. The disappointment in his voice was honed to a razor's edge, and each word was the stroke of a dagger through Doyle's heart. "You're nothing but a shadow of me, a poor sad imitation. Doyle . . ."

"Da, I only tried to get what was yours."

The eyes shut, a furious, fast eclipse. The face seemed to recede, falling away from him. "Doyle . . ."

"Da, I'm sorry . . ." But his da was gone and Doyle opened his eyes, blinking at the pain of the light.

"Doyle . . ."

"Shay?" Tiarna O Blaca was leaning over him. Doyle was lying in a bed in a room he didn't recognize, and someone else bustled about in one corner fiddling with vials arrayed on a small table. "Where . . . ?"

"You're in some foul inn in Ballintubber," O Blaca told him. "And safe as you can be for the moment. I brought in the local healer, not that I think his potions did any good." O Blaca scowled at the man behind the table, who gathered up his bottles, plunged them clinking into a leather pouch, and scurried out of the room. The sound of the door shutting made Doyle wince.

"Edana?"

"She's here also, and the same as she was." O Blaca went to the door, opened it and peered left and right, then closed it again. When he returned to sit on a stool by the bed, his voice was hushed. "Doyle, what happened up there? I saw the lights flashing on the horizon all the way in Lár Bhaile, but Quickship was empty and the mage-lights didn't come, and so I had to ride here. What happened?"

Haltingly, pausing frequently for water and rest, Doyle told O Blaca the tale. "I *had* Lámh Shábhála," he said finally. "I had it in my very hands, Shay. But Ó Riain and that damned Toscaire . . ." He stopped, licking dry and cracked lips, feeling the sense of loss weighing on him. The grief was worse than when his mam had died;

the inner torment was real and palpable, and he found himself weeping. "They took Snapdragon, too. By the Mother, Shay, the pain . . . It's worse than I believed it could be . . ."

"I'm sorry," O Blaca said, but there was a reserve in his voice, an aloofness that made Doyle's eyebrows lower over his eyes.

"What is it?" he asked. "What else is wrong?"

"Godfist, Weaver, and Sharpcut are gone, too; Nyle, Alaina, and Shéfra are dead, so is your cousin Aghy— we found them on the mountain." Shay pressed his lips together, frowning. "That's not even the worst of it," he continued. "I spoke with the Rí Mallaghan before I left. He gave me two messages to give you, depending on what I found here. I won't need to tell you the first, since you don't have Lámh Shábhála. And the second . . ."

"Tell me."

"It was simple. He said to tell you this: 'At the end of the ficheall game, the losing Rí is always dead.'"

Doyle gave a laugh that turned into a protracted and phlegm-racked cough. "I suppose that's clear enough. When are you supposed to do the deed? Should I hand you my sword or would you prefer to use your own?"

O Blaca shifted uncomfortably on his seat. "I was only told to report back to the Rí—I assume that if any of the Rí's gardai find you in Tuath Gabair, they'll have orders to—" He stopped. Took a breath. "The Rí also said: 'Tell Doyle that a good player knows when he's lost and topples the piece himself.' And then he told me that if you decided to take a more honorable and permanent path rather than to live in perpetual shame, I should bring your Cloch Mór back to the Order for a more worthy cloudmage."

"I'm surprised you brought in the healer for me, Shay. Maybe I would have conveniently died for you if you'd left me alone."

A shrug. "You've been my student and then my friend, Doyle. I needed to know if the game was really over first. You couldn't tell me in the state you were in."

"And if I tell you it's *not* over?"

"Then I take my time returning to Rí Mallaghan, and perhaps I'll report to him that you'd already left Ballin-tubber heading for Infochla and your family's holdings when I arrived there, when in fact you take the High Road south to Locha Léin. Tiarna Salia will take you in, at least for a time."

"You'd do that for me?"

A nod.

"You're a good friend, Shay. I'm sorry for what I said earlier. I expected the crows would be coming in to feed . . ." He would have given a wry smile, but the pain racked him again, tightening every muscle in his body, and he groaned.

O Blaca stood. He frowned down at Doyle. "But this is the last thing I can do for you as a friend. And I'm sorry, Doyle, but you have to leave soon. The mage-lights will come tonight; when they do, I'll have to return to Lár Bhaile and give that report. Once I do, I don't know how hard and how fast Rí Mallaghan will send people out looking for you. You lost three Clochs Mór to Ó Riain and Dún Laoghaire, and that means that Ó Riain holds the power in the Tuatha now—so I suspect Rí Mallaghan will be feeling rather vengeful."

"And you, Shay? What are you feeling?"

The frown deepened under O Blaca's dark beard as he pressed his lips together before replying. His eyes glinted hard and cold as marbles. "You may have de-stroyed everything that we've created in the Order of Gabair. I don't know that the Order will survive this crisis and the loss of our clochs na thintrí. I do know that to have any chance, we'll have to appear loyal to the Rí Ard once he's named—and it will be Enean, and Ó Riain will be the Regent Guardian. I'm not the ficheall player that you or Rí Mallaghan are, but I would say that only a foolish player continues a game that's obviously lost, and only a bigger fool continues to follow him." He strode across to the room to the door again, putting his hand on the bronze handle there. "I'm not a fool," he said.

O Blaca opened the door and went out. He closed the door behind him with exaggerated care.

Getting out of the bed was torture. Doyle's body protested every move, and when he stood, the darkness threatened to take him again and he thought he heard the dark laughter of his mam, mocking him. There was a gnawing hunger and craving in his belly, but it was nothing that could be eased by food or drink. His hands shook with it; his body trembled with the need.

He managed to open the door after two attempts. There was no one in the hall; the gardai that Aghy had brought with him were gone. Doyle went to the door to Edana's room. He hammered on the door, leaning against the planks. "It's Tiarna Mac Ard," he shouted. "Let me in."

The elderly maidservant opened the door, fright written on her lined and puckered face, worry widening her rheumy eyes. "Tiarna! I'm so glad to see you. There's been such commotion. All that noise and light on the mountain last night, then the gardai left when those horrible wolves and wild people tore through the village and we heard that the young tiarna was killed and you'd been hurt . . ."

Doyle said nothing, pushing past her and going to the bed where Edana lay. "She stirred last night during all the commotion on the mountain," the servant said behind him. "I thought she was going to wake, I did. I went to her, of course, and held her and talked to her. I could tell she heard me. I thought—"

"For the Mother's sake, woman, shut up and leave us!" Doyle shouted at her. The servant's eyes widened even further and a hand went to her mouth. She fled at the sight of Doyle's face.

He turned back to Edana. There were faint lines on her forehead, as if she were troubled in her sleep. Her arms were at her sides; her Cloch Mór lay on her chest.

Her Cloch Mór . . .

The hunger deepened in his gut. Sweat beaded on his forehead, ran down into his beard. The trembling in his hands increased.

She may never wake up. The person that was Edana may be already dead. That may be only the shell of her body laying there left behind like the husk of a locust. She would want you to have the stone, if that were the case. She would hand it to you if she could. Listen, and you can hear her spirit saying the words . . .

Without realizing it, his hand had gone to the silver-caged jewel of Demon-Caller. His fingers brushed the clear facets veined with purest red, and he could feel the power within it. He could imagine the relief that would flood through him, warm and comforting, once he slipped the chain from around her neck and closed his hand around the cloch to claim it as his own.

All the pain would be gone. He would be part of the mage-lights again. He could seek his revenge for what had been done to him.

If the theft bequeathed the torture he felt now to Edana, what of it? She was already lost. If her face reflected the pain, then it would be a mercy to take the breath from her body and end this sham of a life. Her soul would be grateful for the release; the Mother-Creator Herself would thank him.

Edana would *want* him to have the cloch. His revenge would be hers as well.

The links of the chain were cold on his fingertips. Beneath her léine, he could feel her chest rising and falling. Her mouth twisted as he lifted the chain, Demon-Caller hanging heavy from it. Edana moaned behind dry lips and a hand lifted slightly from the covers before falling back. Eyes fluttered under closed lids. "I'm sorry," he told her.

All that remained was to lift her head and remove the chain.

He stopped. His hands shook, the tremor so violent that the chain slipped from his fingers. His knees folded; he collapsed alongside the bed. *"No!"* he screamed into the fiery, pounding torment. It filled his head, searing, and the apparition of his da threatened to rise from the orange-yellow haze. *"No!"*

Shivering, groaning helplessly, he pushed himself up again. He stood, swaying with eyes closed, trying to push away the stabbing pain in his temples and gut. "I can do this," he said to the image of his parents. "Aye, I can . . ."

He leaned over Edana. He touched his lips to hers. He stroked the hair at her temples. "Come back, Edana," he told her. "Please come back. I need you."

There was no answer. He took a long shuddering breath and stood back, waiting until the room stopped spinning around him. He could still see Demon-Caller glittering between Edana's breasts. He clenched his fists at his sides, unable to stop them from shaking. Turning away with a visible effort, he went to the door and called to the old woman, pacing nervously in the corridor outside.

"Get her ready," he told her. "We'll be leaving in a few stripes."

PART FOUR

TRAITOR

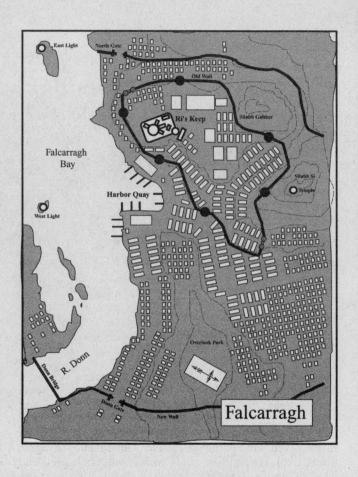

Falcarragh

42

Meeting in the Woods

THEY didn't travel as Riocha, with a carriage and rich trappings and gardai riding alongside. Doyle sold Aghy's horses and carriage to the inn's owner, taking in exchange a sway-backed mare and a ramshackle wagon. Using his dagger, he chopped his long hair close and took his beard down to stubble; he had the servant cut off Edana's tresses as well, leaving her hair disheveled and matted. Edana lay on the wagon on a bed of straw, her fine clothing replaced with simple, undyed cloth and the Cloch Mór hidden underneath. The old woman—whose name he learned was Paili—sat with her; Doyle walked alongside the mare.

They left Ballintubber in the late afternoon. Shay O Blaca emerged from the tavern door to watch them pass; he said nothing to Doyle.

They walked south along the High Road to the Mill Creek, crossing the stream at the foot of Knobtop. Doyle kept his gaze firmly averted from the steep slopes and truncated, rocky summit. He forced his feet to move: one step, then another, watching the dust rise to coat the tattered sandals he wore. He walked like an aged, infirm man. He shuffled along with shoulders bowed and head down, as if the Miondia, the lesser gods who delight in tormenting the living, had heaped a lifetime of abuse and sorrow on him and broken him under it.

It was very easy to pretend. All he had to do was listen to the unending pain inside him.

The road moved slowly under their feet. The sun dropped westward and the shadows of Doire Coill lengthened toward the road. When darkness came, they moved off the road to the east, away from the gnarled oaks that were uncomfortably near. Doyle lit a small, cheerless fire and cooked a thin stew of coney meat and breadroot. As they were eating, the mage-lights began to brush the sky with their luminous hues. Doyle gazed stubbornly down at his plate but the lights gnawed at him.

He imagined Ó Riain, somewhere out under this same sky, holding Lámh Shábhála up to the lights and opening the cloch to himself. He thought of Snapdragon in Toscaire Rhusvak's hand.

With a cry of disgust, Doyle swept the plate off his knees. He hunched over, holding his stomach and retching as the mage-lights strengthened and sent wavering, colorful shadows over the ground. He didn't dare go to Edana, afraid that the temptation of Demon-Caller would be too great for him with the mage-lights flowing above. Setting his jaw and ignoring the cruel pounding in his head, he walked away from the encampment, waving away the cry of alarm from Paili. Not too far south, he could see the swirls of colors coiling like bright thunderheads—evidently someone with a cloch was out there somewhere, replenishing his or her stone. He remembered how it was: connected with the mage-lights, he had been part of a larger whole. Even as they wrapped around his hand as he held Snapdragon, he could sense the tug of others feeding on that same well of energy, had felt the web of all the cloch na thintrí and could even detect, at a distance, the great tidal pull of Lámh Shábhála who had opened the way for the rest of them.

Now, he felt nothing. The mage-lights were a pretty display in the sky, that's all: unreachable, aloof, a reminder of everything he'd lost. They mocked him. The longing and yearning to be part of them again coursed through him as if knives were circulating through his body rather than blood. He sat down heavily on the dew-damp grass and covered his face with his hands until the sheets of light between the stars faded. Then he stumbled back to the cart where Edana and Paili slept. He lay down alongside Edana, listening to Paili's snores.

He slept very little that night.

Doyle woke up in the morning scratching at the fleas and vermin that had crawled into his clothes from the straw in the wagon. The sky spat rain from scudding dark clouds and a looming darkness to the west threatened more. The oilcloth roof over the cart was tattered and thin, and large, persistent drops pooled underneath, gathering and falling. His mouth tasted foul and the water in their skins was stale and bitter. There were no fine clean clothes he could don, no servants to attend to him, no breakfast awaiting, no perfumes, no oil for his hair. There was only a sad, ancient horse to be hitched to the cart and a long, miserable, and nearly hopeless road ahead.

The road that followed the west side of Lough Lár was less traveled and less maintained than that along the eastern shore. There were no large towns on the forest side of the lough, only one sizable village and a few gatherings of a half dozen ramshackle buildings and several farms interrupting the thirty miles of shoreline. Travelers had never been particularly numerous along the road's rutted, grassy length, but in recent years the number had decreased even more.

Before the Filleadh, the coming of the mage-lights, the main danger on that side of the lough had been common bandits and thieves who had taken refuge within the outskirts of Doire Coill, though none of the rogues ever cared to venture far into that forest's heart, for those who did sometimes never returned. Even in slumber, Doire Coill had been a dangerous place. But in those times the forest didn't bother travelers and they came no closer than a few hundred strides from the road, and bandits were readily killed by sword and arrow. The elderly remembered those times fondly, their heads shaking over their stout as they glanced toward the setting sun.

Now the forest had awakened with the Filleadh. Now its outlying trees here and there lifted branches over the road's very edges, and the people who lived between the forest and the lough reported seeing all manner of strange creatures: packs of horse-sized dire wolves, vast herds of storm deer, flocks of wind sprites that would light up entire pastures, and glimpses of other strange and bizarre forms. The trees called loud and strong on windy nights, and sióg mists rolled out from under the oaks with alarming regularity. Ghosts walked in the moonlight, and so did manlike beings who thirsted for the blood of the living. Then there were the Bunús Muintir, who knew the slow magics too well and who hated the Daoine who had nearly destroyed their culture and driven them into hiding.

It was a dangerous time for those who traveled the west of the lough. Even the gardai Rí Mallaghan had assigned to patrol the forest road knew the danger: they'd all seen the horror of one of their own turned to oak; his frozen terror still stood on the road as a warning for all those who saw it.

Doyle had heard of the wooden statue in Lár Bhaile several days before, the tale told to him by a young garda who had just returned from patrol and claimed to have seen it happen. "It was awful, Tiarna Mac Ard. He thrust at her with his spear, a blow that should have ripped entirely through the girl's body, but she just touched him with her staff and the staff went up like lightning, and both Faólan and his horse were caught. There were, oh, a few dozen or more Bunús Muintir with her and they came screaming out of the woods, all of them waving their own staffs. We were outnumbered and they had their terrible magic. We didn't have any choice but to flee. It was horrible!" Doyle had doubted the story at the time.

Now he stared at the truth of it—*"Faólan's Folly, we all call it now, Tiarna . . ."*

Paili wouldn't come near the statue. Doyle didn't know if it was because she was frightened of the statue or because she preferred to sit under the sparse shelter of the cart's oilcloth. "Don't you be touching it, master," she said warningly as he walked up to it in the rain. He ignored her, running his fingertips along the amazingly textured surface, slick and glossy with the drizzle. He could easily believe that horse and rider had once been living. If this had been the work of a sculptor, everyone would have hailed it as a masterpiece. Every detail was there, captured in the oak: the weave and folds of léine and clóca under the leather armor, the belts and straps of the harness, the expression of terror and surprise on the garda's face, the sharp definition of the horse's muscles as it began to rear back. Doyle looked up, blinking into the raindrops: the face of the rider was caught in a moment of sudden fear and surprise, the mouth just opening in what must have been his last shout.

Doyle walked slowly around the captured horse and rider. He glanced toward the nearest trees, no more than a few strides away.

"You there! Get away!"

The shout came from up the road, in the direction from which they'd come. A trio of gardai on horseback had come around the nearest bend in the road, their forms still gray in the mist. Even at that distance, Doyle recognized the one who'd shouted: an officer of the gardai named Bearn whom Doyle had met a few times in Lár Bhaile. The trio cantered up, hooves splashing in the puddle water in the road as Doyle backed away, ducking his head and staring down at the ground like any ordinary tuathánach, not letting them see his face. Bearn came up to him; the other two went to either side of the cart. "That's nothing for you there," the garda snapped at Doyle. He wore a reed coat against the weather; water dripped from the ends. "Keep your filthy hands off that."

"I'm sorry, sir," Doyle mumbled, trying to give his voice the broad rural accent he'd heard in Ballintubber. "I seen it in the rain an' I dinna know . . ."

"Where are you heading on a miserable day like this?" the garda demanded. "Look at me, man." Doyle lifted his head slightly, hoping the dirt and closely-cropped hair would deceive the man. He squinted at Doyle suspiciously, but before Doyle could speak in answer to his question, one of the other men called out from the cart: "Bearn, you should take a look at this . . ."

With a glare at Doyle, the garda yanked at the reins of his horse and went to the cart. Doyle glanced up to see that the other two gardai had dismounted. One was holding Paili's arms; the other pointed to where Edana lay in the back of the cart as the leader rode up. "She'd be a handsome one if you could scrape the dirt off her, don't you think, Bearn? And she didn't stir at all when I nudged her."

Doyle hurried back to the cart. "She's me wife Selli," he told them, "an' she was magicked by an old witch-woman who hated Selli 'cause her husband kept watchin' her. Now she don't wake. I was told there was an herb-woman in Inchigeelagh as could cure her, so me an' her mam Paili are going there . . ." Bearn watched Doyle as he spoke; Doyle kept his head lowered, trying not to let the man see his features clearly. Bearn grunted and dismounted, looking into the cart. He stared for a long time at Edana. Then, with a grunt, he reached over the low rails and grasped the collar of Edana's tunic in a gloved fist. Before Doyle could move or react, he yanked hard. The cloth tore, exposing Edana and the Cloch Mór that lay between her breasts.

"I know you, Tiarna Mac Ard," Bearn said. His gaze went down to Doyle's right hand, and Doyle belatedly pulled his sleeve over the exposed swirl of white scars there. "And my men shall enjoy getting to know Banti-

arna O Liathain as well, I think, after I take the Cloch
Mór. Then perhaps we'll take you all back to Lár Bhaile
for the Rí's judgment."

Doyle had hidden his sword under a rough blanket on
the seat of the cart. He reached carefully under the blanket now with a sense of growing hopelessness and loss.
He had no chance here, not against three gardai in rings
and leather. Doyle's body screamed at the thought of
moving the water-hardened weight of the weapon. *Better
to die here. At least it will all be over . . .*

He drew the sword and swung it at Bearn in one desperate motion.

It was Keira who suggested that they walk down toward
the lough. "Andúilleaf grows best where the soil's moist
and the trees are a bit thinner," she said. "I'm nearly
out of the dried leaf and right now your mam's sleeping.
We should be back before she wakes up again."

Meriel had demurred, saying that she'd wait behind
with her mam—though in fact it was because she didn't
want to see the lough empty of Dhegli's presence and
the day was so dreary and wet. Keira had insisted, however, saying that "three pairs of eyes are better than
one, and the rain won't melt you." Meriel got up with
as much good grace as she could manage and followed
Keira and Owaine back down the meandering path
toward the lough.

"Here," Keira said as they came near the forest's
edge, where the oaks thinned and the brush started to
thicken. Meriel could see the stone fences of the High
Road through one of the gaps between the trees, though
for the most part they were hidden from view. "This is
what andúilleaf looks like," Keira told Meriel and
Owaine, holding out her hand palm up to show them a
small leaf with serrated edges and a small lobe at the
top. "It likes shade and tends to hide under ferns and
the like, since it prefers the same soil. If you're not cer-

tain it's andúilleaf, touch one of the leaves; the plant will curl up as if it were withering before your eyes and you'll smell the same odor you get from an infusion of it. Don't be discouraged if you don't find any—it's a rare plant, and difficult to find, even here where it grows best."

They spread out, moving slowly over the ground, kneeling and crouching in the mud, rain dripping from the branches above. It was wet, dirty work, and—Meriel decided—singularly unrewarding. After a stripe's work or more, she had nothing to show for it but soaked and muddy clothing, hands that were filthy with soil, and several bites from insects who seemed to think she was a roaming breakfast. Keira had found two of the plants and Owaine one small one that Keira had carefully re-planted. "Too young, that one. We'll let it grow some more . . ."

"If she's the only one finding them, why did we have to come along?" Meriel muttered to Owaine as Keira went off again. Owaine grinned and shrugged.

"Practice," he said.

Meriel sniffed at that as Owaine crouched in the mud and starting looking again. She moved off a few feet, brushing dripping curls away from her forehead. From the direction of the road, she heard a shout. Owaine's head had come up; he'd heard it as well. Meriel pushed through the undergrowth in the direction of the road, curious. She stopped alongside one of the young oaks, peering through a gap in the trees as Owaine came up alongside her.

Through the trees, they could see the frozen wooden form of the horse and rider. Near it, a horse-drawn cart had stopped as three gardai rode up. The gardai con-fronted the peasants, dismounting and gathering around the cart, evidently in a discussion with them. Suddenly, one of the peasants reached into the cart and they saw the gleam of a sword in his hand. He swung, but the garda he attacked was quick and had unsheathed his own weapon. They saw the blades meet, then a second later the ring of iron against iron reached their ears. The other two gardai had drawn weapons as well. They heard the shriek of a woman as the peasant retreated, parrying the attack of the garda as his two companions moved to either side, ready to enter the fray.

"That's hardly a fair fight," Keira's voice said from just behind them; neither one of them had heard her approach.

"Can you do something?" Owaine asked the Bunús Muintir. "Some slow magic . . ."

Keira shook her head. "Not from this distance."

"But *you* can, Owaine," Meriel said. The peasant swung his sword again, two-handed, and they could hear the grunt that accompanied it followed by the clash of iron. The other two gardai were laughing now, leaning on their swords and calling out encouragement to their companion. The peasant had gone down on one knee from the impact of the last blow, "You're the only one who can."

"What?" Owaine said, then his eyes widened: "Oh, aye . . ." He reached under the sodden collar of his tunic, taking in his hand the Cloch Mór Meriel had given him. His fingers tightened around the stone. "By the Mother, this feels so much stronger than the clochmion . . ." His eyebrows lowered and Meriel knew that he was no longer seeing only with his own eyes, but also with the power inside the cloch. What happened then surprised Meriel: Owaine raised his hand and scarlet light erupted from it. A trio of fireballs hissed and wailed as they arced away from Owaine trailing smoke. They slammed into earth near the cart: one gouging a hole in the stone wall of the road and sending rock fragments flying; another cratering the middle of the road in a spray of black earth and striking down the decrepit-looking horse reined to the cart; the last hitting the garda as he raised his sword over the peasant. The fireball exploded: an arm pinwheeled away still holding the sword as the man's torso was ripped apart. The bloody, half-corpse remained standing for a second before toppling.

An awful, shocked silence followed. Owaine's mouth was open; Meriel had muffled her shocked cry with a hand. Only Keira moved, walking toward the road from the cover of the trees, her staff raised and an odd ululation coming from her throat.

The remaining two gardai wasted no time goggling at the apparition approaching from the black heart of the forest or waiting for another, perhaps better-aimed burst of magic. They fled. Grabbing the reins of frightened, panicked horses and jumping astride, they galloped north, passing quickly out of sight around the curving road. "Come on!" Keira shouted to Owaine and Meriel. "It's over."

Meriel started to follow, then realized that Owaine wasn't with her. "Owaine?"

He'd released the Cloch Mór, which dangled from its chain. He was staring at his hand. "Owaine?"

His hand dropped. He blinked. A solidity and seriousness she'd not glimpsed in him before set in the lines of his face. "I'm . . . I'm coming," he said.

43

Awakening

THE PEASANT was rising to his feet as they approached, moving as if the effort cost him greatly. He'd dropped the sword and they could see cuts and tears along one side of his body from the rock fragments. He held his arm as if it might be broken. They could see an old woman there as well, a cut along one cheek dripping blood. She screeched at their approach, clambering awkwardly over the stones on the far side of the road. The man didn't move; he stood there, slump-shouldered and swaying as if he were about to collapse.

Meriel caught up with Keira alongside the enchanted horse and rider, the wood of the statue scorched from the blast of the fireball and steaming in the rain. The peasant lifted his head; she stopped. The man's lips curled in a wan smile.

"Hello, Niece," he said. "I suppose I should say it's good to see you again."

Meriel stepped over the wreckage of the wall and the gory remnants of the garda. She stood before him.

She slapped him hard across the face.

She was surprised when he went down with the blow, sprawling in the mud of the road next to the body of the cart's horse. He lay there for a moment before pushing himself up on his elbows. He spat blood.

"This is twice now in the last few days that you've

saved me, Meriel," he said. "I suppose I should be grateful, but somehow that's not what I feel."

She gave him a fierce stare, but she also saw the lines on his dirt-smeared face, the pain that clouded his eyes, the weakness in his limbs. He no longer appeared to be her age; instead, he looked middle-aged and drawn, as if some illness burned deep within him. She turned away as Owaine came up to them. She noticed that he carefully avoided looking at the carnage around them. Keira had gone across the road, calling softly to the old woman to return, who instead bolted for the shore of the lough. Keira sighed and went to the cart.

"Meriel," Keira said. "You should come here."

Doyle swiveled his head around and seemed to notice Keira for the first time. "No!" he shouted. He struggled to rise. "You leave her alone!" Meriel stepped carefully around Doyle to where Keira was standing. She looked into the bed of the cart, where a young woman lay in the straw half-exposed, her clothing torn, and around her neck . . .

"That's a Cloch Mór," Owaine said, coming up. "I know. I felt its presence when I opened mine."

Meriel leaned forward into the cart and pulled the shreds of the woman's tunic over her. She touched the side of her neck. "She's alive, but this isn't a natural sleep."

"Leave her alone!" Doyle shouted again. He'd managed to get to his feet and limped toward them. "That's Edana's cloch."

"Edana? The Bantiarna O Liathain?" Owaine asked. He looked again at the Cloch Mór. "That's Demon-Caller," he said to Meriel. "It used to be the Rí Ard's cloch. Now *that* would be a prize for the Order of Inishfeirm . . ." He reached forward and Doyle wailed, hurling himself at Owaine. Owaine pushed at the man's chest and Doyle went down. Owaine reached for the cloch again, but Meriel touched his arm, stopping him. She shook her head.

"Where are you going dressed like this?" she asked

Doyle. "Why would gardai from Tuath Gabair attack you?"

Doyle had pushed himself up once more, splattered with mud and blood from cuts. He laughed bitterly. "After what happened, I'm hardly in the Rí Gabair's good graces. Quite the opposite, in fact. We were heading for Tuath Locha Léin." He gestured at the dead horse still in the traces of the cart. "Though it looks as if I'll have to carry Edana the rest of the way."

"What's the matter with her?"

"Ask your mam. It's her fault."

Owaine snarled something. Keira only watched, her broad face impassive. Meriel took a breath, not letting herself feel the anger she might have at his tone. "You didn't take Edana's Cloch Mór. You could have."

"And do to her what's been done to me? You don't know me, Bantiarna."

"I know you would have taken Lámh Shábhála from my mam."

"Aye, I would have done that. But I love Edana—she was to be my wife. Your mam . . ." He snorted. "You know the history as well as I do. I can't cause her more pain than she's caused me."

"You can still say that, knowing how you feel now? Knowing that the loss of Lámh Shábhála would be worse?"

Doyle scowled but said nothing.

Meriel glanced at Keira, then again at Edana's still form. She could feel Treoraí's Heart pulling at her as she reached into the cart to touch the young woman's arm. *No*, she wanted to tell the clochmion. *I can't do that again. I nearly lost myself in my mam's madness. She could do the same, mage-snared as she is. I might not find my way out again or be able to help her.*

There was no answer, only the same yearning from the clochmion. Her hand crept toward the gem. "Meriel!" Owaine said warningly, but her fingers touched the stone even as her other hand stroked Edana's arm.

She found herself inside.

There wasn't the blinding maelstrom that had been inside her mam. Here mage-winds howled in the voice of someone lost and trapped, and Meriel felt the panic begin to touch her own mind through her connection with Edana. Meriel moaned and wept, feeling the pain and fear that had driven the woman to this state. Edana crouched inside her own mind, huddled in the dark recesses, and her thoughts mingled with Meriel's. "The lightning," she whimpered. "No more. Please, no more . . ." Around her, the storm still crackled, a looping eternal memory; deeper inside, wrapping around her like dark clouds, were the thoughts and emotions from the moment she'd been trapped. As Meriel became Edana, the emotion buffeted her. She felt them, terribly strong: *She didn't hate the Mad Holder, not like Doyle did with his smoldering loathing. No . . . this was more like killing a wild dog, one that was too dangerous to be left alive. You feared its power and you knew you had to kill it, but you didn't hate it. So strong, so strong . . . Can Doyle handle this power . . . ?* And with the thought of Doyle, there came a feeling of such intense affection and love that Meriel was confused by it, battering against her own loathing of the man. She fell deeper into Edana. *Oh, Mother, I don't think we can defeat her. Don't think I can hold on. Too strong . . .* and then there was a flash of pain so terrible that Meriel screamed, her vision filling with white heat and she felt the last dregs of Demon-Caller's energy fall as Lámh Shábhála tore at her and sent her spinning away . . . falling . . . falling . . .

Meriel/Edana sat in a dark space far, far inside, and remembered lightnings flared all around her. She felt herself holding them away by sheer will, knowing that if they came to her, she would finally die. Meriel fought to retain herself separate from the woman.

"Let me have the storm," she whispered to herself, to Edana. "Let me take the lightning away from you." She felt a sudden faint hope rise within her. "Aye," she said. "We can take the storm away, together. Doyle wants us to come back. He's there. He's waiting."

The hope inside her strengthened. Edana's mind shifted and the memory-storm raced toward Meriel/Edana with a roar. She forced herself to stay there, to let it strike her. She screamed as the lightning flickered around her and fought not to curl into a fetal ball. *It's only a memory, not actually Lámh Shábhála. It's not real. None of this is real. . . .*

The pain was real, however, and it burned and seared her even as Edana cried with relief, even as—with her true eyes—she saw Edana stir, her mouth opening in a gasp, her eyes flying open.

Meriel found herself sagging in Owaine's arms, the vestiges of Edana's turmoil fading in the rain.

"Doyle?" Edana said, her voice ragged and weak. "Where's Doyle? I've been gone so long. . . ."

"Meriel, I'm sorry, but this is stupid," Owaine said when Meriel suggested that Doyle and Edana come into Doire Coill with them. "These are our enemies. You realize that Edana was part of the attack on your mam? By the Mother, Meriel, the woman has a Cloch Mór!"

"Keira doesn't mind," she replied. "And her Cloch Mór's empty. Right now, they can't do much to hurt us."

"It's not 'right now' I'm worried about," Owaine retorted. "It's later."

"Owaine . . ."

He shook his head. "No, you don't have to say anything. I just want you to know how I feel."

"And I do," she said. She smiled at him. Her fingers brushed his hand, taking it in hers. "I know how you feel. I do understand." She looked at him, wondering if he knew what she was saying.

His eyes narrowed.

"I haven't treated you well or listened to you, Owaine," she told him. "I'm sorry for that. But I need you to trust me now in this." He'd pressed his hand around hers. For a few breaths, Owaine stared at her.

"I can see, and I have a Cloch Mór. I'd say you've given me more than I could ever expect."

"Owaine—"

He shook his head. "You don't need to say anything Meriel. I don't want you to say anything." He released her hand then.

They'd followed Keira back into the forest and to the cave where Jenna slept.

"You can't heal your mam the way you did me?"

Meriel shook her head at Edana's question. "It's not the same," she said. "Lámh Shábhála is the strongest of the clochs na thintrí and she held it for years. The loss, the grief, is so strong . . ." Meriel shuddered, remembering what she'd felt inside her mam's mind. "I was able to bring her back to consciousness, and even that was something I wouldn't want to attempt again."

"But you did. With me."

Meriel lifted a shoulder. "Aye. But you had your Cloch Mór when you awoke. Mam didn't. Lámh Shábhála's gone."

"So for Doyle, too . . ." Her voice trailed off as she glanced at him.

She would have tried. She reached for the cloch, but Doyle shook his head—a quick, choppy back-and-forth—the suffering on his face mingled with distaste as he glared at Meriel. Meriel knew that if she offered to try to help him, he would refuse.

She brought her hand back down to her lap. "I could ease his physical wounds, perhaps," Meriel said, "but nothing I can do would replace the cloch he's lost. I can't do anything about that pain."

Edana nodded; Doyle looked down and away again. The rain had stopped with the sunset and the clouds had begun to part, showing the stars. They were seated outside Keira's cavern, eating a dinner of spring water, berries, and smoked meat that Keira had brought out.

There was no fire—Keira would allow no fire out here in the open where the trees could see and feel it. The Bunús Muintir went back inside to watch Jenna. Doyle sat next to Edana, and Owaine stared grimly at the man next to Meriel, his hand significantly close to the Cloch Mór around his neck, ready to act if Doyle made any aggressive move.

Edana closed her eyes and Meriel saw the flicker of remembered pain pass across her face. "I will always be grateful to you," the young woman said. "I was lost and you brought me back." Her eyes opened again, finding Meriel's gaze. "I'll never understand why."

"I can't tell you what I don't know myself," Meriel answered.

"You should know this—the decision to take you hostage—"

"Edana!" Doyle said sharply, speaking for the first time since they'd arrived at the cave. "Don't."

Edana shook her head as she glanced at him, and she smiled softly, touching his hand. "No, Doyle. She deserves to know." She looked back at Meriel, though her hand stayed on Doyle's. "Taking you hostage was my idea. I suggested it first. I knew that you were the only possible thing that could cause the Mad . . . your mam to give up Lámh Shábhála."

Meriel stared. Thoughts roiled inside her, too many and too unfocused for her to speak.

"I didn't know you," Edana continued. "You were just a name. Just the daughter of the Banrion First Holder. I could put you into danger because I didn't know you. Now . . ." She glanced at Doyle as she spoke. "I owe you my life and Doyle's. We won't betray you. I promise you that much."

Owaine sniffed suspiciously; Doyle said nothing. He'd been nearly silent since Edana had awakened, and Meriel could guess nothing of what he might be thinking.

A hint of color wafted between the stars directly overhead. All of them looked up at the same moment, drawn to the sight. Meriel saw Owaine's hand go to his cloch.

Edana's hand lifted as well, then stopped as she noticed Meriel watching her. "I won't betray you," she said again. "But I won't fill Demon-Caller if that's what you want."

Owaine shook his head when Meriel glanced at him. But she also saw the yearning on Edana's face and she remembered the horror that had held her for so long. "I trust your word," she said to Edana. "Go ahead. Take Demon-Caller."

The three of them stood, opening their clochs to the mage-lights as the sky-dance sent bars of light moving over the hillside. Doyle remained seated, huddled in on himself with his head down. Meriel let the cold energy fill Treoraí's Heart, sighing as the clochmion took the power into itself. She could feel, well to the east, Lámh Shábhála's presence, also open to the mage-lights. They *all* felt it, and they all looked that way in anger.

Too soon, the mage-lights faded and they sat once more. Edana took Doyle's hand. "Doyle and I can't stay here," she said. "We can't hide here forever. And neither can you."

"What are you saying, Bantiarna?" Meriel asked.

"Tiarna Ó Riain stole Lámh Shábhála from your mam and Snapdragon from Doyle. He's also duped my brother and taken away a title that should have been mine. All of us here have reason to hate him. He is the enemy of each of us."

"We all have reasons to hate each other, also," Owaine interjected. "Perhaps more reasons than we have to hate Ó Riain."

For the second time, Doyle stirred. His thin, drawn face lifted. "Aye," he said. "But perhaps at this point we make better allies than enemies."

44

Stirrings of War

"LOOK what I have for the new Rí," Ó Riain said as he entered Enean's chambers. Enean clapped his hands with delight at the thought of a gift; Nuala, now Enean's wife, set down her sewing on her lap but didn't move from her seat. Her gaze was flat and suspicious; under her léine, her belly was beginning to round with the child she carried. Ó Riain brought a cloch out from under his clóca, the stone caught in a new silver cage and hung on a wide, ornate chain. "Every Rí should have a Cloch Mór," Ó Riain continued. "Since Edana stole the one that should have been yours, I've acquired this one to give you."

"It's so beautiful . . ." Enean held out his hand and Ó Riain dropped the gem in his hand and let the chain pool around it. Enean took it and held it up to his chest, turning so that Nuala could see it. "Look, Nua. See what Labhrás has brought me. . . ."

Nuala could sense Ó Riain watching her. She kept her face carefully neutral, allowing herself to smile. She knew that Cloch Mór—any acolyte of the Order would have known it. The color of the stone, the shape . . . *It's Weaver, the cloch that Alaina was given. Oh, Mother, what has happened . . . ?* She also knew the smaller stone that adorned Tiarna Ó Riain's chest, the one that made her want to gape in astonishment.

Lámh Shábhála. The Tiarna is holding the first cloch. . . .

She felt a stab of fear touch her swelling stomach. If Alaina was dead, then so also might be Tiarna Mac Ard or the others of the Order, and she must look to her own safety. She knew that Tiarna Ó Riain had his own choice for Enean's wife and had been visibly upset when Enean had made his preference obvious. And the truth was that Nuala found that she liked Enean well enough. He was gentle with her and protective, and if he sometimes seemed to forget her name and call her Sorcha— the name of his dead fiancée—she could overlook that.

But she had no illusions about the situation. Especially now. If something happened to her—and with Tiarna Ó Riain holding Lámh Shábhála, that now seemed far too likely—Tiarna Ó Riain's niece Toiréasa De Danaan would be in Nuala's place as soon as custom and propriety would allow.

Enean was still holding the stone out toward her. "That's wonderful, Enean," she said, trying to hide the tremble in her voice. "I wonder where Tiarna Ó Riain acquired such prizes?" She gave them both the same smile. "You're fortunate to have such a generous Regent Guardian, Enean. Especially one who has the strength to hold Lámh Shábhála."

"Lámh Shábhála?" Enean burst out as Ó Riain raised eyebrows at Nuala. "Is that really Lámh Shábhála?"

"Aye, 'tis," Ó Riain said, though his glance lingered on Nuala too long for her comfort.

"You defeated the Mad Holder, Labhrás?"

"Aye, I did," Ó Riain answered. "Two nights ago, well to the west. She and her cloudmages had come into Tuath Gabair, and I learned of it. I was there to meet her with my cloch and others, as was my duty to you, Enean, as your Regent Guardian." He gave a long sigh, waving his hand. "The struggle was incredible, my Rí, and there will be tales about the terrible lightnings on the mountain generations from now, but finally we prevailed, though many fell. We defeated her and I took

Lámh Shábhála, but only just in time. There were creatures from out of Doire Coill who came to protect her,
awful things from the night, and we had to flee for our
lives without capturing the Banrion."

Enean seemed to have stopped listening somewhere
during the tale. His scarred face twisted as if he were
puzzled. "Shouldn't the Rí have Lámh Shábhála?"
Enean asked. He plucked at the Cloch Mór around his
neck.

"Aye, perhaps you should," Ó Riain told him. "But,
Enean, I had no choice. If I hadn't taken Lámh Shábhála, we would all have died. Wolfen, my old cloch . . .
it was exhausted and useless after the struggle. To save
us, I had to take Lámh Shábhála for myself. And
now . . ." He clasped hands over the gem. "Enean, I
can't give up Lámh Shábhála. It would kill me. Ask your
wife. She knows."

They were both looking at her. "It's true," Nuala answered. She lowered her head so that she didn't need to
meet Ó Riain's eyes. The colors of the sewing thread
blurred on her lap. "Losing Lámh Shábhála would drive
the Holder insane. The pain of the loss is said to be nearly
impossible to bear. I was taught that at the Order of Gabair. The Regent Guardian wouldn't be able to give up
Lámh Shábhála once he took it." She raised her head,
carefully looking only at Enean. "You harm *any* cloudmage
greatly when you take their Cloch Mór," she said. *If Alaina's cloch was taken, who else's might he have?* She wondered if the Order of Gabair even existed now.

At the edges of her vision, a faint satisfaction smoothed
Ó Riain's face. "You see, Enean," Ó Riain continued,
"even though I wanted to give Lámh Shábhála to you,
I *had* to take it or it would have fallen back into the
Mad Holder's possession and everything would have
been lost. Now . . ." His hands lifted. Fell. "I can't give
it up. It won't allow me."

Enean was scowling, the long and jagged scar white
on his face. The burning knot in Nuala's throat grew
larger; she could feel the dangerous annoyance in her

husband, the childish, impulsive rage that sometimes overcame him. Everything had changed now, she realized: Lámh Shábhála had altered her world and she could only try to save herself. "Enean," Nuala said soothingly, "Tiarna Ó Riain is telling you the truth and you have to believe him." She put the sewing aside and went to Enean, stroking his muscular back and putting her head on his chest, placing herself carefully between Enean and Ó Riain. "Remember, your da wore a Cloch Mór and he was the finest and most respected Rí Ard in many generations. You'll be like him when the Ríthe meet for the Óenach again and give you that title. Very soon now. Your da would have been so proud to see you put the golden torc of the Ard around your neck. It's what he would have wanted."

Her voice calmed him, as she'd hoped. She could feel him relax under the influence of her hands and her voice. Her own position was precarious, but she knew that Enean's now was just as insecure. Being Enean's "Regent Guardian" while allowing Enean the title of Rí Dún Laoghaire had been convenient and politically expedient. But now, holding the great cloch . . . if Tiarna Ó Riain felt that Enean was beyond his control or was actively interfering with his plans, she was certain that some accident would befall her husband, and Ó Riain would claim the power that was already his in all but title.

She looked up and her gaze met Ó Riain's. "We should be glad that Lámh Shábhála is in the hands of someone who loves you as much as I do," she said to Enean.

"As indeed I do, my Rí," Ó Riain said quickly with a strange, lopsided smile. "And I will use the power that's been given me to make certain that you receive all that you deserve."

Enean was smiling now, his mood shifting with childish rapidity. "Thank you, Labhrás," he said, plucking at the cloch on its chain. "You're a good friend. I'm sorry I got angry."

"You needn't concern yourself with that," Ó Riain said. He approached them, putting one hand on Enean's shoulder, the other on Nuala's. She forced herself not to flinch. "Tonight, when the mage-lights come, we'll fill our clochs together and perhaps your wife can teach you some of what she learned of the art of the cloudmage, eh?" His voice dropped to a conspiratorial baritone. "It's time the world learned just how powerful you are, Enean. First, we show those on Inish Thuaidh how foolish they were to follow the Mad Holder. Then, when they've bowed to our will, we take our armies and our clochs na thintrí and follow the Toscaire Concordia east to drive the Arruk from Céile Mhór. And who knows, after that is done, perhaps there will be new Tuatha who bow to the Rí Ard in Dún Laoghaire."

"And I'll be the Rí Ard over it all," Enean said. Nuala could see him caught up in Ó Riain's vision, imaging himself in that future.

Ó Riain laughed then, and the self-satisfaction in it made Nuala shiver even as she pretended to smile with Enean. "Of course you will be," Ó Riain said smugly. "The strongest person must always be Rí Ard. . . ."

They shook dust from the earth with booted feet and pounding hooves. The choking swirls rose over them like a dun cloud and their line, stretching for a mile or more, filled the High Road like brightly-clad ants swarming to a nest.

"That's the fourth group I've seen heading north in the last two days," Owaine said. His voice startled Meriel from the half-trance into which she'd fallen, sitting on the slope at the edge of Doire Coill. "The Tuatha are going to war. The question is, against whom?" He sat carefully a few feet from her with a sound of rustling dry leaves that was strangely louder than the distant clattering and pounding of the passing troops. "You shouldn't be out here alone."

"And you came to protect me?" She gentled the comment with a quick smile. She found that she wished he'd sat closer—so she could feel his warmth on a chilly day, she told herself. "Owaine . . ."

"What?"

She shook her head. "Nothing." Her attention returned to the army passing between Doire Coill and Lough Lár. "They're in the green and brown of Tuath Gabair, mostly, but I've seen other colors as well, from most of the Tuatha. Look, that tiarna on horseback and the gardai alongside him are wearing Connachta's colors. If Gabair is marching with Connachta, then the Tuatha aren't warring against each other. And they're going north."

Owaine finished the thought for her. "To Tuath Infochla and the port of Falcarragh, and from there to Inish Thuaidh."

"Aye. And this time, Lámh Shábhála will be riding against Inish Thuaidh and her cloudmages, not with them." Even if she'd never experienced war, Meriel could imagine it all too well: the smoke of the battle, the fires in Dún Kiil, the keep shattered under the assault of thousands of soldiers, the flaring energies of the Clochs Mór sparking all around. Those she knew and loved would be there, grimly defending their land: her da, Bantiarna Aithne and the rest of the Comhairle, Máister Kirwan, Súir Meagher, all the cloudmages of the Order . . . and they would—they *must*—fall, all of them. She could see their bloodied faces, their twisted forms lying on the shattered rocks of Inish Thuaidh.

She must have shivered, must have made some sign, for Owaine scooted over to her and his arm went around her. She looked over at him. "I'm sorry—" he began and started to withdraw, but she took his hand and held it against her shoulder.

"It's all right. It's . . . fine for now." She leaned into his embrace, wanting the comfort of it against the cold vision inside her. "Keira sent crows to Dún Kiil this morning," Owaine said. "I wrote the notes for her, telling them to prepare for war and letting them know that Jenna is here and that Lámh Shábhála has been lost. We don't know if they'll arrive, since Doyle told us how they sent a false crow to trap your mam, but it's all I could think to do."

"Inish Thuaidh can't stand against this," Meriel said, the dark vision still vivid before her.

"No," Owaine agreed, "but we Inishlanders are stubborn and proud and we know our land. We'll retreat to the mountains and caves and hidden places, and we'll come from the darkness like ghosts to ambush the invaders wherever and whenever we can. They might claim the stones, but their blood will stain it for long generations and it will never truly be theirs. And one day, one day, we'll rise and drive them out again."

She could hear the fierceness in his voice, the angry pride of his ancestors singing in the words. His arms tightened around her shoulders, and she curled her own arm around his waist, wanting to believe him, wanting to take some solace and optimism from his words. But the vision wouldn't leave her and he spoke only of more death.

"Edana and my uncle are right," she said. "We need to work together now."

"With that bastard Mac Ard? If he'd succeeded, your mam would be dead and *he'd* be out there at the head of the armies." With his free hand, he gestured at the army crawling before them. "Edana's Cloch Mór would be right alongside him, too. And don't forget that it's her brother who's one of the Ríthe, and most likely to be the new Rí Ard. Where do you think her loyalty would go, if it came to a choice?"

"Right now what Doyle and Edana want is what we want."

"What Doyle wants is to have Lámh Shábhála himself."

"He can't have that," Meriel said firmly. "That's Mam's. But . . ." She could see the train of the army now, a bedraggled caravan of wagon and retainers following in the wake of the soldiers. "I would give him back the Cloch Mór that was taken from him for the promise that he would never try to take Lámh Shábhála again. I believe he would keep his word once he gives it. And I believe Edana's word, as well."

"That's not what your mam believes. She refuses to even see Mac Ard."

"I know. She's wrong in this, though."

"Must you always see the good in people?"

Meriel almost laughed at that. *See the good in people? I think I usually see the opposite.* The lough glimmered beyond the green cover of the trees and the trudging line of the army, and nothing moved on its waters but a few fishing boats. "Don't make me out to be like one of those Mother-touched people, Owaine. I'm not." She scooted away from him slightly, turning inside the half circle of his arm so she faced him. She looked into his face: so plain, and yet, now that she looked . . . "It took me far too long to see all the good in you, Owaine. I was the one with a flawed vision, not you. You're the one who stayed with me, even when I didn't show you much encouragement. After the way I treated you in Inishfeirm . . ."

Muscles tugged at the corner of his mouth. "You treated me better than most of the others."

Meriel shook her head. "No, I didn't, Owaine. I saw the same thing they saw when I looked at you, because I was looking at you with the eyes of the Riocha. Even here, I was still doing the same."

He was staring at her, close enough that for the first time she noticed the flecks of gold in the irises of those brown eyes, that she saw the unmasked affection for her in his face and wondered why she hadn't returned it. With Lucan, with Thady, with Dhegli . . . with them there'd been an intense flare of interest, a searing spark that ignited seemingly the first moment she'd seen them. With Owaine, there had never been such a spark; there had been only a slow, grudging movement toward friendship and trust and appreciation.

But she wondered, now, if there couldn't somehow be more because of that. There was a solidity to Owaine that had been missing with Dhegli, that had never been there at all with Lucan or Thady.

She leaned toward him. She wondered if the touch of his lips would be soft or fierce.

A crow cawed loudly, landing next to them in a loud thrashing of midnight wings, and Meriel moved back, startled. It cawed again, cocking its head to one side as it peered at first Meriel, then Owaine. It hopped backward, turning as it did so. Glancing back at them, it opened its mouth and cried at them once more before launching itself back into the air and landing on a branch a few feet away to stare at them.

"Keira must want us," Owaine said. He hadn't moved. She could feel his hand on her back, his fingers slowly traversing the valley of her spine.

"Owaine," Meriel started to say, but the crow shrieked once more, fluttering its wings impatiently. Outside the wood, the army continued to snake its way through the landscape. She could have leaned back toward him, could have let it happen, but the moment dissolved. Meriel took a breath as Owaine's hand dropped away. He stood abruptly, holding his hand out to her.

"We should go," he said. "Keira wouldn't send the crow unless it was important."

Meriel took his hand, letting him help her to her feet. Doubts assailed her again: *You're too different: a changeling, a Riocha and Bantiarna, the daughter of the Banrion of Inish Thuaidh and the First Holder. This feeling's come only because you've been thrust together out here. You'd be bored with him, once you're back in Dún Kiil . . .* From the east came a din of clanging steel and the shouting of soldiers as an armorer's wagon lurched and rocked over the rutted High Road. The sound was that of war, stretching out and spreading like the gray-black roiling of a thunderhead. It would envelop her, she knew, and with it would come pain and loss, and grief that would only increase the more she entangled her heart with those around her.

She let her hand drop away from Owaine's. The crow, satisfied, flew away with a final cry.

45

Inside the Madness

"IT'S YOUR mam," Keira said as Meriel and Owaine—both breathing hard from the long walk up the slope—approached the mouth of the cave. The Bunús Muintir's face was creased with concern. Past Keira's shoulder, Meriel saw a flash of motion inside the cavern's entrance: Doyle Mac Ard and Edana.

"What are they doing in there?" Meriel asked, unable to keep the suspicion from rising in her voice. "Did he do something to her?"

Doyle slid out of the shadows. He lifted his chin, looking down at her. "I wanted to see her, that's all. I asked Keira if she would bring me in to her. She was with me the whole time."

Edana linked her arm through Doyle's. "Meriel," she said. "It was my idea. I thought . . . I thought we should talk with her, tell how things had changed with us and that . . . that we'd been wrong."

Keira nodded agreement. "Jenna was awake, though groggy with the andúilleaf, and she agreed to see them. Edana went in first and it was fine, then she saw Doyle and . . ." A shrug. "I don't know what happened."

Meriel rushed past Keira before she'd finished speaking. Doyle held out a hand to stop her as Edana bowed her head. "I did nothing to her, Meriel," he said. "Truly. I only wanted to apologize to her." Meriel pushed his hand aside without answering, following the low, wind-

478

ing passage to where it emptied abruptly into the single
large room as Owaine hurried after her. In the flickering
of the peat fire, she saw her mam, standing near her bed
and clutching a blanket to herself. Her hair was disheveled
and matted, her eyes sunken and dark over pinched
cheeks, and she swayed back and forth. For a breath or
two Meriel thought that her mam was singing, until she
realized that the high, continuous keening coming from
her was a whimpering moan, interrupted only when she
paused to breathe. "Mam?"

With the word, Jenna seemed to notice Meriel for the
first time, and she backed away toward the fire. "Stay
away from me!" Her voice was half-screech, half-sob.
"You're one of them. You may pretend to be my daughter,
you may act like you're concerned, but I can see
through you, young woman. I know what you are. I
know what you want."

"What do you think I want, Mam?"

"You want my cloch. *The* cloch. You think I can't see
the puny little clochmion you carry? I know you're jealous
and you want what I have."

"Mam . . ." Meriel started to take a step toward her,
but Jenna backed away again, her clóca and the hem of
the woolen blanket around her dangerously near the
flames. Meriel stopped, her hands out in mute supplication.
She heard Owaine breathing heavily behind her.

"You can't have it!" Jenna's hand clutched together
at her chest, as if she were hiding Lámh Shábhála under
the folds of the blanket.

"I don't want it, Mam. I never wanted it."

Jenna's eyes narrowed, then widened. "You'll take it.
You'll take it from me."

"No, Mam. I won't."

"I can't trust you. I can't trust anyone. They all want
it. They want to take it from me, but they don't understand
how much it *hurts*. . . ." The final word transformed
itself into a long wail and Jenna sank down, the
blanket brushing over coals. Meriel rushed toward her
as she sank backward toward the fire, pulling Jenna for-

ward as Owaine stamped out the sparks on the blanket. She crouched alongside her mam, rocking her in her arms as if Jenna were the child and crooning soft comfort. She caught Owaine's worried gaze.

Treoraí's Heart burned against her flesh. She knew what she had to do and yet it frightened her so much that she could hardly breathe. *It was so awful the last time; this will be worse.*

"Meriel, don't," Owaine said warningly, but she shook her head.

"I have to," she answered. "She's my mam and she's hurting. How can I *not* do it?" The clochmion seemed to pull at her hand. She found herself stroking the gem's cold smooth surface without even realizing she'd moved her hand. And with the touch . . .

She fell into Jenna.

She fell into madness.

This wasn't like the last time at all. Inside, there was no wild chaos or howling storm. Instead, Meriel found herself in a nightmare landscape surrounded by night-shrouded shapes and forms. Fingers reached out from darkness and clutched at her; harsh voices spoke demandingly, eyes peered at her suspiciously. There was little light here and what there was seemed bathed in blood; this was eternal night, a night in which ghosts walked, angry and uneasy. They glared at her as an intruder, all those who haunted her mam's memory. Most of them she didn't know, others she could guess at: the white-haired, stooped Bunús Muintir who frowned gap-toothed at her—that must be Seancoim, or rather not Seancoim but a twisted and misshapen caricature made feral and dangerous by Jenna's insanity. He snarled at her, and arthritic fingers clutched at her shoulder. "I'll tear you apart," he hissed. "I'll open you like a fatted pig and spill your guts on the ground." He lifted an oaken staff, its gnarled head glowing with the power of the slow magic and brought it toward her. She tore herself away from him and he laughed maniacally as she fled.

She was Jenna, swept up in nightmare memories, but she was also herself. She was split, half-complete. She heard Jenna wailing somewhere close by. "Mam?" she called. "Where are you?"

Lost . . . lost . . . "Here . . ."

The call came from within a forest of tangled tree limbs. Meriel pushed through them, the branches snatching at her. She pulled herself away from them and heard laughter. A man appeared before her: first the face, then the rest of the body. He was brown-haired with a beard longer than most men's. He was thin with skin darkened by much sun, and the eyes were a strange, light green. The voice, when he spoke, was deep and graveled. "So this is my daughter," he said. "You looked much like she did, then."

"Da? Ennis?" She knew she was seeing through Jenna's fevered memory, and she wondered if this was what he really looked like, the man who'd been her true father. He wasn't handsome—too unkempt and rough, more like a farmer or fisherfolk than a Riocha. Like Owaine. And yet . . . "Come here," he told her. "I'll take you to her." His eyes were deep-set and sad and she obeyed cautiously, but as soon as she came within reach of him, his hand darted out to grab the front of her clothing. "Where is it?" he rasped. "You have to give it to me."

She struck at him with her fists, and they went through his flesh as if he were made of wet parchment. A wind moved through the darkness and the shards of his body fluttered away, dissolving into the sound of his low laughter.

A pile of stones to her right shifted with a dull, rocky clunking, shifting and rearranging itself, the stone melting as if it were molten and flowing in thick, glassy coils, though Meriel felt no heat. It rose as it moved, forming a creature in the rough shape of a man, but stocky and solid, as wide as it was tall with stony ridges over the caverns of its eyes, its skin gray-brown, glossy and smooth. The thing slammed its hands together. Sparks jumped, and the sound of the clap nearly deafened her, booming like a crack of thunder. The being spoke, its voice sounding like the liquid trill of a dozen bass-voiced birds, the words difficult to understand. "That is *my* heart," it said. "Why would you bring it here?"

"Treoraí?" She lifted the clochmion on its chain. "This is yours?"

"You talk as if it were something I made." Deep in the shadows under the ridged head, there was a gleam as its eyes moved. "That stone is me. I want it back now. Did you really think it could do anything about *this?*" He gestured; with the motion, Meriel's vision seemed to recede as if she were being lifted rapidly into the sky high above the land. This interior world was bathed in bloody red light that seemed only to make the darkness more sinister and deep, and *things* moved in it like white maggots wriggling in rotting meat. Voices—mocking, threatening, arguing—filled the air, and shapes and faces drifted in the winds like clouds. Some of the visages she recognized, though all were warped and changed: Máister Kirwan, her da Kyle, even an angry and sullen version of herself. Others she knew not at all, images from her mam's past and imagination. A strange beast like a gigantic cat with dragon's wings and barbed tail stalked the landscape, crushing things under massive feet, its wings sending blasts of fierce winds across the world. Meriel looked up and saw that the blood-drenched sun was no day star, but Lámh Shábhála itself.

"You can't be here," Treoraí said. He floated alongside her. "You can't affect this, not with my heart." Icy fingers clutched at her, tearing and grabbing. "It's mine!" the Créneach shouted. "I want it back!" he shouted, and they were falling from the sky toward the nightmare landscape, struggling. Meriel screamed, fighting to keep it from tearing away the clochmion. She waited for the horrible impact of the ground; it never came. Instead, they seemed to fall into a thicket with thick, hooked thorns that scraped and tore at Meriel's skin, but that also gouged away huge chunks of the Créneach as they

plummeted through them, until it was only Meriel falling, falling . . .

. . . she was surrounded by cloudy night on the slopes
of Knobtop, and before her there was a young woman
who looked to be in her late teens or early twenties.
Meriel could not see her face, for she held a shield of
polished brass before her, peering over its bright edge.
In the curved, warped surface the world around them
was reflected back distorted and changed. Meriel knew
her, though. She knew her because she could see through
those eyes and see herself standing there. "Mam," she
said. "I came to help us, if you'll let me."

"Can't help me," Jenna said. "Can't. They're all
around me. They all hate me. They all want the cloch
and I won't give it to them."

"Mam, you don't *have* the cloch."

"No!" The denial tore from her throat as the shield
dropped so that Meriel could see Jenna's face. Flecks of
blood and spittle flew at Meriel, spattering her, but she
blinked them away.

"Aye," she insisted. "It was taken from you, Mam."

"No!" she screamed again. "It's here! It's right here!"
She held out her scarred and stiff hand and the hand
was also Meriel's hand. She dangled a chain from her
fingers. There was nothing on the end, but in the surface
of the shield, Meriel could see Lámh Shábhála, larger
than it had ever been and gleaming. She saw it, and she
felt the deep, terrible connection to it. She saw her soul
attached to it, throbbing and bloody.

"It's not there, Mam. I know you want it to be, but
it's not. Mam, let me help us, let me try to heal us . . ."
She closed one hand around Treoraí's Heart and held
out the other, but Jenna didn't reach for her. Instead,
she clutched at the chain as if she were wrenching open
Lámh Shábhála itself, screaming like a Black Haunt calling for a dead soul. The shield she carried swelled, growing huge and rushing toward Meriel with a sound like a
smithy's hammer on glowing iron. She threw up her
hands too late; the shield crashed into her: bearing her

down, crushing her into the ground. Stones ripped upward from the earth, stabbing into her back and spine
like blades. She screamed, and she could see her own
face wide-eyed with terror in the shield as it pressed
down, down, forcing her onto the unrelenting points of
the rocks, relentlessly crushing her.

She was at once Jenna, crushing her daughter under
the shield's horrible weight, and Meriel, underneath.

"Mam!" she screamed, pushing futilely at the shield.
"Mam! You'll kill me!"

"You can't have Lámh Shábhála!"

"Mam!"

The world darkened as pain ripped through her, as
she felt the heat of her lifeblood seeping from her body
from dozens of punctures. She could sense a glowing
azure thread, snaking through the darkness: the connection to Treoraí's Heart and reality. It was fading, thinning, and she somehow knew that once it was gone she
would be trapped here, lost in her mam's madness, one
with Jenna and lost. She pushed again at the shield, desperate, gathering the remaining energy of Treoraí's Heart.
The shield slid aside and Meriel grasped desperately for
her mam with hands glowing blue. Her finger found her
and released the clochmion's power, and at the same
time she let her awareness travel the path back even as
it began to fade and fail.

She didn't make it.

Her mam's mind had quieted; the ghosts haunting her
settling into wisps and vapors, but it was still dark with
whispering voices and the path had faded, the clochmion
emptied. "No!" she cried, and the word came back at
her, mocking: *"No!"*

The night surrounded her, empty. Meriel flailed in
terror.

Scarlet light, different from the blood-drenched sun
she'd found inside Jenna, pierced the veil. "Here," said a
woman's voice. "Feel the mage-power. We're here . . ."

Meriel forced her awareness that way; with a gasp, she
found herself back in Keira's cave, held in Owaine's

arms as Edana released the cloch around her neck. "I was lost," Meriel sobbed, her voice ragged. "Inside . . ."

They were all there: Keira, Edana, Doyle. Her mam stood a step away, her expression confused. She came to Meriel, blinking as if waking from sleep, and brushed Meriel's hair with her scarred and stiff hand. "Thank you." Tears tracked Jenna's cheeks. "You saved me, darling. You did."

"Mam," Meriel said. "I can't do that again. I can't."

"I know," Jenna whispered. "I understand. But thank you, darling. Thank you for bringing me back again." Her skittering eyes found Doyle. "Brother," she said with a mocking little laugh. "I see you didn't hold Lámh Shábhála long."

"I didn't hold it at all," he said. "And now I hold nothing. It was all taken from me."

If Jenna felt any empathy with him, Meriel didn't see it in her face. "And you," Jenna said to Edana. "You were at Inishduán, with Demon-Caller."

"Aye, Banrion. I was. And you defeated me." She nodded to Meriel. "And your daughter brought me back, just as she did you."

Meriel shivered in Owaine's arms. "That was your voice I heard," she said to Edana, "and your Cloch Mór that lit the way."

"I didn't know what else to do. We all saw your panic, and we couldn't get you to release your cloch and were afraid that if we just forced your hand away, we'd harm you . . ." She lifted a shoulder. "I thought feeling a Cloch Mór's power might somehow draw you back."

"It did." Meriel inhaled deeply, held it, let the breath out again. She hugged Owaine, then let go. His arms loosened around her, though one hand stayed gently on her back.

"I'm glad you're back," Owaine told her. "I'm glad you're safe."

She smiled at him, her lips closed. She could still feel the darkness around her, the sounds of madness, the fear, the face of her da . . . "I'm not safe," she said.

"There's no safety for us anywhere now. I think I've finally realized that. What's inside you, Mam, is also all around each of us now and we can't sit here. Edana, you were right. We can't hide here forever, because everything we love will have died out there while we cower under the trees. Then even Doire Coill will fall." She nodded, feeling the resolution harden within her: fatalistic, grim, and certain.

"We go into the storm itself," she told them, "and we'll either fall to it or not."

46

The Sióg Mist

"**Y**OU'RE certain this will work?" Meriel asked nervously, and Keira laughed.

"No," she answered. "But no one seems to have a better idea."

They stood at the northern edge of Doire Coill with the Mill Creek rushing by to its meeting with the Duán. Each of them had a well-stuffed pack alongside them except for Keira, who carried only an oaken staff. A deep, steep-sided valley creased the land there. In the belly of the cleft was a thick marsh, the trees of the wood remaining high on the sides of the surrounding hills. Old Ragan of the Bunús Muintir had come with them, along with a hand of the people from the village. Following Keira's directions, the Bunús stationed themselves around the fen in the predawn light and began chanting in their own language. The chant was long and sonorous, continuing for what seemed a stripe or more as the eastern sky slid from violet to orange to pink. While the sky lightened and the low, droning mantra continued, Meriel and the others saw a thick, white mist rise from the black waters and clumps of rushes and ferns, sliding over the hummocks of grass and loam. The fog was thicker than any natural fog, and when it first rose from the marsh the shapes it made were like those of people that slowly dissolved into the greater cloud. They could all hear whispering, laughing voices.

"Sióg mist," Meriel whispered.

"Aye," Keira said.

Meriel could remember Sevei, holding her back before she jumped into the fog. "The Taisteal . . . my friend Sevei . . . she said that people who go into the fairy mist don't come back out."

"They were right. Usually they don't." The mist was rising now, the Bunús Muintir moving with it, almost as if they were herding it like a flock of insubstantial sheep. The fog climbed, moving against the wind and—impossibly—up the slopes of the cleft toward them.

"You've done this before, though?" The rising inflection at the end of Meriel's sentence made it more hopeful question than statement.

A grin flickered on the woman's lips. "Never."

"Then how do you know it will work?"

"Because Seancoim once told me that it would and Ragan knows the slow magic for it."

"So Seancoim did this?" Keira's face gave Meriel the answer to that. "Or Ragan?"

Another grin. "No. Neither one."

"Wonderful."

"If you want to move quickly and hidden to where Lámh Shábhála is, then you have no choice, at least none that are available to me. If you have another and better plan, now's the time to think of it, before the mist reaches us."

Meriel stared downward at the rising whiteness. She could already feel its chill, like the air during one of Talamh an Ghlas' rare snows, the faint laughter in the air growing louder. She shook her head.

Edana and Doyle were huddled together a few feet away. Jenna stood well away from them, with Owaine beside her. Meriel saw Owaine say something to her mam before coming over to Meriel and Keira. "What's *in* that mist?" he asked Keira. "I hear voices, and look at my arms." He pulled back the sleeve of his léine, showing them the hair rising in goose bumps.

"The fog contains the Corcach Siógai, the swamp folk.
Jenna—or rather, Lámh Shábhála—awakened them from
a long sleep as it did many things. Until now they were
creatures from old legends. The sióg mist is their breath,
and they feed on the hard bones of the living. Dusk and
dawn, they sweep out of the bogs and marshes moving
faster than the wind and bringing back those who become lost in their mist with them, and there they feed.
That's why when you find bodies in the bog, there's
nothing left but an empty skin of leather." Meriel shuddered at Keira's solemn tones. "That's enough to know
about them," Keira finished. "We'll stay together, and
if the warding-and-release spells work, we'll come out
again."

"And if they *don't* work?" Owaine was staring at the
mist as if daring it to come closer. It did.

"Then, Owaine, all your questions about what is inside
the mist will be answered."

Meriel saw Owaine shiver. "I'm finding I'm not really
all that curious." The mist was approaching rapidly, and
Ragan waved to Keira from the edge of the bog. The
chanting of the Bunús Muintir had stopped as the sióg
mist snaked between the trees toward Meriel and the
others. "It's time," Keira called, gesturing to the others.
"Put on your packs. We need to hold onto each other,
or we may be swept up in the mist and lost forever."

They each picked up one of the packs and slung it
around their shoulders. They made a small circle: Meriel
took Owaine's hand and Keira's; Owaine grasped Jenna's, but when Edana—one hand intertwined with
Doyle's—held out her free hand for Jenna to take, Jenna
wouldn't look at it. "Mam . . ." Meriel said, as Edana
reached again for Jenna's hand. Jenna gave Edana a
look of scorn and pulled her hand away. Edana glanced
at Meriel questioningly.

The sióg mist was only a few strides away and rushing
toward them; Meriel let go of Keira's and Owaine's
hands. "Take Keira," she told Owaine, then moved be-

tween Edana and her man. She grasped Edana's hand.
Jenna's free hand was still down at her side. "Mam,
please . . ."

Jenna slowly lifted her hand as the first tendrils of the
mist curled around their ankles, the white cloud of it
rising, rising in front of them. Meriel could feel something like the touch of small fingers on her ankles and
legs and hear the tinkling sound of high laughter.

Then they were inside.

It would not be the last of the Great Sióg Mists (which
would haunt Talamh an Ghlas for long generations), but
it was the first. Those who witnessed it said that the fog
rolled out of Doire Coill like a boiling white wall three
men high, with outrider tendrils that seemed to creep
along the ground like tentacles. The wind was blowing
hard east that morning, but the sióg mist was slave to
no wind and moved northward along the route of the
High Road, gaining speed as it went. It swept over Ballintubber first, enveloping the tiny village in a white
cloud so dense that those who were caught in it couldn't
even see their hands stretched out in front of their eyes
and the sounds of the village were silenced, as if fingers
had been placed in their ears. In the muffled silence
within the cloud, enchanted, high voices called to the
villagers, and those who listened or who allowed the
grasping fingers of the Corcach Siógai to pluck them
away were taken with the mist. In Ballintubber alone,
two children were snatched from their cradles and four
adults were never seen again, including Eliath, the owner
of Tara's Tavern.

The Great Mist was past Ballintubber in but a few
fearful breaths, leaving behind the memory of its dangerous laughter as inhabitants blinked and wondered, as the
first wails arose from those who found loved ones missing. The mist moved on, ever faster, as if desperate to
outrace the rising sun. It passed through Ballyrea, El-

phin, and Garventon and all the villages and farms between, then bent a little more eastward toward Lough
Donn along the High Road to Falcarragh. There, in the
wild landscape of drumlins west of Lough Donn, in the
fens and bogs near the shore, it blended into the more
natural fogs and mists and wisps, falling apart into smaller
mists until the sun, now lifting higher in the sky between
scudding rain clouds, burned it away entirely.

All in all, it was said that a hundred people or more
vanished that morning, though no one would ever know
for certain; of the sióg-taken, none ever returned to their
homes, though workers cutting the turf around Lough
Donn would find brown, leathery bog bodies in the peat
for generations afterward.

In the roiling whiteness, there was only the feel of another hand clutching hers, the terror of the voices and
the fingers that tried to pull them apart and a frightening
sense of far too rapid movement, as if they were flying
blindly as unseen *things* rushed past them on either side,
dangerously close. Finally, when Meriel was ready to
scream herself and let go of the hands to strike at the
clutching fingers of the Corcach Síógai and their derisive
voices, Keira's voice called a command. Mocking laughter answered, and Meriel heard Keira thunder the order
again, then yet again, and this time the Corcach Síógai
shrilled and screamed and shouted and the mist was
shredded as if by a furious wind.

They were standing, wide-eyed and breathless, on a
grassy hummock in a fog-hung swamp with misty gray
hillsides all around. For all Meriel knew, they were still
in Doire Coill, except that the slopes closest to them
were bracken-covered with only a few straggling elms
and maples thrusting upward into the pallid morning.

"That," Meriel said as she released Edana's and Jenna's hands, "was another thing I don't ever want to do
again."

"Agreed," Owaine mumbled. He shivered, shaking dew from his clóca. "Where *are* we?"

"Near Lough Donn, south of Falcarragh," Keira answered. The Bunús Muintir was turning slowly around, gazing at the bogland. "We've traveled in a morning what would have taken us two weeks to walk." She pointed. "The High Road should be over there beyond that hill. You should be able to reach it before the sun goes down."

" 'You?' Not 'we'?" Meriel asked.

Keira shook her head. "I'm the Protector of Doire Coill. That's my task. I have to return there. Besides, your hope now is to be inconspicuous on a well-traveled road—for a Bunús Muintir, that's not possible."

"We need you," Owaine said. "We could travel off the road, moving at night if we have to."

"And as we came closer to Falcarragh, there would be less and less cover, and we'd be traveling over estates and farms and through villages where even in the night we would be seen, by the dogs if nothing else. The tiarna would tell you that; he knows this land." She glanced at Doyle, who nodded. "No, this is your time and your struggle. My charges are the oaks of the Old Forest, and I have to go back to them." She smiled at Meriel, her leathery, dark skin creasing. "It will be a long walk for me. Like you, I don't want to go back the way we came. You have two Clochs Mór and Treoraí's Heart; that's weaponry enough for the road, I would think. What I can do for you, I've done."

Meriel hugged the older woman, who enfolded her in furs and the scent of herbs. "Keira, I'll miss you."

"Make sure you come back to Doire Coill and see me, then, after this is done," Keira answered. Her arms tightened around Meriel before she stepped back. Her regard moved from Meriel to each of the others: Owaine, standing next to Meriel; Doyle and Edana; Jenna, standing apart from all of them and seemingly lost in her own thoughts. "There's andúilleaf in your pack," she said to Meriel, softly enough that Jenna couldn't hear. "Not in hers. She'll need it if she's not to fall back into madness, but don't give it to her more than twice a day, morning and night, no matter how much she asks. For now, you need to be *her* mam." Then she raised her voice, going to Jenna. "First Holder, I wish you luck. You had the strength to bring the Filleadh to us; I know you have that strength still inside you or you wouldn't have been able to survive losing Lámh Shábhála. Few Holders have managed to survive that loss. I hope you hold the cloch again. You have people with you who want the same."

Jenna glanced at Doyle and Edana. "Some, perhaps," she said. "Others might want it for themselves."

Doyle stirred at that. "I don't deny that I wanted to take the cloch from you, Sister. I won't tell you that I don't still want it or that I wouldn't take it if you fall in this gamble. But if we take Ó Riain down and you're there, I'll hand you Lámh Shábhála myself. I promise you that—as payment for what Meriel did for Edana and me."

"I'm supposed to take comfort in your pledges?" Jenna retorted, and Doyle shrugged.

"I don't care if you believe me or not," he said, his voice flat.

"Mam," Meriel said. "*I* trust him, and I trust Edana as well."

Jenna's face contorted and she hunched over with a spasm of pain, groaning. With a visible effort, she straightened. "You may trust them if you wish," she said. She took a few breaths, holding her stomach. "But Doyle's the same man who snatched you away from Inishfeirm. He's the same man who on Inishduán told me that he would kill you, and he very nearly succeeded. Trust him?" Jenna spat on the ground, then groaned again. "I need andúilleaf," she said.

Meriel looked at Keira, who shook her head slightly. "Later, Mam," she said. "First we need to say good-bye to Keira, then get out of this bog. We've a long walk ahead of us yet."

47

Fatal Decisions

UNLIKE the High Road near Doire Coill, the road here was heavily traveled, wide enough that two carts could pass each other and still have a bit of room for travelers on foot, the doubled line of ruts worn deeply in the earth and most of the grass scrubbed away by the soles of boots. Travelers walked carefully around the piles of steaming dung from the horses and other beasts of burden. The area south of Falcarragh down to the drumlins that surrounded Lough Donn was heavily farmed. Well-maintained stone fences lined the High Road with large pastures flecked by white dots of sheep or Dun blotches of cows stretching out to the lines of trees that demarked the property lines, or fields of dusty yellow grain, or long rows of breadroot mounds.

Smaller lanes led off toward the cluster of buildings glimpsed through trees—the estates of the Riocha of Tuath Infochla—and at frequent intervals there would appear the thatched roofs of a small village and the bright signboards of inns and other merchants.

Meriel and the others were unremarkable among those walking the road. Before they'd left Doire Coill, Owaine had followed Doyle's example and shaved his head and beard close as if he were a lice-ridden peasant; Meriel, with Edana's help, had cut off much of her own tresses with deliberate choppiness, then they'd done the same to Jenna. Jenna's mage-light scarred right arm was carefully wrapped, and the others all wore open-fingered and tattered gloves so that their lesser-scarred hands wouldn't show. The trek across the fens of Lough Donn and through the wild brush of the drumlins had given them further authenticity, layering them in the same dirt and grime that coated the legs and clothing of other poor travelers. The Riocha who passed them riding their fine horses or in carriages gave no more than a passing glance at the road-caked group trudging along toward Falcarragh with their heads down: that was the proper attitude for those whose blood was common and whose lives were mundane, short, and toil-ridden. There were gardai and squads of conscripted soldiers passing as well; even as they reached the road, they had to wait for troops to pass, quick-marching north with banners in Tuath Airgialla's red and white.

They followed in their wake.

By evening, they'd reached a town called Kilmaur along the banks of the River Donn, flowing northward to Falcarragh Bay and the Ice Sea. They paid for a room at an inn on the edge of the town; the innkeeper—an elderly man as thin and hard as one of Keira's staffs— eyed them suspiciously and tested the mórceint that Owaine handed him with his few remaining teeth.

"Can't be too careful," he grumbled. "Too many people on the road these days, an' I have to say that you have an odd accent. There's thieves and murderers and worse. And the soldiers all a'headin' to Falcarragh where the ships are waiting. Why, only two days ago, the new Rí Ard passed through on his way to Falcarragh, an' you should have seen the commotion." Doyle's head lifted at that and Meriel saw the innkeeper glance at Doyle's face, his eyebrows lowering. "The two of you should be careful if you don't want to be on those ships yourselves," he said to Doyle and Owaine, but his gaze came back to Doyle and rested there. "I hear that the gardai are pressing men into service if they look like they could handle a pike, and you seem healthy enough for that." Doyle dropped his head and nodded.

In the room, they gratefully dropped the packs from their shoulders and collapsed. After resting a few minutes, Meriel went to the hearth and blew on the coals to get them started again as Edana brought over a few pieces of black turf the innkeeper had provided for them. Doyle and Owaine were talking together near the shuttered window, peering out at Kilmaur's main street and across it to the river and discussing how far it was to Falcarragh.

"I don't like the way he looked at us, especially Doyle," Edana said to Meriel. Meriel poured water into the small black pot on the crane and swung it over the flames to boil.

"There's nothing we can do to change it," she said. "We knew we were taking the chance that someone might recognize us on the way, especially you and Doyle." She rummaged in the pack and pulled out one of the packets Keira had given her. She sprinkled the dry flakes into the water and the smell of andúilleaf filled the room. The aroma seemed to ease some of the aches and pains of the day. Jenna stirred, limping over to the pot and leaning over the water to sniff the fragrance. "I'll bring you the brew as soon as it's done, Mam," Meriel said. "How are you feeling?"

"How would you *think* I feel, after crawling through swamps and trudging miles, you silly child?" Jenna answered angrily before her face softened and she sniffed at the andúilleaf again. "I'm sorry, Meriel. I'm . . . hurting badly, and—"

Meriel touched her mam's face and smiled. "I understand, Mam. The andúilleaf will help."

"We should go down to the tavern," Owaine said. "We might be able to learn something listening to the patrons." He shrugged. "Besides, I don't know about the rest of you, but I'm hungry."

The others agreed, all but Jenna, who wanted to stay in the room after she drank her andúilleaf tea. "I'll be better here, resting," she told Meriel. "Go on. I know where you are if I need you."

They found the owner of the inn in the tavern. He greeted them with a sniff and a lift of his grizzled chin, and poured the round of ale that Owaine ordered only after he paid first. Owaine brought the wooden mugs over to the table Meriel had commandeered in the far corner of the room. "Friendly place," Owaine remarked as he slid onto the bench next to Meriel.

"It's the war preparation," Doyle answered. "Look around; half the women here are clinging to their men like it's the last time they might see them, and they might be right." Meriel glanced around, seeing that Doyle's observation was accurate. There was a forced, deliberate gaiety in the atmosphere, and the smiles on the faces seemed painted there, fixed and unchanging and artificial. Those who looked back at her narrowed their eyes suspiciously at the strangeness of her face and averted their gaze. The conversations they could hear seemed all concerned with the movement of the troops on the High Road and rumors about Falcarragh.

". . . I was told by Tallan, who's been there, that the city glitters in the sun with all the armor and weapons, and that the bay is filled with ships from all the Tuatha."

"Tallan exaggerates, and he's half-blind besides. *I* heard from my cousin that there's an army marching up from Connachta right now, and it's bigger than any of the others. They'll be through here in three days."

"More likely it's a big flock of sheep he saw. They're going to need the mutton to feed all those soldiers in Falcarragh. . . ."

As they listened to the talk around them, sipping at the foamy dark beer, Meriel saw a man enter the tavern. He was dressed in a plain brown clóca and immediately entered into a conversation with the innkeeper, whose gaze kept drifting over to their table though the man to whom he was talking never looked that way. The man in brown paid for an ale and took a stool in the corner of the room. He sat there, his back to the wall, where he could see the whole room. He never looked their way directly, but Meriel frowned, seeing him.

"I think we should leave," she told the others.

"Why?" Owaine asked.

"I just think we should go to another tavern. Maybe we'll hear something different there."

Owaine shrugged. "Fine." Neither Doyle nor Edana made any protest, and after they finished their drinks, they rose and left the tavern.

"My ale's not good enough for the likes of you, eh?" the innkeeper called after them mockingly as they passed. Owaine started to answer, but Meriel put her hand on his shoulder and shook her head warningly. He frowned at her but closed his mouth. They left.

The air smelled of the river, flowing silvered by moonlight across the flagstones and down a grassy verge; a few hundred strides to their left, the town's wharves poked out into the slow-moving water, and a boat was moving silently northward in the flow, the light from two lanterns shimmering on the waves.

The main street of Kilmaur was busy in the darkness: couples walked the street arm in arm; a cluster of drunken gardai in the colors of Tuath Locha Léin stumbled past, talking loudly and laughing. Street vendors hawked their wares; in the shadows, a few women offered less tangible goods for sale. The bright sound of a giotár came to them from up the street where a musician sat on a corner in the light from another inn, the bottom of his felt hat layered with small coins. Meriel could feel a sense of desperate gaiety in the movement and the laughter and the conversations, as if they could banish the reality of the coming war with hilarity, grinning mouths, and alcohol. Or maybe, she admitted to herself, she was only overlaying her own fears on the scene. Maybe this was simply Kilmaur celebrating and none of them were frightened by what was coming at all—they had Lámh Shábhála and their new Rí Ard and saw victory as both certain and easy.

She stood on the street, watching the activity around them and wondering what the truth was.

"I don't know that this is a good idea, Meriel," Doyle

said. Both he and Edana had the hoods of their clóca up, keeping their faces in concealing shadow. "There's the danger of someone recognizing Edana or me, and we're leaving the Banrion all alone in her room." His voice was tired and throaty; his shoulders sagged and he held himself like an ill old man. Edana stayed close to him, her eyes worried. Meriel felt a small stab of guilt. *He's not much better than your mam and you've done nothing to help him.* But the guilt vanished quickly: Doyle had refused her help once and she had no intention of venturing inside the mind of another person gone cloch-mad. Doyle's suffering was far less than that of her mam, and he could bear it on his own—at least, that was how she justified it to herself.

Meriel glanced behind them. "We won't be gone long," she said, and started walking up the street to the corner where the street musician played. She paused to drop in a coin, then led the group quickly around the corner into a tiny, quiet lane with few people about. Meriel led them into the gap between two buildings. "Wait," she said to them, putting her fingers to her lips. Owaine looked at her quizzically, then his eyes widened slightly and he nodded. He placed himself at the opening.

They didn't have to wait for more than a few moments. They heard hurrying boot steps on the flags and the man in brown appeared. Owaine slid from darkness behind him, grasping him by the shoulder and pressing his dagger's blade immediately against the man's throat. "Don't," he whispered warningly as the man started to struggle. Owaine pulled the man quickly back into the gap and pushed him against the wall, his left hand fisted in the man's clóca. The knife flashed in his other hand, high enough that the man could see it.

"If we'd known you wanted to come with us, we would have waited," Owaine said to the man, the tip of his knife just touching the soft flesh where the carotid artery pulsed. Meriel saw Edana's hand slide under the fold of her clóca to where her cloch was hidden; Doyle had straightened, glaring hard at the man with his own knife out. The man pressed his back to the wall, eyes wide, as if he were trying to force his spine between the very stones.

"Who are you? Why are you following us?" Meriel asked him. The man didn't answer, only glared at them with an odd mixture of fright and defiance. Owaine pressed the knife against the skin so that the man hissed as a trickle of blood slid down his neck.

"I'm Bran Mowlan of the Kilmaur gardai, and you're making a horrible mistake here if you don't put that knife down now." Despite the threat, there was no bluster in his voice. The words sounded more like a plea.

Owaine continue to press the blade against him, the line of slow, bright blood soaking into the bunched cloth at the base of his neck. "My friend asked why you were following us," he said. "The mistake would be not answering her."

Mowlan's gaze flitted wildly around them. "Blowick, the innkeeper, he sent word that there were suspicious strangers at his inn, so I was sent to investigate."

"And what did you see?" Doyle asked.

"Nothing worth reporting," Mowlan said. His voice trembled and his eyes were round and huge as he glanced at Doyle without moving his head. "Just some people passing through, that's all." Meriel heard the faint sound of water. She looked down to see liquid trickling down the man's legs and pooling between his feet. The sour smell of urine came a moment later. "Let me go," Mowlan said with a small sob. He sniffed. "Please. I'll say nothing. I swear by the Mother."

"You're right about that," Doyle said. Meriel caught the glance between Doyle and Owaine and the faint nod which was Owaine's response.

"Meriel, take Edana and Doyle back to the inn and see to your mam," Owaine said. "I'll follow in a bit."

"No," Meriel answered sharply. "Owaine—"

"Meriel," Owaine cut in quickly. He glanced again at Doyle. "Watch him," he said, and then took Meriel's arm. Angrily, she pulled away from him. "Then just come with me," he said. "Please." He moved deeper into the darkness between the buildings. She glared at him, then followed.

"I know what you're thinking of doing," she said when she caught up with him, hands on hips. "I won't allow it."

"It isn't just your decision, Meriel. I know you don't want this and I don't either. The Mother knows I've never had to make a choice like this before. It's one thing to defend yourself when you're attacked or to go to help someone else, and another to . . ." He stopped, looking back toward where Doyle held Mowlan to the wall. "I wish we could avoid this, but it's not possible for us to take Lámh Shábhála back without hurting or killing people. How many have already died? If we let this man go, he'll go back to his superiors and tell them what happened."

"You don't know that."

"No, not for certain, but look at him. What's he going to do when his superior asks him what happened? Do you think he'll take the opportunity to have revenge on the people who humiliated him, who made him soil himself? I think he will. Then we won't be facing one person but a squadron and we'll likely end up dead ourselves. I'm willing to trade his life for ours. Think of how many lives we'll save—the lives of our families and friends—if we can stop the invasion of Inish Thuaidh. Leave this man alive, and they die, Meriel. Not just us, but all of *them,* also."

Part of her agreed with Owaine's logic and told her that what he was espousing was the best course. Yet she glanced down the alleyway at the frightened man balanced on the point of Doyle's knife and she couldn't stop wondering about him: did he have a wife? Children? Family? He was obviously terrified and it seemed so utterly wrong to kill him. "We could tie and gag him, leave him somewhere where he won't be found."

"And what if he is found or if he gets loose before

we can leave?" Owaine countered. "Or if he's found the next day and they send gardai on horses after us and also send warnings ahead to Falcarragh, telling them who to watch for." He lifted his hand as if he were going to caress her face and Meriel took a step back from him. He let his hand drop back to his side. "Meriel, I owe you so much and I know this hurts you, but we can't afford mercy here," he said. "We can't afford kindness. Doyle would tell you the same thing, and so would Edana. For that matter, so would your mam."

"Then we're no better than any of the rest of them, are we?" she retorted. He didn't answer. "Owaine . . ." she began. The decision seemed to hang between them, solid. "You've changed so much. Or maybe it's me who's changed. I don't know. I only know that the way I've looked at you has changed." For a moment, she saw the hope in his face, and she shook it away with a motion of her head. "But if you do this," she said finally, "there could never be anything between us, Owaine. I couldn't, knowing what you've done. Maybe you're right; I don't know. You make the decision."

His gaze held hers. She could see the pain in his eyes, in the netting of fine wrinkles that held them. He nodded and slid past her. His knife was in his hand again. "Go on," he said to Doyle, staring at Mowlan and looking at Meriel as she came up behind him, her eyes fierce. "I'll see the rest of you later. Go on."

Owaine returned to the room a little over a stripe later. "As soon as we got back, I told Blowick that we talked to Mowlan," Doyle told him. "I mentioned that Mowlan had said if Blowick ever bothered him again with unfounded suspicions, he would personally see that it was the last time."

"Good," Owaine said with little inflection. His voice sounded dead and void of emotion. "That should gain us a few days, at least." Edana handed Owaine a mug of hot tea. He sipped at it gratefully. Meriel thought that he looked weary and drawn, and his gaze never seemed to find hers. When he opened his clóca and threw it off, there was blood spattered on the front of his tunic. She quickly looked away. "We need to burn these clothes," he said. "Then we should leave tonight, as soon as we can. There's a rear stairs just down the corridor."

She wanted to ask him if he was all right. She wanted to know what he'd done with Mowlan. She wanted to go to him and hold him, to say that she might not like the decision but that she understood. That it didn't make a difference.

She did none of that. "I don't know that Mam can walk right now," she said instead. She hated the rising edge in her voice, didn't like the way it caused Owaine's eyebrows to lower.

"I'll manage," Jenna said. "Just give me a little more andúilleaf . . ."

"More andúilleaf and you'll be in such a fog you won't be able to put one foot in front of the other," Meriel snapped. Jenna glared back at her.

"You forget who's the the Banrion here," Jenna snarled.

"And you forget who has the andúilleaf, Mam," Meriel answered, and she could feel frustration and inarticulate anger coloring her tone. "You also seem to have forgotten what happened when you last were taking it, but Keira hasn't and I haven't either. This isn't Dún Kiil, Mam. You're not Banrion here, you don't have your gardai or Lámh Shábhála to protect you, and you're hurting too much to make good decisions." She looked hard at Owaine, not wanting to glare at him but knowing that she did. "There don't seem to be any good decisions for us."

They were *all* staring at her, none of them saying anything. "Let's get ready if we're going to leave," Meriel finished and went to her own pack, rummaging about in it even though it was as well arranged as it could be. Tears shimmered her vision and she sniffed them away

angrily, her back to the room. She heard the others start
to get themselves ready, Jenna grumbling under her
breath and moaning. Meriel didn't turn around until her
eyes were dry. "You seem to know what you're doing,
Owaine," she said. "Lead us, then."

He'd changed into a spare léine and was crouching in
front of the hearth. She saw him poke at a burning pile
of cloth and straighten. He looked at her with a mute
sympathy in his eyes that made Meriel put her gaze on
the floor. He put on his clóca and pinned its wooden
brooch, then hefted his pack. "This way," he said.

They moved quickly out of the inn and onto the street,
which was deserted except for a few people still going
from tavern to tavern. Owaine kept them in the shadows
near the river, and led them away from the road to the
edge of the river itself. They walked along through
marshy, high grass until they'd left behind the last stone
building of the town, then moved back to the road, staying to one side where they could quickly hop over the
stone fence to the cover of brush and grass if riders
appeared ahead or behind. Owaine stayed at the head, a
few strides ahead of Doyle and Edana. Jenna and Meriel
followed at the rear.

Jenna was struggling to keep up, Meriel could see.
Her mam staggered now and then, her feet dragged the
ground, her left hand clutched at her wrapped right arm
as if it were broken and painful. Her breathing was
heavy and ragged, and she trembled from time to time
from some inner spasm. She seemed to force herself forward only by sheer will. Her eyes were glazed and fixed
straight forward. She seemed to be staring as if pulling
herself along toward a vision only she could see. Perhaps, Meriel thought, that was actually true, and it was
only the faint hope that Lámh Shábhála was somewhere
ahead of them and might be recovered that kept Jenna
from drowning entirely in the black morass of her loss
and physical pain.

For the first time, walking in the cool, moon-dappled
night along that road, Meriel began to see her mam

anew. She realized just how much holding Lámh Shábhála had cost Jenna, how strong her mam had to have
been just to possess that cloch na thintrí, how fierce her
will was not to succumb now that it had been taken from
her. Meriel understood just how much her mam had
sheltered her from the reality of the burden Jenna carried, protecting her not only from the magic but from
the politics that swirled around them. Whether that had
been fair or good for Meriel was something she couldn't
answer, but Meriel understood the choice Jenna had
made; it was the choice she might have made herself for
her own child.

"You can lean on me if you need to, Mam," she said
to Jenna. "I know you're hurting."

Jenna stared straight ahead without answering, plodding along deliberately. "As soon as we stop, when the
sun's up, I'll make some more andúilleaf for you," Meriel offered.

Tiny muscles jumped along Jenna's jawline as she
clenched her teeth. She swept her hair back, and Meriel
saw the silver in her dark hair, far more than Meriel
remembered even when she found her mam on Knobtop. Jenna had aged much since the cloch had been
taken. The lines in her face were cut deeper, with new
channels running out from them. "Why are you doing
this?" Jenna asked. She nodded at Doyle. "I know why
he's here: he has reasons to hate those we're after and
he needs to recover his Cloch Mór at the least, while he
hopes that it will give him another chance to take Lámh
Shábhála. Edana's here because of Doyle, though I don't
understand what she sees in the man. And Owaine; you
do him an injustice, Meriel—he's loyal to those he loves
and more intelligent than you think. I was angry at you
when I saw you'd given him Blaze, but you did well to
give him my Cloch Mór."

"I didn't realize you knew that. I thought you'd be
furious."

Jenna gave a laugh that sounded more like a cough.
"I have eyes, child, and I use them. And I *was* furious.

I gave the cloch to you because it was Ennis'. I gave it to you because I'd loved him and still love him and he was your da. I gave you something of incredible value and you in turn gave it to someone who, half the time, you pretend you don't like. Oh, aye, I was angry."

"You didn't say anything to me."

"It wouldn't have changed anything. Do you think I could take the Cloch Mór away from him, knowing how I feel now?"

Meriel didn't know what to say. "Mam, I'm sorry—" she began but Jenna lifted her hand.

"Stop," she said. "Don't say what you don't mean. You're not sorry about your choice at all. You never knew Ennis, never even knew he existed or who he was to you until recently, so the cloch meant little in that respect. And it wasn't a burden you wanted to take. Having you hold Blaze was *my* desire, not yours, and I understand that. I'm still not entirely pleased that Owaine has it, but at least I know and respect the young man, and he's a cloudmage of Inishfeirm. Ennis would have wanted that, if his own daughter refused to follow his path." Jenna paused, stopping to gather her breath. She leaned with her back to the stone wall of the road as the others kept walking.

Meriel sniffed. "So you're still angry."

"No," Jenna answered. Her eyes were closed, and her mouth tightened as if she were holding back a moan. "It takes too much energy to be angry with those you love. I don't have that energy now; it's all I can do to just keep moving and not give in to the pain." The eyes opened again, clear for that moment, and she inclined her head toward Owaine. "You don't have the energy to waste either, especially against someone you like more than you're willing to admit. Someone whose interests are yours and not divided between the stones and the sea." Meriel could feel the shock on her face and Jenna laugh-coughed again. "Aye, I know that, too. I'd hoped you hadn't inherited that part of me, but you did."

"Mam—"

"Hush, child," Jenna said. She pushed away from the wall. "Give me your arm," she said. "I need it, I'm afraid. It's a long walk to Falcarragh, and I'm too ill to talk at the same time."

Meriel reached for her, and Jenna put her arm through Meriel's. She seemed to weigh no more than the pack on Meriel's back, as if Lámh Shábhála had taken her substance as well as her health.

48

Preparations for War

"YOU SEE, Rí Ard, out there is your Might, your Fist, your incredible strength. No one will be able to stand before you. You will bring the Inishlanders to their knees with one single, awful blow."

Regent Guardian Ó Riain, Holder of Lámh Shábhála, stood with Enean on a balcony of the Rí Infochla's keep in Falcarragh. He gestured at the panorama spread out below them. The keep had been erected high on the broad shoulder of Sliabh Gabhar, one of two mountains that sheltered Falcarragh to the east. Sliabh Sí, the sister peak, was wrapped in high haze to their far left, the great temple of the Mother-Creator on its summit barely visible. Below, Falcarragh itself spread out in the valley. Almost directly below them was Harbor Quay, with several warships docked there. Out where the mouth of the River Donn emptied into the long stretch of Falcarragh Bay, other ships rode at anchor between West Light and East Light, more ships than Enean had ever seen gathered in one place, even in the great harbor at Dún Laoghaire. The streets below were crowded, and on the slopes of Outlook Park to the west the canopies of the troop tents had sprouted like white mushrooms. Over five thousand troops were already encamped there, swelling the population of the town and straining its resources, and more troops arrived every day.

Enean burned to be in the battle that was to come.

In his mind, he could see himself at the head of the troops as they poured into Dún Kiil, his sword raised and dripping blood, and in his other hand, the snarling, glowing dragon of his Cloch Mór. In his vision, all his enemies fell before him as if he were a scythe cutting through ripe wheat. The roar of victory drowned out the wails of the dead and dying, and the Inishlanders who were left threw down their weapons and bowed to him.

Enean smiled. He lifted his chin, as if he were already standing triumphant on the field of battle. "Which ship is mine, Labhrás?" he asked, and Ó Riain pointed to a large, single-masted galley riding the swells near West Light.

"That one," he said. "You see the Rí Ard's crest painted on its bow, and the colors of Dún Laoghaire flying in the rigging. That's where we'll be, Enean, just a few days from now, as soon as the remainder of the troops and ships arrive. Then, not long after that, we'll sail into Dún Kiil Harbor and hear the terror of the Inishlanders at the sight of us. We'll avenge the defeat of your da, and Inish Thuaidh will be another of your Tuatha."

Enean grinned at that, the glorious vision returning to him. Then he frowned. "Da sometimes talked to me about the last time, especially before—" He stopped and touched a finger to the long, ugly scar that disfigured his face. "He said that no army from the Tuatha *ever* managed to defeat the Inishlanders, that it was foolish to try because 'the Mother-damned Inish are too stubborn to know when they're dead and will strike from the very grave.'" Enean shivered. "Can they do that, Labhrás? Can they keep fighting even when you've killed them?" The image of skeletons and rotting corpses swinging rusted blades spoiled the grand vision in his head.

"No," Ó Riain said soothingly, talking to him as his da had. "They're just people like any others, Enean, and when they die, they die."

"Then why would Da say that?"

Enean thought he heard Ó Riain give a sigh of exasperation, but when he looked, the man was smiling at him. "Your da was exaggerating a bit, as people do when they tell stories. You know how tales grow, don't you?"

"MacCamore used to tell me stories," Enean said, but the mention of the man's name dissolved the smile on Ó Riain's face and, with it, the last bit of Enean's vision. He shivered in the cold wind, looking down at the city without seeing it. "Where's Nuala?" Enean asked. "I want to see Nuala."

The frown deepened on Ó Riain's face. "She's just in her chambers across the way, Enean, but I wish she hadn't come to Falcarragh at all. This isn't the place for a woman in her condition."

Enean didn't answer, sweeping past Ó Riain and going back inside. "Nuala!" he called as he pushed past the draperies and into his chamber. One of Nuala's maidservants came to the door, peered inside, then left. A few moments later, Nuala hurried in, still placing a shawl around her shoulders. Her belly had swelled considerably in the last few weeks, and she cupped her hands under her womb. "Enean?"

As always when he looked at her, Enean felt a rush of affection. He strode quickly over to her and wrapped her in his arms, pulling the mound of her belly into him. He kissed the nape of her neck, then her mouth. She laughed under his lips, her hands coming up to tangle in his hair.

Nuala never seemed to care about his disfigured face. She never treated him as some kind of slow child, as some of the Riocha did. And she would give him a child soon: a son, he was certain, who would grow up to be the man that Enean himself might have been had that robber's sword not changed his life forever. Nuala was a gift, one that Edana had given to him.

Edana . . .

He saw his half sister's face in his memory, heard her laughter, mixed with that of Nuala. He released his wife, frowning suddenly. "What's the matter?" Nuala asked.

He saw her gaze slip past his shoulder to where Ó Riain stood watching.

"I was thinking of Edana," Enean answered truthfully. He knew people lied, aye, but he rarely did so himself and not very well when he did. "I miss her."

"You should forget her as if she were dead," Ó Riain said immediately. Enean, looking at Nuala's face, saw his wife stiffen and her mouth pull into a tight moue. "Edana's shown that her loyalty is to that traitor Doyle Mac Ard and the Inishlanders, and she's almost certainly in Doire Coill with the Banrion and her daughter and the wretched Bunús Muintir. I told you how they attacked the Rí Gabair's gardai, Enean, remember? We had Mac Ard captured, and the Banrion's daughter and her filthy band came out of the dark wood and rescued them. Well, they can stay there until we're finished with Inish Thuaidh, and then we'll come back and deal with them."

Enean spun around to face Ó Riain. "Edana is *not* a traitor," he said, irritation at Ó Riain coloring his voice. Sometimes the man seemed to smother Enean, a burden that weighed him down and made it difficult to even breathe. "She *loves* me."

"She loves Mac Ard, and she would kill you in a moment if she thought that it would allow her to be Banrion."

A fury rose inside Enean. He could feel it building, like a dragon's fire igniting in his belly and rising, rising through him so that his hands trembled with it and the lines of his face burned. He glared at Ó Riain, who looked back at him blandly. "That's not *true!*"

"It is true, Enean, and the sooner you realize it, the better. Everyone knows it's true. Ask the Ríthe. Ask any of the Riocha. Ask the cloudmages of the Order of Gabair. Edana might have loved you once, but she loves power more. She and Mac Ard both deserve death— and they'll have it the next time we meet."

"That's *my* decision," Enean insisted, the fury still rising.

Ó Riain merely smiled, and the heat exploded inside Enean. "Enean, please . . ." he heard Nuala say warningly behind him, but it was too late. With a guttural and wordless roar, he pushed Ó Riain, shoving him backward with both muscular arms. Ó Riain tumbled backward, slamming into the wall and sliding down. Enean had his hand on the hilt of his sword; Ó Riain's hand went to Lámh Shábhála, installed on a new, wide golden chain around his neck.

"Enean!" Nuala screamed at him, and her shrill cry broke through the red cloud around him. "By the Mother, no!" She pulled at his sword hand, trying to drag him back from Ó Riain. There was panic and a desperate entreaty in her voice, and a manic strength in her hands. "Enean, please. *Please!* The Regent Guardian has only your best interests in his heart. That's all."

Enean could see a glow enveloping Ó Riain's hand as the man glared at him with slitted eyes. Nuala had moved around so that she was between them, and she hugged him desperately, her hand on his scarred cheek as she stared up at him. "You shouldn't fight with the Regent Guardian, Enean," she pleaded. "He'll keep you safe during the battle. He thinks only of you." She cast a beseeching glance back at Ó Riain. "Isn't that true, Regent Guardian?"

Slowly, Ó Riain released Lámh Shábhála and the glow faded around his hand. He wiped at his lips with the back of his hand, then pushed himself to his feet. He brushed at his clothing. "The Rí Ard is always in my thoughts," he said slowly. "Always."

The energy of Enean's rage was leeching away as quickly as it had come, and his face relaxed into a slight, wan smile. "I'm sorry, Labhrás," he said. Nuala still clung to him. "I shouldn't have pushed you like that." Ó Riain nodded, but the answering smile never came to his face even though his words were honeyed and soft.

"The Rí Ard doesn't need to apologize for anything he does," he said. He rolled his shoulder as if it ached from the impact with the wall. "The Rí Ard need only lead us into battle and to victory. I consider it my duty to show the Rí Ard exactly the right time to strike against those who stand between him and what he desires. And that time is soon. Very soon."

He did smile then, a fleeting tug at one corner of his thin lips before he moved to the door, Enean turning to watch him. Ó Riain knocked and one of the hall garda opened the door as Ó Riain bowed to Enean and Nuala. Then, with a swift adjustment of the folds of his clóca, he left. The garda nodded to Enean and shut the door again.

"Why are you trembling?" he asked Nuala. "I can feel you shivering. Are you cold?"

Nuala held him tightly, laying her head on his chest. "Aye," she said. "That's it, my love. I'm cold." He felt her arms press him to her. "I'm just cold."

"The sweetfish are running in the outflow current. Come swim with me."

Dhegli heard Challa's call, but he didn't immediately respond. He was standing in human form on a foamy shingle of beach, staring inward at Winter Home. He and Challa had been three days moving down the Great Sweetwater from its northern lakes to its long, widening mouth well in the south, and then more days moving up the coast of Winter Home. They were as far up the coast now as they would go, ready to make the crossing across open water to Nesting Land. They were both weary from the travel and the thought of sweetfish made Dhegli's stomach growl, but yet . . .

He could still feel Meriel in his chest. He could sense her, somewhere deep in Winter Home's hard interior, moving. No longer where she'd been, near the north pool of the Great Sweetwater, and not too distant from where Dhegli stood now. He could feel the determination and fire in her, and the fear. Meriel was going to where Lámh Shábhála, the great sky-stone, burned. He knew that the First Holder no longer held the stone; he'd felt it in the mage-lights. And now Meriel was moving to the stone, and he could sense the danger, could feel it as clearly as he saw the foretellings that Bradán an Chumhacht sent to him.

"Dhegli?"

He did turn then, letting his human form go, so that it was another Saimhóir who looked back at Challa, hauled out on a rock in the white surf. "I hear you, sister-kin," he said.

She warbled her acknowledgment, but her gaze went past him to the stones of the Winter Home. "You made your choice days ago, brother-kin," she told him. "You can't be thinking of returning to her." There was pain in her voice, and sadness, and—aye—disappointment and even anger.

"She goes into the heart of danger with little help and little hope. Bradán an Chumhacht—"

"Bradán an Chumhacht is for the Saimhóir, as the sky-stones are for the stone-walkers. Why do you persist in helping them when they don't help us in return? Why do you listen to the stone-walker in your blood instead of the Saimhóir that is your true being?" Her muzzle lowered and she slapped her tail on the wet rock. "You have love *here,* Dhegli, right in front of you. You have love that you can share for more than a few hours a day. You're Water-snared, Dhegli, or you couldn't have swallowed Bradán an Chumhacht. Your duty is to the Saimhóir and our needs."

"I know that."

"Then come with me and eat the sweetfish so that we'll be strong enough to reach Nesting Land tomorrow. We've both been too long gone from the families. They'll be wondering if Bradán an Chumhacht swims free again." She paused. "I need to return to Nesting Land, Dhegli. There is new life within me. *Our* life."

"Ahh . . ." For a moment, Dhegli felt the pall lift around him. "Challa, that is so wonderful. I didn't know."

"You should have known," she chided him, but it was a gentle thrust and her deeper affection for him showed in the shiver of her blue-black fur and the deep night of her eyes.

"You're right. I didn't, and I should have. It makes me wonder, though . . ."

She knew his thoughts. "You wonder if Meriel also has new life." There was no jealousy in her voice, not as the stone-walkers would have understood it—that wasn't an emotion the Saimhóir understood or felt. Dhegli would undoubtedly mate with many of the cows and Challa with many of the bulls. Sexual fidelity simply didn't matter. But there was still friendship and there was still love and Dhegli heard that concern.

"I do," he admitted.

"You can't be with her, not the way the stone-walkers would do it," Challa told him. "And any child that you have might not even carry the blood of the Saimhóir and be able to change. It might not be able to follow you into the sea."

"Our child would carry the Saimhóir blood," Dhegli said.

"You *know* this?" Challa asked, emphasizing the word. "You've *seen* it."

"There's no certainty in Bradán an Chumhacht's visions of the future," he answered. "Only glimpses, possibilities, and choices. But as much as anything in the future can be known, I know that if it *would* happen that Meriel carries my child, then that child would have a destiny for both Saimhóir and stone-walker."

"And now?" Challa asked. "Where do we go now?"

"I don't know," Dhegli answered truthfully. He looked out over the gray, white-tipped waves to where—just over the horizon—the Nesting Land lay in fog and rain, and he could feel the pull. Bradán an Chumhacht was a magic of the WaterMother, and to risk it to help the stone-walkers seemed somehow wrong, when he could use the power for his own people. Yet . . .

He could feel her, also, and in the visions of Bradán

an Chumhacht, he had seen her die—die because he wasn't there to prevent it. *The waters were bright with magic. He could taste the energy in the salty currents as he swam among the floating islands of their ships. Meriel was above him, the magic of the sky-stones flaring around her, defenseless. He swam up, up, holding the power of Bradán an Chumhacht ready, and releasing it as he broached the water, deflecting the bolt that would have killed Meriel. But he had been seen, too, and one of the cloudmages turned his attention to Dhegli and searing red light tore through him, shattering his body. As he sank senseless back into the water, Bradán an Chumhacht swam from his open, bleeding mouth into the sea, free again. . . .*

He didn't know if that was a cost he could pay. He didn't know if it was a cost he *should* pay. As if she sensed the pattern of his thoughts, Challa spoke again. "Any debt Bradán an Chumhacht may owe to the stone-walkers for returning it to life has been paid, many times over," she said.

"I know that," he answered. "That doesn't concern me. But I also owe Meriel."

"For showing her what was inside her?" Challa scoffed. "For coming for her when she called? For returning her love? For bringing that stone-walker cloudmage to find her? I would say the debt is on her side."

"I hear you," he said. "Maybe you're right." He snorted, looking again at the shore and feeling Meriel's presence. "For now, let's swim out to find the sweetfish and eat, and then we'll see. We'll see."

49

Alliances Formed

THEY WALKED the rest of the day, and Meriel noticed that Jenna grew slowly more tired and less communicative as the day went on. By the time that the sun was painting long shadows across the rolling landscape through which the River Donn meandered, Jenna, with Meriel beside her, was trailing well behind the rest of the group. Meriel heard the low drumming of horses' hooves on the roadway, past the curve they'd just rounded. They'd met other travelers on the road that day and had stayed on the road, exchanging greetings and the normal civilities, and attracting no more attention than any other group.

But riders meant Riocha, and they were coming from the south, which meant they might be from Kilmaur and pursuing them. "Mam, we need to get off the road," she said. Jenna stared back at Meriel dully, her gaze listless, her mouth half open. "Mam, come with me," she said more urgently, pulling at her. She could hear the brighter jangling of livery now, and a faint laugh. She half pulled Jenna to the side of the road and over the low stone wall that bordered it, both of them hunkering down in the brush between the stones and the riverbank. She hoped that the others ahead of them heard the riders as well, but it was too late to call to them.

There were half a dozen Riocha in the group, all male, laughing and joking as they walked past, their great

steeds sniffing and blowing and tossing their heads.
Through the brush, Meriel could see that the livery was
in the green and brown of Tuath Gabair, and at least
one of the men had a cloch na thintrí around his neck.
They wore leathers and had swords ready at their sides:
these were not Riocha on a jaunt, but going to war.

". . . If I remember, there's a village just ahead. We'll
stop there for the night," she heard one of them say
as they passed. "We'll be at Falcarragh soon enough
tomorrow. The Rí Ard has said that he wants all the
Clochs Mór there before we take ship. The Inishlanders
will be squashed like bugs under a rock."

Low laughter followed, flowing out over the river. The
riders passed on, and after a time, Meriel helped Jenna
back onto the road. They found the others not too long
after, waiting for them. Owaine pointed northward. "I
went on ahead a bit. There's a village around the next
bend, and those riders are in the inn at the edge of town.
I think we should camp here, up on the hillside in the
trees, rather than going on. The Riocha may have heard
about us in Kilmaur."

No one objected, and they made their way through a
boggy meadow and up the slope until the road was hidden behind the screen of foliage. They sank down gratefully among the leaves, tired and sore. Owaine started a
small fire and Meriel fixed andúilleaf for Jenna, who went
to sleep almost immediately after drinking the brew. Meriel watched her, brushing back her mam's hair and tuck-
ing a blanket around her. She fingered Treoraí's Heart,
feeling the cloch's desire to be used.

"You can't," Owaine said behind her. His hand
touched her shoulder; she didn't move. "Not after the
last time."

"I know," she told him. "But she hurts so much, all
the time . . ."

"You already know that you can't do anything about
that. The best thing we can do for her is take Lámh
Shábhála back," he said.

She almost laughed, looking around them: her mam

moaning in her sleep; Edana hanging a small cook pot
over the fire on a makeshift tripod of branches to make
a stew of dried herbs and some of the smoked meat they
carried; Doyle watching her, his own pain reflected in
the gray cast of his skin and the dark blotches under his
eyes. "Aye, we look fierce and dangerous," Meriel said.
"If I were the Rí Ard, I'd be trembling inside the walls
of my keep with all my armies and all the Clochs Mór
around me, if I knew we were coming."

Owaine did laugh then, and his fingers tightened on
her shoulder. " 'Tis true it sounds foolish, but sometimes
fools do great things."

"Name one who did," Meriel said.

There was silence behind her.

"Usually fools fail," Doyle's voice commented, but
when Meriel glanced over, he was watching Edana.
"Maybe I can snare a coney or squirrel," Doyle said.
He'd yet to shed his pack, standing over her. "It'd taste
better than this dried stuff."

"How are you feeling, my love?" Edana asked him.

Doyle shrugged. "Awful. Worse than ever. But sitting
here won't help. Not me, not us, and not that stew."

"Doyle?" Edana rose from the fire, going to him, but
he shook his head.

"I'm as fine as I'm going to be. Just . . ." He seemed
to shiver. "I need to be by myself. I'll be back in a bit,"
he said, and strode off.

"Mac Ard!" Owaine called after him, but Doyle never
turned or responded.

"Let him go," Meriel said to Owaine.

"We don't know what he's going to do or where he's
going, Meriel," Owaine protested. Edana looked carefully away. "When those men passed us, the riders, I
thought Doyle might know them."

"He did," Edana said softly, without looking at the
two of them. "They were from the Order of Gabair, and
one of them was Shay O Blaca, the head of the Order."

"Then he could be betraying us, right now."

"Not without betraying me also," Edana answered.

Her face lifted, and she looked at Owaine as she might
have at an insolent Tiarna, back in Dún Laoghaire. "As
well as losing any chance he has to gain back the Cloch
Mór he lost."

"She's right," Meriel agreed. "We can't worry about
him, Owaine. Not at this point."

Owaine sniffed, staring into the gathering twilight
where Doyle had gone, but he said nothing.

Doyle stood cloaked in the darkness under an oak tree
near the inn, though he could hear the voices inside and
see the yellow light of the fire and candles through the
half open shutters. A boy of perhaps thirteen summers
wandered down the street from one of the village houses
and Doyle called out to him. "Young sir! I have a favor
to ask of you."

The youth stopped a careful few feet away. "An' what
would that be?" he asked suspiciously, peering slit-eyed
at Doyle. Doyle reached into the purse tied to his belt
and retrieved a mórceint; he flipped the coin once so
that the boy could see the glitter of it in the light from
the inn's windows. "There's a tiarna inside. You'll recognize him easily—a big man, in green and brown, and he
has a Cloch Mór around his neck that's the white of sea
foam. His name's Shay O Blaca. I want you to tell him
that you have a private message, only for him. Get him
away from his companions, or whisper it into his ear if
you must. Tell him that there's someone outside who
would like to speak with him."

"If I were a tiarna, I wouldn't be coming out, not into
an ambush, an' I might be tempted to hurt the messenger a bit, just to see what else he knows."

Doyle laughed. "Ah, you're a wise one, indeed. Give
Shay one more word: tell him it concerns Snapdragon.
Just that. Snapdragon. He'll understand." Doyle flipped
the coin toward the boy; it landed glistening at his feet.
"Can you do that for me?"

The boy stopped, plucked the coin from the earth. From the expression on his face, Doyle knew that he'd been expecting a simple copper. His eyebrows raised at the gleam of gold, probably more money than his family saw in a month. "Aye," he said wonderingly. "Aye, I can indeed."

"Then do it. I'll be here, waiting."

Doyle watched the boy enter the tavern, the light spilling out across the road and the voices rising in volume as he opened the door, then darkness and quiet returning as it shut behind him. Doyle moved away from the tree, going to the side of the inn. A few moments later, the door opened again and he saw O Blaca's broad shadow outlined in the light. The man stood there, obviously peering out into the darkness. "Shay," Doyle called, stepping out so that O Blaca could see him. "I need to talk with you. Alone."

"Doyle?" O Blaca's bass rumble was a half laugh, but there was a bitter tinge to it, a cautious reserve. He glanced over his shoulder into the tavern. "By the Mother, man, you're supposed to still be back in Doire Coill. Someone's information is very wrong."

"And it needs to stay wrong," Doyle told him. "I hope you're still the friend I know you to be. I hope your loyalty's to the Order of Gabair before any oath you've given to that damned Ó Riain."

Shay's face tightened. "The new Holder?" He spat carefully on the ground. "You don't look good, Doyle Mac Ard. You look ill and beaten."

"Ill, aye. I am that. Beaten?" Doyle lifted a shoulder.

"You were always resilient, I'll give you that," Shay said. "Why are you here, Doyle. Is it Snapdragon? The Toscaire Concordai wears your Cloch Mór, and he's with the Regent Guardian."

Doyle shook his head. "Not Snapdragon, though I'll pay back the Toscaire for that."

O Blaca nodded but he looked unconvinced. "So that's it, is it? Still pursuing the chimera. If you've come here looking for help from me, then I'm sorry, Doyle.

Cloudmages need to tread carefully right now, especially when it concerns the new Rí Ard's Regent Guardian."

"Aye, I can believe that," Doyle answered. "But the Regent Guardian might not be the Holder of Lámh Shábhála for long. The winds may change."

"Those are nice and brave words, but you hardly inspire confidence, Doyle. Your last few plans have been . . . less than successful. Damned deadly, in fact, for those in it with you."

Doyle hissed, drawing himself up even though the pain inside made him want to hunch over. "I *had* Lámh Shábhála, Shay," he said bitterly. "You know that. I *had* the cloch and it was only betrayal by that foul Toscaire Concordai and Ó Riain that ruined it. The Order of Gabair would have been ascendant then, Shay, and you and the rest of our cloudmages with it. We *had* it . . ."

"There's no 'we' when it comes to holding Lámh Shábhála. And it's 'had.' Not 'have.' We don't have it now."

"But maybe again."

O Blaca smiled. "Your appearance doesn't say that, Doyle. I see no Cloch Mór around your neck. I see a sick man who looks as if he can barely stand, who dragged himself here from Gabair in clothes more ragged than a field worker's. Do you command an army of beggars, Doyle? Will you come against the Regent Guardian and Lámh Shábhála with pitchforks and torches?"

Doyle nodded. "I will do that if I need to. But, Shay, my old friend, remember that twice now since Knobtop I was to be killed and I'm still alive. Fiodóir hasn't woven me out of the tapestry of life, and so I think the Mother-Creator has a better fate in store for me at the end. Remember the tales you heard of how I vanished into Doire Coill; remember that I'm still supposed to *be* in the Dark Wood surrounded by gardai, and I've escaped. I dress as I do because I want to move without notice, but don't make the mistake of thinking me an old toothless dog."

"And what kind of teeth do you have?"

Doyle glanced up. Tendrils of light were snaking among the stars, brightening and lowering, swirls and coils of gold and blood and deep-water blue. Seeing the mage-lights made the yearning swell in Doyle's chest, made him want to close his eyes and moan with the pain of the loss. He forced himself not to move and to keep the pain inside. "What teeth?" he answered. "Teeth that will chew on the mage-lights. The teeth of a sister. Inish teeth. Cloudmage teeth."

O Blaca made a hissing noise, glancing up at the mage-lights. "You and Edana have allied with the Order of Inishfeirm?"

"I've allied with those who will gain me what I want. I've allied with those who will take down the Regent Guardian-Holder. Understand that I've no quarrel with Enean, though—he's a pawn in this."

"He's more than a pawn, Doyle. He has Weaver." Doyle sucked in his breath at that, and O Blaca nodded. "Aye, a Cloch Mór is around his neck, he has a strong right arm, and the commanders of the armies may know that he's childlike and slow, but they still admire him. If you want Lámh Shábhála, you have to consider Enean."

"Then I will," Doyle answered. "And you, Shay? Where is your loyalty?"

O Blaca sniffed. "I gave my fealty first to the Order, then to the Rí Gabair, then to the Rí Ard. Rí Mallaghan said he would follow the Rí Ard into battle, and so I go with him. I'm just telling you this: Enean could be more trouble than you think."

"And Edana could always handle him. He won't hurt his sister, Shay."

O Blaca glanced up at the mage-lights, strengthening and glowing brighter. In a few moments, Doyle knew, the others would be coming out from the inn so their clochs na thintrí could commune with the power above. But he would not. He could only look at the mage-lights and feel the empty yawning hole inside himself. "Perhaps not," Shay ventured, "but you may have to deal with Enean as an enemy. Are you prepared to do that? Is Edana?"

"We'll do what we need to do," Doyle answered. "Right now I need to know if you'll help. If I ask for your aid sometime in the next few days, will you give it?"

"Recently, when I've done that, the results have been less than spectacular." Doyle saw O Blaca's hand start to drift to his Cloch Mór, and he knew the man wanted to turn his attention to the mage-lights.

"I promise that no one will know of your involvement unless I'm successful, Shay. For what we put together in the Order of Gabair, I ask this of you. *Especially* for the good of the Order."

O Blaca sighed. "Aye. We've always been friends, Doyle. I've thought of you as the younger brother I never had. I'll make no promise, understand, but I'll listen when you call. If I can—*if* I can—I'll do what you ask, especially if it takes down Ó Riain. Right now the Holder's attention is on Inish Thuaidh; when that's over, I suspect he'll look at the Order of Gabair, and I don't trust the man."

Doyle grinned and slapped the O Blaca on the back. "You're a good friend, Shay. I promise you won't regret this."

"Then you'd best be leaving before the others come out for the mage-lights and see you," O Blaca told him. "They might be inclined to claim the reward the Rí Ard's put out for you." He started to close his hand around his cloch, but Doyle interrupted him.

"One more thing," Doyle told him. "You remember the rabbit hutch that sits just outside the eastern gate of Goat Fell back in Lár Bhaile? Aye? Good . . ."

"They're asleep," Meriel said quietly. "Why aren't you?"

Owaine turned. The mage-lights had died and their

campfire had gone to glowing ash. Meriel was a dark shadow under the tree-cloaked and cloud-masked sky. She sat next to him, close enough that Owaine could feel the heat of her body. "Doyle," he said.

"That's what I thought."

"He was gone two stripes or more, Meriel, and he didn't come back until the mage-lights were failing."

"At least he came back with a rabbit. And it tasted good." He heard rather than saw her smile.

"I still don't think he was hunting most of the time he was gone."

"You think he has a cloch he's hiding? That he used the mage-lights out of sight of us?"

Owaine grimaced. "No. I think we'd have sensed that. But I do wonder . . . We're so close to the village where those Riocha have stopped, and Edana admitted they knew them."

"We can't worry about that," Meriel answered. "I think Doyle just needed to be alone as he said: to think, to rage, to suffer in private without people being around." Her shoulder lifted, brushing against his. "I don't know how deeply he's hurt, but I can understand. Sometimes we get angry at those who most want to help us, even when we shouldn't. Even when we realize how stupid we're being."

"You're too trusting and forgiving."

Meriel laughed. "I wish I actually had either of those two qualities. I don't think I've ever forgiven my mam for what I thought was the way she ignored me as a child, even when I finally started to understand why she acted the way she did. And you, Owaine . . . I never trusted you when I should have, all along."

Something in the tone of the words made Owaine lift his head. The affection for her, the feelings that he'd had ever since he met her in Inishfeirm, that he'd pushed down lest they choke him, rose again as they always did, seeming to batter against the bars of his rib cage. "It doesn't matter," he told her, the lie coming automatically. It *did* matter; it *had* hurt, but the ache never altered his feelings, his infatuation with her. He'd raged against himself many nights, angry at his own stupidity for being captured by her when it was so obvious that the affection wasn't—would never be—returned. At Inishfeirm, he had always seen the annoyance that pulled at her mouth whenever she saw him or whenever they spoke or even when he simply happened across her in the halls, and it had hurt. Even after he'd gone after her and found her in Doire Coill . . . "I didn't care."

"I think you should have. I think you did." Her hand touched his. He didn't dare move. Her fingers interlaced with his own, pressing. Slowly, tentatively, he returned the pressure. She was very close to him when he looked at her, and water shimmered in her eyes. "I've been stupid for a long time. I've missed what's right in front of me. I'm sorry."

Her hand pulled away from his; reluctantly, he let it go. He thought she'd rise then, and leave him. But the hand lifted in the darkness and touched his cheek, her fingers curling around the back of his neck, a slight, slight pressure . . .

She brought his head down to hers.

Her lips were wonderfully soft, her breath sweet and warm. After the first touch, he started to pull away, uncertain, but her hand brought him back down and this time he responded as he wished, his arms going around her. The kiss was long and lingering, their mouths slowly opening to each other, and he could feel the tears running down her cheek. Reluctantly, he broke away from her, brushing the moisture away from her skin with his thumb.

"Why?" he asked her finally, not knowing if he were asking her about the tears or the kiss.

"Don't ask questions, Owaine. Just accept it."

"I have to ask," he told her. "I saw you with Dhegli, Meriel. I know how you felt about him because it was the way I felt about you. But you've never felt that way about me. So I . . ."

"Shh," she told him, placing a finger on his lips. "Isn't this what you wanted?"

"More than anything else," he told her. "But I only want it if it's what you want also. For the same reasons." He watched her eyes. Her gaze held his, solemn.

"Owaine . . ."

"It's different, isn't it, Meriel? Different than what you had with Thady and then with Dhegli."

Her answer was a sigh melded with a sob. "Aye," she told him. "But what I had with them . . . Owaine, it didn't last. And Dhegli . . ."

She was crying now, and Owaine had to resist the temptation to just take her in his arms, to try to comfort her. "I realize now that Dhegli doesn't see love the same way that we do," she said finally. "I realize that there has to be more than heat and light in a relationship. There has to be something deeper if it's to last. Owaine . . ." She choked back a sob, gazing up at him pleadingly. "I don't deserve your love. Truthfully, I'm not even really sure what I'm feeling right now. I don't know what it will become or where we can take it. You're right; it is different than what I felt for Lucan and Thady and Dhegli, but maybe it's better that way. I don't know. I know that it feels right to be with you. Here. Now." She pressed his hand. "If it's what you still want."

He could feel his pulse throbbing at the sides of his neck. "Aye," he managed to say. "But only if it's also what you want."

"It is," she whispered. "Aye. Come here, Owaine . . ." She lay back and pulled him down alongside her.

This time the kiss lasted far longer.

50

Into the City

NO ONE remarked on the fact that Owaine and Meriel were sharing a bedroll the next morning. Edana, first up, woke Meriel with the soft noise as she rekindled the cook fire, and the young woman's eyebrows lifted slightly as Meriel peered at her sleepily, but Edana said nothing, not even when Meriel reluctantly left the covers to help her and Owaine also stirred. Jenna also was awake, but she was staring into a distance that none of them could see and only seemed to snap back into focus when the smell of andúilleaf reached her nose. She grasped the cup that Meriel brought her eagerly, her stiff and scarred right hand curling around the mug like a piece of deadwood, bitterly cold to Meriel's touch. Jenna sipped at the brew despite the heat.

"Look," Jenna said, pointing with her chin as she drank. "Over there."

Meriel saw it then: a doe and her fawn—not the storm deer, but the more usual red. They were standing in the shadows of the elms close to the edge of the clearing in which they'd made their camp. Above them, the elm's branches were covered with several long white vines . . . but as Meriel watched, the vines writhed and wriggled, and she realized they were not vines, but pale-scaled snakes, their bodies longer than a human's and as thick around as Meriel's forearms. Even as Meriel opened her mouth to speak, the snakes moved, dropping as one suddenly on the fawn. The doe gave a high bleat and fled into the woods.

The snakes wriggled, wrapping their long, muscular bodies around the panicked fawn's neck, their heads rearing back and biting the animal repeatedly. It was over in a moment. The fawn went down, its legs kicking wildly and then going terribly still after a last, final jerk of its body. The snakes continued to writhe around it, like a nest of impossibly huge worms, their jaws wide as they started to tear away and shred the flesh of the young deer. Meriel could hear the sound of their feeding, a wet, continuous rasping like liquid fire. Muscles moved in waves down the snakes' thick bodies as they swallowed and gorged themselves.

There was a horrible, visceral fascination to it. Meriel stared. "Snakes don't cooperate," Owaine said behind her. "Not like that." His arm went around Meriel and she leaned gratefully into his embrace. He smelled familiar and good.

"Evidently those have never heard that rule," Doyle said. He'd awakened as well. Edana, by the fire, had stopped preparing breakfast. "You know, my love, I think I've just lost any appetite I had."

"What are they?" Meriel asked. "There aren't any snakes in Inish Thuaidh, and they're supposed to be rare even here in Talamh an Ghlas. But I've never heard of any like *those*."

"I woke them," Jenna said, and Meriel glanced over Owaine's shoulder at her mam. She was staring also, with no horror on her face but only a solemn fascination. "Or rather, Lámh Shábhála did, at the Filleadh. As it woke others."

"You could have skipped those, Banrion, and I wouldn't have complained," Owaine said. Meriel felt him shiver. "Let's pack up and get moving." No one objected. They quickly broke camp and moved through the trees toward the High Road, watching carefully above them for white snakes.

"We should come to the Donn Gate of Falcarragh by

the end of today's walk," Doyle told them when they reached the road. The village was just ahead of them, though the Riocha who had ridden past them the previous evening had evidently already left the inn, for they could see that the stables were empty except for a few draft animals. "What do we do then . . . ?" His voice trailed off into the question.

"We lose ourselves in the crowds, first," Owaine said. "We find somewhere where we can be relatively safe, and we see what the situation is."

"There's going to be no place 'safe' in Falcarragh, not with mages everywhere and the combined armies of the Tuatha in town," Doyle answered.

"With all that, it's going to be more chaotic than usual. A few ragged travelers shouldn't attract much attention," Owaine told him.

Meriel listened to the two of them—*just like men, to plan without asking any of the rest of us what we think*— her own thoughts far less certain. She had no plan in mind beyond reaching Falcarragh; in truth, part of her hadn't believed they would actually get this far. It had seemed so improbable, back in Doire Coill. Now, facing the actuality, it looked no better. Jenna, especially, seemed to grow more withdrawn and exhausted as they approached the city. She said almost nothing that morning as they passed through a succession of small villages that seemed to crowd close together along the River Donn as it swelled toward its meeting the with Bay of Falcarragh. Meriel had worried that Jenna, used to being not only among Riocha, but as Banrion someone whose word was to be listened to and obeyed, might accidentally betray them. But she remained silent and hunched over whenever other travelers greeted them or talked to them, and no one gave the woman with the heavily-bandaged right arm more than a glance of pity.

Seeing Falcarragh, late that afternoon, made their intentions seem beyond foolish. . . .

They topped a small hill and spotted the Donn Gate ahead of them, the westernmost entry to the city, where

the River Donn, now wide and slow, made a sweeping
northward turn and opened into the long cleft of Falcarragh Bay, which would finally join the Westering Sea
twenty-five miles to the north. From there, Inish Thuaidh was only thirty miles distant across island-pocked
waters.

Falcarragh itself lay before them, its dwellings sweeping up on steep hills, though the bulk of the city, Meriel
would learn, was hidden from them, nestled in a wide
valley just beyond the ridge to the east of Donn Gate.
But beyond the ridge, the city swept up again on the
shoulder of two tall, rounded peaks: Sliabh Gabhar,
where the Rí's Keep perched in stolid impregnability as
it overlooked the bay; and the taller and steeper hump
of Sliabh Sí, where the Mother-Creator's temple stood.
Out in the misty, blue distance, they could see ships at
anchor, dozens of them slumbering on the waves. And
Donn Gate . . .

Meriel had always thought Dún Kiil, the capital city
of Inish Thuaidh, immense and crowded, especially compared to the towns and villages she'd visited elsewhere
on the island. But this . . . Several roads converged here,
the one they had followed up from Lough Donn, another
coming in from the east and Glenkille, yet another crossing the Donn Bridge from the west and south, leading—
Meriel suspected—all the way down to Tuath Connachta
and Keelballi. The gates themselves were immense iron
latticework doors, fancifully wrought in the shape of animals and vines and leaves, and so large that Meriel realized it must take a dozen gardai to close each of them.
Twin round towers marked the opening, the ledges of
each story adorned with the leering faces of gargoyles
and mythical beasts, the summits—twenty feet above the
road—also populated with stone carvings. A thick stone
wall ran from the end of the Donn Bridge, along the
bank of the river, and then turned abruptly toward the
first of the gate towers. From the other side, a second
wall extended to the south until it swept over the steep
slope of the ridge and vanished in the distance.

"By the Mother . . ." Owaine breathed the exclamation, nearly open-jawed with wonder. They'd stopped, moving to one side of the road to gaze out over the sight as other travelers moved past them toward the gate. Meriel almost laughed, knowing how the city must appear to Owaine's eyes, having never been away from tiny Inishfeirm. "I never thought so many people could live so close together," he said.

"I know," Meriel told him, linking her arm in his and leaning her head against his shoulder. Behind them, she heard Doyle sniff and Edana shush him. "I've never seen the like. Not even Dún Kiil."

"Aye, but you've never seen Dún Laoghaire," Doyle said. "You could fit Falcarragh inside the inner wall there and have room left over."

"Then I hope I never see it," Owaine told him. "I'll be happy to go back to . . ." He stopped and looked around them. *Inishfeirm.* Meriel knew what he'd wanted to say, but it wasn't a name one should evoke here, where there were so many ears to overhear. Owaine sighed. "We should go on," he said.

It seemed that everyone in all of Talamh an Ghlas was trying to cram themselves at once between the massive stone portals of Donn Gate: wagons full of produce from the outlying farms, travelers from each of the roads, a squadron of gardai wearing the red-and-white colors of Tuath Airgialla and marching in solemn formation, Riocha on horseback or in carriages, peddlers, citizens hurrying about on business, even a caravan of brightly-clothed Taisteal (making Meriel think of Sevei and Nico, and starting her wondering what had happened to Clan Dranaghi in the wake of her escape). The visual riot of color was matched by a cacophony of noise: people shouting, animals bleating and grunting, the racket of squealing, poorly-greased axles and wheels, the enticing calls of vendors. The other senses were assaulted as well: the scent of spices and manure and far too many people; the feel of exotic cloths and the salty mist of the bay on their skin. Falcarragh was overwhelming, its sensory input almost too much after Doire Coill and then the long walk from Lough Donn. At least it appeared they could lose themselves easily in the city, as Owaine had intimated.

Assuming that they could first could get through Donn Gate . . . There were gardai there, watching those entering. They leaned against the doors to the towers, appearing to be mostly bored, but their gazes were on the crowds passing into the city. Meriel and the others stayed to the middle of the avenue, trying to hide themselves among the crowd without appearing to do so. Meriel, holding her mam's arm, crowded against a wagon full of melons, the ripe smell of them almost overpowering, trying to shield them from the gardai to their right with the horse.

"Hey! You there!" The shout came from the left, and Meriel's head snapped around. One of the gardai had pushed himself away from the wall and was striding over in their direction with two of his companions. "Aye, you two!" he called, pointing to Owaine and Doyle. Doyle glanced at Owaine, then took a half-step forward to meet them.

"Sirs?" he inquired, his voice a husky whisper. "Is there a problem?"

The gardai who'd hailed them grinned. "No problem at all. In fact, we have a proposition. You two look like fine young specimens, and we happen to have a need for men like you. Haven't you heard that war is about to start? We need good, strong hands on the pikes, and we'll pay you ten coppers a day for the privilege—to you, or to your widows." He grinned again, displaying tilted brown teeth. "You'll be coming with me now—" He leaned forward as if he were about to grab Doyle by the arm as his companions also came toward them.

Doyle coughed, a long and horrible hacking sound, and the gardai stopped. He scowled, looking closely at Doyle's drawn and ashen face. "I have an illness from the marshes," Doyle told the man. "I was bitten by wind sprites, and the next day was like this. The woman with us, my mam . . ." He gestured at Jenna, who glared once but said nothing. "She has it, too." He coughed again, openmouthed, in the direction of the garda, who took a step back.

"Then perhaps you should stay and take care of your mam," the garda said. Then his gaze drifted to Owaine. "But your friend here looks healthy enough. Come along with us, now." He gestured to his men to take Owaine, but Meriel rushed forward, grasping him.

"No, you can't," she cried. "We're . . . we're newly married, and I'm with child. Please, if you have any compassion at all . . ."

The garda laughed mockingly. "Aye, I have compassion. And you have a fine face and talk almost as well as a Riocha. I'll let you give him a last kiss to remember him by before we leave, and then you can give us one, too."

"Meriel!" Owaine said sharply. "It's fine. I'll go with them." He looked at Edana, whose hand had moved to her léine, where her Cloch Mór lay hidden. "Be calm," he said, a bit too loudly. "I don't want anyone hurt."

"What accent is that?" the garda asked, his face suddenly suspicious. "That sounds Inish. Take him," he said to the others. "Maybe we've just caught a spy."

"No!" Meriel shouted. The situation seemed to be worsening with each second. The other gardai at the gate were looking over curiously now, and they found themselves in the midst of an open space at the center of the gate traffic, all the other travelers suddenly giving the confrontation wide berth. Meriel had an image of them having to fight their way out of here, of Edana and Owaine bringing their clochs into play, of fire and magic playing their deadly light over the area, of gardai rushing them with swords or sending a rain of arrows at them from the windows of the gate towers as they tried to flee. She wondered if she could grab her mam quickly enough, if Jenna and Doyle had the strength to run at all, and how far they would get before they were caught and brought down. *It all ends now, before we even get into the city.* She wanted to weep, wanted to undo it all and have just stayed back in Doire Coill, where at least they would have been safe. She didn't know if she could stand seeing her mam cut down, or Owaine . . .

There was a sound behind the gardai, high on the tower: like two rocks slamming hard together. As the gardai turned to look, one of the gargoyles perched on the top ledge leaned forward. It tumbled down as people scattered, landing with a crash on the flagstones not ten feet from them, shards of gray stone ricocheting around the gate. One of the gardai clutched his wrist, a long bloody scratch appearing there, and there were cries of pain from other people around them as they were struck by stony shrapnel. There was another loud *crack* as the gargoyle next to the first broke away. "Someone must be up there!" the garda holding Owaine shouted. "Come on!"

The gardai rushed toward the tower as the second statue hit the pavement with another barrage of rock fragments. Someone in a dark clóca was standing alongside them suddenly. "Follow me!" he said, and moved quickly forward with the crush of people through the gate. "Hurry!" The voice seemed familiar though she couldn't see his face, and Meriel heard Jenna— surprisingly—laugh. Owaine grasped Meriel's arm and they were moving, half running and half walking, caught up in the flow away from the scene. Behind them, gardai were shouting to close the gates; they started to swing shut, but they were already through and the huge iron doors clanked into place behind them. People surged at the gate, but the gardai held them back with pikes, and more gardai were rushing from inside the city and along the walls toward the gate.

The man they'd followed turned and swept the hood back from his face. The features were familiar, but out of context, Meriel couldn't find the name. Then it came to her, suddenly: *Mahon MacBreen, the head of the Banrion's personal gardai, always alongside or a little behind her mam whenever she appeared in public, his dark, keen eyes scanning those around them, his hand always near the hilt of his sword.* Jenna smiled—the first time Meriel had seen that expression on her mam's face in a long time. "Mahon, you're the last person I'd expect to find in Falcarragh," she said.

"I think I have at least one other about whom you'd say the same and more," Mahon answered, returning the smile. "I came to bring you to them. If you'll come with me . . ." He stopped, and Meriel heard him choke back the "Banrion" he wanted to add. "We still have a bit of a walk ahead of us, and I think we should leave this area." He looked at them, his eyes narrowing as he saw Doyle and Edana. "This way," he said.

He led them into Falcarragh through the swarm.

51

Meetings and Plans

"WE'VE been waiting for you for two days. The crow that came from the Protector of Doire Coill said that you'd be coming in from Lough Donn, so we've been watching Donn Gate. I almost didn't recognize you until the gardai stopped you. Stay here a moment."

Mahon MacBreen entered the door of a narrow building set in the warrens of Falcarragh. Meriel could see his gaze sweeping the room before he opened the door fully and allowed them to enter. He brought a chair over to the hearth for Jenna, helping her to sit and then crouching down in front of the banked fire to bring it back to life. "It's not much, but we thought it best to attract as little attention as possible."

"We?" Meriel asked, and Mahon grinned at her.

"You'll know soon, Bantiarna MacEagan. Please, sit and rest. You all must be exhausted." Mahon brought out bread, cheese, and water, and put a pot on the crane to boil for tea. As he bustled about, he told them how a crow had appeared at Dún Kiil Keep with a message wrapped about its leg from Keira, telling them that the Banrion was alive and intending to recover Lámh Sháb-hála, and that she and her companions were walking to Falcarragh dressed as peasants and would be there within a week. "You can imagine how Tiarna MacEagan and the Comhairle were in an uproar. He'd been fighting

with them for days, with half the clans saying you were
dead and we must name a new Rí, and Tiarna MacEagan
and his contingent arguing just as forcefully that if you
were dead, we would have learned of it, that the news
would have reached us from our contacts within the Tuatha. He insisted you were still alive, despite the rumors
that the Rí Ard's Regent Guardian was holding Lámh
Shábhála. He wanted to come here himself, but the
Comhairle refused to allow it, naming him Regent and
charging him with the preparations against the Rí Ard's
invasion fleet. But he sent—"

There was the scrape of a key at the door and suddenly Mahon's blade was out. He crouched as the door
opened, motioning the rest of them back, then sheathed
the blade in one motion as a tall, gray-haired man entered. In shabby clothing, he looked very different, but
both Owaine and Meriel shouted at the same time.

"Máister Kirwan!"

Mundy laughed, shaking his head and lifting a finger
to his lips. "That's not a title to use here," he said. "Too
many ears, and none of them friendly. But it's good to
see the two of you, safe after all this time. I worried, so
often . . ." He looked at Doyle and Edana, then Jenna,
huddled near the fire. "Jenna, it's true, then, that the
Regent Guardian has the cloch? I'm so sorry . . ."

Jenna's mouth turned up in a quick, fleeting smile.
"So am I, Mundy. I should have listened to you and
Kyle, but then you always said I was too stubborn for
my own good."

"Aye, and it's the same quality that made you a good
Holder, and will make you one again."

Jenna gave him the fleeting smile again, but Meriel
saw none of that optimism in her mam's eyes. "So now
we know what happened at Donn Gate," Meriel said to
Mundy. "That was you."

"A bit of slow magic, that's all. Mahon and I thought
that when you came we might need a bit of a diversion,
and rather than unleash my Cloch Mór and alert all of
the Riocha here that an Inish cloudmage was in their

midst, I took the time to prepare a few spells." Satisfaction widened his smile. "You should have stayed around to watch; they were still clambering all over the towers looking for intruders when I left. The gate's in chaos, and I'll bet there's two hands of burly 'suspicious characters' already in custody. Someone in that guard shift is going to be in for an explanation to the Captains of the Gardai, and won't like the experience. But we've got you into the city, and that's the simplest part of the task, I'm afraid." His face went serious, then. His gaze went back to Doyle and Edana. "I don't know the two of you, but I can make a guess based on what I've heard and the lineage I see in your faces. You make unlikely allies, if you're Doyle Mac Ard and Edana O Liathain."

"You guess rightly," Edana answered. Doyle slumped in his own chair, his head down. "In this, we're on the same side. We want the Rí Ard's Regent Guardian brought down."

"And yourself installed as Banrion Ard?" Mundy asked, raising one eyebrow. "And who will hold Lámh Shábhála once it's taken from Ó Riain?"

Doyle's head lifted at that. "My sister will have it again, if she's alive," he answered Mundy. "I've given her my word on that already."

Mundy nodded, a grim look on his face. "That's the right answer," he said. "And she will still be alive, if any of us are after this foolhardiness. Here's what we bring to this: I have my Cloch Mór and any slow magic we can devise; Mahon brings a strong sword and sharp tactical mind. We also have a half dozen other men here in the city with us, none with clochs, however."

"We have clochs to add, Má—" Owaine choked back the title as Mundy smiled. "I have the Cloch Mór Blaze and Edana has Demon-Caller. Meriel still has Treoraí's Heart."

Mundy's gray eyebrows lifted again, and he looked to Jenna. Meriel knew what he was thinking: *Why does Owaine have Blaze and not Meriel?* But Jenna didn't lift her head, and Meriel saw him close his mouth on the question he might have asked. "Three Clochs Mór, then," Mundy said after a moment, "and a clochmion. And one other who is trained as a cloudmage." He glanced at Doyle. "Though not perhaps as well trained as he could be at Inishfeirm."

"Trained well enough," Doyle answered darkly. "The Order of Gabair has no fear of an Order whose time has passed. How many Clochs Mór do you still have, Máister?" The title dripped mockery. "The Order of Gabair has more, even now."

"Stop it!" Meriel interjected as Mundy flushed and Mahon's fingers curled around the hilt of his sword. "Our enemies are out there, not in here. Aye, we have a few clochs, but the Rí Ard commands a double hand of them and more, and enough men to bury us in simple numbers. If we're to have any chance, *any,* then we need to work together here."

"Aye," Edana agreed, looking at Doyle. "Listen to Meriel; she brought us this far, when no one else could have."

Mundy's posture slowly relaxed; Doyle's head dropped again. "You sound like your mam, Meriel," Doyle said. "She's taught you well."

Jenna uttered a short, almost bitter laugh but said nothing. An uneasy silence settled in the room. Meriel could hear the crackling of the fire and the rattling boil of the water in the pot. Meriel moved the crane away from the flames and reached for the tea, putting the leaves in to steep. "So we have a small force here, but a real one. Is it enough?" she asked.

Mundy and Mahon shrugged simultaneously. "The Rí Ard and Ó Riain are in the Rí Keep on Sliabh Gabhar, and rarely come out. The keep's garrison is large and well-trained, and several of the Tuathian mages are there also. We could set a diversion and hope to draw off some of the gardai, but a frontal assault on the keep would fail: too much resistance inside, and as soon as they realized there was an attack on the keep, the commanders of the army would come in full force. We'd be like a spider smashed against a wall, caught between those inside and out."

"Are there hidden ways in?" Meriel asked. "Servants' passageways, or old tunnels?"

"None that I've been able to learn of," Mahon responded. "Perhaps the tiarna or bantiarna, who have been here before . . . ?"

Edana shook her head. "None that I know, either. I've been in the keep as a guest several times, but always entered through the main gates and saw very little of the keep beyond the Rí's Hall and my own chambers."

Doyle remained silent and Meriel looked at him. He finally stirred. "I've the same experience," he said quietly. "Sorry." There was something else in his eyes, and Meriel had the sense that he was holding something back, that he had thoughts or knowledge that he wasn't sharing. Meriel wished she had Siúr Meagher's clochmion here, to hear if Doyle's words were false. She wondered again about his absence the night before—*could Owaine have been right? Could he have gone to the tiarnas we saw on the road?*

Doyle stared at her, his gaze almost challenging. She held his regard for a moment, then broke it abruptly. "Then we can't do anything while they're in the keep," she said. "But they can't stay there forever."

"Aye," Owaine said. "At the least, they'll have to come out to board ship for Inishfeirm."

"And when that happens, they'll have an entire army close around them," Mundy said. "We'd be in no better a situation then. It might actually be worse, considering that our first strike isn't likely to take down Ó Riain unless the man's incredibly stupid—and he's already demonstrated that's not the case. I don't like the man at all, but he hasn't gotten to where he is by being either foolish or incautious."

"Three Clochs Mór might—*might*—be enough to take Lámh Shábhála, but Lámh Shábhála can hold off the three long enough for the other clochs in Falcarragh to come to its rescue." Everyone turned with Jenna's

words. She looked at them with sunken, exhausted eyes.
"I know better than anyone. Three Clochs Mór alone
won't be sufficient to bring Lámh Shábhála down quickly
enough."

"Then what can we do?" Meriel asked her mam.
"What do we need to do?"

A shrug. Jenna's head went back down. She pulled
her shawl closer over her shoulders and turned back to
the fire. Meriel went to her, stroking her hair.

"We'll find a way to do this, Mam. We will," she whispered. Sighing, she straightened again. "We need to iso-
late Ó Riain then, draw him out from behind his
defenses and his people." Doyle was staring at her, and
she pressed her lips together. "That's what you did with
my mam, after all," she said to him. "And I was the
bait."

Doyle's attention went to the window of the small
room.

"*I* can be the bait here," Edana said abruptly. Doyle
spun about, glaring at her, and she looked placidly back
at him. "It's true, and you know it," she said. "Ó Riain's
weakness right now is Enean—my brother's the prop for
his political power, and Enean will come to save me if he
thinks I'm in trouble . . . and bring Ó Riain with him."

"You can't," Doyle said quickly. "Edana, this isn't
anything you need to do."

"No?" she asked him. "I think it is, if I have any
thought of ever being with my brother again or of being
what Da wanted me to be, or of either of us ever having
the life together that we wanted." She gestured with her
chin to Meriel. "Look at her, Doyle. This isn't anything
she *needs* to do, either. Yet she's the one most responsible for us being here."

They were all looking at Meriel now, all except Jenna
who still stared at the fire. Owaine moved closer to her
and she took his hand in hers. They all seemed to be
waiting for her to speak, as if her approval was necessary. Meriel found herself wondering just when everything had changed, when she had transcended her mam

in their eyes. Owaine's fingers pressed hers; Jenna stared
blindly into the flames, lost in her interior agony.

"Then we'll use that," she said to Edana. "If you're
willing."

Mundy and Mahon raised eyebrows when Meriel placed
her and Owaine's few things together in one of the tiny
rooms, but when Jenna said nothing about the sleeping
arrangements, they also remained silent.

The two of them snuggled together as the flames gut-
tered low in the room's hearth, Meriel enjoying the feel
of lying close to Owaine. His finger trailed down the
flank of her body and she shivered, half in delight and
half at the tickling feel of it, and caught his hand as it
reached her hip. She nestled her head on his chest, the
chain of his Cloch Mór under her hair, the jewel itself
large in her sight, only a hand's breadth away. Treoraí's
Heart was a warm pebble caught between her breasts—
neither of them would ever be entirely naked, not by
choice. Their clochs would always be with them.

"What we're doing—it's not likely to work." The
words came low and warm out of the twilight of the
room and she felt the fear in them. "If anything happened to you, Meriel, especially now . . ." She heard his
breath, felt him swallow.

"I know," she told him. "I'm terrified, too."

"Thank you, at least, for giving me last night, and
this."

"Is that what you think it is? Some kind of gift? A
reward?" She lifted her head to look at him. "Owaine,
I would never do that. That wouldn't be fair to either
of us." She stopped, knowing that he still doubted her
feelings for him and wondering how she could tell him,
how she could make him understand. "Mam . . . when
I was inside her with the Heart, I could feel all her
memories, and I saw how it was with Ennis—my real
da—and her at first, how she didn't realize for a long

time what she truly felt for him. When she finally let herself open to him, they only had each other for a short time before she lost him. I don't want the same thing to happen to me. To us. Mam never recovered from that loss, Owaine. Not really. All these years later, she's still grieving for him. I always thought . . . I guess I just believed that most marriages were like hers: cordial and friendly but without any real passion. I thought that was what Mam wanted, thought she was happy with it. But . . ."

She took a breath. Another. She stroked Owaine's cheek, sliding fingers through the wiry softness of his beard. In the dimness, she could see the marks of Treoraí's Heart on her hand. "She lost the person she loved most, but then she shut herself off and never allowed herself to love that way again. My da—Kyle—is her friend but he doesn't want more, either. But I look at Máister Kirwan and the way he watches my mam and talks to her, and I wonder if he doesn't feel more for her even if he can't or won't show it. If Mam would open her eyes, if she'd see it too."

"Mundy Kirwan? And your mam?"

"Is it stranger than you and me?"

He made no answer. Finally, in the quiet, she continued. "I wish I could show you, make you feel what I feel . . ." She could feel Treoraí's Heart: warm, so warm, and she knew. She found the clochmion and took it in her hand. She opened it in her mind and at the same moment she kissed Owaine. In the cloch-world, she fell into him, as if he were smoke and fog, finding her wrapped in soft layers of blue affection and red lust and black fear. She saw the white nodules of his doubt and she gathered them to herself. *Here,* she said to him with her cloch-voice. *Here I am. Become me, Owaine. Become me and feel what I feel . . .* She opened her mind to his, felt him touch her in surprise and delight. She held herself out to him. *This is what I feel,* she told him. *All of it. I hide nothing from you . . .*

She let him look at it all, holding none of it back: the

ugliness of her reaction to him on Inishfeirm; the cold ungratefulness in Doire Coill after he rescued her; her joy at seeing Dhegli again; the slow, halting change as she began to see him anew.

Her feelings now.

"Ahh," he breathed. She saw the moisture in his eyes and she let go of the cloch. She kissed him again, more urgently this time.

And then, for a time, she thought of nothing at all.

52

A Trap Set

"*WHAT!?*" Enean roared. The man before the Rí Ard flinched, hands up, with the sound of ringing metal as Enean drew his sword. Even Ó Riain took a step back. Enean in a fury was dangerous, with the sleek and powerful muscles of a warrior and a child's lack of control. Ó Riain had no interest in making himself the target of a blind temper tantrum, but he also didn't want Enean hacking this man to pieces before they had all the information from him.

"My Rí Ard," he said as soothingly as possible, staying a careful few steps away from the raised weapon. With the sound of Ó Riain's voice, Enean's eyes flicked toward him, angry and wild. "Please," the Regent Guardian said soothingly. "This man did nothing. He came here as a loyal subject should. Let us hear him out, so we can take appropriate action and keep Edana safe. We need to know more. For Edana, Enean. For your sister. We need to listen to the man."

Slowly, Enean lowered the sword, though he didn't sheathe it. The tip clattered against the stone flags as Enean's shoulders relaxed, and Ó Riain permitted himself a small, brief smile. *So like a child . . . It will be good when I'm rid of him. Soon . . .*

"Now," Ó Riain purred, turning to the frightened man in rags. "Tell us your story again, and leave nothing out."

The man was quivering so much that Ó Riain wouldn't have been surprised if he'd lost control of his bladder during the confrontation. The man ducked his head to Ó Riain, though he kept glancing back at the glaring Enean. "Regent Guardian, it was as I said. A man dragged me aside near South Gate. I don't know the man; I've never seen him before. I swear that by the Mother-Creator, Regent Guardian. He was big and rough, like a garda, though he was dressed no better than me." The man opened his arms, displaying his ragged clothing and torn and dirty tunic. Ó Riain could smell the man: the stench of the streets and poverty, the same malodorous air that sometimes wafted over the keep when the wind blew in from the city. "The man put a knife to my throat, he did. Look—" He pointed to his neck below just at the larynx, where a black-red spot beaded on his skin. "See? The point pricked me there. He told me that I had to come here or he'd kill my family, and then he stuck the parchment I gave to your gardai in my hands. He turned me around, pushed me, and when I looked back again, he'd vanished, as if he'd never been there at all." The man gulped, his throat convulsing. "That one was worse than a Black Haunt, he scared me so much."

Ó Riain could easily believe that; the man's face blanched with the memory. "So you came here . . ." he prompted gently, and the man nodded furiously.

"Aye, I did. Ran here right then, I did, and gave the paper to one of the Rí Ard's gardai, and they brought me here." The man spread his arms wide. "I swear to you both, I don't know any more than that. I can't read, so I don't even know what the paper said, though I can see that it upsets the Rí Ard greatly and I'm sorry for that." That last was said with a beseeching glance at Enean, who still gripped the hilt of his sword.

Ó Riain smiled at the man. It was obvious that the man was just a messenger, and a frightened and unwitting one at that, but it was probably best to be certain. "Thank you for coming here," he told the man, opening the door to the chamber. The gardai in the hallway straightened quickly. He nodded to them. "See that this man has food and a reward for his efforts," he said, but he grabbed the shoulder of the second garda as they started to escort the man away. "Peader, take him down to the donjons and determine if he's telling the truth, and send me word. Don't hurt him permanently, but make certain that he's not hiding anything. Let me know what you determine."

Peader nodded, his face carefully neutral. "Aye, Regent Guardian. I understand."

Ó Riain clapped the man on the back and shut the door once more, turning back to Enean, who was standing at the table near the window, staring down at the paper the man had brought. Though he already knew every word by heart, Ó Riain found himself reading it once more around the bulk of Enean.

To the Rí Ard: We have your sister Edana O Liathain and are holding her for ransom. Come to the western pass of Sliabh Bacaghorth where the High Roads cross two mornings from now, no more than a stripe after daybreak. The cost of the bantiarna's ransom is five thousand mórceints—bring them and we will return her to you unharmed. You are to have no more than one companion with you. If we see gardai or mages, your sister will die. This ring is a token that we do have Bantiarna O Liathain in our possession.

The note was unsigned and a golden ring chased with geometric designs had been enclosed—a ring that had caused Enean to wail when he'd seen it. He was holding it now, turning it in the fingers of one hand and gazing at it. Ó Riain didn't believe the note for a moment—Edana had been taken into Doire Coill along with Doyle Mac Ard, and the Bunús Muintir wouldn't write ransom notes asking for mórceints. No, the note was undoubtedly a ruse—but Enean didn't know that, and that was something Ó Riain might be able to use to his own advantage.

"She'll be safe, Enean," he said. "They won't dare harm her."

"If they do, I'll hunt them down," he growled. He opened his fingers, the ring clattering to the table, and lifted the sword again. "I'll gut them and hang them by their entrails until they rot."

"I know you will, and it's only what they would deserve," Ó Riain said. His voice was calm though his mind seethed with the possibilities. He was certain it was no coincidence this would come just as the invasion fleet prepared to sail for Inish Thuaidh. Everything about the note had the smell of a trap about it, and the smell of the Inish as well: Ó Riain remembered his history well and he knew that nearly five hundred years ago, it was at Sliabh Bacaghorth where Lámh Shábhála was taken from Rowan Beirne in an Inishlander ambush, and the cloch removed to Inish Thuaidh. Ó Riain was confident that the choice of locale was no accident; after all, some Inish blood ran in his body, even though his ancestors had chosen to leave the island. No one whose direct ancestor was Peria Ó Riain could fail to know the history of Lámh Shábhála. He could even hear her voice now, whenever he touched the stone.

No—this had the odor of Doyle and the Mad Holder about it. Ó Riain remembered all too well the reports of Doyle being rescued by Inish cloudmages and Bunús Muintir at Doire Coill. Ó Riain was certain that the intention was for Enean to be nicely feathered in arrows from an ambush. With Enean dead, Edana could advance her claim to the throne of Dún Laoghaire, and Doyle as her husband would have her ear. She might even make a play to become the Banrion Ard.

That scenario made sense. After all, that was what Ó Riain would do in the same circumstances, and Doyle was easily as ambitious as he was himself.

This was good, Ó Riain decided. Whether it was an Inish trap or one set by Doyle or both, Ó Riain would use it himself. This was exactly what he needed. It was difficult to keep a smile from touching his lips as he read the letter once more. Traps were far less dangerous for those who saw them, and they could be turned to other

uses. Enean dead *and* Doyle and Edana dead—now that
would be delicious. There would be no obstacles at all
in his path then. The Holder of Lámh Shábhála would
also be the new Rí Ard.

"I will come with you, my Rí," he said to Enean, who
was glaring out at the panorama of the city as if his
burning gaze could find the ones who had sent the note.
"I will come with you, and we will recover your sister
and have our revenge."

Meriel had never seen streets like this. She knew they
existed, even back home in Dún Kiil, but the daughter
of the Banrion was rarely allowed to mingle with the
poor or to wrinkle her nose with the smell of corruption,
filth, and unwashed and unperfumed bodies.

Meriel had been too tired and too fearful to have noticed much of the area the day before, rushing through
Falcarragh's streets behind Mahon and constantly glancing behind to see if they were followed. Now, in the
unrelenting sunlight, Meriel found herself recoiling inwardly.

"Oh—" Meriel bit back the curse that wanted to follow her exclamation, instead covering her nose with
her sleeve.

"I know," Owaine said as he stepped out alongside
her. "It's . . . not what I expected."

The street outside their door was little more than an
alleyway. Though it was straight enough, receding away
in a line in either direction, the houses leaned against
each other and crowded the paving stones, occasionally
bowing toward their neighbors across the street as if
nodding to ancient acquaintances. There were vacant
places along the lane, like empty sockets in a gum line
where rotten teeth had been pulled, where buildings had
succumbed to fire or age or gravity. The street was no
more than three strides across, and the central gutter
was foul with the contents of emptied chamber pots.

Enormous black flies buzzed lazily, biting where they landed, and the air was thick with the odor of rot. There were no crowds of servants here to sweep the pavement clean, to wash away the night soil, to scrub the grimy stones. Here, things lay where they fell and only the rain cleaned the streets.

Children were running through the streets and around the houses, an entire noisy herd of them. They nearly ran into Meriel and Owaine as they stepped off the curb, Meriel lurching backward as a grimy-faced girl struck her leg and caromed off with a shout of apology as she fled.

"Now you know why Mundy wasn't happy with the idea of us going out—he's afraid we'll be trampled by the urchins," Owaine said. He wrinkled his nose, shaking his head as he looked around. "There are times when I wish you'd left my sight as it was, Meriel. The smell's bad enough." The herd of children turned left and doubled back, passing them again and splashing filthy water over the stones. They were chasing a thin, grime-caked boy, it seemed, and Meriel saw genuine fright on the child's face as he glanced over his shoulder. The pack caught him a few houses to their right, the boy going down in a flurry of tangled limbs. Fists flew, and they both heard a sharp *crack* and a high shriek of pain.

"Hey!" Owaine shouted. "That's enough!" He advanced on the fight, waving his arms, and the kids fled, leaving their victim behind. Meriel came over as Owaine crouched down next to the boy. He was sobbing, cradling his left arm, his lips bloodied and one of his eyes already beginning to swell and purple. The child's ribs showed under the torn léine he wore and his features were misshapen, his ears sticking out through thin, brown and mud-stiff hair. "It's all right," Owaine said. "They're gone. What's your name?"

The boy sniffed. "Feiad," he said. "Feiad Sheónin." He sniffed and blinked away tears.

"Are you badly hurt, Feiad?" Owaine asked, and the boy shook his head, but when he tried to stir and move, he cried out, gasping, holding his left arm tightly.

"Here," Meriel said to Owaine, crouching beside him. People were watching from the nearby windows, but no one had come out for the boy. "Let me see," she said, moving Feiad's hand away from the injured arm. They could see the swelling and the slight angle in the middle of the forearm. Meriel moved her hand gently over it, and under her léine she could feel Treoraí's Heart respond to the touch.

"The arm's broken, I'm afraid," Owaine was saying, and Feiad was crying again. "Where's your mam? Where do you live?" The boy couldn't answer him through the sobs.

"He's too frightened to talk," Meriel told Owaine. Treoraí's Heart was pulsing under her hand, the pull of it causing her fingers to close around it, bunching the cloth of her léine as she stroked Feiad's injured arm. "Shh, Feiad," she told him softly. "I can help you. I can make it stop hurting."

"Meriel—" Owaine said sharply, his voice a hiss in her ear. "You shouldn't. Not here. If word gets out . . ."

She didn't answer him, looking instead into the boy's wide, pale green eyes. "The Mother-Creator gave me a Healing Touch," she told the boy, the words bringing back an image of Sevei's face to her. "You know the Taisteal?" The boy nodded, sniffing. "I learned it from them," she told him. "If you lie quietly and let me, I can help. Will you do that?"

Feiad sniffed again. He nodded solemnly.

"Meriel . . ." Owaine was glancing around them. A few people had come out from the houses to watch, sidling closer to them. Meriel closed her hand around the clochmion and the other around Feiad's arm. The boy gasped in pain and fear, but she had already opened the cloch and the cloch-vision overlaid hers. She could *see* the pain, wild striations of red and orange racing along the nerves, traced in jagged lines from the ugly gray fissure of the break in Feiad's arm. With it came the torrent of his thoughts: mostly residual fright, but also an underlying, eternal hunger. Images of his family flashed past—his mam; a grizzle-faced and sour older man who might have been his da; his sibs; a sweet and gentle baby's face laying too still in her crib. *Lheisa . . .* The name came to her, a baby sister who succumbed to childhood illness like too many of those here. The grim weariness of his life weighed down on her, and she forced herself away from the memories, concentrating instead on the pain that made her want to cry with the boy.

Meriel sent the cloch's energy toward the break, imagining it closing and healing, becoming whole and straight again; in the cloch-vision, the bone reacted, the red-orange flares bending away from Feiad and lancing toward her. Meriel gasped as they touched, releasing Feiad and Treoraí's Heart with a cry and clutching at her own arm as she fell backward into Owaine. His arms went around her and she let him hold her, gratefully, as the pain slowly receded.

Feiad laughed, dragging the last of the tears away with the back of his hand. He held up his arm, flexing his fingers as the crowd, fascinated by what was happening in the street, came closer. Some of them were among the group who had been chasing the boy a few minutes before. Feiad shouted, a wordless gasp of amazement, hopping to his feet. "Thank you, Healer!" he shouted to Meriel and then ran off, pushing through the first ranks of the people and vanishing. Meriel and Owaine were surrounded now by a few dozen people. None of them spoke to them, but they could hear the murmur of whispered comments: *"She has the Touch; I saw it . . ."* *". . . the boy's arm was broken so the bone nearly went through his skin, and she made it as if it had never happened . . ."*

"Come on," Owaine said to Meriel. She could feel his hand on her arm as she gazed around them, shaking her head. "We have to go. Now." He led her away, the crowd parting to let them pass. A few followed them for a bit, though most remained behind, talking among themselves, and finally, as they approached one of the market squares to the north, they found themselves alone amidst the crowds of Falcarragh. Owaine bought a few loaves of hard bread and some cheese, and they sat on a stone wall and ate, watching the people pass.

"Mundy won't like hearing this," Owaine said finally, tearing off a piece of the loaf and handing it to her.

"I had to, Owaine," she told him. "I couldn't look at the boy suffering like that and not do something."

"I know." His fingers brushed over hers. "I'm not surprised. It worries me, that's all."

She took a bite of the bread—the taste reminding her of the Inish brown bread of home. Even the accents she heard around them had a tinge of the slow, rolling brogue of the Inishlanders. They were close to home: up the long expanse of Falcarragh Bay and across a bit of ocean, and she could be in Dún Kiil once more. "You're afraid that we'll be caught, that someone will realize that I have a cloch and tell the gardai."

Owaine shook his head. She could see a distorted image of herself in the dark mirror of his eyes. "Mundy and the others can worry about that," he said softly. "I'm worried about *you*, Meriel. I'm afraid because we're here to kill someone—realistically, that's the only way we're going to take Lámh Shábhála from Ó Riain, and I wonder if you truly realize that. If we're going to take the cloch back, Ó Riain is going to die, and probably others who are around him. For all any of us know, you may have to do some of the killing. Watching you with Feaid just now . . ." He lifted his shoulders. "I saw someone I love and admire, but I didn't see someone who could kill. I saw a person who would give away a Cloch Mór because she preferred a cloch that had the gift of healing. I saw someone who was furious with me just a few days ago in Kilmaur because . . ." He looked at his hands and didn't finish the sentence. He took a breath before looking at her again. "I saw someone whose first worry just now was a child with a broken arm, not the thought that it would be safer for her to do nothing. I see that person and I don't know that she can do what we intend to do."

Meriel turned the bread over in her hands, looking down rather than at him. "I know what we're here for, Owaine," she said. "I was the one who brought us here."

"Aye, you did. But there's a vast difference between knowing and doing. When your mam sent me to the Order, all unexpected, it was such a gift that I was certain that the Mother-Creator had a tremendous fate in store for me. I had this fantasy that I would go to the White Keep and the mages there would all marvel at how quickly I mastered their art, and that I would become the greatest cloudmage of all, that—aye—one day when your mam was too tired to bear the burden any more, she would come back to Inishfeirm and give *me* Lámh Shábhála to keep."

He had such a solemn expression on his face that Meriel had to laugh. "You didn't," she said, and he smiled back at her.

"Aye, I did. I *knew* I was blessed and that there was a great fate in store for me. But I found very quickly that no matter how much I wanted to pretend that I was capable of doing all that, I was no better than an average student and maybe less, and that most of the Bráthairs and Siúrs thought that even the clochmion your mam gave me was too good for the likes of me, who couldn't even see clearly across a room."

She leaned over to him and kissed him once on the lips. She pulled back a bare inch, staring into his eyes. "I find you quite heroic enough, Owaine Geraghty. I know what you're saying. I won't deny that I'd prefer to do this bloodlessly if at all possible. That's why I agreed with Doyle's plan—and I'd point out that if I hadn't spared Doyle's life back on Knobtop, we wouldn't have Edana with us nor this chance. There are times when not killing is the right course. But if it comes to it . . ." She pressed her lips together. "I don't want to talk about it now," she told him abruptly, jumping off the wall to her feet. "I suppose we should go back; the others will be worrying."

She held her hand out to him. "Come on," she said. "Mam will be needing her andúilleaf soon, and we have a lot to prepare."

53

Sliabh Bacaghorth

THE MOUNTAIN was a steep, heather-wrapped slope. The road from Falcarragh snaked alongside the river that ran in the valley at Sliabh Bacagorth's feet. The pathway was rarely traveled and poorly maintained— there were few villages here along the craggy eastern coastline of Falcarragh Bay. Most travelers, even those from towns to the north, preferred to continue south a dozen miles to where the mountains gentled somewhat and the roads were better and ran directly to Falcarragh's gates.

Sitting high up on Sliabh Bacaghorth's stony flanks, huddled together in the misty rain shaken from low, slate-colored clouds, Meriel could see the gray waters of Falcarragh beyond the point where the mountain's western ridge fell away suddenly down hundred-foot-high cliffs; at the point where the river in the valley below them met the bay in the foggy distance, there was a small fishing village. The sight of the water made Meriel think of Dhegli, caused the Saimhóir part of her to respond almost as if she felt him near her again. She looked quickly away, turning her attention back to the mountainside. Directly below was a crossroads where the High Road from Falcarragh met the tiny trail that led to the village, and meandered westward to eventually find the High Roads to Glenkille.

In the far distance, as the wan light of the masked sun

began to push away the shadows of the night, they could
see two riders approaching from the south, from Falcarragh. Owaine gave a sigh of relief. "We have what we
asked for," he said. "They're alone."

"And that's Enean on the left," Edana said. "No one
else sits that regally atop a horse."

"And the other?" Mundy asked her. "Is that the Regent Guardian?"

Edana shook her head. "I don't know. It might be,
but I can't tell yet." She shivered in the cold, pulling
her hood closer over her face. "No matter what happens,
Enean is not to be permanently harmed. Remember
that."

Mahon grimaced. "In the midst of a battle, that's
going to be hard to guarantee, Bantiarna. We'll do our
best."

"He is *not* to be harmed," Edana repeated. "If he is,
I swear I'll turn my cloch against whomever hurt him,
no matter what the consequences. He's my brother, and
an innocent pawn in this."

"We promised Edana to keep Enean safe," Meriel
said, looking at all the others, "and we'll keep that
promise." The others grumbled their assent, all but
Jenna, who huddled silently in her oilskin on the damp
ground, staring at the road below. "Let's get into
position."

They scattered, clambering down the hillside in the
shelter of the bracken and pines. Meriel and Owaine
helped Jenna to a scree of rocks near the crossroads;
Mundy and Doyle scurried into brush bordering the road
on the other side. Mahon and Edana stood directly in
the road, Mahon holding Edana's arms as if she were
his captive, a knife held casually at her throat. Meriel
ducked behind the rock as she heard the slow *clop-clop*
of the riders' horses. "Stop!" Mahon called out loudly.
"That's close enough. We have archers ready, Rí Ard.
Come any farther and your sister dies."

Enean's deep voice boomed worriedly as he pulled up

on the reins. Alongside him, the other man also reined his horse back. "Edana! Are you all right?" Enean called.

"I'm fine, Enean."

Meriel heard the sound of something heavy hitting the ground, followed by the bright sound of metal. She lifted her head and saw coins scattered from a broken chest. "There," Enean said. "There's your ransom. Now let my sister go as you promised."

"Thank you for coming for me, Enean," Edana said as Mahon lowered his knife and released her. Meriel saw Edana glance at the hooded figure on the horse next to Enean and give a slight nod. That was Ó Riain, then, his hand at his chest. Meriel knew what the man touched there. They all did. "And thank you, also, Regent Guardian."

It was the cue they'd been waiting for. With Edana's identification of the man, Owaine's hand went to his Cloch Mór, as did Mundy's and Edana's. *Three against one, that I could withstand,* Jenna had told them, and Meriel had seen Doyle grimace at the reminder. *But I doubt the Regent Guardian can do that much, not new to Lámh Shábhála, and not if he is surprised.*

They attacked the Regent Guardian as one, loosing the power of their clochs and hoping to bear the man down in the first wave. Lightning arced from Owaine's hand and Blaze; blue tendrils snapped outward from Mundy's Snarl; the demon wailed as Edana released it to the air. Mahon reversed his knife and threw it spinning toward Ó Riain; Doyle stood with a bow, releasing an arrow and then, rapidly, another.

Meriel watched as did Jenna, though Jenna had risen to her feet and she screamed the caointeoireacht na cogadh, the war cry of the Inishlanders.

But there was no surprise to their attack: Ó Riain seemed to have somehow expected it. Mahon's knife and Doyle's arrows rebounded as if they had hit a clear wall three feet from Ó Riain's chest. Owaine's lightning crackled close enough to light Ó Riain's face but without touching him; Mundy's tentacles of force wrapped around the man but could not tighten about him.

Ó Riain sneered. Edana's mage-demon roared in answer and its red-mailed fist swung. The sound rang like steel on steel and thunder followed. For a moment, Meriel felt a surge of hope and optimism, for Ó Riain went down with a cry, falling to the road as his horse reared and fled. Lámh Shábhála might be powerful, but Ó Riain, as her mam had suspected, wasn't yet skilled at wielding it. They would prevail.

The other clochs gathered themselves and sent their power surging toward him. The mage-demon howled and lifted its foot, ready to crush Ó Riain into a bloody mass in the mud.

Meriel heard Jenna laugh.

But new lines of blue-white force materialized, wrapping about the demon's ankle and pulling. The monster went down, crashing to the earth near Ó Riain.

Jenna hissed. "Weaver," she said. Enean had entered the fray.

"Edana! What are you doing?" Enean screamed, his hand around his own cloch.

"Enean, please! You have to trust me!" she shouted back, and the netting about the demon's ankle loosened somewhat as Enean's face twisted in puzzlement and confusion. But the moment where they might have won had passed already.

Ó Riain pushed himself up and Lámh Shábhála raged. He shouted, and it was as if the sound were a physical blow. Mundy and Owaine were flung backward along with their clochs' manifestations—Meriel crying out in alarm—and Edana screamed, going to her knees as wild light flared around the mage-demon as it roared in agony. The gale that was Ó Riain's shout picked up rocks and stone, sending them smashing against the mage-demon and Edana. Blood ran from cuts on Edana's face and arms; she and the mage-demon screamed together. The demon took a step toward Ó Riain and

was shoved back as wild light poured from Lámh Shábhála, so bright that Meriel had to shield her eyes.

"No!" Enean shouted. "Don't hurt Edana, Labhrás!"
But the assault continued as Mundy and Owaine picked
themselves back up and intensified their attack. Lámh
Shábhála faltered, the storm wind around it subsiding,
but Ó Riain ignored the others except to throw up a
wall against them. Edana was the focus of Lámh Shábhála's fury: light as bright and blinding as the sun erupted
around Edana's mage-demon—burning it, tearing at it,
ripping into its body, shredding its flesh. The demon
shuddered in torment and Edana fell to her knees in the
mud, doubled over in reflected pain.

Meriel could see the valley, bright in the searing new
dawn of Lámh Shábhála. The radiance painted the bottoms of the clouds, made the rain sparkle.

She realized that they had lost. They had lost, and
there was nothing she could do to help. Lámh Shábhála
and Ó Riain were too strong, even for three Clochs Mór.
Yet out of defeat came a sudden glimmer.

"No!" Enean shouted again. The Rí Ard jumped down
from his terrified horse like a vengeful spirit, holding his
cloch high though his other hand was on the hilt of his
sword. He stood over Edana's prone body, glaring at Ó
Riain—and when lightning crackled from Ó Riain's
hands, lashing out toward Edana as a finishing stroke,
he attacked. Weaver's pale net went snapping forward,
joining with Mundy's and Owaine's siege of Lámh Shábhála's wall. The lightning faltered and went dim. Ó Riain
moaned and the mage-demon stirred again as Edana
lifted her head. Lámh Shábhála pushed back at its attackers, but this time they were four, not three, and they
held fast. Owaine grimaced angrily alongside Meriel,
grunting wordlessly as he pushed at the mage-wall. Edana's demon roared and stomped toward Ó Riain, bringing its red fists down to shudder once against the man's
defenses. Ó Riain shoved her back; the demon staggered, then charged once more. Again she was pushed
back and again she returned: as the other clochs tore at

the wall, which suddenly fell in an explosion of sound and light . . .

. . . then . . .

Ó Riain wailed, a thin sound against the din of the clochs. He collapsed, falling into a heap in the mud. His hand opened.

There was, astoundingly, silence punctuated by the rolling echo of the battle rebounding from Sliabh Bacaghorth. The mage-demon vanished as Edana gasped and released her cloch; Enean sank down beside her. Owaine gave a sigh next to Meriel and Mundy reeled backward in weariness.

Stunned and exhausted, no one moved.

No one but one.

Jenna, on Meriel's other side, gave a wordless cry and scrambled to her feet, rushing out from cover and dashing toward Ó Riain's unconscious body as Meriel, belatedly, pursued her. But another did the same.

Doyle.

They reached Ó Riain at the same time. Jenna was crouched, snarling like an animal with hands extended like claws and her eyes glaring wildly at her younger brother. "It's mine!" she hissed, and when Doyle scoffed and reached for it, she slashed at him, drawing blood from his hand. "Mam!" Meriel shouted as Doyle reached for the knife at his side and Jenna crouched over Ó Riain like a wolf guarding its kill. Meriel heard the sound of steel being drawn and a sword cut air dangerously close to Jenna's outstretched hand.

"No!" Enean's voice boomed. "Back away, both of you!"

"Don't make a mistake here, Enean," Doyle answered placatingly, his hands spread wide. "This is our chance. Think of it: you as Rí Ard, Edana at your side as Banrion Dún Laoghaire and me as her husband with Lámh Shábhála . . . Enean, no one could oppose us. No one. Your reign would be the wonder of all time. The songmasters would sing of you for centuries." Meriel saw a slow, childlike grin spread over Enean's face with that, and she also sensed the dangerous vibration of the clochs—Edana's, Owaine's, Mundy's—and she didn't know where they would strike, only that they would.

Enean's sword wavered for an instant, and as it dropped Jenna plunged her hand past the blade, snatching at the chain of Lámh Shábhála. Enean roared, and his sword drew a line of blood down Jenna's white-scarred arm, but her fingers were around the stone now, pulling, and the chain's links flew apart as Jenna opened the cloch with her mind. Ó Riain's eyes flashed open; he gasped openmouthed like a man drowning, reaching for the cloch, but Jenna danced back away from him.

Her cry was laugh and scream and shout of rage, all at once, melded with the fury of Lámh Shábhála's power. Jenna was transformed in that instant. She seemed younger, vital, and terrible.

And insane. Meriel knew what she saw: the person who had once been called the Mad Holder. ". . . *it's those you love you should fear the most, for they hold the greatest danger for you.*" Sevei had told her that what seemed a lifetime ago. Meriel had believed that if they could recover Lámh Shábhála the crisis would somehow end, that with the recovery of the cloch her mam would right the world and everything would return to how it had been. She realized now how wrong she'd been.

"Mam!" Meriel cried again, but her voice was lost. She had thought that Lámh Shábhála had been emptied, but perhaps Jenna knew the hidden places in the stone or how to tap it far more deeply than had Ó Riain. A widening ring of pure energy welled out from the cloch: a wild, rushing storm wind, black and awful and hissing with lightning. Meriel was thrown backward and away, lost in the whirlwind, feeling herself striking rocks and brush. She could hear the others yelling also, and one loud wail rose over the din. Her head struck something hard and for a few breaths or perhaps more, Meriel fell away into darkness. When she could see again, she could hear the sound of hooves and a woman's angry cursing. Blinking, groaning, she lifted her head and saw her mam

riding away south along the road to Falcarragh, and the
wind brought the sound of her voice . . .

"I'll kill them! I'll kill them all!"

"Mam!" she called uselessly, and then groaned again.
She sank back down, trying to hold onto ground that
seemed to be rolling around her. "Owaine? Mundy?"

"Here!" She felt Owaine's hands on her shoulders.
"Are you hurt?" Meriel shook her head and tried to get
up; Owaine helped her to her feet.

"My mam . . ."

"Gone mad." That was Mundy, his clóca and léine
torn, standing a few feet away, blood running down one
side of his face from a long cut on his forehead. He
stared down the road to where Jenna had vanished into
the rain and mist. "And dangerous, with Lámh Shábhála."

"We have to go after—" Meriel began, but a wail
interrupted her.

"*Enean!*" It was Edana's voice. "Oh, Mother-Creator,
no!" Edana was kneeling next to Enean, who lay sprawled
on the ground, his sword broken halfway up from the
hilt. He had the look of a broken doll, his arms flung at
wide, awkward angles, one leg bent entirely backward.
Coins glinted in the mud around him, the mórceints he'd
brought for Edana's ransom. His eyes were open, Meriel
noticed as she sank down beside Edana, but they saw
nothing and his chest did not move. "You have to help
him," Edana said to Meriel. "The clochmion . . ."

Meriel took Treoraí's Heart in her hand and placed
her other hand on Enean. She willed it to open, tried to
force herself into Enean's body. The power within
Treoraí's Heart filled her but she sensed nothing from
Enean—there was no pain, no spark, no thoughts, no
connection at all. She might as well have been touching
a rock. "I'm sorry, Edana," she said. "I'm so sorry . . .
There's nothing I can do . . ."

Edana wailed, her head back. Rain pounded down on
them, as if her cry had ripped open the sky. Meriel put
her arm around the woman, but Edana shrugged her
away angrily. Meriel stood up as Owaine came to stand

next to her. They stared down at Enean, the rain slicking his face, his eyes staring upward. Doyle went to his knees by Edana and held her. She sank into his embrace, sobbing, as Doyle reached out to close Enean's eyes.

"We need to go after your mam," Mundy said to Meriel. She tore her gaze away from Enean to the worried face of the Máister. "There's nothing we can do here, but Jenna is—" He stopped.

"Mad," Meriel finished for him. Owaine's arm tightened around her in sympathy. "I know. I saw it; I felt it."

"She won't get to Falcarragh before nightfall," Mahon said, "if she gets that far at all."

"That's what I'm worried about," Mundy said. "Lámh Shábhála must be nearly drained after this, but when the mage-lights come . . ." He took a long breath. "Far too many could die."

54

Rogue Holder

Ó RIAIN was also dead, Meriel realized when she went to him. His eyes and mouth were open in his last cry, his hands still reaching hopelessly for the cloch he'd lost.

"He wasn't as strong as your mam," Owaine told her. "Losing Lámh Shábhála killed him."

Meriel didn't hear him. She was looking to the west, where the hidden sea surged against the land. Her forehead burned.

Mahon brought their horses from where they'd been hobbled. Ó Riain's body they left on the road; Edana insisted that Enean's remains had to return with them and they laid him across his horse. Edana had taken the torc of Dún Laoghaire from her brother. It now lay around her own neck. She'd also taken the Cloch Mór Enean had held. Mundy had started to protest, but Meriel shook her head at him and he subsided. Weaver now lay on Doyle's chest, the man's face no longer looking drawn and weak. The way he stared at her—cold and almost angry—made her uncomfortable. She looked instead at Edana.

"Mam didn't intend to kill Enean," Meriel said to Edana as the group quickly mounted. "She threw us all back, even me. This wasn't what she would have done if she were thinking rightly. You must know that."

The glance Edana shot toward Meriel was venomous

and sharp. "What I know is that my brother's dead. And I know who killed him." She looked at Doyle, staring now in the direction that Jenna had taken. "I also know that Doyle wouldn't have done that had *he* taken Lámh Shábhála. I know that if she'd killed all of us taking Lámh Shábhála, including you, she wouldn't have cared. That's what I *know,* Meriel, and you know it also. I think too many people have made too many excuses for your mam over the years." Her fierce, grieving stare went over them all: Owaine, Mundy, Mahon, and then came back to Meriel. "You, at least, should realize it. Didn't you taste her madness yourself?"

"Enough talk," Doyle said before Meriel could reply. "We waste time here." With that, Doyle slapped the reins of his horse and moved off quickly. Edana followed, with Enean's horse tied behind. Mahon started after them, his face red and furious, but Meriel shook her head at him. "You three can follow them soon enough," she said. "Let Edana grieve with Doyle for now."

" 'You *three* can follow?' " Owaine repeated, tilting his head toward her. "What about you?"

Meriel looked to the west, where the mountains ended. Ever since her mam had left, she could feel the tug of the water and something else . . . *someone* else . . . "I'm going to Falcarragh another way," she told him. "A way you can't go."

"Meriel," Owaine said. His hand touched her arm and there was pain in his eyes. "Don't do this."

"I'll get there faster that way," she told him. "I may get to Falcarragh even before Mam." But Owaine was shaking his head.

"Is *he* there? Is that why?" She didn't respond, but he nodded as if he'd heard her answer. "Aye, so he is."

"If you trust me, if you love me and you know that I love you also, then you also know you have nothing to worry about," she told him. "This is the best way, Owaine. For me *and* for my mam. For us."

"For us?" Owaine grunted. "Meriel . . ."

"I *have* to, Owaine. I must. I love you, Owaine. That hasn't changed."

At last, his hand dropped away. She leaned toward him, his arms going around her. The kiss was fierce and long, and when he released her, he touched her lips with his hand. "Stay safe, Meriel," he said. "I hope . . ." He stopped. "Go on with you, then," he finished.

"I do love you, Owaine."

"I know. And I you. I found you when Doyle snatched you from Inishfeirm; I suppose I can find you again in Falcarragh." He gave her a quick, lopsided grin that faded as quickly as it had come. He nodded to Mahon and Mundy. "Let's go," he said, and dug his heels into the sides of his horse, the other two following close behind. Meriel watched them go, then turned her own horse's head to the west and the salt water.

"Go!" she cried to the mare.

Dalhmalli was a cluster of half a dozen cottages huddled on a rocky shore with the cliff of Bacaghorth looming over them. The residents were fisherfolk and superstitious, since after all Sliabh Bacaghorth was a haunted place and Falcarragh Bay itself was home to strange fogs and hidden creatures. Today was a day for the truly superstitious, with the gloomy rain and mist and with the strange thunders booming through the valley along the slopes of Bacaghorth and bright, colorful, and impossible colors flickering under the clouds. So when a rider came galloping along the road from the east, not a stripe later than the odd lights, those of Dalhmalli stayed inside, watching fearfully from their small shuttered windows under the thatched roofs as the apparition appeared. They were expecting a fire-breathing stallion, perhaps, ridden by a skeletal soldier—such as some had said haunted the crossroads not far from here. Or perhaps it might be the ghost of old Rowan Beirne himself, wailing for the great cloch na thintrí he'd lost to the Inish.

But the horse was just a plain brown mare, and the rider only a young woman, though what happened afterward would make them wonder if she had not been something mythical herself.

Meriel drew the mare up at the water's edge. A single, sagging wharf ran out toward the water with a few small boats tied to its gray, bowed planks. Here, the smell of fresh rain mingled with the strong odor of brine and fish. The pull she had felt back at the crossroads had grown stronger as she came nearer the water and now it sang in her head, driving out nearly everything else. She knew the villagers were watching; she didn't care.

On the rocks nearby, a half dozen blue-black seals pointed their whiskered snouts and bright, dark eyes at her, and on the wharf itself . . . A naked man stood there, strangely comfortable in his nudity and the cold: his hair slicked with rain and seawater, his body marked with swirling lines of scars like those on her mam's arm. Seeing him both pleased and frightened her. She'd told herself that the old affection for him was gone, that she felt nothing for Dhegli since he'd left her at Lough Lár, that what she'd found with Owaine had driven all memory and traces of it away, burned it away with a new fire and passion . . .

. . . but it wasn't true. Looking at him, she knew. She knew that what Dhegli had told her once was indeed possible—she could feel love for more than one person. The realization was freighted with guilt and sadness. "Hello, Dhegli," Meriel said. "I'd hoped you'd be here." She touched her forehead. "I felt you."

He smiled at her and spoke, though the words were the sounds of a seal. He padded forward, his footsteps quiet on the slick weathered boards. He took her hand; its warmth surprised her. Its softness pleased her. "Hello, Meriel," he said, his voice sounding in her head with the touch. "I saw you, too, in my dreams. I *had* to come."

"My mam . . . Jenna . . . The Holder . . ."

"I know. We felt the power change suddenly, to something wild and dangerous."

"I'm so scared for her, Dhegli." Her heart pounded in her chest, remembering Jenna's wild manic gaze and the awful ease and strength with which she'd wielded Lámh Shábhála. One of the seals on the rocks gave a coughing bark, drawing Meriel's attention. She recognized the seal: the one called Challa. "She came with you." Meriel couldn't keep a slight stress from the first word.

One corner of his lips turned up, dimpling his stubbled cheek. "She told me not to come, but, aye, she followed and we brought the others—several of the Saimhóir who have swallowed the smaller Bradán, the fishes that hold the power of the sky-energy. They have pledged to help me, as we helped your mam once before. I don't know what we can do or if it will save her, but we'll try."

"Why?" Meriel asked. "Why do you do this for me?"

Dhegli laughed at her. He leaned down, his face close to hers. "You know why." He bent his head to hers. Meriel trembled, but she didn't move away, not until his lips touched hers. With a gasp, she leaned away. He didn't move, and finally she brought her head back and kissed him. She tried to pretend it was Owaine and couldn't. She wept, not knowing why.

"Come swim with me, Meriel," he whispered. "Let us have one last time together."

Meriel stepped away from his embrace. She could feel the eyes of the village on them, watching. Slowly, she lifted her clóca and léine above her head and let them fall to the wharf. She stood naked except for Treoraí's Heart.

She walked with Dhegli to the wharf's edge. She felt the change beginning even as she dove with him into the water.

They would say in later years that the mage-lights had never shone brighter or more intensely than they did that night. The first rippling bands of pale blue and green began to appear not long after the sun had set. The rain had passed, finally, and the western sky was a

deep aquamarine in which the first few stars swam. The
mage-lights came from the north, as they always did,
swaying and dancing their way to the zenith as the colors
deepened and became more varied, so luminous that
they put to shame the East Light, the beacon for ships
out on its island in the bay. No ship would need the
beacons that night to guide the way into Falcarragh Harbor: the mage-lights rivaled the day.

They seemed to hover over the city where so many
Clochs Mór had gathered. The guards at North Gate
were particularly alert already: the Rí Ard, the Regent
Guardian, and a few dozen attending gardai had ridden
out from there the night before and were expected back
at any time. The curling fire of the mage-lights began to
snake down toward the waiting clochs, but the guards
atop the gate towers could see another brightness toward
the north, like a great fire burning. It seemed to flicker
like red lightning, growing closer. "It's the Regent
Guardian," one of the gardai speculated. "Lámh Shábhála, it draws the mage-lights more than any other cloch,
I've heard . . ."

He and his companions peered down along the High
Road outside the New Wall, winding at the foot of the
hills that bordered the water. The light crept closer, illuminating the hillsides as if some giant were walking there
and bearing an immense lantern. They could see the
mage-lights spiraling down like a waterspout made of
moonlight and jewels to someone hidden just past the
first bend. They straightened, expecting to see the Rí
Ard and his retinue. But there was only the sound of a
lone horse and rider, galloping madly toward the city in
a blaze of storm-light, the mage-lights a raging tornado
behind. "Close the gates!" the garda shouted in sudden,
tardy alarm. "Send a runner to the Rí . . ." but it was
already too late.

They heard a faint shout from the rider. "Mother-
Creator, who is that?" someone asked in a marveling,
fearful voice. "It's not the Regent—" and a furious
streak of light shot from the rider's upraised hand

toward the gates. It slammed into the New Wall with a boom and crash; the great stones, heavier than any ten men could lift, were flung about like a handful of pebbles. The garda felt the platform under him give way as the towers flanking the gates toppled, and he screamed as he fell the forty feet to the flagstones below, a scream that was lost in the din of the collapse, in the dust of the explosion, in the great shadow of stones that entombed him a moment later.

The rider laughed, a pale sound in the midst of the destruction that was heard only by the terrified people in the hovels outside the walls. Mage-lights rushed back down into Lámh Shábhála, filling it to bursting again; the scars on the Holder's arm seeming to glow as if she were illuminated from inside. She sent a burst of hurricane wind toward the rubble of the gate, sending rock and stone scattering and clearing a path for her to ride through.

"I've come!" she shouted to the city, her voice amplified by the mage-power she bore. "Hear me, Riocha! You stole Lámh Shábhála from me; you would have bloodied my land with the bodies of my people. But your bane and your destruction have come to you! It comes *now!*"

She urged her steed forward, wide-eyed and snorting with its own terror, held only by the power of the woman who rode it.

The Mad Holder rode into Falcarragh and it trembled before her.

55

The Battle of Falcarragh

OWAINE, Mundy, and Mahon had caught up with Doyle and Edana soon after they'd left Sliabh Bacaghorth. The two had stopped perhaps a mile away, and Owaine pulled up his own horse at the sight that transfixed them. Past a bend in the road and a copse of trees there was a boggy meadow, but the heath there had been burned, curling wisps of smoke still rising from the wet ground. Scattered alongside the road were the corpses of two hands or more of gardai and their horses, scattered as if they'd been picked up and smashed again into the ground. Most were charred black beyond recognition; on those few who were not, they could see clócas in the unrelieved dark gray of Dún Laoghaire—the Rí Ard's color: Enean's gardai, then, brought with him as an escort from Falcarragh and kept back while he and Ó Riain had gone on to Sliabh Bacaghorth.

Owaine didn't need to ask what had happened to them. He knew who had done this.

Leaving the scene of the carnage, they'd ridden together toward Falcarragh in silence, each of them lost in their own thoughts. "Where's Meriel?" had been Edana's only question, and she only nodded at Owaine's answer: "She's gone back to the city her own way."

Night began to fall as they came near Falcarragh, still without any sign of Jenna. They were close to North Gate; they could already see the East Light, out in the

Bay. The mage-lights appeared, early and strong, and
they halted for a moment to lift their own emptied
Clochs Mór to the sky. Owaine, Mundy, and Edana all
felt it, then, as their clochs slipped into the web of energy: Lámh Shábhála, feeding at the mage-lights, as
swirling and dark and all-consuming as a maelstrom of
the sea. In Owaine's mind, it was an awful vision, a horror, and he gasped at the sight of it. "What has she
done?" he asked as he heard Mundy gasp.

The Máister's eyes were wide. "She calls the lights
and pulls them in, then throws out their power again,
only to take in more, over and over again."

A flash and boom came then, not far away and in the
direction of the city gates, and they felt a simultaneous
tug at their clochs. "Ride!" Owaine called to them.
"It's begun."

Jenna rode through the wreckage of North Gate with a
feeling almost of exultation. The world seethed in her
doubled vision: the glowing, brilliant colors of the cloch
overlaying her own sight. She could hear the voices inside Lámh Shábhála calling to her, the old Holders. Real
fire crackled around her—the walls of the gate had tumbled into some of the nearby houses, and a few were
now aflame. People were running about, most of them
fleeing, a few trying desperately to quench the fires before they spread.

*". . . Jenna, you've gone mad. Remember the last time.
Remember Lár Bhaile . . ."*

". . . do it! You have the power—use it! . . ."

And a voice she recognized as Riata, sad and forlorn
in the babble. *"Jenna, they will take you down. There
are too many of them . . ."*

She ignored them all. It felt so *good* to be part of
Lámh Shábhála once more, as if a part of her that had
been amputated had been blessedly restored whole and
intact. The mage-lights had cauterized the deep, oozing

wounds in her soul and seared away the pain, and still
their energy flowed in and around her. The sky was alive
with the power this night, greeting and welcoming her.
She could feel the pull of all the clochs na thintrí around
her, so many of them—Clochs Mór and clochmions,
more than she'd ever felt gathered in one place—and
yet they all seemed so puny and insignificant compared
to what she carried. She felt that she could defeat them
all tonight as long as the mage-lights burned with her.
She could gather that strength in the stone in her hand
and nothing could stand before her.

She laughed as she entered the city.

"I am the First Holder!" she called out to Falcarragh,
to its houses and stone buildings, to the crowded hillsides, to the fleet gathered in its harbor. "I've brought
your war to you! This is what you wanted—come and
take it!"

The first of the Clochs Mór struck back then, even as
she stared up at the Old Wall on the slopes of Sliabh
Gabhar and past its stone ramparts to the Rí's Keep.
The mage who wielded it was clumsy and alone: in her
cloch-vision, a skeletal army appeared before her, arrayed in ringed mail and helm and holding swords in
their bony hands. They flew at her, jaws wide and screaming in high-pitched voices. Jenna tossed them aside, shattering bone and steel alike and then following the line
of force back to the mage who wielded the Cloch Mór.
She sent a pulse of raw, unfocused energy from the
mage-lights at him, and the tiarna who held the cloch—
in the nearest tower of the Old Wall, up the hill from
her—was crushed under the barrage. She didn't know if
he died or simply lost consciousness. She didn't care; he
was gone, smashed like an annoying fly. She saw, dimly,
a squad of frightened gardai rushing toward her up the
street. She almost sighed as she tossed the great stones
of the broken gate tower at them: they scattered, retreating in undignified terror.

"Come on!" she raged at them. "You wanted me—
your bane is here!"

Torin Mallaghan, Rí of Tuath Gabair, glanced around the courtyard of the keep as he lifted his Cloch Mór to the sky. With him were three other Ríthe: Brasil Mas Sithig of Tuath Infochla, whose keep and courtyard this was; Harkin O Seachnasaigh of Tuath Connachta, his face looking a bit less toadlike to Torin in the magical light; Mal Mac Baoill of Tuath Airgialla, who seemed sour and irritated even as he filled his cloch. Kerwin Taafe of Tuath Éoganacht and Siobaigh O Treasigh, the Banrion of Tuath Locha Léin, had remained in their own territories, both pleading ailments that would not allow them to travel, though both had sent commanders and armies. Torin wished that the Banrion had come, if only because he enjoyed her company and her support; on the other hand, he hoped Rí Taafe's piles were horribly inflamed and bleeding.

There should have been two others there with them in the courtyard. But the Rí Ard and the Regent Guardian hadn't returned. Torin was beginning to worry about their absence this late, especially with the fleet due to set sail for Inish Thuaidh with tomorrow's evening tide. Neither Enean nor the increasingly insufferable Ó Riain would say why they had left Falcarragh, only that they'd return by nightfall today. Night had come, but they had not.

And the mage-lights felt strange this night. They were glittering madly all over the sky, brighter than he'd ever seen them, and yet the stream that had wrapped about his hand was strangely weak and diluted. He wondered how that could be. From the expressions on the other Ríthe's faces, they were having the same experience.

"*My Rí!*" The captain of Rí Mas Sithig's personal gardai rushed into the courtyard. His sword was out, a terrible breach of etiquette with the other Ríthe present, and that alone told Torin how alarmed the man was. "There's been an attack . . . The North Gate's been destroyed . . .

Houses afire . . ." Out of breath, the man could do no more than gasp the awful phrases.

"Who?" Rí Mas Sithig roared. "The Inish?"

The man shook his head. "The Mad Holder, my Rí," he answered. "Alone. Banrion MacEagan. She has . . ." He took a gulp of air. His voice was tremulous and hoarse. "She has Lámh Shábhála."

"By the Mother . . ." Torin could not help the exclamation. The implications struck him like mailed fists. *If the MacEagan woman has the cloch, then Ó Riain is dead and probably Enean as well.*

Torin had heard the tales of his da's generation, of Jenna Aoire the Mad Holder who would become Banrion MacEagan. His own keep back in Lár Bhaile still bore the scars from the Mad Holder's flight after she'd killed his mam. He'd heard the older Riocha talk of the Battle of Dún Kiil and the awful destruction the woman had wreaked there. Some of the tales were undoubtedly exaggerations, but some . . .

If even half were true, she would be a formidable opponent, even with the Clochs Mór of the Tuatha arrayed against her. A cold foreboding slithered down his spine.

"She is mad if she believes she can stand alone against us all," Mas Sithig said. He brought his hand down, the mage-lights trailing away reluctantly. "She's brought herself to her death, none too soon." His gaze flicked over Torin, and he saw that despite the Rí's brave words, the man was as uncertain as Torin. *Aye, she'll fall, almost certainly, but how many of us will she take to the Mother with her? How many of us will she kill before the Black Haunts come for her?*

But there was nothing any of them could do. The battle had been brought to them, all unexpected, and they had no choice. "Sound the keep bells," Mas Sithig told the garda. "Send runners to Overlook Park and alert the troop captains—have the soldiers arm themselves and come here."

"It's already done, my Rí," the garda said. "And I've placed a squadron of twenty men outside the courtyard who will remain with you."

"Then send a runner to Tiarna O Blaca," Torin told the man. "Tell him to gather the mages of the Order of Gabair and meet us at the Old Wall."

The garda nodded and rushed off.

"No Holder has ever stood against so many Clochs Mór," Rí O Seachnasaigh said. His plump face looked almost eager. If he was shocked or upset by the apparent death of O Riain, the man he'd championed, the emotion didn't show. "One of us will hold Lámh Shábhála tonight."

Those of us who are still alive, Torin thought. "I hope you're right, Rí O Seachnasaigh. Let's go, then, and may the Mother go with us," he said.

He placed the chain of his Cloch Mór around his neck, wondering if he would see the dawn.

They rode into the teeth of a hurricane. They rode into chaos.

Owaine saw the lightning of the clochs and the leaping flames under the swirling mage-lights. He heard the walls tumble and the gardai wail.

By the time Owaine and the others reached North Gate, Jenna had moved deeper into the city. They could heard the sounds of battle; they could feel the tingle of enormous mage-power unleashed; they saw the flashes and forms of the Clochs Mór in battle. Owaine pulled Blaze from under his clóca. Dread sat in his stomach, and worry about Meriel and where she might be tore at him. He gaped at the ruined walls, lit fitfully by the spreading fires in the nearby dwellings and the mage-lights above. The smell of smoke choked him. The scope of the destruction awed him and terrified him at the same time.

The choice before him seemed clear. Jenna may have

gone mad, but she was still the Banrion, and the armies that filled this city had come here to take Inish Thuaidh. He was an Inishlander; he knew what he had to do, as did Máister Kirwan.

"We have to help the Banrion," Mundy said, speaking Owaine's thoughts. "She can't hold off all the clochs alone—they'll kill her. Come on!" He started to ride off, Owaine and Mahon following, but Edana and Doyle sat unmoving on their horses in the midst of the rubble.

"We part ways here," Edana told them. Her horse stamped nervously. "We were allies against Ó Riain and in recovering Lámh Shábhála. That's over now, and I won't save Enean's killer." Her face was grim and set.

"You'll fight with the Tuatha, then?" Mundy asked her. She shrugged. Doyle glared at Owaine silently. Mundy's face tightened and Owaine thought that the Máister might open his own cloch and attack Edana rather than let her leave. Edana must have felt the same, for her hand went to her breast and she frowned. Doyle, too, reacted, and Owaine put himself between the two.

"Meriel would understand your choice, Bantiarna," he said. "Go the way you feel you need to go, and I thank you both for the help you've given Meriel and me. I only hope we don't meet again tonight, Edana. We don't need to be enemies."

"We don't get that choice, Inishlander," Doyle spat back. "Your interests are no longer mine or Edana's. Not if you intend to help my sister survive her murderous folly."

Owaine heard the creak of leather and Mahon reached for his sword at the insult to the Banrion, and from the side of his vision he saw the Máister's hand close about his cloch. "Then we'll end this here and now," Mundy said warningly, but Owaine shook his head desperately.

"No, Máister. Please," he said, but it was already too late. Demon-Caller was open and the mage-creature howled, stamping its feet and shaking the ground. Horses reared, Owaine falling from his mount to land in a bruised heap in the rubble. Arms of light wrapped around the demon from Mundy's cloch, but the demon laughed and vanished. When Owaine looked, Edana and Doyle had fled into the darkness. Gone. Mundy cursed.

"We can still catch them," Mahon shouted, his sword out, but Mundy shook his head and pointed to the west and the hills where the Old Wall sheltered the keep. Owaine could see the mage-lights curling there like a brilliant tornado, and as he touched Blaze with his mind, he could feel other Clochs Mór gathering against it. "The Banrion is in battle," he said. "We can't wait."

Mundy nodded. "Then we'll go to her, and we'll fight and die like Inishlanders," he said.

Edana and Doyle hurried their horses up the street to the gate that led through the Old Wall. They moved against a seething flood of Falcarragh's citizens, all of them rushing away from the center of the battle. On the nearest tower of the Old Wall, Doyle could see Riocha gathered, outlined in the flickering of mage-light. Rí Torin, and Rí Mas Sithig, and . . .

Doyle froze for a moment, then dug his heels into his horse's ribs, nearly running down the people in front of him, who scattered away as best they could. "Doyle," Edana called. "Wait!" She hurried in his wake and they forced their way through the gates even as the gardai were trying to shut them. They were inside, and Doyle stared at the tower, outlined against the fierce mage-lights netting the stars.

Tiarna O Blaca was there, and another . . . Doyle could see the bear's head, silhouetted against the fury of the sky.

"Shay!" Doyle shouted. He let himself half fall from the horse. "Shay! I ask you now!"

O Blaca turned, peering down to where Doyle stood. He seemed to nod, and he lifted his Cloch Mór.

The Toscaire Concordai was suddenly no longer on the tower, but was standing on the ground with his back to Doyle. The man seemed confused and disoriented at the sudden shift of place, his hand lifting with the jewel of Snapdragon.

"Toscaire," Doyle said softly behind the man. "Remember me?"

Rhusvak's head started to turn, but Doyle gave the man no chance to react. His dagger slid quickly and deeply along the man's neck, severing the jugular vein and spattering Doyle in a gout of steaming blood. The bear's skin slipped from his head; the man's eyes were wide with fear as he saw Doyle and he clapped his free hand uselessly to his neck as blood continued to pulse from the wound. Doyle tore Snapdragon from the Toscaire's blood-slick hands.

"This is mine," he said to the dying man. "Be happy I killed you rather than let you live with the pain I've suffered." He pulled the chain of Weaver from around his neck, tossing Enean's Cloch Mór to the ground as carelessly as a chicken bone. He put Snapdragon around his neck, exulting at the familiar feel of it. He lifted his hand holding the cloch, his skin and the sleeve of his léine soaked with blood to the elbow. The dragon roared.

He looked at Edana. She was staring at him as if he were a stranger.

"Damn you! Damn you all!"

Jenna had never felt such power arrayed against her. Even at the battle of Dún Kiil, the focus of the clochs had been scattered rather than directed only at her. Here, she was alone and the clochs struck repeatedly at her, again and again, relentless. She was already unhorsed, the animal lying dead and broken in the street behind her. She should have been lying there with it, but the mage-lights were still twisting above her, feeding Lámh Shábhála, and instead she stood and directed her fury at the ramparts of the keep and the Ríthe and cloudmages who stood there with their Clochs Mór. She pulled the power continuously from the sky as they could not, Lámh Shábhála doing what no other cloch could: remaining full even as the other clochs drained themselves of their power.

In her mind, the mages set against her were dark, gibbering demons. They roared at her, their anger joining the wild jabbering of the dead Holders in her head, the crackling of fires, and the din of the various manifestations of the clochs. Wolves howled, a dragon curled in the sky and spat fire, ghostly armies marched and thickets of spears flew through the air between globes of fire. She broke the spears, cast aside the fire, tore the wings from the dragon, and smashed the wolves even as they tore at her.

Already she had defeated half a dozen of the Clochs Mór, a feat no other Holder in her mind had ever accomplished. Already this night would be legendary. She had come alone against impossible odds and she stood unharmed in the midst of carnage.

But slowly, she *was* flagging, exhausted in body and mind even though berserk mage-power still coursed through her. She could not last forever. She could not stand against them all. A giant fist smashed against the wall she threw up almost too late and Jenna fell to her knees with a cry. The fist rose up again and she dissolved it with a thought, but could not react quickly enough to the red flare of lightning that reached her. She screamed, walling herself inside Lámh Shábhála, wrapping herself in mage-light so the next stroke broke, as did a flight of glowing arrows that followed. She hurled back the gardai—clochless—who rushed her as one, screaming their battle cry, crushing the squadron of soldiers against the Old Wall and then tearing it down to bury them. She heard their wails as they died.

She had killed so many this night: hundreds already. What did a few more matter? She laughed her bitter, mirthless laugh.

The Clochs Mór regrouped and came at her again, striking her from all sides at once. Jenna couldn't contain them all, couldn't put her attention everywhere. She tried to imagine a black, thick wall around herself, but they tore at it and she couldn't put it back up all at once. There were a dozen Clochs Mór attacking now, and several cloch-mions also, buzzing about like stinging, angry insects.

The ancient Holders' voices in her head whispered warnings, but there was also admiration in them.

". . . this is far more than any of us could have held off."

"You wield Lámh Shábhála so well, better than nearly any of us . . ."

"But you'll still die. You'll be with us . . ."

"No!" she shouted at them, all of them. The anger filled her, a blinding blood-red that soaked the world around her in its color. She concentrated, sent Lámh Shábhála's energy out to where most of the Clochs Mór were grouped, and felt at least two more of them go down, the images vanishing in her cloch-sight. "No!" But there were still the others, and they followed her back through the hole in the wall she'd made with her counterstroke. Ghostly spears impaled her; gaping, white-toothed jaws tore at her; lines of energy wrapped around her.

And then: a new Cloch Mór, or rather, a new mage holding it: a gold-and-red dragon appeared in front of her. "Hello, Sister," the dragon said, and struck. The hideous mouth she pushed aside before it closed around her, but the tail, whipping around, struck her hard. She felt ribs break in her chest.

Jenna went to her knees. The mage-lights swam above her, milky and furious.

"No!" she shouted again, but this time it was a shriek of pure agony, and she knew she was lost. "Damn you, Doyle!"

"Has Bradán an Chumhacht given you a vision of what's to happen?" Meriel asked Dhegli as they swam toward Falcarragh.

"Aye," he'd answered. "It has . . ." But he would not tell her what he had seen.

The surface of the water, above them, was bright with the colors of fire and blood, of ice and snow. Dhegli, swimming alongside Meriel, his flippers brushing her side, lifted his snout toward it. "The sky burns tonight as it never has," he said in awe. "Your mam draws it all down."

The pod of Saimhóir had entered Falcarragh Harbor, swimming quickly close by the island of East Light and slipping near to the quays. Around them, even in the blackness of the water, she could sense the barnacled hulls of warships and the long chains of their anchors. The seals moved among them, unseen. Challa hovered near the two of them, and her gaze was not friendly.

Meriel could feel the power of the mage-lights also— Treoraí's Heart was a white-hot ember against her fur, and through it, she could sense the searing pinpoint that was Lámh Shábhála, crowded around by other clochs, all of them arrayed against her mam. The battle had begun, and Meriel knew her mam could not defeat them all. Already, Treoraí's Heart told her, Jenna was injured and in pain. "Dhegli, my mam . . ."

"I know," he said. "We need a diversion that will take the attention of some of the clochs." He swam away, the Saimhóir surfacing as one and she heard his whistling, barking voice speaking to the others. The seals ducked below water again as Dhegli came over to Meriel. His flipper touched her. "Watch!" he said, his muzzle pointing to a warship moored at the Harbor Quay, flying the Rí Ard's colors.

Foaming water erupted around its waterline, and there was a sudden, gaping hole in the wooden hull through which water was rushing. The boat heeled over, sailors shouting alarm on the deck, the masts and lines creaking and snapping, the pier itself shuddering. Lanterns swayed as men looked over the railing at the water and the crippled boat, then there was a great splash near another boat anchored out in the bay, and it, too, began to slowly founder. There were shouts of alarm all around them. Somewhere close by, mage-light flickered and a ball of light rushed past them, falling into the water with an explosion and the sound of hissing steam.

"There," Dhegli said. "The Saimhóir will take away the attention of at least a few of the Clochs Mór. Now— you and I go to the First Holder." He slipped away before she could say anything, moving quickly to the shore. Meriel hurried after him, hauling herself out awkwardly. He was already changing: a naked, dripping man pushing himself up from the mud. A moment later she stood beside him, equally bare but for the gleaming chain holding Treoraí's Heart.

The city was on fire and they could see the shadows of people running through the smoke and haze and mage-lights. They could hear shouting, and the crackling of mage-power. "Hurry!" Meriel said to Dhegli. "We need to find her!"

The dragon that was Doyle coiled above Jenna, leering. The mouth gaped open as the forms of the other Clochs Mór gathered around. Jenna yanked at the tendrils of the mage-lights in her mind, sucking down the energy, but the dragon moved and she saw death snaking toward her.

Before Doyle could strike, blue-green ropes wrapped themselves around the dragon's throat, holding the creature for a moment before it snapped them like threads. But then red lightning erupted against its scaled chest, driving Doyle back and away from Jenna. She knew that energy, knew it very well—it had come to her aid before: the Cloch Mór Blaze. "Ennis?" she whispered, a faint hope arising in her. "Oh, Ennis, is that you?"

She followed the trace of Blaze's power back to its source, looking with the eyes of her cloch-sight, and she saw that it was not Ennis but some young man. She stared at him, uncomprehendingly. *Owaine* . . . The name came to her as if through some dim memory. For a moment, the red haze about her died, the wild madness receding. *Where is Meriel, then* . . . "Oh, Mother," she whispered. "What have I—"

The Clochs Mór gave her no rest. Snapdragon was back, and Edana with Demon-Caller was with him, and the clochs of the Ríthe . . . They came at her again and the mad blood-mist returned, obliterating thoughts of Meriel. She was the Holder—that was all. The Holder . . . There was nothing more.

Jenna pulled at the mage-lights with Lámh Shábhála in furious desperation, pushing herself to her feet again. She could feel Blaze moving to her flank, and Mundy's cloch also. Briefly, she allowed herself to feel some hope.

Jenna raged. She tore at the Old Wall and the base of the Ríthe's tower, and great boulders flew. Two more of the Clochs Mór went silent as the Ríthe and mages gathered there fled for more stable ground. Jenna seized the opportunity—in her cloch-vision, she found Doyle and locked Lámh Shábhála's energy around him. She could see his face, straining with the effort of trying to escape her. The mage-demon howled and charged at her, but Jenna threw the beast aside contemptuously. "Brother," she said. "You've lost a battle with me for the last time. You are your da's son, and I hated that man as much as I loved our mam."

The dragon wriggled in her deadly, tightening embrace as Doyle grimaced, his mouth shut as muscles jumped at his jawline. She watched his struggle, almost lovingly, ignoring everything else but his face. She tightened her hold, then released it slightly. "Scream," she crooned to him. "I want to hear you scream first."

"*. . . aye, that is what I'd do . . .*"

"*. . . is insanity. She's lost herself.*

"*Jenna! You must let the madness go . . .*" That was Riata's voice, the whisper of the ancient Bunús Muintir Holder.

"Be silent!" she shouted back at the ghost.

He would not. "*Your madness blinds you . . .*"

He was right, she realized belatedly. She'd given the other Clochs Mór time to regroup, and they came at her again. She could feel Owaine and Mundy at her back, protecting her, but they could only deal with one or two foes at a time, and there were too many. Too many.

The assault tore Jenna away from the dragon, which hissed in both frustration and relief. She batted at them, clutching at the zenith with ethereal fingers and tearing at the mage-lights there, throwing the energy at her enemies wildly, not caring who she struck or how.

She was tiring rapidly. She could feel the cost of wielding such power for so long. The air crackled around her and she felt stretched and worn thin, as if her soul would tear apart in a harsh wind. The red haze around her was deepening and she could no longer tell foe from friend. She lashed out blindly at the clochs. Her awareness drifted high over the city now, as if she were one with the mage-lights, and she howled down at it with fury and disdain and hatred, knowing that soon, soon, she must fall.

And when she did . . . she vowed that she would take as many as possible with her to the Mother-Creator.

56

A Holder's Death

NO ONE took much notice of two unclothed swim-
mers running up from the water. There was far too
much confusion and fear in the city for that. The city's
attention was on the conflagration near and around the
Rí's Keep, where it seemed that all the clochs na thintrí
were engaged in battle, or out to the harbor where the
fleet of the Tuatha was under attack, with half a dozen
ships already sinking.

As Meriel and Dhegli reached the streets below the
keep, they came across evidence of the destruction Jenna
had caused: Buildings were burning, flames leaping high
in mocking imitation of the cold mage-lights above them.
Stones littered the street, some of them so huge that
they knew only a cloch could have moved them. And
there were bodies . . .

Now that she was back in human form, Meriel was
cold from the wet and the night air. She paused to take
the clóca from a dead woman and wrap it around herself.
"I'm sorry," she told the corpse. She found herself wondering about the woman: who had plaited her long,
brown hair into such intricate braids? She looked, even
in death, fair of feature, and her skin was smooth and
oiled—was she Riocha or perhaps céili giallnai? Did she
have children? A husband? What had she been like in
life? Meriel shook her head, tears starting in her eyes
and guilt washing over her.

This is your fault. All of this is your fault, because you made it possible for your mam to take back the stone. You should have known the andúilleaf had taken her to the edge of madness, should have remembered what happened the last time. You were inside her; you felt the madness yourself. . . . "I'm sorry this had to happen to you," she told the corpse, which only stared back at her. Treoraí's Heart was throbbing, pounding, tugging at Meriel's mind. So many hurt, so many wounded and injured, so many dead . . .

Your fault . . .

Meriel was sobbing suddenly, standing over an unknown dead woman in the midst of smoke and destruction and noise. The grief washed over her, an overpowering tide, and through the shimmering salt water of her eyes, she saw Dhegli move to her, enfolding her in his arms. "There's no time, Meriel," he whispered softly in her head, nuzzling her ear. "Later. Later, you can let your feelings show. If we're to help your mam, we have to go on."

"I know." She wiped at her eyes with a fold of the clóca. It still smelled faintly of the woman's perfume, sweet against the harsher odor of smoke. Dhegli released Meriel: he seemed not to notice the cold or his nakedness or the devastation around them; his attention was only on her. She placed her hand over her breast, over Treoraí's Heart. With the touch, cloch-sight washed over her and she felt her mam's presence, a gigantic whirlpool pulling at everything around her. Circling her were the great lights of the Clochs Mór, most of them attacking the black center of Lámh Shábhála, but a few standing with her: Mundy and . . . "Owaine." She breathed his name.

"Aye," Dhegli said. "He's here and he needs you. Come!"

Taking her hand, Dhegli led her through the streets toward the focus of the fighting. As they approached, Meriel found herself immersed more and more in the cloch-vision, seeing the world through the power of the mage-lights rather than with her own eyes. It was a violently bright world, the colors oversaturated and primary. Treoraí's Heart throbbed under her hand as it never had before. In the past, she had needed to touch another person to feel their pain and make the connection, but not now. Not here in this world where the mage-lights seemed to have come to earth.

Meriel's awareness was a living thing; she could send her thoughts sweeping outward and she could become part of them: Máister Kirwan, wielding his Cloch Mór with the ease and mastery of long study, though she could feel his worry and resignation. He fully expected to die here, and that certainty was a hard, resolute stone in the center of him; there was a deep love for Jenna in him also, hidden carefully away. Mundy was already injured—she could feel that, too, Treoraí's Heart yearning to heal him—his left arm hanging uselessly at his side with an arrow entirely through it. Two Clochs Mór opposed him and she could see the faces of the mages who held them even though she didn't recognize them. One had a torc around his neck: a Rí, then. She wondered if it was Torin Mallaghan.

But Meriel tore her attention away from the Máister, searching . . .

In her normal sight, they ran through the winding harbor street, moving closer to the Rí's Keep and the Old Wall. Fires had broken out in several places and long lines of citizens snaked from the harbor to the burning houses, passing buckets of water. Gardai screamed orders; she saw a squadron of them rush toward Máister Kirwan. He took his attention away from the clochs for a moment and lifted a hand in their direction: some of them went down with the flare of mage-power. She saw Mahon, sword lifted high and battle rage distorting his features, meet the others with ringing steel. As Mahon advanced, she saw another figure behind Mundy and Mahon . . .

Owaine . . .

He was struggling and exhausted, and within him there

was the same dread that filled Máister Kirwan, though
Owaine did not accept his coming death, but railed
against it. He was wrapped in the flames of his cloch,
sending its fire outward in great, searing blasts. Meriel
could feel the heat, could see the fierce light play over
his strained features. And in him, she let herself touch
the love he bore for her, shadowed by his worry for her.
"Owaine!" she cried, and his head turned toward her.

"Meriel!" he called back to her. "Your mam . . ."

*. . . She saw Jenna in her true sight, standing halfway
up the slope to the Old Wall, which had been breached
in front of her. Her mam's right arm was raised high,
and the mage-lights wrapped around it, linking her to the
sky. A wind seemed to rush about her, her dark hair
whipping around. She looked younger than Meriel ever
remembered, beautiful and yet dangerous at the same
time. She, too, was injured: blood streamed down one
side of her face and soaked into the shoulder of her léine;
when she stepped forward, she hobbled on one leg, almost
falling as she put weight on it. Archers were firing at her
from the walls though none of the arrows reached her,
disappearing into smoke and ash. On the wall, Meriel
could see one of the mages pointing at Jenna and looking
backward over his shoulder. . . .*

A shout from Owaine brought her back to the cloch-
vision. A pack of snarling wolves appeared in the air
before him, and though he burned them with Blaze, one
came through the flame and its great jaws closed around
his arm. Owaine bellowed in pain and anger as the wolf's
great bulk bore him down, the beast's head whipping
back and forth. It released the arm and went for
Owaine's exposed throat.

Meriel started toward him, but she felt a cold blue
presence rush past her, leaving the smell of salt in its
wake. The newcomer pulled at the mage-lights with the
strength of a Lámh Shábhála, drinking them into itself.
It flared, the light nearly blinding in Meriel's cloch-
vision, and the Clochs Mór fell back from it. The wolf

was torn away from Owaine and tumbled howling into
the void. The presence laughed, and its sound was
familiar.

Dhegli had brought Bradán an Chumhacht to life . . .

*. . . he was still in human form next to her, his hand
holding hers, his skin marked by the curling mage-scars.
A quartet of gardai rushed toward the two of them, but
Dhegli simply glanced at them and the swords shattered
in their hands; panicked, the gardai fled. "You know what
to do, Meriel," he said to her.*

*"I don't know what you mean," she told him, but he
had released her hand and she could no longer hear his
voice. He stepped forward, bare feet on broken rubble.
He lifted his arms to the mage-lights . . .*

In her cloch-sight, he was magnificent, a form of deepest azure from which aquamarine light flowed outward.
Like the harsher brilliance of Lámh Shábhála, he over-
shadowed the smaller forms of the Clochs Mór around
him. With his appearance, the mages paused in the midst
of their battle, wondering what this manifestation might
be. They didn't hesitate long—a monstrous fist raised
above him; a net of glowing yellow enveloped him. Meriel shouted in alarm; Dhegli laughed again. A tidal wave
rushed outward from him, rushing down the lines of
force that led from the fist to the wielder of the Cloch
Mór—a distant cry came faintly as the fist vanished.
Dhegli took in a long, slow breath and his cloch-form
swelled, the golden lines turning pale white and then
snapping apart. He floated, and now in the midst of the
blue light she saw the shape of a Saimhóir.

"Holder," he spoke, the word like the ringing of some
vast brass gong. "I've come again for you." He and
Jenna stood together and the sky above them rained
light, stormed with brilliance. . . . *The true sight was
almost ludicrous: Jenna crouched bleeding on the ruined
hillside, and alongside her, a scarred bull seal looking out
of place and awkward on the land* . . . "This isn't what
we should be doing, Holder," he said, his voice sad.
"This isn't the time for Lámh Shábhála and Bradán an

Chumhacht to war together. Come, I've brought Meriel and we can leave. We don't need this." Light played around their magnificence, illuminating the wreckage and the destruction. "Come away with us," Dhegli said again.

"Aye, Mam," Meriel shouted up at her, her voice sounding impossibly thin and small. "Please listen to Dhegli." The Clochs Mór circled about, but they were all waiting, none of them daring to attack the two presences. Jenna's head turned and found Meriel. Her face softened and her lips quivered. Something changed in her eyes.

"Meriel . . ."

Meriel held out her hand. "Please come with us, Mam." For the first time, Meriel began to have hope. They could escape this trap. They could go to the water and swim away while Owaine, Máister Kirwan, and Mahon took one of the ships. They could escape alive. They could go home. "Take my hand, Mam," Meriel said. . . . *Jenna turned to Meriel and she reached for Meriel's hand with the fisted hand still holding the cloch. For a moment her eyes went sad and frightened. Her mouth moved with unheard words: "Help me . . ." but then the moment passed and she pulled her hand back.*

She scowled . . .

"You'll betray me like the others," Jenna said, hugging her scarred arm to her body. "That's why you're here. You want Lámh Shábhála, too, but you'll never have it. Never!" Her voice was like the slap of a hand. Meriel could see the words whip red from her mouth, and the impact of them struck Meriel down to her knees. Jenna's presence loomed over her, eclipsing Dhegli.

"No, Mam," Meriel cried. She could taste blood in her mouth.

"Jenna," Dhegli's voice boomed, and blue pressed hard against red as Meriel squinted into the brilliance of the cloch-sight. "Don't."

The bloody light flared, and Jenna shrieked. "You're the same!" she shouted at Dhegli. "You're all the same . . ." and she lifted her hand, pulling mage-energy from the sky and throwing it flaming at Dhegli. Meriel saw the Saimhóir tumble backward with a cry.

The Clochs Mór attacked as one, seeing the two allies strangely at odds. Meriel could barely make out the half-glimpsed forms amidst the lightning and glow. She saw Owaine strike at a gold-and-red dragon with a sheet of fire that burst in rippling fury along the great beast's scales, and Edana's mage-demon roared as Mundy lashed at it with his cloch. Howls and cries erupted, making Meriel want to clasp hands to ears.

She saw her mam surrounded and Dhegli trying to reach her, himself besieged. *Jenna staggered, half falling backward down the slope. A creature from a nightmare raked at her with ichor-dripping talons, opening a gash down the arm she flung up to protect herself. The archers on the wall, sensing weakness, sent a new flight of arrows toward her and though none touched her, several hurtled into the ground alongside her.*

There was nothing Meriel could do. Nothing. Except . . .

She could feel the tug of Treoraí's Heart, surging up through her. It seemed, in her cloch-sight, to burn as brightly as any of the Clochs Mór and she could hear a voice within, a voice created of stone and filled with the wisdom of long ages. "Go into her," it said in a voice of quartz and granite. "Find her and bring her back."

"I can't!" Meriel answered, shaking her head as she remembered the feel of her mam's madness, how she had nearly lost herself twice in it. "I can't. Not again."

The power flared, closing her fingers tightly around the cloch. "You must."

The voice resonated with her own heart; she could feel the rightness of what it said even though it frightened her. Truth was the rich green of spring grass and the gold of sunset. Truth tasted of the salt of the sea and the sourness of fresh bread. She nodded. She held the power of Treoraí's Heart and released it. It twined around the tornado that linked Jenna to the mage-lights and plunged in, heedless of the clamor and destruction around them.

Inside the red wall, there was silence. The roaring chaos was gone. Here, there was a stillness painted with shadows. She tried to merge with her mam, to become Meriel/Jenna as she had the previous times, but though she could feel the touch of emotions that were not her own, something held her away. "Mam?"

A faint sob answered her.

Meriel could see nothing. She drifted in a black void, suspended in the depths of a moonless sea. The sobbing continued and a touch brushed her arm. Meriel gasped in fright, whirling around, but there was nothing to see and the touch was gone. The weeping seemed to come from all about her, directionless. "Mam?" she called again. "Is that you? I'm here. It's Meriel."

The touch came again like the brush of a warm breeze: on her cheek, lifting her hair, and gone. The sound of a breath approached her, touched her ear, and vanished. Indistinctly, Meriel could begin to hear the clamor and confusion of the battle raging in Falcarragh and streaks of wild red rippled and flowed all around her, a scarlet cage. She could feel faint shudders and tremblings, as if something were striking the cage now and again. The breath came again, a bellow's sigh. Yellow splashed on the walls surrounding her, fading to orange and red and finally returning slowly to black, and the colors were accompanied by a wave of pain that made Meriel gasp and close her eyes.

"It's not safe in here, Mam," Meriel called out when she could breathe again. "You can't hide from this."

No answer. But there was a faint thread of white light she could see now. She reached down to touch it.

"Leave her be!" It was the shriek of a harridan, a witch, a demon—hissing and venomous. A face rose from the darkness: her mam's, but twisted and disfigured

and nearly unrecognizable. Pale and sickly yellow light played over her scowling features. "Can't you see she doesn't need you? Doesn't want you. *Never* wanted you. You're a leech, a parasite, as greedy as all the rest of them."

Meriel ignored the apparition. She reached again for the white thread, and this time taloned hands closed around her arm, the nails digging deep into her flesh so that Meriel screamed. Blood welled around the scabrous nails and flowed thickly away as the fingers tightened, digging ever deeper into Meriel's forearm. Meriel couldn't move without ripping out great chunks of her own flesh with those nails; the arm held her. "Now you'll stay here with me," the mam-thing husked. "You'll stay here always."

"You're going to die if you don't stop what you're doing, Mam," Meriel said frantically, trying to pull away, but the hand clenched her more tightly.

"I don't care," it said. "It doesn't matter. We all die. You'll die with me."

"Mam!" Meriel shouted, but the thing only laughed at her.

"Your mam is dead already," it said. "Your mam is gone."

"No." Meriel shrieked the word, as if the force of her voice could shatter the awful mockery of Jenna that hovered in front of her. She ripped her arm away from the creature with the shout, heedless of the terrible wounds it left on her arm as she tore herself from the deeply-embedded claws. *"No!"* she howled again in denial as she took the white thread in blood-slicked fingers.

You should leave now, she knew. The madness had released her and all she needed to do was let go of Treoraí's Heart and she would be back in her own body, away from this. Meriel trembled, part of her wanting to do just that. If she left, her mam would die, but she might be able to save herself. If she stayed here, they both might die. *Let it go,* she whispered to herself, but though her breath came fast and panicky and she whimpered, she could not.

You're lost . . . lost . . .

Edana and Doyle had forced their way up to the wall where they could see, in doubled vision, the battle taking place. Even as Edana set the mage-demon to tearing at the wall Jenna had erected around herself, she saw with her true eyes the slight figure of Meriel rushing up from the ruins of the street below, clambering up the slope through the shattered blocks of the Old Wall and the crushed heather to where her mam stood. The others saw her as well; the Clochs Mór attacked this new arrival, but Owaine and the Saimhóir who had come to Jenna's aid deflected the fury aimed at Meriel. Edana could see Meriel holding Treoraí's Heart aloft to the sky, saw her touch her mam's arms even as Jenna went down under the lash of a dragon's tail.

For a moment, there was little change: Lámh Shábhála continued to battle, continued to throw wild, dangerous lightning everywhere, to pull at the walls and hurl back the clochs of the Tuathian mages. But though the wall stayed up around Jenna, her counterattacks had stopped. Edana stared downward, watching as Meriel's arms went around her mam.

"Hold!" Edana shout to the Ríthe. Near Edana, the mage-demon went still. Brasil Mas Sithig, standing with Torin Mallaghan and the other Ríthe and cloudmages, glanced over to Edana. "Rí," she told him. "Wait! A moment, only. Let her daughter have a chance . . ."

"Bantiarna O Liathain, Tiarna Mac Ard," he said, as if seeing them for the first time. "I am Rí here, not you."

"Aye," Edana answered. "But look—" She pointed down the hill. Lámh Shábhála pulsed in a cage of magelights, but their brilliance flowed around the Holder and then back into the sky—not destructively out to Falcar-

ragh. The manifestations of the other Clochs Mór surged
around her, but Jenna was no longer attacking them.

Rí Mas Sithig raised his hand, as did Rí Mallaghan;
slowly, the din of the battle subsided and Edana's cloch-
vision receded.

Meriel hugged Jenna to herself, and Edana remem-
bered Meriel's touch and the way she had brought
Edana out of her own darkness. "Hold," she said again.
"For a few breaths more . . ."

With Meriel's touch, the white line began to glow, as did
Treoraí's Heart. The new light from the cloch pushed back
the darkness and banished the apparition. It faded like
a quick morning fog, the wispy hands still reaching for
Meriel even as they vanished.

She saw her mam—or some internal image of her—
huddled in a corner of the mind-room. Her face was thin
and drawn, her eyes dark hollows, her hair hanging in
limp strands. She lifted a hand, shining with the light of
Lámh Shábhála and the hand trembled with a palsy. "I
won't let it go," she said. "It's mine. I won't let you take
it away from me. I don't care that you're my daughter.
Lámh Shábhála is *mine*."

"Aye," Meriel told her soothingly. "It is yours, Mam.
It always has been, and I don't want it. I don't. But you
can't use it this way."

"I have to," Jenna answered. "Don't you see? I have
to kill them or they'll kill me. Look! They're all against
me. They want what I have, all of them, and I have to
kill them to keep Lámh Shábhála. I have to."

"They'll kill you either way, Mam. There are too
many of them and the mage-lights will eventually fail.
But there's still a way out, Mam. Dhegli's here, and if
we can reach the water, we could escape as Saimhóir."

"The water . . ." For a moment Jenna sounded hopeful, then she shook her head. For the first time, Meriel
began to slip into her. She could feel the chaotic thoughts,

the contradictory impulses of the madness, and Meriel straggled to hold onto herself. "I can't. I hurt too much. I can't hold on." Jenna began to sob, her chest heaving with the cries. "It hurts so much. Let it end here. At least I won't hurt anymore."

Lost . . . lost . . . Meriel could feel the comfort that the image of Jenna lying dead on the ground gave her mam. *All the pain gone. All the madness, just a long sleep, and then the comfort of the Mother-Creator. . . .*

Meriel/Jenna could hear, faintly, the sounds of ghostly voices in the air, wafting up from Lámh Shábhála: *"Aye, let it go." "Come join us." "We're waiting here for you." "I went mad, too, in the end . . ." "And me . . ." "And me . . ." "It's better to be dead than to bear the stone . . ."*

"The voices lie. They want you to fail," Meriel said, but she could see her mam's head tilt as she listened to them. And Meriel/Jenna listened, too.

"Hold . . ." Edana said, but though the other Clochs Mór paused when Rí Mas Sithig and Rí Mallaghan both barked out the order, one mage did not.

Doyle, with Snapdragon.

The gold-and-red beast snarled and hissed near the wall of Lámh Shábhála, pacing. Its great head reared back as it lifted itself, then snapped down again as it disgorged fire from its open mouth. The shield around Jenna shuddered and began to melt, even as Edana screamed at Doyle, as she turned to strike at him with her bare fists. "Stop it, Doyle!" she yelled at him, but his face was grim and determined.

"Not this time," he told her. He backed away from her assault, though the dragon tore at the black wall with its claws. "Edana, we have Lámh Shábhála in our grasp. *Everything* we wanted could be ours."

"You'll kill Meriel, too. Let her try to stop this."

"Why?" His head whipped around to look at her, and there was nothing but fury in his gaze. "By the Mother,

Edana—look around. How many people has my sister killed here? How much of the city has she destroyed? She *deserves* death, as much as anyone ever did. If Meriel dies with her, well, so be it." He pressed his lips together. The dragon roared and belched flame at Jenna once more.

"I don't want it this way," she told him. She struck him again in the chest with a soft fist. "Not now. This has already cost us too much, Doyle. I don't want to lose the rest of what I once loved. You have Snapdragon and your sanity back. That's enough. If you take Lámh Shábhála, you'll lose me. I feel that. I *know* that."

"Edana . . ." She saw his face soften and the dragon paused . . .

. . . but it was already too late. The strange new power, the one of the sea, hurled itself at the dragon in defense of Jenna. Doyle's face went white, his eyes wide, and he groaned in pain and shock; he staggered, moaning, and Edana saw wounds open on his chest and arms. Rí Mallaghan and Rí Mas Sithig shouted to the other mages, and even as the dragon turned to meet its new foe, the other Clochs Mór also struck back. As one, a half dozen or more of the Tuathian cloudmages struck at the Saimhóir and it could not hold them all back.

Edana saw, in her cloch-vision, the great blue form fall as dragonfire flickered, as ethereal wolves leaped at it, as lightning flared and flights of glowing spears arced, as a black tornado writhed around the power and a wave of sea-green slammed into it and an army of gibbering demons charged. Edana could see Owaine's and Mundy's clochs rushing to help, but they were too few and too late.

There was a shriek, full of torment and loss. . . .

The walls around Meriel and Jenna shuddered with an explosion: white-hot air flared and the pain spread out from its center in writhing tentacles of orange-red. Meriel and Jenna cried out together. Faintly, from outside the wall, she heard voices calling in triumph. Inside, the voices of the old Holders laughed.

"You see! The dragon attacks!"

"It happens now to you as it did to us . . ."

"Your soul will go to the Mother, but part of you will stay here . . ."

Suddenly, Meriel felt a terrifying sense of loss, a feeling of dread and grief that threatened to drown her. *Owaine . . . Dhegli . . .* Something had happened outside, and she was lost inside her mam . . .

"Don't listen to them," Meriel told Jenna, trying to shut it all out. *You can't affect anything outside; you can only do something here.* She crouched alongside the frail figure of her mam. She knew what she had to do, and it terrified her nearly as much as the fear she had for the others. Meriel thought again of fleeing, of leaving here, afraid now that if she chose to use the power of the Heart here, she would have nothing left if Owaine or Dhegli or any of the others needed its power.

You have to choose. You have to choose now. . . .

Meriel closed her mouth, sucked in a deep breath through her nostrils. She tightened her grip on Treoraí's Heart as she touched her mam. "Let me take the pain for you," she said. "Let me . . ."

Her mam's face turned toward her in sorrow and hope.

Then Meriel could say nothing at all. She could only wail in terror.

The horror came at her in a great, rushing mud-brown wave that broke, foaming, above her. Meriel fought against it, but it overwhelmed her, drowning her. She was inundated with Jenna's memories, losing hold of herself entirely. She was no longer Meriel—only Jenna. Here . . .

. . . here was the pain of using Lámh Shábhála; here was the hurt and fear as Padraic Mac Ard became her great-mam's lover; the first, deceptive taste of andúilleaf; Jenna's murderous rage at Lár Bhaile. Here was the horror of seeing Ennis killed in front of her; the black tor-

ture of the Scrúdú. Here was the Battle of Dún Kiil and
its death; here Maeve's rejection of Jenna. Here was the
pain of Meriel's birth; the years of difficult decisions as
Banrion, decisions that inevitably led to suffering for
some even as it helped others. Here was Meriel herself
and the guilt of Jenna's neglect, of not being the parent
she wanted to be. Here was Doyle and the distress of
losing Meriel, and the battle on Inishduán . . .

The misery and anguish consumed Meriel as it rushed
outward from her mam. Image after image pounded at
her as all the bile poured out. Someone was screaming
in torment, and she didn't know whose voice it was.

The flood was more than she could hold. It bore her
under. As she succumbed, flailing, she saw the wall of
Lámh Shábhála shatter. Outside, the storm of the Clochs
Mór was raging, and then it, too, swept over them.

Her last memory was of her mam's wail.

57

The Banrion

IT was as if a hand had wiped her eyes clean of cataracts. One moment, the world had been dark and muddied and strange, and the next it was bright and familiar once more. The cry she made was less of pain than of long-confined grief and relief. Jenna felt light and unburdened, as if the last few decades had suddenly been removed from her, as if she'd been returned to the time before the Filleadh, before andúilleaf, before all the death and strife.

Jenna took a shuddering breath, and it sluiced through her clean and cold. She blinked. "Meriel . . ."

With her true eyes, she saw her daughter crumpled on the broken ground next to her. Farther down the hill a Saimhóir lay, torn and bloody, its sides heaving in distress. Mundy and Owaine gaped up at her; Mahon— spattered with blood and his sword edge chipped and notched, paused. In the cloch-sight, the wall of Lámh Shábhála fell and the clochs rushed at her. She saw death.

Unless . . .

The mage-lights burned like a new sun above her and she pulled at them, not caring that the frigid sky-power burned at her like real fire, tearing open her newly-healed wounds. Jenna screamed with pain and rage and frustration even as she continued to let the energy pour into her, to fill Lámh Shábhála as it had once been filled before at the time of the Filleadh. The cloch was nearly bursting, radiating with a cold so intense that it seemed Jenna's fingers were frozen around the stone. The pattern of scars on her arm shot out rays of mage-light while above there were only stars and the ragged darkness of clouds.

Jenna shone: a sun come to earth. The radiance of the Clochs Mór about her was lost. Sharp, black shadows streaked outward from the center where she stood and she saw the Riocha on the walls above her shading their eyes against the glare. *"Stop!"* she said.

The word boomed like thunder over Falcarragh.

They obeyed, if only from the shock. Even the red-gold dragon held back, though its tail lashed the ground and it growled. Its claws raked grooves in the stone flags of the roadway. "Ríthe!" Jenna called out. "I call for a truce."

She could see them milling above her, figures wrapped in their bright clóca: uncertain. "How can there be a truce, Banrion?" Rí Mallaghan called down to her, his hand shielding his eyes from her appearance. "You brought war here."

"And you would have brought it to Inish Thuaidh if I had waited," Jenna answered. "But we can both end it now." The energy she was holding was ice and fire, and radiance streamed out of her, white and blinding. "I can't hold this power much longer, Rí—all the energy within the mage-lights tonight is with me, and I will let it go—I have no choice. It's your choice whether I release it back to where it came from or if I reduce Falcarragh to ash and ruin." Her body shook; she trembled. "Choose quickly. *Quickly!*"

She could see the Ríthe consulting with each other. Edana was there, too, and Doyle, and she wondered what they were saying. It was Edana who answered.

"You have your truce, Banrion."

"Swear it," Jenna grated out. "Swear it by the Mother. Swear that you will let me and those with me leave freely."

"We swear it," Edana answered, and she saw the Ríthe with her nod agreement. "By the Mother-Creator, we swear it."

Jenna gave a sigh, and the energy within her boiled out again, tearing at her as it left. She howled like a wild beast, her voice lost in the great rushing sound it made. The mage-lights erupted from her, fountaining high and bright above her, streaking in a great, radiant column to the zenith. High above, they spread, fading slowly like the embers of a sullen fire.

The sky went dark, leaving afterimages dancing in her eyes.

"Meriel!"

The name was wrong. She wasn't Meriel; she was Jenna. But she knew the person holding her: Owaine. She could feel his arms, his hand brushing her hair back from her face. Her eyes didn't want to open. She lifted her hand to them and found her fingers sticky with blood. She blinked, her vision smeared red. For a moment she tensed, waiting to feel the horrible pain. But it was gone.

"Meriel!" Owaine said again, urgently. Aye, she knew that name. She knew . . . Her daughter . . .

There was pain in her forehead and she winced, touching it. An ember burned there, and it called a name in a deep, strangely familiar voice: *"Meriel . . ."* She shook her head, but the ember still burned, and with it came the smell of the sea. *"Meriel . . ."* and now it was followed by images and memories, things that seemed to be hers but yet not: swimming with a Saimhóir, a naked man with sea-wet hair and a smile and black, black eyes. A kiss. A feeling of love and longing and lust. *"Meriel . . ."* and she felt the call resonate within her. Her name. Hers. She closed her eyes, feeling the new presence assert itself, breaking through Jenna like a butterfly from its cocoon.

"Meriel . . ."

The ember went cold in her head, suddenly. Treoraí's Heart was heavy on her chest. "Mam?" she asked, the word a bare growl from her tattered, raw throat. "Where's Mam?"

"The Máister's with her. It's over. I think."

Meriel blinked again and her vision cleared a bit. The last residue of Jenna fell from her. She could see Jenna sitting on a boulder from the Old Wall, Máister Kirwan crouching alongside her and Mahon, his sword still unsheathed, standing in front of her glaring outward at the nearby gardai and Riocha.

She saw one more thing: a seal's body, its fur dark and matted with blood and lying very still—*too* still—on the hillside. *The ember cold in her head . . .* "Dhegli!" she shouted and started to get up, but Owaine held her.

"I'm sorry," he said. "There's nothing you can do for him, Meriel. Not anymore."

She wouldn't listen. She pushed herself to her feet as Owaine released her, stumbling over to where Dhegli lay. She fell to her knees next to him. "Dhegli . . ." she whispered. There would never be an answer, she knew, even before she looked at his face: the open mouth, the blindly-staring eyes. She knew because the scale of Bradán an Chumhacht was dead inside her. Where his presence had once been, warm and comforting, there was nothing. *Why did you come here?* she wanted to ask him. *You must have seen this in your visions. . . .*

She knew that answer also.

A drop of salt water fell from her face to the seal's fur. She cradled his head in her lap, not caring about the blood that smeared her clothing. She tried to lift him, and suddenly Owaine was there with her. "He has to go back to the water," she told him, sobbing. "He has to go back now."

Owaine said nothing. He left, and Meriel wondered if he'd abandoned her, but he returned a moment later with a board. "We'll put him on this," he said.

"I'll help," It was Jenna's voice. The Banrion knelt down next to Meriel. She stroked Dhegli's fur, her fingers crackling with static electricity as she brushed the pelt. "I'm sorry, Meriel. If he hadn't come, I would have been dead and you wouldn't have had the chance to bring me back from madness. I'm so sorry; I think I know what he meant to you."

Meriel looked at her mam, at the tears that streaked her own grimy face. The woman leaned over and kissed Meriel on the forehead. "You stopped me from destroying myself and far too many others," Jenna said. "You came and found me when I was lost." She was fumbling with the chain that held Lámh Shábhála. "I came so close here to destroying everything."

Meriel glanced up at her and continued to stroke Dhegli's fur. Jenna didn't seem to be able to hold her gaze, her head turning aside to look around at the carnage. "I destroyed too much as it was. The guilt for this is all mine." She licked her bloodied, cut lips. "Meriel . . ."

"Aye, Mam?"

Jenna knelt beside her. "A Holder *can* pass Lámh Shábhála on voluntarily, when they're at the end of their time and tired of carrying the burden. I'd give it to you, now. I can't think of anyone who deserves to hold it more."

Jenna cupped the stone in the palm of her hand. Meriel stared down at the stone: vibrant green crenellated with white. She could feel its pull. "You'd be a better Holder than me, Meriel," Jenna continued. "You would put it to good use, and perhaps . . ." Jenna shrugged. "Perhaps you'd succeed where I failed." Again, her gaze went to the destruction in the city, and she shuddered with a deep, throbbing sob, her eyes closing as if she couldn't bear to see any more. "Perhaps you can make up for some of what I've done here."

Meriel stared at the stone, at her mam's drawn, lined face, carved by years of holding Lámh Shábhála, of

being Banrion. Of loss and pain. "I love you, Meriel,"
Jenna whispered. "I always have. I wish I'd said it more;
I wish I'd shown it."

"I knew," Meriel told her. "I always knew."

Meriel reached out and closed her mam's fingers
around Lámh Shábhála. Bending down, she kissed her
mam's hand. "I know you, Mam. I was with you. I know
you make the offer, but I also know that Lámh Shábhála's so entwined with you that losing it would kill you.
And I can't do that. I don't *want* to do that. Keep the
stone," she said. "I have a cloch that's better suited to
me."

Doyle closed his hand around Snapdragon. The cloch
was dead and empty, though he could still feel the connection with it. It was as if he'd exhausted all the power
within the cloch. From the expressions on the faces of
those around him, it was the same for all of them. Somehow, his sister had snatched the sky's power from all of
them and sent it hurtling back to where it had come.
The clochs na thintrí were drained, all of them. They
would have to wait for another night when the mage-
lights returned to refill the crystalline wells within the
stones.

Taking Edana's arm, he walked with the Ríthe, O
Blaca, and the other cloudmages down from the Old
Wall to where the Inishlanders had gathered around the
body of the Saimhóir. They were staring at the scene,
all of them: Riocha; the gardai with their swords and
shields; the townspeople peering fearfully from hiding
places in the rubble.

But Doyle stared only at Jenna and the small, seemingly insignificant stone around her neck. "No," he
heard Edana whisper to him. "We gave the Banrion
our word."

"There are only five of them. Five," he answered. He
gestured around them. "Their clochs are as empty as

ours, and we have an army of gardai. She can't stop us now, can't do anything to prevent it. Our swords are all we need, Edana. We're hundreds against five."

"No," she told him again.

He wanted to sweep his arm around, to the Ríthe, the other Riocha mages, the gardai, the people. *"Rí Mallaghan, Rí Mas Sithig, Shay, my friend, don't you see? Lámh Shdbhala is ours for the taking, here in front of us and unprotected!"* he wanted to shout to them. *It should have been mine . . . it would have been mine if she hadn't killed Da. It's my* right *to have it, and I will take it!"*

"Your niece brought me back to you, as she brought her mam back from insanity here," Edana said quietly, as if she could hear his thoughts. Her hand stroked his arm. "She saved your life when the gardai would have killed you. You owe her for that if nothing else." Edana's hand turned him. She looked up at him, her face serious and stern. "Enean's gone because of Lámh Shábhála. I don't want to lose anyone else I love. But you need to choose, Doyle. You can't have me and also have Lámh Shábhála. Not anymore. You have to choose."

She let him go, stepping back to where the rulers of the Tuatha stood, and her hand touched the torc around her neck. "I say the same to the Ríthe," she said. "With Enean dead, I claim the torc of Dún Laoghaire. I am Banrion Dún Laoghaire, and I *will* make war on any Tuath that breaks the truce we have made here." She glared at them. Rí Mallaghan seemed to almost smile; Rí Mas Sithig snorted but also shrugged. Rí O Seachnasaigh of Tuath Connachta started to sputter a protest, but Rí Mac Baoill touched him on the shoulder with a nearly imperceptible shake of his head.

"Not now," Mac Baoill said. "Not here."

"But Mac Ard is right," O Seachnasaigh protested, but his voice trailed off as Doyle moved toward the Inishlanders. Edana felt her heart seem to dissolve in her chest. "Doyle . . ." she whispered.

Mahon lifted his bloody sword as Doyle approached,

stepping deliberately in front of Jenna; Mundy lifted his hand as if he were ready to unleash a spell of slow magic. Doyle stopped two strides from Mahon. The man's stare bored into Doyle's. Doyle silently showed the man his empty hands and finally Mahon stood aside, though the sword never left its ready position.

Doyle stood in front of Jenna and Meriel. "I'll never like you or trust you, Sister," he said to Jenna. "This is not ended between us. That's the only promise I'll make to you. This is not over." Then his gaze went to Meriel. "Edana's right," he told her. "I may hate my sister, but her daughter . . ." He bowed to her, as he might to one of the Ríthe. "I wish you'd taken the stone," he said.

Stepping alongside Meriel, he crouched down and took hold of the board on which Dhegli's body rested. "Let me help you with this," he said.

Out in the dark night of the harbor the hulks of the fleet smoldered, listing and burning, their sails ragged. The Saimhóir had all come ashore, and their shining black eyes watched as Meriel and the others approached with the makeshift bier holding Dhegli's body. Challa was there on the shingle with the waves lapping white and phosphorescent around her. The seal grunted and coughed furiously, and Meriel didn't need to know the language to understand the anger and hostility in the words. "I'm sorry," she said, knowing Challa couldn't understand her but hoping that the emotions came through. "I know you loved him, too."

They carried the bier forward until they were knee-deep in the choppy water, Challa swimming next to them. Then Meriel nodded to the others and they set the plank down in the water. For a moment, nothing happened, then Meriel saw a silver, glowing form flash out from Dhegli's open mouth. Challa moved more quickly than Meriel thought possible, her tail and flippers thrashing water. She dove, and then nearly immediately surfaced again. They could see the bright fish in her mouth. She flipped it up once, and swallowed.

Bradán an Chumhacht had come to a new Holder.

Challa swam back to them, swimming fluidly alongside Meriel. Her flipper touched Meriel's leg; when she spoke, Meriel could hear her words in her head.

"Dhegli had stone-walker blood in him. I do not. He could love a stone-walker. I will not. I tell you now: Bradán an Chumhacht will never come to the aid of a stone-walker again, not as long as I hold it within myself. Tell your mam that the Saimhóir no longer serve at Lámh Shábhála's whim. I will make it my task to warn the Saimhóir against your kind. You may come to the sea, but you'll never swim with me, Meriel, or with my milk-kin. You had Dhegli's love, but you only have my loathing, and I will never, never forget. That is my promise to you."

With that, the touch was gone, before Meriel could reply. Challa moaned once to the others and with a flip of tail, curved quickly away from Meriel. The Saimhóir gathered around Dhegli's body, pushing past the humans and shoving the corpse farther out in the water. They moved away through the surging waves. "No, wait . . ." Meriel started to say, but Owaine held her back. She let him, leaning back against him. The water was cold and frigid around her legs and she told herself that was why she shivered.

Her mam took her hand. Together, she and Owaine led her out of the water.

The Ríthe watched from the shore as the Saimhóir's body was offered back to its kind. They saw the bright flash of Bradán an Chumhacht and its passing to another. "We offer the Banrion and her people a ship to return to Inish Thuaidh," Edana said to Jenna. "But you must leave now."

Rí O Seachnasaigh gave a muffled croak at that. "And

by what right do you order the Ríthe to do anything, O Liathain?" he asked. "Even if you claim Dún Laoghaire, this is Tuath Infochla, and even if you can uphold the claim to Dún Laoghaire, you are *not* the Ard."

"Perhaps she should be," Torin Mallaghan said softly. "She has Enean's lineage, she has proved her worth here tonight, and she had her da's blessing."

"You can't be serious," O Seachnasaigh sputtered. He looked around at the other Ríthe. "Surely none of you are listening to this man's ravings?"

"I am serious," Mallaghan said. "None of us trust each other well enough." He lifted his chin toward Edana. "I would trust *her*," he said.

"It's not for you to decide," O Seachnasaigh retorted. "That's for the Óenach."

"Aye, it is," Mallaghan agreed. "And when we call the Óenach together again, I will propose Edana O Liathain for the Rí Ard." Edana heard a mutter of agreement from Mas Sithig, though Mac Baoill remained silent, rubbing his bearded chin with a thumb. "What do you say, Banrion O Liathain?" Mallaghan asked. "Do you think you'd make a good Ard?"

Edana saw Doyle watching her, saw the Inishlanders also huddled close by. "There are those who *can* be Ard through blood and kinship, or through the spoils of battle," Edana said to them. "And there are those who *should* be Ard. Those are sometimes different things."

PART FIVE:

BANRION ARD

58

The Torc of the Ard

"THERE are those who can be Ard through blood and kinship, or through the spoils of battle. And there are those who should be Ard. Those are sometimes different things."

Meriel remembered Edana's words at Falcarragh. That day now seemed ages ago, the memories dimmed by a month and more at home in Inish Thuaidh: with watching her mam slowly return to herself and take the throne seat before the Comhairle in Dún Kiil; with seeing Inishfeirm again; by the joy of being with Owaine, and with their quiet marriage ceremony in the Weeping Hall; by the bittersweet melancholy that came over her every time she saw seals swimming in the sea.

By the knowledge that she had missed her last two moon-bleedings. She'd told no one that, not even Owaine. She would wait for the quickening or the bleeding, whichever came.

But she stood now in the bright sunshine near the whitewashed splendor of Tuatha Halla on its hilltop overlooking the harbor of Dún Laoghaire. There were several ships in the harbor, flying the banners of all the Tuatha. The banner of Inish Thuaidh fluttered on one mast as well—that of *Uaigneas,* the ship that had brought Meriel and Owaine here. Edana had told Meriel that their ship was the first Inishlander vessel to have been in the harbor for over a century. Meriel hoped that it was an omen, and that Inish trade ships would now ply back and forth from the Tuatha.

Across from Tuatha Halla, on its own low hill, stood the Keep of Dún Laoghaire, its massive walls girdling the slopes. The towers were decorated with banners displaying the colors of all seven of the Ríthe who were in attendance and the keep's great wooden gates were open and welcoming. The keep was not a fortress today, but a home for the Riocha who had come for the Óenach.

" 'Tis a beautiful sight," Owaine said. He was clad in the white clóca and léine of the Order of Inishfeirm, Blaze gleaming a brilliant red on his chest. Owaine linked his arm with hers and pressed her to him, leaning closer to her ear to whisper so that none of the Riocha could hear. "But 'tis not as beautiful as Dún Kiil, I think. This land is too flat and too tamed."

Meriel grinned at that and leaned her head against his shoulder. They stood among the crowd of Riocha waiting for all the Ríthe to enter the sacred hall before they filed in to listen to the Óenach. Meriel was already tired of the polite conversation and careful smiles, and she would be glad when she and Owaine could return to their chamber in the keep. Though that would be stripes from now, after the celebratory supper for the new Ard. She was tired of the whispers and the half glimpsed pointing of fingers. *"That's the Mad Holder's daughter, and the Inishfeirm cloudmage with her is her husband. They were both there at the Battle of Falcarragh. I wonder how many they killed . . ."* Meriel would glance at them and they would quickly stop the whispering and smile back, as if they'd been discussing the weather. The whisperers were bad, but the ones who came fawning up to her were worse. *"Ah, I heard the Banrion Mac Ard talk of how you ended the battle at Falcarragh with your cloch. We're all so grateful to you, Bantiarna. I wonder . . . my niece is ill, and if you could see her, then perhaps . . ."*

They smiled at her, too, those who wanted Treoraí's Heart.

All the Ríthe had entered but for the Banrion of Dún

Laoghaire, last as custom dictated. Her retinue was just cresting the hill, with banners fluttering in the strong wind off the bay and horns blaring to announce their approach. The Ríocha and—behind them—the tuathánach around Meriel cheered as the Banríon's carriage reached the entrance and Edana disembarked on Doyle's arm, the gold-and-silver-chased torc of Dún Laoghaire around her neck.

Meriel whispered up to Owaine through the noise of the approbation. "Amazing how they cheer now, isn't it? Only a few months ago, she and Doyle were hunted criminals, and these same people were howling for them to be killed."

"As they did with us," Owaine reminded her. "Those with power are always cheered to their faces, no matter what the people really think. But you . . ." He grinned down at her. "Anyone who knows you would shout 'huzzah!' and mean it."

Meriel smiled and hugged him. Edana and Doyle were walking toward the beckoning doors of the Halla, but Edana stopped as they came abreast of Meriel and Owaine in the crowd. She motioned to them to come to her, and released Doyle's arm to take Meriel's. "Come," she said. "Let's walk over here for a moment, away from the crowd. Doyle, if you'd stay with Owaine; you can tell him what we're discussing."

Doyle, to Meriel's eyes, didn't seem happy with the request, but he nodded and clapped Owaine on the back. Edana led Meriel a few paces away, putting the carriage between them and the crowd of Ríocha, watching curiously as their Banríon spoke to the Inishlander.

"Are you nervous, Edana?" Meriel asked her. "You'll make a fine Banríon Ard. I know this."

Edana smiled back at her, pressing her fingers in Meriel's hand. "I'm pleased that you think so. Your approval means much to me." She paused. "The decision for the Ard won't be unanimous, though. Ríthe Taafe, Mac Baoill, and O Seachnasaigh will vote against. But Ríthe Mallaghan and Mas Sithig, and Banríon O Trea-

sigh and myself are in agreement. Four against three—
it's a slim margin, but enough. It won't stop the arguing
or the disagreements, however, and the Tuatha will take
time to accept the decision made today."

" 'The Tuatha are in agreement as often as the sun
rises in the west,' " Meriel said. "That's one of Mam's
saying, and I've heard others in Inish Thuaidh say the
same. But you'll manage to win them over."

Edana laughed, then her face turned somber. "No, I
won't. I'm not to be the Ard, Meriel," she said. "I will
be Banrion Dún Laoghaire only; that's enough for me.
I spoke with Malaghan, Mas Sithig, and O Treasigh last
night and we've all agreed on another."

"Edana, no . . ." Meriel could feel the shock and disappointment on her face. She and Owaine had come at
Edana's specific request to see her take the torc of the
Ard, and now . . . Meriel felt the joy in her dissolve.
With Edana as Ard, there was at least some hope of
peace between the Tuatha and Inish Thuaidh. With
any other . . .

Meriel remembered the horror of Falcarragh, and
could imagine what would have happened had the armies of the Ríthe actually come to Dún Kiil. Edana, she
knew, would never fully forgive Jenna for her part in
Enean's death, but she would at least seek to keep peace
between their countries. Meriel dreaded having to bring
this news back home to her parents and the Comhairle.
"If not you, then who? Torin Mallaghan? My mam said
his da certainly had aspirations for the throne—"

"No," Edana interrupted. She seemed strangely undis-
turbed by the news she'd brought. A pale, soft smile
brushed her lips, genuine and almost amused. Meriel
wondered if she wasn't simply relieved at not having to
take on the burden of being the Ard in addition to her
duties as the Banrion Dún Laoghaire. "Not Rí Mallaghan. In fact, the person we intend to nominate isn't
a "Rí or Banrion at all."

"Then who?" A sudden, horrible suspicion came to
her and she glanced quickly over to Doyle, still talking

with Owaine. Edana saw the direction of her gaze and laughed gently.

"No, not Doyle. He would not be anyone's choice. In fact, as much as I love him, he would not even be my choice. I've also seen his flaws."

"Then who . . . ?"

Edana was staring at Meriel. The odd trace of a smile on her face was reflected in the shining metal of her torc. "You, Meriel," Edana said. "You."

Meriel started to speak, but no words came out. She gaped, too shocked to think. "Me?" she said finally. "Edana, this is nonsense. It's worse than nonsense—it's rash insanity. You can't be serious."

"I am. We are. Very much so."

Meriel was still shaking her head. "My mam's the Banrion Inish Thuaidh, whom the Ríthe still consider an enemy, and I'm . . . I'm not . . ." Meriel had a sense of disorientation, that this was all some odd, intensely real dream. She blinked. "This can't be. I don't want it."

"Please, listen to me for a moment," Edana answered. "This is something I've thought about for weeks now. Aye, your mam's an Inishlander and the Mad Holder besides, and that's why Taafe, Mac Baoill, and O Seachnasaigh will squawk and scream and turn red and vote a forceful, loud nay. They'll be furious and feel that they've been betrayed, and they will try to make your reign as Ard difficult."

"All the more reason—"

Edana lifted a hand. "No, listen. What they would do with you is no more than they'd do with me. But let me also be honest about the others' feelings. Rí Mallaghan thinks that because you're young and inexperienced in the intricacies of politics, you'll also be pliable and easy for him to control. He'll find out that he's wrong, but by then it will be too late. Rí Mas Sithig looks at the ruin of Falcarragh and then at how near his Tuath Infochla is to Inish Thuaidh. He'll be too afraid to insult the Inish to vote against you once you're nominated. Frankly, he needs the aid and money your mam has promised to

Tuath Infochla after her return to Dún Kiil, in repara-
tion for the death and damage she caused. And he also
wonders if Falcarragh wouldn't be the first victim again
if Jenna becomes angry at the Tuatha or turns mad
again. Banrion O Treasigh only sees your gender and
the fact that her hated cousin Rí Connachta will be
mightily upset, and she takes delight in that. She will
vote 'aye' for sheer perversity, and because Locha Léin
is a long way from Dún Laoghaire and the Ard's seat."

Meriel gave a cough of disbelief. "If that's how everyone feels, why would you even be thinking of me as
the Ard?"

Edana's smile widened. "Because *I* know the true reasons. I know what I saw in Doire Coill and in Falcarragh.
I witnessed courage and bravery, determination and loyalty. I saw someone who is compassionate but who's also
not afraid to be strong when strength is needed. I saw
someone to whom I could kneel as Ard and be proud
to do so. It took me time to see it, after Falcarragh and
poor Enean's death, but I have. Give the Ríthe time,
and most of them will realize that also."

"But *me . . . ?*"

"Why not you? You're Riocha. Your pedigree is as
good as most of them here. The MacEagan line is well
known; the Aoire line connects to the Mac Ards. Your
mam is the Banrion Inish Thuaidh and the First Holder
besides."

"Owaine has no connection to the blooded families,
and he's my husband."

A shrug. "No, he's not Riocha, but he's a cloudmage
of the Order, a Holder of a Cloch Mór, and Inish—
everyone knows that Inish are different. Owaine isn't to
be Ard. You are."

Meriel's head was shaking as if of its own volition.
"*You* should be Ard, Edana. Not me. You were born to
it, your da and your great-da were both Ard. You *understand* the politics; you're part of them. I don't. I was
never even part of it back home. Be the Ard, Edana, as
you should be."

"I wanted it," Edana admitted. "Part of me still does. But I *do* know what I'd face and I know the limitations I'd have. I'm afraid I'd be little more than the holder of the title. I don't know how much I could accomplish."

"I'd be no different. I'd be worse."

"No." Edana laughed again and Meriel could hear a tinge of bitterness in the sound. "If I were Ard, I'd simply be one voice among the seven Ríthe, and the Tuatha would squabble and fight and even war among each other no matter what I said. I worry about that. I worry about what's happening in Céile Mhór with the Arruk— you didn't see the creature that the Toscaire Concordai brought, Meriel, but I did and I wonder if we won't be facing them soon. I worry about Inish Thuaidh, too. I think it's time that the Inish and the Tuatha try to work together, not apart. But old sentiments and grudges and hatreds run deep in the families, and my lone voice as Ard won't be enough. I have Dún Laoghaire, the weakest of the Tuatha, and I have two Clochs Mór. That's enough to make me Banrion Ard if I say that I want the title; it's not enough to do more than give me the name." Edana spread her arms wide. "I thought about all this," she continued, "and I knew I couldn't be the Ard I would want to be. But you . . . you could. You bring with you Lámh Shábhála's reflected power and the immediate support of Inish Thuaidh. You'll have Dún Laoghaire with you as well—and that is enough to give you the votes of other Ríthe like Infochla, if only in fear of the consequences if they oppose you. You have the potential to actually unite the Tuatha, Meriel, and I'm afraid that will be necessary if we're to survive."

"I don't hold the kind of power you seem to think I have," Meriel protested. She lifted Treoraí's Heart. "I don't even hold a Cloch Mór."

"I wonder if you don't hold more," Edana answered. She touched the scars on Meriel's arm with a finger. "But Owaine holds a Cloch Mór, and I do, and Doyle. Your mam holds the most feared cloch of all. Meriel, even the Bunús Muintir would stand with you. I promise you that Dún Laoghaire will always be your ally, and you know Inish Thuaidh will. And you . . . you will also have the people of all the Tuatha: the tuathánach." Edana cupped her hands around the one with which Meriel held her cloch. "The people will respond to an Ard who heals rather than hurts, a ruler they can love rather than fear. That will scare and impress the Riocha more than anything. You may need no more than that."

Meriel was shaking her head. Her heart pounded against her ribs; her breath came short and fast and the Tuatha Halla threatened to begin dancing around her. "Edana—I didn't ask for this. I don't *want* this."

The smile on Edana's face creased itself deeper. "I know, and that's another reason you should have it. Too many people—even my da and his da before him—wanted it too much, and it consumed them. Too many people want it *now*."

To be Banrion Ard . . . The thought still made her dizzy, but Treoraí's Heart pulsed warm in her hand— *. . . the people will respond to an Ard who heals . . .*— and the fear no longer burned in her stomach.

You're not fighting this, she realized suddenly. *You're frightened at the thought, aye, but at the same time you're actually considering it.* She looked over to where Owaine and Doyle stood talking. Doyle glanced over at them, and his stare was hard and grim. "What of Doyle? Does he agree?"

The smile faltered slightly at that. "My dear husband? No, he doesn't. But he can say nothing here and he won't. And you will change him, also, Meriel. You will."

"How could you say nothing of this to me?" Meriel looked around, bewildered. "How could you let me come here thinking you were to be Ard?" Everyone seemed to be staring at them and she wondered what she saw in carefully smiling faces.

"If I'd said it, would you still have come, or would I have had to find a way to pry you out of the White Keep at Inishfeirm or Dún Kiil?"

"You sound so certain of all this. I'm not."

The smile returned. "But I notice you've stopped protesting."

Meriel made no answer. She glanced over again at Owaine. He was staring in her direction and grinning widely. Edana tilted her head quizzically at Meriel. "If you say no," Edana said, "I will understand."

"And you would become Ard?"

"No." Edana spoke the word like a curse. "To convince the others to stand with me, I had to insist to them that I had no ambition to be Ard, and I can't tell them differently now. They're already in there, waiting. If you say no, our alliance is broken and someone else will be Ard. I don't know who that would be, but I'm certain they won't be as kindly disposed to Inish Thuaidh as you are."

"That's blackmail."

A shrug. "Call it a final inducement. Come," Edana said. "It's time for the Óenach. Come inside with me and we'll begin this together."

Edana lifted her arm in invitation. Meriel stared at her for a breath, then at Owaine. Finally, reluctantly, she put her scarred left hand through the circle of flesh.

Together, they left the warm sunshine and entered the hall.

APPENDICES

The Rulers ("Ríthe") of the Tuatha (in Year 1148):

Tuath Airgialla: Mal Mac Baoill, Rí Airgialla

Tuath Connachta: Harkin O Seachnasaigh, Rí Connachta

Tuath Dún Laoghaire: Nevan O Liathain,* Rí Laoghaire

Tuath Éoganacht: Kerwin Taafe, Rí Éoganacht

Tuath Gabair: Torin Mallaghan, Rí Gabair

Tuath Infochla: Brasil Mas Sithig, Rí Infochla

Tuath Locha Léin: Siobaigh O Treasigh, Banrion Locha Léin

Inish Thuaidh: Jenna MacEagan, Banrion Thuiadh

* also Rí Ard (High King) of all Tuatha

CHARACTERS (in order of appearance):

Jenna MacEagan (nee Aoire)	The Banrion of Inish Thuaidh and Holder of Lámh Shábhála
Doyle Mac Ard	Jenna's half brother, the son of Maeve Aoire and Padraic Mac Ard
Maeve Aoire (nee Oldspring)	Jenna's mam
Padraic Mac Ard	A tiarna from Tuath Gabair and lover of Maeve Aoire, killed by Jenna in the Battle of Dún Kiil

Nevan O Liathain	The Rí Ard, the ruler of Talamh an Ghlas and the Tuath
Ennis O'Deoradháin	Jenna's lover and biological father of Meriel; killed by Tuathian sympathizer before the Battle of Dún Kiil
Meriel MacEagan	Daughter of the Banrion of Inish Thuaidh
Lucan O Dálaigh	Meriel's boyfriend at Dún Kiil
Mundy Kirwan	Máister of the Order of Inishfeirm
Barra O Dálaigh	Lucan's father and a tiarna in Kyle MacEagan's townland
Nainsi	Meriel's attendant/companion
Kyle MacEagan	The husband of Jenna and father-by-marriage of Meriel, a tiarna of Inish Thuaidh from the townland of Be an Mhuilinn, Bay of the Mill
Aithne MacBrádaigh	A tiarna of Inish Thuaidh from Rubha na Scarbh, also on the Comhairle
Mother-Creator	The Goddess: creator of the world
Máister Cléurach	Previous head of the Order of Inishfeirm
Owaine Geraghty	A Bráthair of the Order of Inishfeirm
Faoil Caomhánach	Meriel's roommate at the Order of Inishfeirm, daughter of Tiarna Odhrán Caomhánach
Alexia Meagher	A Siúr of the Order of Inishfeirm who holds a clochmion that can tell truth
Iosep O'hEagjra	A tiarna on the Comhairle

Aisling (nee O'hEagjra)	Iosep's sister, married to Odhrán Caomhánach
Odhrán Caomhánach	Faoil's da, and a holder of a Cloch Mór; from Tuath Infochla
Peria Ó Riain	A long-dead Holder of Lámh Shábhála who died attempting the Scrúdú
Mahon MacBreen	Captain of Jenna's personal gardai
Enean O Liathain	The feeble-minded son of the Rí Ard
MacCamore	Enean's "keeper"
Labhrás Ó Riain	A tiarna of Dún Laoghaire and a rival of Doyle Mac Ard
Edana O Liathain	Daughter of Nevan O Liathain, betrothed to Doyle Mac Ard
Vaughn Mac Ard	Doyle Mac Ard's uncle and once captain of the gardai in Tuath Gabair; dead at the time of *mage of Clouds*
Shay O Blaca	The Máister of the Order of Gabair, who holds the Cloch Mór called Quickship, and an ally of Doyle Mac Ard
Thady MacCoughlin	A third-year student within the Order, from Tuath Gabair
Siúr O'hAllmhurain	A teacher at the Order of Inishfeirm; has a room at the end of Meriel's hall
Siúr Bolan	A teacher at the Order of Inishfeirm
Severii O'Coulghan	Son of Tadhg O'Coulghan and Peria Ó Riain, and Last Holder of Lámh Shábhála
Tadhg O'Coulghan	A long-dead Holder of Lámh Sháb-

	hála, lover of Peria and founder of the Order of Inishfeirm
Maitias	Librarian of the Order of Inishfeirm
Dhegli	A Saimhóir who is the possessor of Bradán an Chumhacht, the Saimhóir equivalent of Lámh Shábhála
WaterMother	The chief god of the blue seals
Khennhi	A Suir of the Order of Inishfeirm and the Order's apothecary
O'Therreagh	A Bráthair of the Order of Inishfeirm
O'Flagherty	A Siúr of the Order of Inishfeirm
Kharidi	Thady's roommate in the keep
Ulán Rhusvak	The Toscaire Concordai (delegate) from Céile Mhór
Aerie MagWolfagdh (the Third)	Thane (High King) of Céile Mhór
Kiernan O Liathain	The previous Rí Ard, the da of Nevan O Liathain
Kerys Aoire	Meriel's great-great-mam (great grandmother), who fled from Inishfeirm when she became pregnant
Niall Mac Ard	An acolyte of the Order of Inishfeirm who fell in love with Kerys Aoire; Meriel's great-great-da (great grandfather)
Treoraí	One of the creatures called the "Créneach"; Meriel holds a clochmion called "Treoraí's Heart"
Nico Dranaghi	The head of one of the Taisteal clans

Sevei Dranaghi	A member of the Dranaghi clan
Keara Dranaghi	Nico's wife
Cailin	Meriel's name among the Dranaghi clan
Seed-Daughter	In Daoine and Bunús Muintir mythology, the daughter of the Mother-Creator, who planted the first seeds
Salia	A tiarna of Tuath Locha Léin
Toma Macsnei	The Ald of Ballicraigh
Áine Martain	A little girl cured of a lung illness by Meriel
Léimard	The squirrel companion of the Bunús Muintir Cataigh
Cataigh	The Bunús Muintir Protector of Foraois Coill
Greatness	The Bunús Muintir term for the Mother-Creator, the God who made the world.
Fiodóir	In Taisteal mythology, the son of the Mother-Creator, who weaves the tapestry of Fate
Cianna	A Banrion of Tuath Gabair, killed by Jenna almost two decades before
Sorcha	The fiancée of Enean O Liathain, killed in a robbers' attack
Toiréasa De Danaan	Niece of the Rí Connachta and cousin of Labhrás Ó Riain
Nuala Chathaigh	A bantiarna loyal to Edana O Liathain
Nyle O'Murchadha	A tiarna loyal to Doyle Mac Ard
Keira	Protector of Doire Coill, once the pledge-daughter of Seancoim

Arror	Head of the pack of dire wolves in Doire Coill
Garrhal	Arror's mate
Challa	Milk-sister of Dhegli
Aghy O'Máille	Cousin of Doyle Mac Ard, holder of a clochmion
Torin Mallaghan II	The Rí Gabair, son of Torin Mallaghan and Cianna (killed by Jenna)
Harkin O Seachnasaigh	The Rí Connachta
Brasil Mas Sithig	The Rí Infochla
Mal Mac Baoill	The Rí Airgialla
Kerwin Taafe	The Rí Éoganacht
Siobaigh O Treasigh	The Banrion Locha Léin
Ragan	Ard of the Bunús Muintir in Doire Coill
Alaina Glanchy	Cloudmage (female) of the Order of Gabair
Shéfra Cahill	Cloudmage (male) of the Order of Gabair
Eliath	Son of Tara, owner of Tara's Tavern in Ballintubber
Paili	An older servant woman who cares for Edana
Faólan	The garda Meriel turns to wood with Seancoim's staff; the resulting "statue" is called Faólan's Folly
Bearn	A garda of Tuath Gabair
Blowick	An innkeeper in the town of Kilmaur in Tuath Infochla

Bran Mowlan	A garda of the town of Kilmaur in Tuath Infochla
Feiad Sheónin	A boy Meriel heals in Falcarragh

PLACES:

Ahmaci	Southernmost city of the Daoine in Lower Céile
An Cnocan	A townland in Inish Thuaidh
An Deann Ramhar	A townland in Inish Thuaidh
Áth Iseal	A village on River Duán, where the High Road crosses the river
Bácathair	Capital city of Tuath Locha Léin, on the west coast of the peninsula
Ballicraigh	A small village in Tuath Infochla
Ballintubber	The village where Jenna was born
Banshaigh	A village on Lough Glas in Tuath Connachta
Be an Mhuiliann	A townland in Inish Thuaidh
Bethiochnead	The "Beast-Nest": the location in Thall Coill where the Scrúdú takes place
Cat's Alley	A back street in Lár Bhaile
Céile Mhór	The far larger peninsula to which Talamh an Ghlas is connected by the Finger, a strip of mountainous land
Croc a Scroilm	The "Hill of Screaming," the mountain that faces Dún Kiil Bay
Dalhmalli	A small village north of Falcarragh on Falcarragh Bay, next to Sliabh Bacaghorth
Doire Coill	The "Forest of Oaks"

Duán Mouth	The mountain-girdled and long end of the River Duán, which ends in an island-dotted bay
Dubh Bhaile	A city in Tuath Gabair, south of Lár Gabair on the Lough Dubh
Dún Kiil	Chief city of Inish Thuaidh
Dún Laoghaire	Main city of the peninsula, seat of the High King
East Light	A small island in Falcarragh Bay where a lighthouse stands
Falcarragh	Capital city of Tuath Infochla
Glen Aill	A fortress mansion in Rubha na Scarbh (Inish Thuaidh)
Glenmill	A village in Tuath Infochla
Ice Sea	The sea to the north of the peninsula
Ingean na nUan	A townland in Inish Thuaidh
Inish Bideach	Literally, "tiny island"
Inish Thuaidh	A large island off the peninsula of Talamh an Ghlas, home of the "Inishlanders"
Inishduán	A small island off Inish Thuaidh, where Jenna once gave the body of Padraic Mac Ard to Maeve Aoire, Jenna's mam
Inishfeirm	A small island off Inish Thuaidh, home of the Order of Inishfeirm and of Jenna's great-mam and great-da
Kirina	A village in Tuath Infochla
Knobtop	A small mountain outside the village of Ballintubber, on whose flanks sheep are often grazed

Lár Bhaile	A city on Lough Lár, the seat of Tuath Gabair
Lough Crithlaigh	A lake on the northwest border of Tuath Gabair
Lough Dhub	A lake on River Duán. Scene of one of the final battles between the Bunús Muintir and the Daoine
Lough Donn	A lake in Tuath Infochla, from which the River Donn flows northward to Falcarragh Bay
Lough Glas	A lake on the coastline of Tuath Connachta
Lough Lár	"Center Lake": a large lake nearly in the center of the peninsula, very near Ballintubber
Maoil na nDreas	A townland in Inish Thuaidh
Néalmhar Ford	The crossing of the River Néalmhar, the Gloomy River, in Inish Thuaidh
Rubha na Scarbh	A townland in Inish Thuaidh, home of Áron Ó Dochartaigh and Banrion Aithne MacBrádaigh
Sliabh Bacaghorth	A mountain in Tuath Infochla near Falcarragh, where Rowan Beirne lost Lámh Shábhála
Sliabh Colláin	A mountain in a southern county of the peninsula; also the title of a song
Sliabh Gabhar	One of the two peaks sheltering Falcarragh to the east. Literally, "Goat Mountain"
Sliabh Míchinniúint	The battle at the end of the previous incarnation of the mage-lights where the forces of Infochla were defeated by the Inishlanders

Sliabh Sí	One of the two peaks sheltering Falcarragh to the east; literally, "Mountain of the Fairy Mound"
Talamh an Ghlas	"The Green Land": the peninsula on which the events of the novel take place
Thall Coill	The "Far Forest"
Thall Mór-roinn	The "Far Continent": the distant mainland, of which Talamh an Ghlas is a peninsula of yet another larger peninsula, Céile Mhór
The Black Gull	The only inn on Inishfeirm
Thiar	A city on the west coast, the seat of Tuath Connachta
Tuath Airgialla	The Tuath in the northeast corner of the peninsula
Tuath Connachta	The Tuath to the immediate west of Tuath Gabair
Tuath Éoganacht	The Tuath in the south of the peninsula
Tuath Gabair	The Tuath in the center of the peninsula, also where Jenna Aoire MacEagan was born
Tuath Infochla	The Tuath in the northwestern corner of the peninsula
Tuath Locha Léin	The Tuath in the southwestern corner of the peninsula
Valleylair	A location in Tuath Connachta, famous for its ironworks
West Light	A small island at the mouth of the River Donn in Falcarragh Bay, where a lighthouse stands
Westering Sea	The ocean to the west of the peninsula

TERMS:

Ald	The "Eldest," a title of respect for the local repository of history
Andúilleaf	A plant from which an addictive narcotic can be obtained
An-tUasal	"Mister"
Arruk	A race of belligerent creatures invading Céile Mhór
Badger, the	A constellation used for navigation, as the snout of the badger always points to the north
Banrion	Queen
Bantiarna	The feminine form of tiarna, "lady" rather than "lord"
Before, The	The time of myths, when magic ruled
Black Haunts	The spirits of the dead who come and take the souls of the living when it's their time to die
Blue seals	Intelligent seals, black, but with a sheen of electric blue in their fur
Blood Wolves	Huge wolves that walk upright like people and prey on unwary travelers; possibly mythical
Bóruma	Tribute paid to a Rí by those under his rule
Bradán an Chumhacht	"Salmon of Power": the blue seals' analogue to the clochs na thintrí. It is through eating one of the Bradán an Chumhacht that a Blue Seal can tap the energy of the mage-lights

Bráthair	The title for males who have dedicated themselves to the Order of Inishfeirm.
Breadroot	A tuber plant grown in "lazy beds" (soil mounds over limestone rock) as a food staple
Bunús Muintir	The "Original People," the tribes who first came to Talámh an Ghlas, and whose remnants still can be found in the hidden places
By the Mother-Creator . . .	A familiar mild curse, as we would say "By God . . ."
Caointeoireacht na cogadh	The war-keening. The ululating and terrifying war cry of the Inishlanders as they charge their foes. The cry in conjunction with their ferocious aspect has sometimes sent foes retreating in panic
Céili giallnai	The lower grade vassals of the Rí
Cinniúint	Máel Armagh's ship
Clannhra	The Taisteal title for the female head of the clan
Clannhri	The Taisteal title for the male head of the clan
Clóca	A long cloak worn by the Riocha over their clothing, usually in the colors of their Tuath
Cloch Mór	The major clochs na thintrí, the ones with large abilities
Cloch na thintrí	Literally, "stone of lightning," the stones that gather the power of the mage-lights
Clochmion	The minor clochs na thintrí with small powers

Clock-candle	Device used to keep time: a candle of standard diameter with colored wax at fixed intervals. One "stripe" equals roughly one hour
Cloudmages	Sorcerers of old who took power from the heavens to create their spells
Colors	The various Tuaths have colors that show allegiance.

  Tuath Gabair = green and brown
  Tuath Connachta = blue and gold
  Tuath Infochla = green and gold
  Tuath Airgialla = red and white
  Tuath Locha Léin = blue and black
  Tuath Éoganacht = green and white
  Tuath Dún Laoghaire (and the Rí Ard) = dark gray
  Inish Thuaidh = blue and white
The banner of the Concordance of Céile Mhór is a stylized dire wolf on a field of blue

Comhairle of Tiarna	The Council of Lords, the actual governing body of Inish Thuaidh
Comhdáil Comhairle	The "Conference of the Comhairle," the meeting of all chieftains in Inish Thuaidh
Concordance of Céile Mhór	The confederacy of kingdoms on the larger peninsula to the east and north of Talamh an Ghlas
Coney	Rabbit, from the Irish Gaelic "coinín"
Corcach Siógai	Literally, "Swamp Fairies," the creatures who create the dangerous sióg mists
Corn Festival	Autumn feast in Ballintubber

Corrthónach	The Bunús Muintir term for the Taisteal
Crannog	An artificial island built on a lake and used as a safe dwelling place
Créneach	Literally, "Clay Beings," a race of sentient beings who inhabit the mountains near Thall Coill
Currach	A small, dug-out boat used by the fisherfolk of Inish Thuaidh
Da	Father
Daoine	Literally, "The People," the society to which Jenna belongs
Dire wolves	Large, intelligent wolves that speak their own language
Draíodóir	Those consecrated to serve the Mother-Creator, in essence, the priesthood, though it is not restricted by gender; the plural is Draíodóiri
Drumlins	Low, steep-sided hills packed closely together, often with bogs, marshes, and small lakes at their feet
Eneclann	Honor-price, the amount a person can owe by his/her status
Éraic	Payment of blood-money from a slayer
Feast of Planting	One of the great quarterly festivals, taking place in late March
Fia stoirm	Storm Deer, a giant deer, previously thought extinct
Ficheall	A board game similar to chess

Filí	Poet
Filleadh	The "Coming Back," the prophesied return of magic
Fingal	To slay your own kin; one of the worst crimes
Foulweed	A common weed in gardens
Freelanded	A term meaning that the land is owned by the person living there; to be freelanded is to be one step down from being Riocha, or nobility
Garda	The police of the large cities, or the personal protectors of a tiarna, also a term for "guard"; the plural is gardai
Giotár	Stringed instrument, guitar
Great-da	Grandfather
Great-mam	Grandmother
Iníon	"Miss"
Is ferr fer a chiniud	"A man is better than his birth"
Kala bark	An analgesic used for headaches and minor pain, non-addictive, but not anywhere near as strong as andúilleaf
Klaastanak	The "meeting of the clans" for the Taisteal, which takes place once every decade in Thall Mór-roinn; it is at the Klaastanaks that the business of the clans takes place
Knifefang	An extinct or mythical carnivore of the land
Lámh Shábhála	The cloch na thintrí that Jenna holds
Léine	A tunic worn under the clóca

Maidin maith	"Good morning!"
Mam	Mother
Marbhsháinn	In the game of ficheall, "check-mate"
Milarán	A breakfast griddle cake from Inish Thuaidh, sprinkled with molasses and spices
Miondia	The lesser gods
moj ljubav	"My love," an endearment in the Taisteal tongue
Moon-time	The time of a woman's monthly menstrual flow
Mórceint	A fairly large denomination coin
Óenach	An assembly held on regular occasions to transact the private and public business of the Tuath; after the death of a Rí Ard, a special Óenach is called by the Ríthe of the Tuatha to confirm a new Rí Ard, although this is often only a formality
Oscail	The verb "open"
Pauk	The Bunús Muintir spider-god, who weaves the web of fate
Pledge-son/daughter	A Bunús Muintir term, a younger person adopted by an Elder as his or her successor
Quern	A stone mill using for grinding grain and corn
Rí	King, the plural is "Ríthe"
Riocha	The royalty

Saimhóir	The name the blue seals call themselves
Scrúdú	The test which allows a Holder to fully open all of Lámh Shábhála's capabilities, often fatal
Seanóir	The Eldest, the oak trees of Doire Coill and the other Old Growth forests
Seed-Daughter's Star	The evening/morning star, brightest in the sky, that appears just after sunset or before sunrise
Sióg mist	"Fairy mist": according to legend, those lost in the sióg mist never return to their own land, but are trapped forever in another world
Siúr	The title for females who have dedicated themselves to the Order of Inishfeirm
Sochraideach	Mourner
Stirabout	A meat stew
Svinja sin od pas	Taisteal phrase: "Bastard son of a dog!"
Taisteal	The "Traveling," an itinerant group of peddlers of anything, from orphaned children to hard goods
Tanaise Ríg	The Heir-Apparent
Thane	The High King of the Concordance, a title roughly equal to the Rí Ard of Talamh an Ghlas
Tiarna	The title "lord"
Toscaire Concordai	"Delegate of the Concordance," a title used for representatives of the Concordance of Céile Mhór

Tuath	Kingdom; the plural is "Tuatha"
Tuathánach	"Peasant" or "commoner": those without royal blood in their lineage
Tuatha Halla	The ancient hall where the Ríthe of the Tuatha meet to certify the election of a new Rí Ard
Turves	Turf cuttings, peat.
Uaigneas	The Banrion's ship: "Loneliness"
Uisce Taibhse	Literally "Water Ghost," a race of intelligent creatures living in freshwater loughs; sometimes antagonistic to humans
Wind sprites	Nearly transparent, small and sentient herd creatures, once thought to be entirely mythical; nocturnal
Witchfire	A fire made through slow magic and the use of certain herbs; a witchfire lasts far longer than a torch, and gives off a brighter light

SAIMHÓIR TERMS:

Bradán an Chumhacht	The "Salmon of the Mage-Lights," the analogue of a cloch na thintrí
Bull	Adult male seal, bulls are less common, and are "shared" by several adult females
Cow	Adult female seal
Great Sweetwater	The River Duán
Haul out	The term for leaving the water for the shore
Land-cousin	Those humans with Saimhóir blood in their ancestry

May the currents bring you fish	A common polite greeting
Milk-mother	The cow who suckles a youngling, not necessarily the same cow who gave birth to the infant. In Saimhóir society, the young are often suckled by another cow. There is generally a stronger attachment to the milk-mother than the birth-mother (unless of course they happen to be the same)
Milk-sister/brother	A seal who has shared the milk of the same mother
Nesting Land	Inish Thuaidh, it is only on this island that the Saimhóir breed, on the northwest shores
Saimhóir	The name the blue seal call themselves
Seal-biter	The shark, which feeds on seals
Sister-kin	A term of endearment
Sky-stones	The cloch na thintrí
Stone-walker	A human
Sweetfish	Any of the small fish that make up the bulk of the Saimhóir's diet
WaterMother	The chief god of the Saimhóir. It is possible, though not proved, that the WaterMother is simply another manifestation of the humans' Mother-Creator
Winter Home	The peninsula of Talamh an Ghlas, where the currents are warmer and

the fish more plentiful during the
coldest months

THE DAOINE CALENDAR:

The Daoine calendar, like that of the Bunús Muintir, is pri-
marily lunar-based. Their "day" is considered to start at
sunset. Each month consists of twenty-eight days; there is
no further separation into weeks. Rather, the days are
counted as being the "thirteenth day of Wideleaf" or the
"twenty-first day of Capnut."

The months are named after various trees of the region,
and are (in translation) Longroot, Silverbark, Wideleaf,
Straightwood, Fallinglimb, Deereye, Brightflower, Redfruit,
Conefir, Capnut, Stranglevine, Softwood, and Sweetsap.

The solar year being slightly more than 365 days, to keep
the months from recessing slowly through the seasons over the
years, an annual twofold adjustment is made. The first decision
is whether there will be additional days added to Sweetsap;
the second proclaims which phase of the moon will correspond
to the first day of the month that year (the first day of the
months during any given year may be considered to start at
the new moon, quarter moon waxing, half-moon waxing, three-
quarter moon waxing, full moon, three-quarter moon waning,
half-moon waning, or quarter moon waning). The proclama-
tion is announced at the Festival of Ghéimri (see below) each
year—any extra days are added immediately after Ghéimri and
before the first day of Longroot. All this keeps the solar-based
festivals and the lunar calendar roughly in line.

This adjustment is traditionally made by the Draíodóiri of
the Mother-Creator at the Sunstones Ring at Dún Laoghaire, but the Inish Thuaidh Draíodóiri generally use the Sunstones Ring near Dún Kiil to make their own adjustments,
which do not always agree with that of Dún Laoghaire.
Thus, the reckoning of days in Talamh an Ghlas and Inish
Thuaidh is often slightly different.

The year is considered to start on the first day of Longroot, immediately after the Festival of Ghéimri and any additional days that have been added to Sweetsap.

There are four Great Festivals at the solstices and equinoxes.

Láfuacht: (7th day of Straightwood)	Marks that true winter has been reached and that the slow ascent toward the warmth of spring has begun. Generally a celebration touched with a somber note because the rest of winter must still be endured.
Fómhar (11th day of Brightflower)	Marks the time to prepare for the spring planting to come and the birthing of newborn stock animals. This festival was an appeal to the Mother-Creator and the Miondia (the lesser gods) to make the crops grow and the livestock fertile. A time of sacrifices and prayer.
Méitha (19th day of Capnut)	Marks the height of the growing season. In good years, this is the most manic and happy festival, celebrating the plenty all around.
Ghéimhri (28th day of Sweetsap)	Marks the onset of autumn. This is a date fraught with uncertainty and worry as the crops are harvested and the colder weather begins. Though this holiday often spreads over more than one day, it is also laden with solemn rites and ceremonies to placate the gods who awaken with the autumn chill.

The following is a sample year with corresponding Gregorian dates. However, bear in mind that this is only an approximation and will differ slightly each year.

1st day of Longroot (New Year's Day) = September 23
1st day of Silverbark = October 21
1st day of Wideleaf = November 18
1st day of Straightwood = December 16
    Festival of Láfuacht: 7th day of Straightwood (December 22)
1st day of Fallinglimb = January 13
1st day of Deereye = February 10
1st day of Brightflower = March 10
    Festival of Fómhar: 11th day of Brightflower (March 20)
1st day of Redfruit = April 7
1st day of Conefir = May 5
1st day of Capnut = June 2
    Festival of Méitha: 19th day of Capnut (June 20)
1st day of Stranglevine = June 30
1st day of Softwood = July 28
1st day of Sweetsap = August 25
    Festival of Gheimhri: 28th day of Sweetsap (September 21)

A BRIEF HISTORY:

Time of Myth

Though details and sometimes names vary, similar tales are shared by both the Bunús Muintir and Daoine people, which indicate a common mythological base and possibly a shared tribal ancestry. The following tale is just one of many, and is the primary Daoine Creation Myth.

*   *   *   *   *

The Mother-Creator had intercourse with the Sky-Father, and gave birth to a son. But their son was sickly and died, and she laid him down in the firmament, and his skeleton became the bones of the land. In time, the Mother-Creator overcame her grief and lay again with Sky-Father, and gave birth to Seed-Daughter.

Seed-Daughter flourished and in time became as beautiful as her mother, and she attracted the attention of two offspring of the Sky-Father, Cloud and his sister Rain. From that triple union came the plants living in the soil that covered her brother, the earth. Seed-Daughter was also coveted by Darkness, and Darkness stole her away and took her in violence. When Seed-Daughter escaped from Darkness and came back to Cloud and Rain, sorrowing, she was heavy in her womb, and from her time of confinement would come all the Miondia, the Lesser Gods. The Miondia spread out over the earth, and from their couplings emerged the animals in all their varieties.

After the rape by Darkness, Seed-Daughter could conceive no more. She wept often, sometimes fiercely, which we see even now in the rain that falls.

Year –2500 (approx.)

The first of the Bunús Muintir tribes reach Talamh an Ghlas, after traveling from Thall Mór-roinn, the mainland, into Céile Mhr, the larger peninsula to which Talamh an Ghlas is attached. These Bronze Age people created their society where no human had ever walked, which lasted until the arrival of the Daoine tribes in Year 0.

Year –75 (approx.)	The final disappearance of the mage-lights for the Bunús Muintir people. The mage-lights would not reappear again until after the arrival of the Daoine and the collapse of Bunús Muintir society.
Year –70 (approx.)	Death of Bunús Muintir chieftain and cloudmage Riata, Last Holder of Lámh Shábhála.
Year 0	The first of the Daoine tribes enter Talamh an Ghlas, crossing over the "Finger," the spine of mountainous land connecting Talamh an Ghlas to the peninsula of Céile Mhór, and also arriving by ship at Inish Thuaidh, on the western coast at Bácathair and in the south at Taghmon. They would encounter and eventually displace (and interbreed with) the Bunús Muintir people.
Year 105	The Battle of Lough Dubh, where Rí Crenél Dahgnon defeated the last Bunús Muintir chieftain Ruaidhri.
Year 232	The first mage-lights appear over Inish Thuaidh in the reign of the Daoine people. Caenneth Mac Noll becomes the first Daoine cloudmage and First Holder of Lámh Shábhála. This is the beginning of what will be popularly called "The Before."
Year 241	Caenneth Mac Noll dies in Thall Coill, attempting the Scrúdú.
Year 711	Máel Armagh, Rí of Tuath Infochla, sets out to conquer Inish Thuaidh, and is defeated and killed in the Battle of Sliabh Míchinniúint by Severii

O'Coulghan, the Inishlander who would be the Last Holder of Lámh Shábhála.

Year 726

Last reported sighting of mage-lights over Inish Thuaidh. End of the "Before." Over four centuries will pass before the mage-lights return.

Year 1075

A cloch reputed to be Lábh Shábhála is stolen from Inishfeirm by an acolyte named Niall (last name unknown) and is given as a pledge of love to Kerys Aoire.

Year 1111

Niall Aoire, son of Kerys Aoire, arrives in Ballintubber and meets Maeve Oldspring, whom he will marry.

Year 1113

Jenna Aoire is born in Ballintubber

Year 1129

On the 18th day of Longroot, mage-lights reappear over the village of Ballintubber in Tuath Gabair. This heralds the beginning of Filleadh—the "Coming Back." Jenna Aoire becomes First Holder of Lámh Shábhála.

Year 1130

25th of Redfruit: Doyle Mac Ard born to Maeve Aoire.
5th of Sweetsap: Jenna Aoire marries Kyle MacEagan.
21st–23rd of Sweetsap: The Battle of Dún Kiil, where the forces of Inish Thuaidh defeat invaders from the Tuatha, led by Nevan Ó Liathain.

Year 1131

10th of Longroot: Jenna becomes Banrion (Queen) of Inish Thuaidh.
18th of Deereye: Meriel MacEagan born to Jenna.

Year 1135	11th of Conefir: Nevan O Liathain becomes Rí Ard after the death of his father.
Year 1148	2nd of Silverbark: Meriel MacEagan is sent to the Order of Inishfeirm.

THE HOLDERS OF LÁMH SHÁBHÁLA

(Dates given in Daoine years and in chronological order. Entries in **boldface** indicate the cloch was active during the time of Holding.)

THE BUNÚS MUINTIR HOLDERS (from Year 160)

–160 to –144	**Lasairíona (F)**
–144 to –129	**Óengus (M)**
–129 to –113	**Dávali (M)**
–113 to –70	**Riata (M) The last Bunús Muintir Holders of an active cloch. The magelights failed in the last years of his Holding, and Lámh Shábhála would rest again for three centuries.**
–70 to –63	None—during these years, the cloch remained in Riata's tomb.
–63 to –63	Breck the Tomb-robber (F)—for two days, until she was caught and executed.
–62 to –60	None—again, the cloch rests in Riata's tomb.
–60 to –53	Nollaig the One-Handed (M)— Nollaigh, like Breck, stole the cloch from Riata's tomb but held it for years, until he was caught pilfering other items from the chieftain Lobh-

aran's clannog. The cloch and other
items once belonging to Riata as well
as from the other tombs there were
found among Nollaig's belongings.
Some of the treasure was returned to
the tombs, but Lobharan kept the
stone. Nollaig lost his hand.

-53 to -27   Lobharan (M)

-27 to -15   Ailbhe (F)—Lobharan's daughter

-15 to 11   Struan (M)—Ailbhe's son, father of
                        Cealaigh

11 to 37   Cealaigh (M)—first war chief of the
                        Bunús, who were now actively fight-
                        ing the Daoine in the north of Ta-
                        lamh an Ghlas. He would wear the
                        cloch in battle under his armor, and
                        was never defeated on the field—he
                        died of an illness.

37 to 42   Mhaolain (M)—Mhaolain was Cea-
                        laigh's successor as war chief, who
                        (like Cealaigh) wore the cloch as a
                        talisman for victory. When he was fi-
                        nally defeated by Dyved of the North
                        Holdings' army, the cloch passed
                        from Bunús Muintir hands to those of
                        the Daoine.

THE DAOINE HOLDERS

42 to 57   Dyved of the North Holdings (M)

57 to 59   Salmhor Ó-Dyved (M)—Dyved's son,
                        killed in battle against the Bunús
                        Muintir. The cloch was among his ef-
                        fects, but none of Salmhor's heirs

seems to have inherited the cloch. From here, it passes out of history for nearly two centuries until the mage-lights come again in 232.

59 to 232

The Lost Years—sometime during this period, the cloch was moved from the North Holdings (a small kingdom in what would later be part of Tuath Infochla) to Inish Thuaidh. No one knows for certain who held the stone during this time, though several people in later years would claim that their ancestors had been among them. Since none of the Daoine had seen the mage-lights, it's doubtful that they understood the significance of the stone beyond its recent history as a talisman of the Bunús war chiefs.

There is a legend that the Bunús Muintir recovered the cloch after Salmhor's death on the battlefield, and that the Bunús themselves took the cloch to Inish Thuaidh to hide it. Another legend claims that the cloch was thrown into the sea, and that a blue seal brought the cloch to Inish Thuaidh. The truth of any of these claims can't be verified.

232 to 241

Caenneth Mac Noll (M)—the first Daoine cloudmage, and the return of the mage-lights in the skies. Caenneth was not of royal lineage, but a simple fisherman of Inish Thuaidh, yet he would come to understand the sky-magic, and would reactivate the other clochs na thintrí. Caenneth would die in Thall Coill, attempting the Scrúdú.

241 to 263	Gael O Laighin (M)
263 to 279	Fearghus O Laighin (M)
279 to 280	Heremon O Laighin (M)—died testing himself against the Scrúdú
280 to 301	Maitlas O Ciardha (M)
301 to 317	Aithne Lochlain (F)
317 to 329	Nuala Mag Aodha (F)
329 to 333	Ioseph MacCana (M)—died testing himself against the Scrúdú
333 to 379	Lucan O Loingsigh (M)
379 to 382	Naomhan McKenna (M)
382 to 392	Kieran MacGairbhith (M)
392 to 401	Eilís MacGairbhith (F)—killed in the Battle of Lough Lár by Aodhfin O Liathain, and the control of the cloch moves south from Inish Thuaidh to the mainland of Talamh an Ghlas
401 to 403	Aodhfin O Liathain (M)—Rí of the small kingdom of Bhaile
403 to 416	Dougal Woulfe (M)
416 to 432	Fagan McCabe (M)
432 to 459	Eóin Ó hAonghusa (M)
459 to 463	Eimile Ó hAonghusa (F)
463 to 480	Dónal Ó hAonghusa (M)
480 to 487	Maclean Ó hAonghusa (M)
487 to 499	Brianna Ó hAonghusa (F)
499 to 515	Lochlainn O'Doelan (M)
515 to 517	Maitiú O'Doelan (M)—perhaps the only Daoine from Talamh an Ghlas

to attempt the Scrúdú. He came to Thall Coill stealthily via ship in company with his good friend Keefe Mas Sithig. He did not survive the attempt.

517 to 529	**Keefe Mas Sithig (M)**
529 to 541	**Conn DeBarra (M)**
541 to 577	**Barra Ó Beoilláin (M)**
577 to 591	**Uscias Aheron (M)**
591 to 597	**Afrika MacMuthuna (F)**
597 to 612	**Ailen O'Curragh (M)**
612 to 622	**Sinna Mac Ard (nee Hannroia) (F)**—the young lover of Ailen O'Curragh who, after O'Curragh's early death, married Teádor Mac Ard, then the Rí of a fiefdom within what is now Tuath Gabair. After Teádor's death in 622, the children of Teádor's former marriage demanded that the eldest of them (a son) should be the new Rí. Sinna took ill during this period (rumors abound that she was actually poisoned) and died, at which point Teádor's son by his first wife was named Rí. However, Bryth, then only thirteen years of age, took Lámh Shábhála from her mam's neck.
622 to 648	**Bryth Beirne (nee Mac Ard) (F)**—daughter of Sinna and Teádor Mac Ard. It is during Bryth's holding that the Inish cloudmages began to secretly plot to bring the cloch back to the island. Negotiations were begun with Bryth, including possible arrangements of marriage to the Rí of

Inish Thuaidh, but she refused despite Rí Mac Ard's interest in that political union, and eventually married Anrai Beirne, a tiarna of Tuath Infochla.

648 to 651   Rowan Beirne (M)—Bryth's son Rowan foolishly allowed himself to be drawn north out of Falcarragh to a supposed parley with the Inishlanders, where he was ambushed and murdered by assassins in the employ of the Inish cloudmage Garad Mhúllien. Lámh Shábhála was taken from Rowan's body and brought to the island.

651 to 662   Garad Mhúllien (M)—the cloch returns to Inish Thuaidh. Garad would die testing himself against the Scrúdú.

663 to 669   Rolan Cíleachair (M)

669 to 671   Peria Ó Riain (F)—mother of Severii, lover to Tadhg O'Coulghan. She died in Thall Coill testing herself against the limits of the cloch with the Scrúdú. Tadhg would take the cloch from her body and become Holder himself.

671 to 701   Tadhg O'Coulghan (M)—founder of the Order of Inishfeirm based on the tiny island of the same name just off the coast of Inish Thuaidh. Tadhg was the da of Severii, the Last Holder. It was Tadhg who began the process of codifying and bringing together all the lore of the clochs na thintrí, as well as Lámh Shábhála.

701 to 730   Severii O'Coulghan (M)—the last person to hold an active Lámh Sháb-

hála until the mage-lights returned in 1129. The mage-lights had ebbed to nothing by 726.

730 to 731   Lomán Blake (M)—lover of Severii, and a wastrel who sold Lámh Shábhála to pay off gambling debts.

731 to 741   Donnan McEvoy (M)—kept Lámh Shábhála, hoping that the mage-lights would return. They didn't. Donnan, a gambler, was killed in a tavern brawl in Dún Kiil, after which the stone passed into the possession of Kinnat Móráin, who owned the tavern and confiscated the dead McEvoy's belongings.

741 to 753   Kinnat Móráin (F)

753 to 779   Edana Ó Bróin (F)—the daughter of Kinnat Móráin, who found the stone in her mam's jewelry chest after her death due to the Bloody Flux. Edana and her husband took over the tavern. She had no idea that the stone was Lámh Shábhála; she kept it only because it had been her mam's. She happened to be wearing it on the day Doyle Báróid came to Dún Kiil on business and stopped in the tavern for a drink and a meal.

779 to 831   Doyle Báróid (M)—a Bráthair of the Order of Inishfeirm, who recognized that the unprepossessing stone around Edana's neck was similar to the description of Lámh Shábhála in the Order's library. He purchased it from Edana, and brought it back to Inishfeirm. He would eventually become

Máister of the Order. On his death, the cloch was put in the collection of the Order.

831 to 1075   During these two and a half centuries, there was no single Holder of the stone. The stone resided in the Order of Inishfeirm's collection of clochs na thintrí.

1075 to 1093   Kerys Aoire—Kerys fell in love with a man named Niall, one of the Bráthairs of the Inishfeirm Order. Niall, as a pledge of his love, stole the cloch and gave it to Kerys. Because the Bráthairs were contracted by their families to the Order and were forbidden to marry, Kerys and Niall fled Inishfeirm. Their small currach foundered in a storm; Niall drowned, but Kerys, pregnant, survived. She would give the cloch to her son, also named Niall.

1093 to 1113   Niall Aoire—in traveling, he came to Tuath Gabair and the village of Ballintubber, where he fell in love with and married a woman named Maeve Oldspring. Niall would lose the stone (or perhaps the stone lost him) while walking on Knobtop, a hill near Ballintubber.

1113 to 1129   None—during these years, the cloch lay on Knobtop.

1129 to ????   **Jenna MacEagan (nee Aoire) (F)**

A Partial List of the Clochs Mór:
Their Current Manifestations & Holders (Year 1148)

Stormbringer (color: smoky-gray)	Inish	A Siúr of the Order of Inishfeirm	Ability to control weather within a small defined area. Able to call rains, gale-force winds, and lightning. Though the direction of the winds can be controlled, the lightning cannot—it will strike randomly and unpredictably.
Blaze (color: bright red)	Inish	Held by the Order for Meriel	A fireball/lightning thrower.
Snarl (color: blue-green)	Inish	**Mundy Kirwan** of the Order of Inishfeirm	Capable of putting out ethereal, constricting tentacles with strength well beyond anything an unaided human could resist.
Firerock (color: ruddy)	Inish	**Kyle MacEagan** of Inish Thuaidh	Creates a creature of glowing lava
Scáil (color: reflective silver)	Inish	**Aithne MacBrádaigh** of Inish Thuaidh	Can mirror the effect of any other Cloch Mór, mimicking its power.
Demon-Caller (color: clear with red veins)	Tuatha	**Nevan O Liathain, Rí Ard**	Creates a winged demon-creature
Waterfire (color: sapphire)	Tuatha	**Mal Mac Baoill, Rí Airgialla**	Produces blue streams of fiery, arcing energy.
Snapdragon (color: yellow laced with red)	Tuatha	**Doyle Mac Ard**	Creates a whiplike dragon whose tail wraps about its opponent, causing incredible pain as it chews at the flesh.

Rogue	Tuatha	**Torin Mallaghan, Rí Gabair**	Creates a tsunamilike burst that crashes over its target, inundating it.
Sharpcut	Tuatha	A tiarna of the Order of Gabair	Calls into being dozens of glowing, yellow spears that slice through flesh as if wielded by an unseen infantry.
Weaver	Tuatha	A tiarna of the Order of Gabair	Creates a stinging web of force that constricts around its victim.
Nightmare	Tuatha	**Harkin O Seachnasaigh, Rí Connachta**	Gives the Holder the ability to read the mind of an enemy and create images of that person's worst fears or greatest loves.
Wolfen (color: amber crackled with black)	Tuatha	**Labhrás Ó Riain**	Calls into being gigantic, ethereal wolves which attack at the Holder's command.
Tornado (color: black)	Tuatha	**Siobaigh O Treasigh, Banrion Locha Léin**	An energy-sucker. Does no damage, but pulls power from another Cloch Mór, eventually draining it.
Quickship (color: seafoam white)	Tuatha	**Shay O Blaca** of the Order of Gabair	Has the ability to transport one person (either the Holder or another) to a site of his/her choosing, and bring them back again.
Blackcloak	Tuatha	A tiarna of the Order of Gabair	Can cloak itself and chosen other people/objects within a few dozen feet of it so that others can't see them.